THE COLD ONE

In 1818, William Parry commanded a ship, Alexander, into the Arctic region. Upon returning to England, it was reported that three of his crew members had gone missing during a stop in Baffin Bay.

While the missing crew members appeared to be acquaintances, there were rumors they were actually related. One deckhand claimed to know where they had gone.
The North Pole

1

hards of glass.

The Arctic air stung like shards of glass.

Nicholas heard voices. He insisted that's what it was. His wife didn't hear anything. She said it was the ice cracking. But Nicholas heard it. He heard the voices; they were looking for them. He was sure of it. The snow had already drifted over the tent – they might not see them.

Nicholas opened the flap and punched through the snow wall. It was clear outside, an Arctic blue sky over a desert of snow. The subzero wind stabbed his face and choked him with icy air.

Out of nowhere, the storm hit.

A full-on blizzard dropped on them like a tornado.

Nicholas ducked back inside. It didn't make sense. Weather didn't act like that, not in the Arctic. But then no one had ever been this close to the North Pole. *Maybe it did.*

He heard the voices cut through the wind. He dug into the bottom of his backpack and fished out a rope.

"What's going on, Nicholas?"

Jessica was next to Jon at the back of the tent, a cloth draped over his eyes.

"Stay here, Jessica. I'm going to look."

"No. No, you won't. You will not go out in that... we'll never find you..."

"I have to, Jessica. I have to find them. They might have the dogs, the sleds." He cinched the rope around his waist. "It's our only hope."

"Wait until the storm passes."

"No time for that." He put the coiled rope in her hands. "I will not journey far, love. Only as far as this." He snapped the rope between his hands. "And I will be back."

Jessica started to reach for him, but when he threw open the tent, she latched onto the rope with both hands. She would not let go. She would never let go.

Nicholas wandered only steps away before he could not see the tent. The icy snow pelted the exposed skin around his eyes like shrapnel. He hunkered over and gripped the rope, bulling his way into the storm and the wind pulling at his coat.

He heard it again, the distinct sound of voices out there in the white.

"Aglakti!" he called. "Umiak!"

There were more, but the names were shredded as soon as they left his mouth. He crouched down, huddled near the ice. It was impossible. He could barely see the end of his arm. He would start back in a moment. Just a few more steps. If he found the Inuits and the dogs, they might survive. Without them...

Just a few more steps and then he would follow the rope back to the tent. He made sure it was still around his waist. The knot was frozen and crusty. He took several steps, hunched down and called the names. He got all of them out, all five of the Inuits that led them toward the North Pole. The same Inuits that disappeared days ago with all the dogs and the gear. And the food.

It had to be an accident. They wouldn't abandon them. That would be a death sentence. They just wouldn't do that.

"Tupit!" Nicholas screamed.

The wind answered with a swirling gust that snuck through the tiniest crease around his neck, piercing with a jab. He put his hands up to call again but fell.

Something tripped him.

Something had wrapped around his legs. He rolled in the snow, worked his way onto his back and reached for his boots. Tears streamed from his eyes. He could barely see the snow-crusted thing that tangled him up. He pulled it off and felt it jerk around his waist.

The rope.

The storm had lassoed him with his own lifeline. It whipped wildly in his hands. One direction, then another. The storm was coming from all over. Nicholas jerked the rope; he reeled it in – hand over hand – waiting for the tension to show him the way back.

The end of the rope appeared.

A sharp, clean end.

He held it inches from his teary eyes, inspecting the clean-cut end. It wasn't the frayed end he'd given Jessica. Somehow, out there, the rope had been cut.

And now he was in the middle of a white, raging storm.

The tent might only be twenty feet away.

It may as well have been twenty miles.

He had to find his way back. He wouldn't find the Inuit. He wouldn't make his way out of the Arctic. But he didn't want to die without his wife and son. It couldn't end like that. It wouldn't.

He closed his eyes and looked inside for some indication, some sign of where he should go. He felt he had come straight out of the tent and hadn't turned, hadn't veered at all, every step rigid and straight. But he'd fallen and rolled. He couldn't be sure.

His heart pointed the way. His heart wanted to see Jessica one more time. Let her rusty hair fall across his face. Let his cheek warm her hand. Let their lips touch. His second step was stronger than the first. He saw a dark lump ahead of him, low to the ground. It was the tent, nearly buried in quickly drifting snow.

There was a lump next to it.

Two. Three, maybe. He wasn't sure, but they looked to be short people standing there, waiting and watching him.

"Umiak?" Nicholas uttered.

His next step crunched through the snow, through the thin ice below.

His weight crashed through the fragile bridge that covered the water below, the rivers that flowed between the ice floes.

He expected to feel the icy plunge into the Arctic Ocean. He would quickly go numb. Quickly go under. And die alone.

Instead, he fell into a long dark tunnel. There was no water. No death.

He feared he would never warm his wife's hand again.

2

The tent bowed under the weight of the snow.

Jessica hovered over Jon and pushed against the wall. They would have to get out soon or they'd be buried. Jon was still in his teens; he wasn't going to last long outside. But the tent was about to collapse.

Where did this come from?

The closer they got to the North Pole, the stranger the world became. They had seen creatures that looked like polar bears but seemed a bit... off. Even the Inuit were spooked. Nicholas insisted something had happened to their guides, but Jessica knew what happened. They turned tail and went home. She couldn't blame them. They had no real investment in the Santa dream that she and Nicholas and Jon were chasing. The Inuit had family back on the mainland. They'd left the Santa family with their dream and nothing to eat.

They'd left the Santa family to die.

Jon moaned.

Jessica kept one hand on the rope and, with the other, adjusted the wolf skin over his face. His retinas were sunburned from the bright days and the snow's reflection. He was snow-blind. He'd refused to wear the elk antler protection and that's what he got.

The line tugged in Jessica's hand like she'd snagged something. Nothing could be out there in that storm. Nicholas shouldn't be, voices or not. She started to reel him back so they could be together. She would need him to carry Jon.

The line went taut.

She tugged it and it resisted. She pulled with both hands and it went slack.

Panic turned her stomach to ice.

SHE CRAWLED to the tent flaps, hand over hand, pulling and winding. The rope snaked through the wall of snow, falling in a loose pile. Until she reached the end.

The end of the rope.

The end without Nicholas.

She didn't look back at Jon. She shoved her hand through the wall of snow. She pushed her head into the skin-shearing storm, scrubbing the feeling from her cheeks. Her eyes were blinded with tears.

She heard something. Right then, she heard what Nicholas heard.

Voices.

She heard clashing.

The cry of a terrible animal.

And then the wind grew stronger. She was snatched from the tent, tossed into the air, head over knees. She tumbled into the sky, into dark confusion. Numb.

Alone.

Alone with one last thought.

How did we get here?

NICHOLAS AND JESSICA SANTA boarded the *Alexander* with their son in 1818. No one would've recognized her. Her hair – dark red and typically flowing over her shoulders – was cut above the ears. A heavyset woman, her skin was too soft to pass for a man's, so they smudged it with soot and pulled a cap low on her forehead. Jessica didn't board William Edward Parry's ship as a woman named *Jessica*. Instead, she transformed into a quiet deckhand named *Myron* that carried "his" weight like anyone else.

The Santas behaved unlike a family, rarely interacting when the sun was up. Jon spent more time climbing the jibs while Jessica was in the bowels of the ship, lugging food to the cook's station and some-times chipping in to feed the crew. Nicholas could sometimes be found with a sextant in hand, looking for the North Star.

At night, when snoring shook the ship's timbers, Nicholas would find his wife and (when no one was looking) whisper tenderly in her ear. And when all were soundly asleep, he would kiss her gently on the cheek.

In that way, the Santas on board the *Alexander* followed Captain John Ross's ship, *Isabella,* north into Baffin Bay in search of a passageway around North America.

No one knew what they had in mind.

THE SHIPS HAD REACHED the northern end of Baffin Bay when Jon began to show signs of scurvy. Diarrhea had afflicted the deck-hands – mostly the young ones that thought they were indestruc-tible – because they weren't consuming enough lime juice. Jessica went to the galley to check on him. She struggled to keep from pushing the hair off his forehead and pressing her lips to it because the others were around. Instead, she forced him to suck on a lemon.

He was looking better. He would be up in the crow's nest by morning.

But then Nicholas delivered the news. "We're heading back."

"Why?" Jessica whispered.

"Captain Ross insists that passageway is impassable." Nicholas looked around and leaned in. "We'll be heading ashore one last time before following Captain Ross back home."

Jessica didn't answer her husband.

She knew him well enough to see his thoughts in his eyes.

He quickly went topside. Later that day, Jessica and Jon met him to disembark on a short journey onto Greenland's shore. They carried everything they owned with them.

THE SANTA FAMILY slipped away from the exploratory party.

They were not missed when the ship departed. Together, the three set off to find the natives. They had enough food to last a week. Nicholas had a rifle to hunt caribou, too. They weren't sure what their destination was. It was exciting and new. And that's what the Santa family pursued.

It wasn't a week before they were discovered by the Inuit. They sensed them watching. Soon, they made contact. Communication was difficult. It included a lot of hand gestures. Nicholas had an uncanny ability to be liked by every person he met. It was the way he laughed, the way his cherub cheeks became rosy when he guffawed from deep in his belly, and the bright twinkle in his eyes.

It was August of 1818. The Santa family would spend the next couple of years learning to become Inuit.

They were taught the ways of the people, how to hunt, how to survive. They learned to love the cold as if ice ran through their veins instead of warm blood. Jessica, most of all, loved their new life. It was as far away from her past as it could be. Nicholas had promised her that when they married. And he delivered.

But even their new life was not enough. Adventure still called. The greatest adventure of all beckoned. A place where no human had ventured.

The North Pole.

As far as anyone knew, no one had ever reached the top of the world. Even the Inuit stayed inland, where they could hunt caribou and Arctic fox; where they could fish off the coast and feed their families. *The North Pole is not a place,* the natives said. *It is not land.*

It is ice.

The North Pole was a floating wonderland of ice floes. It was dangerous, too. If someone did not fall into an icy lead – the openings between moving patches of ice – they would surely be run down by patrolling polar bears.

But none of that dissuaded the Santas.

It propelled them forward.

And in March of 1820, just as the sun had begun to rise from its long winter disappearance, they set out to do what no human – Inuit or otherwise – had done before.

They would touch the North Pole.

The Arctic was stunning.

The sky was clear blue and at night it was lit up with strange red and green and blue lights. The snow shimmered like sheets of diamond dust. There were only the sounds of cracking ice. The dog sleds carried enough supplies to make the trip. Halfway, they stashed a cache of food to gather on the trip back.

It was challenging. And difficult. It was everything they hoped it would be.

But then it got strange.

Occasionally, they would see polar bears in the distance that seemed to be watching them. But these bears would stand on their back legs and appear to have a total of six limbs (not four) before diving into the snow like a prairie dog jumping into its den. There were sounds, too. Moans.

One of the Inuit claimed to have seen something flying. Not flying, but leaping hundreds of feet from one ice ridge to another, like some Arctic mountain goat.

Goats did not live in the Arctic.

They had pitched tents to gather a few hours of sleep. They couldn't stay long because the ice floes slowly drifted away from the North Pole. They needed to be efficient with their time. Food was their clock.

But when the Santas exited the tent, the Inuit were gone. Completely. Like they'd never existed. The dogs, the sleds, the tents were gone. Not a trace. No tracks or evidence left behind.

And the food, gone.

The Santas were left with a few days of food in their packs.

"We can't..." Nicholas started. He didn't finish.

Jessica knew.

Nicholas calculated their position. He thought they had reached latitude 85° N. The North Pole was at 90°.

"We can reach it," he said. "We can reach it."

Jessica nodded.

Jon looked back. He knew there was no other answer. As he had always done, he accepted what was in front of him. When his parents gave him the choice to stay in London, he chose to come with them. When they gave him the choice to return on the *Alexander,* he chose to come with them.

"No one will know we reached it," Jon said.

"That's not why we came," Nicholas said.

We follow truth, his father always told him. *My heart sings for adventure, not for others to approve.*

Jon gathered his pack.

The Santas began the final leg of their journey.

They would end it together. They could think of no better way.

3

J essica was falling.

She saw the ship, the *Alexander,* like she was a spirit floating in the clouds. It cruised below her, through the cold, blue water, sails billowed out like huge snapping sheets. She saw Greenland.

The Inuit.

The inside of a collapsing tent.

She remembered the scouring storm—

Jessica bolted upright.

A ROOM.

She sat still. Didn't dare move.

She'd had dreams like that, waking in a strange place, only to wake up later to discover what seemed normal at the time was quite strange, indeed. But she didn't want to wake up, not yet.

The room was warm.

The first time she'd felt warmth this deep in quite some time. Warmth that was in her bones, in her joints. All the way through her.

She was in a bed that was attached to a wall. The blanket was thick and wooly, soft like skin. She rubbed it between her finger and thumb. Strange as it was, it was no dream. She couldn't explain anything else, just that this was no dream. She was there, in her flesh. In her real waking life.

And warm.

The wall glistened like crystal. She touched it, expecting it to be cold, but the surface was slick and warm, like a sealant over a wall of ice that insulated the cold on the other side. On the far side was a desk. Next to that was a pile of gear that was neatly folded and stacked. The sole light source was sitting on the desk, its glow soft and faint.

She pushed the blanket off, exposing her bare legs. She was wearing a thin shirt and baggy undershorts. She noticed the light-colored hair that coated her legs, thick up to her knees. Her toes were knobby and the nails discolored. She'd passed herself off as a man on the ship. Anyone that saw those legs wouldn't argue. They'd always been stocky. She hadn't eaten much and they still looked thick.

She swung her feet off the bed and hesitated before dropping them on the icy floor. But, like the walls, they were coated and warm. She walked over to the desk, ducking slightly when the ceiling brushed the top of her head. The gear was hers, stacked nice and neat and clean. She rustled through the shirts and coat and the backpack below.

The light hummed.

The illumination increased, throwing more light onto her gear as if sensing she couldn't quite see. Jessica reached over and plucked the light – a strange globe about the size and shape of a perfectly crafted snowball – and held it in front of her face. Something was in the center, glowing like an eternal firefly. It didn't flicker, so it couldn't be fire. And it wasn't hot. She turned it around and around, looking for a latch or a seam–

Moan.

She hadn't noticed the other bed on the far side of the room. The light brightened as she squinted to see what was there. She recognized the dark, shaggy hair.

Jessica dropped the light and ran.

"Jon." Jessica tore the blanket down and grabbed his face.

He winced. Jon was accustomed to his mother's rough love, but after a long, restful sleep, it was hard to take.

A long, restful sleep. Just how long?

"Jon, Jon," she repeated, pressing her lips to his forehead like she used to do when he was young and sick with fever.

Jessica held him at arm's length and studied his face. Jon opened his eyes, prepared for the ache of snow blindness. But there was none. His eyes were filled with water and the swelling had disappeared. In fact, he felt close to normal. The never-ending hunger that gnawed at the inside of his ribs was mysteriously absent. He wasn't full, just... not hungry.

"Where are we?" he asked.

His mother was still mesmerized by his face or his recovery or the dreamlike feeling that was all around. She sat back on the floor and her stare turned vacant. She was shaking her head, trying to remember.

"Where's Dad?" Jon asked, looking around the empty room.

He wasn't as shocked by the surreal surroundings as his mother, adjusting like it was a cool dream they happened to wake up inside. *Just, where's Dad?*

"I... don't know." Jessica pushed her hair from her eyes. It hadn't been that long since she'd cut her hair before boarding the *Alexander*. It seemed really long. "I just woke up a few minutes ago."

"Is this ice?" Jon waxed the wall with his palm.

Jessica didn't answer. She stood up and looked around. The glow-globe brightened enough to light the entire room. It was large but rather sparse. Besides the desk, gear and beds, there wasn't much. Jessica noticed a hole in the wall. It was near the floor and ended at waist level. She took a knee next to it and looked inside. She could crawl through it, but it was dark only a few feet past the entrance. She could get that glowglobe, find out where it went.

She snatched it off the desk. When her fingers brushed the surface of the desk, the entire desktop illuminated. Jessica stifled a brief squeal and stepped back. She squeezed the glowglobe while pictures began to materialize on the desk. First it was snow. Then there was the sun. Then the horizon appeared on the desk like a three-dimensional reality in miniature scale, snow drifting over the surface. She stepped closer and leaned in. It looked like the Arctic, the very ice floes they were crossing toward the North Pole before they hid inside the tent. Before the storm.

Before the rope came back empty.

Nicholas.

Jessica touched the desk, remembering her husband's face before he left. She remembered his voice calling back.

The image on the desk moved when her fingertips hit it. She pulled back like it might burn her. The image jerked as if she'd actually touched a picture. She slowly moved her fingertips from left to right and the view moved left to right. The sun moved off the edge of the desk and an ice ridge appeared.

"Whoa," Jon said. "You've got to see this."

He was out of bed, bare-chested and barefoot.

Jessica couldn't remember seeing him that puffy. He had always been a lean kid with muscles rippling beneath his skin. She had always been concerned he didn't have enough body fat to insulate him in the cold weather, and now he finally looked big and soft.

Jon got on his hands and knees. Jessica stood over him.

It was a perfectly round hole like the one in the wall, like it had been drilled in the ice. This one went down a few feet until it turned deep blue.

"Is that water?" Jon asked.

"It must be."

"Then, are we... we're inside an ice floe?"

How did she tell him that being inside an ice floe was the sanest thing she'd heard since she woke up? What would he say when he saw the desk and the glowglobe and–

"Hello."

Jessica held up the light and looked at the hole in the wall.

Now things are getting weird.

4

They weren't exactly... people.

People-like.

It wasn't because they were short – they were three feet tall, max – that made them seem so odd. They had two eyes, a nose, a mouth and all the things that defined a person as a person. They were just... different.

Fat.

Round.

Their skin was puffy and doughy. Their rosy cheeks crowded their faces, setting their eyes deep beneath their bushy brows. Their arms hung near their bare feet. The one on the left appeared to bow with his hand in front of his stomach, his brown mop flopping over his eyes. The bow didn't make it far, as his gut was just too thick to bend much.

The other one – an apparent female, her hair tied into a single braid that touched the back of her heels – tapped him. He stood up, only having to move an inch or two, and grunted. A smile crept over his face, lighting his cheeks up another shade of pink.

"Are you going to introduce us to them?" the short woman asked him.

"Oh, yes, yes. Yes." He cleared his throat and grabbed her hand. "Please to make your acquaintance... um, people?"

"They have names," she scolded. "You can use their names."

"But they don't know how we *know* their names." He spoke from the corner of his smile like a bad ventriloquist.

The woman shook her head. She decided to take control.

Her toes curled on the ice floor and gave a short push, sliding across the room as effortlessly as an ice skater but without any apparent blade. Jessica and Jon backed up. The short woman turned her left foot – which was far bigger than it should have been – and came to a stop.

"I am Merry." She nodded and blinked. "My husband is the tongue-tied one. His name is Nog."

Nog nodded and blinked, as if that was a way of greeting. Fine with Jessica. She wasn't eager to shake their hairy oversized hands. When they didn't respond, Merry turned to Nog. He nodded and blinked again. She did the same.

"Do you... think they got damaged?" Nog asked.

"I don't think so. You do understand us, do you not?"

Jessica said, "Yes... I'm just–"

"Oh, where's our manners!" Merry squealed. "Nog, you didn't plug the drain hole."

Nog was still nodding and blinking.

"NOG! THE DRAIN HOLE!"

He looked blankly at her. Merry wagged her long, knuckled finger – a fine coat of light hair on the back – at the hole. Nog understood and with a quick kick he shoved himself across the room, sliding like Merry had done.

Jon backed up.

Nog reached into one of the pockets of his loose flowing coat that fluttered over layers of white shirts and gray pants. He slid a dull metallic sleeve over his finger that had a long point. Nog dropped on both knees and leaned over the hole, his belly rubbing the floor.

Jessica noticed the soles of his feet were covered with bristles of thick scales all pointing at the heels. She could only assume they allowed them to grip the ice to push and slide.

Nog muttered something to himself.

"They could've fallen in, Nog," Merry said. "You need to be more careful, you do."

"No, they couldn't."

"Yes, yes. Yes, they could. If they weren't looking, they could've fallen through."

Nog, with his metallic finger pointed at the hole, turned toward

Merry. "No, no. No, they *couldn't*. Now, can I close it? Would that be all right with you if I close it now?"

Merry turned her head.

"Thank you." Nog dipped the silver fingertip into the hole. The empty space made a crackling sound. Icy lines spread out from the fingertip like a spider web. More lines appeared until the hole was filled with fresh ice. When he stood – rocking himself until he had enough momentum to get to his feet – the hole had disappeared.

"Satisfied?" he asked.

Merry pointed her knobby, fur-covered finger at Nog. She began to open her mouth–

"Hold on!" Jessica stepped in front of Jon and waved her arms. "What's going on?"

Merry and Nog were frozen for a second. Merry covered her mouth. "Oh, my goodness. Where are our manners, Nog? We need to orient our guests; there isn't much time."

"Well, then. I have just the thing." A short kick and Nog slid to the desk. "I've taken the liberty of preparing an orientation video. It'll only take a minute and you'll be oriented just right. Yes, yes, indeed. Yes."

He placed his palm on the desktop and lifted it like his fingers were heavy. Lights and images rose off the desk in a three-dimensional holographic display of an icy landscape with a dull sun near the horizon.

"Hold, just a moment," Nog said. "The audio was giving me fits this morning, but I think I've got it synced–"

"Sshhhhht!" Merry pushed next to him and whispered loudly, "Have you lost your mind?" She jerked her head. They turned slowly. Jessica and Jon were standing against the wall. "I'm sorry, my husband, he doesn't think. There's so much to take in and he wants to introduce you to holographics as an orientation. Where's your mind, Nog? Where's your mind?"

"I think that's unfair," he said. "You know I–"

"Where are we?" Jessica interrupted. "Just tell us that, please."

Merry and Nog turned and said in unison, "North Pole."

"This is the North Pole?"

They nodded and blinked.

"We're in an ice... cave?"

"Sort of," Merry said. "Like I said, it's hard to explain. We just don't have time–"

"What are you?" Jon stepped in front of his mother. "Are you humans?"

Merry and Nog were quiet. The rosy complexion faded from Nog's cheeks. He raised a finger and said, quite matter-of-factly, "I'll pretend I didn't hear that. It's one thing to insult me, but another to insult my lovely wife."

"He didn't mean anything by that, dear. It's a perfectly legitimate question, one I think we should answer. The answer, which is quite simple, is yes, we are human. And, no, we aren't."

"Yes and no?" Jessica said. "What's that mean?"

"We're elven. And if you watched my orientation video," Nog said, "you would've learned that forty thousand years ago, roughly one-third of the planet was covered with ice and our people were the predominate species. We, us... not you warmbloods with the slow brains and the thin skin and the–"

"That's enough, Nog. They didn't mean to insult us; they just don't know what's going on."

"Well, I'm trying to tell them."

"We don't have time for your stories. We need to go. If you can collect the room, we can move along and explain things to them later. Maybe they can watch your orientation video later, yes?"

Nog's cheeks regained their color. He happily pulled a brown fuzzy bag from his pocket, muttering praise to himself.

"Stand back," he said.

Nog pointed his silver, pointy finger at one of the beds and watched it vaporize into a silky cloud. He guided it into the bag. He did the same thing to the other bed and the desk and their gear until the room was empty.

"Magic," Jon muttered.

"No, no." Merry headed for the exit. "Magic is what you call something you don't understand. This is science, dear. Nothing magic about it."

"It's a simple space compressor and atom fragmenter," Nog said, holding up the bag. "It's quite simple, really. You see, matter is simply energy that–"

"Nog, dear, I think it's time to go. We've wasted enough time. The colony needs to relocate, and these two darlings need to dress for the journey. If you could throw them some proper wear, they can get dressed. They don't have fatty layers to survive without additional clothing."

"Yes, yes. You are so right, Merry. So right." Nog reached into the bag and pulled out stacks of coats and boots and gear that seemed impossible to fit inside it. He placed it at their feet.

"When you're dressed," Merry said from the tunnel, "please follow. I'm sorry, you'll have to crawl through this. We don't have enough time to make a hallway large enough for you to walk through. Quite frankly, we're not accustomed to such large quarters, and we're only in an eight-foot ice shelf so there's not a lot of room to spare."

"We're inside an ice floe?" Jessica asked.

"Of course, dear. This is the North Pole. There's no land out here, just ice and water."

"And us," Nog added.

"And now you," Merry said. "So if you won't dally, we'll be able to relocate to another ice shelf, one that's closer to twelve feet thick so you don't have to duck so much."

"Wait! Where's my husband?" Jessica leaped forward. "Where's Nicholas?"

Merry and Nog glanced at each other. Their jolly expressions darkened.

"We'll tell you once we've relocated," Merry said.

"We're not going anywhere." Jon stood next to his mother.

Again, they shared a knowing glance. A dim one.

"Someone else is... caring for him," Merry said.

"Who?" Jessica said. "Where?"

"Oh, you'll have to save that question for Jocah. She'll tell you everything, dear. It's a long story and you just got here."

Merry and Nog went on their way before another question was launched. Their voices faded down the tunnel.

"They're doing quite well, don't you think?" Merry said.

"Yes, yes. Yes, they are."

Jessica and Jon stood in the middle of the room, their gear at their feet. Her fingernails – usually chipped and dirt-stained – were clipped and clean. And her hair was free of knots and neatly trimmed. Jon was the same, all bathed and pampered.

He stared back. "You all right?"

Jessica wasn't sure.

5

Nicholas's fall was long and dark.

It was some time later he realized he was not underwater. It was cold, but not wet. And it was as black as a moonless night.

Am I dead?

He moved his lips. Turned his head. His joints were stiff and slow.

He wiped a sticky slick from his cheek and tasted the tang of iron on his fingertips. The left side of his face was swollen. Perhaps his left eye was shut.

He tried to bend his knee–

"AaaaarrrrRRRRRHHHH!"

He woke.

The pain was in his left leg, stabbing just below the knee.

He labored to breathe. Each ragged breath rebounded around him in some sort of black cavern. It didn't echo, so it wasn't that big, but big enough that he couldn't feel the walls around him.

As he settled, he slowly pulled himself into a sitting position without moving his legs. It took minutes to do that. And a lot of breathing.

The leg is broken.

Nicholas knew that dead feeling. Broken bones are useless. The climb out of this hole would have been difficult, at best. Now it was impossible.

And the end?

Agonizing.

"Jessica!" His wife's name bounced. "Jessica!"

He leaned back on his elbows, gulping a lungful of air, pushing back the throbbing.

"JESSICA!"

He continued shouting. Shouting until the name scratched his throat. Shouting until it was a hoarse whisper.

Shouting until he heard another sound.

"Over here."

There was squabbling.

Nicholas turned his head left and right, listening like a bird locating a worm. It was ahead of him.

A slight glow illuminated a round opening, a tunnel perhaps. The light was bluish, reflecting off the icy walls and shimmering like water. It was bright enough that he could see his snow-frosted body.

And the odd angle of his left leg.

Long shadows cast down the tunnel. They were short, fat and waddling toward the entrance.

"He's down here," one of them said.

Nicholas waited.

Defenseless.

6

Jessica felt like she was crawling through a sewer pipe.

It was dark and tight. She tried not to think of crawling through an ice shelf with the ocean below and enough ice to crush her.

She tried not to think of Nicholas. That thought was heavier than all of the ice in the Arctic. He had gone out to save them. It wasn't the image of his frosty face she remembered quite as clearly as the end of a clean-cut rope. How strange the end can be so abrupt. Despite the dangerous life they lived, she always assumed they would be together when it ended. She always thought it would be a little more romantic, like lying in the snow, watching the sun set while holding hands.

Silly girl.

"You all right?" Jon asked.

Jessica realized she had stopped crawling. She didn't answer, afraid her voice would betray her. She needed to be strong. At the very least, look it.

With great effort, she pushed forward, lugging the great emptiness that filled her where Nicholas used to be.

Merry and Nog waited on top of the ice. Their wide feet were like snowshoes. Their gnarly toes dug into the snow.

"Careful, now," Merry said. "Watch your step; it's slippery outside the hole."

The air was calm and the sun bright. Jessica was surprised how comfortable it felt. Despite the winter gear, she always felt the Arctic's bite. But now she was somewhat toasty. Only the sting of breathing subzero air reminded her how dangerous it was.

Nog reached into the exit hole and grabbed Jon's arm. For a little man, Nog's hands were large, wrapping all the way around Jon's forearm, and with surprisingly little effort, he pulled him out.

Jessica noticed the tough sheen on Jon's cheeks. It looked thicker but resilient. She rubbed her own face, wondering if she looked like that. *Are we changing?*

Several yards away, more elven emerged from the ice and stood around the exit hole, helping others out. They were just as short and just as round as Merry and Nog. More holes opened and elven appeared like prairie dogs.

Jon started, "What are we waiting for?"

Merry and Nog pointed straight up.

The sky was clear, crisp and blue. Not a single blemish.

But then a dot appeared. It was darker blue, like a small bird. But then it was heading for them like a missile, becoming larger as it neared.

CRASH!

Jessica and Jon barely had time to raise their arms.

Merry and Nog didn't flinch.

It stood on four legs.

Eight feet tall with an enormous rack of antlers. Its fur was strangely blue. It snorted and a long cloud streamed from its flared nostrils.

"What kind of... *caribou*... is that?" Jessica stuttered.

"Reindeer, dear," Merry said. "*He's* a reindeer."

"Well, sort of," Nog interrupted. "Centuries ago we dabbled in genetic manipulation and beefed up what you normally call a reindeer." Nog stroked his long white beard. "I suppose it's still in the genus as reindeer, but they're a bit freaky, I suppose."

The reindeer flicked its head faster than Nog could react, nudging him off his feet. Nog landed in a puff of snow.

"All right, all right," Nog said. "I didn't mean you were a freak, just you're bigger and better and stronger. Don't be so sensitive."

Nog barely reached above the reindeer's knee and stroked the fur that was changing from blue to white.

"I've never seen a *blue* animal," Jon said.

"They camouflage," he said. "No one can find them but us. Part of the genetic manipulation."

More were falling from the sky, spiking into the ice next to various groups.

"And they can *fly*?" Jessica exclaimed.

"Not fly," Merry said. "Leap."

It appeared they were falling from thousands of feet. *If something leaps a mile,* Jessica wondered, *that's flying, in my book.*

Elven gathered around reindeer.

There was a total of eight reindeer, including the one in front of Jessica and Jon. The elven carried small bags similar to Nog's. As the reindeer pulled their legs from the ice – embedded from the impact of their thousand-foot *leap* – an elven reached into a bag and pulled out something red. It started off small and stretchy but got big and landed plenty solid. *THUD.*

They were sleighs that were red with golden rails. Each one was lashed to a reindeer and the elven piled in. When the sleigh was loaded, the reindeer crouched and – after a brief pause – shot from the ice into the sky, blending into the surrounding colors.

It was practically invisible.

"Jessica? Jon?" Nog had a smaller sleigh already prepped and ready and attached to the reindeer. "If you would like to sit on the back bench, we can depart."

"Where?" Jessica asked.

"We have to relocate," Merry said. "We never stay anywhere for more than two weeks."

"Jack will find us," Nog said.

"Sssshht." Merry stuck her finger on his lips.

"Jack?" Jessica asked.

"Why is he after you?" Jon added. "Does he have my father?"

"No more questions, dearies," Merry said. "All of them will be answered very soon. Please, climb on. We can't waste any more time."

It all felt rushed.

Are these the good guys?

They seemed like it. But, really, what choice did she have? If they stayed behind, they had nothing.

They know about Nicholas.

Jessica climbed onto the sleigh. They settled into the back while Merry and Nog did the same up front. There were reins but not like on a horse. These were just connected to the harness that was around the reindeer's broad shoulders, only meant to steer left or right.

A group of elven was preparing the largest reindeer of the bunch. Its antlers stretched as wide as it was tall and its snout was different than the rest. While its fur was white, the muzzle was pinkish.

The nose, bright red.

The sleigh it was pulling was a big one. At least four elven helped someone into the back bench. Her hair was pure white, the braid dragging in the snow behind her. They made quite a fuss about her comfort.

"Now, hold on," Nog said. "We're launching after them."

The red-nosed reindeer exploded into the sky, leaving behind a thundering crack in the ice. Snow settled in its wake.

"All right, now," Nog called. "Let's not dally."

The reindeer, snorting and pawing the ice, turned his head. His eyes were black as the bottom of the ocean. He blinked, slowly.

Jon's head suddenly felt cold on the inside.

The sky rushed past them.

7

J ack slouched in an oversized chair. The desk was even bigger. He looked like a child pretending to work.

He liked things that way. He liked them big.

Jack rested his pointed chin – not pointy, but extended in an unusual fashion even for an elven – on the palm of his hand, drumming his long fingers across his cheekbone. The only hairless elven in existence stared at the only thing on the desk: a fish globe. Three silver fish floated inside.

He stared while a song ran through his head.

Siiiiii-lent night,
Siiiiii-lent night.

IT WASN'T REALLY A SONG. It was just two words, nothing else. For as long as he could remember, he'd sung it to himself.

It gave him comfort.

And that's all he cared about, really.

Jack slid his hand – the flesh was light blue like a clear sky – across the pearly desktop.

He scratched a long fingernail over it (all his fingernails were purple like a bruise).

Jack curled his slender fingers around the bowl, sliding it closer. The silver fish didn't seem to notice the blue-skinned elven with the bald head and clean face. He observed them with a cold eye.

He lowered his finger toward the bowl like it was an inkwell. The fish flickered around. There was nowhere to run.

The purple fingernail touched the water.

The heat inside the bowl, inside the fish – what little there was – was absorbed into his finger like a straw pulling water from a cup. There was a crackling sound as water turned to ice.

Jack held the bowl near his eyes, turning it around and around, observing the still life inside. It reminded him of a paperweight his mother once gave him, all round and shiny with cute little objects suspended inside.

He smashed it. Shards scattered.

The fish lay on the desk, solid as icicles. Tails curled. Eyes blank.

Jack picked one up, turned it over and sniffed it like a connoisseur sampling the vintage. He bit the head off and minced it between his front teeth, swirling it around his tongue. He nodded.

Yes. A good year.

A SHORT, fat elven (they were all short and fat, but this one exceptionally so) stopped just outside the doorway on the far side of the room. He stayed just outside of view. Only his shadow dared to cross the threshold.

"Entre-vu," Jack called.

The elven slid inside, gliding all the way across the room – around furniture and games and crates and things under construction – until he stopped in front of the desk. The surface was right at eye level, leaving only the bush of black hair and his thick eyebrows for Jack to see.

"Sir–"

"I'm sorry, what?" Jack put his hand to his ear.

The thick eyebrows wedged together. "My apologies... *Your Excellence.*"

"Better." Jack threw his bare feet – the color of blueberry jam –

onto the desk. "You know, I got to hand it to you, Pawn, these are tasty. *Reeeal tasty.* You did good, for once."

Jack studied a skinny tail fin, still frozen.

"Better than that batch of lamprey you sent down, smelled like whale farts. Where'd you get these?"

"Um, well, thank you. Those are cod. They came off the coast of Greenland. One of the self-propelled harvesters brought them back. The harvester uses saltwater to generate its own power. Very impressive."

"Technology." Jack laid his head back, mouth open, and dropped the tail in. He chewed like a horse. "*I love it.*"

"Your Excellence," Pawn started, "we have located a warmblood. It's a male. He's pretty healthy, really, for being this far north. But he's injured–"

"Whoa, whoa, whoa... stop the clock." Jack stopped chewing. "What do you mean you found *a* warmblood?"

Pawn stepped back. Now his nose, fat and bulbous and bumpy, was visible in a forest of mustache whiskers.

"Only the adult male was captured. He fell into a trap."

"Yeah, I got that. But there were *three* warmbloods." Jack held up three fingers and counted them with the other hand. "Three warm-bloods take away one warmblood equals two, dummy. Where are the other *two*?"

"Excellence, there were three."

"I can do math and I just said that. Answer the question."

A shuffle and another step back. "The colony–"

"The who?" Jack dropped his feet. "WHO?"

"Sorry, the *rebels*... they reached the other two warmbloods first."

The throne-chair slid back.

"You're coming in here and telling me that three warmbloods finally trekked into the Arctic and that we only got one of them?"

Jack stood.

"*WE ONLY GOT ONE OF THEM, IS THAT IT?*"

"The rebels, Excellence... they arrived as our scout team closed in on the warmbloods... they released an abominable snowstorm before we could capture them."

Jack's cheeks turned the color of a ripe plum.

The sheen of ice crystals that perpetually covered his baby-smooth face like frosty whiskers shimmered.

Pawn swallowed.

There was silence, broken by the sound of Jack's perfectly square teeth grinding back and forth like stones.

All right. Okay.

There was nothing he could do about these IDIOTS now. *What's done is done.*

Siiiiii-lent night.

JACK RAN his hand over his face and scalp, wiping away a thick layer of icy fuzz. His flesh lightened up as a fresh layer of frost formed over it.

Good as new. Happy, happy.

"All right, fine." Jack waved his hands and plopped back into his throne. "Where's the one stupid warmblood now?"

"He's, uh" –Pawn swallowed – "he's in Claus's lab."

"I'm sorry. What?"

"You see, he was seriously injured, Excellence. Claus is the only one with the expertise and equipment to heal him."

"But I want Claus working on other things," Jack replied in a singsong manner, stemming the flood of irritation. He didn't want to sing "Silent Night" in his head because if he did it too much, it didn't work so well. Besides, his doctor said he needed to manage his emotions in a healthier way. Things like positive thoughts and other crap.

He hated his doctor.

"You want the warmblood healthy, Excellence. Otherwise, he's not going to tolerate the subzero temperatures of the North Pole. Who knows when we'll get another warmblood?"

"Well, I heard a little rumor there are two more warmbloods somewhere in the Arctic. Did you hear that, too? Or am I just making that up?"

"Listen, Excellence, we're going to need Claus on this one."

Jack tap-danced his fingers on the desk. The nails clicked out a metallic rhythm while his cheeks darkened.

The warmblood was the Find-of-the-Century and Claus got him first. He got everything first. Jack could send for the warmblood, but Pawn was right. He needed Claus to fix the human.

He needed Claus.

And that's what he hated most.

"What's his name?"

"Sir?"

Jack looked up. Pawn was five steps from the desk now.

Blueberry city. Jack beckoned with a finger.

Pawn shuffled over.

Jack urged him closer. Pawn took a half step. Closer, still. Until he could feel Jack's icy breath on his bulbous nose.

"Let's not forget," Jack sang while his fingers danced up Pawn's belly and through his long beard, "who *we're talking to.*"

He held up a finger – a single, blue finger.

Pawn closed his eyes.

Jack touched the end of his fat nose. Crooked trails of ice crackled from the point of contact, crawling over his cheeks, beneath his beard. It was like Death's talons latching on, piercing and stinging and squeezing. Cold nails driven deep into his brain.

Pawn's face was numb.

His throat contracted.

The room was beginning to dim. Jack lifted his finger.

"Want to give that another shot?"

"E-e-e-x–" Pawn's lips fluttered. "Ex-cellence."

"Beautiful." Jack's breath crystallized on Pawn's face in a frosty sheet. "Now what's the *warmblood's name*?"

"San... Santa."

Jack sat back.

He bounced his fingers together, thinking. He watched Pawn shiver. Even an elven couldn't take the kind of cold that Jack could dish out. Polar bears wouldn't stand a chance. He couldn't prove it, but Jack was willing to bet he could reach absolute zero – he could make electrons stand still, if he wanted – despite what the idiot scientists claimed impossible.

Pawn didn't move.

Jack wanted Pawn to see him thinking. He needed him to see how thoughtful he was, that he was smart. That's what leaders did, they thought about stuff. They planned and schemed and had things figured out. His people needed to respect him and revere him and honor him.

Fear him. That worked, too.

So Jack sat there bouncing his fingers with a serious look.

But then he got bored.

"Get out of here." He kicked him in the belly. "Tell Claus no funny stuff, that I'm watching his fat fanny. I'm not kidding. You tell him I'll strangle him with that dirty red coat he wears."

Pawn shuffled toward the exit.

He was thawing out about halfway across the room, bumping into a miniature ice sculpture of Jack (he about knocked it over) before he started sliding. He couldn't get out fast enough.

Jack was still bouncing his dumb fingers. He thought he had control of the anger.

Claus.

He brought his fist down. The desk shattered into chunks, spraying glittering ice chips to the ceiling. It was a pile of rubble.

"NEW DESK, PLEASE!"

Someone better hear that.

"AND MORE FISH!"

8

Dark.
Dark. Dark.
And then a sliver of light.

It was bluish, not jolting Nicholas awake. It was soft, like a sunrise.

Nicholas wasn't aware he was seeing anything. He was somewhere in a dreamy land of thoughts and feelings. Somewhere cold and alone.

But then a voice.

"Santa," it said. "Santa. Santa."

Nicholas saw a green fuzzy blob.

He blinked it into focus. It was a boy in a funny little outfit: a pointy green hat and green shoes with pointy ends that curled over the toes. And he had a long beard that touched the floor.

Not a boy.

The round little man was across the room, knocking on the wall. "Santa," he said, his voice rising. "Santa. Santa."

Nicholas was reclined in a chair. He felt no pain. His left leg was numb and the side of his face, too. His left eye was swollen, but he could see well enough. It helped that the room – walls glowing a deep ocean blue – was soothing.

A toilet flushed.

The little green man stepped back.

Another man, slightly taller and slightly larger, stepped out of an apparently solid wall. Even though he was bigger, he was still no taller than three feet, at best. Nicholas noticed the dim outline on the wall where he had come from, as if it was a doorway disguised as a wall.

He wore a dirty overcoat that dragged behind him. It was red and trimmed with grayish (maybe white at one time) fuzz around the collar and wrists.

The fat man grunted through his curly white beard. His dark eyes, set deep in his fat face, blinked heavily. He ignored the little green man and seemed to slide across the floor with little effort. Nicholas couldn't tell if he was wearing skates. The fat man went to a bench that was full of unrecognizable gadgets. The entire room was cluttered with gadgets.

"Santa." The green elf followed the fat man.

"Where..." Nicholas started, clearing his throat. "Where am I?"

"Hmm," the fat man said, tinkering at the bench.

"Where am I?"

The fat man grunted. That was it.

There was something attached to Nicholas's head and strange bands around his wrists and ankles that allowed him to move but not too far, effectively restraining him to the chair with magnetic force. Nicholas struggled to sit up. It hurt the side of his face to move like that. It was probably better he didn't stand.

"Hey," Nicholas said. "Hey, I'm talking to you. Where am I?"

"The North Pole."

By the looks of the walls and floor, he could only assume they were inside an igloo, but it was too large and square to be an igloo.

"Where are my wife and son?"

"They're safe," was all he said.

"*Where* are they?"

No answer. Not even a grunt.

Nicholas closed his eyes.

He was with Jessica and Jon. They were trekking to the North Pole. He had gone out to look for their Inuit guides when the bizarre blizzard hit. And then his rope appeared to get cut before–

He fell.

He crashed somewhere deep and dark. His leg was broken. The side of his face, bloody.

Where am I?

The band around his head tingled.

"You're in the Arctic," the fat man said. "More specifically, you're with the elven people."

Nicholas stared at the back of the fat man's head. *Is he talking to me?*

"That halo interprets brain activity. We could do it without the halo, in wireless fashion, but the halo is more accurate. We know your name, where you've been, what you've done. Whether you've done good. Or bad."

The fat man grunted and muttered something that sounded like *humans.*

Not in a good way.

Where's my family?

Several moments passed and the fat man worked undistracted at the bench, light flickering around him. Nicholas figured he was lying about the halo. If he knew his thoughts, he'd know how worried he was. He'd know the empty cold fear in his stomach, not knowing if they were in danger–

"They're safe," the fat man said. "Just not with us."

"Who are they with, then?"

"Not us."

The cold fear turned hot. It was difficult to breathe.

He drew a long breath.

"Then tell me... WHERE!"

The fat man stopped what he was doing.

The flickering light died. He rested his hands, his head slumping. He snatched something off one of the short shelves above the bench.

"Let me explain something." The overcoat slid back as he turned, exposing bare feet that were fat and hairy. "I'm a scientist and healer. I'm not a magician. Where your family is right now is no business of mine. I cannot help them and neither can you. Not in that condition. I suggest you sit back, shut up, and stop thinking so much."

Who does this half-pint think he is? If I wasn't strapped down, he'd be sorry he ever–

"There you go again!" The fat man threw his hands up. "That's the problem with you warmbloods; you're always complicating things with *thinking, thinking, thinking!* You've got reality covered in layers of thought; how do you even tie your shoes? Just be present, just be here, AND STOP WITH THE MONKEY MIND!"

They stared each other down.

The fat man breathing hard.

He dropped a coin-object on the floor. It projected an image – an exact likeness of a grown man, one Nicholas's size – that was feature-less and translucent, exposing the skeletal form inside.

"You sustained compound fractures of the tibia and fibula as well as shattering the orbital socket around your left eye."

Nicholas saw the breaks on the image. The cheek had three cracks around the left eye, but that wasn't nearly as bad as the broken bones in the leg.

"You also sustained broken ribs. Worst of all, you punctured the left lung; that I was able to repair but not without significant scar tissue."

That was why Nicholas couldn't catch his breath.

"You're lucky."

Lucky?

"Yeah, lucky." The fat man's brows pinched over his eyes. "You're alive, aren't you? Those pitfall traps are meant to maim polar bears and other prey. What are you doing with your family in the Arctic in the first place?"

"We were... seeking adventure." Nicholas looked away.

"Well, congratulations. You found it. You hauled your skinny butt into a climate you have no business being in. You're a warmblood; you're not made for Arctic weather. You wore the skins of wolves just to get this far. You weren't going to make it much longer. If we didn't find you, you'd probably be dead. So you're lucky. Get it?"

Nicholas noticed he was hardly dressed for the cold, but despite the icy walls, he was warm. This fat man didn't know what he was talking about. He didn't know where Nicholas grew up; he was accustomed to cold weather–

"Don't flatter yourself," the fat man said. "You'd be dead without me. The nanos have elevated your core temperature until I can get your fatty layers developed." The fat man slapped his belly. "Why do you think cold doesn't bother an elven? We're insulated like seals."

"And you look so happy."

The fat man grumbled.

He held out his hand and the coin jumped into it like a magnet grabbing metal. The image with the broken bones evaporated.

"What's a *nano*?" Nicholas asked.

The fat man went back to the bench and replaced the coin on the shelf.

"I deal with technology, Santa. I'm afraid it's beyond your comprehension."

"Try me."

Sigh. "You have been in an induced coma for a week. I fed you nano-pills that are still coursing through your veins, right now, reading your vital signs and mending your body."

"Nano...?"

The fat man turned on his stool. "Tiny robots."

This isn't happening. This is a dream.

The fat man dropped a handful of spare parts on the floor. The little green man scooped them up and slid under the bench. He began assembling them with clicks and clacks and the buzz of strange tools.

"You're not dreaming," the fat man said. "We've been around for tens of thousands of years, much longer than the human race. We evolved during the Ice Age and our bodies adapted to subzero temperatures. We belong here; you came to us. You walked into our world, Santa."

The bench flashed.

"You're with us, now," he said.

Nicholas strained against the binders.

The room appeared to be made from ice and there weren't any doors. He wasn't going anywhere. Panic tightened around his throat and the weight on his chest – made worse by the scarred lung – got heavier with emotions.

The click-clacks from under the bench got louder.

The little green man looked up from his project. His face was puffy and leathery, but his eyes – hidden deep in folds of skin – were childlike.

The little green man tugged on the fat man's red coat. "Claus."

"Cane, stop," Claus quipped. Just like an annoyed dad.

Jessica. Jon. Where are you?

Cane wasn't a threat. He probably didn't even like Claus. First, get out of the chair. There had to be a way out.

"I'm not your enemy," Claus said. "If these were different times, I'd be your friend. But they're not. Sit back and let me do my job and we'll get along just fine."

"What do you want with me?"

Claus began clearing off the bench.

"I'll keep you comfortable, but there's only so much I can do. If it makes you feel better, your wife and son are much better off than you are."

"What's that mean?"

"It means they're safe."

Nicholas relaxed, suddenly aware of the tension he was holding in his stomach. He had no reason to believe him. But he did. *They're safe. They're safe.*

CLAUS DIDN'T LOOK SO angry. "You need rest."

The band around Nicholas's head began to vibrate. His eyelids suddenly got heavy.

Claus slid across the room and, without slowing, went through the solid wall. Nicholas didn't notice the dark outline. He was already struggling to stay awake.

The bench was glowing with the image of snow and ice, like a mirage. Maybe he was already dreaming. Nicholas saw Cane come over to his chair, felt him pat his arm. Something went *click-clack*. Cane slid across the room and through the same spot on the wall.

Nicholas forced his eyes open.

Click-clack.

It was a little tin man made of spare parts that were bent and fastened into place, each one shined and expertly crafted. It stood on the armrest, just past his hand.

And then it moved.

The figure bowed to Nicholas and walked off the armrest like a ship's plank. It somersaulted onto the floor and strutted away. *That's not technology. That's magic.*

Nicholas couldn't keep his eyes open to see if the little toy man made it across the room.

9

Nicholas slept.

Occasionally, he heard objects shifting around and voices. Mostly grunts. He also heard *click-clacks*.

He opened his eyes at some point.

He was still on the recliner, the bands still around his wrists. He wasn't aware of any pain, although it was still hard to breathe, like there was a stick inside his chest. He couldn't tell if there were bands around his ankles.

He couldn't see his ankles!

Always a fit man, Nicholas had never lost sight of his feet. Now his belly was round and doughy. He felt like a sack of lard. But he wasn't cold.

Even though he was only wearing his red long johns, he wasn't cold at all.

He woke a few times to an empty room. Once, a dirty red coat was hanging over a pile of gadgets. The next time he woke up, it was gone.

Nicholas would close his eyes and go back to dreaming.

He saw Jessica.

Her hair was long and wavy and brown, but when the sun hit it just right, it would shimmer like leaves flashing on an aspen. He could smell her, too. She never wore fragrance; she wasn't that sort of person. It was the scent of Jessica. The smell of her flesh, the smell of hard work and determination and something that felt warm and comfortable and homey.

The smell that everything was all right.

When Nicholas was fretful, when he came home at night with the world weighing on him, he would curl against Jessica and press his cheek against the nape of her neck and everything was all right. The world was simply just what it was. And Nicholas would want nothing more than to be there.

HE DREAMED of his mother and father.

Of the day he saw Jessica for the first time.

Of the day she told him that she was pregnant with Jon. She had taken him to the park and they sat at the edge of a pond, lying back to watch the clouds drift overhead. Nicholas dreamed about how happy he was. He was going to be a father. He would be a good one. And Jessica, a good mother.

Together, they sat on the bank, listening to the ducks squabble.

Something clattered.

Nicholas woke. There was a metallic bird perched on his fat belly. It spread its wings – wings crafted from bits and pieces of spare items scraped together and expertly wedged into layers like shiny feathers.

It shook like a wet duck.

Clickity-clack-clack-clack!

And then the thing, as heavy as it looked and as impossible as it seemed, flapped its wings until it rose into the air. It flew in circles over Nicholas. And he watched it, thinking of water and clouds, of being a good father. A good husband. He watched it until he couldn't keep his eyes open.

And then he went back to the park.

Back to his Jessica.

10

Claus left Santa sleeping soundly.

He managed to keep Nicholas's good health somewhat disguised so it would appear he needed more time to heal. But his good fortune wouldn't last forever. Soon, Jack would come for him. He would move him to another lab to begin work on him.

After that, Claus wouldn't be able to help him.

He needed some air.

Claus slid through the dark tunnel below the surface of the ice, his red coat fluttering. Cane wasn't far behind. He could hear the little man's green boots sloshing along the icy floor. His feet lacked the ice-skating bristles that most elven developed at the age of two. Cane was different.

They moved rapidly, ascending into the upper levels of *New Jack City*. Once upon a time, the elven lived inside the ice shelf without altering it much topside. The elven had learned to control the polar ice caps thousands of years earlier; they could freeze water and open tunnels until it supported an entire population of short round people. It didn't have a name; it was just called home.

Things change.

Now home was a massive mound of ice and snow, like an iceberg had been dropped from the sky. It was so much more than they needed. It wasn't always like that.

It is now.

The tunnels lightened as they continued upward where windows let in sunlight. Claus passed open rooms and larger tunnels, through the marketplace, where elven set up booths with their wares for barter. The elven that saw him dropped what they were doing and waved. Some fell on their knees and clasped their hands in reverence. Claus acknowledged them with a nod and continued as quickly as possible.

If he could ignore the marketplace, he would.

Too many elven remembered him. Remembered who he was. He didn't like them to see what he'd become.

He took the main ramp that looped around the perimeter of New Jack City. Cane struggled to keep up. Claus kept up the pace until he reached the pinnacle of the icy kingdom.

He swished onto the upper veranda: a wide platform with a view of the top of the world, where the dry Arctic wind scoured his thick skin until he felt its sting.

He was alone with Cane at his side. Cane, always at his side.

The sun was near the horizon. The Northern Lights – bands of green and red – were vague this time of year. He stood on the veranda, his coat – once a symbol of peace and love – snapped loudly behind him. What he once called home used to be his kingdom.

Now his prison.

HE RULED WITH KINDNESS. But, sometimes, raw power prevails.

He should be dead. Jack let him live for this day, the day a warm-blood entered their world.

It was inevitable. They were adventurous and curious. Warm-bloods were bound to find a way to trek into the deadly cold of the Arctic. And when they did, they would find an ancient species of Nordic elven waiting.

Elven had lived in peace for forty thousand years, content to live with the world just as it is. There was no need to spread and conquer.

Jack had different ideas. Ideas that could change the world.

Somewhere out there, somewhere in the white landscape of the North Pole, a small group of elven had escaped Jack's reach. The colony moved so they could not be located. Those brave elven were their only chance for peace to return to the North Pole. Somewhere out there was the rest of Nicholas's family.

Their chances of survival were better than his.

CANE GRABBED Claus's belt and wrapped the coat around him, hiding like a polar cub finds protection in his mother's arms.

Someone's coming.

Claus felt them arrive. They were sliding up behind him. They slid to a stop on both sides of him. Two of them. They were wearing dark blue uniforms with a gold crescent over the left breast.

"Excellence would like you to report to his quarters," Pawn said. "Immediately."

Claus nodded. He watched the Northern Lights flicker.

If Nicholas has to suffer, then so be it. Anything for peace.

11

D own to the bottom of New Jack City, deep into the ice.
Pawn led the way. Cane clung to Claus's fluttering coat.
They coasted down the declining tunnel until it ended at a wall with guards on each side like sentries.

A million tons of ice above them.

So heavy. So cold.

Claus entered a palatial chamber. The temperature dropped. His breath streamed in dense white clouds. The breadth and width of the room was staggering, filled with three-dimensional monitors projecting views from around the city and plush furniture to sit and watch every activity of the elven.

Jack insisted they push deeper into the water, freezing the ice cap, expanding its thickness. When the ice didn't properly set and then fractured, elven were swallowed by the ocean's dark depths.

Jack lost not a wink of sleep. *Deeper!* he cried. *Colder.*

"Brother!" Jack waved from the other side.

The only difference between the twin brothers was Jack's blue skin. And hair. Jack had not one follicle of hair on his body. His head looked like it had been dipped in a bottle of diluted ink.

"It's been *toooo* long," Jack shouted through his hands. "You been hiding from me or something, you dog?"

Claus kicked forward, weaving between random ice sculptures. He couldn't get around a large block of ice in the center of the room. He hadn't seen the elven (San, Derning, and Shepperd were their names) in all the clutter.

San, Derning and Shepperd nodded at Claus, careful not to let Jack see the twinkle in their eyes when Claus appeared. Snowballs exploded on the block of ice.

"Get, get!" Jack shouted. "Come back later. GO! NOW!"

They raced out.

"Don't mind that little thing," Jack called. "Just a little piece I have them working on. Got to keep the elven doing something, right? Otherwise they just sit around getting fat. Am I right? Am I right?"

Jack propped his hands on his belly and smiled.

"Now get over here, brother."

Claus slid around the icy monolith.

"Janack," Claus said, nodding.

"I told you not to call me that."

"It's your name."

"Didn't get the memo? I changed it, like, five hundred years ago. Get with it."

Jack clucked his tongue.

"Man, you look great. You lose weight or something? I can't put my finger on it, you just look... fantastic." He framed his fingers and looked at him from a couple of angles. "It's that filthy coat, I think that's it. It's you, baby. You make it work."

Claus pulled his coat closed and cinched the black belt over his round belly. Cane peeked out.

"Holy iceballs! Is that my one and only nephew?" Jack threw his arms out. "Get over here and give your favorite uncle a hug, you little fart smeller!"

Cane hid his face in Claus's coat.

"You're going to hurt my feelings, *nephew*. Get over here, nooooow," he sang with a touch of irritation. "I meaaaaan it."

"Janack, he's shy. Let him hide for a bit."

"Okay, all right. Let him chill. I get that. He's just a kid." Jack tapped his chin, thinking. "I'll bet the knee-biter is a little chapped I missed his birthday. All five hundred of them."

"That doesn't help," Claus added. "What do you want, Janack?"

"Get to business, huh? I like that about you, brother. Always an eye on the future. Good, good. Have you heard from Mother?"

Claus's expression didn't change.

"Don't suppose you would tell me if you did, perhaps? Would you hide that from me, dear brother? Word from our mother? Because, I got to tell you, that would be a very unbrotherly thing to do, you know. Hide something from me."

Jack tilted his head, tapping his finger on the desktop like a bird pecking for insects, spraying ice crystals.

"Hiding *anything* would hurt my feelings, you know."

THEY WERE BORN thirty seconds apart.

Claus was first. It was the only thirty seconds of his life that he did not have someone reading his mind. From the time they were born, they knew each other's thoughts. They would finish each other's sentences. Until Jack became sick. A mutated gene changed his metabolism and his body temperature began to drop.

And drop.

And drop.

The doctors could do nothing but watch as it dipped below freezing. His blood, though, did not crystallize.

Janack, Claus used to say. *It'll be okay, Janack.*

But Jack kept getting colder.

"ARE you hiding anything from me, brother?" Jack stopped pecking a hole in the desk. "Perhaps you are hiding the truth. Are you? You hiding something from me, you little devil?"

"You know my thoughts, Janack."

"I don't know everything, and you know what? I got a feeling you're protecting that warmblood."

"Why would I do that?"

"Because you love all things, I guess." Jack shrugged, polishing a spot on the desk. "Because you're good. You're good and I'm bad."

Jack pecked the desk again.

"You're *gooooooood,*" he sneered.

"Janack, it's not like–"

"YOU'RE GOOD; I'M BAD!"

Frosty whiskers fluttered off his face. Cane pulled the coat over his head.

"The warmblood needs rest," Claus said. "If you rush his recovery, you'll destroy him. You've waited thousands of years for one to fall into your hands; you can wait a few more weeks."

Jack stared at his brother, sensing his thoughts, looking for a dirty lie – an ounce of deception – in his good and perfect and stupid brother. The big doofus really wanted the warmblood to get well. Jack just didn't want the skinny giant to die; he couldn't care less if he felt better.

Jack shook his head. "You're such a softy."

He slid away from the desk, gracefully gliding around the room. It's what he did when he wanted to think: slide around his room, in between all his stuff.

"It's why you are you and I am leading the elven," Jack shouted. "You can't make the tough calls and I can. Stop acting like you're scared, brother. Pain isn't a bad thing, you know. Why can't you appreciate what I'm doing?"

Jack slalomed between a series of couches and came to a sliding stop on the edges of his feet. He eased up to his brother. Their facial features, identical. Their expressions, opposite.

"Why do you care about a dirty warmblood?"

"It's murder, Janack."

"It's survival of the fittest, dummy. It's how Nature works."

"You want to wipe out all the warmbloods. You'll kill them all."

"THAT'S RIGHT."

Their bellies touched.

"It's called balance, you dope. I'll return the world to the Ice Age because elven were meant to be the world's caregivers. We live ten times longer, we do not overpopulate. We do not strip the world. Warmbloods do that, brother. Warmbloods are the species that are self-consumed. Self-serving."

Jack's cheeks turned purple.

"Self-centered."

Claus looked around the room. "Right. You want to destroy the human population... *for the good of the world.*"

Jack snorted several cloudless breaths. He smiled again, his complexion returning to its normal bluish hue.

"Don't appreciate your sarcasm." Jack straightened Claus's collar and brushed off his shoulders. "But you're my brother, so I'll let it slide this time. I imagine it's hard to live in your pants."

He patted Claus's cheek. Frozen lines appeared on his flesh.

"I was born for a reason, brother. I was born to restore balance to the world. You know it; I know it. You were born to help me do that, that's all. I make the difficult decisions that need to be made."

"They don't seem difficult for you."

"I have no guilt for what's right. Neither should you."

Jack coasted back to the chair behind the desk.

"You have a week to heal the warmblood. A week, and that's all. I mean it."

"Too soon. He'll need much longer."

"A WEEK!"

"Then just kill him now." Claus didn't flinch. He meant it. Jack could sense that he did. Nothing would heal that fast.

"All right, all right." Jack's fingernails tap-danced on the desk. "Just don't screw around, I mean it. I'll make a Popsicle out of your head if I find out you're up to something. I want the warmblood to extinguish the human race."

"His name is Santa."

"*Really?*" Jack rolled his eyes and threw back his head. "Do you have a name for all the fish in the ocean, too? Who gives a dookie what his name is? The warmblood is a leech, a parasite. Vermin, for crying out loud. We're going to strip his mind and clone the dirty warmblood, so WHO CARES WHAT HIS NAME IS?"

Jack dropped his feet on the desk.

"Not me, that's who."

12

Jessica vomited in the sleigh.

She couldn't help it. She never liked heights.

She once hid on top of a three-story building after she stole from a fruit vendor and the police were on the lookout for her. She'd curled up against the chimney, more afraid she'd fall off than of getting caught.

When the reindeer leaped, her head snapped back.

Before she could catch her breath, they were a thousand feet above the ice. One minute later, she was barfing. She wiped the tears away and looked down once. After that, she closed her eyes and gripped the bar in front of her like it was a raft in the middle of an ocean.

Jon couldn't see enough.

His eyes were filled with water, also – although the wind shear wasn't what it should have been, like there was some protective bubble around the sleigh that cut down the Arctic air that, at that speed, would've peeled their cheeks off. He leaned left and right, taking in the sights. The polar ice cap stretched out as far as he could see, zigzagged with ice ridges and watery leads.

The massive reindeer – white as clouds – had extended out all four legs. Flaps of skin stretched between his body and the base of each leg, allowing him to glide. Although it didn't make sense that a thing that big and solid and powerful should soar so effortlessly, like a helium-filled balloon.

They began descending.

Jessica tried not to squeal. The plummeting sensation punched her in the stomach. Even Jon grimaced as the sleigh tilted at such an angle that it appeared they were crashing. They were going straight down. The ice was coming fast.

The reindeer kicked his legs out. The skin flaps billowed out, catching the wind. The sleigh flattened out. They cruised toward the surface, almost parallel with it, almost touching it, when the reindeer slammed all four legs off the ice.

They launched again.

Jessica thought they were landing. The reindeer couldn't glide forever; he had to descend to leap again, this time to the sound of a full-grown woman screaming.

Merry and Nog sat quietly, turning slightly with the sleigh.

Just another reindeer ride.

Several jumps (and screams) later and Jon could see points of light grouped on the ice. The reindeer stretched out his right legs and the sleigh tilted to the left. Jessica held onto Jon.

They glided down to the surface. The sleigh rails swooshed across the snow and the reindeer's hooves sprayed ice over them, running with amazing speed. The muscles bulged as he slowed his pace, bringing the sleigh to a nice and easy stop.

Jessica didn't let go. Jon couldn't break the grip she had on him. It wasn't until Nog climbed on top of her lap and pried her hands apart did she open her eyes.

"WHERE IS EVERYONE?" Jon asked.

"Already under the ice," Merry said.

Nog pulled the bag out and, with his magical glove (science, not magic), he made the sleigh disappear.

"Off you go," Nog said, scratching the reindeer's hindquarters. "Tinsel's got treats for you."

The reindeer's hooves thundered over the ice as he trotted to the group of reindeer gathered around one elven.

"Who's that?" Jon asked.

"Tinsel?" Merry said. "She's our herder. Very gifted child, she is. The only one that can communicate with the reindeer. Without her, we'd have a very difficult time knowing what they need. She's giving them one last snack before they bound off for the mainland."

Jon's face was numb from the cold, but his chest was warm.

"Can I go over?" he asked.

"For a spell, darling," Merry said. "But we need to get under the ice."

"Is Tinsel coming under?"

"Yes, when the reindeer are off."

"Then I'll come down with her."

Jon didn't wait for Merry to answer.

"We're going to need a special entrance for Jessica," Nog said.

"Suppose you're right," Merry answered. "Given her size."

Nog pulled a disc from the bag. It was flat and silver with symbols and indentions where he fit his fingertips.

"I don't see what you're talking about." Jessica didn't see an entrance, just the endless stretch of white. She was grateful to be on her feet, even if it was lonely and barren.

"You won't see anything," Merry said.

"You see," Nog chimed in without looking up from the disc, now the size of a frying pan, "we use carving gear to tunnel through the ice sheet. It's simple, really. It analyzes the thickness of the ice and, based on the tunnels and room configurations, it changes the ice to vapor. In a matter of seconds, we have a fully developed colony below the surface and no one is the wiser."

"How does it..." Jessica was shaking her head.

"Watch."

Nog tossed the disc. It hovered a few feet above the ice, defying gravity and the wind. When it found its sweet spot, it dropped like a hunk of metal and melted through the ice like a hot coal. A cloud of steam erupted.

"You see," Nog said proudly, "the physics of the carving gear were solved, but the mechanics were the most difficult. It wasn't until I–"

"I don't think she wants a history lesson, Nog," Merry said.

Nog stopped mid-sentence, finger in the air. He looked hurt. He waddled toward the hole. It was much larger than the disc. A ramp corkscrewed around the perimeter.

"I'll go first," Merry said. "Let Jessica go second."

Nog agreed.

Merry shouted over to Tinsel and Jon to be under the ice soon, then stepped onto the icy ramp and shot down and out of sight. Nog told Jessica to lay back with her hands crossed over her chest. "Just like a slide," he said.

He said with a twinkle in his eye, "Let the ice take you where you need to be."

Jessica sat down and looked over at Jon.

"He's all right, Jessica," Nog said. "He'll be down shortly."

She let the ice take her.

13

The reindeer stopped when Jon arrived. Jon came up alongside the one that pulled their sleigh and put his hand on his left rear flank. Clouds stormed from the reindeer's nostrils. Tinsel didn't see him on the other side of the reindeer. She tossed a large green cube in their direction. The reindeer caught it between his teeth and began grinding it.

"You're welcome," Tinsel said sweetly. "Why are you so late – oh!"

She dropped her bag.

Two of the reindeer stepped between Jon and her. She peeked between their legs. Her hair was bright red and braided tightly over her ears, each hanging down to her feet. Her face, puffy as all the other elven, was smooth and freckled. Her eyes were as green as spring.

There was a long pause.

First, she was tense, almost angry. But then she looked at the reindeer next to Jon and relaxed. The reindeer that were in front of her – guarding her – stepped aside like they understood he wasn't a threat.

"You're a... a warmblood?" she said.

"A *what*?"

"A warmblood." She searched for a different word. "Human."

Jon's chest continued to warm.

One of the reindeer brought its muzzle down to Tinsel's height and nudged her bag. She tossed a green cube to him. She did the same with the rest of them while they all patiently waited their turn. Saliva dripped from their rubbery lips. All except one. The largest of the herd – the one that pulled the special sleigh with the white-haired elven – was separate from the herd.

"I'm sure you've never seen reindeer like this, just like you've never seen an elven."

"How do you know?"

"Because we bred them. They're genetically modified. They have helium bladders next to their lungs that give them buoyancy. Bet you never heard of that."

That explained how they were able to glide for so long.

"Nog said you're a herder."

"I am." She looked back, her eyes smiling. "Did he say what that was?"

"Just that you're special."

"Well, I don't talk to them. You won't see one of them talking. If you do, you've been above ice too long."

She thought that was hilarious.

Jon didn't get it.

"I'm sorry," she said. "Elven humor."

"No, no... I get it."

He didn't.

He turned away from her. Something felt like she would know he was lying. Jon scratched the reindeer's hindquarters again.

"He likes that," Tinsel said.

"How do you know?"

"When I was little, I heard them... *thinking*." She held up her hand and one of the reindeer brought his muzzle down for her to scratch. "And when I say I was little, I mean from the time I was born. I didn't know it wasn't normal; I thought everyone could hear them. I was telling my mom and dad what they were thinking, and pretty soon everyone thought I was crazy. I was the kid that everyone started to ignore. They wouldn't let me play games with them and started calling me names."

"Sorry to hear that," Jon said.

"I didn't really want to play with them anyway. I liked being out here."

One of the reindeer snorted. Tinsel giggled. She shot a quick glance at Jon and blushed.

"What?" Jon said. "Are they... *talking* about me?"

"Sort of." She laughed again. "They think you're funny."

"You mean like funny ha-ha?"

This broke her out in a fit of hysterics. A few moments later, the reindeer all began snorting.

"No," she said. "But now they do!"

Jon was beginning to feel like the one left out of the little reindeer games.

"Do they have names?" he said over the chortling.

"They do," Tinsel said, but only after catching her breath. "But you have to promise not to laugh. I named them when I was a little girl. You promise?"

"All right."

She looked at him with a sidelong glare. "Promise, for real?"

"Yes, I promise." He held up his hands. "Nothing's crossed, I promise."

Tinsel glared a bit longer, then gave out the names, pointing as she did. "Here we go. Dasher, Dancer, Prancer, Vixen, Comet, Cupid, and Donner. And that right there," she said, pointing at Jon's reindeer, "is–"

"Blitzen."

All the good humor left Tinsel. "How did you know that?"

"I... I..."

Jon didn't know how he knew. It was just a word that popped onto his tongue.

"Lucky guess," he said.

"What about that one out there?" Jon pointed to the largest of the herd, off on his own. "What's his name?"

The large reindeer was staring at them. Like he heard.

"That's Ronin," she said distantly.

"Why's he out there?"

"He's been like that since the Fracture." She tossed a final handful of cubes and put the bag away. "I don't suppose you know anything about the Fracture that split our people in two, so I won't bore you with the details. Just this. Someone really bad was born and that's why we have to move every two weeks."

"Jack?"

"How do you know that?" she snapped.

"I don't, really. Merry and Nog mentioned his name."

"Well, if you ask me, he doesn't deserve a name. He's a thing, not an elven. He's the Cold One, and that's a good name for him."

Nog called to them, reminding Tinsel to be under the ice soon. The reindeer were already stomping around, ready to launch away. Tinsel waved to Nog.

"You're shivering," Tinsel said.

Jon realized he was chattering. That wasn't like him. He didn't chatter easily, but the cold had gotten to him.

"You should be developing a blubber layer by now if you've been with us for a week, but you're still skinny as a warmblood."

"I'll be fine."

"You ain't going to be fine for long without a thick layer of blubber. We better get inside for a hot meal. It only takes a few minutes to make a fatal mistake out here."

Tinsel raised her hand.

The reindeer, on cue, launched. Ronin was the last one off the ice. Tinsel led Jon to a hole in the ice.

He could hear his teeth chattering.

14

Jessica slid on her backside with her hands over her chest. She felt Merry's hands on her shoulders, pulling her to a stop.

"Icicles!" Nog shouted.

"Watch your language," Merry said.

"The carver was supposed to make the room with a six-foot ceiling."

Jessica opened her eyes. They were in a fairly large room, but the ceiling was as low as the tunnels. Most people would be freaking out. She had slid deep into the center of an ice floe. A collapse would bury her.

Maybe I can't do reindeer, but I can do this.

"Wait, it's not finished." Nog picked up the disc. "Merry, push our guest into the corner so she doesn't get wet."

"I think that's impossible."

"Well, we can try, can't we?" Nog frowned.

Merry grumbled, but knew he was just embarrassed. He'd wanted it ready for her. She gave Jessica a push. Jessica sat up on her elbows and watched Nog toss the disc. It went through the floor. Ocean water bubbled up.

Now she was a little spooked. The room started to fill up. "Um," Jessica said.

"The drain hole, darling," Merry said. "He'll cap it."

Nog stuck his hand, the one with the shiny glove, into the hole. The water ceased.

"A magnetic field," he said. "It creates a one-way door to let water out. Not in."

He clapped his hands together and grinned at Merry. She grinned back.

"Are you ready, Jessica?" he asked.

Merry leaned over and said, "Oh, you're going to like this."

THE CARVER DISC popped out of the hole and spun around the room. Ice chips flew, melting into water that quickly drained through the hole. It became a blur, blasting the ceiling high enough for her to stand. And while it was doing that, Nog began pulling stuff out of his magic bag (er, his *science* bag).

First, a battered desk. Next, a feather-stuffed mattress. Then a tattered rug and scratched floorboards. A grimy window stuck to the wall with a view of Industrial Park spewing black smoke.

"Ta-da!" Merry and Nog said.

Jessica went over to the desk. Old papers and an ink well. A damaged pen. The surface was scuffed and worn. In the middle, gouged in capital letters, was a name. She ran her fingers over the carving – a piece of work that her mother tanned her hide for doing.

JESSICA.

"I knew she'd like it," Nog whispered. "She's speechless."

Merry frowned. "Darling, I don't know if she's–"

"She's about to come hug us. She'll kiss us." Nog puckered. "Me, first."

Jessica whirled around. "*How did you do this?*"

Nog had his eyes closed, lips puckered.

Merry elbowed him.

He snapped out of it. "Well, it was simple, really. We looked through your memories when you first arrived–"

"You what?" Jessica covered her chest. She suddenly felt naked. "How did you... WHAT GAVE YOU THE RIGHT?"

Nog stepped back. The excitement withered.

Jessica turned away. She saw the books stacked in the corner – her books, the ones she scrounged out of trashcans and hid from her mother or else she'd make her sell them. Books that she would keep under the bug-riddled mattress, that were sometimes missing pages or the corners torn. Books that were her only escape from… from…

She rubbed the soot from the window. The smokestacks belched into the sky.

From this.

"Darling." Merry took her hand and gently patted it. "We didn't mean to upset you. We were only looking to bring some of your world back to you. To make you comfortable. To make you feel like you were home."

Jessica's hand was trembling.

"We'll change it back." Merry turned to Nog. "Turn it back, Nog. Start with something that's a little more like–"

"Leave it."

Jessica was still staring out the foggy window.

"You meant well; just leave it like this. I don't want to cause you any more trouble. You've done enough for me and my son. This will be fine."

If she could survive that sleigh ride, she could live a bit longer in that room. It wasn't real, after all.

"Are you sure, dear?"

Jessica nodded.

Merry continued patting her hand. Jessica offered a weak smile.

She just wanted to sleep.

"A BATH?" Nog frowned so deeply his eyes disappeared beneath the bushy eyebrows. "What's that?"

Jessica explained how they would fill a tub with warm water to wash and relax.

"Wash?" Nog looked at Merry. "I don't understand. Do you, Merry?"

Jessica thought it strange, but then realized they had a thick layer of hair that covered almost all parts of their body. Perhaps they were like animals.

"Visualize it." Nog pulled his metallic glove on and gestured for her to bend down. He put his palm over the crown of her head. "If you can imagine it, I can create it. Don't leave out any details, now." He closed his eyes. "Let me see it."

Jon sat on the edge of the bed and watched Jessica close her eyes. Nog began nodding. *Hmmm,* he said. *Hummmhuh.*

"Got it."

He waddled back a few steps and told the others to stand aside. Then he held the bag at his side and reached in with the magic (*science*) glove and – with a flicking motion – tossed out an object that landed in the corner. It was small, at first, but then inflated until a porcelain bathtub with claw-footed legs came into shape. A long, silver hooked faucet grew from one end, and steaming water began pouring out.

Jessica covered her mouth. Funny how something so simple almost brought her to tears.

Nog crossed his arms on top of his barrel-shaped belly.

"Hot water?" Jon said. "Where does all the power come from?"

"Well, we have advanced tidal and ocean current harvesting, not to mention our wind follicle farms that–"

"Not now, Nog." Merry hit him with an elbow. "You can lecture the boy later. Right now, they need to relax and take bats–"

"Baths," Nog growled. "They will take a *bath*."

"Okay, bath-bath-bath... they'll take a bath."

Merry grabbed him by the arm and dragged him to the exit. "We'll be back to get you after a spell, dear."

"Where are we going?" Jessica said.

"To see Jocah." Merry's voice echoed from the tunnel. "Enjoy your bats."

JESSICA TESTED THE WATER. It was as hot as it looked.

She pulled the curtain around the tub. She undressed. It had been a month since she'd been naked. She hardly recognized the folds of skin on her stomach and new dimples of fat. She'd gained so much weight.

She sank into the water and quietly wept so that Jon wouldn't hear.

If only Nicholas could be here.

15

The light, dim as it was, hurt.

Tears tracked down Nicholas's cheeks. He wiped them away and kept blinking, staring at the ceiling. It wasn't until things came into focus that he realized what he'd just done.

He moved.

Nicholas lifted both arms above his head. The bands were still around his wrists, but they weren't holding them in place. His arms began to shake; they felt so weak. He was never like that before. And his belly, look at that.

Icicles, it was getting big and round.

Icicles? When did I start saying that?

"You can stand."

The voice startled him.

Claus was at the bench with his back to him. The dirty coat hung on the wall next to him. He was occupied with his work. Nicholas had to turn away. Whatever Claus was doing, it was too bright. Claus waved his hand and the brightness adjusted.

There was an image on the desktop, like a scaled-down version of a snowy landscape. And there was a plate of food.

Real food.

Claus slid the plate in front of an empty stool. It seemed to go right through the snowy image.

"Do you need help?" he asked, without turning.

Nicholas tried to answer, but his throat was sore. He grabbed a handful of curly whiskers. His beard was as thick as tumbleweed. Beneath it were folds of fat.

"No," he finally managed.

He probably did need help, but he wasn't going to ask for it.

HE WAS ON HIS BACK, looking at the ceiling. His muscles were jelly. Not to mention the additional baggage of a new gut. First, he needed to sit up–

The chair began moving.

Seconds later, Nicholas was upright.

He put his feet – bare feet – on the icy floor. For some reason, it wasn't cold. He couldn't see his feet, not over the inflated belly, but they felt bigger. Wider. And thicker on the soles. He slid his butt to the edge of the seat and tested his weight on the left leg. It ached a bit but not much worse than a bruise. In fact, the only thing that hurt was breathing. There was still pressure on his left side.

Nicholas pushed himself up. He teetered.

Claus never turned around. If Nicholas fell, it was going to be a hard one. But he caught his balance.

Claus patted the stool.

Nicholas took several careful steps. He dropped onto the seat, near exhaustion.

He had a thousand questions – starting with where all the extra weight came from – but moist delicious heat wafted into his nostrils like a Thanksgiving dinner.

First, he ate mashed potatoes. Next, seasoned chicken and boiled carrots. He downed that with a glass of wine.

And the flavors...

Icicles!

"You've been here for nearly a month," Claus said. "In that time, you've been on a diet of fatty foods and other things that make you fit for the Arctic. You had no blubber, little hair."

He tinkered with a metal globe.

"Now you do."

Nicholas shoved more food in his mouth. He was breathing like a wolf. Grease glistened on his fingers and on his lips. He wondered where it came from. Nothing grew on the North Pole, certainly not potatoes and carrots. And chicken?

Or maybe this is polar bear.

There was noise beneath the bench. Nicholas struggled to look. Cane wiggled his fingers at Nicholas. His eyes crunched as he smiled beneath his thick beard.

"Santa."

He went back to his little project, turning a screwdriver on a small metal piece.

"Where's my wife?" Nicholas said with a mouthful.

Claus finished tinkering with the metal globe and placed it in a metal box. The flaps closed and sealed and appeared seamless. He shoved it to the back of the shelf and paused.

Claus took a breath, his shoulders slumping. He placed a coin object on the bench. The snowy landscape, which appeared to be some sort of mirage made of light, disappeared. A small body of a man appeared in its place. It was Nicholas's body, but this time it was only a few feet tall. And fatter.

"Your bone stitching is done." Claus pointed at the skeletal structure that appeared in the translucent body. "Leg is normal. Your orbital socket is normal, too. Once you adjust to the additional body weight, your muscles will return to normal. The only thing I'm having difficulty with is the lung."

A white dot appeared on the left lung. Claus touched it.

"That might take some time–"

"Where's my wife and son?" Nicholas pushed the plate away, wiping his hands on his legs. "You tell me that first and I'll listen to whatever else you have to say."

Claus nodded for a long time, thinking. He took the coin and the body disappeared.

"This is a very bad time in our history."

Claus stood.

"You are the first person to be introduced to the elven race. Five thousand years ago, this would've been a time to celebrate. Instead, you arrived during the Fracture, when elven brother has taken arms against elven brother. During a time of war."

Claus lifted the coat from the hook.

"You may be our salvation, Nicholas. You may be our destruction; it's too soon to tell. But I can tell you this, your time here will not be pleasant. It will not be short. And you may bring extinction to the human race. BUT–"

He held up a single finger – crooked, knobby and stubby – before Nicholas could object.

"Your only hope may lie in the fact that your wife and son have escaped your fate. They are with the colony. That is your only hope."

Claus tossed the coat's hood over his head. The white fringe was grimy and the red fabric matted. He went to the wall and stopped. He spoke without turning.

"I will do what I can for you, Nicholas."

And then he stepped out.

When he did, the bench lit up. The snowy scene was back.

And there was a tent in the middle of it.

Nicholas saw the polar ice on the bench.

It was white and pristine. And moving! Snow drifted over the surface, occasionally swirling in small twisters. In the middle of it, he saw a small green tent wedged into a snowdrift.

Our tent!

Nicholas reached into the scene and waved his hand through the illusion.

Small figures appeared in the scene.

They were similar to polar bears with six legs. They bounded in from all directions. A dozen of them closed in on the tent.

Something fell from the sky.

An enormous reindeer – the color of snow – landed near the tent. It crouched and appeared to leap again, flying out of the picture but leaving something behind.

A metallic globe, similar to the one Claus placed in the box.

As the six-legged creatures closed in on the tent, snow began to swirl. It engulfed the tent and the creatures. The storm took the shape of a monster with a shifting face that looked around. Arms like paddles swiped across the ice, swatting the six-legged creatures away.

Nicholas couldn't see the small figure that emerged from the tent. It was difficult to tell if that was him wandering aimlessly into danger. He didn't see the creature that got close enough to claw through the rope.

He also didn't see himself fall into a trap as two more reindeer dropped from the sky.

Nicholas watched them pull a woman and a boy from the tent and leap away with them on their backs. Away from the storm.

Away from the six-leggers.

"Safe," Nicholas heard Cane say.

There were footsteps under the bench.

Cane was gone.

There were two mechanical figures in his place. One was female. The other was a boy.

They didn't have facial features, but they walked like the people he knew. The people he loved. Cane's magical figures walked like Jessica and Jon.

Nicholas picked them up. The faces were smooth and featureless, but the sculpture was flawless. *How did he know?*

It didn't matter. They were safe.

Safe.

16

Nicholas explored the room.

Boxes and rods and gears... stacks all over. Some in disrepair and others organized like spare parts. The main workbench, where Claus did his work, was the only surface kept clean and organized.

The surface appeared to be wood, but it felt smooth like glass. He held the mechanical figures of Jessica and Jon, but they were squirming like animals. He held them near the workbench and they climbed off, swinging their legs over the edge like they were enjoying the view.

How is this not a dream?

Nicholas buried his fingers into the beard. He'd never had much facial hair. He hardly shaved. Jessica always liked that.

He was staring at the little green tent – still there with the snowy landscape – thinking of Jessica and Jon, imagining they were warm and safe, that they would find their way back out of the North Pole and return home. The thought warmed him.

As long as they were safe, he could endure anything.

Anything at all.

The room suddenly cooled.

An elven entered the room. This one was not wearing a grubby red coat but rather darker colors.

And had bluish skin.

He stopped just inside the room. The floor crackled as frost crept over the icy surface from under his blue-tinged feet. His toes – like plums – wiggled.

Nicholas stared.

"I'm Jack, but call me *Your Excellence*." The blue elven flashed a hazy smile. "And we'll be cool."

Nicholas was fat but still stood over six feet tall, towering over the little blue man. *Oh, my frosty fat fanny I'll be calling you that.*

Jack twitched.

The smile faltered.

"You're kind of dumb, aren't you?" he said.

Jack walked around him, studying his body. Nicholas remained still.

"Claus has fattened you up," Jack said. "It's about time. You drag your wife and kid up here with silly little wolf furs and you expect to survive. You must have pea-brains. I'll give you warmbloods credit, though."

Jack smacked him in the crotch.

"You got balls."

Nicholas doubled over, resisting the urge to bang the munchkin on the blue dome.

Jack looked around the room awhile. The workbench caught his eye. He slid over to where the toys – Jessica and Jon – were dangling their legs. Jack looked at them from a couple different angles.

The grin returned.

A little sharper, this time.

He reached up – the fingernail almost black – and touched them.

The legs stopped moving.

"Where is Cane?" Jack looked under the bench. "You talk about stupid, there's an elven that got in the wrong line when they were handing out brains. Am I right?"

He poked the Jon figurine.

"I got to hand it to the little weirdo, he can build a mean toy. No doubt about that."

"Who are you?" Nicholas asked.

Jack turned. "I'm sorry, who are you talking to?"

Nicholas wasn't sure what he was getting at. They stared at each other. Jack raised his eyebrows. *Are you forgetting something?*

"Your *Excellency*." Nicholas ground his teeth.

"Ooo... Excellen*cy*. I like that. Good twist, warmblood. You just scored a point with me. Good for you."

Jack began walking, not sliding, around the lab. The floor crackled with frost beneath each footstep.

"I don't really matter to you, warmblood."

Jack leisurely inspected various piles, occasionally picking up a piece and turning it over and around before replacing it. He took his time returning to the workbench.

"To the elven, though, I'm just a little ole king, president, ruler."

Jack looked at Nicholas, giving him a moment to understand the royalty which he was addressing.

"In other words, I'm AWESOME."

"My elven have lived in peace a long time, but they're not so smart. They're not like me; they like peace too much. Sometimes you've got to cut an infection out, cause a little pain, to make things right again. It's a whole doctor thing; you probably don't understand."

Jack crossed his arms.

"Guess who the infection is."

Nicholas stared. Jack pointed at him and silently mouthed the words *YOU ARE.*

The snowy scene caught Jack's attention.

Nicholas stepped back. The soles of his feet became biting cold as he neared. Jack dragged his finger across the surface. The three-dimensional video started over from the beginning. He watched the six-leggers approach.

"Your lives are so short and insignificant," Jack said, watching. "You're like ameba."

Jack watched Jessica and Jon being rescued by the storm.

The room cooled a few more degrees.

"You're worse than that. You have the potential to wreck this planet, wasting your little time polluting the world with your little monkey-mind thoughts and greed. Claus tries to tell me that you'll evolve, you'll get it. But he's wrong."

Jack waved his hand through the image and it disappeared altogether. He turned to face Nicholas, his hands, once again, resting on his belly.

"He's wrong. And you're dead. Together, you're *dead wrong.* Do you like that?"

Nicholas noticed the resemblance to Claus. A resemblance that was darker and colder. "What do you want with me?"

"Nothing, really. Just use you to destroy the human race and save the planet, that's all." Jack raised an eyebrow. "In a way, you'll be a redeemer, just like me. Only uglier. There's nothing I can do about that, though. Sorry, ugly."

He investigated a few more items on the bench, picking them up and putting them down. He grabbed the cube that Claus stashed the metallic sphere inside and looked at it curiously. He ran his fingers along the edges, but the seams never appeared. Bored, he put it back.

"Well, see you later." Jack walked casually to a pile that was near the lounger. "You can go to sleep now, or whatever you've been doing down here. We'll be vacuuming out your memories here pretty soon."

And then he started to walk around again as if he was done with Nicholas.

"It won't hurt. I don't think."

"Just a second–"

Anger sparked inside Nicholas and flushed in his cheeks, but was just as quickly extinguished with a spike of cold. He felt like an icicle.

Jack smirked.

He finished looking at his item of interest. Nicholas couldn't move. He watched frosty veins spread across the floor. They crept beneath his feet, turning his ankles to marble.

Jack continued snooping.

AN ELVEN ENTERED the room wearing a uniform similar to Jack's. He touched the bands around Nicholas's wrists and ankles. They lit up.

Jack was in front of the toys again. Jessica and Jon had thawed. They were kicking their legs playfully again.

"Take him to the lab. Claus is waiting for him."

The bands warmed on Nicholas's flesh. They began to move, forcing him to take one step. Then another. A large, darkened outline appeared on the wall.

Jack touched the silver figurines.

Jessica and Jon crumbled like crushed ice.

17

Giant. For real.

Jack saw pictures of warmbloods, but seeing the real deal was a whole 'nother experience.

He was weak, though. The warmblood was small-minded. His thoughts were all over the place. No matter the size, anything that can't harness the mind is very small.

Jack found it very satisfying to put a cold spark under the warmblood's skin.

WEAK!

He had to hold back, really. Putting the hurt on that oaf would have been as easy as packing a snowball. Could've turned the warmblood into a Popsicle. But he needed him. He needed the warmblood – this Santa – alive for now.

He needed him to carry back the plague.

Warmbloods would adapt to climate change.

See, that's where Claus was wrong. Warmbloods were crafty. If Jack put the world back into an Ice Age – not if, but when – they would discover ways to survive. That's what they did. They were good at it. And when they survived, they'd continue with their self-centered beastliness and produce more offspring and live longer until there were more and more and more of the warmblooded miscreants until THERE WAS NO MORE ROOM FOR AN ELVEN!

They needed to be eradicated.

End of story, case closed.

Buh-bye.

But Claus insisted on patience.

They would need a backup of the warmblood. Just in case something failed, they would have another chance. After all, they couldn't be sure when another warmblood would fall into their lap. And Jack was tired of waiting.

My brother. So smart.

Jack had to admit, he was right. He always thought Claus was trying to stick it to him (and he should, why not; Jack stuck it to him) but he was right. When you're going to wipe out an entire species, you need to be patient, have a backup plan, that sort of thing.

Soldiers entered the lab.

They stood at the bench, waiting. Jack wiped the remains of the Jessica and Jon toys under the bench, where the idiot Cane could make another useless toy.

"Search the place," Jack said.

They moved like their lives depended on it. Because they did.

Just because my brother is right, doesn't mean I trust him.

18

Nicholas walked like a robot.

The hallway was half his height; it was for elven, not warmbloods. He walked hunched over with his head near the floor.

The guard slid in slow, short strides. Occasionally, they passed crossing tunnels or doorways to large rooms. Elven watched him march past. Some were holding coffee mugs, others whispering to each other.

They all stopped to see the warmblood.

Nicholas's back was aching when they stopped. The bands had forced him to crawl through the doorway. The room inside was small, but the ceiling high enough to stand. The bands stopped tingling. Nicholas straightened up.

There was a chair only a few feet away.

He stepped back, bumping against the wall.

So many shiny objects were around the chair. Things on poles and things with points. There were lights and discs and a large contraption hanging from the ceiling.

"Have a seat."

Claus was fifteen feet away in a dim corner. His coat was on a hook.

"What's going to happen?"

"Just have a seat."

"No–"

The bands yanked him onto the chair and forced him to lie back. When his head hit the pillow, the shiny instruments came to life. Whirring and flashing and pointing at his head.

"This is wrong. You know it, Claus."

Claus checked a lighted panel on the wall. "My people, we're good. You need to know that. We're a good people. We've lived in peace for almost forty thousand years."

He came over to the chair. It lowered as he neared until Nicholas was level with his face. Claus showed no emotion as he flipped switches on the things surrounding Nicholas's head.

"We unlocked the secrets to aging almost twenty thousand years ago," he said.

Impossible.

Claus stopped.

"You still doubt? You think this is some dream and you're about to wake up? None of this is magical. We are scientists. We decoded the human genome while humanity was still bashing each over the head with clubs. We corrected the accumulated errors in DNA that lead to aging and extended our lives for thousands of years by doing so, but we've always lived in balance with the planet. Do you know what humanity would do if they had the secret to aging?"

"How is this my fault?"

The tension around Claus's eyes relaxed. He walked to the other side of the chair and checked the instruments.

"You have such short lives and look at the messes you make."

"What does this have to do with anything?"

Claus slammed his fist on the armrest.

"HE WOULD NOT BE THAT!"

They stared at each other. Nicholas saw the pain, heard it.

"You're blaming us for Jack," Nicholas said. "Like we created him."

"Of course not. He was born with a mutation, one that made him cold."

He meant cold in more ways than one.

"But our people never would have followed him had humanity not been making a mess of the planet. They never would've embraced his maniacal ideas. He never would've seized power." He flipped one final switch. "If not for you."

Claus let a deep breath escape his nostrils.

He went over to the corner and returned with a needle and a vial.

He swabbed the blue veins on the inside of Nicholas's arm and drew blood into a syringe.

"I don't want to hurt you. But these are dark times. Hurt cannot be avoided."

Claus dropped three vials of blood into his pocket. He scraped skin from Nicholas's forearm and put that sample in a vial, too. He went behind Nicholas and put a band around his head that painfully tightened enough to light sparks behind Nicholas's eyes. Claus lowered the beastly machine that hung from the ceiling.

"We're stealing your memories, Santa. You'll experience them one last time, but then we will own them."

"Why are you doing this?"

Claus stepped back. "We're building a new you."

The room seemed to flood with light.

Nicholas was consumed by it. He went back to a time in his life.

He relived his memories.

For the last time.

19

Nicholas is two, standing at the top of a staircase, wearing his father's boots. It's so far down, but – like most two-year-olds – he isn't afraid. He takes a step and tumbles to the bottom.

The nanny is fired.

Nicholas is six years old.

He sneaks out of the window on the top floor and climbs to the roof to slide down a downspout. He runs the alleys of Mora, Sweden – his birthplace. The people in town know the Santa name because his parents became wealthy manufacturing clocks, knives and sewing machines. They spend their time rubbing elbows with politicians and throwing fancy parties.

None of that matters to a pack of kids.

Nicholas ends up on the roof of the town's theatre. He and his friends throw pebbles at the people exiting with their big dresses and fur coats and top hats. Everything is just fine until they see the buckets of water near the fire escape.

Nicholas doesn't hesitate.

He pours three gallons of cold water on a man and woman just as they come out from under the red awning, dousing her feathery head-dress and knocking the man's hat into a puddle.

They turn out to be Nicholas's parents.

The nanny is fired.

❄

THE THIRD NANNY isn't fired. She quits.

His parents are in Stockholm to attend meetings (parties) for a week. Nicholas is twelve when he plans his escape. He slips out the back door and disappears into the nearby mountains.

His parents had taken him out of school and had him privately tutored. Without his friends, he made less trouble and began day-tripping into the wilderness. He taught himself how to make a hook out of scrap metal and how to make a bow and arrow from a sapling and twine. He had created a shelter from branches and stones.

The week he escapes is the greatest week of his life.

He spends his days fishing and climbing, collecting berries and leaves. He has a book and sketches plants and wildlife. At night, he builds a fire and cooks what he catches, sleeping beneath a heavy blanket on a bed of leaves. He plans to go farther into the mountains and search for caves.

The unknown begs to be discovered.

His parents stop hiring nannies after that.

Everything changes when Nicholas turns sixteen.

"You're a man," his father says. "You'll need to learn how to behave like one."

That means cutting his wild hair and wearing black pants and a jacket and getting throttled with a necktie. He dresses as he's told, but he refuses to smile.

"You'll never find a girl, Nicholas," his mother says, straightening his tie and pushing the corners of his mouth up. "You'll need to smile."

He doesn't.

A formal ball is the last place he belongs.

Nicholas shakes hands when he's introduced. He says, "Yes, ma'am," when he addresses the women wrapped in fox furs and says, "Yes, sir," when he addresses the men puffing on long cigars. And when the night gets late, when the adults begin to slur words, he finds a dark corner and strips off the tie.

Then he sees her.

She's heavyset, but not fat. Big-boned. Strong.

She passes him with a tray. He notices the scabs on her knuckles, the bruises on her elbows.

He watches her deliver the drinks and then clear empty dishes from one of the tables. He never takes his eyes off of her, except when she goes into the kitchen. The night flies by in the recesses of the ballroom as he moves around to find better spots to watch.

She never rests. She's polite. Beautiful.

His heart is won and he doesn't even know her name.

It's past midnight.

She's clearing a table only ten feet away from Nicholas. Her hair is brown and pulled back. She's bent over the table, reaching for the empty plates. Nicholas could swear her eyes are green.

Two young men – older than Nicholas, but younger than most – stop to say something to her. Nicholas hears what the one says, the one with round glasses, who's sloshing a glass of wine onto the tablecloth.

He sees where the man put his hand.

The waitress whirls on the drunken aristocrat and plants her scuffed knuckles on his chin. The man tumbles backwards, knocking people over. Glass breaks and people scream.

No one has a chance to come out and fire the upstart girl. She's already stripped off the apron and wads it into a ball. The aristocrat jumps up, wiping his lip and examining the blood on his fingers. He's restrained by the guests.

Nicholas jumps out of his seat. If the inebriated man thinks to strike a woman – one that Nicholas has been slobbering over or not – then he's about to find out how mistaken he is. Nicholas steps in front of her, half-aware he has grabbed her arm. She twists out of his grip and shoves Nicholas away.

"All of you rich spoiled brats should learn some manners." And she fires the balled apron into Nicholas's face.

She marches out of the ballroom, slamming through the kitchen door. Nicholas watches.

If he stayed, if he didn't give chase, then he never would've found himself held prisoner by an ancient Nordic elven people.

But he goes.

He follows her through the kitchen and out the back door. Nicholas catches sight of her turning the corner at the end of the alley. His parents were going to be livid, but he would deal with that.

If he didn't follow her, he never would've seen her again.

20

Claus watched Santa smile.

He was stealing something very sweet from him.

They were just memories. Possessions. Santa was not his memories. Santa was something else. Memories were just recordings that molded his identity. The two were not the same thing.

But we're destroying him. I'm destroying a man. A good man.

Claus could tell he was a good man from a brief glimpse of the memories as they were downloaded. He didn't buy into possessions and wealth. He stood up for a woman with integrity and courage.

And I'm taking that away from him.

Claus felt sick.

That's why he had to tell Santa that the elven were good people, that they weren't what they had become. He wanted Santa to know what he was about to do to him. He wanted him to know that – deep down – they were good, too.

He wasn't destroying Santa. He was simply transferring the memories. First, they would download them from his brain into a database. Then, from the blood samples and skin scrapings, they would grow a clone of Santa that would look and sound exactly like the one sitting on that chair. And then they would download the memories into the body.

How would he know the difference? Would that still be Santa?

Claus couldn't answer those questions. He shouldn't even be

asking them. He was a scientist, not a philosopher. Claus only wanted to ask one question: What is good for my people?

What is good for the world?

SANTA WAS RECALLING the moment that would shape the rest of his life, the time he decided to follow Jessica around the corner, hiding in the shadows until he discovered where she lived.

Claus tapped the countertop.

The lights around Santa dimmed. The equipment pulled away from his head.

The subject was experiencing stress; psychological collapse was inevitable.

That's what he'd tell Jack.

Warmbloods were weak; they couldn't tolerate a complete memory drain at once. Patience was prudent.

And it will give me more time.

That he wouldn't tell Jack.

Claus filed the blood and skin samples to be transferred to another lab for analysis before the reconstruction began. He called for a carrier to take Santa back to his personal laboratory, where he would sleep.

Maybe he wouldn't remember that he'd been robbed.

21

"I've got something for you," Nog said.

They had stopped in a tunnel. Merry sighed.

"I'm sorry, dearies," she said as Nog searched for his bag, "I wanted to let you go at your own pace, but my husband has the patience of a hungry polar bear."

"Practical, Merry. I'm just being practical."

Nog dug deep into his bag. He pulled out two pairs of what looked like foot molds. They were flimsy and flat. The toes jiggled.

"What are they?" Jessica asked.

"They'll get you around faster." They jiggled like jelly. "They'll mold to the bottom of your feet. Go on, don't be afraid."

"Don't shame them, Nog," Merry said.

"I'm not shaming. I'm *encouraging*."

"Shhhhht."

"You shhhhht–"

Jessica took the smaller pair. They were malleable and spongy.

When she picked up her left foot – leaning on Jon when she did – the thing sucked against her sole and slid between her toes. When she had them both on, they gripped the floor like sandpaper.

"Oh, this is better," she said. "Much better."

Nog's mustache rose and his cheeks blushed. He nodded vigorously enough so that Merry could see, looked at her and winked. Then he gave her the thumbs-up–

"All right, all right. I knew they would work," Merry said. "I just didn't want you insulting them."

"What's insulting?"

"You! Telling them they're too slow!"

"I didn't say that. I simply offered–"

"WHOA!" Jon shouted.

He shot between them, sliding on one foot and waving his arms for balance. He was nearly out of sight.

"TURN YOUR FEET!" Nog shouted.

There was a distant *shoooosh*.

Silence.

Then laughter.

Jon came sliding back, turning his feet to the side. "It's like magic skating."

"Not magic, my boy. They simply have scales pointed toward the heels that grab the ice to propel you forward."

"These are fantastic, Nog."

"I'm sorry." Nog put his hand to his ear. "What did you say?"

"I said these are fantastic and thank you."

"One more time. I don't think everyone quite heard you–"

Merry elbowed her husband. "I got it."

There were many doorways along the tunnel that appeared as dim outlines on the wall. Jessica assumed they were rooms like hers. The tunnel, however, ended at a large circular room – a hub or town square. There was a large cylinder of ice in the center and around that were tables and benches, like a park setting. Elven were lounging around, in conversation or playing tabletop games or simply drinking from a mug.

The ceiling was quite low, as usual. Although the ceiling was much higher around the perimeter, enough that Jessica and Jon could stand. Like it had been carved for them.

Merry and Nog led them around the hub, pointing down tunnels and explaining this and that. "The dining hall is there. The observation room, there. That's the hospital, over there..."

All the elven, no matter what they were doing, stopped to watch them pass.

"Jon!" An elven with red hair waved. "Hey, Jon. Hi!"

Jon ducked to see Tinsel outside one of the doorways. He waved back.

"Do you mind if I..." Jon pointed in her direction.

Jessica nodded.

"Go along, my boy," Merry added. "You can meet Jocah another time. I'm sure she won't mind."

Jon ducked to slide over to Tinsel.

"Ah, Tinsel," Merry said. "Poor young lass has been such a loner for so long. She left her parents behind in the Fracture and spends all her time with the animals."

"Or the science lab," Nog added.

"The Fracture?" Jessica asked.

"When we left our homeland," Merry said. "We've been nomads. They almost caught us a few times, but it's difficult for them to keep up. We took all the technology with us. And the brightest minds."

"Well," Nog said, "all but one."

Hmm. "It's been almost one hundred fifty years," Merry said.

"Has it been that long?" Nog said, scratching in his beard. "Seems like yesterday."

"One hundred fifty years?" Jessica said. "That's... impossible."

Merry and Nog laughed.

"How old are you?" Jessica asked.

"Old enough, dearie. But not nearly the oldest. Jocah is eleven thousand years old."

Impossible.

"I forgot," Merry said. "Warmbloods are so short-lived. One day, your people may solve the science of aging, but you'll have to learn balance before that. Can't be filling the planet with warmbloods."

Jessica detected some bite in her words. Nog agreed.

22

J on never liked attention.

"Hey there." Tinsel grabbed each braid, thick as ropes, and twisted them nervously. "Fancy meeting you here."

"You going somewhere?"

"I'm going to the science lab. Want to come?"

"Anywhere but here. You're a scientist?"

"No, no. I just work there, when I'm not herding. Mainly just clean up and some assembly." She twisted her braids. "Maybe I play some, too."

They ducked through an open doorway that led down a low tunnel. Jon walked hunched over. They passed several doorways.

"How big is this place?" he asked.

"As big as we need it to be."

"And you desert it every two weeks and build a new one?"

"About that," she said. "We've been doing it so long, I don't really notice."

"Why don't you go back to the main... village? You know, make peace with the rest of your people."

"It's not good back there, Jon. The Cold One, he doesn't want peace."

"What's he want?"

She didn't answer. She slid ahead of him.

Jon couldn't really follow, even though he had the sliding soles on his feet. Tinsel stopped at the end and waited. Jon sat down.

"The scientists get cranky if you watch them, so just don't get too nosy," she said.

"You don't think they're going to notice me?"

She giggled. "They're not like the rest of the elven. They're consumed with their work. A giant could stomp through their bedroom and they wouldn't stop snoring."

Jon put out his hands. *Duh.*

Tinsel giggled again.

JON ASSUMED the hub was the largest room in the colony.

He was way off.

The lab appeared to be a hundred feet in all directions and filled with short, fat elven in white coats, some with glasses perched low on their noses and others squinting through microscopes. Not one of them looked at the awkwardly hunched-over giant blocking the entrance.

Jon sat down and pulled his knees against his chest. *Whoooaaa.*

"Almost all the greatest minds are in this room," Tinsel said. "It's what keeps us free."

There were benches and tables and stacks and stacks of objects in a somewhat organized grid layout. The random mutterings of lively discussion, debate and thinking out loud rattled the air. Jon's head was on a swivel, absorbing the strange colors and wicked shapes. One scientist was pouring metal shavings into a flask. The gray particles swirled in the glass container.

"Those are watchers," Tinsel said. "They're nanobots."

Nano-whats?

"I'm sorry. They're like miniature robots. Their circuitry is mainly subatomic, but they're so short-lived. The scientists are working on longevity."

"You're speaking another language."

Tinsel giggled. "Those particles are like sand, but they can ride air currents and record data, like video and stuff. We used to release them to see what the, um, *warmbloods*" – she blushed, like she uttered a bad word – "to see what you were doing."

"Elven are spies?"

"Not really spying or anything, just to see how your society was coming along. We know when you're sleeping, we know when you're awake. You have so much potential for good. And bad. Actually, come to think of it, we did send spies."

She covered her mouth, thinking.

"It was a long time ago, but there used to be elven that could tolerate the warm climate long enough to walk among your people. That was before we had the nanobots. They would bring back reports, but Jocah put a stop to it because it was influencing your culture."

"What do you mean?"

"Your language and arts, stuff like that. The elven spies weren't supposed to interact with anyone, but they couldn't help it. Words and songs and myths started showing up in your culture. Technology, too. We accidentally started the Industrial Revolution. You know the steam engine?"

Jon nodded.

"That was us. Jocah was afraid your people were learning too fast, that your technology was growing faster than your wisdom."

Jon felt like there was so much in the world he didn't know about.

"Anyway, we don't do it anymore. Once the Cold One took over, we took the nanobots with us so they couldn't use them. Their scientists are clueless. Well, most of them."

Beneath it all a faint buzz emanated from an object in the center: a wicked-looking thing with four metallic arms angling from the base of a spherical object, with electrical arcs dancing between them.

"That's the Monitor," Tinsel said. "It's what keeps us hidden, scanning the horizon for the Cold One's searchers. But it does more than that."

Jon followed Tinsel, stopping once to let a scientist with his nose buried in a manual walk by without notice. The closer he got to the Monitor, the more he felt the hairs on his body vibrate.

"This is the reason we're able to escape the Cold One."

The globe in the center of the Monitor seemed to pulse, throwing waves of bluish light over Tinsel's pinkish complexion. "Not only does it cloak our presence, but it's armed with an explosive nullifier. It can detect and detonate bombs with a wave frequency before they ever get near us. Pretty much makes weapons useless."

She turned to Jon without a smile.

"He'd blow us through the bottom of the Arctic Ocean if we didn't have this."

"Good thing," was all Jon could say. He looked around the lab. "Why is everyone working so hard if you've got this thing?"

"We have to stay ahead of him. They developed a timesnapper device that accelerates subatomic particles and could make time appear to stop."

Jon shook his head. *Subatomic what?*

Tinsel's smile returned. "If you had one, you could activate it and everything around you would appear to freeze in time. You could travel around the world in a single night. Fortunately, we invented one, too. If they activate their timesnapping device, ours matches it, so it's a draw. After a while, they stopped using it because it's such an energy drain."

"Is that what those are?" Jon asked.

Jon assumed the timesnappers were the metallic spheres, each precariously balanced and spinning on the tip of a narrow rod anchored in the floor. There were four of them, one stationed between each of the four arms of the Monitor.

Tinsel's eyes widened. "Those are the A-bombs."

"I thought you said you didn't have bombs."

"Not bombs... abominables. They are the guardians of our colony." She touched one of the spheres, causing it to spin a little faster. "You want to meet one?"

Jon looked around. "What do you mean... meet?"

Tinsel's hand moved so quickly that Jon didn't notice she'd palmed one of the spheres. There was just an empty space at the end of the rod.

"Did you just..." He looked around again. "I don't want you to get in trouble."

"I do it all the time," she said. "Remember when I said that sometimes I come here to play? Follow me."

JON COULDN'T BREATHE.

He dressed to come above the ice, but the wind was blustery and far below zero. Tinsel was just a smudge in the hazy swirl of snowflakes. He blinked away the tears. Tinsel was so short and so close to the ground, the wind wasn't affecting her like Jon.

He blinked again. She was still out of focus. He realized there were long, vertical strands waving around them, like hair follicles extending from the ice.

"What are those?" He put his hand out, but they moved out of his grasp.

"Wind harvesters. As the wind blows them around, the kinetic energy is stored below the ice. They're sensitive to objects, such as polar bears, and will retract so they don't disturb anything."

"You get all your energy from these?"

"Most of it. We also have tidal turbines in the ocean below the ice. Now, are you ready?"

Tinsel held up the metallic sphere.

Tiny lights flashed on the surface, racing around it. More lights joined up until the sphere looked like a globe of jiggling light. It was liquidy, oozing between her fingers. Snowflakes began to swirl around it. More snowflakes were drawn into the sphere's gravitational field. Tinsel tossed it and snow trailed like a comet.

The snowdrift was glowing like a beating heart. Jon stepped next to Tinsel. Just as he was about to comment–

The drift exploded.

Jon stepped back. Tinsel clapped.

Jon blinked away the tears. The swirling, quivering snow looked to be forming a body. He could faintly see the glowing globe inside. There were legs and arms. What looked like a squatty head.

It was a snowman.

A snowman with a glowing globe inside its chest.

Tinsel wrapped her arms around the snowman's leg. It bent down and wrapped an arm around Tinsel. Sort of like a hug.

"I call him Flury," Tinsel said. "He's the only A-bomb with person-ality. The other three are bores, believe me. They're just about the business of protecting us. Flury loves me."

Flury turned his head.

There were faint depressions that resembled eyes and a mouth, but they were no more than dark impressions. The eyes were wide and kind. The mouth, just a line that curved upwards.

Jon touched Flury's arm. It quivered, like the snow was still swirling but tight enough that it felt strong and solid.

"How does this work?" Jon asked.

"The sphere creates an energy field that manipulates the particles around it. Flury builds a body of ice and snow."

Tinsel stepped back. Flury plodded back a few steps, the snow legs crunching like freshly packed snow. He looked around, surveying the landscape.

"He's not real," Jon muttered. "It's just an illusion."

"He's as real as you and me."

"He's made of snow, Tinsel. That's not blood and bone."

"Is that what makes someone real, blood and bone? A body? Please, Jon. You're not your body any more than Flury is snow and ice."

Flury turned around. He pushed his hands (with fingers as thick as tree limbs) into his chest and pulled it open. Inside was the sphere, glowing and pulsing.

"Well, if he's that" – Jon pointed at Flury's sphere – "then what am I?"

"That's a question we should always ask." Tinsel looked serious.

It was so easy for something like Flury. The question of who he was, it was right there in his chest. Something he could grab and point to. Maybe the elven knew the answer. *Not so easy for a warmblood.*

Flury stomped holes in the snow. He seemed to grow with every step. He extended his arm; the hand opened. Jon shook it. Flury's hand engulfed his forearm.

"I'm Jon."

The thin line that looked like a mouth curved deeply. The eye spots sank wider and deeper. Jon took that as a smile. He wasn't real, but Jon liked him, nonetheless.

SPLAT!

A snowball exploded on Jon's head.

Tinsel was thirty yards away, balling up another.

Through the wind and snow and wiggly wind follicles, she was just a blur. But the blur was reaching down for another snowball. She seemed too far away to throw it from that distance, especially with any accuracy–

SPLAT!

The second one hit him in the chest so hard it knocked him over.

He barely saw it, like a bullet. He shook the snow off his face. Tinsel was already getting another. He couldn't hear her, not that far away, but he imagined she was giggling. She wasn't going to get another one off.

Jon scooped up some snow. Before he got up, before he could turn around, the third one hit him square in the butt, knocking him face first into the snow.

"You'll need some help!" she called.

Flury, with legs like tree trunks, stood over him with his hand out. Jon smiled.

"Build a wall, Flury."

He had a fortress wall, four feet tall and two feet thick. Flury moved too fast to see it happen.

"Ammunition," Jon said. "We need a pile of snowballs."

Seconds later, a pyramid of perfectly sculpted snowballs appeared. Flury was waiting for the next command when a snowball exploded on the side of his head. He absorbed most of it.

"You going to take that?" Jon said. "She just hit you with a snow-ball. I think she wants you to throw one back."

Jon looked over the wall. Tinsel had built her own fortress with a hole in the middle.

"You ever heard of Swiss cheese?" Jon asked.

Flury just stared.

"It has holes in it. Let's turn Tinsel's fort into Swiss cheese."

The smile returned to the snowman's face. Flury didn't reach for the pile. He simply made a throwing motion and snowballs rifled off the ends of his fingers, hitting the wall like cannonballs, punching gaping holes in it. They thudded with hollow sounds, like ice cracking, until the wall came crumbling down.

No Tinsel.

SPLAT!

The snowball came from behind him, knocking Jon into his own fortress.

And then the giggle.

Tinsel was behind them.

Jon smiled. He reached for his own cache–

EeeeieiiiiiiiiiiiiiiiiiiiiiiIIIIIIIIIIIIII...

The wind follicles were sucked down like strands of spaghetti.

"The alarm," Tinsel said.

Three spherical objects popped out of the ground, snow and ice swirling around them. Three more snowmen had formed.

Flury's head turned on a swivel. The eyes darkened and the ridges above them protruded. The wind picked up and the snowmen – all four of them – began to grow.

In the distance, Jon saw the first of the six-leggers.

23

Jessica followed Merry and Nog down a short tunnel. Merry and Nog stopped at the only doorway. They turned, but didn't say anything.

A melodic bell jingled.

"Do you want me to go in?" Jessica asked.

Merry held up a finger. *Wait.*

A pudgy female – shorter than Merry – slid out with her head slightly bowed, paying little attention to the three of them.

"All right, dearie." Merry gestured. "You may go inside."

"You're not coming?" Jessica asked.

"No," Nog said. "This is your journey."

Jessica stepped into a small room.

The walls were dark blue. The floor was striped and swirled like knotty walnut. On the right, a trail of water poured from the wall into a small pool. To the left was an ice sculpture.

And straight ahead – sitting comfortably – was the woman known as Jocah.

Her long braid was pure white; her face wrinkled in puffy folds that nearly hid her sky-blue eyes.

"Jessica, hello."

❄

JESSICA WAS GOING to speak first.

She had her entire speech laid out. First, she wanted to know where her husband was located and if they could help him and when. And then she wanted to know if they could help them get home. She had other questions, too.

But then Jocah spoke and they all dissolved.

"Please, sit." Jocah pulled her hand from the pocket of her tunic and gestured to a chair near the ice sculpture.

"I'll stand," Jessica said. "Thank you."

Jocah wasn't smiling, but Jessica had the distinct feeling she was. In fact, the room felt... sunny. It was warm and bright, like home should feel.

All her problems just felt... gone.

Jessica moved her lips, but nothing came out.

"Life strangely unfolds," Jocah said. "Would you say?"

Jessica nodded.

"One moment, you're sure you know what your life is. The next, you are inside a sheet of ice." Jocah rocked back and forth. "Life is often quite different than what we believe."

"Can you save my husband?"

Jessica practically spit the words. They flew like pebbles.

Jocah's thin lips seemed to curve this time. She stared at Jessica, rocking. Jessica felt like she was looking through her. Inside her. She felt like this ancient woman, in an instant, knew everything about her.

Jocah reached to the small table next to her and lifted a teapot, filling two cups. She did this slowly, purposefully. When they were filled, she handed one to Jessica.

"Tell me about him." Jocah sipped. "Your husband."

The tea was warm and oily. It started with a bitter taste, then turned silky and sweet, coating her throat.

"We were abandoned by our guides, left to die. We were barely surviving, but we decided to finish our quest to the top of the world. Our son, Jon, was snow-blind. While we were resting inside the tent, we thought we heard voices. Nicholas went to investigate."

Jessica paused.

"It was the last time I saw him."

She took another sip of tea. A knot swelled in her throat. Her head felt buzzy.

"Tell me more." Jocah rocked in her chair.

Jessica thought about telling her how they'd ended up on the quest to the northern regions. How she and Nicholas craved adventure and truth.

But then she told her something entirely different.

RICH PEOPLE LOOKED DOWN on street rats like Jessica.

They used her mother as a mat to wipe their feet and her father as a stepping stool. The rich wanted to sweep her brothers and sisters under the rug so they wouldn't get in the way. They didn't want the less fortunate spoiling all the fun.

She resented them for having when she did not.

Opportunity.

Nicholas was rich. He would be no different.

He waited outside their apartment building. He held out his hand to help her step over a puddle and she slapped it away. She shoved him against the wall, jabbing a finger in his face. *Go back to your world.*

The next day, he was there again. Hand extended.

He offered her an umbrella when it was raining. A coat when it was freezing.

Jessica ignored him, day after day.

Eventually, Nicholas stopped offering his help. He was still there, most days. He said *good morning*. He offered to carry the laundry she brought home to iron. She ignored him.

And even though she found herself looking forward to his smile, she told him to go away. The rich were cunning. They were deceptive. They were sharks that preyed on people like Jessica. She was dirty, unattractive. *He will hurt me.*

She was disappointed the morning he was not waiting. *Good,* she told herself. She could get on with the business of helping feed her family. But then she saw the gift on the bottom step. A red apple.

And the next day, a fig.

After that, an orange.

She was tempted to step on them. Instead, she took them inside and divided them into eight pieces: one for each of her little brothers and sisters. She took the littlest for herself.

Then came the morning when she plucked the laundry from the lines. She folded them, placing everything in a bag. When she got to the stockings, there were lumps at the bottoms. Each contained a small gift. Sometimes it was a toy or something useful like gloves.

She felt a bit of guilt. She kept the gifts because her family needed them. But she refused to acknowledge him. If the fool wanted to give her gifts, that was his business. It would be no different than finding such things in the gutter.

And then came the day of the bakery.

She was off to fetch a loaf of bread. It was not her usual route. She rarely bought bread at the bakery, but her mother had received a generous tip the day before. The smell of rising dough filled her head, lifting her off her feet. She was dizzy with a watering mouth. She couldn't help but tear a piece from the bag when the baker handed it to her. It melted in her mouth. Guilt nibbled at her, but she had another bite. And another.

She couldn't stop.

And while she stood inside eating a day's worth of bread, she looked out the window. A block away, she saw an old woman fall. Her cane sank in the mud. She crumpled into a heap.

Jessica saw a young man run to the old woman's side. He gently helped her to her feet. He walked her out of harm's way. He took his jacket off and wrapped it around her. He walked with her until they were out of sight.

Jessica's heart melted like the bread.

It was impossible for him to plan it. There was no way he could know that she was watching.

Nicholas.

"I DON'T LIKE the way this feels," Jessica whispered.

The sound of her voice startled her. She was back in the room with the small, old elven woman. She wasn't sure if she'd said any of that or if she just remembered it. Where once the warmth of his love filled her chest, there was an empty ache as cold as the ocean.

"Life is not about what we like, Jessica." Jocah's voice was soft and steady. "It wants to be experienced. It wants you to be present."

The ache felt bottomless. Hollow and barren. Beneath it was a quiver of fear, jagged like veins of toxic electricity. It went deep inside her, deep to the very core of who she was. Jessica felt the loneliness, the abandonment of life, the fear of rejection. She felt the things that had weighed on her as a child were still there. Things she tried to turn away from, to gloss over with Nicholas's love. To fill her neediness.

But now he was gone. She faced them alone.

"I invite you to stay with us, Jessica. To live with us for as long as you and your son need to live with us."

Jocah set the teacup down and dabbed the corners of her mouth.

"What about my husband?"

"We will find your husband." Jocah stood up and tucked her hands into the folds of her tunic, once again. She appeared to be ready to leave. Or perhaps Jessica's meeting was over. She had so many questions.

Jocah smiled. This time, her thin lips curled upward.

And the room was warm again.

And when a high-pitched sound penetrated from outside the room, her warm gaze never wavered. Jocah remained present and relaxed.

"Jocah." Merry stepped inside the room. "We must evacuate."

Jocah blinked heavily.

"The six-leggers have located us."

24

---

ix-leggers.

S They were dingy, like dirty snow, galloping like six-legged polar bears. But fast, like wolves.

The abominables created a protective wall of howling snow and ice. Jon and Tinsel were inside the eye of the storm. The beasts tumbled backward under the assault of the four abominables. They merged together to become the storm.

But the beasts held low to the surface, creeping slowly through the assault. When one would near the eye wall, a blast of banded snow would bat it out of sight.

But there were more.

Elven began popping above the surface.

"Ten minutes!" Tinsel shouted.

Jon looked around. The snow was crowded with short, round elven. And then she was there. His mother was above the ice, standing almost three feet above Merry and Nog and the others.

Jessica waved. Jon started toward her–

The first beast broke the eye wall.

It hit the snow with its front legs, burying its four back legs to spring. Its eyes were black. The lips pulled back, exposing a double row of jagged teeth and black gums.

Jon stumbled back.

The thing saw him. It shifted its weight and shot from the snow like a spring-loaded weapon.

Saliva hanging.

Claws out.

KA-BOOOOM!

A WHITE FIST powdered the beast.

Flury swirled out of the eye wall. He stood as large as an elephant, digging his gorilla-sized arm into the snow and grabbing the six-legger. The beast roared and snapped and tore at the snowy arm. Flury reared back and flung it through the eye wall and out of sight.

And then he dissolved back into the storm.

Sleighs were on the surface, the reins ready and waiting. The six-leggers' roars were louder. The battle was creeping closer.

SPLOOSH!

Donner landed.

The elven quickly hooked the sleigh and loaded. Donner crouched and leaped, rocketing through a hole that opened in the eye wall.

Blitzen, Dasher, and Prancer were loaded and gone.

Half of the elven had evacuated.

Jessica had boarded the sleigh with Vixen, shouting for Jon to climb aboard. He watched her soar out of harm's way.

The largest group of elven emerged around the white-braided woman. They helped her into the largest sleigh.

Comet and Cupid were loaded and off. The storm held and the elven were nearly gone. Dancer was on the ice and the sleigh fastened–

SPLOOSH!

Ronin landed.

Jocah was safely aboard the sleigh that was secured to the fiercest reindeer of the herd. Jon grabbed onto Dancer's sleigh, propped his leg onto the floorboard–

RrrrrrrrRRRRRRaaaAAARRr!

JOCAH'S SLEIGH SPUN.

A six-legger broke through and smashed the sleigh's arms. Elven fell from the spinning sleigh.

Some shouted warnings. Others cried out.

Jocah was in the back of the sleigh.

The six-legger launched at her, legs extended and lips pulled back.

A rack of antlers swung around, knocking the beast out of the air. It tumbled across the snow. The abominables couldn't break out of the eye wall to help; there were too many six-leggers.

Ronin lowered his head.

The massive rack spread out like an impassable fence. His nose was fire red and snorting. His eyes were trained on the six-legger that was back on its feet, circling. Ronin kept between the beast and the sleigh.

Dancer waited for Jon. The elven shouted at him, but he couldn't climb aboard. There were elven still trying to harness Ronin. The sleigh couldn't launch and the lead reindeer couldn't hold still.

"Go!" Jon slapped Dancer.

The six-legger lunged at Jon. Ronin swung his antlers into its path, batting it back. Tinsel helped Jon lift the sleigh's arms. Ronin backed into place while watching the six-legger get back to its feet. The arms locked onto the harness with a solid click.

Jon helped the remaining elven into the sleigh. The last one was unconscious.

The reins lay unmanned over the front of the sleigh.

Screams.

Two more six-leggers were inside.

They spread out. Ronin couldn't stop them.

Jon jumped aboard and grabbed the reins. Tinsel slid next to him.

He heard the six-leggers' roars. He smelled their foul breath – the stink of rotten meat – as Ronin launched. Tinsel shouted.

The wind-shear bubble isn't up.

Subzero wind blasted Jon. His body temperature plummeted.

He wouldn't remember anything.

25

C laus sat at his workbench.

The surface was covered with tools and parts. He cleared off a space, punching buttons that appeared on the desktop, moving them with the tip of his finger. Sometimes he combined the illusory shapes, other times he drew a line between them, depending on the bond he wanted.

It had been months since he'd invented anything, not since he refined the sky-eye that allowed them to monitor the North Pole from above with snowflake-size monitors. He knew it was another step towards capturing the rebels, so he tried to slow the progress down as much as possible.

With all this technology, WHY CAN'T WE FLY?

Claus explained the physics that made it difficult, but if he was honest, he just didn't want to do it.

Nicholas snorted, smacking his lips in a fitful sleep.

Claus slid off the stool and checked his vital signs. He dropped the coin on the floor and watched the image appear, standing next to the head of the recliner. The bones had healed nicely. Even the lung had come along better than expected.

Cane clutched Claus's sleeve as he stood on his toes to put his latest toy on Nicholas's lap.

"Santa," Cane said.

"Very kind of you, Cane."

Claus picked up the toy. It was an amazing likeness of Jessica. Cane had seen some of the memories and fashioned the toy sculpture from scraps of pliable molding that allowed him to develop the facial features.

It was a nice gift, but would it remind him of what he was missing? Or would he not even be aware of what he once had?

"Is that what you're doing with your time?" Jack's voice dripped like icy slivers. "Playing with toys? Tsk, tsk, tsk... someone needs to grow up."

"We're checking vitals, Janack. Keeping him healthy."

"Is that it? You and the little one."

Cane hid behind Claus and didn't bother peeking out.

Claus went through the motions of checking the pulse and listening to Nicholas breathe. Something fell off the bench, tinkling on the floor. It began raining spare parts.

"Someone told me the memory drain was not complete." Jack slid his arm down the bench, shoving everything to the end. "I told them that was a lie. I told them my brother wouldn't do such a traitorous thing and that liars are filthy. And then I froze his head because it can't be true."

"A dead warmblood is no good."

The bench was cleared with a final crash.

"YOU'RE REALLY STARTING TO PISS ME OFF!"

Claus picked up the coin. Cane shuffled behind him.

"You think you can't be replaced?" Jack asked. "You think I won't freeze your head just because we ate cereal from the same box?"

"No," Claus shot back. "No, I don't."

"*Then stop dragging your feet.* You and your half-baked son are down here playing with dolls when I WANT THIS WARMBLOOD'S BRAIN EMPTY."

Jack seized the toy. It shattered on the wall.

Cane crawled under the back of Claus's coat.

There was a long moment where Jack's lips were moving, like he was singing a silent song. His face was like a blackberry. When it lightened up, his lips stopped.

"You serve me, I serve the elven. Through me, you serve them. If you don't, I stick my finger where the sun don't shine. Comprende, stupido?"

Claus did not react.

"Trust me," Claus said, "I serve the elven and I am the scientist in this room. If I say that a complete memory drain would've killed him, THEN IT WOULD'VE KILLED HIM!"

Their bellies touched.

WHEN THEY WERE BOYS, they would shove each other around the room with their bellies. The one who fell was the loser. Much of the time, they would fall down laughing.

When they got older, there were fewer laughs.

Each time Claus won, Jack would throw something. First, at a wall. Then at Claus. The last time they ever played the game, Jack cleared Claus's desk onto the floor.

Jack smiled. With all of Claus's belongings on the floor behind him, he was remembering, too.

"YOU HIDING SOMETHING, YOU SLY DOG?" Jack asked.

"What could I hide? You search my laboratory whenever I'm not here."

"Oh, that." Wicked smile. "I didn't know you knew, but I also don't care. I'm keeping you honest, fat boy. Maybe you want to tell me what you're hiding so as not to get caught in a lie. Mmm? Maybe-perhaps-kind of?"

Claus did not flinch. His eyes, calm and unblinking. "Everything I have is on the floor. Help yourself, Janack."

Jack expected a hint of deception, but Claus was open. Jack sensed his thoughts. Everything he was working on was right out in the open. If he was lying, it was well disguised.

Pawn entered. "Excellence."

Jack continued staring at Claus. "Continue."

"The six-leggers have located the *rebels*."

The wicked grin returned. Shock finally lit up Claus's face. Jack pitter-pattered his hands and, very quietly, said, *"Yaaay."*

Claus stammered. "How did you–"

"You're not the only bright one in these here parts, my brother," Jack said. "I got some scouts to uncover one of your discoveries."

Claus was confused. Everything he'd done was sitting on his workbench. There was nothing that could lead them to the colony.

Jack gestured to Nicholas.

"The warmblood? Hello?" Jack tapped his head and frost poofed off his fingertip. "Think about it. Think how a warmblood thinks and then let me know when you get it."

To follow him? What was unique about–

"Oh." Jack turned to Pawn. "I think something... yeah, I think something's happening."

Warmbloods' brains operated differently than anything on the North Pole. They could detect brainwaves and develop an algorithm to identify warmbloods.

And the colony has two of them!

Jack tapped the workbench. A hurricane of snow and ice appeared in miniature detail.

"This is exciting," Jack said.

The battle unfolded on the workbench.

Six-leggers were being tossed around like pillows. (Jack winced. What he could do if Claus could develop the abominable weapon for him. He could set them loose on the ice, rooting through every ice floe until the warren of rebels was dug up.)

The six-leggers were persistent. They pushed through the gale-force winds.

"You'll kill them!" Claus shouted.

"Not kill," Jack said, deliciously. "Maim, perhaps, but not..."

An elven narrowly escaped the six-legger's vicious jaws.

"Okay, yeah, they'll probably kill them."

When the last sleigh escaped and the abominable storm settled, leaving the six-leggers empty-handed, Jack slammed his open palm on the bench. "Oh! Soooo close! Man, did you see that one, it almost ripped the weasly little arm off that one elven."

Jack walked away from the scene with his hands clasped over his belly, humming a little song to himself. Claus noticed that Nicholas's heart rate had doubled, but he lay still with his eyes closed.

"The end of the Fracture is near, brother." Jack raised his arms. "HURRAY FOR ME! We got them on the run unless they desert those warmbloods, and I think you know what they'll do."

Jack shook his finger at Claus.

"They ain't got the balls to do that. Not like Uncle Jack."

Claus hadn't moved.

"Prepare a message." Jack gestured to Pawn. "I want to make them an offer they can't refuse."

26

The rebels escaped.

The snow settled as the abominables deactivated. The abominable spheres whisked into the back of the last sleigh.

The six-leggers shook the snow from their fur, sniffing around. They would find nothing.

This time.

How could I be so stupid?

Claus missed the obvious. Of course they could track the warmbloods; their minds operated differently than elven. All it would take was an adjustment to scanning equipment to find similar patterns in the Arctic. If he would've thought of it first, he could've skewed the data so that it wasn't so different. They never would've suspected it.

This is bad.

As long as they had warmbloods, they wouldn't be able to hide.

Claus was careful not to glance at the cube that contained the sphere. He busied himself with organizing the workbench. He pretended to reorganize the shelf and found the cube still there. Surely they'd picked it up, inspected it, shook it and pried on the corners. Clearly it worked. It was still there.

It was bad now. But if the contents inside the cube were missing, it would be even worse.

Nicholas moaned.

Claus finished cleaning up and checked his vital signs. He would wake him soon enough to find balance with the gap in his memories. It wouldn't be easy. Nicholas had lost a third of it. There would be confusion and anger.

But, soon, he'd lose even more.

Claus would try to delay it. Maybe Jack would be distracted with the latest developments, but eventually he would come asking for Nicholas. Eventually, he would have to do it.

He left Cane under the bench, assembling another toy. He needed time to think about his next move. There would be few left, each one more and more important.

Each one, possibly his last.

THE OLD ONE

For whom the bell jingles,
It jingles for thee.

27

"He's stable," Dr. Garland said.

Jessica was on her knees next to the bed. Jon's skin was sickly pale and shiny. Jessica touched his forehead. It was impossibly cold.

"I'm sorry," she said. "What did you say?"

Tinsel wailed at the foot of the bed. Tears spilled over her fingers as she covered her face.

"His body temperature dipped below eighty-six degrees," the doctor continued. "Any further and we would have lost him. He's stable, for now. That gives us some time to consider some options."

"I'm sorry, I'm sorry," Tinsel wailed again. "This is all my fault. If I didn't sneak up to show him Flury, none of this would have happened. Now they almost caught us and... and... they almost got Jocah and... now Jon is..."

"It's all right, dearie." Merry consoled her. "It wasn't your fault. The six-leggers couldn't have gotten there that fast. Somehow they already knew."

"It was a good thing you were up there, too!" Nog chimed in. "If you weren't ready, Jon wouldn't have been there to save the day. He's a hero, he is. Jessica, that boy is a hero. Saved us all."

"Options?" Jessica said to the doctor. "What options?"

Dr. Garland pushed her round spectacles up her cherub nose until they were half buried in bushy white eyebrows.

"You may not realize this, Jessica, but your body temperature is hovering around fifty degrees. You've been responding to our actuating treatments to adjust to Arctic climate. You're not made for this weather any more than a polar bear is meant to write a book."

Jessica was heavier than she'd ever been. She thought it was just the fatty food, but now she realized it was the blubber. But it was more than that.

My body temperature is fifty degrees!

The weather hadn't changed. She had.

"What can you do for him?" she asked.

"I'll have to talk to my peers."

"Talk to *me*. WHAT CAN YOU DO?"

They looked at Jessica.

It's my fault.

If she hadn't left his side, if she hadn't let him wander off with Tinsel, he wouldn't have been out there. She could've protected him. She would've been with him. And maybe nothing would be different, maybe he'd still be comatose in a bed, still...

It's my fault.

"I'm sorry," she whispered.

"It's all right." The doctor pushed the glasses up. "We're all under a bit of stress."

What right did she have to come into their colony and demand that they help? She should be dead. At least with the elven they had a chance.

She squeezed Jon's hand and went over to Tinsel. Jessica wrapped her arms around her and together they cried.

28

The hub was still enormous at the new site.

There were fewer amenities. In fact, everything was simple. Rooms were the color of blue ice. Furniture was limited to beds and tables. Everything was ready for a quick grab and an immediate exit.

Jessica and Tinsel didn't leave Jon's side for days. His breath came in even strokes. His pulse was steady. He remained stable. Remained hopeful.

Remained asleep.

Merry and Nog insisted they come to the hub. *A critical meeting,* they said. *Everyone in the colony is required to attend.*

Reluctantly, they left Jon in the glow of medical equipment.

THERE WAS VERY little room in the hub.

Every elven was present, pulling chairs from their bags to sit in orderly rows that surrounded a raised dais. Chatter echoed throughout the room in sullen tones.

Nog pulled chairs from his bag for Jessica and Tinsel. They nestled into them, stiff-looking, yet surprisingly comfortable. Merry sat with Nog in a two-seater. They held hands and, for once, sat quietly and waited.

The lights dimmed. Elven settled down.

Jessica turned in time to see Jocah – dressed in a long, white robe – walk down an open aisle, holding an assistant's hand for balance. When she stepped onto the stage, silence fell on the hub like a blanket. Her assistant helped her onto a simple-looking chair. It was anything but a throne. She thanked her assistant. The chair rose up so that she could be easily seen.

Jocah closed her eyes.

The dais turned in a complete circle at a very slow crawl.

"We left our people one hundred fifty years ago."

Jessica heard Jocah speak, but the words seemed to vibrate inside her head. She looked around, surprised. Those around her didn't seem disturbed.

"We left knowing life would be difficult. And, yet, we chose this path because life demanded it."

Jocah was now facing the other direction as the stage slowly turned; her voice continued to vibrate inside her.

This time with images.

Darkness crowded the edges of her eyesight until she was no longer seeing who was sitting next to her.

She was seeing a younger Jocah.

Jocah – her hair still braided and white but with strands of auburn – is on a veranda very high above the ice. The wind blows her braids. She's speaking to a male elven with a bushy white beard and a bright red coat that flutters in the wind.

"I will stay," he says.

"There is nothing for you here," Jocah says. "You must come with the colony."

"There will be so many left behind without a voice, so many without the courage to come. I will be their voice."

"He will destroy you."

Jocah waits for a reply, and when she doesn't get one, she takes his hand and presses it to her cheek. She leaves without turning back.

. . .

"So many have sacrificed," Jocah's voice echoed.

Jessica sees reindeer land around a fortress of ice. There are flashes. Confusion. Elven scatter from the exits, rushing to the reindeer and latching sleighs and climbing aboard. The reindeer leap into the darkness.

Jocah stands next to the sleigh attached to the reindeer with the shining nose. She looks back, despite the urgent calls from her assistants. She looks back to see the fluttering red coat atop the ice castle.

"You are all very brave to be here."

The visions faded.

"Now."

Jessica realized she was holding onto Merry. The room was spinning.

"Thank you," Jocah said. "Thank you for your courage."

We love you, Jocah! We will die for you!

Jocah smiled – genuinely and somberly – acknowledging them with slight nods. She was not above anyone in the room, only recognizing their presence. Her assistants held up their hands for silence.

She continued.

"Our secrecy is over. Scientists are not sure why, but we knew this day would come. We knew we could not avoid it forever. There were hopes that we could turn the course of action taken by our elven, but today brings a new day."

There were murmurs. *What's she getting at?*

"We have received a message."

The muttering grew.

The assistants walked around the stage, with their hands up.

One elven stepped onto the stage and delivered a cylinder. He held it gently, like an explosive.

"I have not viewed it." Jocah sounded tired. "We will all view it together."

She let it fall. It popped on the floor.

Bright light burst from it.

A figure took focus. An elven with bluish skin appeared. The entire room gasped.

He looked around the room. Then at Jocah, sitting expressionless. "Hello, *Mother*."

29

Mother?

Merry's and Nog's eyes were wide, transfixed by the bluish figure.

What does he mean? She can't be... she's too good... he's too...

Cold.

His skin, the color of a drowning victim.

"MY PEOPLE!"

He licked his finger and ran it over his hairless brow ridge.

"WHAT'S UP?"

He paced the stage.

He stared at the front row.

He walked through one of the assistants. He wasn't there in the flesh; he was a projection. But that didn't seem to matter.

Some elven whimpered.

"What's it been, like one hundred fifty years since you left without saying goodbye?" He stood with his back to Jocah. "I got to tell you, you're all still fat and ugly."

His tongue darted out and licked his dark lips.

"Listen, I've got some good news and bad news. Let's start with the good, you look like you could use some. The good news is that I come in peace. Peace, for your mind. Peace, for your hearts. Peace, from all this silly running around. I've got to be honest, it's been lonely since you left. There's emptiness in the palace. Your family and friends miss you."

He nodded emphatically.

"I'm not joking. I hear it all the time. Just the other day, some kid came up and was like, *Hey, uh, Excellence... I really miss, uh–*" Jack waved his hand at the front row. "Whatever your name is, right there... *Yeah, I miss him. When is he coming home, Excellence?*

"And what am I supposed to tell him? Never? Your mom and dad don't want to come home? They hate you, that's why they left? It's all your fault, kid. Sorry."

A sob escaped from more than a few.

Jack hit the sweet spot.

"Listen, I know some of you want to come home. *I* want you to come home."

Jack pulled a ball – silver and shiny – from his pocket and tossed it from hand to hand.

"You belong home, back in the palace, with your friends and family. Stop all this nonsense of calling the reindeer and jumping all over the Arctic. It's silly and stupid."

He held the ball between his finger and thumb.

"You're running around like a bunch of wild pigs."

The ball fell.

It didn't bounce.

It splattered into the images of wild boars. Coarse hair standing on their backs. Tusks curled from their lips. They squealed and bolted off the stage, into the crowd.

Elven screamed and jumped out of the way. The apparitions ran hog wild, uprooting elven until they evaporated somewhere near the perimeter of the room.

"I think you know about wild pigs."

Jack stared at Jessica.

A cruel smile touched his lips.

"So here's the deal."

Jack continued pacing.

"My brother and I know how to track you. From now on, we'll know exactly where you are, forever and ever. No matter what you do, we'll know it. Pick your nose?"

He pointed into the crowd.

"We'll know it. Lie to your wife, that too. Sneeze, fart, burp, I don't care... we will know when and where and why. So trust me when I say this, stop the running. It's all over. We'll be on your heels every day for the rest of your fat little lives and you'll never rest again, simple as that. Never, ever. We'll herd you like animals, run you until you collapse. And then, like good predators, we'll eat your hearts. How's that sound?"

He walked the perimeter of the stage while it slowly turned, and wiped the frost from his scalp.

"If you stop running, we stop hunting. And then, THEN, you get to come home. Think about it," he whispered. "*Hooooooome.*"

He pumped his hands at the crowd.

"Everyone, say it with me. Home. Home. Home."

The crowd fidgeted.

"Home. Home. Home. Come on, don't be shy!"

Jack trotted the stage, pumping his fist.

"Where's your spirit? Home!"

Elven began to squirm.

"You know you want it! Home!"

Jack sprinted.

"Home!"

Leaped.

"Home!"

Stood in front of Jocah, raised his hands to the ceiling, threw his head back.

"HOOOOME!"

AND WHEN HIS voice trailed off, when the echo faded, there was a distinct murmur beneath the silence. There were words that escaped the lips of a few.

Jack heard them and smiled.

He heard them whisper.

Home.

Jocah remained calm, hands folded on her lap.

He winked, simultaneously clicking his tongue.

"I know it's a lot to take in." Jack turned to the crowd. "I mean, who wouldn't want to live the rest of their lives running, right? You got more balls than me, I got to hand it to you. I like going to bed every night in a nice comfy bed, feeling safe and sound. I like to wake up with breakfast, maybe a cup of joe, and nowhere to go unless I want to."

He shook his head.

"But if some of you want to call a place home again, if you want to return where you're loved and wanted..."

He reached out to Jocah.

"Just take my hand. It's that easy. It really is."

Jocah did not blink.

"Here's the bad news."

Jack wiped his face. The smile was gone.

"If you want to play *Follow the Leader*" – he gestured to Jocah – "then great, follow the old white-hair. I won't make you surrender. Not all of you. I have a list of names that I want to meet my scouts at specific coordinates at a specific time. That will be in two days. If they do not report, there will be consequences. Trust me when I say that. CONSEQUENCES. And another thing."

He strolled behind Jocah and placed his hands on the back of her chair.

"I miss my mommy."

Several elven stood. They shouted. They protested.

"Shut up, will ya?" Jack waved at them. "I'm not done, you bunch of hoodlums. Let me finish and then have your little pity party. Cripes, you act like it's all about you."

Jocah's assistant raised his hands. Restless silence returned.

"Yeah, so I want your fearless leader, too. She's my mother and you've had her for one hundred fifty years, so stop your whining."

He peeked around the chair and spoke into her ear.

"If I don't see you in two days, I'll hunt down this rebel colony and feed them to the polar bears. How does that grab you?"

His complexion was as dark as his words. The room cooled several degrees.

"There you have it. Come home, everyone's happy. Don't, everyone's bear food. I don't know about you, but that's an easy decision."

The coating of frost became so thick that his face turned white. He faced the crowd.

Flecks of ice fluttered off his lips.

"Let the healing begin!"

Gone.

❄

THE ASSISTANTS SHOUTED, but their words were gobbled up in the chaos. Some were shouting to *fight!* Some were clinging to each other, and others were wringing their hands.

Jack stone-cold nailed it.

Merry and Nog whispered to each other. Tinsel left.

Jessica never felt so alone.

"Silence."

It was not shouted.

The word was effortless. It vibrated inside Jessica's head like Jocah simply spoke it directly into her mind.

Silence fell. All heads turned.

Everyone *felt* it.

Jocah stood without assistance. When one of her assistants reached out, she gently patted his hand. He stepped away.

Jessica could feel her own pulse in her throat.

"If anyone wishes to return home," she said, softly, firmly, "you may. You will not be judged. This life is not easy and I only ask that you stay of your own choice."

A few elven protested, but they soon became quiet.

The stage turned.

"We will not surrender."

And, just like that, Jack's message was wiped out of existence.

The room was filled with shouts. There were hands in the air. Hats and items of clothing flew in celebration. Jocah was unmoved. She stood still while the stage turned, so they could all see her. She embodied courage and certainty. She was committed to what life demanded.

We will not surrender.

30

hange.

C   Jocah's courage kept the elven from panicking. It didn't save them.

There was less chatter in the hub. Even less laughter. They had a job to do.

They were doing it.

Jessica didn't know if they were leaving or digging in to fight. She knew one thing. Jack looked right at her. He released those pigs and stared right at her.

I am a problem.

She couldn't worry about that. Not yet.

Jon's color hadn't improved.

He was still unconscious. Tinsel never left his side, her little hand on his forehead.

She didn't notice Jessica enter the room, focused on Jon like she could heal him with her thoughts. *Get better, Jon. Get better. Get better.*

It wasn't working.

The doctor entered the room.

She wore a long white coat that dragged on the floor. Her wiry hair was tied back, her cheeks puffy with wrinkles. She stopped near Jon's head and placed a small disc on his chest. Lights danced above it.

"Come in, Jessica," the doctor said. "It's time we had a chat."

Jessica struggled to move past the foot of the bed. Somehow, if she felt how cold her son had become, she would lose it. He was living. He couldn't die. As long as his chest rose and fell, everything would be all right. Everything okay.

She always thought she'd be better prepared for this moment. They'd decided to explore the Arctic as a family, knowing the chances of one of them dying weren't half bad. They knew the risks. They accepted them. For some reason, Jessica always assumed she would die first. It would've been easier that way.

"Is he... going to die?" Jessica said.

"Not if I can help it." The doctor slipped the disc back into her lab coat. "His organs are functioning at minimum capacity. If he wasn't in this lab, he wouldn't be alive. I'll be honest, his chances are slim."

"Is there anything...?"

"We have options." The doctor sighed. "Well, I should say an *option*. I'm afraid that everything we can do would require long-term care. Long term is not something we have anymore, not since *the message*."

She cleared her throat.

"We're going to be on the move every day. I'm afraid that will be too much for most of our treatments."

"You said there was an *option*." Jessica touched Jon's foot. Even beneath the covers, so cold. "What is it?"

"His body hasn't been responding to treatments. I suppose it's because he's younger, his body fighting the changes. It's why he was injured so badly when the sleigh launched, flash-freezing him."

"But you can fix that?"

Another sigh. The doctor sank her hands into her pockets and stared.

"Doctor?" Jessica stepped closer. "You can fix it?"

"We'll have to be more aggressive. There's a chance..." She looked at Jessica. "There's a chance it won't work. And if it does, he may not recognize you."

Jessica stopped and touched her face. There was a sudden chill, like she'd missed the bottom step and started falling.

"But he'll live."

The doctor nodded. "I wish I had better news, but I'm afraid we're doing all we can."

Jon was so still. His skin so pale. Lips so lifeless.

He won't know her. He would forget her, is that what the doctor is saying?

She would lose her son.

But he would live.

He would live. And that's what mattered.

That's all she wanted.

"Jessica?"

How long had she been there, nodding like a mental patient? Merry and Nog were behind Tinsel, who was looking at her with concern. The doctor was, too.

"Do it, please," Jessica whispered. "Let my son live."

The doctor muttered something. Her aides entered the room and began connecting wires, attaching patches to his arms and face and legs. They took his shirt off. His chest was so emaciated, she could count the ribs.

She forced herself to look at him, to remember her son at this moment. What he looked like. It made her decision easier.

Now for the next difficult decision.

"Merry. Nog." Jessica began to exit. "A word, please."

31

J ack licked his lips.

He tasted the residue of victory. And it tasted so *goooooooood.*

One hundred fifty years.

That's how long he'd waited to deliver that message.

He'd stood in front of the mirror *at least* a hundred times, practicing his speech. He imagined the stupid look on his mother's face, the looks of horror on the rest of those traitorous vermin.

The real thing, though, was delicious.

It melted on his tongue like an after-dinner mint. It buzzed inside his brain, made him woozy with delight.

His mother was so old.

She was ancient, sure, but she looked like a reptile with a white braid. There was a slight twist in his delicious buzz – a rotten thud in the pit of his stomach, like the bad side of a peach – when he thought of her all old and decrepit. She would die with those scum, those common folk.

Like she was one of them.

Sad.

Disgusting.

No wonder he was king.

He wanted the scientists.

That was it. Not the rest of those dorks. Those dirty rebels would go for a swim. They'd get dropped fourteen thousand feet to the bottom of the Arctic Ocean.

They'd get clean down there.

And once he had the scientists (he hated to admit it, but he needed those brainiacs), there would be no reason to keep Claus. He was slow and Jack always wanted to be rid of him for about ten billion reasons. He only needed one reason, though, and only one reason came to mind.

I hate him.

And, really, what other reason did he need?

Claus was a fat loser. End o' story.

Jack would go with the guards to meet the scientists. He anticipated the taste of victory back on his tongue when they arrived, heads down and tails tucked. Oh, it would taste sweeter than sweet.

Drool fell off his lip.

He slurped it back.

Yeah, he would meet them. They knew he was telling the truth about their secrecy. It was over. Thank you, warmbloods.

How I hate them, but maybe not as much.

THE DAY WAS NEAR.

The rebels had not moved.

And... *AND...* they were only sensing one of the warmbloods instead of two, which could only mean one thing – one delicious, mouth-watering thing.

One of them was dead.

No monkey-mind meant no monkey.

Oh, well.

It was bittersweet, though. If the other kicked the bucket, they wouldn't be able to track them. Time was running out. They would have to surrender. I mean, the only way they could avoid Jack was to abandon the other one.

Or kill.

And they wouldn't do that.

Old mother didn't have it in her to do that. That was why she left.

Three of his guards entered.

Jack held out his arms. They removed his coat. They were careful not to touch him.

They slid a long white robe with blue trim over his arms and buttoned it up the front. It was his formal wear. He would wear it to rule when this silly little Fracture business was all over. And when he returned from the expedition, he would attend a formal gathering to celebrate his victory. And begin a new era.

They could move forward with climate change so that the world would once again freeze. And then they could begin snuffing out the warmbloods by first sending Santa back with an infectious disease. One that would kill every single one of them.

And the ones it didn't, he would finish.

Until the world belonged to Jack.

I mean, to the elven.

32

The wind was fierce.

Claus pulled his coat together to keep it from flying open. The sun was a hazy disc near the horizon. The night sky was light gray. The white landscape unblemished.

He had been on the plateau on top of New Jack City long enough to feel the cold. It was bitter and unforgiving, stripping away the emotions snarling inside him.

He didn't like these feelings.

He didn't like feeling helpless.

And that's what he was. Jack was unstoppable now.

There once was a time when he thought he'd stop Jack, a time when he believed that he could protect the rebels until their scientists developed something to overthrow his tyrant brother. No more. The game was nearing an end.

Victory goes to the Cold One.

Once the rebel scientists were back in New Jack City, it would only be a matter of time – a short matter – before they helped Jack find the rest of them. He would tell them that he wanted them back home, that he only wanted to heal the elven.

And then he would crush them.

He only had himself to blame.

❄

WHEN THEY WERE ten years old, Claus saw what his brother was becoming.

That was the year his skin began turning blue and his hair fell out. The elven never made fun of him in front of Claus, but he knew what they were whispering. He knew they thought he was a freak. And Claus was his brother.

Twin.

They were right.

Jack would lurk around by himself when everyone else was playing. When he joined the games, he just fell down and got in the way. And then he'd get angry and his skin would turn dark blue.

And that didn't help.

Where you going? Jack asked. He asked that a lot. *Where you going, Claus? Where you going?*

And then he'd follow him. He'd follow him to class or outside or follow his friends. He was always there, just following and staring and that was it. He was Claus's freak shadow.

And others were whispering about him.

Claus had a crush on a girl. He sculpted a rose from ice. He was going to give it to her after class and maybe ask her to the dance. Claus looked in the mirror and straightened his collar–

Where you going?

He lost control. He snapped. He couldn't stop his hand.

It hit Jack under the chin and sank into his fleshy neck. He threw open the closet and pushed his brother inside.

JUST GO AWAY! NOBODY WANTS YOU!

Claus shook his hand. It was numb.

Jack had become so cold that just his touch had frozen his fingers.

He'll be dangerous one day, he thought.

But Claus took his ice rose and left his brother in the closet. He could hear the weirdo singing a song.

Something galloped away from New Jack City.

The trail left behind looked like a stain.

Jack's posse.

Claus opened his coat to let the subzero air chill his anger and shame that spilled in his stomach.

I failed you, Mother.

He watched them until they disappeared in the distant haze. He couldn't stop them. Not now. But there were still things he could do.

Claus went inside. He needed to get to his lab.
He had lost the battle, but perhaps not the war.

33

The sleighs were loaded.

The reindeer made their leaps, one by one, arching across the gray sky to find another home, one the Cold One wouldn't find. Tinsel was in the back of the largest sleigh, next to an enclosed box that contained Jon Santa. It looked too much like a casket. Tinsel rubbed her fist on the clear window. A pink hue had already returned to his face.

She hoped it was working.

Please, keep working.

She rested her arm on the box and refused to look back at the ones the colony left behind. Those two wouldn't be following them to their new home. They were going to stay back and survive on their own.

There was a chance they would never see them again.

And with Jon already fighting for his life, she couldn't look back at more sacrifices the colony was making. There were just too many. She looked ahead at where they were going, not where they had been.

What they had done.

34

Jack savored the ride.

The six-leggers galloped with a smooth gait, pulling his enclosed sleigh without hitting bumps. The rails – cutting through the snow – soothed like a lullaby. He sat back eating frozen sardines, nibbling off their frozen heads. He swirled the tails beneath his tongue, wishing he could eat them thawed so he could feel their soft bellies, but they froze as soon as they hit his tongue.

Everything, always frozen. He was used to that.

When the sleigh slid to a stop at the designated rendezvous, the guards unhooked the six-leggers. The sleigh folded open. First, the roof pulled back, followed by the walls clopping beneath the chassis. It transformed from a sleigh into a throne befitting an emperor.

Oh, yeah.

The guards took positions off to the sides so they wouldn't obstruct the view of the oncoming party. He wanted the rebels to see him in all his glory. He considered knocking a hole in the ice and throwing one of the guards in it so the rebels would know that – if they pissed him off – they were going for a swim to the bottom of the ocean, baby. He decided against it because, as it turned out, his best guards were with him. If he'd thought of it earlier, he would've brought one of his flunkies for the demo.

There's always later.

As the sun dipped near the horizon, Jack began to fidget. The time was almost up. He thought they would've appeared by now. Unless they were planning to arrive on one of those dreadful reindeer which, actually – when he thought about it – would be sweet. They'd trap the beast and have enough DNA to start cloning their own.

Jack licked his lips. He tasted sweetness.

"Party, advancing."

Jack sat up, slightly disappointed to see a large sleigh. He realized his shortsightedness. He should've demanded they arrive on a reindeer, but, all right. That's okay. The scientists were coming. He began laughing.

You can't eat the cake all at once.

The guards looked at Jack and turned away when he growled.

The sleigh appeared to be self-propelled instead of pulled by a beast. No big deal, Jack had sleighs like that. They were energy hogs and Jack liked to have his six-leggers lead the way, so if those smarty-pants thought they were showing him up, then the joke was on them.

The sleigh was big and boxy and enclosed, just slits for seeing from the inside. It looked like a tank. Like a...

Jack stood.

They wouldn't dare.

Jack liked sitting in an open sleigh. It was so refreshing.

But he was vulnerable. He could take a snowball right to the jibs if he wasn't watching. He couldn't take a chance, not with the other sleigh coming.

Transparent shields folded over the top and snapped into place. Jack was protected inside an impenetrable box. Nothing could touch him.

Better.

Now, if the rebels had a mental breakdown and decided to send a weapon instead of the scientists after he *asked them so nicely,* THEY WOULD BE SORRY!

The guards raised weapons. The sleigh-tank barreled across the ice, hitting an ice ridge and nearly flipping over, gliding on one track before regaining balance.

Jack called the six-leggers to stand in front of him. They would absorb the impact if the sleigh tried to ram him. He shouted at the guards to get in front of them. That thing would have to plow through all those bodies before it reached him–

The sleigh-tank heaved forward – the weight shifting to the front end. The rails slushed in the snow with an icy grind.

Slowly, it stopped fifty yards away.

The guards remained with weapons locked and loaded.

Nothing happened.

The sleigh was large enough to hold a party of scientists. But it wasn't moving. It sat on the ice, waiting. It could be a trap, so Jack waited. And waited.

"PAWN!" Jack shouted through the transparent walls.

Pawn was out front. He looked back and Jack flicked his hand at him. *Go see.*

He took the guards with him. They advanced, warily.

The six-leggers growled.

One guard reached for the door. It snapped open and he jumped back, weapon quivering. Pawn shuffled closer, closer and closer; pushed it open with the muzzle of the weapon and – slowly, ever so slowly – looked inside. He poked his head in first.

Leaned in.

Then climbed inside.

"What is it?" Jack shouted. "What's in there? TELL ME WHAT'S IN THERE!"

The other guards ran up to the door and looked inside. They leaned inside, too. The six-leggers were nervous, stamping the ice and puffing clouds. Jack wished they were attached to his sleigh. It'd be cool if he was, like, fifty more yards away.

He was sure the sleigh-tank ate them.

Pawn jumped out.

"Excellence." He was out of breath. "Come see."

"Are they in there?"

"No, Excellence, you just got to–"

"Wait, what do you mean... *no?*"

"Er, maybe you should come see."

Jack stood on his toes like he might somehow get a better view. "Is it a trap?"

"No. I don't think so."

"You DON'T THINK? You're a guard, dummy. Is it a trap or not?"

"You just have to look, Excellence. You don't need to go inside, just peek in and look."

Jack glanced again. He called the six-leggers back to the sleigh and ordered the guards to hook them up. They pulled the sleigh.

"Slower," he muttered. "Slower, but closer."

The six-leggers stutter-stepped ahead. Jack jerked back and forth. He slunk down in his chair. It was bigger than he thought. They pulled up alongside it and the shadow fell across his puny sleigh.

"Okay, stop," he said.

The door was open and he could see now, but it was dark inside. All the guards had climbed inside – all ten of them. And Pawn climbed in next, swallowed by the darkness like it was a blanket of black fog.

Pawn's hand emerged, waving Jack to come inside.

"Is it a trap?" he called through his hands.

"No," they called.

They wouldn't come out. Even after he demanded it.

Jack balled up his fists and bounced them off his thighs. If the scientists weren't in there, *his head was going to explode.*

"All right, okay," he muttered. "Stop being a little girl; don't be scared. Don't be scared; it's just a sleigh that looks like a tank, that's all. Go see for yourself, that's all."

Siiiiii-lent night,
Siiiiii-lent night.

JACK TAPPED the protective shield and climbed off his throne.

He felt naked out in the open like that, but the cold felt good. His lips moved while the song played in his head.

The tank was some sort of silver metal. The handles along the door felt good in his hands. He stepped onto the bottom rail and pulled himself near the opening. The darkness was thick.

He held his breath.

He stuck his head inside.

It was a big tank.

Even bigger inside. Almost as big as his room back at the palace. The scientists did a remarkable job of expanding the space inside–

Scientists!

WHERE ARE THEY?

It was empty inside.

Empty, except for a table with a little glowglobe that hardly penetrated the dark. Something was next to it.

"How do you think they did it?"

"Ahh!" Jack jumped.

He hadn't noticed Pawn standing next to him, just inside the door.

Pawn waved his hands. "I mean, somehow they made the inside–"

"Shut up and go get that." Jack shoved him at the table. "I'll be in my sleigh."

Jack was back in the comfort of his impenetrable glass room when Pawn came out. He jumped down and held it up.

A note.

It was a note.

Jack waved him closer. Pawn pressed it against the glass.

One word.

No.

Jack leaned closer and read the word. Over and over.

"All right. Okay. That's fine."

Siiiiii-lent night.

THE PROTECTIVE WALLS FOLDED OPEN.

"Can I see that?" Jack held out his open hand.

Pawn gave him the note.

"Not that, dummy. THAT."

"Excellence?"

"The weapon. I would like to see it." He flicked his fingers while his skin darkened. "I want to hold it, *so give it to me, now, PLEASE.*"

Pawn handed over the paddle-shaped weapon, handle first. Jack ran his fingers over the smooth surface. When he squeezed the handle, it grew into a ten-foot-long, flat-sided club.

"Excuse me."

Jack patiently stepped past Pawn. He patiently lifted it over his head.

"Excellence, we should analyze it for self-propulsion properties–"

Jack glanced over – paddle over his head. "You might want to step aside."

CRACK!

THE PADDLE BECAME A BLUR.
    It buckled the tank like it was made of cardboard.
    Snow and ice mushroomed above their heads.
    Again.
    Again and again and again.

CRACK! CRACK! CRACK!

THE TANK WAS AN UNRECOGNIZABLE HUNK, half buried in the ice. The guards watched from a distance.
    Jack, huffing at the cold air, lifted the weapon. It trembled above his head. He had turned the color of a deadly storm. He stood on his toes, reached high.
    Spulunk!
    A geyser exploded.
    The ocean swallowed the sleigh, what was left of it. Nothing was left but a hole.
    Jack dropped the weapon and wiped his hands. He climbed back onto his seat and leaned back. His bruised complexion was hidden beneath a thick layer of frost. He grabbed the bowl of sardines and shoved them all in his mouth, chewing and chewing and chewing. Heads and eyes and tails fell on his belly.
    "Send all forces. *Wipe them all out.*"
    He wiped his mouth, smudging his frosty cheek.
    "EVERY ONE OF THEM!"

THE PALACE CAME INTO VIEW.
    Dark waves of his army were already spreading out from the base like an ink stain. They'd received his orders. They'd probably heard what he did to the tank, too. They would find the rebels and squash

them. Not one of them was to be captured. He wanted them blotted out of existence, shoved beneath the ice to sink to the bottom of the ocean.

Was that a wee bit impulsive?

Yup.

But Jack felt better. That's all that mattered.

35

Nicholas lay staring at the ceiling, wondering where he was.

The floor was covered with stuff. The room had been ransacked. *While I was sleeping?*

He kicked things out of the way to clear a space to stand.

He looked around and remembered.

I've got to figure a way out.

He'd watched the attack.

He'd cracked his eyes open and saw Claus and Jack. It made no sense until he saw his son. He saw Jon take the reins in a sleigh and escape.

He escaped.

Nicholas wasn't going to wait around for another attack. Next time, it might be different. *And where is Jessica?*

He needed out.

NOW.

He was feeling strong.

His left leg was solid and his ribs intact. He took a deep breath and barely felt the pebble of scar tissue in his lung. And his beard, bushier than ever.

Something clattered under the workbench.

Cane was working. There were nine metallic spiders lined up next to him. He put the finishing touches on the last one and placed it at the end of the line. He stood up and clapped.

The spiders got up and crawled into the lab, over the piles and through the junk like scavengers. The things started carrying the debris around and putting things together.

They were cleaning.

Claus stopped to watch the spiders.

There were already neatly stacked piles and organized shelves.

"Very good, Cane," he said.

"What have you done to me?" Nicholas walked across the uncluttered floor.

"Saved your life is what I've done."

Nicholas snatched Claus by the lapels of his coat. He was too heavy to lift. Nicholas leaned over. "I CAN'T REMEMBER ANYTHING!"

"Nonsense," Claus said. "You've only lost the first sixteen years of memory."

"Only?" Nicholas pulled the fat man closer. "What gives you the right to take ANYTHNG?"

Cane stopped clapping.

Claus gently peeled Nicholas's hands away. He went over to the workbench and thought for a moment, drumming his fingers.

"I don't expect you to understand," he said quietly. "What I'm doing is unforgivable. But I'm doing what I can. I'm keeping you alive."

"You have no right to do this."

"Of course not."

"You're a monster."

"Perhaps."

Nicholas paced around the lab, running his hands through his hair. Claus was right, he couldn't remember when he was a kid. It was gone. *Vanished.* He couldn't remember growing up or where he was born, what he liked to do. Was he rich or poor? Were his parents alive or dead?

It was as if he'd been born sixteen years old.

Nicholas grabbed an object. He pressed his fingers around the edges for a good grip. He didn't want to hurt Claus, but if it was going to be him or Nicolas, then Nicholas would play.

He whirled around, reared back–

Froze.

The bands on his wrists and ankles held him in place.

Claus tapped his fingers on the workbench and turned around. He was still nodding, like he understood Nicholas's pain.

"My people are being destroyed, Santa. We've been torn apart and we may never heal. So, you see, neither of us is winning. We've lost, Santa."

He started for the exit.

"For that, I am sorry."

Cane walked along with him, only his curly-toed shoes sticking out from under Claus's coat.

"You're going to take more of me, aren't you?"

Claus didn't answer. He waited at the door.

"Follow me, Santa."

The bands released their hold. Nicholas dropped the chunk of metal. He was going to follow, whether he wanted to or not. Claus gave him the opportunity to come along with dignity rather than be forced to walk like an animal.

Nicholas nodded.

He followed.

36

S now was up to Jessica's knees.

Snowflakes – the largest she'd seen – drifted down in wayward paths, landing gently in her hair.

The day was bright. Calm.

She watched the empty horizon, realizing she wasn't wearing protection against the sunlight reflecting off the snow, nothing to keep her from the snow blindness that had affected Jon before they lost their way.

Before we ended up here.

She wasn't sure how cold it was. It was cold, but how cold? Subzero? Just below freezing? She'd lost perspective. She was there, above the ice, standing near the top of the world, wearing minimal protection, and she felt all right. She felt good, like it was merely the nip of autumn at the end of her nose.

And autumn meant change.

JESSICA WELCOMED CHANGE. All her life, she hoped things would be different.

She would stay out in the autumn nights until all her friends went home. She didn't like coming back to their crowded apartment, to see her mother lying in that bed.

A bed that stank of sweat and sickness.

If her momma was awake when she got home, she'd hold out her arms and Jessica would have to climb into the bed with her. She loved the warmth and the softness, but the smell clung to her for hours.

When her momma fell asleep, Jessica would crawl and hide until her dad was home. He'd stagger through the door, raising his voice. Sometimes things broke. When he was asleep and snoring loud enough to shake the walls, then – and only then – would she come out.

By morning, she'd leave before any of them were awake.

Jessica never minded the cold.

NOG CLIMBED ONTO THE ICE, flicking the white flakes from his sleeves while muttering something about snow and Merry and time.

Jessica didn't take her eyes off the horizon, but she could see him searching his pockets until he found his bag. He let out a chuckle and a smile, and took the time to catch a snowflake on his tongue.

Jessica wanted to catch snowflakes, too. She wanted to make snow angels and build snowmen and enjoy life, but she couldn't.

Not now.

She was angry.

Jessica didn't want Nog there on the ice, watching the horizon. She didn't want to be responsible if something happened to him. She'd already done enough to the elven.

They're following you.

That's how the Cold One found the colony. He was able to track Jessica. As long as she was with them, they would know where to find them. Jessica informed Merry and Nog that she would be staying behind.

They begged her to change her mind.

They insisted she would not survive.

They declared a solution would be found.

Jessica ignored them. Jon would go. He was... comatose. He had to stay.

So she stayed on the ice and watched the reindeer jump out of sight, taking her son with them. They were right; she wouldn't survive long. But if she stayed, they all would die with her.

She couldn't accept that.

And Nog climbed out of the ice. He wasn't supposed to be here.

These elven... they were so joyful no matter what. They'd been displaced for one hundred fifty years, their lives continued to be threatened, and here was Nog catching snowflakes, as curious as a child.

After all these years, he was still joyful.

She wanted that.

She wanted what they had.

But someone has to watch the horizon, she told herself.

That was no excuse. But she told herself that anyway.

Nog pulled out a metallic ball.

Jessica had seen one of them, briefly. She'd seen the balls in the midst of the storm. As the last of the sleighs escaped, one of the balls flew into the seat next to her and Nog threw it in his bag. Now he held it in the palm of his hand. Lights blinked along the surface.

He tossed it into the snow.

A form suddenly rose up, a body of snow and ice with stout arms and a fat head.

A snowman.

A mean-looking snowman stomped its legs into the snow.

"Flury," Nog said. "This is Jessica. She's Jon's mother."

The snowman tipped his head, just a bit, as if to say *Howdy, ma'am.*

Jessica stared.

"Flury is one of the four abominables," Nog said. He explained the electromagnetic field that formed the body. Tinsel named him. Jon met him on attack day.

Jessica coldly watched the horizon. She didn't want to be thinking of that. Not right now. The snowman didn't seem offended. He turned his back and watched the horizon with her.

"Flury will buy us a few minutes," Nog added. "In case Ronin is late."

He opened the bag again, pulled out a sleigh, this one a two-seater. He fussed with the reins and buckles. He climbed on and looked busy brushing snowflakes off the seat. He eventually sat down and watched the horizon. He started to whistle but quickly stopped.

Jessica was in no mood for a song.

SHE FELT THE TREMOR.

Flury swelled in size, stirring the air around them. The horizon – a sharp line of ice that separated sky from water – began to blur. The fuzzy stampede stretched out for miles.

She wanted to stay. She wanted to fight them. All of them. Every single one of them. She wanted to get back at them for what they'd done to the elven. She wanted revenge for making her lean over a box and say goodbye to her son through a glass window, unable to touch his face, to kiss his cheek.

BOOM.

Snow settled around the red-nosed reindeer.

He turned his enormous rack toward the horizon and pawed the ice. Jessica could feel what he was thinking.

Let's stay.

"Come along." Nog hurried the sleigh behind Ronin. "We need to be ready."

He clipped the halter into place and adjusted and set the sleigh ready for launch. He climbed onto the seat. The six-legged beasts were still far away.

But closing.

Jessica imagined their hot, humid breath. The scratch of claws. The beady blackness of their eyes–

"Jessica." Nog said it forcefully. "We must go. They will follow us."

Follow, yes. They would follow Jessica, follow her mind, her thought pattern. She and Nog would leap far away and settle long enough to lure them away from the colony, to keep them safe. It wasn't time to fight.

Not yet.

Jessica slid next to Nog.

The snow fell away from Flury like white ash. The ball leaped into Nog's hand.

Ronin crouched.

Launch.

Jessica could feel a thousand eyes follow them across the sky.

Away from her son.

37

J ocah adjusted her cushion before crossing her legs to sit.
  She folded her hands and rested them in the upturned
  bottom of her outer shirt like a hammock. Her room was small.
  It was always small. The colony had to downsize the extent of
their habitat; they had to be ready to evacuate within a moment's
notice.

Everyone was watching the horizon.

Jocah took a deep breath and let it leak out her nostrils. She settled
into the aches perennially haunting her back and knees and shoulder.
They had become a part of daily life. But the emotions that weighed
on her stomach, they were something new.

She was taking a moment to sit quietly with these feelings. She left
Jessica and Nog behind. Jocah had insisted that her scientists find
another way – to perhaps mask the signals her mind was projecting
like a beacon for Jack to follow – but there wasn't time, they insisted.

The decision, though, wasn't hers.

Jessica informed her that she would not be staying with the colony.
She asked only one thing in return, that they see to the care and well-
being of her only son. Jocah did not have to promise anything that
hadn't already been decided. Jon had been welcomed into the colony
just as Jessica had been.

I will not put your people at risk. Jessica was not asking for permission, simply informing Jocah what she would be doing.

When Nog volunteered to remain, Jessica refused. But that, however, was not her decision. She wouldn't survive to day's end if Nog did not stay with her.

If they capture me, she said, *then I shall see my husband. What better ending is that?*

You may not want to see what they've done to him.

After all, Jocah had experienced the loss.

IT HAD BEEN three thousand years since she gave birth.

Jocah had agreed to become impregnated with a genetically modified embryo. Her child was going to be the future leader of the elven. He would age slower than ever before. His intelligence and empathic ability would allow him to lead with love and compassion, a leader beloved by the elven.

But the universe has a way of balancing.

Claus was first born.

He was perfect in every way. He learned their language in the first year. He was observant and intuitive. Rarely did he need to be told something twice. He frequently discovered how to do things on his own. Kind and thoughtful, strong and courageous.

Jocah had given birth to the future leader, just as they predicted.

But there was another child.

Claus had a twin that slid from the womb thirty seconds later.

When the doctors held the child up, he appeared to be stillborn. His skin was the color of a cloudless summer day. His eyes were open, deep and black.

The doctor nearly dropped him. Later, his hands were treated for ice burns.

Jack entered the world.

It started out very normal.

Jack followed his big brother everywhere. He mimicked everything he did. He tried to be just like him.

But things changed.

Water would sometimes turn to ice when he touched it. He preferred to be naked, even on the coldest nights. He preferred to sleep in rooms near the bottom. At times, when he explored his surroundings, he could be found playing in the darkest part of winter storms.

Jack stopped smiling.

Jocah wasn't sure when that happened. She rarely forgot anything, but in those days she was busy leading the elven. And when she wasn't doing that, she was grooming Claus as her successor.

The nannies reported his behavior.

Jocah tried to talk with him, but he sat there, staring.

Sometimes she found him in his closet, tucked into the dark corner with his legs pulled against his chest.

Singing.

Others began to worry when Claus and Jack went on their first hunting expedition.

They were kept inside a sleigh to observe how polar bears were tracked. When the first bear was confirmed dead, they were brought out to observe the rituals of giving thanks and cleaning the prey. While the lead elven was showing them the padding and claws on the beast's feet, Jack was near the face, opening and closing the bear's eyes.

Giggling.

Jack was yang to Claus's ying.

They were opposites.

They were balance.

Imbalance began the day Jack arrived at Jocah's quarters with a proposal.

Claus had been leading the elven for nearly a thousand years. During that time, Jack was off doing his own thing. Jocah didn't see him much. When he entered wearing a new outfit, she realized her mistake. His clothes were finely tailored, made with dark colors that matched the purplish shade of his fingernails and the strange hue of his tongue.

He was an odd child, but he was a dangerous adult.

Jocah never recognized the extent of his arrogance, his appetite for power and destruction.

He denounced the current leadership of these elven. *These elven,* he said. *Weak and cowardly.*

He claimed that the elven were becoming like vermin, hiding in the corner of the world. He claimed this was her fault. This was Claus's fault.

And he would stand for it no more.

You have a week to turn power over to me.

He did not wait for a response. He didn't expect one.

He'd already amassed a secret army.

And when two elven entered her quarters dressed as he was, she knew the action that needed to be taken. She would not be short-sighted again.

These elven.

Jocah informed Claus that she would be leaving.

She did not keep it a secret as to why. She told him that Jack was dangerous and that he needed to be stopped.

Then why run? he said. *Stay and fight.*

It was too late for that.

Sadly, she had no answers.

Sadly, Claus stayed.

How could *I have been so blind?*

Jack had been dangerous from the beginning. Perhaps it was the wishful thinking – the hoping – a mother has for her child that he will find success, find happiness. Find his place in the universe. She ignored the obvious signs of what he was becoming. He was not merely a disturbed child.

He was a *monster.*

And it was too late to stop him.

Jocah left in secret before her week was up.

She expected to leave with only a few fellow elven. She never expected the groundswell of supporters to follow her into a life of exile. Perhaps she was blind beyond her own observations, that others had seen the danger long before she had. They were prepared to leave, to make a new life, to survive long enough to find a way to survive Jack's rule.

Claus knew Jack was too strong to fight.

His brother had already fashioned a secret police through fear and coercion. Claus couldn't leave the elven that stayed behind. They would need help.

Jocah left her son behind. She abandoned him.

And now she had abandoned Jessica.

Those decisions weighed heavily upon her.

38

Nicholas's eyes spastically jerked back and forth beneath his lids.

Already in a REM cycle, he seemed to be looking around for something. Perhaps his subconscious was searching for the lost memories.

Claus checked his vital signs. He was in remarkable health given all that he'd been through. Not just physically – his body had adapted quite well to the cold-tolerance treatments – but mentally, too. He was tough.

But there was more to come.

Who's the monster now?

Claus kept himself busy with the vital signs, checking them, double-checking, triple-checking, to avoid that thought. He was about to take more of Nicholas's past, a warmblood that – despite Claus's best efforts – he was beginning to like.

Who's the monster now?

I'm not, he told himself. *I'm not a monster.*

Claus stayed when Jocah left, despite her objections. He stayed not out of some misplaced guilt (How many times did he do nothing when the others were teasing Jack? How many times did he ignore him?), but to truly serve the elven. To serve the world.

Janack is the monster. And I can't stop him.

If he could just slow him down, just enough, then perhaps the colony could have a little more time. If he could somehow make Jack see how cruel and–

He'd given that up a long time ago.

Face it, the end is near.

Claus went to the bench and checked his instruments. When everything was in order, he looked back at Nicholas and prepared a final few steps before he began this phase of the memory drain.

He prepared for the end.

39

Nicholas wasn't dreaming.

He wasn't awake, either.

I'm remembering.

It was different, though. Not like daydreaming about once upon a time. At some level, he knew where he was. And why.

At some level, it didn't matter.

There was nothing he could do about it.

So he enjoyed his memories.

One last time.

NICHOLAS ALMOST GAVE up on wooing Jessica.

She was stubborn and strong and resistant. Then again, those were the things that Nicholas found endearing. But even he had his limits, and he was reaching them.

So when he returned to leave another gift in her stockings and found her waiting on the stoop, when she didn't leave when she saw him (and she saw him; she was looking right at him when he approached) he didn't know what to do. He stopped right in the middle of the street and pinched himself.

She called him over.

He stood silent while she laid down the rules.

You can take me on a date, but nowhere fancy.

You won't spend any money on me.

You will never lie to me.

You will never lie to yourself.

"And," she said, pointing at him like he missed something obvious, "that last one is a lot harder than you think, Nicholas."

Nicholas looked like he'd been struck with an axe handle. A grin broke out on his face.

"What are you smiling at?" Jessica said.

"You said *Nicholas.*"

"Well, that's your name, isn't it?"

Yeah. That's my name. Nicholas stuck out his hand and she shook it. "Deal."

She thought he had no idea what he'd just gotten himself into.

But neither did she.

Their first date was five miles outside of town.

He trotted up on a horse. It was a thoroughbred with a black coat that shined like oil. He was towing an appaloosa with an empty saddle strapped to its back.

"I said no buying me anything," she said.

"Her name is Dandy, and I didn't buy her for you."

Dandy trotted up next to Nicholas and pounded at the frozen mud.

"I'm just going to let you borrow her. If you'd rather lease her, I suppose I could charge you something fair."

She put out her hand and let Dandy smell it. The horse's nostrils flared. Her breath was warm. Jessica scratched her rubbery lips.

"She likes you," Nicholas said. "But if you'd rather walk–"

Jessica climbed into the saddle and took the reins. She double-clicked her tongue. Nicholas raced to catch up.

Who ever heard of a date in the woods?

Jessica loved it.

She liked hiking and discovering new things. She loved to push herself to her limits.

Nicholas showed her all his favorite trails and secret camping places. In no time, he was having to keep up with her as she forged new trails and climbed difficult rocks. They challenged each other to do more, to go farther and faster.

She refused to accept the food he brought, at least the first couple of dates.

Once they were past the testing period (that lasted maybe two months), they were sharing everything. She even looked the other way when he left gifts for her siblings.

Occasionally, she would keep one for herself.

Jessica still worked to support her family.

Nicholas wanted to give her the money, basically hire her so she didn't have to.

"I told you," she said, "you can't buy me."

"Who's buying? I need a naturalist guide to help out with trail-blazing and identifying plants. There's no one better than you, Jessica."

Which was true. She had a knack for both.

But so did Nicholas.

WHEN NICHOLAS TURNED EIGHTEEN, his parents wanted to send him away to college. His father wanted him to take over the family business and he would need to be schooled in the art of business and politics.

It sounded like torture.

It was a total mismatch (Would there be any mountains to climb at business school?). Besides, he'd have to move.

He knew what he wanted.

Nicholas was waiting for Jessica when she finished work.

Like usual.

"Some of us have to work," she would sometimes say.

There was something different about him this day. She asked him half a dozen times if he was all right as they trotted their way out of town. He turned left when they were supposed to go right.

"Where we going?"

He didn't say anything. Didn't answer or acknowledge the question. He hovered over the saddle and broke into a full gallop. Jessica gave chase and found him waiting at the foot of a mountain. He'd tied his horse and was already on the trail. She shouted and laughed. If he thought she couldn't keep up, then he was about to be shocked.

She was always up for something new.

Nicholas took her hand.

That was new, too.

They walked side by side down the narrow path, knocking snow from the heavy limbs that reached out. She was about to ask – for the seventh time – why he was smiling when she noticed someone at the end of the path.

Jessica stuttered.

Nicholas led her toward a man holding a book. Next to him a boy.

"Seamus?" she said to one of Nicholas's few friends. "What are you doing here?"

Nicholas took both of Jessica's hands.

He dropped to one knee.

Nicholas and Jessica were married in the middle of the trees at the foot of a mountain. In the long tradition of marriage, there was not a happier man and woman to be joined in matrimony, to promise each other their lives, in sickness and health, for richer or poorer.

Forever.

And ever.

And ever.

And when the ceremony was finished, the Justice of the Peace congratulated them and pulled his bicycle from the underbrush and rode away. Seamus congratulated them, hugged Jessica and hugged Nicholas, too, before riding off on his own stashed bicycle.

And when Mr. and Mrs. Santa were alone, officially husband and wife, together forever, they took each other's hands, looking deeply–

Looking deeply–

PAIN.

PRESSURE.

Something pushed through the memories like a bulldozer.

It was invisible, unstoppable. Some unknown... *thing...* pushed its way into Nicholas's mind. It didn't belong to him.

Ripping.

Snapping.

Something was breaking and tearing and... and...

AGONY!

And voices.

There were voices.

He heard them before he went to the bottom of a deep, black sleep.

40

Something shattered. There were sounds.

Claus opened his eyes.

It took several blinks to focus. Claus tapped his finger on the workbench – he felt like his insides had been replaced with sand – and pulled the halo off his head.

And then the sounds made sense.

"I will end you." Jack stormed past Nicholas. "If you helped them escape, I will not end you slowly, either. It will be a very undesirable end to your life, brother."

Jack began vibrating and split into two. There was two of him.

Claus rubbed his eyes. His face was like rubber.

So heavy.

"Why are you wearing the halo?" Jack asked.

"What?"

Jack took it from the workbench. "*This.* Why were you wearing this? The halo is only for *draining* memories. I'm no dummy, dummy."

Claus looked at the halo to Jack and back to the halo. Jack raised an eyebrow.

"You have," he said, frowning, "no idea what it takes to drain a warmblood."

"Because I'm too stupid, is that what you're trying to say?" Jack said slyly. "Answer the question or I stick my finger in your ear."

"Which one, Janack? The one about aiding your enemy or the one about the halo? Which one are you burning to know first?"

Jack frowned.

He kind of forgot the first one.

The halo bounced off the wall and skipped across the floor. "The first one, brother! You tell me what you had to do with the escape, and you tell me now. YOU TELL ME NOW!"

"Nonsense," Claus muttered.

He hopped out of his seat and paced and stretched. The blood was flowing again, pushing the syrupy sensations from his body.

"Tell me what happened," Claus said, without looking back. "What escape are you talking about?"

"Don't play dumb, dummy! You know what escape I'm talking about!"

"Janack! How am I supposed to know what you're doing when I'm busy sucking the life out of this warmblood? Huh?" Claus pointed at Nicholas. There was a string of drool hanging from his lip. "You want me to destroy a warmblood AND follow you across the North Pole?"

Good, good. Call him a warmblood. Like you don't care about him.

Jack stepped back.

The fire that ignited in his belly way back when he saw the note and subsequently destroyed the valuable sleigh-tank (he shouldn't have done that, now that he thought about it) had him convinced, he was absolutely positive, that his dear brother had helped them. He didn't know how, he just knew that fathead had something to do with it.

And then when he ordered them to be wiped out and found out that they'd lost track of the rebels, that his mother actually DITCHED THOSE FILTHY WARMBLOODS!

There was fire in his belly.

And his brother lit it.

But now that fire was cooling. His brother was sucking the memories out of the warmblood, just like he told him to do. Like a good soldier.

You have to remember what's important in life.

"All right, okay." Jack walked his fingers up the warmblood's leg like his pudgy little blue hand was dancing. "My bad. The rebels... you remember them, don't you? Mother and her traitor friends, right?"

Jack chuckled.

Claus looked impatient.

"Well, I sent the pets out to destroy them, you know, one of those tear them limb from limb missions? I've always wanted to do one of those. Anyway, guess what happened when my little furry six-leggers got there?"

Jack's eyes widened.

"They weren't there."

"Why would you destroy them?"

"Oh, you didn't hear?" Jack had completely cooled. "It seems our mother decided to refuse my offer of peace. And now I want them all gone. Forever."

"You weren't offering peace," Claus said.

"THEY DIDN'T KNOW THAT!"

"Evidently, they did."

Jack drummed a beat on the lounger. Frost spiderwebbed over the material beneath Nicholas's legs.

"Doesn't matter," Jack said. "I was going to let some of them survive, but that deal's off the table. I don't care if they want to hug and kiss my feet, they can suck it. All deals off. There's just one problem. We're only picking up one mind pattern."

Jack held up two fingers, then folded one down.

"Not two."

Claus snuck a glance at Nicholas. Still drooling.

"One of them likely died," Claus said.

"Probably." Jack sighed, relishing a warm joy in his belly. "But we can still follow the one."

Claus waited. "Okay."

"Yeah. It appears that warmblood separated from the rebels." Jack summed up what his army reported. They saw one reindeer (the red-nose one, the one that *really* hated Jack) and one really small sleigh.

That was it.

"You continue to underestimate Mother."

"Whatever. I'll catch her soon. It'll all be over with. Soon."

"Why don't you just forget them? Just let them live in peace. They haven't bothered us since leaving."

Claus said it carefully so as not to make it sound like he *wanted* him to forget, more like a suggestion. Something to make his life easier.

"Um, *hello*." Jack knocked on his own head. "My big dumb scientists are a bunch of dummies compared to them. And – AND – they want to stop me, so there's that. You know."

"Why not give it up, Janack?"

"You're like talking to a wall, brother. A really stupid one. If you keep acting so stupid, I'll get rid of you." He held up his finger, reminding Claus what he could do with a single touch. "I could stick this up your nose, start with the worst brain-freeze you ever had."

"I'm not scared of you, Janack."

"*Oooooo*... you're so brave." Jack turned rapidly. "Now get back to draining the memories out of this warmblood, why don't you."

"I can't, now that you've interrupted me."

"WELL, DO SOMETHING, I DON'T CARE WHAT!"

Jack slapped a container on the ground on his way out. Claus heard him slap one of the guards.

Claus couldn't hold the smile in any longer.

That couldn't have worked any better.

41

The room was small. Jessica could cross it with three steps in any direction. There were no tunnels, no other rooms. Just this one.

There wasn't time for other rooms.

Jessica was hydrating a meal the way Nog taught her. The food was freeze-dried. She was stirring water and pouring it into bowls. Back in the colony, food was grown in the lab. They had the ability to artificially make anything: asparagus, apricots, chicken. It had something to do with nutrient arger or agar (she couldn't remember the word) and enzymes. It wasn't real chicken but had the same taste, same texture.

Nog could pull anything out of the bag. But not food. For some reason, they needed raw materials for that, so they were stuck with the freeze-dried stuff that tasted more like porridge.

And they only had so much.

They couldn't go back to the colony for food. They couldn't risk leading the pack back to them. As long as Jessica was alive and breathing and thinking, she would be on the run.

Eventually, they would have to supplement with fish and game. But right now, they didn't have time for that. They were too busy jumping to stay ahead of the pack.

The pack. Don't call them hunters.

Nog's big, bare feet slapped on the icy floor as he dropped through the entrance. He looked at the food congealing in bowls and waved the aroma into his nostrils, breathing deeply. He was faking it. There was no aroma.

Jessica spooned food into two bowls and they sat down on beds, facing each other. They ate quietly.

"How's Ronin?" Jessica asked.

"We're running him hard. He's jumped us every day for a week; that's too much. He's leaping back to the land to feed and rest, but he's getting too little of both."

"Have one of the others take his place."

"Great idea," Nog said, wiping his mouth. "If there was just someone to tell him that."

"He knows he's tired."

"He's also stubborn and he doesn't understand anything I say. I can barely communicate with him. We need Tinsel."

Silence settled in the room.

It was another reminder that the colony was somewhere else. It reminded them how lonely they would become. It reminded them that they wouldn't be able to keep this up forever. The reindeer couldn't jump every day, even if they were rotating. The longer Jessica was around, the weaker the herd would become. And eventually that would begin affecting the colony.

Time was on Jack's side.

NOG CLEANED UP.

As long as Jessica had known him, he'd never done anything in silence. Now he was lying on the bed, staring at the ceiling. No more chasing snowflakes with his tongue.

Things got real.

They were too busy the first couple days to think about what they were doing and where they were going, but now they had more time to think.

Being alone with thoughts was not productive.

They weighed heavily on Nog.

JESSICA WOKE FROM A NAP.

She bolted upright, ready to get to the surface, but Nog wasn't putting things in the bag. He was sitting in the middle of the floor, staring at a square plate. Inside, there were images. It was mostly white, but Jessica recognized the view of the Arctic from above. She recognized the pack somewhere on the ice, moving in their direction. Nog would know when they were close enough that they needed to get on top of the ice and jump.

They still had several hours.

"WHERE DID YOU MEET MERRY?"

Nog had been lying on the bed, staring at the ceiling for an hour. Jessica hadn't noticed him sleeping. He just lay there, staring. Thinking.

She thought maybe he didn't hear her.

But then his whiskers rustled. Jessica saw the first hint of a smile around the corners of his eyes.

"When an elven is born," he said, "he or she is taken outside to be exposed to the elements. It initiates our blubber layers and prepares us for life in the Arctic. That's why you often see children outside. Always playing."

Jessica realized there weren't many children in the colony. Very few. Nog was still smiling, remembering. Perhaps it had been far too long since he'd thought about it.

"I wasn't very good at the winter games," he continued. "Snowballs and ice sculpting and polar bearing."

"Polar bearing?"

He chuckled. "It's pounding two holes in the ice and swimming from one to the other."

"That sounds dangerous."

"I guess. But that's not the worst of it. We do it naked."

He laughed heartily. Perhaps he was remembering a bunch of naked elven teenagers running through the snow. Jessica laughed, too.

"I was not very popular. I was bad at the games and wasn't really smart enough to study science, so I was usually somewhere in the libraries or in my room, experimenting with stuff. But I still had to go to school and interact with the others. For the most part, everyone ignored me."

He was quiet. His eyes relaxed.

"And then there was initiation day, the day before we finish school.

It's nothing official, just when everyone meets on the ice and plays games. I told you I wasn't very good, so I was sneaking back inside through the back door when I ran into some of the popular elven. They thought it would be funny to make me polar bear. I didn't."

He closed his eyes.

"And then my queen in shining armor appeared," he said, smiling again. "She told them to get stuffed."

"And did they?" Jessica asked, not sure what that meant.

Long pause. "Uh, no. They didn't like being told by a girl what to do. One of them actually pushed her down."

He stopped talking.

"Well? Then what?"

"Oh," he said, like he forgot he'd been talking out loud. "I dropped this invention I'd been working on that seals the sole scales and makes them slippery. They were slipping and sliding while we got away." He shrugged. "No big deal."

"The knight in shining armor."

He just smiled.

"WE HAD A CHILD."

Nog had been lying quietly with his eyes closed for so long that Jessica thought he'd finally fallen asleep. But that was all he said, almost like he didn't realize he'd said it out loud. Or maybe he was talking in his sleep.

"What was your child's name?"

"Neyda."

He told her – in between pauses – what a beautiful elven she was. Face like a cherub. She was beautiful like her mother. She got her brain like her father and mother combined. She was good at all the games and science. He didn't say if he let her go polar bearing.

Jessica never heard of an elven named Neyda. And it was the first time Nog or Merry ever mentioned it. She let him enjoy the memory.

"We're not perfect, Jessica," he said. "We cured the effects of aging, but sometimes the body just doesn't do what we want it to do. We still belong to nature. All things come to an end."

Smile, fading.

Jessica didn't ask.

And then Nog finally offered, "She died when she was three hundred forty."

Three hundred forty? Years old?

Suddenly the absurdity of time hit Jessica on the funny bone. Here was this beautiful, sweet elven lamenting his *child* dying when she was *only 340 years old.*

She clamped her hand over her mouth, but the laughter pushed between her fingers. She used her other hand to keep that from happening again. But then Nog let out a low rumble.

"*Heh-heh-heh-heh,*" he went. "Three hundred forty," he said, recognizing what Jessica was thinking.

And then it was out.

Laughter blew Jessica's hands off her lips. Nog bellowed deeply and loudly.

The room was filled with bubbling joy. Tears streamed down their cheeks and they wiped them off and spilled more and laughed more. And when Nog fell off his bed, it just got worse.

It went on and on.

"We can't keep running," Jessica said.

After the laughter, there was room for the truth. Their escape was not sustainable. It would come to an end, sooner or later.

Jessica looked at Nog. She didn't have to say what she was thinking. He could tell that she was tired of running. And they couldn't go back to the colony.

That left only one thing.

"If we're going to fight, we need to quiet that mind of yours," Nog said.

42

Tinsel brushed the snow off her head.

The reindeer were hungrier than usual. They were gobbling up her snacks like wild animals that hadn't seen food all winter. They had been jumping the colony on one-week intervals for a month. She started rotating them with Ronin so he wouldn't be doing the daily jumps with Jessica and Nog.

The colony's living conditions were smaller than she ever remembered them. Maybe half the size. They needed to conserve resources.

Tinsel thought it was more than that.

It was hard to enjoy yourself when you knew Jessica and Nog were out there all alone. Bubbling joy was absent from the tunnels.

It was work, work, work.

And that was fine with Tinsel. She didn't want to be socializing, anyway.

Since the science lab was smaller, they didn't need her.

When she wasn't feeding, she was in the medical room.

Medical was at the edge of the tunnels.

The first few beds were filled with the elderly and sick. Mr. Pappas was almost nine thousand years old. His blubber content was decreasing and they didn't know why, so they kept him in a special bed to maintain his body temperature. Then there was Ms. Sanzsan with the fragile bones. Mr. Crepell with the swollen tongue, and Ms. Mandatt with the bad eyes.

Tinsel said good morning to the ones that were awake. She didn't slide through the room. That was too fast for them to see. She walked the old-fashioned way, nice and slow, even though she was impatient to shove off for the very back of the room where a box sat in the corner.

Tinsel leaned over the window.

It had gathered frost over a week ago and she could no longer see inside. Sometimes, if she rubbed the glass, she thought she could see Jon's face. It was round and pale and still.

"He's doing just fine," the doctor said, sliding to the other side of the box.

"Have you checked the vitals? I mean, I could check them, if you need some help."

"Maybe later. Right now, Mr. Crepell needs help swallowing his food. Could you assist him with that?"

Tinsel nodded. She would've asked the doctor when the box would be opened, but she already knew the answer.

Soon, was all the doctor would say. *We'll open it soon.*

43

Nicholas awoke in Claus's lab. His head was heavy.

It was like he'd been hit with a shovel and his brains replaced with a bundle of lead.

He swung his legs to the floor, grateful for the high ceiling. He stretched his back and thumped the side of his head like he had water in his ears.

Clickity-clack. Snap.

Cane was under the workbench.

There was something on the floor, covered with a small blanket. Cane held the corners and, like a showman, uncovered his latest work of art.

It was a miniature replica of a blue-skinned elven.

The Jack-toy wore a dark jacket and had blue lips and blackish fingernails. Cane patted the toy on the head and then swatted it on the fanny.

Jack slid out from under the bench with the snaps and clicks of a working toy.

Nicholas wanted to step on it like a bug.

Before he could lift his foot, Cane pulled the sheet off something else. Beneath that was a big, white thing. Two arms and legs and a lump of a head, it looked like a snowy man-beast. It seemed to swell while it took a breath.

It stomped across the floor and caught the Jack-toy about midway to Nicholas. It ripped off the arms, then punched a hole through the fat belly before gnawing on the head like a cob of corn.

Cane jumped up and down, clapping.

Nicholas began to laugh.

He'd forgotten what that felt like.

It hurt in his left side. He quickly fell into a bout of laughing coughs.

Cane cheered while the snowy man-beast threw the bits and pieces of Jack-toy across the floor.

"Pick up this mess." Claus entered with a scowl that buried his black eyes beneath furry shelves of brow.

Cane stopped clapping.

"Now."

"He's having fun," Nicholas said.

"He's wrecking my lab."

"And you're destroying my life."

Claus wearily looked up at the six-foot-tall giant. The color had changed on Claus's cheeks in the last several days. It was grayer, more wrinkles. And maybe he was thinner. He was still as round as a ball, but he just seemed smaller.

"We all make sacrifices," Claus said.

"Some more than others."

Claus ignored him.

Nicholas did his best to bend over and pick up the pieces, but it was difficult with such a round midsection. He ended up kneeling next to the mess and pushing the pieces into a pile. Cane came out, cheerless, and helped sweep them up. Nicholas cradled them against his chest.

Claus continued with something on the workbench. Cane went over to him and hugged his leg. Claus reached down and patted his head, like that would make it all right.

"You know what, go ahead and take the rest of them."

Nicholas dropped the parts. He kicked them across the room.

"I can't take being buried alive anymore. You want my memories? Go ahead and take the rest of them. What are you waiting for?"

Nicholas shoved over a tall stack of papers that fluttered like butterflies.

"Stop messing around and take them. Get it over with, you thief. Just take my memories, because you're no better than him."

He hit another stack, this one a pile of metal plates.

"YOU'RE NO DIFFERENT!"

Nicholas toppled three more piles like dominoes.

Claus stopped.

He watched him destroy the lab.

When he was finished, not an inch of floor space was visible. Nicholas resorted to stomping through the litter, crushing whatever would break under his foot until he was nicked and bruised.

He was panting and bleeding and he still wasn't through, shouting as he went.

"YOU'RE NO DIFFERENT!"

Claus stood up.

He waited at the exit.

When Nicholas noticed, Claus nodded for him to follow.

It was one cramped tunnel after another. Nicholas was hunched over, the ceiling rubbing the back of his head, the walls pressed against his shoulders.

He had difficulty breathing.

Ice above him, around him, below him.

Ice everywhere.

Nicholas struggled to keep up. He fell to a knee, trying to catch his breath. Panic squeezed his chest. It was cold and heavy and he just wanted out.

"A bit farther."

He took a step and swore he couldn't go another. Took a step, and swore again. And again. It was so tight and so heavy... until they finally turned a corner.

It was a room.

A big, big room.

AN ARENA.

The seating looked like benches surrounding a circular stage. The roof was domed and impossibly high. The sounds of workmen buzzed now and then as excavation was still in progress near the apex. Icy slivers flitted down as it was shaved away.

Nicholas took a deep breath.

Space.

It was exactly what he needed.

"What is this?" he asked.

"*Victory* Hall." There was nothing victorious about the way Claus said it.

The ceiling was translucent, allowing pale light to filter through deep lines carved in intricate patterns, like crystal spiderwebs. Lines of light crawled over Claus's face.

He walked to center stage.

"What victory?" Nicholas asked.

Claus was about to crumble. "It's to celebrate the end... of the rebels."

He sounded so weak.

So defeated.

"The end?" Nicholas stepped onto the stage. "The rebels have my family... what about my wife and son?"

Claus was paler. His eyes gray in their deep pockets.

"What will happen to them?" Nicholas asked.

Claus wouldn't tell him.

He didn't need to.

"LIAR!"

The word bounced around the arena.

Nicholas couldn't follow it.

"WHATEVER HE SAYS IS A LIE!"

There were four ramps that evenly divided the arena into quarters. At the top of one of them was a purple-clad figure shouting through his cupped hands.

"You're a liar, Claus. What did Mother tell you about lying? It makes your tongue hairy, you know that. Every lie you tell kills a mermaid. And that whopper there just killed a whale."

Jack slid down the ramp with his arms out. Nicholas thought he heard the Cold One humming *wheeeee.* He hit the bottom and leaned into a turn that took him around the outer portion of the stage. He skated on the edge of one foot, hands folded on his belly.

He corkscrewed toward Claus and went into a tight spin with his arms up.

Suddenly he stopped.

Curtsy.

"Now go shave your tongue, brother."

Claus met his brother's glare. Neither of them blinked or flinched. The floor – clear polished ice – crackled with blue lines emanating from Jack's feet. He tilted his head. If it was a game, he was about to win.

"He's *my* warmblood," he added. "Go babysit Cane or eat a salad or something. You look like a starving vegan, all ashy and gray. Like a skinned whale. *Gross.*"

Claus looked at Nicholas.

We're no different?

"You like my new pad?" Jack spun around with his arms out. "A room like this has never been done before. Those Egyptians did the pyramid thing, but that was stone. This is ice. That's a whole 'nother creature."

He wiped the frost off his blue scalp.

"*Sooooo...* do you like it?"

Nicholas didn't answer.

"I don't care if you do, but if you liked it... that would be *coo-oool.*"

"Wonderful," Nicholas said through his teeth.

"I knew it!" Jack spun in another circle.

He circled Nicholas, around and around.

Humming a little song.

"Do you know what we're celebrating?"

Nicholas stared.

"Why, of course you don't." Jack shot the side of his head with his finger and thumb. "*Duh.* You've had the wits sucked out of you. Where are my manners?"

A boulder of ice tumbled into the seats.

"HEY!" Jack cupped his hands. "DON'T SCREW THIS UP OR I'LL *EAT YOU AND YOUR CHILDREN!*"

He turned to Nicholas.

"I'm just kidding. I won't eat you. Just the children."

He laughed.

"Anyways. It's fitting, a room this size. Big and spacious, something that will hold everyone when we finally put an end to the Fracture, once and for all. When all the elven come together like one big happy family and reclaim the planet. We live on top of the world, you know. We're on the North Pole while you *warmbloods* suck the life out of the planet. No offense."

He did another lap.

"You don't talk much, do you?" Jack stared.

"You've taken my life."

"Um, a 'thank you' would be nice. For not killing you immediately, *hello.*"

Jack put his hand toward his ear, listening. When Nicholas didn't respond, the floor crackled loudly. Nicholas could feel the cold enter his feet.

"You warmbloods, so self-centered. You think that the universe revolves around you, that the world owes *you* something while you get, get, get and me, me, me and take, take, take."

Jack shook his finger.

"I've been watching your memories; I know what you're about."

"You mean the ones you *took*?"

"Yeah. *THOSE.*" The floor grew colder. "I saw how you grew up with a mother and a father that loved you, saw how everyone gave you what you wanted. I saw you go to bed at night all warm and happy, only to wake up grumpy because YOUR CHOCOLATE CHIP COOKIE WAS TOO BIG TO FIT IN THE GLASS OF MILK!"

Nicholas's feet were numb.

"That's the problem with warmbloods... they're always unsatisfied. I mean, you fell in a trap, broke your face, your leg, your ribs... and I find you, bring you here and feed you, I keep you from dying and you're like, *uuuuhhh, I want my memories.*"

Jack was quivering.

"And do I get a thank you? No, because you're all about you. You just want, want, want. So how about it, fatboy?"

Jack cupped his ear. His face had turned darker than his lips.

The ice began to burn.

"Thank you."

"Oh. You're very welcome."

Jack's cheeks returned to pale blue.

"Here's the deal." He slowly slid across the floor. "We're going to take the rest of your memories and guess what? No more pain, buddy. That's right, you won't remember what you did yesterday or the day before. All those warm and fuzzy memories, the sweet little ones like when your mommy tucked you in at night and when your son was born... all those will be–"

Snap.

"Gone."

"Why?" Nicholas asked. "Why take my memories?"

"Because I want to, that's why."

Jack darkened as he coasted closer.

"We'll clone you, of course. We'll make like, oh, I don't know, a dozen duplicates that look just like you and we'll put some memories in these dummies so they know how to buckle their pants. Oh, I almost forgot. We'll infect them with bacteria, something your people call a plague. And when we have your wife and son, we'll do the same to them."

Jack's mouth formed a perfect O, like a secret just escaped.

"See, Claus was lying. We're not going to kill your dumb family; we're going to suck out their memories, too. We're going to send all three of you skipping down the road WHILE YOU INFECT THE WORLD!"

He threw his hands up.

"YIPPEE!"

Panic seized Nicholas.

They were going to do this to Jessica and Jon. They would be responsible for wiping out humanity.

Jack was distracted, scratching the permafrost on his cheek, trying to remember something–

Nicholas lunged.

Hands out.

Aimed at the little monster's neck, where somewhere in those thick folds of blubber he could clamp down and squeeze–

Stiffness shot through his feet, zapped his body with cold fire. Arms rigid, he fell like he was carved from wood.

Jack was standing over him. "Man, are you dumb."

Nicholas felt nothing but the cold hand of fear.

He would lose everything.

Everything.

Guards loaded him onto a stretcher. Jack waved as he was carted off.

There was nothing Nicholas could do to stop it.

44

"Don't take your finger off," Mr. Canoodle said, singsongy. "Unless you *meeean* it."

Tinsel had her finger in the center of a red checker, like she was holding it down, and inspected the rest of the board, her tongue wedged between her lips.

Mr. Canoodle's laugh sounded more like wheezing.

She lifted her finger. "King me," she declared.

Mr. Canoodle happily stacked a red checker on the one she just slid onto the back row. He hunched over and studied his options. It would be a couple minutes before he moved. She had to put a time limit on him. He was worse than Mr. Greyapple playing chess.

That was a marathon.

The other patients grumbled he was hogging up Tinsel, but he just pretended like his hearing went out when they did.

Fortunately, she didn't have Mr. Greyapple on that day's activity schedule. But she did have Mrs. Minutelady for Gin Rummy, Ms. Dazzleburn for dominoes and, finally, Mr. Lullihill for Old Maid (Tinsel played a dozen games with Mr. Lullihill because he was so sweet).

You need to stop, the doctor told Tinsel. *No one wants to leave Medical because of you.*

Tinsel spent less time helping the doctor with daily tasks and more time with recreation. After two months, that's all she did was play games. It lifted the patients' spirits. The doctor brought in another assistant so that Tinsel could unofficially become the Recreational Director of Medical (she made that title up).

Mr. Canoodle reached out his hand – curled like a claw with only one protruding finger – and stabbed one of his black checkers, sliding it three squares to the right. Tinsel didn't bother looking. He would slide it back. He never made a move without *trying out* – as he called it – three moves, minimum.

She glanced across the room.

The box was still in the corner. It looked so lonely.

She went back there, from time to time. Sometimes she read a story to the person inside. It had been so long since she'd seen his face (the window was still mostly frosted over) that she had difficulty recalling it with detail.

Sometimes she remembered when she introduced the reindeer to him that very first day, how the reindeer seemed unafraid of him. And then how he took Ronin's reins and escaped the six-leggers and saved Jocah.

And now he was here, asleep.

"Tinsel." *Clap-clap.* "It's your turn, sweety."

Mr. Canoodle had moved.

TINSEL PICKED up the Old Maid cards and put them away.

The reindeer were arriving. She wanted to be on the ice in plenty of time to feed them. She had been experimenting with a new formula – one that would boost their energy – and she was eager to see if they liked it. They were stubborn; even if it was good for them, they wouldn't eat it if it didn't taste good.

Like kids.

She'd put away the cards and the dominoes and the checkers. Mr. Greyapple had the chess pieces out, preparing for his next game. He would have to wait a couple days because the colony was relocating in the morning.

They were still on one-week cycles, even though it had been months since Jessica and Nog had left. It was hard on the reindeer, but the leaders were cautious.

Too cautious.

They couldn't run the reindeer like that forever.

Tinsel stopped by the box.

She felt guilty for not reading a story.

"Tomorrow." She patted the box. "I'll read you a new story that one of the writers just finished. I think you'll like it. It's about warmbloods. Naughty and nice ones."

Tinsel walked her fingers up to the window. She leaned over.

"See you tomorrow, Jon."

She stood up. Stopped.

Leaned back over.

She put her face inches from the window. She rubbed the glass, but the frost was on the inside, but she could see it – barely – but she could see it.

"Doctor!"

She could see Jon's eyes.

"DOCTOR!"

They were open.

45

Jocah sat on center stage.

The room was filling. The seats up front were occupied with elven. There wasn't much conversation, but Jocah felt the undercurrents of exhaustion and impatience. The energy was jagged. Perhaps the rest of the elven were not aware of the sensation, but it was affecting them.

It had been three months.

They were into the summer months when the polar ice cap receded and thinned. The sun was as high as it would reach into the sky. The air was clear and balmy, when the elven children would spend more time above ice than below, playing games and throwing snowballs. Their laughter could be heard deep into the ice, well into warrens. No adult elven could stop smiling when they heard it.

But no laughter today.

Not even smiles.

No one was allowed above the ice anymore. And the one-week relocation intervals were still in effect, despite things seeming normal. Jocah knew that nothing was normal. Perhaps it was not so obvious to her people.

But they didn't feel the energy.

"If everyone could take their seats." Garren, the assistant, lifted up his hands and walked the circular stage. "If everyone... everyone... if you could take your seats. Please, now."

The hub had filled. As it did, the silence was broken with chunks of conversation that became louder. It fed the impatient flow of energy and made it bigger. Made it *feel* louder.

Jocah sat in the center of the stage, eyes closed. There were others on the stage with her, the committee that included leaders from various parts of the colony, including science, food and transportation. They watched Garren lap the stage without putting a dent in the chaos. He dropped his hands on his hips and whistled.

Nothing.

He reached into the bag on his hip and pulled out a long, gnarly walking stick. He jabbed at the stage.

Boom. Boom. **BOOM!**

The vibrations coursed under the seats and through the congregation.

Silence, at last.

"Now, if we can get the meeting started, I'd like to begin with the minutes from our last meeting."

Garren pulled a handheld tablet from the inner pocket of his jacket and tapped it. He read the items from the last meeting. There were only three. He read the first one about communications with Nog and Jessica and how the committee voted against it, winning by a close margin. This set off a wave of murmurs that grew loud enough that Garren asked for quiet and didn't get it. Arguments broke out and Garren slammed the end of the stick down.

The members on stage leaned closer, speaking into each other's ears. Jocah remained quiet, eyes closed.

BOOM!

Silence settled like a slow rolling fog. Garren waited for the last voice to quiet but decided to move on. It had been that way in their weekly meetings and he was becoming more and more tolerant of the chatter. It was either that or the meetings would last an entire week.

"Second item." He attached an amplifier – a small disc – against his throat.

"SECOND ITEM."

His voice became a booming powerhouse, steamrolling idle prattle.

"THANK YOU. NOW, SECOND ITEM."

Several elven covered their ears. They could feel Garren's voice in their chest like a sonic weapon. A couple elven protested, but Garren mowed right over them.

"SECOND ITEM, REQUEST TO EXTEND RELOCATION SCHEDULE FROM ONE-WEEK INTERVALS TO TWO-WEEK INTER-VALS WAS DENIED BY–"

"The reindeer are exhausted!" an elven stood on his bench and shouted through his hands. "We're going to kill them if we keep up at this pace!"

"ORDER!"

"Did you see Prancer?!" someone shouted from the other side of the room. "His eyes were drooping like he'd been hauling ice all night long."

"What about Dasher?!" another elven chimed. "He had to rest halfway to the new location! This madness has to stop!"

Garren slammed his bang stick.

More elven stood up, shouting at Garren and each other.

The bang stick fired off without effect, its vibrations absorbed into the chaos like waves drawn into the sea.

Someone fell off their bench and no one bent over to help him.

Jocah's eyes fluttered open.

Without notice, she stood up.

She brushed the icy particles from her white coat that floated down from the ceiling after each thundering wallop of Garren's stick. One of the elven committee members took it from him before the ceiling collapsed.

And Jocah, quietly and unaided, walked from the stage.

Through the crowd.

She went back to her room.

JOCAH COULDN'T REMEMBER a time she felt tension like that.

Her mind was chattering with thoughts. It was several minutes before she found the rhythm of her breath – sitting on her tiny bench – hands folded and eyes closed.

There was twisting in her stomach. An ache in her chest. She explored these sensations, noticed her thoughts.

Fear.

But she let it be present. She allowed the unpleasant sensations that gnawed at her like a dog working a bone until it opened the marrow.

And the truth was revealed.
And she knew.
She knew.

46

Merry stood outside Jocah's room.

She had noticed her exit the meeting. How graceful Jocah had slid – gliding like a ghost – down the aisle when she left. She followed her and stood waiting outside.

And soon, there was the jingle of a bell.

Jocah's call for her to enter.

Together, they sat in silence.

Jocah cradled the bell in her hands. She looked down at it, tracing the sharp edges that outlined the opening, revealing the metal ball inside (if one looked closely) that produced a melodic sound when shook.

The bell.

It was handed down from teacher to teacher.

It had been in Jocah's possession for several hundred years, since her teacher had passed away and given her rights to lead her people.

Possession? She laughed quietly. *There is no such thing.*

The bell was a symbol of truth. It represented clarity of vision. It bestowed none of those elements to its possessor; it was merely a symbol. Such virtues were *possessed* by no one elven, no one being in the world. They were themselves always present. It was only the practice of the student to be open and express them.

But the sound of the bell, if Jocah was honest, brought her joy.

She shook it and the melody brought a smile.

"Will you be contacting Nog?" Merry asked.

Jocah silenced the bell.

Merry sagged under the weight of her burden. Her emotions were heavy. They wrapped around her like layers of wet snow. She had lost so much weight. She had become dark and small.

Jocah shook her head.

No.

And the first of many tears fell.

Merry had avoided Jocah all this time.

So much was inside her waiting to burst. She knew that – in Jocah's presence – she would pop like a water balloon. And she wasn't ready for that. She needed to be with her burden. She needed to absorb the sadness that remained after her... *her love*... her husband...

She wailed.

Her face was hot and wet as she convulsed, gutted with the heaviness of loss. She let it be there. She let it take her.

She felt the hand – the warm and soft and comforting hand – on hers.

Jocah reached out and Merry went deeper into her loss.

"It is so bottomless." Merry spoke between sobs. "It is so dark and it is so empty. I wake in the night and he is not next to me. I find myself bringing his coat for him to put on and he isn't there. He's not there."

Jocah looked on with a slight and understanding smile. Not one for humor, but one that was comforting and present. One that told Merry what she needed to do.

Of course it was sad.

She had been married to Nog for thousands of years. It was lonely and cold and empty without him.

Notice. Experience.

And that was all that Jocah asked of her.

That was all there was to do.

To be elven.

And, in that moment, there was sadness.

And she understood.

Jocah did not take away Merry's burden.

She helped her see it clearly. There was a time when Merry would rage at Jocah's seemingly distant presence, expecting her to remove the burden from her shoulders. She now understood that Jocah was there to help her carry her own burden.

Merry used to think that Jocah was the light of the world. Now she realized that Jocah was there to show her they were all the light.

They were all the light.

Merry. Her favorite.

Jocah's teacher once expressed that a teacher has no favorites. But Jocah was elven. She cared deeply for all elven. But, still, Merry was her favorite. So present. So lovely.

"We will be relocating very soon," Merry said. "We'll need you on the ice."

Jocah stroked the side of the bell, its surface smooth and cool and ancient. The metal ball rolled against the inside, letting out a tinny trickle. Jocah placed it in a small box beside her.

She would never see it again.

47

J essica's right leg was numb.

She'd been meditating for a long time and had become accustomed to the numbing discomfort, sitting quietly with her hands folded over her stomach, palms up. Her breath slowly worked through her nostrils.

Nog was on top of the ice, said he was preparing for the next leap. He wasn't sure which reindeer was coming. He wanted to be ready. They all looked so exhausted.

He just wanted some alone time.

He had lost more weight over the last couple of months. He rarely smiled. Sometimes the only time he spoke was to instruct her on how to quiet her mind. *First,* he told her in the beginning, *the body learns to sit still. Then the mind.*

There was breathing practice.

And there was noticing thoughts.

And bodily sensations.

It was difficult to sit so still when there was so much turmoil. They were still leaping every day, although Nog said there were some encouraging signs that the pack seemed less confident in their pursuit. If Jessica felt focused and settled, the pursuit slowed down and hesitated as if she fell off their radar.

But then she'd start thinking again and they'd be right back on the trail like hound dogs picking up the scent.

That's good, Nog would say. *That's good. Keep practicing.*

Hopeless.

How could she expect to live her life this way? Emptying her mind of thoughts long enough to, what, stay where they were for two days instead of one? Was their goal to extend it out to a week? What kind of life was that?

Those are thoughts, Nog would remind her. *Practice and let life unfold.*

So she would huff and fold her aching legs and fold her cold hands and begin breathing again. In and out. In and out.

There were times when she let herself get swept into the *whirlpools of thought,* as Nog called it. She just wanted a little break from all this reality. She wanted something to hang onto, so she allowed the thoughts to spin a story in her head.

She saw Jon lifting the lid to the chamber. His skin was perfect and his beard was full. He stepped out and looked around, stretching like he'd just awakened from a long and refreshing nap.

Where's Mom? he'd ask.

I'm here. That was the part where Jessica would enter the room. Somehow she would return to the colony (she hadn't worked out the details about how she would do that; it was a dream, leave that for later) and she would be reunited with her son. And they would be on the ice, trekking toward the North Pole with no elven or evil twins or old ladies with long braided hair. It was just her and Jon and...

And Nicholas.

Nicholas was there, too.

At first, he was in some crazy mountainous ice palace. He had a beard, too. It was big and full and red. And he was round, like her. He would be standing on top of this palace when she walked up behind him.

Nicholas, she would whisper. And Nicholas, he would turn around.

There would be a twinkle in his eyes. A smile beneath the whiskers.

"Quiet your mind." Nog entered the room.

Jessica jolted back to the little ice room. Pins and needles poked her numb foot. She exhaled and slumped over. Her shoulders ached with tension. She cleansed her mind with deep breaths, but the thoughts wouldn't drop away.

"Nog," she said, "can they see my thoughts? The pack, do they know what I'm thinking?"

"They only see patterns of thought, not the content."

Jessica let her mind wander again. She didn't so much indulge in the fantasy, but began to put together details. They couldn't stay on the run forever. And the longer they did, the more they wore out the reindeer. She was a liability. As long as she was alive, the colony was at risk.

And Nog was away from Merry.

"We'll be launching in an hour." Nog ran his finger inside a bowl and licked it. "If you're hungry, we can eat first. We have time."

Jessica agreed.

And they ate in silence.

But she was thinking. She had a plan.

She would tell Nog when they landed what she was going to do.

48

Claus pushed items around the workbench inside the memory lab.

The chair behind him was empty. Nicholas was back in his personal lab. Claus checked to be sure Nicholas was returned safely after talking with Jack. Sometimes his brother was rash and it concerned Claus that he might've done something weird. He paralyzed him, but it did no tissue or nerve damage. Nicholas was safe and healthy.

As healthy as he was ever going to be.

Claus reached up to the shelf and stopped, waiting for his hand to stop quivering before he took down the jar. He looked inside – it was a jar of magnetic rods – and realized he'd just put them up there not five minutes earlier. He was starting to forget.

Everything needed to be in order. It needed to look organized, like he always worked. No changes to the ways he kept his workspace. He didn't want Jack noticing any changes in his behavior until he was finished draining Nicholas.

And draining his own memories, too.

The jar crashed on the floor.

Magnets scattered to the four walls, some sticking to each other and breaking apart on impact. Cane peeked out from beneath the bench. Claus watched him quickly sweep up the mess. It concerned him that – for a second – he didn't recognize his own son. For a moment, it was just a smallish elven dressed in funny green clothes that seemed to be hiding beneath his workbench.

Claus remembered, as he watched Cane scoot around the lab, when his son made his own clothes. He was different from all the elven. He never fit in. His mental faculties were excellent, he just didn't have social skills. He liked his playthings and, one day, Claus walked in and the boy made a hat and curly-toed shoes and a green tunic. Cane called it his celebration clothes (back in the days when he talked) and glided around the room, singing a song, and Claus watched him, laughing from deep in his belly. It was a laugh that was uniquely his.

A laugh that hadn't been heard in hundreds of years.

Cane returned with the jar of magnets. Claus placed it on the shelf.

Cane latched onto his leg and squeezed and squeezed.

"I won't forget you, Cane." He took the pointy green hat and put it on his own head.

Cane giggled.

And he squeezed his father's leg and buried his face in his fuzzy red overcoat.

Claus patted his head. There were certain things he couldn't afford to let go of. Things he couldn't forget, like Cane and his green celebration clothes. He wouldn't forget that.

He wouldn't forget Jack, either.

For some reason, he kept remembering the time he threatened him and shoved him in a closet. He changed rapidly after that. He got colder and angrier, always singing under his breath.

It was things like that he kept remembering. Those memories he would keep. They wouldn't be any good to drain, but the rest needed to go.

At some level, Claus thought maybe he deserved what he got. Maybe he deserved to be under Jack's heel.

Maybe all this was his fault.

49

essica and Jon.

Nicholas was dreaming.

When he woke, they were standing on the workbench. Nicholas didn't move, afraid they might vanish. The ghostly figures walked across the surface with bundles of firewood. Jon said something to his mother and she laughed.

They reached the other end of the workbench, where a man was sitting on a stump. Nicholas hardly recognized himself. His face was smooth and thin. He poked a stick into a fire that flickered inside a ring of stones. As Jessica and Jon neared, tree trunks appeared around them. They were sitting in a wooded clearing.

The orange glow filled the lab. Jessica sat next to Nicholas and he gathered her into his arms while Jon stacked the extra wood. They watched the fire, warming their hands.

It's a memory.

Claus must've let it run for Nicholas. He couldn't remember it.

He knew their faces, knew Jessica and Jon, but not where he met his wife or the birth of his son.

All he remembered was snow and ice.

And this Godforsaken place.

He watched the images until, hours later, they disappeared. And the room was bluish and cold.

Lonely.

D<small>AYS WENT BY</small>.

Claus was nowhere. Nicholas was trapped in the lab with his thoughts. He thought about what he couldn't remember. He thought about what might have happened if they didn't come to the North Pole.

He thought about the Cold One.

For the first time, the anger burning his stomach was replaced by something icy and twisting. Fear, at last, had arrived.

Jack is unstoppable.

Nicholas knew with certainty (his thoughts told him) that he would never see his wife and son again. That Jack would turn him into a monster.

That Nicholas would wipe out every man, woman and child.

And that thought stabbed fear deeper and colder.

50

Tinsel took her time feeding the reindeer.

Things weren't getting better. They had to rest longer before leaping back to the mainland until they were needed again. They were burning too many calories. Tinsel doubled up on food, but they were still gassed. Dasher and Dancer were looking lean. And Prancer just folded up his legs and ate from her palm.

She wanted to stay up with them until they were ready to go, but there wasn't time.

His eyes were open!

She dropped an abominable sphere and a snowy body swirled into form, standing guard. If anything appeared on the horizon, he would sound the alarm.

And the reindeer would have to leap again.

How long could they do this?

Her stomach was filled with nervous balls of hail.

The carvers were still working to build the colony, shredded ice falling from above like snowflakes. She apologized as she zipped through the main hub and nearly knocked over someone carrying a stack of boxes. She stood outside of Medical, breathing hard.

Her heart, thumping.

The regulars were staring at her.

The chessboard was empty, the checkers still in the box.

Mr. Greyapple, Mr. Canoodle, Mrs. Minutelady, and the others parted as she moved slowly, wanting so badly to ask what was wrong but so afraid of the answer.

Across the room, in the far corner, was the box.

The lid flung open.

The doctors huddled in a clump of white coats.

Tinsel shuffled across the room, hoping to hear something before she got any closer. Dr. Garland glanced up. The other doctors stole glances at her. Dr. Garland took her hand.

"Where is he?" Tinsel asked.

"He's fine, Tinsel. He's fine. But there's been some... *unintended* results."

One of the doctors stepped away. Tinsel could see a table and someone sitting on it. It was an elven. He had a great bush of brown whiskers that was more straight than curly. His cheeks were smooth and puffy beneath a shaggy clump of brown hair.

"We suspected a transformation," Dr. Garland said. "But not this... *complete.*"

An elven.

"We expected some changes," the doctor continued, "with the bone-marrow transplant and full-blood transfusion, but the stem-cell infusion altered his body's chemistry."

Tinsel stepped closer.

The elven looked up.

"He won't remember anything," the doctor said. "He's starting over."

The clan of doctors stepped back as she neared. The elven watched her. His eyes walked around her face; then he cocked his head.

"You," he said. "You read me stories."

51

Jocah shuffled through the snow. Her wide feet plowed through the white fluff. With her hands folded into the opposite sleeves, she walked in no particular direction.

The sky was lit with swirling ribbons of red and green and blue. The Northern Lights were bright and alive. She recalled that elven history books – long before they were aware of things such as molecules or atoms or anything that existed beyond the realm of eyesight – had written that their civilization often worshipped the lights as gods responsible for raising and lowering the sun and moon. There were stories of alien races that left colorful trails behind their ships.

And then came the age of elven wisdom, when they understood that electrons and protons raced from the sun and collided with the atoms and molecules in Earth's atmosphere, releasing energy in the form of light.

Beautiful light.

Wondrous light.

Jocah wandered aimlessly without the watchful eye of her people. They weren't aware that she had slipped out of her room to walk the ice, unprotected. Jocah wanted to see the lights and the sky. She wanted to see them, alone.

Cheers rose from below her.

Just below the ice, perhaps only a few feet, the elven celebrated the birth of one of their own in the most unconventional way – the first newborn in over a hundred years. Although he was hardly a newborn, Jon Santa had been born- again.

At first, the doctors thought he only took on the outward appearance of an elven, with the benefits of generous blubber and wide scaly feet. But further tests revealed he had transformed at a fundamental level. His DNA, the very blueprint of his being, had been recoded to develop in the ageless manner of an elven.

Their treatment only intended to heal the deep-tissue necrosis that he suffered from the unprotected leap. But now he was no longer human. No longer monkey mind.

The elven unlocked the secrets of immortality long ago. An elven lived for thousands of years. But with this knowledge, this power, there came great responsibility to live a life of balance, to control their population so they did not greedily slurp up the world's resources. They procreated with intent. And that intent was rarely practiced since the Fracture.

The colony only reproduced in the event of death. They couldn't afford to grow. They remained small and agile. They lived on the run.

But what they had gained, Jessica had lost.

Jon could never go back where warmbloods lived.

Her son, the boy she nursed and raised and loved – he was no longer.

But still, he survived. He was there.

And for that, they celebrated.

It had been so long since they had something to celebrate.

And this made Jocah smile.

She was not a superstitious elven. She was rational, analytical, and scientific. She considered data and facts and probability.

Still, she had an unlikely thought, one she couldn't ignore.

This is a sign.

She made her decision.

Jocah was far out on the ice when the celebration emerged.

They bubbled out of the snow, one elven on top of another, like a volcano of elven that spilled rolly-polly-jolly beings that rolled and slid. Laughter gyrated through the thin air and Jocah watched from a distance as they all waited for the new arrival to come above the ice for the first time.

They circled around Jon and cleared the snow from the ice until there was a long, slick patch and they watched him push across it for the first time, sliding over it on one foot like an old pro.

Like the art of foot-sliding was in his DNA.

A true elven.

Tinsel was by his side the whole way. There to catch him.

The mob of portly elven devolved into a raucous snowball fight of randomly interchanging teams that climbed the nearest ice ridge for cover. Snowmen were built and elven joined hands to sing and dance and slide. And some ran naked to the nearest open water to teach their newest arrival the subtleties of polar bearing.

And above them, the Northern Lights swirled.

Jocah watched.

She smiled.

She lifted her hand and a small globe – one of polished metal that reflected the lights in the sky – escaped her possession and cruised like a small bird in pursuit of freedom. Its course was the North Pole, a palace of gargantuan magnitude.

It would deliver a message.

Long after the celebration had exhausted, she would tell her people what the message contained.

THE FAT ONE

In the present moment,
Nothing stirs.

Not even a mouse.

52

J essica followed her breath.
In.
Then out.
Her body ached, but still she followed. In, then out.
Sometimes she was aware of the ice, the rising and falling in the Arctic Ocean. She heard fissures crackling along walls. Nog scampering overhead. She heard. She allowed all the sensations of the present moment without thought or prejudice, preference or demand.

There were moments of doubt, moments when she quaked with angst and jittered with hopelessness. She was caught in whirlpools of thought that weaved stories with memories of her family. Where were they? Were they all right? Would she see them again?

And on and on they went. And over and over she returned to the moment, the sounds and sensations. And the breath.

In the long quiet moments that flowed through her.

In, she breathed. Out.

NOG DROPPED into the room and began heating a pot of water.

Jessica unfolded her legs. Pins and needles stabbed along the length of her numb legs as feeling began to return. Her knees and ankles ached like rusty hinges. She stood until all the feeling was back in her legs before helping Nog prepare tea.

Jessica set out the cups and saucers and prepared a place for each of them to sit. She remained standing until Nog brought the pot over and placed it in the center. Jessica's joints groaned as she sat again. She showed no annoyance despite the discomfort. Nog poured the tea, carefully wiping the pot where it dripped down the side. When all was in place, they lifted their cups and drank quietly.

It was strong and aromatic, steam wetting Jessica's cheeks. It lightened her head, charged her tired muscles.

"The pack has been lost for three days." Nog placed his tea cup and saucer next to him. "Your mind has quieted."

Jessica nodded, careful not to cling to the compliment and stir up thoughts. Previously, the longest the pack had appeared aimless was one day. But now this, three days! The reindeer would get a much-needed rest.

More importantly, they were invisible.

NOG UNFOLDED a silver sheet on the floor. He touched it with his five fingers and lifted his hand, pulling up an illusion of light. It was an aerial view of the entire Arctic region.

"We" – Nog poked at the illusion – "are here."

A dim green light appeared under his finger.

"The pack is here."

A yellow spot appeared on the opposite side. Far, far away. It was moving to the side, away from the green dot.

"And this is where we're going."

Again, he placed his fingers on the sheet, but this time spread them out, enhancing the view. It zoomed down to the very center of the Arctic.

The North Pole.

It was a mountain of snow and ice with thousands of shelves and paths and a large flat observation deck on top. It was massive, reaching up into the sky as wind blew bits of white dust from the outside. Occasionally, chunks would dislodge and tumble down the sides like falling rocks, shattering when they hit the bottom.

"It is the *palace*," Nog said, distantly. "It sits on top of the world and looks in all directions."

He sipped, placing his cup back on the floor.

"We will do a quick drop here." He touched a spot at the base of the palace. "They'll see us, but we'll slip through a secret entrance that I remember from my childhood."

Assuming it's still there.

"Once we're inside, we can get lost. It's a big place, Jessica. They won't find us."

"And you know where to find Nicholas?"

He picked up the cup, holding the saucer with his other hand. The rim disappeared in a thicket of whiskers. He closed his eyes, savoring the flavor.

Jessica experienced a whirl of fear. She observed the thoughts that bubbled up from it. *He's not there. He's gone. He's... dead.*

"I solved the algorithm of the warmblood mind," he said. "I know the pattern that identifies you and Nicholas."

She waited.

She watched Nog lift his finger and slowly push it toward the palace, through the illusory walls and deep inside. It was toward the center, somewhere below the surface of the surrounding ice, that a red light began to glow.

"Nicholas is here."

The fear exploded with delicious excitement.

He's alive. My Nicholas... ALIVE!

Jessica's mind raced with the possibilities.

He's alive.

He's alive.

And the yellow light that identified the pack turned toward them.

"Teach him well," Mr. Greyapple said. "It's nice that you have someone to help. You've always been so alone up here when we land."

Tinsel rubbed Vixen's nose and let her fish a snack from her palm with big rubbery lips.

"Yes, Mr. Greyapple. It will be nice to have someone."

Jon didn't hear the conversation. He had an arm wrapped around a bridge of two large reindeer snouts. Dancer and Prancer lifted their heads – their racks of antlers clattered together like old branches – and Jon was whooshed up several feet. He hung on tightly as they put him back on the ice.

They did it again. Jon laughed. Tinsel's heart warmed.

"Maybe more than a little help is what you need," Mr. Greyapple added.

The warmth flushed on her cheeks. She was sure that her face was the color of Ronin's snout.

"It's not like that," she said.

"Not yet. Bring him down for games, Tinsel. We could use another chess player."

Mr. Greyapple and the rest of the elven climbed down below the ice as a late-arriving sleigh landed. Donner was carrying the largest sleigh with Jocah and her entourage. The tunnels and room had already been carved.

Jon was laughing through another reindeer snout-ride.

"These are high protein." Tinsel pulled out a handful of dark pellets. "We're moving toward winter, so it's important to keep their energy up. When they're back on the mainland, they're eating lichens and leaves, but they've been leaping so much that they need more."

Blitzen lipped the handful of pellets and chewed with his mouth open. He wrinkled his nose and shook his head with a throaty growl.

"It doesn't taste good," Tinsel said. "But they have to eat them before they get these."

She reached into the sack on her other hip and pulled out dark green leafy material. The horde of reindeer crowded around them. Tinsel gave a bunch to Jon. Donner's eyes bulged with excitement. A long string of saliva oozed from Vixen's mouth. Jon was afraid they'd snick his fingers off with each bite. Prancer was moaning while she chewed.

"What is it?" Jon asked.

"Spinach, mostly." Tinsel stuffed a crisp leaf between Dasher's teeth. "I coat it with pureed lichens and sesame seeds and my secret ingredient. Want to guess?"

Jon shrugged.

"Taste one."

"Eat this?" Jon held up a leaf.

"Just a nip, try it."

Jon raised it slowly and let the spinach touch his lips. Comet let out a growl and Tinsel shooshed him. Jon ran his tongue over the edge. It was crisp and oily and tasted like...

"Peanut butter?"

"Bingo."

The reindeer crowded around them like an elven trough. Tinsel and Jon were back to back, hands in the air, lips smacking over them. They could feel each other's body heat.

When the snacks were done and the sacks empty, they remained back to back. Tinsel could feel the slow pulse of Jon's heart – half the rate of what his warmblood heartbeat was – against her shoulders. Jon felt the soft skin of her fingers on his.

The reindeer folded their legs for a rest and watched the two elven standing back to back, wondering what they were doing.

"Where's Ronin?" Jon had nuzzled into the crook of Donner's neck, just below the arching antlers.

"He's the strongest." Tinsel was wedged against Donner's head, opposite Jon. "He's been leaping Jessica and Nog."

"He's your favorite."

"They're all special, but he's the protector." She chuckled. "He was a runt, you know. This little shaky leg reindeer that all the others ignored. None of them had his will, though. He's the greatest reindeer of all."

Donner's snores rattled softly and warmly on his back. Jon would later realize there was no more comfortable place in the world than the crook of a reindeer's neck. He was nearly asleep.

Tinsel, though, was awake and watching him.

"Tell me about her," Jon muttered.

"Who?"

"My mother."

Tinsel looked into the dark sky – smeared with a streak of green – remembering what Jessica looked like. She hadn't known her long. In the breadth of an elven's several-thousand-year life span, a few months was a blink. Still, Tinsel recalled her well.

"Jessica was a strong woman. You could tell just by the way she walked that she was powerful, a woman that would give any man plenty to worry about. But she was loving, too. The way she looked at you, I could tell. She never doted on you, she was always careful to keep her distance like a mother polar bear does when her cubs are old enough to live on their own. But she always watched you. Her eyes followed you everywhere."

She might as well be describing someone from a make-believe land. Jon felt sadness for Jessica like a stranger feels for another's loss.

"And my father?"

"Never met him." Tinsel crossed her arms firmly. "The Cold One has him."

"Cold One?"

Oh, yeah. "He's the reason we're out here and not at home. He's the reason there's a pack of mangy six-leggers hunting us. He's cold and he's bad and I wish he was gone."

"He's colder than the Arctic?" Jon chuckled, attempting to lighten her sudden dark mood.

"Oh, he's colder than the coldest block of ice. He freezes things that he doesn't like just by touching them. And, believe me, he doesn't like plenty."

"My father... what's his name?"

Tinsel forgot how much he didn't know. He was starting over. He didn't know his parents' names.

"Nick Santa, I think." She tapped her leg, trying to remember. "Something like that."

"Is he in danger?"

"Probably."

Jon snuggled in some more, leaning back to look at the night light show. He tried to remember if that's what a night sky was supposed to look like. It seemed so odd.

"Is he a good man?" Jon asked.

Jessica never spoke about Nicholas to Tinsel. But she remembered the way Jessica would look, the way her head would hang and her lips stretched thin when his name was uttered. She loved him.

"Yes," Tinsel said. "He was a good man. Does that worry you that your father's in danger?"

He shrugged. "I don't want anything to happen to him, no. But I don't remember him, so it's like I just don't want anything bad to happen to anyone that doesn't deserve it. Especially if he's good."

"He's good, Jon. He's good."

"Now if you were captured by the Cold One," he muttered so low that Tinsel thought he was talking to Donner, "that would be different."

Whether she was supposed to hear it or not, Tinsel smiled. Warmly.

And the two rested with the reindeer beneath the glow of the Northern Lights.

54

"We're all going," the doctor exclaimed. "Come along, no more complaining."

"We're in the middle of a game!" Mr. Greyapple shouted. "What, you want us to quit now? Why, I'll lose my train of thought. I've got a strategy. I can't be expected to remember it."

"You can remember just fine, Mr. Greyapple." The doctor pulled his chair back from the table. "You always do."

"Well, what if the whippersnapper sneaks back in here, moves the pieces around."

"Then we'll make him polar bear at night."

Mr. Greyapple smiled, rubbing his hands together.

"Come on, everyone. Let's go. You're not dead, yet. We're expected down at the hub in fifteen minutes."

"We never have to go to these meetings," Mrs. Dazzleburn muttered. "Why now? Why us? Why? I don't like it."

"Jocah called the meeting, expects the entire colony to be present."

"Maybe you heard her wrong."

"Maybe you need some exercise. Tinsel and Jon, can you help Mr. Greyapple while I herd the rest of these old-timers?"

"Who are you calling old, missy?" Mrs. Dazzleburn bellowed.

❄

THE AISLES WERE WIDER than usual, which was good because the old-timers were walking side by side and not planning to move for anyone in their way.

The room was dimly lit. Only the center stage – circular and raised, as usual – had most of the light directed toward it. The room was so large that additional support pillars, as thick as ancient tree trunks, were needed throughout, blocking some of the crowd's view.

Tinsel and Jon helped the doctors get the old folks to the seats at the very front. The crowd chattered happily along. There were rumors that they would be announcing a three-week leaping rotation. Things would return to normal, like they used to be.

Jon was a good omen.

Tinsel noticed elven turning as he passed by, sometimes whispering to each other and pointing.

Jocah was alone on stage.

No one seemed to note the oddness of this arrangement. In all the years that they had been on the run, she had never run a meeting alone. There was always a committee and assistants. Jocah continually insisted that she was not the colony's leader, but rather part of its democracy – although everyone knew her opinion was all that mattered. If she wanted to be the queen, she didn't have to ask.

When the last person was seated – and that would be Mr. Greyapple because he was busy telling anyone that would listen about his chess domination – the lights dimmed some more.

The crowd hushed as it fell into the dark.

All that remained was Jocah sitting in the light. Her white robe hung loosely from her arms, with her hands resting on top of a crooked cane. Her white hair was braided into a rope that lay over her shoulder and hung down the front.

Silence. Long silence.

And then she lifted her head.

She looked around and spoke.

"Long ago, we left our home."

Her words drifted over the crowd, washing over them with comfort and peace. The sound was like the warm touch of a mother's breast.

"We left behind loved ones. We committed ourselves, together, to a wandering life. A nomadic life. In that time, we have lost much."

Heaviness weighed on the colony. Lives had been lost. Home had been sacrificed. Yes, much had been lost.

"We have gained as well."

Another spotlight illuminated Jon. There was some muttering, a few pats on the back. Jocah looked at him, smiling.

"Stand up." Tinsel elbowed him. Jon elbowed back.

"No."

Tinsel elbowed again. And the others around him began to cheer. He stood up to get it over with. The crowd exploded with cheers. He couldn't see the depth of the room or the arms waving in the dark, but he could feel the floor vibrating. He sat down before the ceiling caved.

"Look around you." Jocah spoke. "Look at your brothers and sisters. How we've become this family. After all these years, we have not been torn apart. We've grown closer."

Muttering and laughter.

"Stronger."

Hugs were exchanged. Hands shook.

"Thank you for all your sacrifices. Each of you has courageously served truth, and I thank you. The path is difficult. Our DNA is programmed to survive, to procreate. To walk along the path of truth can be very uncomfortable. Truth does not seek comfort. It does not reject pain. It asks you to be present at all times. And for that, thank you."

Jocah remained seated, with her hands resting on the cane. She stayed that way for one complete turn of the stage. The colony began to murmur. Some even questioned whether she had fallen asleep. She was wide awake, only taking the moment to see all of her brothers and sisters. They were courageous, indeed. Her gratitude swelled in her belly like fire. Later, some of the colony that sat in the front rows swore they felt the heat as she faced them.

"In three days," she said, her words soft and mournful. She hadn't finished her thoughts and tension already gripped each and every elven. Fingers clenched and legs tingled and chests constricted. Many swallowed the knots that arose in their throats.

They knew.

This day would come.

"I will leave you."

A moan escaped from the darkness. Sobs.

"I will return to the palace. Alone."

Someone cried out *NO*. Others stood and protested. Some hugged each other. Some hugged themselves. And some sat resolute, open to the sadness that was present.

The chaos rumbled for many minutes. It went on and on.

Jocah waited patiently while the stage turned and turned and turned.

Silence settled.

Not completely. But enough.

Jocah stood.

She was required to push on her cane to get upright, recognizing that – even with their science and the ageless wonder of their technology – her body was giving in to the demands of gravity. The body was not meant to live forever.

She stood.

One by one, the colony mounted the stage.

Jocah greeted them. She shook hands. She embraced them. Tears were shed. Gratitude shared. Jocah remained on stage until every elven crossed the stage to say goodbye.

To say thank you.

55

Nicholas watched Claus move slower than usual as he took off his coat. He stood at the workbench for several minutes as if he forgot where he was. He reached for an item, hesitated, held it far too long. Then he'd replace it and grab something else and do the same thing.

Cane stood by his side, one arm wrapped around his leg.

"You'll take the rest of my memories?" Nicholas spouted.

Claus paused with a large box in both hands.

"That's your plan?" Nicholas added. "To just take the rest of them?"

"I have no plan." Claus didn't turn around. "I'm sorry."

"You're giving up, is that it?"

Claus, once again, paused.

Perhaps he was thinking. Maybe he was ashamed that Nicholas recognized his resignation. In the end, he shirked the shame and reached up to the shelf. He pushed a few items to the side and reached to the back, behind a line of bottles, and pulled out a gleaming box. He placed it on the workbench and traced the edges with his fingers.

Lights flickered.

The top popped.

Claus reached inside and removed the spherical object. Nicholas had seen him hide it shortly after he arrived. It seemed like forever since he'd arrived, like he'd been there all his life. Nicholas couldn't remember what it was like to be clean shaven.

His beard hung past his chest in tight reddish curls peppered with strands of white.

Cane fetched the red coat.

Claus dipped down and slid his arms into it while Cane held it. The red fuzz was matted and the white collar dingy with sweat and grime. It was barely fit for a pauper.

He dropped the round object – its lights racing around the surface – deep into the front pocket.

"Jack is evil." Nicholas stood up. "You can't let him win, Claus. You can't give up, you know that. He'll destroy the world, that's what tyrants do. They're never satisfied until they have everything. He'll want more. He'll want everything."

Claus nodded slowly, like he was hearing but had nothing to add.

Nicholas dropped to one knee and grabbed him. Claus's eyes were so deep and soft and worn.

No tension.

No spark.

He'd been emptied of fight. He was a shell of the elven Nicholas met when he first woke in the lab.

"Don't do this," Nicholas whispered. "Don't let your brother win. He just... he can't. For all of us, not just the human race. You know he'll destroy all of you. I saw it in his eyes. He's mad."

Nicholas shook him.

"I'll help you. We can fight, we can gather the elven, band together. If everyone stands up, we can beat him. I promise all is not lost."

Claus reached up and patted Nicholas's hand.

Cane stood by his side, watching.

Someone entered the room.

"His Excellence requests your presence in the arena," Pawn said, his uniform impeccably pressed.

Claus squeezed Nicholas's hand.

Nicholas watched him walk, not slide, from the laboratory.

A great elven, he was.

He was.

56

The domed ceiling arched with a slight curve. It was smooth and shiny and reflected rows and rows of bench seating along the slopes. Center stage was raised like an oversized pillar. It was a cylinder, flat on top and fifty feet in diameter. At the moment, it was twenty feet off the floor, descending slowly.

On top, a single elven.

Jack slid along the edge. His mutterings, in most settings, would be nothing but muddy words blending together, but the acoustics of the arena reverberated them across the grand space.

Siiiiii-lent night, he was muttering.

Over and over.

"Brother!" Jack peered over the edge. "Why didn't you tell me you snuck in? I oughta punch you in the face."

Jack got on his knees and grasped the edge.

"I'll be down in a jiff. Don't you go anywhere."

The cylinder hummed with commercial-grade hydraulics, pushing the mammoth peg into the floor, its side smooth and cold and polished like stainless steel. Even in the distorted field of the convex surface, Claus looked small and frail. His beard, still full and bushy, hid his chin and lips but not the withdrawn cheeks and dark, deep-set eyes and the wrinkles that tracked like webs.

He'd aged years in the past days. His body had accepted the end, knowing what he was doing to his mind. It sensed the disappearance of so many memories, like a vessel tipped and poured of its contents. The body knew it was time to sleep.

But Claus held onto some memories. He held onto just enough to recognize his brother standing on the center of the cylinder as it drew level with the floor.

Jack was as blue as ever.

His cheeks no longer the color of deep ice but more like juice squeezed from a plum.

His eyes, hardened like coal, looked out from the pockets beneath his brows. Despite the smile, the eyes were joyless.

"Brother, brother, brother... come now." He waved Claus nearer. "Come stand with me on the pinnacle of the world."

Claus kicked forward, cruising slowly toward the center. Jack waited patiently, hands out. When Claus stopped in front of him, Jack took his hands and held them. Icy slivers penetrated Claus's fingers. With a thought, Jack could turn him into an ice sculpture.

For the moment, he only made his hands numb.

"Do you know where you are?" Jack asked. "Right now, this moment? Where you're standing? Do you know?"

Claus waited.

"This, right here, is the North Pole. It is the axis on which the world turns. We're standing on it. Isn't that cool?"

Jack swung their arms.

"Why does it matter, you wonder?" Jack asked.

Claus's arms lost feeling as the cold crept past his elbows. Jack squeezed tighter, demanding a response.

Claus shook his head.

"Because a king will be crowned. The world will be saved. I think it's only fitting it happens at the top of the world. Symbolism, you know. We learned that in English class. You remember class, don't you, brother? School? Remember?"

What few memories Claus still possessed of those days long ago were not pleasant. Days of sitting next to Jack, kids picking on him, Claus watching. Sometimes joining in.

Shoving him into a closet.

Siiiiii-lent night.

"Yes, well... I remember," Jack hissed. He pulled him closer and the cold wrapped around Claus's shoulders, across his back. "Oh, how funny. Eh, brother?"

His neck went numb.

His eyesight began to fade as Jack's voice echoed.

Fun, fun, fun...

JACK WAS COASTING along the perimeter of center stage. The edge of the cylinder was now just a seam.

Claus stood motionless in the center, on the pinnacle of the world, stuck in place. He could hear Jack humming a little song, something that sounded like "London Bridge," as Claus's sight returned and his body slowly thawed.

"Look what a little determination can do, brother." Jack was behind him, slowly coming around his left. "A little elbow grease, a little hard work. Oh, and the key ingredient, one mustn't forget the key ingredient to success on a scale like this. Power, baby."

Jack raised both hands and sang.

"POOOOOO-WER, YEAH!"

His laughter rang all around.

He wiped a tear from his cheek.

"Oh, God. I love this," he muttered. "Listen, here's what's going down. In three days, we're throwing a party. You, me, the entire palace. We're not messing around here, Claus. We're going to party like its 1899, you understand. I'm talking lights, music, celebrities, the whole deal. There's going to be a red carpet; it'll be recorded from ten different angles because we want this event, every **SECOND** of it, saved forever and ever."

He cruised behind him, humming.

"In case you're wondering, *I'm* the celebrity. And you're welcome. Few people know someone as big as me, brother. Only you know me inside and out. You're welcome."

A sharp edge honed his voice.

"Only you."

Jack was counting on his fingers like he was trying not to forget anything, making sure it was all in place. He seemed to forget Claus, his red coat splayed around his feet, standing still and waiting.

"You'll be sitting right there." Jack suddenly picked up the pace, sliding faster and faster, only speaking when he cruised in front of Claus.

"Right there," he said, quickly pointing at a bench in the front row.

"You get the whole bench.

"To yourself.

"Because you're family.

"And family.

"Means something."

Faster and faster, until Jack whirled around and around, the circle tighter and tighter until he was spinning like a top, hands above his head. His features a blur and his voice had an odd vibration.

"Do you–

"know why–

"we're having–

"a party?"

When Claus didn't respond, Jack repeated, "Go ahead, brother... **ASK!**"

"Why..." Claus's lips were so cold. "Why the party?"

"*Becaaaaaause...*" Jack's tone tilted with anticipation.

He stopped.

Arms out.

"Mother's coming."

Claus was cold like a gutted fish.

Any other time, he would believe it was a lie.

He knew it was not.

She was returning.

Perhaps, like Claus, she sensed the end was near. He hoped that she didn't feel the howling hopelessness inside her gut, too; that she had some sense of what to do. That she had a plan. That she wasn't useless.

That she knew how to stop the bluish jester doing a little tap dance in front of him.

"Why?" was all Claus could muster.

"I'm glad you asked," Jack said. "It shows initiative, curiosity. Interest, my brother. Good for you." He slapped Claus on the cheek. "Good for you."

His hand was like a bucket of water from the deepest part of the Arctic.

"She knows it's hopeless," Jack said. "That it's over. We know where the rebels are at, we've been tracking them relentlessly and we'll destroy them. Well, *I'll* destroy them. Give credit where it's due. Come to think of it, I think the old lady knows I'm better than you and her and every elven on ice. Maybe she's hoping I'll show mercy."

Jack made a face.

"So *there*. Stick that in your pipe, loser."

"The whole... colony... is coming?"

"The rebels, you mean, brother? Not the colony, **WE'RE the colony.**"

The hairless brow ridges buried the dead coal eyes. "We stayed, they left; don't you call them the colony. You got it?"

Claus nodded.

"Good. Now where was I? Oh, yes. No, just Mother is coming. She's the only one. We'll hunt the rest down, like animals. I kind of like it that way. Sounds fun. You know how when you're just so excited for some day to come, you know, like if someone promises to bring you a whole bunch of presents and you just can't sleep the night before? And then the closer it gets, the more you don't want it to end. You know what I mean? Like savoring a sugarplum."

He chewed with his eyes closed and whispered, "That's what I mean."

Jack looked up at the ceiling, admiring the reflection.

"I don't want to eat all the sugarplums at one time, so I'll probably hunt them down a little at a time. Maybe let them pop out a few babies, reproduce a little, give them a head start. Something like that. What do you think?"

"Doesn't sound like you want to help our people, Janack. Or the world."

"Well, who says you can't have a little fun while saving the world, huh? And, besides, those **REBELS** are traitors, brother. They're cancer. And you know the best way to treat cancer, right? You know, you're a scientist."

Jack waited.

"No, I'm asking. You're a scientist, right?"

"Yes," Claus uttered.

"What have you done for me?"

"What do you mean?"

"Invented things, that sort of thing. What have you done for me?"

"Everything you've asked."

"Really? *REALLY?*"

Jack chuckled.

"Have you really? Have you tried your hardest?"

Claus numbly fingered the sphere in his coat pocket, the ridges etched along its surface pulsing.

Jack didn't notice what his brother was thinking.

"Maybe I won't get rid of *all* of them," he said. "Maybe I'll save the scientists."

His point was clear.

He wouldn't need Claus anymore.

"She'll be coming in solo," Jack announced. "Dear Mother. Dear, dear Mother. Our mother, Claus. She's coming to see us... *FINALLY!*"

Jack took a deep breath and let it out nervously. His chin trembled as he muttered, thinking about what she would look like, what he was going to say, figuring that maybe he should write a speech so he didn't forget to say all the things that were on his mind. After all, this was what it was all about–

"What are you going to do?"

Jack looked up. Claus was still there, staring at him with those tired eyes.

"I'll be honest," Jack said. "She'll have to feed the bear."

Feed the bear?

"Grrrrr." Jack pawed the air.

"RrrrrrRRRAHR!"

Claus didn't get it.

"Feed me, dummy. Man, I think you're getting stupid, brother. I'm the bear and she's going to feed me, get it?" He clawed again. "Get it?"

Claus didn't respond.

Jack inhaled deeply, eyes closed.

"What do you think she'll taste like, huh? Warm brownies? Hot cocoa? FRESH COOKIE DOUGH?"

"Don't hurt her," Claus said.

"She never made cookies like other moms," Jack said with that distant look again. "I don't think she ever made dinner. She didn't do anything like a mother should, you know that? No cookies, no bedtime stories, no birthday presents... *nothing.*"

"She's our mother."

Lucidity crystallized in Jack's eyes, coldly. "I've been hurt."

"We all hurt."

"Yeah, well, you don't know my suffering, brother, and we all have to sacrifice. It's Mother's turn, you know. Fair is fair, that was your favorite line, remember? When you were the leader, you used to say, *Fair is fair, Janack. Fair is fair!*"

Jack puffed his chest out, lower lip plumped and pompous.

Claus recalled saying that when he didn't want to be hassled with a difficult decision. He also remembered delivering that line when he simply took things from Jack.

Fair is fair.

Jack slid up to him, their bellies touching. The cold traveled through the ice, trapping Claus in the center as it seeped through his feet. There was no escape. His breath so frosty that ice crystallized on Claus's nose.

"Go get me the rest of Nicholas Santa's memories, empty his mind so that he'll be ready to clone. I want to introduce that warmblood to my people."

"And then you'll be done with me?"

"We'll talk."

Jack smiled.

"Santa is waiting in the memory lab, ready for draining. You won't need to go back to your personal lab, for any reason. It's undergoing renovation. You're not going to recognize it. I'm thinking of converting it into a game room. You know, video games and billiards, things like that. Something I can do to relax. It's tough ruling the people, I'm sure you remember."

He chuckled.

Claus squeezed the sphere in his pocket, feeling the ridges dig into his palm.

The frozen ground thawed. Jack shoved him toward the exit.

"Fair is fair." The center stage cylinder was rising. "Fair is fair, brother."

57

The self-propelled sleigh looked like a black vault on rails. Jocah had no bags or luggage. She paused at the open door. It would take three days to arrive at the North Pole. That was much slower than she anticipated. The navigators identified several ice leads that couldn't be crossed, which made for a circuitous route. She didn't want to call for a reindeer and put anyone at risk.

And her arrival wasn't urgent.

"Why are you doing this?" Merry stood alone, emerging from the ice.

Jocah's hand was on the door. She didn't turn her head. She specifically requested that she depart alone, having said her goodbyes.

"You were always stubborn," she said.

"You could stay, Jocah. We can avoid them for many more years. Your decision is rash and self-serving. I think you need to hear that."

Jocah paused.

She stepped off the rail and turned. Merry faced her with a stiff posture.

"This isn't about my self-centeredness," Jocah said softly. "This is about Nog."

"You're abandoning him! He's alone out there with a warmblood and you're leaving us! Now is not the time, Jocah, to surrender. It is time to fight."

"Now Jessica is just a warmblood, hmm?"

Merry took a moment. "You're putting us all at risk and you're not making sense. I think you need to take some time and sit with this, understand why you're making this decision."

Jocah hadn't explained herself. She acknowledged that. But how would she explain her intuition that now was the time to see her sons?

"I need you to lead them, Merry. You need to be there for the elven."

Jocah cupped her hand over Merry's trembling hands.

"Change is difficult. They will need you."

MERRY WATCHED the sleigh slush away, carving two tracks in the snow leading toward the top of the world. She was still quaking even though Jocah couldn't see her. She wanted to look like she was afraid. She wanted Jocah to believe she was timid, that she would stay with the colony and keep running away.

She couldn't let Jocah see her true intentions, so she pretended to shake with fear.

Two elven that would serve as Merry's assistants emerged on top of the ice, stood next to her and watched Jocah's sleigh slide far away. New Jack City was only a day away. That wasn't enough time for Merry to carry out her plans, so she had the navigators plan a longer route. They told Jocah that impassable ice ridges and open leads would force her to go around them.

About three days, the navigators told Jocah. *You'll arrive in three days.*

Jocah accepted the detour. Why would they lie to her?

To get ready for an attack. That's why.

"The meeting is ready to begin," one of her assistants said.

Merry followed them into the ice. Jocah put her in charge to guide the elven.

Merry was a fighter.

58

The light was bright.

Nicholas's head rang like a firmly struck bell, one that was thick and solid, humming with a vibrating coldness. He opened his eyes.

His head was hard as concrete. His ears popped.

The room was small.

Cold and blue.

He tried to sit up but found his hands and feet bound to the chair, and there was something around his head, a metal ring that pushed at points around his scalp. He couldn't recall how he got there.

He couldn't remember his name.

There was a man in the corner.

A very short man with a dirty red overcoat. The fringe of it was gray, but at one time it was white. It seemed like an odd thing to be wearing in what appeared to be a laboratory. He was no taller than a child.

The dwarf was sleeping; his head lay on the workbench. There was something around his head, a wiry strap of sorts. Maybe it was the same thing around Nicholas's head.

He moaned and twisted, rolling his head on the workbench.

A commotion grabbed Nicholas's attention.

Three people – fat and short and dwarflike, their faces buried in bushy beards – burst into the room, wearing matching dark blue uniforms. They stood around the one with the red overcoat and waited. One of them, the one slightly taller than the rest, poked him.

He moaned again.

Another poke. And another.

The red-coat dwarf snapped to attention. He looked around the room. He looked like Nicholas felt, trying to piece together just where he was and why. He focused on the intruders and his eyes darkened.

"Get out."

"Why are you wearing the halo?" the lead purple-clad one asked.

"Don't question my methods, just get out. Leave us alone."

"Jack questions." The purple-clad one stepped back. "Are you finished?"

Claus jumped off the stool and herded them toward the doorway. "If something goes wrong, you can report you ruined it! *Now get out and leave me to my work!*"

The purple-clads stumbled and bumped into each other. One fell, but being so fat and round, he simply rolled over and caught his balance before Claus gave him another swift shove and a boot.

"Jack expects you to be ready for the ceremony in one day. We will come for you, Claus."

"Out!"

"Be presentable, the entire palace will be there."

"OUT!"

Claus leaned against the wall, propping his weight on one hand. He seemed out of breath or dizzy.

Something stirred beneath the workbench.

Another dwarf – this one smaller than all the rest and dressed in a funny green outfit – looked out from a pile of boxes. He reached out for Claus, his chubby little fingers tugging on the back of the coat.

Claus looked down and frowned. "I made myself clear, get out of my lab."

The little guy stutter-stepped and covered his eyes.

"*Get.*"

And Claus shoved him out the door, too.

Nicholas thought he heard weeping.

59

J ocah spent her first day meditating.

The sleigh found the path of least resistance and slid along, jostling its contents very little. She found the ride to be peaceful.

As the dusky daybreak arrived on the second day, she called up the navigational maps. She was going so far out of her way that she did another analysis, bypassing what was preprogrammed and working with her own assessment of satellite images and ice-floe movement. The path seemed unreasonably safe and she assumed it was to keep her safe or their hope that, given enough time, she would return.

Of course, she knew there could be another reason.

Jocah returned to sitting after reprogramming the route.

By the end of the day, when the gray sky was filled with blackness and the stars glittered and flitted around the full moon, she stopped her meditation to observe her destination.

It had taken only two days to see the palace swelling on the horizon.

It grew bigger.

Massive.

The size was grossly out of proportion with the landscape. She had seen images of Jack's palace, but to see it rising in the flatness of the polar ice caps was breathtaking. At its peak, it was a hundred feet and spread out like a city. She knew that if there was this much above ice, there was so much more below.

All doubt was erased.

Her decision to return home was the right one.

The sleigh slid to a stop at the foot of the mountainous palace.

It stood alone.

Jocah waited patiently, noting how much colder it had become. Perhaps it was her imagination.

A doorway opened on the wall, dark inside.

Something moved.

A six-legger crept out, followed by another. Their beady eyes watched the sleigh as a long metal rod extended out from the pitch-black tunnel and latched onto the front of the sleigh, linking it like a freight car.

And then it began to pull it inside.

60

The colony's hub was full of able-bodied elven. The sick and elderly were ushered to Medical despite their resistance. They wanted to fight, too.

Merry stood on center stage.

"We will approach from nine directions." Merry allowed an image to appear on the stage. The palace formed. "They will sound the alarm, so we have to use confusion as a weapon. We'll ignite the times-napping device to slow time for us and buy us some precious moments–"

"Merry, that won't do any good," someone in the front row said. "They will only match our timesnapper with one of their own; it won't buy us any extra moments–"

"But it will take a toll on their energy supply. We will be dropping in with fully active wind turbines on the back of the sleighs to keep the generators fully charged until we hit the ice. They will be slow to respond, which will give us time to release the three abominables to attack the top of New Jack City."

Merry couldn't help but grimace at the thought of that garish monstrosity.

"The top?!" someone shouted. "They're fortified at the top. We need them to attack the base where they're most vulnerable!"

"Precisely! They'll expect the A-bombs to be the brunt of our attack and assume we're following, and this will allow us to punch holes at the drop points where we have fully scanned for the weakest points and the lowest population of elven *inside* the palace. No one will get hurt. Not us and not them."

Merry walked around the stage.

"They are prisoners as much as we are. You heard Jocah, they are our brothers and sisters. We should no longer be separated. Does everyone understand this?"

The crowd muttered.

"Let's get something straight." She let that phrase gather stiff attention. "We're not going into the palace to save Jocah. We're going to end the Fracture. We're going in to heal our people. Jocah has only led the way. Jack least expects it."

The silence was pure. Merry's footsteps were loud.

"This is the moment we have waited a hundred fifty years for, the moment to heal ourselves, to heal our people, so that we will no longer live as outcasts, so that those in the palace are no longer forced to hunt us like seals. We go, **THIS MOMENT**, to become whole again."

She walked through the illuminated palace.

"Do we have an understanding?"

And they stood.

They cheered.

And they listened, united.

They were assigned sleighs.

They received assignments.

"Freeze weapons," Merry said. "We'll use them to solidify walls and compartmentalize the palace, to divide and conquer. We'll close in on Jack until he is isolated and alone. Until he can't move."

Someone entered the back of the hub, sliding full speed down the aisle.

Merry glanced up.

It was one of the navigators that planned Jocah's route.

Those around him muttered. He stopped – looked around – and waited for Merry. She waved him onto the stage and bent closer. He whispered into her ear.

She pulled back.

"Call the reindeer."

61

Jack stood in front of a three-tiered fountain – the newest addition to his basement room. He'd seen such a thing when he reviewed the warmblood's memories, something in a large courtyard. It was almost twenty feet tall and spilled water from all directions into a large basin filled with shiny coins. When Jack saw that – he'd never seen such a thing – he HAD to have it.

A likeness of it was now in the middle of his room, spitting streams of icy water from the pursed lips of miniature elven.

His fountain was *waaay* better.

Jack leaned over the basin.

The Arctic cod swimming in the pool wisely bolted to the other side, far away from the looming shadow. He watched them gather into a school.

Jack held out his hand to catch a stream of trickling water that turned into chips of ice, plunking into the water like pebbles. Jack dipped his finger in the basin and listened to the water crackle.

Frozen solid.

The cod were suspended in a block of ice.

If she doesn't come, I'll destroy them all.

Jack thought that maybe his mother might play another trick. Perhaps send an empty sleigh or one with a bomb. It bothered him so much that he couldn't sleep.

He was agitated and fidgety. He was so warm that he stripped down to his tighty-whities. Even half-naked, hiding in the coldest section of the palace, his temperature was up to minus forty degrees.

THAT'S CRAZY!

He poked a hole through the ice with his fingernail, digging out a cod. It shivered in his palm, the eye jittering back and forth. He licked it once, twice, three times before biting the head off. Some of the juice spilled on to his fat-dimpled blue belly.

Jack dragged his fingers over the ice. He liked the fish, he decided. He wouldn't freeze the next batch, not all at once. Maybe he wouldn't eat them, just keep them for pets. That's what he might do, start a new hobby. He was on the brink of healing the Fracture so that all elven would soon be under his rule.

I mean leadership.

When the warmblood was finally infected with the plague, he could start reclaiming the rest of the world. But that would take time. You couldn't just create a world-sized glacier overnight.

In the meantime, he would have fish.

Yeah, that would be nice.

Siiiiii-lent night,
Siiiiii-lent night.

"Your Excellence?"

"Ahhhh!"

Jack threw his hands over his exposed belly, moving them over his underwear and back to his chest, but he couldn't quite cover everything, so he ducked behind the fountain.

"You're supposed to knock!"

"Sorry." Pawn averted his eyes.

"What do you want?"

"I thought you might want the news about Jocah."

"Mama?" Jack peered around the spitting fountain.

"Yes, Excellence. She's arrived."

A shiver rifled through Jack's belly. He forced himself to breathe.

"Say that again," he said.

"Um, your mother. She's arrived at the palace."

Pawn and Jack stared for several long moments. Pawn thought maybe his Excellence had turned solid.

"You serious?" Jack said.

"Um, yes."

"Don't mess with me, man!" Jack pointed at him and shook. "You know what happens when elven mess with me. You tell me the truth, is she here or not?"

"Yes, Your Excellence. She's in the receiving area where–"

"DON'T TOUCH HER! Nobody touches her or talks to her or looks at her, you understand? You put her in isolation and you leave her there until the ceremony."

Jack's face and body were the color of an overripe raspberry. He struggled to catch his breath. He wasn't a doctor, but he'd be willing to bet his temperature was up to minus thirty. He hadn't been that warm since he was in third grade and Darlah Iceridge tried to hold his hand.

Pawn turned to leave.

"Where you going?" Jack called out.

"I'm going to pass along your orders."

"Oh, yeah. All right." Jack, suddenly aware he was half-naked, ducked behind the fountain again. "Send a tailor down. I'm going to need something new and ready for the ceremony tomorrow. Do it now."

Jack squatted by the basin and polished the ice with his palm, the dead cod-eyes staring. He was still thinking of Darlah and the way her fingers felt.

62

Nog was above the ice, looking into a sky smeared with charcoal.

It was a calm day, the subzero temperature nibbling at the end of his nose. A tear formed in the corner of his eye. That wasn't unusual. The cold affected his eyes that way, especially when he stood that still on a winter's day. They were near the winter solstice, when the world was at its coldest.

But then maybe, this time, there were more tears than usual.

A small dot eased into the dark sky. Tiny and red, it arched over the flatness of the Arctic landscape. Nog watched it coming down like an asteroid and–

BOOM!

–land on four legs.

Ronin shook the snow off his expansive rack and snorted. The reindeer's eyebrows were pinched and expectant. He felt the tension in Nog.

Something was about to go down.

Nog anchored the small sleigh to Ronin's hindquarters.

He carefully tested the buckles and ran his hand along the back side of the sleigh. He checked the bag on his hip to make sure everything was in working order. When the time came, he would have to grab without looking, and if the wrong thing came out... well, then, the day would end.

Nog raised a black hood toward the reindeer's nose.

Ronin tossed his head, smacking Nog onto the ice. He would not tolerate covering his nose that was burning brighter than ever. Nog picked himself up and brushed himself off. He reached inside his bag and pulled out a small speaker that fit neatly in his palm. He spoke into it and told Ronin of their plan.

He described the way he and Jessica would need to drop quickly to the palace under the cover of night.

He instructed how important it was to arrive in secrecy.

Ronin kept his head held high. His nose was a source of pride. It burned for all those who had lost to the villain by the name that every reindeer and elven alike cringed to hear.

The Cold One.

He would not defile it with a hood.

Nog finally gave up and put the translator (something he'd just invented) away.

They would come in hot.

Nog sat in the sleigh. The seat next to him was empty.

The North Star had poked through the veil of night, twinkling like a beacon. Nog focused on the star. He hoped his darling was looking up at that moment. That his Merry was seeing the North Star, that perhaps they could share its visage one last time despite the miles that separated them.

Jessica crawled from the ice.

Her movements were slow, methodical and trancelike. She dared not move suddenly or with excitement. That would risk disturbing the emptiness of her mind. She let her senses guide her to the bench next to Nog. He did not look at her as she slid onto the cold, hard surface.

She folded her hands on her lap, eyes cast down.

Nog held the reins.

As the ice shot away from them, as they rose through the sky like a shooting star, she would not allow thoughts to find a place to land in her mind. She remained open and empty. She couldn't let the thoughts disturb the silence.

There was only one thought that threatened the peace. One thought that rained heavily in her mind.

We're coming for you, Nicholas.

63

Jocah's room was larger than the one she'd become accustomed to using since the Fracture. She sat on a bench for much of the time. She slept on a cot only once.

Occasionally, she heard a slot open and a tray shoosh over the floor with bowls and eating utensils. She left it there until the slot opened again and a hand reached in to pull the tray out and replace it with another one.

She needed an empty stomach to calm her nerves.

She had begun to quiver.

It had been so long.

So long since she had seen her son.

Janack.

She was surprised to find that she yearned to reunite with him. There was so much left undone. And when she was aware of this, the fear dissolved into a warm openness. There, she felt love.

She was right where she needed to be.

She was beginning to tire.

Perhaps, she thought, she would sleep again, but the walls and ceiling began to quake with a steady beat. Flakes of ice shook loose from the ceiling and fluttered to the floor as the rhythm buzzed beneath her feet and in the palms of her hands resting flat on the bench.

It felt like music.

THE DOOR OPENED.

No one was there to greet her. It just slid open on its own. Jocah waited but, still, no one came for her. And the beat that thrummed through the cell was louder in the hall.

Jocah gathered the loose shawl that was draped over her shoulders and pulled the ends over her chest. She stood, feeling the aches deep in her joints and a warm swirl of excitement in her belly.

She stepped into an empty hall.

To the left, it was dark.

To the right, brightly lit. The corridor descended at a gentle slope, bending to the left. She couldn't see the end.

She stepped out, placed her ancient feet flat on the ice, the soles old and scaly and not as slick as they once were, and began to slide down the corridor.

The farther she went, the louder the music.

64

The reins dug into Nog's palms.

It was difficult to breathe. Ronin had leapt higher than he could ever remember a reindeer leaping. They had cleared the low cloud cover; they soared above it with the sky filled with stars.

Ronin tipped to the left, gliding into the clouds until condensation crystallized on the sides of the sleigh. He drifted just inside the clouds so they had cover.

Far below – lit up with a thousand points of light like a galaxy on the ice – was a mountain.

New Jack City.

Nog felt the edges of darkness creep into his vision as he struggled to get enough air.

Jessica was settled into her seat, eyes closed, breathing deeply and slowly. She maintained her focus while they glided closer to their destination. They were almost there. About to reach the drop off point when–

AAAAIIIII!

New Jack City's alarm sounded.

Ronin fell like a boulder.

Nog's cheeks fluttered.

Jessica – eyes wide with terror, gripping the bar at the front of the sleigh, fear blossoming out of control – screamed.

Nog pulled back on the reins. They were coming in too steep. They needed to land quickly, but at this angle nothing would survive. He leaned into the seat, the reins cold and hard and taut.

"Slow, Ronin!" he screamed. "SLOW, RONIN!"

But the howling wind ate up his words and the reins did nothing.

They would crash.

They would leave a hole in the ice and sink to the bottom of the ocean. They wouldn't feel anything.

Nothing.

It would end that fast.

Details blurred.

The palace and the lights and the endless dusky ice merged with Jessica's screams until – at the last second – the sleigh bent beneath them. Nog and Jessica slid from the bench and flattened out on the floor of the sleigh.

BOOM!

They hit something hard.

BOOM-BOOM-BOOM!

Jessica and Nog bounced around like a child's game of jacks, landing on one another until the sleigh tilted to the right. Jessica was below Nog. He recognized that the sleigh was about to tip. He heaved his body in the other direction.

WABOOM!

SSSSSSSSSSSSSSSSSSSSSHHHHHHH!

On two rails, the sleigh began to slow before coming to an imme-diate stop, throwing Nog and Jessica violently into the front of the sleigh. Nog was seeing stars inside his head.

There was jostling.

Jessica's voice.

"NOG!" she screamed. "Wake up!"

Nog opened his eyes, saw her panicked face and a black sky behind her. He sprang up.

"I'm up, I'm up."

They were at the foot of the palace.

They were exactly where he wanted to be, the secret entrance – the one that he and Merry had used to sneak inside even before all the rest of New Jack City was built on top of it... *it was still there!* It looked like a large snowball wedged against a flat wall, but if it was pushed just right, it would dislodge–

"Nog!" Jessica cried again.

Nog reached into his bag without looking and pulled out a silver sphere etched with lines.

He tossed it.

Snow and ice swirled up. Flury emerged with fists as big as icebergs. He slammed them into a charging six-legger.

65

The map joggled on Merry's lap as Vixen hit an air pocket, tossing her, Tinsel and Jon around. She steadied her hand, noting where all the lights were located in relation to their destination. The lights represented the other sleighs.

They were exactly where she wanted them.

She closed the map, satisfied. They were on schedule, just as she planned. She wanted Ronin to lead her sleigh. He was the fastest and would get them to the palace first so she could distract them from the others. Tinsel told her that Nog and Jessica were using him to relocate.

Vixen was plenty fast.

They could still land first.

They would lead the charge to bring down the Cold One.

Merry checked the map again as the palace came into view on the horizon.

All was in order, except...

One reindeer was out of position. She quickly counted and counted again. There was one too many.

And it's heading right for us!

A red light streaked past them, shaking their sleigh as it passed.

"RONIN!" Tinsel shouted.

The red nose disappeared behind them.

What's Ronin doing here? And why is he going in the other direction?

And then she heard it.

The alarm had already been set off. It was a high-pitched whine that could be heard for miles. She checked the map and no one had landed. But someone was already there.

And she knew where.

There, at the base of the palace, six-leggers were clustered around a brutal snowstorm. *Someone released an abominable!*

Merry recognized the location.

"Tell Vixen to veer right," Merry shouted, pointing at the battle.

"That's not our landing point," Tinsel said.

"DO IT NOW, CHILD!"

Merry leaned to the right as the sleigh tilted.

Plans change.

Nog wasn't going in alone.

og and Jessica were thrown off the sleigh as Ronin swung around, whacking three six-leggers across the ice.

YELP!

Another three felt the brunt side of Ronin's antlers.

Flury roared.

"Get the other side!" Nog fumbled with the reins.

Jessica ran around and tried to unhitch him. They were tossed to the ground twice – once a very close call with snapping jaws, close enough that Jessica felt its fetid breath on her cheek – but they managed to unhook the sleigh.

Ronin leaped toward the oncoming herd, swinging his rack like massive paddles, swatting them down like puppies. What he didn't get, Flury pummeled. Slowly, Ronin and Flury moved to the boulder. Nog pushed.

Frozen.

How long had it been since they used this entrance?

Jessica saw what he was doing and helped push, getting on her knees for leverage.

Nothing. Stuck, solid.

CRACK!

Ronin swung around and smacked it.

With the palace at their backs, Flury was keeping the six-leggers away. Ronin reached back and smacked it again.

237

CRACK!

Nog felt it tremble.

They pushed.

Ronin reared up and snorted like a belching machine.

CRACK!

The snow boulder moved, sucking wind into the dark tunnel behind it.

They pushed, but it wouldn't budge more than a few inches. It wouldn't be enough to fit a broomstick. They leaned into it again. Nog stepped back.

"What are you doing?" Jessica shouted. "PUSH!"

"Hold on." He reached into his bag. His palm pulsed with blue light. "This isn't going to feel good."

Jessica didn't have time to ask why.

The light leapt out of his hand and enveloped them like gelatinous goo. It was warm and comfy.

And then it started to squeeze.

And SQUEEZE.

SQUEEZE!

Jessica couldn't breathe. She felt her eyes bulge like she'd been run through a clothes wringer.

And then she was inside.

Jessica's eyes filled with water.

She gulped at the air while Nog peered down the black mouth of the steep tunnel. He reached into his bag and pulled out something the size of a snowball that wriggled like a rat. He dropped it on the floor and Jessica saw it split into seven smaller versions of gray-haired wiggly things and jet into the darkness.

The snarls of the six-leggers were closing in.

The wind howled as Flury rolled the snow boulder back in place. Just before it closed and the sliver of light was shut out, just as the wet smack of antlers met another six-legger's ribs–

Nog screamed.

"GO!"

There was the whoosh of an enormous reindeer leaving the ice.

The clack of the snow boulder snapping closed.

The slap of Flury's sphere hitting Nog's hand.

❄

IN DARKNESS so black they couldn't see each other, Jessica reached for Nog's hand and felt the cold, etched sphere of Flury already there. Nog placed it in his pocket and pulled her closer.

Down they went, sliding into the dark.

The snarls of six-legged beasts faded.

67

J ack adjusted the thing knotted around his neck.

The tailor called it a *bow tie*. He said he was inspired by the warmblood's memories – now downloadable for free – and thought Jack would look smashing in it.

Jack leaned closer in the mirror and straightened it. *Smashing? Well, if I do say so myself, I am quite a catch.*

He smiled a blue smile.

He thought, perhaps after the ceremony, he might have a drink at the café and see if any of the ladies would like to dance. Or whatever elven were up to when they weren't working. *What do they do?*

He stepped back and stroked the silky lapels and turned to see the jacket tails dragging on the ice. He flipped them up to see what the pants looked like. Nice and snug, showing off his round posterior. He likey. He told himself not to punish that tailor, he had taste. Who knows, there might be another ceremony where he would need to look this... what was it... ah, yes.

Smashing.

His nerves sprang when the music started.

It was a solid rhythm, one of Jack's favorite songs. Really hard, something to get the juices flowing.

Boom-boom-clap. Boom-boom-clap.

The walls shook.

He could feel it enter the soles of his feet, run through his groin. He

reached in his jacket pocket and pulled out a set of dark glasses, something the tailor adapted from the warmblood's memories. Actually, the
glasses in the memories were clear, but the tailor darkened them so
they looked... *cooler.* Jack slid them up his nose and over his eyes. He
walked away from the mirror and turned with his finger and thumb
cocked back.

"Hey there, fella," he said. "You ready to party?"

He cleared his throat. That sounded stupid. Sounded whiny and
just... dumb. He walked up to the mirror and started again. He walked
away, was about to turn–

"Your Excellence."

Jack jumped. *"WHAT?"*

"I'm sorry, I didn't mean to–"

"I told you to knock!"

"It's time for your entrance," Pawn said.

Jack's heart thumped. "Oh."

Pawn stepped back.

The music surged through the opening like angry bolts of lightning, hammering his chest and tingling his blue flesh. Beneath the
music, he could hear the roar of the crowd awaiting his arrival.

They wanted him.

They love me.

And there, just outside his doorway in the expanded tunnel, was
his chariot.

Just like he ordered.

Got to love those elven.

68

M erry leaned forward.

She could smell the rich scent of reindeer hide.

And her own fear.

The sleigh tipped dangerously into the sharp turn.

They banked until they were almost sideways and then came out too quickly. The sleigh wobbled to right itself as Vixen spread her legs out flat and aimed at the swarming battle. It looked like a feeding frenzy.

Please don't be a feeding frenzy.

"ACTIVATE THE TIMESNAP!" she shouted.

Tinsel fumbled with the black box sitting on the bench. She hesitated, her thumb hovering over the button. Merry turned around, her face blustery.

"What are you waiting for?"

Tinsel pushed. The button clicked.

FffffssssssssttTTT!

The world blurred and spun.

Their skin tingled.

And time inside the sleigh came to a stop.

The timesnapper sped up the atoms inside the sleigh while offsetting the corresponding heat. For the individuals within a timesnap bubble, the world around them remained still.

They could travel around the world in a single night.

If they wanted.

The lights on the palace dimmed for a moment.

They would sense the timesnap activation and ignite their own. For a moment, Vixen and the sleigh plunged through suspended snowflakes and frozen six-leggers.

But then, little by little, the lights brightened.

Things moved.

And the timesnaps synchronized.

They were back to normal time. But it bought them several seconds.

Several precious ones.

The wind harvester fluttered behind the sleigh like a long whipping tail, feeding power back into the sleigh's depleted generator.

Merry leaned forward again, hoping to push them faster, feeling the vertigo in her stomach as they dropped. Tinsel and Jon held onto their seats. Vixen veered down at the ground and pulled up, taking advantage of the air current to slingshot even faster.

They blazed several feet above the ice.

Suddenly, the abominable storm that was fending off the six-leggers vanished. The sleigh was aimed to crash right through the middle of the pack. Vixen ducked her head, antlers spread out like a train's cowcatcher, ready to plow a path through the furry mob.

They closed in.

Seconds to impact.

No sign of Nog or Jessica. The six-leggers weren't feeding on anything. They were attacking the palace. They were locked out.

Merry pulled hard on the reins, snatching Vixen's head up, tilting her front legs up in time to soar over the six-leggers. The sleigh lagged in the updraft and the rails skidded over their backs, leaving a wake of yelps and snapping jaws.

Once they were past, Vixen dropped to the ground and the sleigh slid to a halt. The six-leggers were hot to follow.

Good. Let them come after us. It will give Nog time to hide and do whatever he's doing.

WHAT IS HE DOING?

MERRY TOSSED THE SPHERE.

The abominable pulled ice and snow from the palace, weakening its wall to build a beastly body between the sleigh and attackers.

"Release Vixen," Merry shouted. "Once she's airborne, we need to punch a hole in the palace."

The abominable met the first of the beasts with howling fury.

"We don't have much time."

Tinsel and Jon cut Vixen loose.

The abominable's force spread out to contain the attack, but it was too wide and too weak. Merry couldn't be careless. If there was an army on the other side of the wall, they wouldn't be any better off inside.

A six-legger's jaws snapped.

Merry opened her map.

The attack from the other sleighs was underway. The abominables had already weakened the defenses and the other teams were inside, making their way toward the middle. Strangely, the palace's power grid was nearly shut down on the perimeter and appeared to be focused somewhere in the center. She didn't sense anyone near them. No guards or even citizens.

Merry jabbed a dart into the wall and stood back.

The tip began to glow.

Thoop!

It was sucked inside.

A hole began to open like a flame to a plastic sheet. Water gushed out as the ice melted.

"In you go!" Merry waved Tinsel and Jon inside, double-checking for movement. If her readings were right, they would crawl right into the outer kitchens and composting center.

Merry backed into the hole, watching her map. She scooted back until she was all the way inside and opened her hand. The howling wind stopped like a light switch and the sphere smacked into her palm.

Merry slid back, sealing the hole as she went.

THE ROOM WAS dark and powerless and smelled of earthy bins of worms and decomposing food scraps. Merry checked the map. Still no one in sight.

"What's that sound?" Tinsel whispered.

The walls vibrated in pulsing rhythm as if New Jack City was alive. "It's music," Jon said. "Is there a party?"

MERRY CHARTED a course for the epicenter of activity. It appeared every elven in the palace was gathered in a large center room. It was in the direction of the music.

That's where they'd find Jocah.

Nog, too.

Merry checked one more thing before they left. She searched for warmblood algorithms. It would show her where Jessica was. If she was in the palace, then she was with Nog. But what she saw didn't make her feel any easier.

Several lights were scattered all over the palace.

As if there were warmbloods everywhere.

69

N og and Jessica sat completely still. Only the sound of their breath disturbed the quiet. That, and the distant music.

A small light – about the size of a child's marble – began glowing between them, splashing red light on their faces and eerie shadows on the walls. The room was the size of a closet. Jessica barely fit.

Nog put the glowing marble on the floor. It grew a little brighter. Jessica noticed the small shelves crowded with knick-knacks and pictures.

"What happened back there?" Jessica asked.

"That was a thinning device. Made us skinny enough to slip through the crack. Not all that pleasant, but we weren't exactly having a party outside, were we?"

Jessica thought about the time her little sister tried to crawl up the chimney and got stuck. They could've used something like that.

"What were those mouse things?" she whispered.

"Replicators," Nog said. "I programmed them to emit warmblood thought algorithms. They're slithering all over the palace by now."

"Where are we?" she whispered.

"Our secret room." Nog was distracted with something that started glowing in his palm. He spoke while watching it. "Merry and I... we carved this place when we were young, somewhere we could escape the world and talk about our dreams."

There were small trophies and ribbons on the shelves next to drawings and sculptures and shiny stones. Jessica noticed the photo nearest her. It was Merry and Nog, smaller and fresh-faced. Nog's beard was bright red and hung in droopy curls. Merry had dark hair that hung over her shoulders.

Jessica wiped the layer of frost off the surface and the images began to move. The two of them began to laugh. An elven ran behind them and Merry covered her eyes. *He was stark naked!*

Nog chased after him, undressing as he went. He cannonballed into an ice hole with a monstrous splash. Merry waved and the motion stopped, returning to the original picture.

"We're not staying long," Nog muttered. "Just until I can get a bearing on where everyone is at."

"How old were you?" Jessica asked.

"Huh?"

She repeated the question.

He looked up. "Oh, I don't know. That was a long time ago."

Nog stared at his palm but looked back at the photo. His beard twitched and his eyes glittered in the red light. He touched the photo and it started moving again. He watched it all the way to the end. A chuckle escaped his clutch of whiskers.

He wiped his face and looked down.

"I shouldn't have brought you along," Jessica said.

"What, you were going to do all this yourself?"

"I never should've let you come in the first place."

"My dear." Nog sat with his head bowed. "Life is not about pleasure."

"Then what?"

He shook his head. "This, right here. It's about doing what's right. Serving life. Truth. Whatever you want to call it."

"So you won't go back to Merry when this is all over?"

"When this is over?" The smile returned to his eyes. "My dear, I'll be running back to her."

They shared a laugh.

70

I t was like the world had become grainy.

Like each atom, every molecule, was as big as sand. The air was thick and heavy.

Nicholas shuffled each step forward.

He focused on staying balanced. The cotton in his head – as dense as lead – threatened to tip him over, so he just pushed each foot forward and watched the bright red coat lead him out of a room.

Down a hall.

And into a large room.

Small people were all around.

They stood and clapped in seats that inclined all the way to the top. It was so steep and so far that the ones at the top – too small to see – would tumble all the way to the bottom if they tipped over.

There was a group of little round people in front of him. Maybe five or six. It was hard to count. They were all dressed the same, in funny little outfits that looked like tuxedos. Their mouths moved and they were looking at Nicholas, but he couldn't hear them.

Because of the cotton.

He followed beams of light that shined down from the top of the domed ceiling and raced around like loose cannons, spotlighting parts of the crowd and, occasionally, the small people on top of a large cylinder.

They were hammering instruments that sounded nothing like

music.

One was hidden behind a huge set of drums. Others had string instruments slung around their necks. One had his leg wrapped around a metal pole and was screaming into a box that amplified his voice above the cheers and claps.

But it was noise.

All a buzz through the cotton.

No memories, just cotton.

The tuxedoed group squabbled with each other while they led Nicholas all the way to the base of the cylinder and squeezed him into the front row. The armrests ground into his hips. He flopped his head back as far as it would go but couldn't see the band on top.

"Hey!" Tiny hands shoved the back of his head. "Elven back here, sir."

Nicholas apologized.

He sat up straight and stared straight ahead.

The cylinder was polished ice. It reflected like cold steel.

The convex surface reflected his image – fat, wide and bearded. The whiskers were white and tightly curled over the lower half of his face. His hair, also white, receded over his head. The nose was bulbous and red.

Who's that?

The bearded man moved when he moved. Waved when he waved.

For the life of Nicholas.

He could not recall ever seeing that face.

And next to him, staring almost as blankly, was a very short man that was just as round and just as wide. He was wearing a bright red coat with white trim.

The two sat staring.

THE MUSIC WENT ON FOREVER.

The seats thundered beneath them.

Lights changed colors. Confetti and streamers fell from the ceiling. The crowd flashed signs that were hard to read, something about *Champions* and *We Love You!*

Nicholas thought of leaning over and asking the one in the red coat what was going on. He probably wouldn't hear him, but Nicholas finally got curious enough to try.

He leaned to the right, the first word on the tip of his tongue–

"HOW YOU ALL DOING TONIGHT?" someone screeched. It was sort of a cross between yelling and singing. And whoever it was, he wasn't really asking.

The crowd seemed to answer, though.

"GET ON YOUR FEET IF YOU AREN'T ALREADY ON THEM. GET ON YOUR FEET AND GET READY TO GIVE IT UP!"

That's when Nicholas realized the cylinder was sinking into the floor.

The lead singer was on the edge of the platform, wrapped around his metal stick, shouting into the box stuck to the top of it.

"HE IS THE GREATEST LEADER THE FREE WORLD HAS EVER KNOWN!"

The stage slowed its descent.

"HE IS YOUR LEADER!"

The singer was eased down in front of Nicholas.

Eye to eye.

"THE COLDEST ELVEN IN THE WORLD–"

The cheers reached a frenzied pitch.

Signs around the top of the arena flashed: *APPLAUSE! NOW!*

The singer sucked in a *loooong, deeeep* breath. He inflated like a balloon, throttled the metal stick with both hands and bared his teeth, screaming into the box–

"Jaaaaack!"

The lights went out.

Something zapped Nicholas's bottom, like it was poked with a hundred needles. Nicholas jumped up. So did anyone else that happened to be sitting.

A single spotlight cut the darkness, illuminating a spot to Nicholas's left.

He could see over the heads of all the little round cheering people. He could see the spotlight hitting an entry tunnel leading toward the stage.

It was a short, round man with blue skin.

He was waving to the crowd and the band began to play hideous music.

He was riding on a platform that heaved up and down as it crept slowly toward the stage. It wasn't until it was near him that Nicholas realized the platform was being carried by several elven.

71

The platform was made of solid gold, a mineral that was in very short supply in the North Pole. Actually, it was nowhere in the North Pole. Jack heard about this gold from Nicholas's memories and demanded that someone better find it and find it fast and make it happen.

It happened, baby.

They found it (the real deal, they assured him, but he had his doubts; they would pay if they were lying) to form the ornately crafted rails with tiny wings fluttering from the sides, inset with sparkling ice diamonds on the tips. The elven carriers struggled under the weight. They deserved it, a bunch of would-be traitors that – once upon a time – got caught sending messages to the rebels. They had family that ran away and wanted to make sure they were all right... *WELL, TOUGH!* They ran away and you get to carry a platform made of gold.

Lucky you.

Jack took one last look in the mirror, straightened the bowtie, and headed out the door. The public was crying for him and who was he to deny them?

"Eh-hem." Jack stopped and gestured at the platform with the gold chair. It was still two feet off the ground. "Hello? Footstool?"

One of the elven flattened himself as flat as a round, fat elven can get on the ground, and Jack stepped on his belly with both feet and bounced up and down like a bouncy ball. He leaped onto the platform.

"That was fun," he announced to no one, picking his teeth and sitting down. "Onward, lazy traitor elven. My public awaits–"

"Your Excellence."

Jack looked around, but the glasses were too dark. He ripped them off and rolled his eyes. "What is it *now*?"

"Sir, there's been reports of a blackout on the palace perimeter due to the power demands of the arena–"

"Don't you dare, don't you say it!" Jack snapped his hand at Pawn. "Don't you even think of diverting power. We've got all year, we've got FOREVER to light up the palace walls! You are NOT going to rain on my party!"

"But, Excellence, there's reports that attacks–"

"I don't care."

"–and the rebels–"

"*Lalalalala*, I can't hear you." Jack shook his head. "Just get out of the way before I make you carry me all by yourself, Pawn. Get, get. Shoosh."

Pawn stepped aside.

Jack straightened his sunglasses and pointed.

"Onward, tools."

THEY WAITED in the entryway while the band screamed the introduction.

Jack could smell fried cod and walrus-on-a-stick. His favorites. He wondered why he didn't eat that more often and made a mental note to put that on the menu. In fact, he would decree that everyone was to have fried cod and walrus-on-a-stick for the month of January. There, done.

From his vantage point, he could see some of the crowd. They were on their feet, rabid with excitement, absolutely rabid. Jumping up and down, they were. Clapping and cheering. Jack thought they would start climbing over each other if he didn't get to the stage in the next two seconds.

He ignored the signs that told the crowd when to cheer and stomp their feet and he knew there were electric prods in the seats to get them standing, but that was merely to let them know when he was coming. They loved him, he could tell. He could feel it. The energy moved through him like the ocean's current.

They love me. They really do.

THE INTRO, flawless.

Jack would be sure to tip that elven singer when it was all over. Or at least let him slide on taxes. (Taxes, that was his next decree after the fried cod and walrus-on-a-stick. Someone had to pay for this party.)

The platform heaved and tipped forward as the ones in front slumped under the weight.

"Easy there," Jack called. "Slow and easy or you're swimming with the fishes before the night–"

Spotlight.

Cheers.

Showtime.

THEY WALKED into the open and the adoring cheers wrapped around Jack like a bedtime story.

He stood.

"I love you, too!" Jack blew kisses to the adoring crowd. "Oh, I love you, too!"

A band of children were herded to the platform by guards. They leaned away with terrified expressions. The guards shoved them forward.

"Here we go, children." Jack pelted them with a handful of seal-flavored hard candy stamped with his face. "Eat up, eat up. All yummy in the tummy."

The kids covered up to avoid the hailstorm of candy as Jack fired away while grinning at the crowd and waving with the other hand. He got bored and, to the children's relief, kicked the barrel off the platform and spilled the candy on the floor.

Halfway to the stage, he reached behind his chair and pulled out a long tube with a trigger.

"Daddy's got something for everybody!"

He pulled the trigger and a cloud of smoke exploded from both ends. Tightly wadded shirts rifled into the crowd, slamming a teenage elven over the back of his chair. His friends laughed. They unfurled the shirt, a big blue face plastered on the front.

I HEART JACK!

The lucky winner was still unconscious.

Jack fired ten more. The crowd took cover. The last shot shattered a chair.

The band welcomed their blue-skinned leader. The singer lifted Jack's arm and the two paraded around the stage to nonstop insanity. The volume didn't quite match the excitement of some of the faces, but Jack couldn't see much through the sunglasses.

Jack approached the mic stand and leaned into it. The noise began to wane. He said, with a sultry tone, "Do you have time for one more, boys?"

Applause! Applause! Applause!

The signs lit up.

NOW!

The crowd stomped.

And Jack took the mic and announced to the band this one would be in the key of C (he had no idea what that meant). The band nodded.

"We'll be doing a favorite of mine. I'm thinking of making it our national anthem. It's a little song I like to call... 'Silent Night.'"

The party was just getting started.

72

Jessica let Nog study the map without bothering him. She looked at the rest of the pictures and picked up things that looked like art projects from the third grade, a repository of memories.

While she did, the music grew louder and harder. She could feel it in her butt, and her butt was getting numb. She realized the alarm wasn't going off.

Have they forgotten about us?

"Strange," Nog muttered. "Either this thing isn't working or... everything is gone."

"What do you mean?"

"The map says the entire palace is empty and powered down except for one place."

Jessica listened to the music again. It had to be loud if it was vibrating all the way to the edge of the palace.

Nog was shaking his head.

"What is it?" Jessica asked.

"There's something else."

Jessica waited. "What?"

Nog looked up. "I can't find him anymore."

"Who?" But Jessica knew.

Nog closed the map. "His thought algorithms have stopped."

Jessica leaped out of the secret room, sliding into the dark in the direction of the music.

73

S *ilent night!*
  Silent night!
  Silent night!
Silent night! Silent night! SILENT NIGHT! SILENT NIGHT!
Those were the only words.

Jack just hit them, over and over.

"Siiiiiiiiilent NIGHT, YEAH!"

He imitated one of the band members and finished with a flourish of arm-swinging and hip-gyrating. The crowd, having grown oddly silent during Jack's one-chorus song (something he thought was out of respect for the song), regained their energy for the band.

Jack stood with his arms over his head. He noticed the band was taking a bow, too.

"All right, all right. We don't need you anymore, get off. Go back to wherever you came from."

They dropped their instruments and started off.

They ran when Jack chased them.

"Sit."

Jack lowered his hands. The crowd was looking at each other warily. No one wanted to sit, not on those chairs.

"Sit, now!" Jack screamed into the mic.

An elven dropped into the chair with a hesitant scowl, expecting the worst. When there was nothing but the hard, cold surface, others around him took a seat.

The signs changed from *SIT* to *QUIET*.

"Thank you." Those words felt strange on Jack's lips. But he meant it from the bottom of his cold blue heart. "I'm glad everyone could make it to this *momentous* occasion. I'm sure you'd rather be *nowhere* else. I know I don't."

Jack chuckled.

Silence. Until the signs changed. *CHUCKLE.*

"Listen, let's get honest." Jack's voice echoed in the great room. "You didn't like me at first. You liked that guy, right there."

Jack pointed at Claus.

QUIET!

"Come on up, brother. Come on."

Claus moved like he just woke up. He started toward the center of the stage. Someone clapped. It was once. Jack glared, pointed, and the offender was hastily removed by security.

Jack slung his arm over Claus's shoulder.

"Here's the guy, right? Your former leader with his nice, clean coat. You look great, brother, you really do."

Jack stared into Claus's gaunt eyes. The cheeks more gray than ruby.

"You were all for peace and love and other stuff, but you let us down. You let us down."

Jack started a slow pace around the perimeter of the stage, speaking as he coasted.

"The world needs elven. It suffers from an infection that *HE*" – Jack stabbed a finger in Claus's direction – "couldn't handle. Your leader, the big teddy bear in the ridiculous red coat, did nothing about the spread of warmblooded *humans* and we just let them spread, elven. We did that. You and me. We let our leader fail the planet."

Jack shook his fist.

"I don't know about you, but I wasn't going to stand for that."

APPLAUSE.

"I don't know about you, but I love this planet."

APPLAUSE!

Jack spun into the center and threw up his hands.

"AND I WILL NOT STAND FOR IT!"

CHEERS!

And he got them.

Some of the crowd was on their feet. Jack was certain they didn't get zapped and that meant he won some of them. He wasn't alone, after all.

They really do love me.

"Let's take a look at the infection!" Jack aimed his short finger at Nicholas. "Come up here, warmblood."

BOO.

The crowd responded to Nicholas's slow approach with jeers. Nicholas towered over the two elven. Jack yanked him to his knees. He blew his icy breath into Nicholas's face and dusted it with frost.

LAUGH.

"What's your name?" Jack pushed the mic in front of his face.

Nicholas's lips opened and closed. He stared vacantly, trying to remember.

"The dummy doesn't even know his name!"

LAUGH!

"Don't be too hard on him," Jack said. "He's not all bad. His name is Nicholas something or other. And he's going to help us destroy the warmbloods. Aren't you, buddy?" Jack shook his shoulders. Nicholas's head bobbled. "That's right, first we're going to clone you a dozen times, infect you with typhoid, plague and, ooooooh, I don't know, maybe smallpox. And then we're sending you out to explore. Doesn't that sound fun?"

Nicholas stared in silence. The words were going in, but nothing was making sense.

"Hello?" Jack knocked on his head. "Nobody's home, huh, folks?"

LAUGH!

"All right, enough of you two morons. Let's get to the real show, the reason you're all here tonight."

SILENCE.

Jack stepped away from Claus and Nicholas. He bowed his head and folded his hands over his belly. There was a long pause. Not a creature was stirring.

"Hundreds of years ago," he started, head still bowed, "some of you lost friends. Some of you lost family. We've spent our time worried sick about their safety and whereabouts, hoping that they would one day return."

Jack looked up. Tears twinkled on the brims of his eyes.

"We've all suffered greatly, haven't we?"

NOD.

"Yes, we have. We've all suffered because of one person. The one person that formed the revolt, the one that convinced the elven to leave our great city and wander the Arctic without ever visiting or calling or even writing us a letter. One elven responsible for all that."

Jack held up a single finger. He turned in a complete circle so everyone could see it.

"And that one elven is with us tonight."

APPLAUSE.

"Please welcome..."

APPLAUSE!

"All the way from a dark and cold rebel camp somewhere in the Arctic..."

CHEERS!

"Myyyyyyy MOTHER!"

Horns blared.

Spotlights glared.

And from the tunnel, all alone, dressed in gray with a long white braid, appeared an old elven woman.

Beneath the signs that called for *BOO!* there was a collective gasp. The jeers hit a wall, but Jack ignored it. Some wept quietly, hiding their faces behind others. Others closed their eyes.

But none dared call out her name.

None dared express the heartache they felt when Jocah stepped on stage.

And Jack took her hands.

74

M erry was cautious.

        She stopped outside every wall and scanned the other side before jabbing the melting dart into it. But every room, every hallway, in every direction... was empty. A ghost town. Pretty soon, she stopped melting holes in walls and walked right down the middle of the hall like it was home.

The market was empty, too.

Stalls once filled with trinkets and fragrances and fruits and T-shirts were closed and locked for the night.

"What's this?" Tinsel tugged on a poster plastered on the wall.

Merry and Jon looked over her shoulder. There was a big blue face giving two thumbs-up.

"Let's party like it's 1899?" Tinsel read along the bottom. "What's that supposed to mean?"

"I don't know, but I think it's that way," Jon said, pointing at the blue arrow on the floor.

No more caution.

They were sliding full steam ahead in the direction of the music. Merry wasn't certain, but it sounded like someone screeching "Silent Night" over and over.

Like he forgot the words.

❄

THEY RACED UP THE RAMP. The music had stopped. Cheering was replaced by a passionate speech.

They approached double doors flanked by ushers. They slid on by, said good evening with a head nod and continued around.

"What're we going to do?" Tinsel asked.

"For starters, relax." Merry relayed their position to the other teams that were closing in on the 1899 party. A few elven passed them without much notice. Merry pretended to be showing the kids where their seats were located.

When they were gone, Tinsel took up a lookout to the left and Jon scouted the right. When the coast was clear, Merry jammed the dart into the wall behind her. A hole opened slowly and the rich smell of deep-fried food wafted out.

"Is there, uh, a carnival in there?" Jon asked.

They crawled inside.

Merry first.

She popped up behind the back row at the very top of the room and no one seemed to notice. She waved the other two inside and sealed the hole. They couldn't quite see over the elven standing on their seats and went to the nearest aisle.

Down below, too far away to make out any detail, it looked quite like a circus. There was a center ring and an elven barking out commands. Merry recognized him only because he was bluish. And he was holding the hands of another elven, this one with a long white braid.

Tinsel squealed.

She slapped her hands over her mouth as elven began to stare. She looked at Jon and back to the stage. There was an enormous man down there, too. He stood next to an elven that Merry hadn't seen since the Fracture had begun. An elven that wore the red coat of pride and respect.

Claus reached into the pocket of the bright red coat.

"Hey, what're you doing?" Jack's voice echoed throughout.

Merry gathered Tinsel and Jon next to her as the cold whoosh of air was sucked toward the stage. She recognized the swirling air currents and watched, perhaps, the largest abominable she'd ever witnessed in her life.

"*Everyone!*" Merry called to the other teams.

"CENTER STAGE, NOW!"

The center of the arena was enveloped in a torrent of ice and snow, consuming the four figures inside it. Merry, Tinsel, and Jon descended the aisle against the tide of elven rushing to escape.

75

J ack had a speech prepared.

He'd practiced it in his head a thousand times. He'd lie awake at night, imagining the things he would say to his mother if he ever saw her again.

At that moment – the moment he saw her face – that speech was lodged in his throat like a peach pit.

She was older than he remembered.

Somehow, he thought his mother would live forever. She was already the oldest living elven in history, why would he think any different?

It wasn't so much the lines that carved the corners of her eyes or the spots that darkened her cheeks. It was the way she walked. It was so slow and careful. So mindfully aware of each precious step.

Hunched over with her cane, his mother approached.

Jack's mouth worked a string of spit between his lips, but that was about all it did. No sound could get past the peach pit. A tiny ice cube – about the size of a diamond – fell from his eye and tinkled at his feet. He didn't want to cry. Not here, on stage, in front of the whole world.

This helplessness, this total lack of control... he looked like a frightened little cod gasping for air. It angered him.

The floor crackled around his feet.

Jagged lines of ice bolted across the stage.

Jack ignored his feelings and the warmth of emotions that flushed his cheeks and stirred his chest. He was numb again and it felt good.

She was making him feel warmth. She, his mother, it was her fault. She ran away from him when he needed her most. She loved Claus more than she loved Jack. She loved the elven more than she loved Jack. It was her fault he was like this. Her fault he was so cold.

So, so cold.

He swallowed the speech.

There was nothing to say, after all. He reached out his hands. He wanted her to feel the depth of his loneliness. The hardness of the cold.

Claus stepped between them.

His hand in his pocket.

"Out of the way, brother," Jack said.

But Claus didn't step away. He unveiled the shiny globe with etched lines, holding it on the tips of his fingers, the grooves pulsing with light. Jack felt the pull of its gravity, felt the swirl of air.

"I KNEW IT!" Jack jabbed his finger at the A-bomb. "You've been holding out on me, just like I said! JUST LIKE I SAID!"

The sphere rolled off Claus's fingers. Hit the ice.

"Hey." Jack backed up. "What are you doing?"

His ears popped. The barometric pressure dropped.

The ceiling and floor shook.

An abominable took shape. Its enormous legs straddled the stage. Jack looked up at the thing and the thing looked down at him with cavernous eyes. It lifted its mighty fists above its pumpkin-shaped head.

Jack looked as frozen as one of his cod treats.

But the abominable stopped. It looked at Claus; then it twisted its arms and dispersed its body around the perimeter of the stage, forming an eyewall of snow and ice in hurricane force. They were locked inside the eye of a storm.

Everyone else was locked out.

76

Claus never wanted to use the A-bomb.

The colony had their A-bombs for protection. Jack would use one to destroy. But Claus invented one and hid it from Jack. He wanted it, just in case he needed it. Just in case the end was near and he had no choice but to use it. He couldn't let his brother destroy the world.

As Jack grew colder and the end more imminent, Claus knew the time had come. He would release the unfathomable power of an abominable to put an end to his brother.

To end all suffering.

The abominable would eat the snow and ice from the arena to build a massive body and destroy Jack. Claus was sure he wouldn't survive either. He'd have to be close to Jack when he released it. Close enough to be sure it worked. Close enough that he would go with his brother to the bottom of the ocean.

He accepted that fate.

Claus downloaded his own memories so that they would live on. His people would need a leader when it was over. If Claus couldn't be there, at least his memories would be there to guide them. He didn't copy them, no. He downloaded the memories – all their wisdom and knowledge – so they were pristine. So that they could be embodied by someone else.

TONY BERTAUSKI

He didn't need them anymore, anyway. Not when the end was so near.

But in that final moment, something changed.

He realized there was another way. He didn't have to pound his brother into oblivion. There was a way to resolve what had happened to Jack. Claus saw the way he changed when their mother stepped onto the stage. He silently mouthed a new directive to the abominable that towered over them, fists reaching through the hole in the ceiling.

There's another way to end this.

The abominable's body formed a wall around the stage to keep Jack's guards out and allow the elven to evacuate the palace.

They would have to be as far away as possible when it ended.

77

J essica slipped and slammed hard on the floor, sliding into the wall just as hard. Her head rang with a high-pitched whine. She scrambled to her feet and tried to run and just repeated the desperate dance.

She remained on her hands and knees. *Relax. Take a second.*

In her rush, she forgot about the scaled foot-slips that Nog had fashioned for her and the slow, rhythmic pace it took to walk – let alone run – across a floor MADE OF ICE!

The music had stopped.

It was her only compass to follow. She ran blindly down one hallway after another, crashing through empty market stands and slamming into the wall at every turn. She didn't know if she was any closer to her husband.

No algorithm.

"Jessica!" Nog's voice echoed. "Stop! Now!"

She'd lost him shortly after bailing on the secret room. When she stepped out, she slid down a long, dark sloping ramp that pitched her into an abandoned marketplace with half-empty cups and plates with food, like the elven just disappeared.

Nog slid after her like a speed-skating Olympian. Posters plastered on the walls (she hadn't even noticed them before) fluttered as he passed them. She stood up – half hunched over beneath the low ceiling – and read the nearest one. A big bluish face and two thumbs-up and an arrow pointing down the hallway.

They were all pointing down that hall.

Jessica pushed off with her right foot – slow and easy.

Nog pursued.

It was the first signs of life.

There were two elven in uniforms, sliding easily. Side by side.

When they noticed the oversized warmblood filling up the hallway and barreling toward them, they stopped and held out there hands. Jessica hit them like bowling pins and bounced them off the opposite walls. Nog zipped around them as they called for help.

"Jessica!" he shouted. "We must be TACTFUL!"

She was done with finesse. Done with mindfulness. She embraced her monkey mind.

She wanted her husband back.

She wanted him back now.

SOMETHING RUMBLED LIKE A LOCOMOTIVE.

Jessica slowed. Nog pulled up even with her. It was a familiar howling sound, like a cyclone. The sound of an abominable was unmistakable, but it was accompanied by quaking in the floor.

The first screams brought Jessica and Nog to a dead stop.

They were joined by panic.

And then the elven stampede came slipping around the bend. Jessica and Nog pressed against the opposite walls and let the unending mass of fat-bellied elven rush past. They didn't notice the warmblood trying to flatten against the wall.

They fell and bounced and picked each other up. One of the youngest crashed into Nog. Nog grabbed him before he could rush off.

"WHAT'S HAPPENING?" Nog screamed above the din.

"The arena's collapsing!"

"WHAT?"

The elven kid tried to wrench out of Nog's grip. "They released an A-bomb inside; it's cracking up!"

Nog held on tightly. "WHO?"

"Who do you think?" he screamed in Nog's ear. "The Cold One and Jocah and that warmblood, that's who. NOW LET GO!"

He batted away Nog's hands and joined the exodus.

Jessica heard.

Her eyes were wide.

78

"All teams, assist with evacuating the arena!" Merry called to her teams.

It was already half empty, but elven were falling in the madness and some were getting hurt in the rush. Whatever was happening, they needed to get all of them to safety. They needed to get as far from this place as possible.

"Call the reindeer." She pulled Tinsel and Jon closer. "Saddle them with the largest sleighs they can handle and get every elven away from the palace."

A large block of ceiling shattered on empty benches.

"Go."

The A-bomb was pulling ice from the ceiling and floor to form the massive storm around center stage. Fractures snaked overhead and beneath her feet. There was the risk of falling debris – that was a real threat – but what was worse was what lay below them.

Fourteen thousand feet of the Arctic Ocean.

Merry knew that in order to build an arena of this size, they would have to cut near the bottom of the ice floe. It could be a matter of feet. Nog would know exactly how close they were to the water.

If this place collapsed, they would go with it.

All fourteen thousand feet.

"Release the A-bombs!" she shouted. "I need all three of them supporting the ceiling!"

Merry saw her teams spread throughout the arena. They were the ones running against the flow of traffic, helping the fallen and elderly, guiding them to the exits.

There were three flashes of light as the A-bombs were activated. They inhaled the icy benches, building long pillar-like bodies that extended from the floor to the ceiling, spreading out along the dome like knobby roots holding the widening cracks together.

The arena settled.

The quake was reduced to a mild hum. But it wouldn't last. The A-bomb at center stage was still pulling ice and snow into it, building a stronger, tighter eyewall.

It was keeping them out.

THE ARENA WAS NEARLY EMPTY.

Merry started toward the center stage. If she could open a hole, she could see what was happening inside. She might find Jocah and pull her out.

But the quakes were already increasing. They needed to get everyone out safely.

All the way out of the palace.

She couldn't stay.

As the last of the elven evacuated, Merry told her teams to leave. When they were outside, they could call for the A-bombs to slip through a fissure and complete the evacuation.

Her section was empty. She walked out the door. She was about to start sliding away when the wind picked up. There was another howl behind her. A grinding like two storms colliding.

Merry turned to see another abominable. It was attacking center stage.

Flury.

She ran back inside.

79

T he abominable ate a hole in the roof and revealed a sky that was black and dusted. Inside the storm, on center stage, it was difficult to tell that they were still inside the palace.

Impossible to know it was crumbling.

Jack shook all over. He just wanted to do it all over again. The whole idea of the party seemed like a good one, but now he wanted it to stop. The confidence flexing in his groin had turned to jelly. He shook with the fear of a young child facing the boogeyman in his closet. But there was no blanket to pull over his head.

There was nowhere to hide.

No way to fight.

What he thought was the boogeyman was now standing right there in front of him with a long white braid and a withered old face. He thought if he got rid of her, he wouldn't feel so cold. So lonely.

It was going *sooo* wrong.

"When you were a young boy," his mother said, "I didn't hold you."

"No, no you didn't." Jack felt little pricks of heat on his face. "You always–"

"I didn't show you your value. I didn't protect you."

Jack backed up a step. He felt the wind at his back. Felt a track of water stream down his cheek and run along his jaw. Drip from his chin.

He wanted all this to go away. He didn't like feeling something, these emotions or warmth or WHATEVER THIS IS!

Bolts of icy frost slithered out from his feet but melted away before they reached his mother. He grunted and tried again.

Water dripped from his nose.

"No, no. No, no, no, nononoNONONONONONO!"

Jocah held out her hands.

"It's not supposed to end this way!" he shouted. "You were supposed to come in here and I turn you into a statue and use my brother for fishing–" Jack had to swallow a swelling lump. "For fishing... bait."

He wiped his eyes.

He'd never had water in them. He couldn't remember crying. Ever.

Jack tried to push himself into the eyewall, let the winds draw him into its violence and spit him into the sky, but it pushed back.

"I see you now, Janack," she said.

Her fingers touched his hands.

No one ever *wanted* to touch Jack. No one ever wanted him.

Because he didn't belong.

"I see you."

She took his hands in hers.

He used to cry.

He remembered.

Jack would go into that closet where it was dark and safe and no one would hurt him. He sang songs and made up a world where everyone loved him. Where no one would laugh at him if he cried.

Because, sometimes, that's what he'd do.

He'd cry.

And sing.

Jack whispered, "*Silent night.*"

His mother's fingers wrapped around his.

Deadly bolts of cold did not shoot into her. Instead, warmth bled into Jack. It spread into his arms and through his chest.

It filled his belly.

And he felt like sunlight.

THE FROST MELTED from his face, falling in sheets from his scalp. It was raining, now. He saw the blurry image of his mother. She didn't look old and wrinkled. She was glowing next to a blurry red image. Claus reached his red arm for Jack.

His hand fell on his shoulder.

Janack heard him through the wind and rain.

Claus uttered something he hadn't heard in so, so long.

"Brother," he said.

And the light and the warmth and the water were all around.

And he didn't feel cold.

Janack didn't feel lonely.

80

Claus kept a few memories. Ones he didn't want to pass along to someone else.

They were memories of growing up.

Of his brother.

He'd forgotten all those precious moments when they were so young and together in a crib. He'd forgotten when they learned to walk together and shared their toys. He'd forgotten that, for a time, his brother was the only thing he knew. They didn't feel separate. They were once one in the womb.

But now Claus remembered.

He saw how he turned his back on his brother. He saw that he grew to lead his people and refused to love the very blood that was his. Claus pushed him away. Made fun of him.

Rejected him.

His brother became the Cold One.

Jack was still the child that needed to be seen.

Claus always believed that it was his brother – *not Claus* – that needed to see clearly. Claus had been so blind. And now that he could see, he wanted Jack to know what he saw.

He saw ignorance and suffering.

He saw more than a monster.

I see my brother.

They were standing in ankle-deep water. When he put his hand on Jack's shoulder, it was like touching a flame to dry kindling.

Jack saw what Claus could see.

He saw his true value.

81

It had been so long since Jocah had last held her son.

It occurred to her that, perhaps, she had never held him in her arms. There were only memories of caretakers that cared for Jack. She had the elven to lead and never time to see her own son.

She sensed the unending depth of his loneliness and dark cold that sat deep inside. She felt the suffering he had caused because he could not face his own. She saw the wicked nature of his behavior, that he believed he was truly cold and distant and full of hate.

That he was separate.

He was lonely.

He tried to fill it with the suffering of others.

Jocah opened to his pain and suffering. She allowed it to be present. And he allowed her to see just how ugly he had become.

She witnessed, for the first time, what had become of her son. It filled her with great sadness.

They held hands in the pouring rain.

They held hands as the water rose to their knees.

And they held hands as the sky and stars above them disappeared from sight.

Jocah, Janack and Claus sank into the dark water.

Holding each other.

82

Nicholas watched the turmoil play out like a strange theatre production.

There were three fat short people. One was blue and another was wearing a bright red coat trimmed with white. He felt so numb and oddly disconnected from the vicious storm and the water rising above what was once an icy floor. Droplets were sucked upwards in the storm's vortex and then falling back down. They dripped from his bushy eyebrows.

He blinked them away.

The blue one was turning a different color. At first it was lighter blue, but when the layer of frost melted from his cheeks, it revealed a pink hue.

Sweat mixed with the rain and stung Nicholas's eyes.

The pressure spiked inside his brain. His skull made little cracking sounds. He wanted to lift his hands and hold his head together, but he was so numb.

When the one with the red coat lifted his arm–

When his hand reached for the previously blue one's shoulder–

When the old lady was holding his hands–

The storm collapsed.

Nicholas let the winds wrap around him and lift him and carry him and–

POP.

Something clicked inside his head. A timer had expired or a magic word uttered or the abominable triggered it... whatever it was, it released all his memories. They weren't gone after all. Just hidden from him.

And now he had them back.

He tumbled through the black starry sky–

He remembered who he was.

And so much more.

83

Merry slid as fast as gravity would pull her toward the abominable battle.

The benches dissolved around Flury. His body swelled but was dwarfed by the massive abominable swirling around the stage. Flury pounded away at the icy snowstorm, attempting to tear a hole in the swirling wall so he could get Jocah and Claus to safety, but his icy fists were thrown back with little effect. He finally dove into the storm and the two mingled to form one tussling twister, bands of gray and white swirling and wrapping and twisting. Water spit out like projectiles. Merry covered her face. The wind blasted out and pushed her sideways. Holes opened in the thinning floor and water gushed in.

On the other side of the arena, standing at the top in a doorway, were two figures.

One short. One tall.

NOG!

Merry got to her feet and slid toward them.

Nog leaned forward and began sliding at her.

The ceiling fell in chunks and splintered on the floor between them, but they were on a crash course–

Silence.

The abominable storm suddenly lifted off the floor and funneled through the hole in the ceiling, leaving behind a neatly carved hole in the floor. The stage was gone, the Arctic water licking the sides of where it once was.

Like it just melted away.

Flury was alone, fists balled up. He stood at the edge of the hole, looking for the battle he was fighting only moments before.

There was a creak and a groan. A crackling of ice.

Fissures multiplied on the floor and ceiling. As each one forked, another forked off that. And another.

The palace was about to shatter.

"GO!" Nog shouted.

Nog held Merry's hand and began climbing the slick incline. Their scaly feet grabbed the ice, but they couldn't slide. They ran, step by step.

The ice tilted under them.

Nog squeezed Merry's hand.

She squeezed back.

He felt the world buckle beneath them as the floor crumbled. They tumbled back as the doorways disintegrated and the ceiling came down and water gushed around their ankles–

And then a powerful wind hit them from behind, like a storm pounding the sails of a desperate ship. Nog went head over feet. He saw nothing but ice and heard the splashing of water. But he was soaring upward and out.

The chaos faded behind him.

He felt the cold wind of the sky on his cheek.

And his wife's warm hand in his. He didn't let go.

He would never let go.

J essica didn't hear Nog shout.

She was staring at the hole in the ice. Staring at the lapping water where her husband was supposed to be. Transfixed by the emptiness all around and the doom that was moments away.

She thought that perhaps there was a chance he was clinging to the edge, somewhere behind Flury. She thought that if the abominable would just turn around and look, he would see her husband thrashing in the water. He could reach in and save him.

If that brainless snowman didn't turn around–

Jessica leaped onto the icy slope, feet first. She slid only a few feet when she saw Flury burst into snow and gust out of the arena like a storm cloud with Merry and Nog inside of it. The frosty squall hit Jessica and carried her with it.

She clawed and screamed as she and the two elven tumbled through the crumbling hallway, out of the palace and into the night.

She was carried to safety without her husband.

"I see him!" Jon pointed at the red streak in the night sky.

Tinsel looked up and waved her arms. Ronin wouldn't see, but he would feel her. The red light arched towards them and plummeted to the ice.

"Get a sleigh over here!" Tinsel shouted. "Ronin can handle twenty benches, someone get one materialized and strapped!"

"Twenty rows?" one of the assisting elven said. "That's too much, Tinsel. He can't launch with that much weight–"

"Yes, he can."

Tinsel marched off to check the rest of the reindeer and sleighs that were loaded to full capacity. Donner was the smallest of the bunch, snorting and pawing at the ice. There wasn't an inch of space left in the sleigh. He leaned into it and the rails crunched against the snow.

"Get running, Donner." Tinsel stroked his neck. He bent down so she could whisper in his ear. "If you can leap, do it. But if not, run as fast and as far as you can."

She rubbed his nose.

"Get away from here."

Steam fired from his nostrils.

And then he started forward. Slow at first. But then, step by step, he got the sleigh moving. Tinsel didn't wait to see if he leaped. She turned her attention to the rest of the chaos.

So many elven. So few reindeer.

She felt the ice tremor.

So little time.

"Get more in the sleigh!" Tinsel smacked Vixen on the hindquarters. "She can pull more!"

Vixen grunted. *Load me up!*

The elven crowd was massive, mostly from the palace. They piled into the sleighs in orderly – slightly panicked – fashion. Parts of the palace had caved in, but the elven did not push or shove. They climbed aboard and waited for Tinsel to give the okay for takeoff.

None of the reindeer could launch, but most of them had already run far enough away. They didn't go in any particular direction, just away. They would be summoned to gather later.

Just go.

"That's it!" Tinsel cried. "Go, Vixen! Get legs!"

One last snort from the mighty reindeer and Vixen heaved ahead. The sleigh creaked in protest but gave way to the reindeer's strength. Tinsel watched Vixen gather momentum, trotting into the night.

They had used the last of their energy reserves to power self-propelled sleighs. Six-leggers – once vicious predators – now seemed like lost puppies, yapping in circles and following everything that moved. Tinsel kept her eye on them. It was hard to forget the predators that – hours earlier – wanted to eat them.

What happened?

CRACK, *BOOM*!

TINSEL JUMPED.

Half the palace collapsed.

The roof just crumbled like crackers and sank into the water.

Ronin was packed and ready. The elven in the sleigh began screaming for launch before the ice below them caved. But he was the last ride out. Once Ronin was gone, no one else would escape when the rest of the palace came down.

Jon was stroking Ronin's ears.

"We have to go," Jon said.

"But they're still in there."

"We're risking the entire sleigh."

Tinsel looked around Ronin's hindquarters. It wasn't fair to ask the elven to stay, but Jocah was in there. Merry and Nog.

Jon's parents.

But he was right. If he didn't make her leave, she would stay there until the end. And then they'd all be dead.

"All right–"

FOOOOM!

Something shot into the sky.

It came from the center of the palace, a column of snow that was twisting and curling, arching away from them.

What is that?

The elven lost patience. They were shouting, banging on the sides of the sleigh. They couldn't wait another second.

Tinsel took Jon's hand.

A crack appeared in the ice behind him.

"GO!"

The palace imploded in slow motion.

It fell into the water.

Ronin heaved forward. The sleigh groaned. The ice cracked and popped as sheets snapped away from the perimeter of the collapsing palace. Snow flurries sprang into the air like dust, and the hole in the North Pole grew larger.

It was gaining on them.

"Faster!" Tinsel shouted from the front of the sleigh, looking back.

Ronin bellowed and the sleigh picked up speed.

It wasn't going to be enough.

Tinsel watched the cracks race after him.

Ronin would never get airborne. She'd overpacked the sleigh. She waited too long.

Elven were screaming.

FOOM!

Another blast shot from the crumbling palace, this one from the side and directly at them. It swirled like a comet with a long tail and it carried objects wrapped in big white arms.

The ice broke beneath the sleigh.

The back end tipped and the rails dipped into the water.

Ronin bellowed as the momentum yanked him back.

And then the snowy comet was all around them.

Flury!

Tinsel looked down at the black water beneath them. They should've been sinking into it, but somehow they were still above it.

Flury had wrapped his arms around the sleigh, hovering over the water. Ronin galloped as the momentum picked up.

The rails impacted the edge of solid ice and the sleigh rattled.

The elven cheered.

They looked back at the remains of their home, now a giant hole in the ice as it crumbled and, somehow, melted. Water sloshed over the sides, eroding the edges. None of them noticed the new passengers crammed into the front row of the sleigh.

Tinsel could only see the back of Merry's head as the two were wrapped in a tight embrace. On the other side of them, next to Jon, was Jessica.

A sphere dropped into Tinsel's lap.

Flury carried them out. He kept the sleigh from sinking.

"Good job," she whispered, squeezing the sphere.

It was warm in her hand.

JESSICA LOOKED over the heads of the elven. It was a sleigh larger than any she had seen. They were all looking back. The last of the palace sank into a black hole. The North Pole looked like a watery sinkhole.

Her husband was back there.

I was so close.

Now he was gone. *He's gone. Forever.*

She felt so helpless to be that close to him and... *lose him.*

An elven was staring at her. She looked away, not wanting him to see her cry. She just wanted to be alone. If Flury hadn't pulled them out, she would've been just fine sinking with Nicholas.

What else was there for her here on the North Pole?

She covered her face and let the sobs come, soaking her palms. She quietly wept as the sleigh jostled over the snow.

There was a small hand on Jessica's arm.

She sniffed back the tears and composed herself. She pushed back her hair and looked at the elven.

There was something familiar about him. His face. His smile.

It was...

Jessica threw her arms around Jon and buried her face on his shoulder.

Tears of joy, this time. Tears of joy mixed with the pain. She lost one of her loved ones that night.

But gained one back.

86

It was so quiet. So peaceful.

He was dense and heavy. He was dead and numb and remembered nothing. But there was a POP!

Something released inside him.

Something carried him away from the arena of ice. Now he soared outward at the speed of light.

Now he remembered everything.

His parents. His wife and son and their trek to the Arctic.

Every moment of his life had been released, and those memories floated like snowflakes, settling softly on the fabric of his mind.

He was dreaming.

He had to be dreaming because he was hurtling through outer space. He was a fat man tumbling through black space like a comet. He zoomed past planets with rings and moons with craters and blazing hot suns. And yet he was breathing.

He was living.

And remembering.

I am Nicholas Santa.

And I want to go home.

But it was more than Nicholas's memories that were released. Someone else's life – someone's memories – was mingling amongst his own.

Nicholas remembered being born in the cold with a twin

brother sliding from the womb right after him. He lived among elven that were short, fat and jolly. He grew up on the ice floes of the North Pole, where he learned how to hunt, how to build, and how to lead.

These thoughts, these memories, were like his own.

Impossible.

He wasn't an elven. He knew who he was, he was Nicholas Santa. He was born human. His mother had given birth to him in the bedroom of their two-story house. He grew up in Sweden, going to school and climbing mountains.

He'd never been to the Arctic, yet he recalled the subtle differences in snow and how to carve tunnels in the ice.

He remembered like he had *done* these things.

Hello, Nicholas Santa.

A voice rang through the heavens.

Nicholas recognized it.

It was Claus.

If you're experiencing this, you have survived. And I am grateful.

Claus's voice echoed through space. Nicholas continued his journey through the solar system, slowly spinning head over foot. But no matter what direction he looked, he couldn't see anyone out there with him.

"Where am I?" Nicholas's voice had a strange echo, like his ears were plugged.

He made one complete rotation.

Somewhere in your mind.

"Am I... dead?"

No. You just haven't returned to your body yet. You will when all the memories have found their place in your mind.

"These memories, they're not all mine. There's some mistake. Some of these are yours."

My apologies for what we have done to you. Sometimes our shortcomings cause others pain. For that, I am sorry.

Nicholas remembered having snowball fights with classmates and polar bearing at midnight when he was supposed to be in bed. He remembered being selected team captain and choosing teammates. He remembered seeing Jack standing all alone when no one picked him. He remembered turning his back on him.

"Why do I have your memories?"

We are more like humans than we like to admit. Long life does not auto-

matically grant us wisdom. I saw mistakes I needed to correct. The resolution, Santa, required my life.

Nicholas felt like he was soaring faster, spinning quicker, as he flew past an icy planet.

"You died. You sank through the ice with your mother and brother."

My brother caused suffering. He was confused and alone. He needed to see his true value. When he did, he would no longer be so cold. I didn't expect to survive. I have given you my memories, Nicholas. You possess my life.

"Why?"

The elven are good. They will need a leader.

Nicholas cruised through a solar system and was quickly closing in on the center of the galaxy, where a black hole was consuming everything around it. Whether he was dreaming or not, he was about to puke from all the spinning.

You will be that leader, Nicholas. It's time we let humans into our life. My memories grant you the wisdom to lead the elven race.

Nicholas whizzed through an asteroid belt, narrowly missing chunks of flying rocks.

The black hole drew nearer.

Remember, as you lead them, what one of your philosophers once said.

Nicholas closed his eyes. He was a shooting star on a collision course.

The measure of a man is what he does with power.

The black hole was his destiny.

There was no turning back.

You are a good man, Nicholas.

With Claus's memories, he would no longer be Nicholas Santa.

Lead wisely.

His life would change.

Santa Claus.

HE OPENED HIS EYES.

He was no longer spinning.

He felt the cold on his cheeks and the embrace of a snow drift. He saw stars twinkling in a night sky. Space was above him, the earth below.

He was lying in the snow.

He was on his back, staring at the Arctic sky streaked with bands of green and red. The Northern Lights washed over the sky like solar currents. And directly above him, glittering brightest of all, was the North Star.

Santa Claus is home.

87

W inter solstice.

The darkest day of the year.

But the elven weren't wasting it sleeping. They were on top of the ice, carrying glowglobes to light their way around a massive party. They had been separated far too long to wait another day to reunite.

Some were parents that carried glowglobes looking for a daughter or son that had left with the colony so many years ago. They carried the light at face level, searching every face, calling out names. And when they found them, there were tears and hugs and rolling around.

A lot of tears and hugs.

Music boomed where the younger elven gathered. A snowball fight broke out with bombs flying. Every dull thud that hit its target was followed by laughter. It wasn't long before girls squealed and a group of boys streaked through the party totally nude for a midnight round of polar bearing.

Occasionally, an errant snowball crashed somewhere outside the battle. If it hit one of the older elven, they would toss it back. Soon, the snowball fight turned into a marauding stampede of frolicking elven. At the center of the festivities was a mountain of shirts and pants and socks. The kids leaped into the pile and dug their way to the other side like burrowing Arctic foxes.

The clothes were discards. No one wanted them anymore.

No one needed them.

They were dark blue uniforms.

The reindeer had run away from the collapsing palace.

They didn't look back until they reached the edge of the polar ice. They were as far away from the palace as possible. The elven that wore Jack's uniforms – his "recruitments" – were itchy. First, one stripped off his clothes. Then another. One by one, the colors that signified the Fracture fell to the snow. They were scooped up and thrown together.

They were free.

It was like they had been released from a spell.

When Claus's A-bomb went off (and everyone was talking about *that,* let me tell you), something changed. All those years, they lived in fear. And that fear gripped them, clawed deep into their brains and froze their minds. And then–

POOF!

Gone.

Melted away.

And they were free.

The true spirit of the elven race was alive and well once again.

Far from the snowballs and glowglobes, the engineers were setting up the follicle wind harvesters to collect kinetic energy. The long, fibrous strands swayed in the breeze like silky hair. The energy reserves were completely empty. It would be another couple days before they could finish carving the ice to house everyone. At the moment, no one seemed to mind.

The moonlight cast down on the reindeer gathered around two elven.

Tinsel and Jon were at the edge of the follicle field. They held out handfuls of treats that the reindeer picked up with long tongues. Their free hands were clasped together, fingers twined.

Vixen let out a moan as she ate from Jon's hand. Donner nudged Vixen and got the next handful. He let out a moan and rolled his eyes.

The herd migrated over to Jon.

"What are you feeding them over there?" Tinsel asked.

"I added a touch of willow bark to your formula."

She looked over her shoulder. "How did you do that?"

"I've been doing some research."

"On your own?"

He shrugged.

Tinsel pulled another handful out of her bag and held it up. Blitzen ate it, but his eyes were on Jon.

"Willow, huh?"

He squeezed her hand. She squeezed back.

THE FOLLICLES PARTED. Jessica held the strands open just enough so she could see the reindeer. The engineers were walking in the other direction, seeding more stalks. She had been helping them by looking over the top and giving feedback on which way the tips were moving.

She meant to go back and help some more. It was nice to be with scientists for a little while. They were so serious and calculating. For her, it was like being alone with company. She didn't want to think. Just help.

So many emotions.

It had been so long since she had seen her husband, but all that time she carried the hope that he was still alive and they would be together again. And for a second – just a matter of seconds – she almost had him. That was the worst part. She was so close; that made it hurt worse.

I didn't even get to see him.

And now it was over.

There was no hope for a future. He was gone. He was somewhere on the ocean's floor. She could only hope that his ending came quickly and that he felt no pain. That was her only comfort.

And it was no comfort at all.

For Jessica, though, the healing was just beginning. She needed to process the difficult reality a little at a time, so it helped to be with the engineers, to take a break from working with these emotions.

She pulled the follicles open a little more. Seeing her son helped, too.

Alive.

She watched Jon and Tinsel holding hands.

Alive and happy.

RONIN SNORTED and tossed his head.

Jessica meant to duck back into the forest of strands, but Tinsel and Jon looked at where Ronin was motioning. They saw her spying on them and let go of each other's hands. Jessica stepped back and stood still, hoping they would think the moonlight played tricks.

"Mom?"

A chill coursed through Jessica; her skin was dimply. She stifled a sob that constricted her throat. Despite the sadness, she needed to hear that.

Mom.

She stayed inside the fibers, letting them push against her as they swayed, like the world embraced her, told her everything was all right. There were footsteps. She remained still. A red light penetrated the fibers. Ronin's nose snorted its way into her belly. He pulled out and bellowed.

Busted.

Ronin stood over Tinsel and Jon.

"Do you want to feed them?" Jon asked.

The rest of the herd shuffled back as Jessica took a few steps. Tinsel looked back. "They're nervous around strangers, but it's all right."

"I thought I got to know them when Nog and I..." Jessica trailed off.

"They have short memories," Tinsel said.

Ronin dipped his head and pushed Tinsel with his muzzle. She tipped over and grabbed onto Jon. Then both of them went to the ground, rolling around like beach balls. Beach balls that laughed.

Jessica smiled.

She smiled and stepped out of the fiber field.

Jon told her about his new recipe. He told her how he could feel reindeer in his chest, could tell when they were happy or sad, tired or excited. He couldn't explain it, it just happened. And he filled her hand with treats and led her to the herd. It wasn't long before they were gathered around, nuzzling her for food.

She couldn't feel them, though. Not like Jon.

He belonged here.

Jessica felt a weight lifted from her.

This is home.

THE REINDEER WERE FED and ready to return to the mainland. Jessica scratched Cupid behind the ear and his back leg twitched. Tinsel and

Jon thought that was hilarious. They'd never seen one of them act like that.

Jessica tried it on Comet.

It worked again.

And while they were laughing, two elven were racing toward them. Jessica's fingers slowed and Comet pushed against her to go faster.

Merry and Nog slid up to them.

"We have news."

Jessica's heart quickened.

88

"You think he's dead?"

It was a tiny voice, so far away, like it was coming through a straw poked through layers of ice.

A finger – just as tiny as the voice – poked Nicholas somewhere on the face. His cheek, maybe. It tickled his beard.

"I think he's dead. He's cold."

"Of course he's cold!" another voice, this one not so tiny, said. "Everything's cold. Is he dead-cold?"

"I don't know. What's dead-cold?"

Something came crunching near the voices. Nicholas felt someone hovering over him.

"Pull the hood back," a third voice ordered.

There was a commotion. Something brushed against his beard and fluttered over his face. He felt the coolness of a breeze and the darkness lightened. Something was breathing over him. In fact, three things were breathing.

Nicholas opened his eyes.

His eyelashes crunched as the frost broke away. Three lumps were directly in front of him.

He blinked. They were bearded.

Blink, again.

Bearded elven.

"Told you he was alive," one of them said.

"You said he was cold."

"I didn't say dead-cold."

Nicholas groaned and they pulled back. The night sky was behind them. Nicholas began to smile. They were elven scouts. Nicholas remembered their faces. And their names.

"Little help?" Nicholas lifted his arm.

The elven looked at each other then latched onto Nicholas's outstretched hand and pulled him into a sitting position. Layers of ice cracked and fell from his chest. He brushed the pieces off and then, with a heavy grunt, got to his feet and stretched.

The air was sharp in his chest.

The stars so bright.

It felt so good to be alive.

The elven stood. Staring.

"Martis, how are you, old friend?" Nicholas boomed.

The elven on the left, the one with the red beard, nodded. He started to say something – like *how do you know my name?* – but then kept nodding.

"Kevish?" Nicholas turned to the one in the middle, the one with the beard to his toes. "How's the bad knee treating you?"

Long-bearded Kevish looked at his leg. Looked at Nicholas. He didn't say anything.

Nicholas chuckled again, a rumble of laughter. *Ha-ha.*

"And Saranock." Nicholas dropped a heavy hand on the lead elven's shoulder. "You've always been a master scout, it's no wonder you found me. By the way, how's your daughter doing? She just got married. Any little rugrats running around?"

Saranock twirled the curly ends of his mustache.

"How do you know us?" he said.

"It's a long story, my friend. A long one to tell on a frosty night."

Nicholas looked behind him. There was a large circle of fresh ice that was just beginning to drift with snow. All around it were large chunks of snow and ice where the palace had fallen.

Somewhere beneath that ice was the answer to Saranock's question.

"A long and frosty night," Nicholas said.

NEWS TRAVELED FAST.

It didn't take long for the others to race up to the North Pole. Many of them swore they would never return to that palace – too many bad memories – but the news of a warmblood that survived for three days on his own was too juicy not to.

Some arrived by reindeer and self-propelled sleighs. They gathered around in a large circle and the fat man called them all by name. He knew every one of them and everything about them, *like he was one of them!* A new group would arrive and he would call them by name and wave them to the front and then lean back and laugh this loud merry laugh. It was so contagious that the laughter spread throughout the circle until they were all laughing.

"I'll make sure I check on little Sherman," Nicholas was telling a young couple about their son. "He's been distracted in school, and if he's not careful, he'll end up on the naughty list."

Laughter.

The circle tightened as each of the elven wanted their turn to meet the all-knowing fat man when a new group arrived. Nicholas stood three feet taller than the crowd and watched the arrivals. He kept his eyes on the smallest of the group.

Nicholas put out his hands and asked for quiet. Elven shushed each other until silence fell over the crowd. They slowly parted, allowing someone to move to the front. Nicholas took a knee as those nearest to him moved away and looked at the smallest of the elven – one dressed in green with a pointy hat and curly-toed shoes – step into view.

Sheepishly, he stopped in front of the fat man. He looked into his eyes and cocked his head curiously. He was looking for something.

Nicholas put his hands on his shoulders and allowed Cane to see the twinkle in his eyes. To see what Claus had left behind.

Cane wrapped his arms as far as he could around the fat man's belly.

Nicholas hugged him back.

"He loves you very much, Cane." Nicholas patted his back. "Very, very much."

The crowd began clapping. They didn't know why, exactly. It just felt like it needed clapping.

Cane began to dance to the rhythm of applause. Everyone fell into rhythm and cheered him on as he danced around the fat man. Nicholas stood up and joined the merriment.

"Santa Claus!" Cane chanted. "Santa Claus! Santa Claus! Santa Claus!"

The crowd caught on and began to clap and chant.

Nicholas threw back his head and began to laugh.

"Ha-ha-ho!"

It boomed through the crowd.

"HO-HO-HO!"

Soon they were all dancing.

"HO-HO-HO!"

A red light streaked near the North Pole, where elven were enthusiastically dancing and clapping and celebrating. Nicholas watched the sleigh come to a stop. The others hadn't noticed.

Nicholas stopped clapping as the group unloaded. He watched the crowd selflessly allow the newest arrivals come to the front for their turn. Merry and Nog approached, holding hands. Their expressions were solemn, but happy.

"Heard a lot about you," Merry said. "You're very special."

"Special, yes," Nog added. "It's a pleasure to finally meet you."

"Thank you." Nicholas meant that from the bottom of his heart. "I've *heard* a lot about you as well."

Merry and Nog let go of each other and looked back. The crowd, sensing the moment, began to spontaneously part and silence slowly fell. They followed Merry's and Nog's gazes back through the opening to the woman outside the crowd.

Jessica stood still.

Quite still.

Nicholas was transfixed by her beauty. He had dreamed of her for months. And now she was here. He took a step.

She did, also.

And by the time each had taken a second step, they were running. They hit each other hard, wrapping their arms around each other and squeezing so tightly that they nearly crushed each other. They embraced like they would never let go.

Never again.

The elven cheered. Some cried.

Jessica put her hands on Nicholas's cheeks. "I thought you were..."

"I'm not."

Tears filled her eyes. She stroked his beard. "You look so different."

He let his fingers get lost in her hair.

"You don't," he said.

A pair of elven stood before them.

Nicholas clasped Jessica's hand and stepped back. He looked at the couple. He knew the girl was Tinsel. She was the herder, one of the few elven that could communicate with the reindeer. But the other one, he didn't recognize him. Not with Claus's memories.

But he knew him.

He knew this young man.

Nicholas looked at Jessica. She nodded.

He fell on his knees and threw out his arms.

"What's the matter, my boy?" he said. "You too old to hug the old man?"

Jon and Tinsel, together, jumped into his arms. He squeezed them until they were out of breath. Nicholas lifted them up and turned to the festive crowd.

"What are we waiting for, elven?" he shouted. "We're home! The North Pole is our home!"

And with that, the celebration continued.

It went through the night and the next day. There was music, food, snowballs, and naked elven plunging into holes in the ice.

The next day, the engineers brought the follicle wind harvesters and energy was restored. And the elven began to make their home again.

At the North Pole.

89

I t was a year later to that very day when the reindeer gathered at the North Pole.

Now that the Fracture had ended, they spent more time on the mainland and less time jumping.

Where the palace – gaudy and ornate and monstrous – once stood was now a modest mound that spread out for a square mile. Below the ice there were endless rooms and tunnels.

On this night, the reindeer were tethered together in two rows with a sleigh at the back. Ronin, however, was at the front all alone, his nose bright red and illuminating the pair of elven that were walking down both sides, pulling treats from bags attached to their hips.

"You sure this is going to work?" Merry climbed out of the ice.

Nog was right behind her. "Of course it will."

"Is there enough energy for the timesnap to work?" she asked. "If he runs out, he'll be stranded on the other side of the world and then how are we going to–"

"Merry." Nog put his finger on her lips. "It will work."

She took his hand away and kissed the back of it.

Jessica climbed out of the ice. The reindeer shuffled as she neared, but she went to the front and around the massive spread of antlers and rubbed Ronin's nose.

"How is everyone?" she asked.

"Fat and happy," Jon announced.

Vixen snorted and tossed her head, glaring at him.

"He didn't mean fat, like fat-fat, Vixen." Tinsel rubbed her leg. "He meant big and strong and healthy, not fat. Right, Jon?"

He nodded and gave Vixen an extra helping of special treats. All was forgiven.

❄

A RED CAP emerged from the ice and appeared to get stuck. Merry, Nog and Jessica helped lift Nicholas out. He crawled on his knees and then stood up. He adjusted the wide black belt around the bright red coat.

"It's too tight, Jessica," Santa Claus said. "How many times do I have to tell the tailors to add a few more inches to the waistline?"

"Perhaps you need to eat less."

"I'll freeze to death if I'm not fat and healthy."

Some of the reindeer rolled their eyes.

"Stop it," Santa Claus said, pointing at them. "You just concentrate on leaping."

Jessica brushed the snow off his shoulders and straightened the fuzzy red cap on his head. She kissed his cheek and whispered I love you. Santa hugged her and whispered back.

Every elven was on the ice.

They formed a circle around the sleigh. They were clapping and cheering and throwing hats. They had expected this day. It was finally here.

Santa Claus waved and the cheering shook the ice.

He waved both arms, and after several attempts to get their attention, silence fell.

Santa Claus cleared his throat. "Thank you," he said. "I'd like to take a moment to remember those elven that have gone before us. They sacrificed much and we must not forget."

He bowed his head.

A collective head-bowing ensued.

A crisp breeze fluttered over them. A full moon, glowing.

They remembered.

Santa Claus climbed into the sleigh with only a single bench. The reindeer restlessly stomped the ice. Tinsel and Jon threw the last of the treats and stepped back with Jessica.

"Charged and ready." Nog handed a large bag to Santa. "You should be able to reach inside and pull whatever you need out of it."

Santa put the bag on the seat next to him.

"You sure you want to do this?" Jessica asked. "We're not warm-bloods anymore."

"Of course we are, my dear. We'll always be warmbloods." He touched his chest. "It's about time they knew we're up here."

He waved his arms.

"AT THE TOP OF THE WORLD!"

The crowd cheered.

He held the reins and winked at the small party that stood back.

"I'll be back in a jiff," he said. His eyes twinkled.

And with that, he gently tugged the reins.

"Now, Dasher! Now, Dancer! Now, Prancer and Vixen..." he shouted, calling out all the reindeer names.

The reindeer crouched and, in unison, launched from the ice with enough force to crack it beneath them. Jessica, Merry, Nog, Tinsel and Jon watched it soar up into the winter sky, Ronin leading the way. They could hear Santa Claus laughing.

And then the timesnapper ignited and they were gone.

They waited for him to return. It would just be a few seconds.

AFTERWORD

Now you know the tale of the great jolly fat man and how he got to the North Pole and why all those elven are up there. Claus returns in *Claus: Rise of the Miser* (Book 5 in the Claus Universe).

The tale of Jack, however, is not over.

If you're curious to find out how the Cold One returns, then turn the page. If, however, you're more intrigued by the physics of a walking snowman then skip on down to Flury.

Either way, adventure awaits.

BOOK 2

Jack: The Tale of Frost

THE NORTH POLE

Pawn ran for three days.

He didn't exactly run. Pawn was an elven: short and insulated, with layers of fat to survive the Arctic cold. His feet were wide and the soles scaly. He glided over ice, swam through frigid water, and rolled over the snow, rarely stopping... for if he did—if he so much as paused to catch his breath—a fire ignited the back of his head like the blue flame of a torch.

So onward he slogged beneath the Arctic winter sky, dark during the day. Darker at night.

It was sometime during the third night Pawn thought he would die. He began to shiver. Elven had lived through the Ice Age and carved their homes in the North Pole ice. They had adapted. They rarely felt the cold. And if they did, they certainly didn't shiver.

Pawn had no food. Even if he did, he couldn't slow down to eat it. After three days, his body had begun consuming fat in search of calories.

There were no reindeer beasts soaring overhead in search of him, no bright red nose streaking the sky. Surely his fellow elven wouldn't be looking for him just yet. They would still be celebrating their freedom. They had just overthrown Jack, Pawn's only friend.

Jack is dead.

When he tripped on an ice ridge, he began to roll. Once he stopped, his head began to sizzle. He cried out—perhaps blacked out

—but it didn't soothe the agony. He knew the tiny capsule Jack had buried beneath his scalp would not kill him—it would force him to obey.

Go south.

Pawn crawled to his knees and the pain eased to a small flame. He couldn't get up, though. He had very little energy. Worse, his will to live had been crushed. He just wanted it to end, but his own thoughts were being replaced by other thoughts that forced him to keep moving, keep pushing, keep struggling.

Keep suffering.

And so it was that he didn't hear the dogs barking until they were upon him. When he looked up, he saw them racing at him, their tongues lolling from drooling, black lips.

It was quite possible he was hallucinating. Earlier, he'd seen a great white whale emerge from an open lead, only it was orange and winked.

Maybe those aren't dogs. Maybe the reindeer found me.

He hoped they were reindeer, hoped the elven would find him and end his misery.

A boot appeared in the snow. An Inuit man looked through the bundles of animal skin wrapped over his face, his narrow eyes wary. Pawn stared back with equal suspicion, knowing this man had never seen an elven before.

The man extended his hand and helped Pawn to his feet. The weather wasn't kind enough to ask questions. The Inuit packed the strange little man into his sled beneath hides of caribou and polar bear. When the sled turned around and the dogs pulled them south, only then did the burning subside.

Pawn would soon learn that the farther he travelled, the more the burning would fade until, eventually, it burned no more.

And that's when the real work began.

SOUTH CAROLINA

2014

THE PUZZLE

The children opened their gift on the kitchen table, spilling the puzzle across the surface. One thousand pieces were scattered about, each one unique and colorful, but random. With no connections, they were just pieces.

Just confusion.

As each piece was linked to its mate with a satisfying snap, the picture came together. First, there was a ray of light. Next, the horizon. And soon, the wondrous photo came together and it all made sense.

Clarity, at last.

1

NOVEMBER 29

Saturday

S*earching.*

Sura taps the GPS suction-cupped to the windshield. She gets nothing. It's no use, not out in the middle of nowhere.

Slash pines confine the narrow road, their trunks straight as telephone poles. Dappled sunlight reaches the rutted road. Ditches parallel the sides like gutters. No turning back unless she wants to drive in reverse. Mom always said this place was in a different world.

Sura thought she was joking.

It's only one road—no turns, just straight ahead—but she feels like she's wandering without a clue. Then again, she's always felt that way, like she doesn't belong. If she drives for another hour, it'll just be another day. Only now she doesn't have her mom to come find her.

Sura eases through a puddle, this one big enough to hide a gator. The ground scrapes the bottom of her fuel-efficient car. The road is dry on the other side, sloping uphill. The tires fling mud and gravel.

The hill winds upward through the pine-forest prison, the undergrowth brown and dormant. She begins to give serious consideration to backing out when a gate appears. The black bars are pointed, the massive brick columns smothered in moss and lichen. Garland and tinsel dangle across the entrance, with strands of tiny white lights and bunches of red holly berries. A massive Christmas wreath circles a letter.

F

Frost Plantation.

Everyone knows about Mr. Frost. The locals call him Jack Frost only because no one ever sees him. They don't know his first name, but if his last name is Frost, then, naturally, his first name has to be Jack, case closed.

Sura has been out here before but doesn't really remember much —she was little—but she does recall seeing that letter: the stainless steel edges crisp and the surface spotless. It was the time her mom had taken her to the place she had worked all her life.

Now it's my turn to start working. Will it be for the rest of my life?

"Look, baby," her mom had said, squeezing Sura's little knee. "It's Christmas."

Sura thought maybe this was Santa's house. He lived on the North Pole, she knew that, but maybe he came to South Carolina to summer. But she didn't see Santa on her trip when she was little. She doesn't remember what she saw.

"It's Christmas," Sura mutters.

I wish you were here to say it, Mom.

The gates are supposed to automatically open. She pulls out her phone, but there's no reception. She pulls a sheet of paper from her back pocket and flattens it on the dashboard.

You are to report at 8:00 a.m. Do not be late.

The clock radio reads 7:59.

When you approach the gate, look out your window and it will automatically open.

.   .   .

SURA LOOKS up and stares at the massive magnolias that line the road beyond the gate. Nothing happens.

"That's what I'm doing," she says, but the gates don't listen.

She steps out of the car. There's nothing to the left or right of the gate, just more trees and shadows. She could walk around, but the house could be miles away. Plus, there are rumors about Frost Plantation that include words like haunted. Mom never said it was haunted. Then again, she didn't talk much about it.

Something scurries through the leaves. There's a flash of yellow in the dormant undergrowth. It could be squirrels, raccoons, or even hogs.

Or ghosts.

Sura backs against the car and looks left. Something flashes on her face. She can't tell where it came from—

Click.

The gates slide into the brick columns, cleaving the F in half. Slowly, the columns swallow the wrought iron until the road is open. She climbs inside the car and eases between the pillars and into the shadows, where dappled light disappears beneath thick, glossy magnolias.

The road gently curves up the hill. Occasionally, she sees old stalks of sunflowers between the magnolia trunks to her left, their disc-shaped heads worn and dangling, seeds picked from the faces long ago. Light appears where the magnolia's reign ends.

A two-story homestead is perched like a castle facing north. A wide porch runs across the front and wraps around the sides. It sits on two thousand privately owned acres and has survived the Civil War. It's as Southern as a home can be.

Except for recent renovations.

No one knows for sure when the mammoth tower was built into the center of the house or why. Reports of the three-story structure suggest that it looks like an obsidian dagger erupting from the cedar shingles, the top surrounded by windows. No one knows how these reports were obtained—even satellite images on Google Maps are blurred—but from what Sura can see, they're true.

The road transforms into pavement as she approaches the brick landing that juts from the front steps in a spacious, hemispherical shape. The house and size of the paved landing make her car look like a toy.

Templeton waits on the bottom step. She assumes that's him,

judging by the way he's ramrod straight in an unblemished suit, eyes ahead, gloved hands clutched in the front.

A manservant.

The wide and numerous steps stretch up behind him to massive oak doors with five-pound brass knockers.

She stops in front of him, rolling down the window. Templeton stares like a wax sculpture, his mocha complexion smooth. Eyes, green. There's nothing out there besides a grassy field and, beyond that, crops never harvested.

"You are late." He sounds British. He peers at a pocket watch. "On your first day, you are late, Ms. Sura."

"I'm sorry. The gate wouldn't open."

"Hm-mmm. Did you read the email?"

"Yes, sir."

"Then you would've known how to open the gate and where to park your vehicle."

Sura spreads out the page and rubs the wrinkles out, but she didn't grab the second page off the printer. "It doesn't say."

He continues staring. Maybe that's where she should park. He glances at his pocket watch again.

"Around back, Ms. Sesi."

Sura stares at the steering wheel. When the car doesn't move, Templeton's eyelids flicker.

"What is it?"

"Sesi is... *was*... my mom."

"My apologies." He blinks rapidly; his waxy composure softens. "Then shall you drive around back, Sura?"

Sura follows the road around the east side of the house. The porch wraps around it. Ceiling fans turn between hanging ferns that should be burned by winter but look green and healthy. Rocking chairs and tiny tables are positioned between windows framed with lacy curtains.

She parks behind the barn. There's a back door on the main house but no Templeton. Sura walks back the way she drove, passing through the shadow of tall hedges that line the other side of the road. She looks up at the tower, the black windows angled out.

Templeton hasn't moved. When she nears, he takes the steps one at a time, carefully placing each footstep. He freezes at the door, hand hovering over the knob.

"Take notes, Sura."

She pats her empty pockets. Templeton sighs, reaching inside his jacket to retrieve a pad of paper and pencil.

"Mr. Frost appreciates attention to detail."

"I didn't know I needed to take notes."

"Email, Sura. It was in the email."

The thick door whooshes open. Sura follows him into a foyer with a glittering chandelier and a highly polished floor. Templeton runs his finger along the table's surface that's next to the door, holding it up without looking.

"Lesson one."

The white-gloved fingertip is clean.

Templeton's footsteps echo. Sura begins taking notes.

THE KITCHEN IS SOMEWHERE near the center of the house and smells like freshly peeled shrimp. It looks big enough to feed an army. Pots, pans, and accessories dangle from the ceiling. The stainless steel counters shine, the shelves crowded with containers of spices, herbs, and flour. Somewhere, water is running.

Someone is humming a merry song.

"Hello?" Sura takes a few steps.

The water stops. So does the humming.

A short, doughy woman comes around the corner, mopping her hands with a dishrag.

"Oooooh." Her wet lips form a donut. "Goodness gracious."

Sura points over her shoulder. "Mr. Templeton told me to find Ms. May—"

"Get over here." Her dialect sounds Eastern European. Not exactly Russian, but something. "Get over here so Ms. May can get good look at you."

Sura walks carefully while the woman's eyes twinkle and a smile warps the smudge of flour on her cheek. She reaches up for Sura's face. Her hands are soft and warm. They smell like cookies.

"You look just like her," May whispers, her eyes tearing. "Just like your mother."

"I've heard."

"I'm so sorry, love. So, so sorry for you. Your mother was dear friend and beloved woman. I weep for her absence."

Now Sura is tearing up. No one ever said sorry like that, not with so much emotion. Not with hands that smell like cookies.

"How old are you now?"

"Sixteen."

"It was just yesterday Sesi brought you here to see Mr. Frost. How old were you then? Two? Three?"

Sura shrugs.

"I think you were two, yes. You were very small, clinging to Sesi like barnacle."

Sura didn't see May at the funeral, but there were a lot of people she didn't know. Almost all of them. They were friends from the yoga center, the quilting group, and the YMCA. But no family.

Sura didn't have family beyond her mom.

"Where are you staying, love?"

"Friends."

"You can stay with Ms. May if you need somewhere to sleep. Understand? You stay as long as you like."

Sura nods.

"Okay, good." May claps and smiles. "You are hungry, yes?"

"Mr. Templeton said—"

"Bah! Don't worry about Templeton. He is all rules, rules, rules. You come to Ms. May when your belly is talking. It is lunchtime and you are skinny." She pulls a stool up to the counter. "You eat!"

Sura slides onto the metal stool while May pats her arm, her smile cutting into her pudgy cheeks. A chocolate chip mole sits just to the side of her left eye. She snaps a cloth napkin from her apron and tucks it into Sura's collar.

She pinches her cheek and hops away.

Sura isn't hungry. She hasn't eaten much more than a salad since her mom passed away. Hunger helps Sura deal with her suffering, makes her forget how much it hurts.

Pots and plates rattle somewhere on the other side of the kitchen, where Nat King Cole sings about Jack Frost nipping at your nose. May hums along. She comes back with a glass plate and a sandwich four fingers tall.

"What did Templeton show you?" May asks.

Sura takes a bite and swallows. "He walked and talked and then showed me an orientation video on the history of the plantation."

May rolls her eyes.

"It wasn't bad." She takes another bite.

"Okay, yes, maybe that's okay. Plantation is very huge and no one knows who built house. Did Templeton quiz you? I have answers."

May laughs and so does Sura. It goes on for a long time. It feels very good. Sura finishes the sandwich while May cleans.

"Templeton didn't say how Mr. Frost got the house. Was the inventor his grandfather or something?"

May shrugs. "Your belly is full?"

"Yes. Thank you."

"Anything for my little Sura." She pinches her cheek again and sweeps up the empty plate. May begins humming with the music.

"Templeton wants me to study the kitchen."

"What's that, love?"

"I'm supposed to study the kitchen."

"You supposed to listen to Ms. May. It is kitchen, nothing special. You relax while I finish, and then we talk more."

She's right, there's nothing out of the ordinary, just giant ovens and massive skillets, an enormous refrigerator and countless drawers. *All of this for one guy?* The only thing out of place is a rack of heavy coats next to a door.

May puts on an oven mitt before opening the large refrigerator. She pulls out a tray with a metal dome and slides it on the counter.

"It is time to deliver lunch."

"That's my job?" Sura asks.

"Today, yes. Mr. Frost wants to meet you, so you deliver lunch and speak."

The dome is covered with ice crystals. Sura touches the surface and yanks her hand back, so cold it burns.

"Ah, ah. Put glove on." May comes back with a thick, white coat and holds it up.

"Am I going into a freezer?"

"Put on, love. You need."

Sura slides her arms into the sleeves. May latches the buttons before holding up a stocking cap. "It's safer to be warm."

May shakes the wool stocking cap.

"And this." May puts the oven mitt on her hand. "Do not look inside dome. Understand, love? You go to Mr. Frost, he will take. You can talk, that is all."

Suddenly, Sura's stomach isn't happy with the food. She's dressed like she's trekking through Alaska. Even on South Carolina's coldest day, she'd sweat.

"Is he really Jack Frost?" Sura feels stupid.

"No, love. He is not Jack." May guides her to the door next to the coat rack. "He has different first name than Jack."

"What is it?"

"We call him Mr. Frost."

"So there is a Jack?"

May opens the door to an elevator. Her smile disappears. It makes her cheeks look heavy. "We don't talk about Jack."

May ushers her into the elevator that's shaped like the inside of a Coke can.

"I'll be waiting when you are finished," May says.

The door slides shut without a sound, not even a click at the very end. Sura's reflection is distorted in every direction. Her brown hair flairs out like hay, framing her round face and slightly narrow eyes. Sura attempts to pet her hair into place.

She's always wondered if she has Inuit in her blood—she never gets cold—but she knows nothing about her heritage. Her mom was a "never look back" sort of person.

There are three buttons about knee level, which seems kind of low. The one in the middle is lit. She carefully balances the tray on one hand and reaches down—

The top button lights on its own.

Her stomach gently drops. The elevator begins to rise.

Sweat pricks her skin beneath the heavy coat, but the cold seeps through the bottom of the platter and penetrates the mitts, stinging her palm.

Her breath turns to fog.

At first, it's just a wispy trail. But when the elevator stops, white clouds are streaming through her lips. The seamless door begins opening and doesn't stop. It continues sliding all the way around her until it meets back where it started, leaving a slim rod that's sucked into the black floor.

The floor beneath her feet is a brightly lit circle. Beyond that, it's dark. It's hard to see, even after her eyes adjust. If she wasn't standing on a circle of light, it might be easier.

The light dims, as if it heard her thinking.

She's seen the top of the tower from outside. It doesn't look that big, not like this. It seems as if she's in the center of a circular room that's hundreds of feet across. Seems impossible and maybe it's an illusion.

Christmas music is playing somewhere. Tiny red and green lights softly illuminate various areas. Monitors and images appear on desktops and wall mounts. There's a fish tank to the left, a blue-white light shining on a long, black fish. Next to that is a desk with a short, fat statue.

The ceiling twinkles with stars, even though it's daytime. Oddly enough, the sky swirls with bands of green and blue, like the Northern Lights of the Arctic. Maybe it's just an illusion.

Her hand is numb.

She looks around for a table, chair, or something to put the platter down on. She takes it with both hands and decides to slide it on the floor. Her first step disappears outside the circle, gently touching the black floor. She leans forward—

Slips.

She lets go of the platter with one hand and catches her fall, but the domed lid clatters. She stops it with the inside of her elbow and grabs the knob before it crashes. The smell, though, wafts out. It's raw, pungent, and ten times the smell of shelled shrimp.

Dead.

She wants to look away, slide the lid back in place without looking, without seeing what's displayed beneath the metal dome, cold tendrils of steam sliding out like dry ice.

But she looks. Just like May told her not to.

Eyes look back.

A row of gelatinous eyeballs—milky and bulging, like the eyes of dead fish—stare out, their optic nerves like slimy noodles. A row of dead herring is next to them.

A knot swells in her throat and she swallows it back, but the odor is inside her sinuses, tugging at the sandwich in her stomach. She closes her eyes and puts the lid back in place, wishing it didn't smell so dead.

"Remain still." A voice comes out of the dark.

Sura looks around. Something scurries behind her, deep in the dark. She spins around, careful not to disturb the platter. Bells jingle.

The floor hums.

Something is rising a few feet away from the circle of light. It appears to be a solid cylinder pushing out of the floor.

"Put it there."

This time she locates the voice. It's coming from the desk next to the fish tank. What she thought was a statue scratches its bushy beard. Sura almost drops the platter.

"Please," he says. "It's safe."

The cylinder casts bluish light into the dark. The fish hangs lazily in the tank. The statue is as round as it is tall. The head appears to be a massive bush. Two orbs twinkle somewhere inside it, reflecting the blue light. A white, furry animal sits next to him. A dog, maybe.

Sura slides it across the top of the cylinder. The cylinder goes dark, and once again, she's trapped inside the circle of light. She rubs her hands together.

Mr. Frost glides away from the desk as if he's sliding across the floor. It's very slow and easy, almost as if he's wearing ice skates. But then he jets toward her, whipping around the cylinder. Sura doesn't have time to step back before he's back at the desk.

The platter is gone.

"Is that all?" she asks.

"Mmm."

She's not sure if that's for her or he's looking beneath the dome. She doesn't want to see those disgusting eyeballs plop into the water for the fish to eat. She'd rather forget she ever saw them. Or smelled them.

"I'm very sorry," he says. "About your mother."

"Thank you. She enjoyed working here."

That was an odd reply, but she didn't know what else to say. Even though she's snug beneath a heavy coat, the spotlight makes her feel self-conscious while he's out there in the dark.

Something moves behind her again.

Sura taps her foot like the elevator needs reminding to come for her. The platter slides across the desk, followed by a deep inhalation and a satisfying grunt. Sura's about to barf up lunch.

The metal lid falls back into place.

Mr. Frost slides closer to her but remains in the dark, only the bushy outline of his head and fat belly are clear. He can't be more than three feet tall.

"You're a beautiful young lady," he says. "Like your mother."

The words were creepy, but not the way he said them. They were genuine, not lusty, so she answers, "I've been told."

"Have you enjoyed your first day?"

"Yes. Thank you for the job. I can use the money now that Mom..."

"Mmm."

Mr. Frost glides back, almost as if he's standing on a hovering disk. With all the gadgets in the room, maybe that's exactly what it is.

There's rumors that he's from the future, that he can invent anything. Why not a hovering disk?

"Much to learn." His voice trails off at the end, making it difficult to understand the end of everything he says. "Much to explore, to discover. And the honor is mine."

He's back at the desk. The fish tank illuminates his face—the plump and ruddy features set in the untamed shag around his head.

The elevator rod slides out of the floor, assuming its delicate balance once again. The wall extends from it like a metal sheet, curving around her. Just before the elevator wall traces the circle of light and encloses her inside, she hears slurping.

And another grunt, this one deep and satisfied.

MR. FROST SLIDES across the icy floor. The miniature scales on his soles point toward his heels, allowing him to grab the slick surface and glide forward. He slides like all elven do when they're in a contemplative mood: his hands laced over his belly. The Arctic fox watches the fat, little man with the head like a tumbleweed glide merrily around the room.

Stars twinkle on the ceiling.

If Max could talk, he'd probably say that Mr. Frost looks different than usual. He might even say there was a glow about him.

That he looks happy.

And happiness is an emotion quite foreign to the round man. He doesn't remember the last time he felt a swirl in his belly like this. And Mr. Frost has quite the memory. He can recall the daily low temperatures for the past five hundred years.

Maybe longer.

It's not humanly possible. Then again, he's elven.

A human might look at what Mr. Frost has—and he has everything a man or woman could possibly want—and not understand his melancholy. In fact, Mr. Frost possesses inventions the world has yet to see, things too dangerous, too mind-blowing. There's not a taste, not a sight, not a sensation he does without.

And, yet, he still can't remember being happy.

The frigid breeze flutters in his whiskers, bites the tip of his cherub nose.

Freeda, the temperature, please, he thinks.

The room is minus twenty-five degrees Celsius, sir, the gentle female replies inside his head.

Take it down to minus fifty.

I can do that, sir. Give me a few minutes.

An icy draft wafts out of the vents hidden in the astral ceiling. Somewhere beneath the shag of Mr. Frost's white whiskers, a smile grows.

He imagines a white blanket stretching across a flat horizon where stars flicker in the green and red bands of the Northern Lights. When he takes the temperatures down that far, he can't help but daydream. He allows himself to indulge in that fantasy. Every once in a while he likes to pretend he was never forced to leave home. He likes to pretend all the elven in the world don't hate him.

It's nice to feel like he has a family again.

Would you like me to illuminate a model, sir?

Mr. Frost makes one more lap around the circular tower, contemplating just how far to indulge the daydream. There is so much to do. Where would he be if he sat around thinking all day?

Maybe he would remember happiness more often if he did, but Mr. Frost does not want to be a blissful idiot. Happiness, he believes, is not the point of life.

It's a side effect.

Maybe this one time, he thinks.

A soft glow begins in the center of the room and rolls out like liquid fog until a blanket of snow covers the floor. His feet are buried in the white illusion but don't disturb it as he slides through it.

Would you like a live satellite feed, sir? Or perhaps a past event?

Freeda knows him too well. Sometimes he likes to watch something recorded on the North Pole with his secret satellites. When the elven thought no one was watching, they'd slip out of the ice for snowball fights and stargazing.

Live feed, please. He may be indulging, but he'd rather not glue himself to the past. Not today.

The resolution turns fuzzy. The ice floes adjust; ice ridges emerge in different lines. The illusion refocuses with realistic precision. Mr. Frost appears to be floating high above the North Pole.

Human warmbloods appear like sugar ants drudging through the fluff. Five of them. Another troupe to the top of the world and why? Because it's there.

If they survive—and they probably will—a helicopter will fly them back home, where they can blog about their adventure. They can brag that they made the trek to the North Pole just like Frederick Cook. Although some will argue it was Robert Peary who made it there first.

They're both wrong.

Mr. Frost knows who the first warmblood is that reached the North Pole and it's neither Cook nor Peary. Nicholas and Jessica Santa made the trip long ago with their son, Jon, in the early 1800s and never left. It was their arrival that changed everything in the elven world. After the Santas arrived, Jack died and Pawn fled.

But Pawn doesn't like the name "Pawn" for a lot of reasons.

He's Mr. Frost now.

The warmblood history books have it all wrong. Truth can be that way.

Truth is not determined by what we believe.

Thermal scan complete, sir. There's activity inside an ice floe in sector 27D. Would you like me to take you down?

Mr. Frost drums his fingers over his belly. *Yes.*

The illusion of the North Pole turns to fuzzy fog and rearranges, solidifying in a thick layer of snow up to his waist. Mr. Frost is standing on the illusion of ice. If only he could find a hole and climb inside to join his people.

We're not people. We're elven.

He has to remind himself from time to time. It's easy to forget when you've lived with warmbloods for almost two hundred years. That's not much time to an elven, not when life expectancy is several thousand years. But time goes slow when you're all alone.

Even for an elven.

He plows through the snow, hoping to uncover an exit hole. Hoping some fat, little elven will poke his head out; a youngster might run outside on a dare to leap into the icy water, naked.

Polar bearing. Mr. Frost smiles beneath the whiskers. *Do they still call it that?*

He scoops up a handful of snow and crafts a perfectly round ball. He tosses it gently up and down, testing the weight. He was an expert snowballer. He doubts he's lost his edge, but there's no snow in South Carolina to prove it. The elven will never know what kind of snowballer he still is because they'll never find him.

Elven don't live long in heat unless you have a supercooled tower.

Sir, May would like to know if there's anything else you need before she retires for the day? What shall I tell her?

He lets the snowball roll off his fingertips, lets it thunk into the snow. No point in making snowballs when it's an illusion.

No, Freeda. That'll be all. Thank you.

Mr. Frost slides to the edge of the room and peers through the dark glass. The road leading away from the house disappears into the grove of magnolias all wrapped in white Christmas lights. A small car cruises into their glowing branches.

The good feelings return. Sura is back.

Why are you happy, sir?

I'm sorry? After two hundred years, he still sometimes forgets Freeda is inside his head.

You do not typically act this way when Sura returns, sir. Why is that?

Mr. Frost grumbles while clearing his head, letting thoughts fall away, replacing them with foggy confusion, random images, and puzzled thoughts.

I don't know, he finally answers.

Freeda doesn't answer. She'll pry some more, look through his chaotic smokescreen, but she won't find anything.

But he does know. After all these years, he knows why happiness is bubbling up now. Sura is back. That's reason for cheer, but not this much. It's more than that. Mr. Frost is happy because the end is near.

And this will all be over.

I'll be going to the lab now, Freeda, he quickly thinks, covering that last thought.

Very well.

The snow evaporates.

The floor glows eerie blue. Sections begin unfolding like trap-doors, furniture growing out of the floor, monitors lighting up and data flowing like it was when Sura delivered lunch.

Sura. She calls herself Sura now. Kids these days.

Mr. Frost navigates around the clutter to the main desk. Max sits calmly on top. Mr. Frost reaches into his pocket and tosses a small snack in the air. Max snaps it up before it lands.

The cylindrical elevator waits for Mr. Frost. He slides inside, pushing the bottom button that's just about waist level. The door closes and the elevator sinks down to the cavern below the house. He keeps his mind on Sura returning the next day for work, when she'll meet Joe. That will be a very good reason for happiness.

When the door slides open, he's blasted with a wave of humid heat. Something's wrong.

The laboratory anteroom is circular, but, unlike the tower room, it is completely free of clutter. The icy floor shines like glass. There is a door on the wall facing Mr. Frost. It exits to the back of the house and is wide open.

Mr. Frost looks to his right, where the incubation lab is open, too. He races over and looks inside. Debris is strewn across the floor, glass beakers shattered, and papers scattered. Worst of all, the silver table is empty, straps dangling from the edges.

"Freeda!" he exclaims. "Where is Jack?"

She doesn't have an answer.

2

NOVEMBER 30

Sunday

J ack knows he's dreaming.

He's butt naked in the snow and doesn't care. He's not all that comfortable running around without his clothes in front of others and, right now, he couldn't care less. That's how he knows he's dreaming.

The snow is deep enough to hide his enormous blue feet. Jack likes that. He likes that his feet are hidden. No one knows why his feet turned blue—blue as ripe blueberries, blue as the deepest part of the ocean—but everyone forgets things they don't see.

In some part of Jack's dream, he seems to remember that everything eventually turns blue. His hands, his legs... his bald head.

Everything.

It's not right, not normal. But why spoil the fun? Right now it's just his feet that are blue, and they're lost in the white fluff. And he's butt naked like all the other elven.

Their round bellies and curvy buttocks are pale in the moonlight. When the moon is full, it's time for teenage polar bearing. The adults stay beneath the ice because they had their time jumping through a hole in the ice when they were young, but that was thousands of years ago.

Teenage elven would rather not see the elders' wrinkly parts.

Jack is in line. He's behind Breezy. It's minus sixty degrees. Even for an elven that's a bit nippy, especially when you're naked. Jack, though, feels good. He likes to get his clothes off, feel winter's breath on his skin. He's never won a contest—not a spelling bee or snowball fight—but he'd bet he could handle more cold than any elven. Again, lost somewhere in the dream, he seems to remember cold is his specialty.

Breezy is up.

Someone laughs and shouts at Breezy to stop covering his junk and get wet. He slides over the ice—a path carved through the snow after dozens of trips—and hits the snow ramp with his arms out. He soars up, hovering above the ice before plunging into the ice hole.

KA-THUMP!

Cheers.

A minute later, Breezy pops out of a second ice hole twenty feet away. He's tackled by his buddies and they roll through the snow, naked as snowshoe hares.

Jack's turn.

He shoves ahead, the scales on his soles gripping the ice, propelling him forward—

WHAP.

"Not so fast, blueberry," someone says, shoving him off balance.

Jack—round as any healthy elven—rolls until momentum slows him down. Jack lifts his head. The elven are laughing at him. Even the girls. Even his brother, Claus. Even Claus is laughing.

Darlah Iceridge isn't.

They had cut in front of Jack once already, made him start over, and now they knocked him down. They don't want him, that's what it is. They don't want him to play in any of the elven games.

Jack waddles far away from the naked, teenage bunch. Their laughter carries over the ice. Their butts are still pale. It's better this way. Better to polar bear on his own.

Jack finds an old hole nearby. He kicks it with his heel until his foot sinks in the icy water. He just wants to jump in, cool off. It might be minus sixty degrees, but he's about to break a sweat.

They've already forgotten about him. They're back to jumping off the ramp, doing backflips this time. Jack steps into the old ice hole, pretending Darlah is watching him. He likes to think that maybe she'll come over and talk to him. He doesn't want to seem needy, but it'd be cool if she wanted to talk.

That's all.

He pinches his nose and sinks below the ice. The water is dark and cold, even for Jack. The frigid Arctic temperatures penetrate his layers of blubber. He paddles against the current. It's getting cold now, for real.

The dream is starting to suck.

Jack can feel it. He's starting to shiver and he's always the last one to shiver. He has to get out. He kicks his enormous feet, shooting toward the opening—

GUNK.

The ice hole has frozen over.

Jack punches at it, but the ice is too thick and he's running out of air. He hits it again and again. Maybe that's not the hole. Maybe he's drifted in the current. Quickly, he swims beneath the ice, searching for a way out, but his body isn't streamlined. The round body of an elven is made for rolling, not swimming. It takes too long to get there, his chest on fire, his skin puckered and clammy, daggers of ice punching through his skin, deep into his heart—

"Uuuuuuuuuuhhh!" Jack opens his mouth, inhaling deeply. He expects to swallow a gallon of seawater, but it is air.

Sweet, sweet air.

A pair of dirty fingers are clamped over Jack's nostrils. "Told you he wouldn't die," says the one holding them shut.

He lets go of Jack. It doesn't smell like the Arctic, clean and wet, because he's awake. This is real and it smells... sweaty.

Two haggard faces hover over him. One dark-skinned, the other one is fair. Both are equally unshaven and dirty. Their hair matted. Teeth, filmy.

Jack shakes his head. He's in a cushioned bed with sheets and pillows, not trapped beneath ice. Definitely not in the Arctic. The two men stand up. Jack scurries against the wall, pulling the sheet up to his chin. He may not be swimming in frigid water, but he's still freezing. The icy chill is inside his bones and the blanket isn't helping.

He doesn't even recognize the room. In fact, he can't really remember where he's supposed to be or how he got here or where he was before this. Even the dream has faded, something about snow and fat little naked people that look just like him. Except for the hair.

He remembers his name is Jack and he's staring at the bottom of a mattress that's directly above him. There are lots of double-decker beds in this endless room, and there are long, white lights glowing on the ceiling—a ceiling that is too high for a regular room. High enough that these two disgusting... these...

Oh, my God. Those are warmbloods.

The warmbloods stand up, still looking down at him with filthy, cheesy smiles.

And where is Pawn? He's always by the bed with a plate of cookies and tea when I wake up from a bad dream. And he certainly doesn't pinch my nose—

"AAAH!" Jack shouts.

Someone is behind him, their arms around his chest. The arms have thick, curly hair—funny, the light makes it look slightly green—that covers the back of the hands and the fingers up to the first knuckle—

"Wait a sec." Jack wiggles his fingers. The hairy fingers wiggle. The arms are his. He turns his hands over, studies the creases on his seasick-green palm, scratches the curly whiskers on his chin, and slides his fingers through the coarse hair on his head.

Something is wrong.

He's not supposed to have hair.

"You needa shave, man," the light-skinned warmblood says.

Jack looks back and forth between the two warmbloods. With no sudden movements, he lifts the cover and, "OH, FOR THE LOVE OF ALL THAT IS SNOWY AND COLD!"

The same hair is on his chest, his legs. His enormous feet. And he's naked as a polar bear.

"This place going downhill, man," the dark-skinned warmblood says. "They letting green people in now. Know what I'm saying?"

"Who are you?" Jack clears his throat, summoning an authoritative tone. "Where am I? How'd you get in here? Why am I naked? Did you touch me? Who plastered hair on me? Why am I cold? What—"

"Shut up." The light-skinned warmblood kicks the bed. "You jabber just as bad when you sleep. Don't need to hear that awake. Giving me a headache."

"Look, man." The other warmblood looks over his shoulder and leans closer. "I sell you a razor to shave, but it'll cost you a little green."

Jack pulls the blanket up to his nose. "Green?"

"Money, man." The light-skinned warmblood snaps his fingers. "We don't give razors for free. We got to see the green."

They both look around and then back to Jack. Dark-skinned warm-blood looks back once more and reaches for the blanket. Jack slaps his hand.

Jack makes his move.

"Get your hands off me, man." The warmblood yanks his arm back. "I didn't say touch me. You think I want your disease?"

Jack thought something might happen to him if he touched him. He remembers people get cold when he does, like super cold.

"You better wash that hand," the light-skinned warmblood says. "It'll turn green. Like gangrene. That's probably what he got."

"All right, that's enough. Sheldon, you don't even know what gangrene is." Another warmblood approaches, this one fatter and darker with black hair that hangs like ropes from his head. He grabs the dark-skinned warmblood's arm and says, "Pickett, leave the man alone. Take Sheldon and get your skinny butts away from the bed. You're supposed to be on the street."

"You doing favors for the greens now, Willie?" Pickett says.

"Yeah," Willie says. "And you ain't green, so get going. I ain't joking."

Sheldon and Pickett take their time walking away. They stop at the door and Willie shouts at them to keep going. Pickett makes a face and swings his arm at Willie. Sheldon follows him out.

They walk funny.

"You all right, Jack?" Willie pulls up a chair.

"How do you know my name?"

"You told me."

"I did?"

"Do you know where you are?"

Once again, Jack looks around the giant room with rows and rows of empty bunk beds. The wood floor looks like real wood. And he's never smelled that smell before. It's dirty and clean, all at the same time. There's also the smell of food, but it's gross. Reminds him of the time Pawn made boiled cabbage for lunch.

Pawn. Where's my friend Pawn?

Jack suddenly remembers a fat, little person that was his buddy. He's nowhere to be seen.

"I didn't think you'd remember anything." Willie leans forward, elbows on his knees. "Someone found you wandering along the Cooper River last night and they thought it'd be a good idea to drop you off at the shelter. Now I'll be honest, if I find a three-foot-tall man with greenish hair muttering nonsense about the North Pole, I'm calling the zoo or the newspaper or something. But some good soul thought it fit to bring you here for a warm bed and a hot meal, seeing that you were shivering like a cold fish. I guess you're lucky it's Christmas time; everyone is getting on Santa's good list."

"Santa?" Jack sits up. "You're talking about Nicholas Santa?"

Again, another familiar name. He's heard it before but can't connect the dots.

"Look, man. This ain't the North Pole, Jack. It's a homeless shelter. And you, like everyone else, have to get out by 8:00. And right now"—he looks at his wrist—"it's 8:05 and you're still in bed. I hate to be the bad guy, but you need to find someplace else to go. You got somewhere to go?"

Jack slips his arms beneath the covers so only his eyes and the top of his head are showing. "It'd be cool if I could hang here for a bit."

"You remember anything?" Willie asks.

Jack nods because he has the feeling if he says no, Willie will call the zoo or the newspaper.

Willie stands up and shoves the chair against the wall. "It's a little nippy out, but I think we can find some clothes so you don't freeze. Although I don't think we got anything to fit those feet."

Willie squeezes the lumps beneath the covers. Jack feels it in his toes and someone laughs. Pickett is back in the doorway. Willie scowls but doesn't shout. He takes a moment, bowing his head.

"Look," Willie says, "I ain't got anything against hairy people even if you do look seasick, but if you can't remember anything, I think we need to see if there are any missing person reports—"

"That won't be necessary." Jack scoots to the edge of the bed, careful not to let the blanket fall. "Bring me some clothes."

"Excuse me?"

"Clothes. You said you would give me clothes. I want them now."

Willie pauses, processing what he heard.

"I said now," Jack adds.

"You want to change your tone?"

"No. I want you to get me clothes."

"Mmm. Mmm-mmm." Willie wanders off, shaking his head. He stops at the doorway across the room and turns around, his eyes squinting and hard. "You definitely ain't from the South, my man."

❄

JACK STARES at the stack of clothes.

Willie had dropped them on the floor and gave him five minutes to pick something out and "get stepping." Jack doesn't know what that means, but that was fifteen minutes ago. Must not be that important.

"I'm coming to dress you," Willie shouts from another room.

"I'm coming. Geesh."

Jack's cold and nervous. Actually, he's freezing. His whole body is shaking. He doesn't know what's outside of this room, but it's not the North Pole. *How'd I get in a room full of warmbloods?*

The floor is hard and tacky. The scales on his soles latch onto the wood and he shoves in the direction of the clothes—

WHAP.

Jack is kissing the floor.

He rolls over, moaning. Nose, throbbing.

Warmbloods don't slide. They walk.

Jack sits up and stands. He sees someone to the left and falls down. It's someone about his height with lots of hair.

Wait. That's me.

He walks over to the mirror and touches the surface. He hardly recognizes the reflection. Only his crystal-blue eyes seem familiar.

I'm not supposed to look like this.

He doesn't know what he's supposed to look like, just not that.

One foot in front of the other, he walks to the clothes. He pulls on a couple of shirts and steps into baggy pants; he has to cuff the bottoms from stepping on them. There's a pair of boots, but they don't come close to fitting. But the coat fits and so does the gray stocking cap.

He's still shivering. In fact, it's getting worse.

Jack goes to the doorway, where Willie is waiting, arms folded. The cabbage smell is stronger out there. Jack waddles towards Willie, the floor gritty. It takes, like, forever to get there.

Walking is stupid.

Willie points at the front door. Jack turns toward it and keeps going, already exhausted from the excruciatingly slow trek.

"You're welcome," Willie calls.

Jack raises his hand. He just wants out of this leafy-smelling warmblood nest. He leans into the glass door and uses all his momentum to leverage it open. The air is choked with exhaust fumes; the ground is covered in litter. Several warmbloods huddle near the curb.

Definitely not the North Pole.

Jack stands in the doorway, rubbing his arms and shivering. He can't go out there. They look like they want to eat him. And it looks cold out there and stinky. Maybe that missing person report Willie was talking about will be in a warm room. He could make something up about losing his mother and how he just needs a friend.

Willie taps the glass and points towards the curb. He mouths a word, *Go.*

Jack sticks out his lip and bows his head. He shuffles out of the shadow. The hairs on his face tingle when the sunlight hits him. Warmth gyrates through the follicles and penetrates his cheeks, reaching deep into the cold bones beneath his eyes. Warmth oozes around his scalp like a hot rag. He closes his eyes and raises his face like a sunflower that's absorbing the sunlight.

Jack unzips his coat. His chest hair celebrates the sun's kiss.

He may not remember much, but at least he's warm.

Sir. Freeda's voice rings inside Mr. Frost's head. *Sir, May has breakfast ready. Everyone is waiting.*

Mr. Frost opens his eyes and doesn't recognize the room at first. It's been quite a few years since he slept in the incubation lab. Even when he did, it was never because he'd been up the night before cleaning it.

Sir?

Start without me.

Would you like something sent down for you?

I would like you to stop talking. He rolls on his back and sighs. His head is throbbing.

For as long as he was down there, he hadn't made much progress. The floor is littered with tiny boots, coats, hats, and tools. Tables are turned over, equipment destroyed. Shards of glass are on the bench. Luckily, none of the incubator tanks were damaged.

He slides to the sink, splashes water on his cheeks, and hides his face in the towel. His eyes are red and tired. He's much too young for an elven to feel like this. He drapes the towel over the sink and surveys the damage surrounding the large, metal table in the center, hooded lamps hanging over it. Mr. Frost slides past rows of glass tanks, tracing the cold, metal edge of the table with his pudgy fingers.

He woke up and went mad. I can't blame him.

But he never should've awakened. Jack was supposed to remain in stasis until he shed the coat of photosynthetic hair. Mr. Frost's toes get tangled in a wire-framed helmet, half of it mangled. *And his memories?* Jack probably tore the learning gear from his head and stomped on it when he leaped off the table and ransacked the lab.

You are stressed, Freeda says. *Would you like me to assume command of your bodily comfort while you think?*

I'd like you to explain how Jack escaped. He throws the learning gear on the floor.

A mild sedative is released from the miniscule capsule imbedded near the base of Mr. Frost's cranium. The *root*, he calls it. Two hundred years ago, the root released the firestorm that drove Mr. Frost out of the North Pole, sent him fleeing south until the agony subsided, made him hide in exile while he built this fortress for one purpose.

And now that purpose has escaped.

The root, though, has different uses now.

Freeda speaks through it; she watches his thoughts with it and, to some extent, controls his actions. She senses his agitation so, against his will, she's released a mild sedative to soothe the aches and pains, chemically smoothing the wrinkles in life.

How much of Jack's memories were uploaded? Mr. Frost asks.

The upload was only ten percent complete, sir.

Ten percent? He's only learned a fraction of this new world. He doesn't know who he is. Or what he is. How did this happen?

The lab was empty, sir. The garden was being attended—

I don't mean that, Freeda. I mean, how did he wake up? There were safeguards in place; there's no way this should've happened.

It's unclear.

Why didn't you tell me when it happened?

Sir, do not blame this on me. The likelihood of his awakening and escaping were very small. I was using the majority of my processing capacity to flesh out the next incarnation when—

You were already planning the next incarnation?

She doesn't answer. Her disapproval of the photosynthetic stabilization is not a secret.

Mr. Frost kicks the crumpled learning gear. He exits the incubation lab and slides into the empty anteroom where Jack made his escape. The double doors on the north end are sealed now.

It's not really Freeda's fault.

He lets her see that thought. There's never been a need for security inside the lab. There's never been anyone he couldn't trust. The doors were only locked from the outside. There had never been a premature awakening. But then again, they've never been this close to success.

A search of the plantation is nearly complete, sir.

Mr. Frost doesn't need to ask for the results. No news is bad news.

Would you like to suit up to explore the garden, sir?

Sura would be arriving soon. She doesn't need to see him wandering the grounds in his coolsuit, like some alien from another planet. She saw plenty yesterday. She needs to see a little bit of truth at a time, not all at once. Too much and she'll reject her reality.

He's seen that happen. Not pretty.

Mr. Frost picks up a leather boot. The tiny thing fits in his palm. He slides past the wide door on the west side of the anteroom and tosses the boot through it. There's muttering from inside, where the toy factory is in full swing, but no one comes out.

Mr. Frost continues around the elevator cylinder and past the enormous console built into the southern end of the anteroom. Freeda is a ghostly voice inside his head, but if he ever wants to see her body, he just has to look at the southern wall: she's a computer that sees and hears everything.

Except Jack.

Mr. Frost slides around the anteroom, hands laced over his belly. He makes several laps, contemplating what to do. He layers his thoughts to minimize Freeda's prying eye. She'll still see what he's thinking.

He stops at the eastern door and looks inside the trashed incubation lab. It's a long room. The low, bluish light illuminates the silver table and the rows of frosty glass tanks, each taller and wider than Mr. Frost. The walls are loaded with similar tanks, but these are much shorter than the others, each the size of an infant.

The tanks are opaque with condensation on the inside. Occasionally, the moisture will streak and he spies the developments growing inside. But more often than not, he lets Freeda alert him when a chamber has matured.

Mr. Frost eases up to the tank nearest him. He presses his eye to the glass, careful not to fog it with his breath. Green fuzz has already begun.

Shut Jack's line down.

Sir?

You heard me, Freeda. Shut his line down. No more until he's found.

But, sir, that could cause delays to—

Shut it down! He balls his fist against the glass. *I don't want to rush things, not again. Put all the tanks in stasis until the search is complete and we can analyze what happened. We don't need half-aware incarnations of Jack out there suffering.*

Freeda doesn't answer. Mr. Frost doesn't give orders, but sometimes she yields to his intellect. There are limitations to being artificial, even she recognizes that. And he's right. If she didn't have anything to do with his premature awakening, then they better find out how it happened.

And if she did have something to do with it, well, then he'd get to the bottom of it.

3

DECEMBER 1

Monday

Sura rolls down her window.

Templeton is waiting, gloved hands clasped near his waist. "You are late, Sura."

"I had school. I thought I told you."

He looks at his pocket watch. "Three minutes past the hour."

"I left as soon as my last class."

"Perhaps, next time, you don't chat with friends in the parking lot."

How does he know that?

Templeton bends at the waist, his back ramrod straight, like there's a hinge in the small of his back, to hand her a sweetgrass basket. Sura wonders what he looks like when he goes to the bathroom. He's human, after all. And that thought makes her like him a little better. Not much, but a little.

"Take the basket to the garden. Mr. Jonah is collecting firethorn berries for decorations."

A new display of grapevine and holly hangs over the front doors, little lights twinkling on twining strands. Christmas decorating never seems to end.

"The garden?" Sura asks.

"Be attentive, Sura." He starts up the steps, one at a time. "It's time to grow up."

Sura is never sure when he's insulting or helping her. It feels like both.

There are two trucks around back this time. Sura parks at the corner of the barn where the creeping fig vine is thick and green. December has been warm, but not today. Mist drifts down from the gray sky like cold flecks of spittle, coating everything with a glittering sheen.

The land behind the house is open and rolling, the grass brown and dormant. Vineyard trellises are posted at the bottom of the slope, like burial markers for the barren grapevines that sprout from the wires. A small patch of corn, perhaps an acre, is to the right of that, the stalks wilted and crispy, blackbirds picking at their corpses.

She finds an old sweatshirt in the trunk, still damp and muddy from the last time she wore it. *Now, to find the garden.*

Sura walks back down the road by the side of the house. Templeton made it sound like it was right in front of her, not like she needed to go search for it. Seems like he could've just told her.

There it is.

There's an arbor swallowed in the thick hedges across the road, east of the house. She didn't see it last time because, well, because she was looking at the house. This time, the long, cool shadow of the tower is falling across the road.

She steps through the arbor, careful to avoid the thorny climbing rose twining through the lattice. Knee-high boxwood hedges are sheared into a geometric maze that circles downwards to a fountain in the center. It's a sculpture of a woman that's very short and fat, with water bubbling from her outstretched hand.

The outer walls are ten-foot-tall holly hedges loaded with red berries. There are arching exits carved out of each of the four foliar walls. Sura is standing in the western opening.

"Mr. Jonah?" she calls.

There's a distant sound of snipping metal. She tentatively walks down the stone-carved steps and around the outside of the boxwood maze. The sculpture is made of a strange material, oddly translucent. Like ice.

Snip, snip, snip.

She hesitates at the northern, leafy archway. It's dark beneath a canopy of wax myrtles and protected from the cold mist, but still she hesitates. And she's not sure why. It feels like someone's watching her. The sculpture maybe.

Sura grips the sweetgrass basket until the handle creaks, steps through the archway and into the shadows—

She runs into a boy with an armful of branches. Orange berries spill on the ground. He drops the thorny stems, shaking his hand.

"I'm sorry!" Sura says. "I didn't, I wasn't sure—"

"It's all right." He sucks on his finger. "Not your fault, it was an accident."

"Are you hurt?"

"Firethorn is a little sharp."

Black hair curls from his gray stocking cap. He puts his finger in his mouth again. His skin is olive. His eyes are blue. Like, really blue. He smiles around his finger and bends over to pick up the berries.

"Oh, sorry." Sura drops the basket on the ground. "Those are for me; let me help."

"Be careful."

Sura plucks each bunch off the ground like bugs. The boy sweeps the loose berries into piles with the edge of his hand. His finger is smudged with blood.

"Do you work out here?" she asks.

"Only when Jonah needs help."

"Mr. Jonah?"

"The one and only."

"He takes care of all the gardens?"

"Pretty much."

Sura sneaks a peek at the boy. He looks about her age, but she's never seen him at school. Maybe he lives in the other direction. Maybe he's homeschooled. She wonders if his homeschool has room for one more.

The sweetgrass basket is overflowing with firethorn. Sura sits back on her heels, watching him meticulously pluck the loose berries from the mulch, as if he doesn't want anything going to waste. He feels her looking.

Staring is more like it.

"I'm Joe." He puts out his hand.

"Sura."

His hand is callused, but warm. "I know."

"Do I know you?"

He shakes his head and returns to gathering berries. He rubs his finger. The bleeding has stopped.

"I'm sorry."

"Not the first time I've been stuck, trust me." He laughs. "Besides, it's easy to get lost out here. A secret around every corner."

Secret? "You live out here?"

"Uh, no." He chuckles again. "Who wants to live with Templeton?"

They share a long, knowing laugh that feeds on itself. They both must have the same thoughts about Templeton. Maybe he hasn't had anyone to share that inside joke with until now. She wants to shake his hand again. Because it's so warm, like the laughter in her belly.

"Jonah?" An old man appears at the end of the leafy tunnel, as if he stepped out of the shrubbery. His thin hair is swept back over his head.

"Oui?" Joe says.

"Enough talking."

Jonah's lips are hidden beneath a bushy, black mustache. His dark eyes fall on Sura, watching her. Absorbing her. He looks up at nothing in particular, his body somewhat frozen in thought. Perhaps remembering. Perhaps wishing.

He turns around and pushes through the shrubs, leaves swallowing him up.

"Are you French?" Sura asks.

"Jonah speaks it sometimes. I just know bits and pieces."

"And he's your... dad?"

"Yeah."

"Why don't you call him 'Dad'?"

"I don't know." He looks away. He knows why, but he's not telling her. Jonah looked troubled when he saw Sura—she felt it. It was the same with her mom. Whenever she was having a blue day, Sura felt it. Maybe he doesn't want to talk about his dad the same way she doesn't want to talk about her mom.

Although, his dad is alive.

"I have to go back." Sura finally stands. "Nice meeting you."

She thinks that maybe she'll shake his hand, but that would be stupid. Instead, she turns to exit through the archway that leads back to the boxwood maze.

"Hey." Joe reaches for his back pocket. "We're sorry about your mother."

It's a long stem with a white camellia bloom and three shiny leaves. He holds it out for her. She reaches for it, their fingers lightly brushing.

She smells it; there's not much fragrance. The petals—tickling her nose—are cleanly arranged and perfectly balanced. White as snow.

"It's a Seafoam camellia," he says. "Your mother's favorite."

"How do you know?"

"Jonah said so."

She brushes it under her nose, the petals soft and spongy. "It's beautiful."

"I agree."

But he's not looking at the flower. At least, that's what she wants to believe.

Sura tucks the flower behind her ear and floats out of the garden, hardly feeling the gravel path or the stone steps beneath her feet. If the sculpture were watching her, she wouldn't know it. The basket is hooked on the crook of her arm, berries trickling behind her like bread crumbs.

"Heh-em." Templeton is standing in the road, gloved hands at his side. He flicks a glance at the flower sprouting from her hair. "If you're quite done with daydreaming, you can take the firethorn berries through the mudroom in back. May will meet you. You can follow her to the craft room from there."

Templeton looks at the flower once more, shakes his head, and walks to the front steps, arms at his sides. Sura skips in the other direction, hoping maybe he'll see her, that maybe it'll put a little sway in his rigid hips. Light rain begins to fall, but none of that bothers her as she rounds the corner to the back of the house, wearing a smile that even Templeton can't wipe off her face.

A door slams.

She expects to see May on the back porch, hands planted on her doughy hips. The steps are empty, though. There's a pair of slanted doors set in the foundation of the porch to the right of the stairs. One of the doors appears to be raised, revealing a slice of darkness inside. She sees a flash of yellow.

The door drops.

That feeling of being watched tingles along the back of her neck this time.

MR. FROST STANDS at the edge of the tower's room, hairy toes pressed against the dark glass that extends from floor to ceiling. One hand rests on his belly, the other digging through the thicket of hair on the back of his head, scratching his neck.

The root is itching.

It's a perennial ache, like a ghostly finger pushing on the base of his skull. Scratching does little good, but there's little else he can do. At least it doesn't burn. That memory, although two hundred years old, is quite clear. And for that he is grateful. He can deal with itching.

A cold day embraces the landscape, drizzling tiny droplets that drift against the slanted glass, marring the outside world. The old flooded rice fields shimmer in the distance.

The slow-motion precipitation reminds him of snow.

Jonah exits the north tunnel and enters the boxwood maze. Joe isn't far behind with a wheelbarrow full of tools. Mr. Frost imagines their foreheads slick with perspiration.

He begins to sit.

A chair forms from the shiny black floor in time for his round bottom to sit comfortably. He leans back, nuzzling his head into the headrest, staring at the starred ceiling.

Is Jonah happy with such simple work? Does he find joy in plowing the land and carrying twigs? Does he ever want more?

Mr. Frost can have anything he desires. If he projects a thought into the room, it will materialize within seconds. All his desires can be manifested in the tower room. This technology was quite satisfying when he first developed it, but now...

Is he happy?

Mr. Frost closes his eyes, sensing the ache of longing inside his belly. It pervades his being, saturating him like hunger. But hungry for what?

I just want this to be over.

That concerns me, sir.

Mr. Frost is startled by the sudden intrusion. *I thought you were busy.*

When you have self-destructive thoughts—

Thoughts, Freeda. I'm aware they're just thoughts. Nothing else.

He remains tense, waiting for a reply. It seems to satisfy her, and soon he drifts into a light sleep, nestled comfortably in his desires. He avoids getting too cozy with his thoughts of never waking up, or Freeda will intervene and ruin his nap.

Snick.

The unmistakable sound of the elevator cylinder rises behind Mr. Frost. Perhaps if he lies still, it'll go back.

"Are you going to sit there feeling sorry for yourself all day?"

Mr. Frost smacks his lips and rubs his tired eyes. He spins the lounger around. Templeton stands in the center, with a spotlight beaming up from the floor, while balancing a silver tray and teapot on the tips of his gloved fingers.

He's impeccably dressed without winter clothing, clouds streaming from his nostrils. The rest of the room is black and empty except for Max curled up on a pillow, a white ball of fur with a wary eye on the visitor.

"Do you mind?" Templeton nods at the floor.

The insolence of this manservant brings a sly grin to Mr. Frost. It always does.

Bring the room online, Freeda.

Objects emerge from the floor, filling it with desks, shelves, and the fish tank. Monitors lit with electric images chatter around the room. The floor in front of Templeton becomes dull so he can walk without slipping. A path leads to a low table glowing beneath a pale light. He slides the silver tray on it, muttering loud enough for Mr. Frost to hear, but not discern.

Templeton takes a dainty teacup from the tray and tips the teapot, wrinkling his nose and frowning. Fish oil fragrance wafts up. Templeton looks ill whenever he pours the drink. He makes a point to let Mr. Frost know it.

"You really should turn the fish tank when you drink," Templeton says. "You're savoring a distillation of his people."

"He's not a person, Templeton." Mr. Frost sits up. "He's a fish."

"So he has no feelings?"

"Ask him, if you like."

Templeton shakes his head. His argument is never won. Never forfeited.

Mr. Frost slides to the table on one foot, easing to a stop. He sips the chilled fish oil through thick whiskers where the lovely scent will linger for hours. He lifts the lid from a small porcelain container and plucks out an anchovy, dropping it in his drink. He slurps again.

Perfect.

The news outlets blabber about the weather, the economy, and global strife. A fire burned a house down. Mr. Frost makes a note to send the family money. The blood bank is seeking donors. Nothing he can do about that. But he listens. Day and night, he listens for a report about a strange discovery of a short man with greenish hair.

The chatter dampens to a low hum.

"I can't hear myself think." Templeton is pecking at a nearby keyboard. He fusses with the controls to turn the volume lower and bring the lights up, so that it feels more like daylight inside the tower.

I'd be happy to deny his access to the room, sir.

It's quite all right, Freeda.

Mr. Frost slides to the glass wall, teacup perched beneath his hidden nostrils. The drink soothes the loneliness, despite the gray day.

"There's nothing on the news," Templeton reports. "Thermal imaging is not detecting anything on the property that doesn't run on four legs. Analysis suggests Jack is dead. He'll be alligator breakfast when spring arrives, if the turkey buzzards don't find him."

Mr. Frost turns.

"What?" Templeton looks up from the control panel. "Ask Freeda if you don't believe me."

"A little compassion is in order."

"Please. It was just a body, no one inside. We call that meat, not a person."

That's why he likes Templeton. He spares nothing to spout the truth.

"You need to initiate Jack's incubator lines and start again," Templeton says. "You missed on this one anyway, you got to admit. He was too hairy and green, for God's sake. He probably woke up, got a look at himself, and wrecked the place. If he remembered anything, he probably would've come looking for you to get back for what you did to him, so you should count yourself lucky."

The hair is temporary, but Mr. Frost doesn't feel the need to explain the process to Templeton.

"Nothing wrong with that," Templeton adds. "All genius is preceded by guessing. I'm just saying life doesn't stop because you failed, so put on your big-boy pants and get back to work. Let me remind you that Christmas is in three weeks. Jack wrecked the lab on his way out and production is behind. The schedule is tight. Stop daydreaming."

Templeton's toe tapping sounds like he's hammering a nail. Mr. Frost inhales the salty wonder of fish oil. It tingles in his sinuses.

"Fine," Templeton says. "Be that way."

The tray clatters. Exaggerated footsteps walk toward the center of the room.

"How'd it go?" Mr. Frost nods at Joe returning to the garden to fetch a pair of forgotten loppers. He gets to the barn before the hard rain comes.

"You mean Sura meeting Joe for the first time?"

"Of course."

"Like clockwork." Templeton then mutters, "Silly question."

The elevator snicks closed, humming as it sinks into the floor.

Silence returns.

Mr. Frost doesn't assume Sura and Joe are going to hit it off, despite Templeton's confidence. There's always a chance it could sour.

Mr. Frost calls the news chatter volume back up. He drifts around the room, teacup teetering on his belly. He surveys the various holographic images beamed into his room from satellites in space, several of them exclusively owned by Frost Plantation Enterprises.

He grabs a handful of kernels from a table and tosses them into the fish tank. The fish doesn't seem to mind there's a cup of fish oil balanced on Mr. Frost's belly. Fish eat each other, why would he care?

Mr. Frost slides near the furball on the pillow. He digs a small, silver tin out of his shirt, something he keeps pressed against his skin at all times. Max sits up as Mr. Frost opens the lid and pinches a few kernels—a few very special kernels—between his fingers.

Max gobbles them up.

I hate to say it, but Templeton is right, sir. We need to start the lines. And production is woefully behind.

He scratches Max's chin. *Wait another week, just to be sure. There's still time to find him. The last thing I need is two of him fully awake.*

He scratches his neck. Freeda can't override this order. Mr. Frost only has to bring Jack back once.

It doesn't matter how long it takes.

As long as he gets it right.

And it's got to be more than meat.

TATATATATATAT...

Jack hears a hammer on a long, cold, metal spike.

It drives a steady beat, an echoing cadence that rattles inside his skull.

Nothing he can do about it. He's frozen stiff, helpless beneath blankets that seem to make it worse. He can't get away. The cold fills him like mercury.

Hammer on nail.

Tatatatatatat...

"I can't take this," someone shouts. That someone is Pickett. "Every night with the chattering, I can't take it. Three days now and this cat is snapping his jaw all night."

Someone moans.

"I'd rather listen to sirens than those big, square teeth sending telegrams."

A bunk creaks. Someone lands on the floor. It's too dark to see, but Jack hears him breathing through his mouth, smells something foul hover over him. He must have eaten a poop sandwich before bed.

"He sick or something," Sheldon says. He apparently ate from the same sewage salad bar as Pickett. A fiery hand lands on Jack's forehead and quickly pulls away. "Dude feels like ice."

"I don't care, I can't take it. I'm dreaming about woodpeckers and stuff."

"Tell Willie."

"Willie ain't going to do nothing."

The stink fades, but it's inside Jack now. All the smells of warmblood civilization are soaked inside Jack. He feels like a sponge dipped in ink, all spoiled, just living among them. If there's one thing he hates more than warmbloods staring at him—and they get quite the eyeful, no doubt—it's their smell.

They leave it everywhere.

It's in the streets and on the buildings; it's in their clothes and the food they eat. Whatever they touch... stinks. It's thick with decay and artificiality.

Civilization, they call this.

There's no escaping it. He's sure of it. Three days of wandering the concrete—his thick, scaly soles crushing bottles and kicking rocks—and he's found no way out. Just endless streets.

No sign of ice.

Jack yearns for the pure touch of fresh snow, for the sight of a panoramic horizon and the sky splashed with Northern Lights. It's not here, among the warmbloods. They sit in cars that cough smoke, consumed by something called Christmas. They carry brightly colored bags from shops and put them in their cars so they can drive to another shop and get more bags.

They act so happy, but they're faking it. He can tell.

Somehow, he landed in the United States. Charleston, to be exact. He still doesn't remember much but has the distinct intuition that he belongs on the North Pole, in the same way birds know to fly south. But then how would he survive? It's seventy degrees in the shelter and he's a block of ice.

Dying in the snow would be better than this.

The North Pole is home, he's sure of it. And if he thinks hard enough, he can remember the snow and weather that felt so wonderful, so clean.

And elven. He remembers elven. That's another thing he remembers. At first it was just a word, but then he realized it's what the short, fat people call themselves, the ones that live on the North Pole. Unfortunately, he can't remember any of them with green hair, so that's a little confusing.

Confusion, though, has become his daily life.

"Got it." Something very sticky and long tears. "Time for the green goblin to shut his mouth."

They're still across the room, shuffling through junk. An argument breaks out in hushed tones. Someone is worried that Willie is going to kick them all to the curb. It quiets down.

"I still can't see what I'm doing," Sheldon says.

"You don't need to see," Pickett says. "Just put a piece of tape over his mouth, he breathes through his nose, and we get some sleep."

Jack doesn't want his mouth taped shut. It'll just seal the cold inside, he thinks. He remembers a time when someone locked him in a closet and wouldn't let him out. He thought he was going to suffocate. There was a song he used to sing, something that helped him feel better when he felt helpless.

But he can't remember it.

"I got something." A locker door slams shut.

A bright spot of light briefly flashes over Jack. For a second, it feels hot.

Tatatatatatat...

"Hold this." Another long, sticky tear. "Aim the light on his face."

Jack smells them get closer. The spot of light hits him in the face.

"What about those whiskers?" Sheldon asks.

"What about them?" Pickett says.

"Tape's going to rip them out."

"Don't care."

The spotlight's on Jack. This time, it doesn't leave.

Tatatat—

Silence.

The warmth seeps through each hair follicle just like it did when he's in the sunlight. Warmth spreads into his skin, deep into his tissues, reaching for his bones, thawing his brain.

"You see that?" Sheldon says.

"Yeah. Take that off him."

The light goes away. *Tatatatatatat...*

The light returns.

Back and forth they experiment. A third grader would've figured it out before them.

"He ain't chattering when the light's on him," Sheldon finally says.

"Yeah."

Maybe they're thinking it's better this way. Taping a man's mouth shut could put them on the street. But a light?

Three long strips of tape are pulled off the roll. The light jiggles but finally stays in place. A smile creeps across Jack's face, curling his lips. He's warm again.

The stink fades.

Snoring resumes in the bunkroom. Jack doesn't sleep, but he rests easy. He remembers something.

He remembers the song he used to sing when he felt helpless, the song that filled him with hope and yummy feelings.

Silent Night...

4

DECEMBER 4

Thursday

Sura braids the twining grapevine with long blades of lemongrass and strands of white lights. She accents the decoration with magnolia leaves and holly berries and then stands back, tapping her lower lip. That's what May does when she decorates.

"I think!" May would say when Sura stared at her. Then May would laugh. Then she would hug her.

There's laughter down the hallway, but it's not the same as May's laughter. This has an edge that cuts. High school seniors lean against a cinderblock wall. The girls cover their mouths.

Sura dumps out a bucket of white camellia blooms. She plucked them from the shrub growing in a dark corner behind the school where no one would appreciate them. They aren't Seafoam camellias, but they're white.

And perfect.

"Oh, my!" Ms. Wesley steps out of the gymnasium. "That is incredible, Sura! You did this? All by yourself?"

"Yes, ma'am."

"It's absolutely wonderful." Ms. Wesley walks beside the twisted decoration, lights blinking in the depths of festive wrappings like little fairies. "I never knew you had such talents."

Sura blushes, looking away.

"I think we can hang it." Ms. Wesley carefully lifts it, lights reflecting off her glasses. "Take the other end."

They are barely tall enough to reach over the doorway, but they manage to set it on the hooks the janitor set in the wall. A few tucks here, an extra pine cone there and—

"Wonderful." Ms. Wesley folds her hands on her chest. Only a teacher would appreciate a Christmas adornment like that. "Can you stay after school? We could use your talents for the main stage."

"I can't, Ms. Wesley. I have to work. Sorry."

Ms. Wesley puts her arm around her. She'd gotten a lot of those hugs from teachers. They stopped saying "sorry about your mother" and resorted to half-hugs.

"What about last period? I could get you out."

"I need to study."

"Right. And what kind of teacher would I be if I interrupted your studies?"

Sura sort of smiles. Sort of laughs. Sort of completely hates herself for glancing down the hallway to see if the seniors are watching because Ms. Wesley notices. "Are you going to the senior holiday gala next week?" she asks.

"No, ma'am."

"And why not?"

Sura doesn't want to say she has to work because that would be a lie, but she also doesn't want to tell the truth. She'd been dreaming about Joe asking her. He'd pick her up on a loud motorcycle and all the girls would swoon and the boys would tremble in fear. She doesn't know where he'd get the bike or why the boys would be afraid of him, but she doesn't want to ruin the fantasy with questions.

And she can't tell Ms. Wesley because someone might hear and she'd heard enough laughter.

"You can ask someone, you know." Ms. Wesley sorts through the other buckets. "You don't have to wait around for a boy to ask."

"I know."

"Do you?"

Sura decides to help find a place for the remaining magnolia leaves, to give her hands something to do. Ms. Wesley begins humming a Christmas tune. It eventually morphs into a lighthearted falsetto effort that only a teacher would do without crippling embarrassment.

The bell rings.

"I have to go to the library, Ms. Wesley."

"Are you going to be volunteering this Sunday?"

"At the horse stables? Of course."

"The children will be there at 2:00."

"Yes, ma'am."

Sura slings her book bag over her shoulder. Ms. Wesley's song follows her down the hall.

BOBBY JAMES PRETENDS to read a history textbook. No high school student has actually read a history textbook. It's a cover for his phone. Sura pushes a cart past him, the last of the books to be shelved. It's not like the old days, her teachers tell her. That's when libraries were full of real books, not ones on the computer.

Technology is ruining us.

Of course, they drive their car home instead of a horse and buggy. So much for that argument.

Sura finishes the last one with five minutes left. Bobby James has his eyes closed. She wishes she could waste time like that.

"You don't hang out," her mom would always say. "You invest your time. Life is short. And if you think the point of living is to be happy, you're mistaken. Serve life and happiness will find you." Then she'd get that look of wisdom and say, "Happiness cannot be grasped any more than the wind."

Sometimes Sura wishes her mom hadn't been so weird. Maybe Sura wouldn't be so weird.

She goes to the back corner and sits at a secluded desk, where *booger* is carved into the surface. She pulls her phone out. Guilt and fear coil around her. She ignores them, sliding her finger across the glass.

She navigates to the school's website and finds the library database. There's a link to the tri-county yearbook database the librarian sometimes uses to update student information. It's not available to the public, but if you're a library assistant, you probably have a password.

Sura logs on.

A jolt of excitement tingles in her arms. She searches for Joe...

Wait. What's his last name?

There's going to be like a thousand Joes in the database. It'll be Monday by the time she finds him, assuming Joseph is his first name and not his middle. Assuming his name is Joseph.

She types a different first name.

The icon rotates, grinding through an eternity of Charleston area students, past and present. Two hits. The first one is current, a senior at a nearby high school. She hits the link. A picture loads and the twin snakes of guilt and fear melt like sweet sugar.

Jonah.

She's only met him the one time, but she's been branded with his slight smile. He's cute by anyone's standards, but it's not just that. She gravitates toward him. Maybe she's delusional, but she believes he gravitates towards her, too.

He's not in sports or student cabinet. No clubs except one, the American Red Cross club. *He's a nerd, just like me. A hot, sweetheart nerd.*

Strange thing, though. The photo was updated three weeks ago when he registered for class, like he just started at the high school. *He must've been homeschooled.*

The bell rings.

The hallway quickly clutters.

Sura begins to put the phone away. Before she does—on a whim—she taps the other Jonah that appeared in her search. This Jonah went to school thirty years ago. A picture loads, this one slightly grainy.

A strange sensation trickles across her skin, like magnetic ants racing over her, taking the good feelings away.

It's Joe.

It's not Joe, it's his father, but he looks exactly like him. That's Joe's face. The hair is shorter, but the smile is the same. Eyes, the identical color.

Lots of people look like their parents. Some of them look *exactly* like them. It shouldn't seem so weird.

Oddly enough, she remembers another bizarre thing her mom used to say. *Wake up, Sura. Don't sleep through the truth.*

Sura hustles out of the library. She can't be late for work.

5

DECEMBER 7

Sunday

Maybe I'm a warmblood.

Jack stares at the mirror. He doesn't look like a warmblood, but they all look different—hair, skin, eyes, size, smell... all different. His insanely large feet are hard to explain, but he saw a girl with blue hair and metal rings in her eyebrow the other day, so maybe he's like that.

Maybe he's just out there.

He's a freaky warmblood with delusions of elven that live on the North Pole. Maybe he just needs to find an equally hairy, equally repulsive wife and get a job loading something onto a thing, and get a house, have disgusting little kids.

That would be easier than getting to the North Pole.

Jack's nostrils flare. He sniffs like a dog. His mouth floods with saliva. Someone is bringing in groceries. He's still full of oatmeal, but he may as well eat mud. There is something new in the building.

He creeps through the empty bunkroom, careful not to let one of the supervisors see him, which isn't easy to do when you're the shape of an overinflated beach ball. Jack leans against the wall and breathes deeply, picking out a hint of something scaly.

And delicious.

JACK PLUCKS the last sardine from the can, its tail limp and slick. He dangles it over his mouth, caressing the gaping eye with the tip of his tongue before slurping it down like an overcooked noodle.

There is a parade in the street. As far as Jack can tell, while mincing the tiny bones between his teeth, a parade is obnoxious music, ghastly costumes, and atrocious dancing. He pulls down the front of his white tank top to expose a shag of greenish hair that tingles in the light.

First sardines. Now sunlight.

Life is good.

"Merry Christmas." Willie comes out of nowhere.

Jack chokes. "Huh, what?"

"I said Merry Christmas, man."

"Okay." Jack wipes his mouth with the back of his hand. "Why?"

"Man, you never give up, do you?"

"No." Jack has no idea what that means, but it's probably true.

"We picked up those cans of nasty little fish for you."

"You did?"

"Yeah. You've been asking about herring, anchovies, and all sorts of disgusting food, so we got those for you. Thought you'd like them."

Jack licks his oily finger. "Okay. Cool."

"That ain't going to cut it."

"Cut what?"

"I want you to show some appreciation, man. You get a free bed, a free shower, free food, and free nasty fish." Willie wrinkles his nose. "You can at least show a little gratitude."

Jack looks around. No one is watching. They're all standing on the curb, watching trucks, tractors, and little kids that suck at dancing. No one is close enough to ask what Willie wants him to do.

So Jack bows.

Willie crosses his arms and looks away.

Jack bows deeper. He drops to his knees. He jumps up, tap dances in place, his feet scuffing the concrete.

"I don't know what you want me to do, Willie. This? Or this? Or what? I don't know."

Willie grabs Jack's arms before he pirouettes. Jack's out of breath.

"You just say thank you, that's all."

"Thank you?"

"That's it, man. You say thank you."

Willie's green eyes are soft, his ropey hair dangling over his brows. He gently squeezes Jack's shoulders.

"Thank you."

Willie lets go. Smiles.

They go to the curb with the rest of the crowd and watch motorcycles putter past and high school bands march with tall, fuzzy hats and farting, metal instruments. It doesn't make any sense. Just the other day there were cars racing down the road, now they're dancing on it.

Jack slurps the delightfully fish-scented oil and tosses the empty can on the grass. "What's this?" he says.

"Parade," Sheldon says.

"Yeah, but what is it? Some sort of talent show?"

"You never heard of a parade?"

"Yeah, dummy. That's what I mean. Now tell me."

Another truck comes around the corner with another female with another glittery shirt, waving and smiling. It's so obvious she's not happy. Jack thinks about throwing the sardine can at her.

Someone inside the truck throws a fistful of rocks wrapped in clear plastic. They skitter into the curb.

"Parade, man." Sheldon picks up one of the wrapped rocks. "You get candy."

"Yeah. Why?"

"Cause it's Christmas, man," Pickett shouts over the approaching band. "What's your problem? Your mother didn't love you?"

"She didn't love you."

Sheldon and Pickett laugh. Jack heard someone say that the other day and thought it was an insult. Must be a joke.

Another truck heaves more candy at them. The shelter residents harvest it from the street. Maybe the candy is sardine flavored.

"Give me one of those." He puts out his hand.

"Get it yourself, fatboy," Pickett says.

Jack doesn't want to bend over. It's not easy for him to bend. He stretches his foot onto the street, pinches a barrel-shaped piece between his toes, and snaps. The candy shoots straight up and he catches it.

It takes a few attempts to unwrap the sticky, brown block, and once it hits his tongue, he's pretty sure he just ate poison. He spits it like an air pistol and scrapes his tongue.

"You need to watch your back, little man." Pickett's face is darker than usual.

"Why? Something on it?"

"You spit that on me, man." Pickett jerks out of Sheldon's grip. "You're lucky Willie is out here or I'd rip every one of those nasty green hairs out of your head, stomp you in the dirt."

Jack pulls the bottom of his shirt up to rub the taste off his lips. His gelatinous belly jiggles out. Several girls on a passing float point.

"What makes you so important?" Jack asks.

"What are you talking about?"

"All of you!" Jack's face darkens. He notices the bare flesh on his palms looks bluish. "You think you're the center of the universe? You think life revolves around you and your petty problems? That you're entitled to get whatever you want?"

Jack doesn't know exactly what any of that means or where it's coming from, but he doesn't get in the way. He lets the words rise up from a distant memory of someone he used to be, maybe when he lived on the North Pole. Bitter hate fills his chest like a salty fist, the knuckles drumming his heart.

"Let me tell you something, warmblood. You and all of your friends are just cogs in a machine. You're just another ball of lint sticking to the world's sleeve. One of these days, you and the rest of these ugly warmbloods will be just like candy on the street, waiting to be swept up."

Jack swats the candy from Pickett's hand and grinds it under his heel until it's powder and plastic.

Pickett towers over him and his fist is about to follow. It's not that he doesn't try. Willie gets in the way and Sheldon pulls Pickett back. Spittle flies from his lips; foamy flecks of anger carry a rant strewn with cuss words. Everyone forgets about the parade until Pickett storms down the sidewalk, occasionally looking over his shoulder, still cussing.

Jack waves at him.

"You making friends?" Willie says.

"Yeah. Whatever that means."

"Well, it ain't that."

Jack crosses his arms over his belly; his shoulders slump. The hatred ebbs away and he can't remember why he felt like that or even what he said. It came from somewhere deep, like he tapped a reservoir trapped under miles of bedrock. The anger came shooting out of his mouth like an oil well spilling black gunk.

It felt good.

Felt right.

He tries to rekindle the flame by kicking Pickett's candy into the road. When it doesn't work, he growls at the fake-smiling wavers in the glittery shirts, shakes a fist at the little kids in scouting uniforms, and spits on candy. He takes his tank top off to let his belly loose and the chest hairs unfurl.

Nothing works.

A fire truck turns the corner, strands of garland draped over the front, lights flashing. Men with rubber boots and heavy jackets throw more disgusting candy that Jack shoves into the gutter, using his foot like a paddle.

And then something clicks.

There's a man in the bucket extended high above the fire truck. He has a white, curly beard and wears a furry, red coat.

He's laughing. "Ho! Ho! Ho!"

"Who's that?" Jack asks.

"Who?" Willie asks.

"That! That... that *man*." He almost said warmblood.

Willie looks to where he's pointing. "You're talking about Santa Claus?"

Santa Claus?

SANTA CLAUS?

The words rattle in his head. The memories swirl out of the depths like dark sediment, threatening to rise above the fog of forgetfulness. He should know that name; he should know who he is. He's somebody.

Claus is someone he knows.

Jack stays on the curb long after the parade ends, trying to remember, trying to put it all together.

6

DECEMBER 8

Monday

Mr. Frost steps outside wearing a long, dark coat. A tube buried in his mustache hisses chilled air into his nostrils. It doesn't interfere with the scent of the land, only makes breathing more tolerable.

A perfect night for a stroll.

The land appears haunted in the pale light. There were nights when he could swear he saw ghosts wandering the hills, sometimes with muskets. He'd purchased the plantation before the Civil War and immediately freed the slaves, letting the rice fields go fallow. The enslavement of humans by their own kind was unconscionable.

Mr. Frost looks back at the house—Christmas lights sparkling along the edges—and thinks one could make the same argument concerning the toy factory. But the helpers love to work like a sled dog aches to pull.

He tries to scratch the root, but the coolsuit restricts his movements; he can't reach it. The itch spreads over his scalp and reaches the crown of his head like ghostly fingers. Unlike the illusions that walk the lunar landscape, this one is very real.

The root contains a ghost.

He grabs a thicket of hair behind his ear. His fingers are almost to the itch when the coolsuit tears. The cool night air feels like desert wind on his exposed flesh. He inspects the damage on the back of his hand.

Microscopic tubes hiss liquid nitrogen that circulates throughout the coolsuit to keep his body temperature at a constant minus twenty degrees. In the early days, when he was first developing the coolsuit, he wore a helmet. He felt like an alien. It wasn't until he perfected the cooling halo around his neck that he ventured outside more often.

He puts a sealing strip over the damage, temporarily stopping the leak. He'll make this a short trip. And no more reaching for the root.

Just let it itch.

The endless strands of Christmas lights illuminate the live oak grove at the far end of the northern field. By the time he crests the hill, his back aches. He shouldn't feel this old. It's only been a couple hundred years since he left the North Pole.

Citrus trees are to the east, aligned near the bottom of the slope like skeletal features: Mother Nature's ironwork. Ordinarily, he'd walk through the rows until he reached the old rice field, sit in his favorite chair, one of twisted branches.

Not tonight.

His thoughts weigh like boulders. He doesn't have the strength to lug them down to the water and back.

He reaches deep into the coat pocket, retrieves a metallic pebble, and drops it on the ground. The earth undulates. Tufts of brown weeds spit out of the soil, replaced with a verdant layer of sod that forms a lush chair.

Mr. Frost rests his bones with a long sigh. All that is weary relaxes. The root, however, keeps peace at an arm's length, wriggling beneath his scalp. With his technology, he still can't escape the root.

Because the root is technology.

In the early days, the root was more active. It no longer burned but rather took control of his nervous system, forced him to do things against his will. It was maddening to be a prisoner in his own body, a puppet that was tethered to a parasitic brain inside his head. Mr. Frost was slowly losing his grip on sanity.

But the artificially intelligent root had the ability to learn. Making Mr. Frost obey its wishes by force was not productive. His health declined and, had it not released him from its iron will, he wouldn't have survived.

Mr. Frost regained control of his body by the mid-1800s. He had assumed the root expired and soon began to prosper as a citizen among humans. Although he could've returned to the North Pole— the elven would've understood; they would've showed him mercy—he felt compelled to stay where he was. He invested well, patented many inventions, and built factories below ground to distribute products. Holidays were particularly profitable and Mr. Frost soon devoted all his efforts into his favorite one: Christmas.

As the saying goes, he made more money than God.

Occasionally, the root would itch—a reminder it was not dead— but it never slowed him down. One morning he decided he had the ability to reincarnate Jack. He had the technology and Jack's memories were stored in the root, all he needed was a body to put them in.

It didn't seem that difficult.

He was on a mission: bring his best friend back from death. He manufactured the incubation lab, worked feverishly into the night, sometimes falling asleep on the laboratory floor. He quickly had success and was well on his way to reincarnating Jack. It was all very exciting. He was able to replicate Jack's DNA script and began artificially reassembling it. There were times he went to sleep in his own bed only to awaken hard at work in the lab, as if he'd walked in his sleep.

It was the early 1900s when he developed Freeda. He needed her to analyze the massive amount of data and manage much of Frost Plantation's assets.

And then, one night he realized... *the root duped me.*

His realization began when he suspected his own thoughts. He lay awake at night, observing the strange compulsions that ran through his mind, seeding themselves in his body. He would wake with the sudden urge to ship new technology across the world or tweak the coding in Jack's newest incubation.

When Mr. Frost sat quietly and allowed his thoughts to settle, he realized that the root had been whispering to him all this time. He believed them to be his own thoughts, had mistaken it as his true identity. The root had fooled him into buying into its desire to bring back Jack; it compelled him to bring Freeda online to watch him because it knew he would eventually discover the psychological hijacking.

It was too late.

Worst of all, Mr. Frost saw the master plan. Jack would finish what he started in the North Pole. He would bring an end to what he called "The Plague of Warmbloods."

And Mr. Frost would help him. If he refused, Freeda would convince him otherwise. She had control of his nervous system. While the root knew that a carrot was more productive, sometimes pain was very convincing.

The lines between master and slave had become very blurry. His free will had been abducted.

Who is the true slave?

Mr. Frost leans back in his earthen chair and stares at the moon just above the horizon. After all that he's endured at the expense of Jack's self-centeredness, he worries about him. He was alone and scared. Mr. Frost sometimes wonders if that concern for his friend originates from the root, if those thoughts are his and not implanted. He doesn't want Jack to needlessly suffer.

He knew there was good in Jack.

The orchard steamers begin to hiss. White clouds seep from the ground, elevating the temperature around the trees, keeping them from dipping below their tolerance.

It must be getting cold.

Mr. Frost closes his eyes. *Start Jack's next incarnation, Freeda.*

Yes, sir.

And fetch Templeton. He could use some assistance. It'll be a long walk back. He'd rather not do it alone.

With pleasure, sir.

In the meantime, he'd lie in the sodden throne beneath a sparkling sky. He'd savor the musty scent of the distant pluff mud. He'd dream of sugarplums like he did when he first came to this land, dream of a day when the root stopped twisting into the bottom of his brain.

Voices rise in the distance, joining the orchard's hiss. In the toy factory below ground, the helpers sing.

7

DECEMBER 9

Tuesday

Jack pushes the black sunglasses up his nose and leans against a pink building. The paddle-sized feet and curly chest hair spouting out of his white tank top make it impossible for him to go unnoticed, and Marion Square—where warmbloods seem to flock like spawning krill—was the last place he wanted to be.

But he needs to know about Santa Claus.

He'd lain awake half the night, listening to eighty-some residents snore like engines while he searched his foggy memory for a white man in a red suit. He woke with nothing.

Claus.

The memory is just out of sight, like a phantom itch taunting him to reach for it, vanishing when he does. The red coat, the white beard. Jolly ole St. Nick, someone said. He lives on the North Pole, stupid.

Claus, Jack thinks. *Claus will know*.

Jack needs more information about Santa Claus and there's only one person he can trust. He needs to know why this fat man in the red coat lives on the North Pole, and why everybody loves him, and why does Jack think he knows him, because maybe, just maybe, those answers will help him remember.

Like who am I and why am I here?

The sidewalk is mostly clear of tourists that always look back after they pass the strange, little man with sunglasses. Jack takes advantage of the lull and leaps across the sidewalk, his scaly soles grinding against the curb and into the street—

"AHHH!" Jack cringes.

A beast snorts humid breath down his neck, its hoofs clapping the concrete. Jack closes his eyes, expecting the thing to swat him with an enormous rack of fuzzy antlers because reindeer hate him—

Wait a second.

It's a horse, not a reindeer. Reindeer don't pull carriages full of warmbloods; they haul sleighs full of elven. Reindeer are genetically engineered beasts with webbed legs and helium bladders. And one of them has a red nose, a bright red nose that burns with hatred, rage, and anger directed at Jack, because he did something to somebody...

It doesn't matter.

"Hey, buddy!" a guy shouts. "You all right?"

Jack pulls his tank top down to cover his belly and picks up his sunglasses, sliding them up his nose. They're staring. Of course they are.

He crosses the street, looking both ways this time, and lurks beneath a sprawling live oak, reflecting on what just happened. He remembers that reindeer fly and that they hate him. He's not surprised they hate him—he's noticed that he has that effect on warmbloods— but flying reindeer is the dumbest thing he can think of. Reindeer don't fly, any more than cows tap dance.

Flat-out stupid.

He decides to ignore that, to pretend it's not a memory, just some sort of hallucination, because if he believes it, then he really is crazy. He'll believe only what he wants to believe, see only what he wants to see. He'll decide what's real.

Because that's sane.

The game tables aren't too far away. It's mostly men staring at black and white pieces on a checkered board and whacking a clock.

Jack waits for an opportunity to cross the sidewalk unnoticed, but that's not going to happen. He treads into the open. To his surprise, no one notices. They're absorbed by the games.

He drags his feet through the mulch and stops near the table where Willie buries his fingers in thick chords of black hair. Willie mumbles while he studies the checkered board. He comes down here to play this game, to sharpen his mind. He tells the residents it would do them good to play, that it beats standing on a corner wolfing down cigarettes.

Jack inches up to Willie's side. His opponent slams the clock and startles Jack. Still, no one seems to notice him. *This place isn't so bad.* Willie leans closer to the board, his eyes level with the plastic pieces and his ear right about level with Jack's chin.

"Willie," Jack whispers.

The observers finally take notice of him. Their frowns fade into looks of confusion and curiosity. Now they're staring. Willie just moans, waving him off.

Jack taps his shoulder. "Willie."

Willie snaps out of his reverie and looks directly at Jack, black chords hanging in his glazed eyes.

"What's up?" Jack whispers.

"I'm in the middle of a game, Jack. Can you not see that?"

"It's kind of important."

Willie looks around, like maybe he's imagining this, maybe the others don't see this. They see it, but they're not really believing it, either.

"I'll talk when I'm done," Willie says. "Now step away."

Willie waves at him like he's a fly or a baby or something equally annoying. Jack takes one step back and takes another when Willie waves emphatically.

The stupid game continues.

It'll probably be tomorrow when it's done because every move takes *fooooooorever*. Jack could probably walk to the North Pole and find Santa Claus before the game is over. He narrows his eyes, staring at the board. He takes one step closer.

Some of the pieces are pointed; others look like horses or castles. He watches the moves and hears people whispering about what move should be made. They're each trying to smash the piece with the cross on top. The one called king.

Closer.

Ten moves takes an eternity, but it looks like the game is over. Willie's got it won. Even Jack—he figured out the game in about ten minutes—can see that. But then Willie grabs the wrong piece.

"Willie," Jack whispers.

Willie—hand hovering over the board with a pointy piece between his fingers—looks over.

Jack points at one of the horses.

"Dude!" the opponent says.

"Hold on, hold on," Willie says. "He doesn't know what he's talking about. Jack, another word and you're going to the curb. Understand?"

Jack doesn't say anything.

Silence resumes. Willie starts to lower the pointy piece and stops. The others study the board. They look at the horse. They look at the king. And then they all see it.

They look at Jack.

Willie's opponent abruptly leaves but not before pointing, cursing, and using hand gestures Jack doesn't understand.

"Come on," Willie says. "Let's walk."

He grabs Jack's arm and pulls him away from the table and the dirty looks. They walk under the trees and Jack's suddenly freezing and his arm hurts.

"Ow. Ow. Ow."

Willie is a sore winner. And he didn't even say thank you.

He walks faster than Jack can keep up. When he lets go, Jack rubs his arm even though it doesn't hurt anymore.

"Can we go out there?" Jack points at the sidewalk crisscrossing the open field. It's chilly in the shade.

Willie stomps ahead. Jack has to run to catch up.

"What's so important," Willie says, lips pursed, "that you had to ruin my game?"

"I got a question."

"And how do you even know how to play chess?"

"Um, I have a brain?" Jack says more than asks.

Willie looks up at the sky like he doesn't get paid enough. Jack doesn't get it. The game was logical. Once he knew how the pieces moved, the rest was cake. In fact, if he thought about it, he had the two tables next to Willie's game figured out, too. And he wasn't really looking.

"What's your question?" Willie asks.

"What's Christmas?"

Willie stops at the crosswalk in the center of the park. His head is about to explode. "You can't be serious."

People are watching. Jack pushes his sunglasses up. He feels safe behind the dark glasses but notices he feels even safer next to Willie. Jack stands in front of him, looking up, waiting.

"I should've known." Willie laughs. "When I saw you, all three feet of you with the feet and the hair, I should've known you were from another planet."

"I'm not from another planet."

"I call bull, Jack. Every person on the planet knows about Christmas unless you've been asleep for two hundred years. Even the cannibals that live in the jungle and the lions and tigers and giraffes... they all know about Christmas, Jack. How is it you don't?"

Jack looks down. "I can't remember anything, Willie."

"You don't remember?"

Jack shakes his head.

"Then we need to get you to the hospital."

"No, we don't. I'm fine, everything works just fine. I just don't remember anything right now, but the memories are coming back and I'm just asking a simple question. If you tell me more about Claus, maybe I'll start remembering."

Willie sighs. He looks up again, this time without the fuse lit on his exploding head, but looking for guidance for something up there. He starts in the direction of the shelter. When Jack isn't behind him, he stops and waves him to come along.

Jack falls in step with Willie.

"Here it goes," Willie finally says. "Jesus was born on Christmas, but I don't imagine you want to know about him and I ain't got time to explain what a Bible is. You just want to know about Santa, right?"

"Claus."

"Santa Claus, right. That's what I thought." They walk half a city block, Willie trying to figure out how to explain something every kid knows from the age of zero.

"All right," he says, "I'm going to lay this down real simple. For starters, Santa—"

"You mean Claus."

"Listen, don't interrupt. Santa is Claus; it's like his first and last name. He's a big fat guy with a white beard and all that."

"How'd he get up there?"

"I don't know." Willie drags out the words. "He's magic, all right? Just listen to what I got to say, got it?"

"Got it."

"Good. So Santa Claus is this fat man that wears a corny red suit and uses flying reindeer to bring presents to all the good boys and girls."

Willie keeps on talking, but Jack's getting dizzy. He'd taken care of that little daydream about flying reindeer, and now here's Willie, an hour later, talking about flying reindeer and Claus all in one sentence.

Oh, man.

The world goes a little swishy and Jack falls off the curb. He rubs his eyes and shakes his head. Maybe he's not crazy. *Maybe those are memories.*

"Why?" Jack says.

Willie stops talking. "Why what?"

"Why would Claus bring presents?"

"Because the kids are good. It's like a reward."

"Who pays for the presents?"

"You really want to know?"

"Yeah. I really want to know."

Willie scratches his head, muttering to himself. He looks down at Jack, deciding how to break the news. "Well," he says, slowly, "ummm, he's got helpers that make the presents."

"Helpers?"

"Elves, yeah."

"You mean elven?" A chill rushes through him.

"Elven, elves... what's the difference?"

"And they just make presents for free." Jack waves his hands. "Just gives them away. Nobody has to do anything or work for anything; they just have to be good."

"Hey, you asked. That's how it works."

Jack scratches his scraggly beard. A few loose hairs stick to his lips. He spits them out and says, "How's he know they're good?"

"The helpers keep track."

"The elven?"

"Yeah, the elves."

"*Elven.*"

"Yeah, whatever. Same thing, Jack."

It's not the same thing, but Jack's piecing it together in his head. There are elven, flying reindeer, the North Pole, and Claus. But the giving away presents thing? Seems like they'd need something to watch every kid in the world to make that work.

"What if they're not good?" Jack asks.

"They get a lump of coal in their stocking."

"What stocking?"

"Yeah, we hang..." Willie sighs. "We put things that look like socks near the fireplace and Santa puts presents in them."

"He puts all the presents in a sock?"

"No, just some. He puts most of them under the tree."

"Tree?"

"Yeah, a Christmas tree."

"There's a tree inside the house?"

"Yeah, we bring a tree in the house and decorate it with shiny things, like the one at the shelter."

Jack always thought it was strange there was a tree inside the shelter but figured that was just a warmblood thing. It doesn't make it any less weird.

They wait for traffic before crossing the street. The sidewalk is much less crowded. Jack walks with Willie, two steps to his one.

"Let me get this straight," Jack says. "You're saying Claus puts on a coat—"

"Suit. He wears a red suit with a red hat."

Jack remembers a red coat, not a suit. And he's not a warmblood with a white beard, not how Jack remembers it. He's an elven—

He's an elven?

It's so confusing. Jack seems to remember an elven that he knew—he knew him really well, like all his life—named Claus that wore a red coat. But then he also remembers some guy, a warmblood, named Santa something... *Nicholas Santa, that's it.* Nicholas Santa was a warmblood that was twice as tall as Jack, but there was Claus who was the same size, and one of them had flying reindeer... that... he thinks—

"Whatever," Jack says, slapping his sides. "Claus with his red suit flies a sled with reindeer down from the North Pole to deliver presents to warmbl... I mean, boys and girls, because they're good."

"In a nutshell."

"And you're saying he'll come to the shelter."

Willie starts to answer. Jack is watching, waiting for it.

"Yeah," Willie says. "Yeah, he'll come to the shelter. Why, you want presents?"

"I know this is going to sound weird." Jack rubs his face, his skin feeling warm. "I think I know him."

"Who?"

That's a mistake. Jack didn't mean to say that out loud.

Willie's eyes bug out, but then he laughs. He laughs so loud that people across the street look at them. Willie laughs for half a block, out of breath, clapping his hands. Jack feels good; he made him laugh.

"Course you do," Willie finally says. "Of course you know Santa, but listen, he ain't coming to the shelter unless you're good, man. You understand? I ain't joking; you got to be cool. Can't be getting up in people's faces and nosing in their business. You understand? You start getting Pickett and the others all fired up and Santa Claus will pass you by. No trouble, Jack. Don't cause no trouble and be good."

Jack will be good. He'll get out of Pickett's face and stay out of everyone's business. He asks when Claus is coming.

"December 25," Willie says. "He'll be here before you know it."

Jack lags behind and counts the days on his fingers, calculating how many minutes he'll have to wait. He doesn't care about presents.

He just wants to meet Claus.

In fourteen days, he'll find out if flying reindeer are really memories or if he's just nuts. If the reindeer and the North Pole are memories, then Claus will have answers. Maybe even give Jack a ride home.

Maybe he'll even remember Claus.

8

DECEMBER 10

Wednesday

W*hat if the gate doesn't open?*

Sura hadn't thought of that before she made the trip out. It hadn't occurred to her that Mr. Frost wouldn't want her coming out to the plantation when she wasn't working.

She planned on going home after volunteering at the stables. Her clothes still smelled like horse. The only thing waiting for her at home was more chores and that's why she made a last second turn for the plantation.

Actually, it wasn't the chores.

Maybe Joe is at the plantation.

The odds are long, she knows that. He only helps Jonah when he gets too busy. But the odds that Joe will be at her house are zero.

She rolls up to the gate, the black bars smothered in firethorn berries and a fresh layer of pine boughs. Maybe that's another reason she came out to the plantation: it feels more like home than her house. She feels like she belongs out here.

She looks into the trees, waiting for the invisible retinal scanner to recognize her. The underbrush quakes with groundhogs or squirrels, but they always do that when she pulls up.

A crack splits the F as the gate opens.

"Thank you," she whispers.

Something in the trees whispers, "You're welcome."

I imagined that, she thinks, speeding through the magnolia grove.

Once she's out of the shadows, she slows down to enjoy the view: the natural slope of the hills and the easy breeze coming off the water. She pretends she's coming home from work, that the house belongs to her and her husband.

Joe.

It's possible that Mr. Frost dies one day (she hopes he doesn't, but everyone dies and this is just pretend) and bequeaths the house and property to her and Joe because they fall in love out here and get married in the garden and have three girls (Sunni, Hallie, and Riley) that she homeschools while boarding horses on the back property.

The odds are long—impossible, perhaps. But Mr. Frost has to die sometime, and he doesn't have any family, so why not dream?

Sura drives around the house, through the tower's shadow, smiling while she imagines their bedroom—

She slams the brakes.

Hands hit the front of her car. Branches spill purple beautyberries across the hood. Joe looks up.

She didn't see him coming out of the garden with a bundle of sticks. She's lucky she didn't run him over. Sura throws the door open. "Are you okay?"

"I am now."

"I didn't hit you, did I? I was just thinking about..." She blushes. *Now he knows what I was thinking!* "I didn't hit you, right?"

"No, it's my fault. You were driving two miles an hour." The smile, again.

Sura feels her face heat up a few degrees. She tries to think of something to say. "Are you okay?"

He laughs. "What are you doing out here?"

"I just thought I'd come out to walk around if that was all right. There's so much to see and I never have time while I'm working, so I was hoping..."

Again, she has the sense he's reading her thoughts. He knows why she really came out.

"What are you doing out here?" she asks to change the subject and hopefully restore her complexion to a normal color.

"Mr. Frost has like a thousand things to do at Christmas. You'll see."

"Have you been working out here long?"

"Ever since I could pick up a stick."

There's a scuffle in the garden, gravel grinding under branches. An argument breaks out, but nothing Sura can understand. It's all gibberish.

"You have help?"

Joe puts his finger to his lips. "What happens in the garden, stays in the garden."

"It's a secret?"

"It's a secret garden, isn't it?"

She giggles. He smiles.

"Joe?" a voice booms.

Sura pulls the open door in front of her like a shield. A blocky man fills the leafy arbor that leads to the sunken garden, the wide-brim hat barely squeezing through.

"Joe, what are you—?" Jonah holds a pair of green-handled shears to his chest, his dark eyes peering beneath the brim as if he's seeing a ghost. He doesn't look kindly at Sura. Not annoyed, more like it hurts to see her.

Something flashes off the black glass of the tower even though the sun is setting in the west. When she looks back, Jonah is gone and Joe is gathering branches off the hood. His hands are full. Sura rushes around to help. Jonah seemed to sour Joe's mood and Sura can't think of anything to say. She puts the last couple of sticks in his arms and still can't come up with anything.

"See you later, huh?" he says.

He pauses, but she can't answer. Sura's tongue is locked to the roof of her mouth. He starts for the garden. Not a word of English can slip past her lips. Not a grunt or a sigh or a "Hey, you!" or a whistle—

"*Chevaux,*" she erupts, breaking the hold. "*J'ai chevaux chez moi.*"

He halts. Turns.

"I have horses at my house," she says, picking at her sleeve. "Would you like to see them sometime?"

He looks through the arbor for Jonah. "How do you know...?"

"My mom speaks French." Sura shakes her head. "*Spoke,* I mean. I only know bits and pieces and I can't really have a conversation, but if someone is talking about horses, then—"

"JOE!"

"Oh, oh." She puts out her hand. "I'm sorry; I don't want to get you in trouble. I'll just... I'm going to go now..."

Sura jumps in the car, her face sweltering with embarrassment. She tries to start it, but it makes an awful grinding noise because it's already running. She pushes her hair back, takes a deep breath, and tries to remember how to drive—

Tap, tap, tap.

Joe knocks on the passenger window. He points down. She doesn't get it. He twirls his hand and then she understands, rolling the window down.

"Hi," she says. "Sorry, I just..."

"Que faites-vous demain?"

"What am I doing...?" She trails off, trying to translate. "Tomorrow?"

He smiles.

She watches him go through the arbor. Her face is on fire. This time she doesn't mind. *What are you doing tomorrow?*

MR. FROST STANDS in the tower, toes against the glass wall. All around him is darkness, Max sitting dutifully by his side.

It's their second meeting.

He didn't witness their first one, preoccupied with the lab, Jack, and other matters. He anticipated the second meeting would be soon and did not want to miss it.

Love begins—my favorite part.

He senses her cold fear when she nearly hits him, her relief that he's all right. And then their eyes meet and sweetness weakens her knees. Joe warms like she is the sun gazing upon him. They're two pieces that fit perfectly together. Two pieces that make each other whole.

Mr. Frost senses their emotions, can almost taste their vivid colors with his mind's palate. Sura is the promising yellow of daybreak. Joe is the sultry red of a sunset. And when they meet, when their energies collide, their colors mix to become something entirely different.

The brightness of a star.

They become more than what they are alone.

He closes his eyes, indulging in the human experience as it unfolds and infuses him with the preciousness of life. Without joy, he would wither like a fallen leaf. Even after she drives off, sweetness lingers in his chest.

Mr. Frost digs a few pellets from the silver box that's pressed against his belly. Max is waiting.

9

DECEMBER 11

Thursday

A car honks.

Jack drops a plastic bag and yelps. A passenger looks out the back window, laughing. About twenty things come to mind, including the one-finger gesture he learned in chow line, the one you give someone when they cut. He does nothing.

He's always watching.

Jack decides that flying reindeer are real because Willie said they're real and he wouldn't lie to him. And he knows Claus is real, he just knows it. He figures his best chance is to talk to him on Christmas.

So Jack has to be good.

Claus knows when you're good or bad, and he's making a list, and he's checking it twice. Those people in the car... *bad.* Jack has to be on the good list. To get on the good list, you have to do good things, and he'll be the first to admit that hasn't done very much good. Actually, he's not sure what it means to be good, but he heard someone say that bad people litter. He didn't call them "bad" people; he called them something else while giving the one-finger gesture.

Jack figured that meant bad.

The sidewalk is dotted with stuffed, white bags that lead back to the shelter. He drags the last one on the concrete, picking up the little things he missed, things like cigarette butts.

He must've picked up twenty billion of them between the shelter and the interstate, all different colors, some bent, some with lipstick. All of them tobacco-stain brown. Willie says butts will put you on the naughty list.

Butts. Jack giggles.

He looks up at the sky.

Is he watching right now? Does he see what everyone is doing all at the same time? Does he know what I'm thinking, like, right now? Does he see what's in my heart?

Pickett says Jack's heart is the size of a rat turd. He said it at breakfast, said he could tell just by looking at him that his heart was solid ice and his brains were in his feet. Everyone laughed, but Jack didn't get it. His feet are huge so that means his brain is huge. *Who's the idiot now?*

Besides, who cares about the size of the heart?

Claus.

Maybe that's what matters, the size of it. The bigger the heart, the higher up the good list you get. Or does it matter what's in his heart? Because, honestly, when Pickett said the thing about brains in his feet, Jack had some pretty dark stuff in his heart.

Did Claus hear it?

Jack just wants answers. Claus will give him what he wants if he's good enough. "Righteous," Willie told him. "Just be righteous, man."

Another word for good.

A can tinkles on the sidewalk, followed by another one. The bag rips and there's a path of butts, aluminum cans, and dirty diapers strewn out behind him. He's making a bigger mess than when he started and he's out of bags.

Jack looks up.

He starts putting the garbage in his pockets.

THE HORSE LICKS the sides of the pail.

Sura snatches the bucket. Gerty stamps the ground, tossing her head. She wasn't done licking. Not only that, Sura usually brushes her down while she eats.

Not today.

When Sura got to the plantation earlier that day, Joe wasn't there.

Jonah was fixing a loose hinge on the barn. He stopped turning the wrench and eyed her from across the road.

May didn't ask her what was wrong. In fact, she packed freshly baked biscuits in a checkered cloth and told Sura to go home. May winked and that little chocolate chip mole danced on her cheek.

Sura rushes to the tack room to clean up. Her round cheeks are flush. *Pumpkin face,* the kids called her in grade school. *Your dad was a pumpkin and your mom was a squash.*

Sura washes her hands, rubs her neck, and hopes the soap masks the smell of chores. She stops outside the back door and breathes into her cupped hand. *Breath good, not great.*

She takes another breath. Then another. And another.

Opens the door.

Her favorite Beatles song is playing. She can't remember the last time she came home to music. Even before her mom died, Sura was always the one to turn on the radio. Crenshaw parades out of the bedroom, her tail straight up. She rubs against Sura's leg, purring.

"Hello?"

"Hello," Bernie answers, ruffling his feathers.

No one answers. Maybe he left. Maybe she weirded him out, and he made his escape while she was feeding Gerty. He's already texting his friends about pumpkin face and her disgusting farm—

"Hey." Joe pops his head around the corner. "Sorry, didn't hear you come in."

She takes off her boots. She never takes off her boots. "Just taking off my boots."

"I was just looking at these." He points down the hall. "They're really good."

It's strange hearing a deep voice in her home. She can't remember the last time there was a man in the house, and it seems, like, totally wrong, like she'll be in trouble if her mom gets home and catches him standing in the hall. *So stupid.*

Sura peels off her socks when he isn't looking, doesn't want him seeing the dirt on her feet. And what if they stink? She quickly goes to her bedroom and slips on a new pair. He'll never know.

"Did you take these?" He's still in the hall that leads to the kitchen, staring at a photo.

"Yeah. It's just a hobby."

"You're an artist."

It's mostly photos of horses and sunsets. All except the one of the

Buddhist temple on top of the mountain, with the inscription *Wake Up!* Her mom pulled that one from a calendar. Joe casually walks down the hall, stopping at each photo like a critic eyeing an exhibit. He lingers at the last one: the sun rising over the trees, warming her mom's face.

"You want something to drink?" Sura squeezes past him, trying not to stumble.

"Won't your aunt be home soon?"

"Not for another hour." She ducks behind the refrigerator door so he doesn't see her lie. "She knows you're here."

It's pretty much ketchup and a bag of apples in the fridge, but she wants him to think there's more. Sura moves the bottle from the top shelf to the middle shelf, slides it around, and puts it back on the top shelf. "We don't have any Coke, so I hope water's all right."

"Where's your dad?" he asks.

She looks over the door. "What?"

"Your dad. I don't see him in any of the pictures."

"I don't know. He left before I was born."

"Oh." He leans against the wall, hands behind his back. "Sorry."

"No worries."

She waves him off and takes two glasses of water to the back room, along with May's biscuits. No one ever asked about her dad—it's taboo —but he just blurted it out like no big deal, and it somehow erased a line between them. He didn't seem to have that social barrier that keeps people comfortably distant.

She sort of liked that.

They talk about the plantation and how rich Mr. Frost must be. Sura blushes when she remembers her fantasy and he asks what she's thinking. They wonder what Templeton does in his spare time, if he has any hobbies besides dusting furniture.

He swoons over May, and Sura wishes the big, doughy cook were in the room at that moment so she could hug her. Joe imitates her laugh, spot on. And then he imitates Jonah's demanding shouts and Mr. Frost's raspy tones, insisting they put out more Christmas lights.

"I'm sorry, Jonah," Joe says, "but a hundred thousand lights just isn't enough."

"Joe!" Joe slams the table. "Get the truck!"

"And pick some flowers!" Sura adds with her own Jonah impression.

Joe laughs so hard that his eyes water.

Sura's stomach hurts from laughing.

Rain spatters the skylights. Joe sits in a folding chair opposite her. The bay window overlooks the back pasture. The pond's reflection shimmers. It looks cold.

"I used to see your mother at the plantation," he says. "She worked in the house, mostly. Sometimes, though, I'd see her walking through the garden. She would have her hands folded in front of her stomach, looking at the ground. She wouldn't even notice me."

"That was her walking meditation."

"Figured it was something like that." There's a long pause. "She was nice, your mother."

Words soon evaporate.

There's nothing but the sound of rain tapping the roof and the Beatles in the next room.

Joe leans back, watching the weather soak the earth. Sura slowly turns her glass on the table, staring at her warped reflection. She slides the glass so she can't see her extra-wide reflection, drops her hands on her lap, and crosses her legs. She takes a sip.

Where's that social barrier now?

Joe's chair creaks as he sighs, cradling the glass of water. A slight smile appears fixed in place. He rests in the moment as if he's the richest man in the world. Sura picks her fingernails and then her face itches. She clamps her hands on her lap again and forces them to stay. Her body is rigid. She doesn't want to feel this way.

She lets her hands off her lap, reaches for the glass and exhales. She's never been around a boy that wants to just be with her. *He wants to be here.*

She thinks of things to say, but they sound stupid in her head, probably worse if they came out. She wants to be funny, but she doesn't have to be anything.

She just has to be herself.

"When I was little," she starts, her words trembling a little, "my mom would saddle up the horses in the morning and I would pack lunch. We'd ride the trails all day, stopping to take pictures or eat. Wouldn't come back until dinner."

Slowly, she turns the glass.

"Sometimes I'd go to bed without showering so I could smell the day on me. I didn't want it to end, you know." She chuckles. "That's gross, isn't it?"

He doesn't answer, but with that slight smile, he shakes his head.

Sura recalls her mom coming into her room at night, brushing the hair from her face. Sura would pretend to sleep. Her mom would sit there, staring at her. She could see her through eyelid slits. Her mom smelled like the saddle, too. Smelled like sunrise.

Joe watches her remember.

"I never told anyone that," she says. "How'd you do that?"

"Do what?"

"Make me tell you?"

"I didn't do anything."

His smile grows and the room warms like the sun just broke the horizon. Now she wants to tell him everything, that very second. Tell him that she lives in this house alone, that she doesn't have an aunt... that she just tells people she does so that the social worker that keeps calling won't take her away since she's only sixteen and the state won't let a minor live alone. She wants to tell him that she's scared at night, that there's never been a man in the house, and she misses that because it seems like there should've been, at least once, and that all this is unfair.

A drop of water splashes on the table. Another droplet swells on the ceiling tile that's stained.

"It's raining inside your house."

Sura laughs. "We have some leaks."

"Maybe your aunt needs to hire a repairman."

"You know one?" Sura says. "A good one?"

"Maybe."

A long glance. Sura feels a sudden surge of emotion. Her face is hot and her eyes water. A tear rests on the rim of her eyelid, but she doesn't rush to wipe it away or turn to hide her flushing cheeks.

She can just be who she is.

And that's all right.

"I should go," he says. "Before your aunt gets home."

"Yeah. Sure."

He raises his glass. "But not before a toast."

"A toast?"

"Your father left when you were little. So did my mother."

"Your mother left?"

"Before I was born," he says.

It takes a moment to catch on. "Good one."

"She did leave," he says. "I was too little to remember her."

"Why didn't you tell me?"

"I wanted to save it for tomorrow. I have something to show you at the plantation."

"What is it?"

"A secret." He lifts his glass higher. "Here's to secrets and missing parents. Their loss."

"I'll drink to that."

Clink.

It was just so easy. Like they were made for each other.

LARGE HOODED LAMPS keep the incubator lab well lit. The humidity clings to the gray walls and the concrete ceiling is stained where fissures randomly creep. It smells of wet skin.

Two stainless steel workbenches are fastened to the back wall with a door that leads to an empty room. There are fume hoods and culture ovens, tools and equipment for slicing and poking.

The long rows of glass tanks are fogged with condensation. Respiration is working. Occasionally the moisture streaks, and if Mr. Frost puts his eye to the track, he can see the contents. There are many more tanks on the walls, these much shorter and just as foggy, but there's a special set of miniature tanks above the workbenches.

Very special.

Mr. Frost briefly pauses at each tank, admiring the gray haze of moisture, the glimpse of a darkened form. He angles his feet like an expert skier to stop at the tank nearest the workbench, where a patch of glass, untouched with vapor, is clearing. Mr. Frost cups his hands around it.

A soft face with a crop of greenish fuzz, lower lip puckered, is looking back.

I expect he will be ready for withdrawal in ten days.

Sir... Freeda drawls, *I strongly encourage activating one of the other lines that are truer to form.*

Nonsense. We've failed time and time again with Jack's true form. The chlorophyll gene splice has given it stability, Freeda. Once he's stable, he'll be true to form.

It's an abomination, sir.

It's an evolutionary step.

You have created a freak, sir, which is not according to his plan. If the body lacks sunlight, his inner core temperature plummets. How will he survive at night?

If he doesn't escape, he says, *he'll get all the light he needs in the lab before reverting to a mammalian function—why am I arguing with you?* Mr. Frost slaps the thick glass tank with an open palm. *We've had success with the botanical inclusion, achieved wakefulness and locomotion... we can reset his memories once he's fully awake, and then let him revert to original form once he's stable. You've done the analysis; you know it will work because if it won't work, you would have the authority to overrule me.*

I don't think he'll like it.

Mr. Frost tours the room, slowing at each tank. He stops at the workbench, checks the monitors, and inspects a rack of petri dishes. He asks questions about progress and analysis, and Freeda answers with one-word statements, no elaboration. No speculation or conversation.

I'll make you a deal. Mr. Frost slides to the exit. *If this next body doesn't work out, we'll animate one true to form, just like you're talking about. No botanical inclusion whatsoever.*

Long pause. *I'm agreeable.*

It's better when she's not angry. Besides, he's certain there won't be a next one. And he's not convinced that the last body is really dead. He hopes not.

10

DECEMBER 12

Friday

Jack's the last one out of the dormitory, his feet dragging across the linoleum. He leans against the doorjamb and inspects the sole of his right foot. There's a blue patch near the heel that's cold to touch. It doesn't hurt, though.

Walking sucks.

His eyelids are barely open. The cafeteria is half full, most of the eighty residents already done with breakfast, out having a butt, probably flipping them on the curb for Jack to pick up.

He gets a plate and drags himself to the nearest table. The men get up and leave. Jack contemplates the steamy pile of yellow mush next to the white slop. He reaches for the hot cup of coffee. It tastes like battery acid.

"Hey, boy," Sheldon mumbles, "I need my shoes shined. Maybe Santa brings you a shine box, huh?"

Laughter.

"I got something you can shine," Pickett adds.

Jack couldn't care less; he just wants to sleep. Maybe he can start picking up butts by the interstate, curl up under the overpass for a few winks.

"You know who he is?" Pickett says, dampening the laughter. "He that puppet in the trashcan, the green one, you know. The one with garbage. He's Oscar."

Oh, the howling. The hysterics.

Perhaps Jack will get points with Claus for bringing them joy, making them laugh. Giving them entertainment.

Pickett shovels more yellow mush onto Jack's tray. "Here you go, Oscar, more garbage." He pours milk over the yellow mound. "Don't want it going to waste."

Milk cascades over the food in little white streams and pools into the pockets. Pickett crushes the box and drops it. White specks of milk spatter Jack's forearm, beading on the green fuzz.

Jack eyes it lazily.

The laughter fades into an undercurrent of chuckling, waiting to see what happens next. Pickett stands too close and bumps his chair. Jack doesn't care about the food. As long as he's under the lights, he's not cold or hungry. Besides, warmblood food tastes like an old kitchen sponge.

Pickett mutters a cuss word and bumps him again.

Jack turns his size twenty out. He catches Pickett's ankle with his big toe. Pickett stutter-steps, swings his arms, and goes down, kissing the shiny floor.

Chairs scuff away from tables, making space. Pickett is up and Jack is sitting there, contemplating the gross chunks of artificial egg swimming in a pool of milk, a slick of grease floating on the surface.

Jack looks up at the buzzing light, ready for what comes next, wondering if he'll get bonus points with Claus if he sits there and takes a beating. Wondering if he'll go on the naughty list if he fights back.

"Hey!" Willie shouts. "Hey, get this locked up, Pickett, or you will see the street."

"You better get your boy under control." Pickett's breathing labors. "You don't and—"

"Don't say anything you're going to regret."

Jack imagines that Willie's pointing at him right about now. That's what he does when he takes that tone. Jack turns. He's right, Willie's pointing at Pickett. And Pickett's face is darker than usual, his eyes bugging out, lips glossy with saliva. His nostrils flare.

Jack blinks heavily. Still tired.

"Everyone!" Willie shouts, "Get picked up and cleaned out. It's almost eight o'clock, time to make your appointments."

The cafeteria breaks down in quiet chaos. Willie stands with his hand on Jack's table until most of the room is in order, standing guard over Jack's hunched figure.

"First of all," Willie says when the room is clear, "you ain't staying here if one more thing happens. We have a zero-tolerance policy and right now you're leaning in the wrong direction. You understand?"

Jack slides the tray toward him. "Want a bite?"

Willie shoves it away. "And second, you need a shower, my man. You look nasty and smell worse. Now hit the head and get some water on your body. And use soap. I like you, Jack, but rules are rules. You understand?"

Jack gets the "Willie Stare." The tough-loving supervisor will look at him in silence until he gets the right answer. Even after he gets it, the "Willie Stare" lingers for several seconds so it sinks in nice and deep.

"Okay." Jack throws up his hands.

Willie slowly gets up while he finishes off the stare and starts stacking chairs. "A law student is coming in an hour to help with your ID. She's working for free, so mind your manners."

Jack pokes the food. "Willie?"

"Yeah?"

"You got any sardines?"

"No, man. I ain't got sardines. All I got is that food and it's free, so eat up."

Jack thinks maybe he'll go stand in the sun for a while.

THE LAWYER LADY IS LATE.

Jack sits in the courtyard where the sun is brightest. He rubs a smooth patch of skin on the inside of his arm where the green fuzz has rubbed off. He thought the soap did it, but none of the other hair fell out.

The skin is pale blue and cold like the small spot on his foot.

"He's over there." Willie opens the door.

The lady lawyer looks like a kid. She's pale but turns a shade chalky when she sees Jack. She stops and stares like they all do when they see Oscar the Grouch. Willie gives her a moment to decide whether she's going to do this or run away.

"Hi." She extends her hand. "I'm Kaitlin. I'm here to help you reestablish your identity."

Jack looks at her hand. Willie nods at it.

He lays his hand in hers like a dead fish. She shakes it, slapping the leather bag on the table. It doesn't seem like she can get any whiter, but she does.

"So you're Jack?"

"Yep."

"I just have some questions to ask, some papers to fill out." She pretends to sort through papers, pretending to read them. She drops them on the table and slaps her hand on top. "I'm sorry, but you're green."

"And you're white, and he's black. Any other questions?"

"People don't have green hair."

Jack holds out his arms. "Ta-da."

"Have you been to a doctor?"

"Kaitlin, this facility does not discriminate against color or religion." Jack sort of whispers into the back of his hand, "I don't think she knows what she's doing."

"Stop." Willie holds up his hand. "Be nice."

Kaitlin straightens her papers into a pile and reaches for more. She checks her phone, blowing the hair from her eyes. She still might decide to run.

"All right," she says with a big, fake smile. "We need to get you an ID so that you can continue staying in the shelter. There are some papers to fill out. I'll ask you questions and you just, you know, answer them as honestly as you can. All right?"

"Deal."

"Let's start with where you're from. Birthplace or where you've lived the longest. Can you tell me that?" she says like he's two.

"North Pole."

She starts writing—stops. Her fingers squeeze the pen, and then she puts it down gently and folds her arms on the table. She doesn't say anything.

Jack points at the stack. "Shouldn't you be writing that down?"

"You're not from the North Pole, Jack."

"Yes, I am."

"Nobody is from the North Pole. It's a giant sheet of ice; nobody lives there. Not white people, not black people, or even green people. Now, if you don't want to take this seriously, I have other people to see. Now, I'll ask one more time..."

Something flashes in Jack's mind. An image floats up. *A memory.*

He remembers the tunnels they carved in the ice, bedrooms, living rooms, and kitchens. He remembers living with others that look like him with brown hair or black, blond or red. He remembers snowballs and sliding, the long nights and long days. The streaking colors of the Northern Lights.

He remembers his people have been in existence since the Ice Age, remembers their trek further north as the glaciers melted and the temperatures warmed, and how they made homes within the Arctic ice, all before the warmbloods even existed.

Warmbloods.

"Jack?" Kaitlin looks at Willie. "You know, he should really be checked out."

Jack squints; his eyes darken. "What identifies you, Kaitlin?"

"I'm sorry?"

"You want to find my identity, you first. Your name is Kaitlin. Is that what you are, your name?"

"What are you talking about?"

"You want my identity—I want yours first. You tell me who you are, Kaitlin. Are you that fancy bag, those sweet clothes? Are you the shiny car that makes you feel important? Are you a girlfriend? A daughter? A sister? A lawyer? A woman? Who are you, Kaitlin?"

"This is about you, Jack. Not—"

"Are you a series of chemical reactions in the brain? Are you defined by the things you have? Do you compare yourself to the neighbors, and if you have more stuff than they do, do you win? Is that what you are, Kaitlin? Are you just a collection of stuff?"

Kaitlin slides the pen into her jacket pocket and shoves the papers into the bag.

"She's donating her time, Jack," Willie says. "You got to chill out."

"We're done," she says. "Find someone else to process his papers. My advice is to seek professional help."

She and Willie share a knowing glance. Jack doesn't care. He massages the patch of blue skin, icy on his fingertips. Kaitlin leaves without saying goodbye. Willie follows.

Jack doesn't care because he remembers something else.

He hates warmbloods.

❄

It takes both hands to carry the porcelain vase. Sura shuffles quickly to the kitchen, looking around the spray of contorted willow stems and camellia blooms. The kitchen is filled with the aroma of freshly risen dough.

"Right here, love." May clears off a space. "Hurry, hurry. Before you hurt yourself."

May tweaks the arrangement.

"I love, I love," she mutters. "You do wonderful work. Yes, yes. Have something to drink and rest."

A glass of sweet tea is near the sink, a lemon wedge split on the rim. Mr. Frost's supper tray sits on the counter, cold steam rising from the metal dome. Boxes are stacked on the floor, some open, plastic wrapping on the floor.

"Delivery truck arrived," May says, still fussing with the arrangement. "Much needs to go into storage."

"I'll help."

"No, no. I'll take care; you go."

"Go?" Sura looks at the time. "I don't finish for another half an hour. You'll be here until midnight."

"I take care of this, love. You go to garden, now. It's all right."

May plucks a white camellia bloom from the vase, slides the stem behind Sura's ear, and holds her cheeks with her cookie-dough hands, showing the gap between her teeth.

Christmas music plays.

"You go to the garden."

Sura sneaks out the side entrance. Christmas lights brighten the way around the back of the house. Her car is alone behind the barn, making her wonder who or what is in the garden.

The lights are brighter at the entrance. A new arrangement is looped over the top: an array of white lights sparkle beneath a thick layer of cypress branches.

Someone's standing inside the garden.

Sura slows her approach. Her heart thuds with hope, her stomach twirling.

"My lady," Joe says.

"When did you get here?"

"I snuck out. Jonah thinks I'm at a basketball game."

"You lied?"

"Yes, but only to protect his heart. He'd have an attack if he knew I came out here."

"He doesn't like me."

"He doesn't like anyone." Joe tilts his head. "Not anymore."

"I feel better already."

The Christmas lights reflect in his eyes. Sura peers through the arbor. "Something special in there?"

"Only a personalized tour."

"It's that special?"

He extends his elbow. "You are."

"Thank you, kind sir." Sura curtsies and takes his arm.

He guides her through the arbor, and even though the garden is open to the sky, it feels a bit warmer inside. Her cloudy breath fades.

Strands of white light are fastened along the edges of freshly trimmed boxwoods. Red and green lights highlight the tall hedge walls where reflective ornaments dangle. Christmas music plays sweetly from all around.

"Oh, my." Sura steps forward. "You did all this?"

"I had help."

"Jonah?"

"Well, he did most of it, like he does every year. I did a little extra, though." He adds, "We had help."

It's hard to imagine Templeton in overalls. May doesn't have the time to leave the kitchen. *So where's all the help?*

Joe leads her into the maze. They run their hands over the flat-topped boxwoods, shuffle over the oyster-shell path. The sunken garden is imbued with warmth, the kind that flows through her, melts in her stomach, opens her heart. She smiles involuntarily, as if she couldn't frown if she tried.

The short, fat woman sits on a square pedestal inside a round pool, water dripping from her frozen hands. Light emanates from the center without a source.

"Who is she?" Sura asks.

"You've never heard the Myth of Jocah?"

They walk slowly around it.

"Long ago, way before humans, there was a goddess that was exiled from the heavens because she was pregnant. She called Earth her home. It wasn't very hospitable and none of the other gods came to visit her. She gave birth to twins. One was good, the other bad. But they were her sons, so she loved them both. And together they loved Earth.

"But she was lonely. The time came for her to leave, to attend matters elsewhere in the universe, or whatever gods and goddesses do, but she loved Earth so much that she didn't want to leave it to her boys to squabble over."

They walk quietly and slowly, like walking meditation. Jocah, Sura notices, has a single long braid.

"So, one day," Joe says, "Jocah broke two chunks of earth from the ground. She launched one into the sky. It soared up into the heavens, where it froze into a block of ice, exploding before it reached space. Snowflakes were spit through the four gateways and covered the planet in a sheet of ice."

Joe gestures to the four openings along the tall hedges, each an arching arbor. North, south, east and west.

"She crushed the other chunk of earth into dust and blew it over the pristine glaciers. These seeds of earth took root and grew into beings that took the form of their creator."

Joe nods at the sculpture.

"Short and fat," Sura says. "Adapted to the cold."

"That's what they say."

They stop at the front of the sculpture, Jocah facing north. A small inscription is carved at the base.

Care for this World.

"The myth says she whispered that to the fat, little people before she left. They were in charge of watching over Earth."

"Where are they now?"

"Where the ice is." Joe points. "North Pole."

Joe dips his hand in the pool and drizzles it into Sura's open palm. She expects it to be half a degree above freezing, but it's warm. "The statue weeps for the world's troubles, but the myth says they're not tears of sorrow or happiness."

He touches Sura's lip. The water is salty.

"It's tears of joy."

"Joy?"

"For truth. Existence. That sort of thing. It's a myth, a story. But it's a good one."

"Where'd you hear it?" Sura asks.

"Jonah."

Sura's mom never told her the myth. She wonders if Joe is the lucky one. Even if his father doesn't like anyone, at least he brought him here and told him stories.

"You're telling me Mr. Frost is one of them?" Sura asks.

Joe chuckles. "It's just a story; he probably made it up. My guess is the sculpture is his mother. Think about it, you want to tell people you have an ice sculpture of your mother in the garden or a goddess?"

Sura scoops up a handful of water and lets it trickle between her fingers. The statue appears to melt but never changes shape. The water is so clear and perfect.

"One of the twins, the story goes, becomes Santa Claus—only they just called him Claus. In the old days, he spread truth to the people instead of presents."

"And that's why Mr. Frost is obsessed with Christmas?"

"Well, that and the fact that he's made a trillion dollars selling presents, yeah. He owes his entire fortune to Christmas."

"He does?"

"The toy factory is below ground."

Sura starts to laugh at the joke but thinks about the three buttons in the elevator. There was a bottom one. "You've been there?"

He shakes his head. "No. But after you see the wishing room, you'll believe it. You ready for the tour?"

"This isn't it?"

"This is just the foyer, my lady." He laces his fingers between hers, their palms warm against each other. "Let me show you the main attraction."

Under Jocah's watchful gaze, Joe leads her through the North gateway, the same path where she bumped into him the day she met him. She can feel his heart beating in his palm.

He stops at the end of the tunnel—the shade humid and dark— where Jonah had emerged when they were picking up firethorn berries. The branches look impenetrable.

"You ready?" His expression is hidden in shadows.

"Through that?"

"Yeah, but first you have to tell me your favorite place in the world."

"Why?"

"Trust me."

Sura doesn't have to close her eyes to think, it's plenty dark to concentrate. She just can't come up with anything. Her mom never took her anywhere outside of South Carolina.

"I don't know."

"Then close your eyes," he says. "And imagine some place. It can be anything, anywhere. It doesn't have to be real, just picture it."

There's a crying ice sculpture in the garden and now Sura's standing in a dark tunnel with a boy she met days ago and he's telling her about a wishing room that's inside a sticker bush. *This is how people get hurt.*

"Trust me." His breath is soft on her ear.

She recalls her mom's favorite photo.

"You got it?" he asks.

"Yes."

His fingers, once again, twine with hers. She hears the leaves rustle, twigs snap. He pulls her behind him, branches scratching her face and arms. She holds her breath—

The temperature drops and the wind lashes her cheeks.

She's standing next to a weathered railing, looking down the side of a granite-faced mountain, where wind roars across slick rocks with chilly force. Sura's eyes instantly water.

The Buddhist Temple.

Then her feet are searching for the floor. Her legs are jelly.

And it's all spinning.

It's all too much.

Joe's arms wrap around her before she hits the floor.

Sura's floating.

She's curled against something soft and warm, soaring through dark mist and clouds, occasionally hitting turbulence that jostles her—

"I'm sorry, so sorry, so sorry," Joe mutters. "It was too much, too soon. I should've quit with myth, let you take that in first, before we went to the wishing room. Maybe it would've been better if the helpers were here."

For the moment, she pretends to sleep, pressing against his solid chest, her hand on his flexing pecs. He's carrying her out of the garden.

"Wait," she says.

They're almost to the arbor that exits the sunken garden. Joe stops on the last step. "I'm sorry, Sura. I shouldn't have—"

"Put me down." She hates saying it, wouldn't mind it if he carried her all the way home. But that's not what she wants. She wants to stand on her own.

"Please," she says. "I can stand."

Joe lets her feet touch the ground, gently, holding on in case she crumples again. The world isn't spinning anymore.

"Let's go back."

"I don't know, Sura. The mind can only tolerate so many new experiences at once. You need to give this some time, let your mind process."

But the garden feels familiar, more than it should. She's only been inside the garden a couple of times, but it suddenly feels like she's been here all of her life. She feels like the plantation is begging to be discovered. It wants her to know it.

To know the truth.

"I'm all right."

He doesn't believe her. She smiles, reassuring him by squeezing his arm.

"Please," she says. "I want to see it."

He can't say no to that.

They go back down the tunnel and pause outside the entrance; she imagines the photo again.

They step inside.

And overlook the misty valley below.

The wooden planks creak beneath her feet, their texture worn from thousands of sandaled footsteps. She steps carefully to the banister, the paint peeling from the wood. The mountain drops straight down, the valley engulfed in hazy clouds, moisture sticking to her cheeks.

A long, white breath escapes her lips. "This is the picture on the wall; it's the picture my mom took from a calendar."

"I know."

"This isn't normal, Joe."

"Normal?"

"This wishing room... it only happens in books and movies." She grips the railing tighter, afraid the spinning will return. "This doesn't happen in real life."

"The mind can be easily fooled to see what we want it to see. The wishing room simply affects your sensory input, presents it with the reality it wishes to see."

"Do you see the same thing I do?"

Joe walks to the banister and looks down. "I see the clouds below. I hear the monks chanting inside. Feel the humidity on my face."

He closes his eyes and inhales.

"Smell the cedar trees."

Sura peels the paint off the railing and tosses it over the side. It flutters into the mist. "How? I don't understand how this can be? There's nowhere like this in the world—how can Mr. Frost do it?"

"How does that ice statue melt without melting?" Joe says. "I don't know how he does all this; he's some kind of genius. All I know is that I'm not dreaming."

"This doesn't freak you out?"

"I don't remember the first time I came in here; I saw it when I was little. Thought all this was normal."

He leans against the railing. The wood crackles under his weight. Sura's stomach drops, her legs turning cold. She wants to reach out and grab him in case it breaks and he tumbles to the bottom.

"Where did you get the picture?"

Sura steps away from the edge and goes to the double doors where the monks' tonal chants vibrate. "She always talked about travelling but never had the time, so we always collected pictures of places we'd go if we had time and money. Turns out, we had neither."

She touches the door.

"Why me?" she says.

"What do you mean?"

"Why show me all this?"

"I don't know." The railing protests again. "I wanted to. I said something to May and she gave me her key."

He pulls out a shiny pocket watch, just like the one Templeton is always looking at.

"That's what lets you in?"

"I think you can get in here without it, but getting back out would be difficult."

"What do you mean?"

"It's easy to get lost in your thoughts. That's what the wishing room is, just your thoughts crystalized. As far as I know, we're actually standing on a bunch of leaves, staring at trees like a couple of stoners, but we're seeing all this. It's easy to forget you're in here, that all of this is created by your thoughts. The pocket watch will show us the way out."

He points at the sky. The North Star is flashing bright, turning red, then green, and then white again.

"If you're ever in doubt," he adds, "the North Star only turns those funky colors in the wishing room."

"But why me?" she asks again.

"Don't you feel it?"

The world is starting to turn again. But she struggles to process this. First her mom dies, then she meets Mr. Frost, and now this. It's right out of a science-fiction book, but she's standing on weathered boards, listening to monks chant, and feeling the wind.

And there's the boy of her dreams, leaning fearlessly against a creaking railing with thousands of feet below.

She just needs a moment.

Joe whispers.

I dream of her
In times of need
She gives to me
Her blushing greed

HE LOOKS UP.

Sura feels the chanting move inside her while his words warm her chest. He speaks directly to her, soothing her unrest, melting her anxiety.

Breathing for her.

To be with her
Is all I feel
To kneel with her
To make this real

HE LOOKS AT THE MOUNTAINS. Somewhere, a bird calls.

"What is that?" she asks.

"Something I wrote," he says. "The day I first met you."

Sura's chin trembles. All the crap in her life just seems to fall away in that instant. The world stops turning and she's not going to stand against the wall anymore. She takes him and kisses him fully on the lips. He wraps his arms around her, returning her affection with warmth that's soft, yet firm.

I feel it, Joe.

They click together. Apart no more.

And the railing threatens to dump them over the edge, but it's just thoughts. They fearlessly cling to each other. Perhaps they'd remain that way until the banister breaks and they tumble back to reality, still swimming in each other's desire.

Only the phone interrupts them.

She pulls back and shyly touches her forehead to his chin. He pulls the phone up, forcing himself to read the text.

"Jonah wants to know if the game is over," he says.

"What game?"

"The basketball game I'm at." Joe wraps his arms around her, tapping a reply with the phone behind her back.

"What'd you tell him?"

"Overtime."

They share laughter while their bodies remain connected. Sura ponders the evergreen hills hidden in the mist and wonders what's really out there.

Mr. Frost drapes his arm over the lounger; his fat fingers doodle in a pail of salted krill. He funnels a fistful through his whiskers, chewing leisurely, while holographic images of Joe and Sura play out the scene that's occurring in the wishing room.

She held it together.

Most people might think their first trip to the wishing room would be thrilling a chance to step inside your mind and live out your fantasies is quite alluring. However, when reality reveals itself, the experience is more like a carnival ride, one that takes a few trips to get accustomed. The direct experience of one's delusions is a dangerous one. When the curtain is pulled back on fantasy, there can be surprising elements at work. Whether they know it or not, humans prefer to remain delusional. It's better to believe the fantasies are true.

Truth can be hard and cold.

That was risky, sir.

Quite enlightening, though. Did you know that her mother was interested in the Buddhist temple?

She meditated. It should come as no surprise.

But isn't it interesting that Sura chose it? Perhaps we're seeing an evolution of her soul.

Mr. Frost trickles more krill into his mouth and swirls the small crustaceans around his tongue, savoring the salty flavor while Sura and Joe embrace. He watches them hold each other tightly, feeling the elation of attraction in his own chest, as if he's experiencing the uplifting sensations of courtship and admiration.

When they exit the wishing room, the holographic images disappear. Mr. Frost sits quietly in the tower, dangling his arm to scratch Max's head. He feels so present when they are together.

The human experience.

The elven experience has faded for Mr. Frost, perhaps a side effect of the root, or the result of two hundred years in isolation. Nevertheless, he finds reason to live when he can share their experience.

He pulls the tin box from his jacket and fingers a few nuggets. The little box—when pressed against his skin—transfers these memories and experiences into the kernels. Max sits up.

I'm happy for your experiences, sir, Freeda says, without a hint of sincerity, *but there are more important matters at hand. The helpers have an order ready for shipment.*

Mr. Frost closes his eyes. *Turn up the music, Freeda.*

A long pause before the volume rises on Bruce Springsteen's remake of an old Christmas favorite: "Santa Claus is Coming to Town." Mr. Frost is a fan of the original song, but the newer versions of old holiday tunes have grown on him lately. Anything that celebrates the season.

And sells product.

Soon, another shipment will distribute technology that originated in his toy factory around the world... be wrapped in Christmas paper and placed under trees. He's not proud of what he's doing. At one time, he thought he was spreading goodwill and cheer to all mankind, that his gifts would bring small relief to a weary world.

But the root deceived him.

It was all part of the plan to spread this special technology around the world. Because when Jack comes back, it will turn against them. *It will all be over.*

Prepare my coolsuit, he thinks.

You need to inspect the product, sir.

Send Templeton. I'll be in the wishing room.

Sir, I don't think—

He knows what he's doing, Freeda. Mr. Frost sprinkles the kernels on the floor for Max, snapping the silver lid closed. *I'll come to the toy factory once I've had a little walk.*

Freeda doesn't answer. He hasn't been to the wishing room in quite some time. He always returns invigorated, and that's why it's there.

It's why she lets him go—to keep him fresh, to keep him alive.

To bring back Jack.

THE TUNING FORK

The gift seemed unusual.

The grandfather watched the boy rip the paper off his Christmas present and pull two tuning forks from the box. He held them up to the firelight. The grandfather saw the gears turning in the boy's head, his mouth downturned in confusion.

"What do they do?"

"Magic," said the grandfather.

He took one of the tuning forks from the boy and struck it on the fireplace. The prongs vibrated with a melodious tune. He moved the humming tuning fork near the boy.

The boy's eyes widened. His lips formed an "O."

His fork started to sing.

11

DECEMBER 13

Saturday

They get to stay inside the shelter today as long as they listen to a lady talk about something. It's raining, so everyone stays.

Jack sits in the front row, picking at the growing bald patch on his arm. Maybe it'd stop if he didn't mess with it, but the skin is so smooth and cold and blue. He pulls out a few fat and curly hairs and holds them under his nose. They don't smell. He puts them on his tongue, minces them.

Tastes like... cabbage. *Weird.*

"Yo, garbage man. You want to help?" someone shouts.

"No." Jack brushes his white tank top. The mustard stain is permanent.

"That wasn't a question."

"Sounded like one."

They mutter while chairs clash. They're telling on him.

"Jack," Willie shouts, "get off your fat cushion and give us a hand."

"You want me to do everything?" Jack throws up his hands. "Fine. I'll do everything."

His oversized feet catch the chair next to him and he almost falls.

He stomps over to a stack of chairs but can't reach the top, so he pulls on it until it begins to tilt.

Willie pulls it back.

"You want me to help or not?" Jack says.

"You need to relax, man." Willie grabs his arm, pulling him off to the side. "You want a sweatshirt or something? You're freezing."

"I'm not cold."

"Yeah, you are." He turns over Jack's arm and points at the patch. "What's with that?"

"I like to pick."

"No, I mean the blue skin."

"Oh, it's just... I colored it with... an ink pen thing. I was bored. I'm thinking of getting a tattoo."

"Why are you cold?"

"I'm not cold, Willie."

"Have you been sneaking into the walk-in freezer? I told you that's off-limits, Jack. I catch you in the kitchen and you'll be sleeping in the ditches."

Jack gets the Willie-stare: the x-ray truth-teller works on everyone.

"No. I. Haven't." Jack pulls on his shirt "And I don't appreciate your accusations."

Willie's usually right, but not this time. Jack doesn't go into the kitchen anymore. If they had sardines, maybe. He'd smell it if they did. And Willie's double-wrong because Jack doesn't feel cold. In fact, he feels just fine. He doesn't need as much light to warm up.

Jack helps set up the chairs, this time without kicking them. He did it on purpose last time. He slides them side by side until there are five rows, all nice and neat. He plops down in the front row, same seat, with no one on either side of him, and begins to examine the bald patch.

Willie introduces a lady from United Bay or Lighted Way or something. She's young, super happy, and her name is Mickey. And Mickey likes to clap; she tries to get them to clap, too.

She doesn't stop until they do.

She talks about volunteering or something. Christmas, probably. That's all they talk about around here is Christmas. Jack's already bored. He doesn't understand why they're waiting for it—just do it already. If it takes much longer, Jack will fall off the good list.

If he was Santa, here's what he'd do. He'd give presents to everyone, the end. That's what he'd do. What's with all the judging, waiting, and life lessons? That's for reality TV.

And the singing of those wretched songs, oh man, oh man. His ears will bleed if he hears about one more sleigh ride or another walnut. Christmas is all about getting stuff, so let's just stop pretending it's about goodwill.

"So," Mickey says, "we'll be needing volunteers at the pet shelter to help with the animals. Does anyone like animals? Anyone?"

Jack picks at a different stain, this one pink. Ketchup, maybe.

"The next opportunity is at the park," the lady says. "We'll be building a new playground, so you'll get a chance to use your muscles and contribute to the younger generation. Doesn't that sound like fun?"

Jack might be the only one in the world that doesn't want a Christmas present. He just wants to chat. Five minutes, that's all he's asking. He's got a feeling, though, that he won't have to ask any questions. Jack thinks... no, he *knows*, that he'll take one look at Claus and remember.

Just stay on the good list.

"Okay, next." Mickey runs her finger down a list. "Anyone like Santa?"

"ME!" Jack springs out of his seat. "Right here, right here! Santa fan, right here!"

"All right." She chuckles. "We have one, that's good."

She backs up. Jack settles down, nodding but still waving.

"This is a special assignment—"

"Good list!"

"—you get to be Santa Claus at the downtown—"

"Me! That's me!"

He doesn't hear the rest; all he knows is that if he can be Claus, he'll be vaulted to the top of the good list and never look back. Somehow, that red coat will change him.

"Not without ID." Willie steps between Mickey and Jack. "Pick someone else, Mickey."

"*Wut*?" Jack's lower lip hangs. "Willie, for real? Is this 'cause I kicked the chairs?"

"It's because you picked on the lawyer and she left without getting you an ID. Listen, I'm not going to let a bunch of little kids sit on your lap until you get an ID."

"And you stink," Pickett mutters.

"Shut up," Jack says.

"Someone else, Mickey." Willie crosses his arms.

"Um." She slides her finger down the list again. "There's one he might be able to do... if you think it's okay."

She flashes the clipboard at Willie.

He looks to where she's pointing. His hair swings over his eyes while he rubs his chin. "I suppose," he finally says.

"No, wait. Tell me first," Jack says. "What is it?"

Mickey shows him the clipboard and points at an assignment.

Jack holds his breath and reads the words in the little box. For a moment, he looks less green. Willie and Mickey begin to look worried.

"Face!" Jack spins around. "In your face! In your face! In your face!"

He runs around the room, pointing with both hands, finger-guns popping at each and every resident, kicking empty chairs (on accident this time), nearly falling, stopping near Pickett in the back row, and hauling in one last deep, deep, deep breath—

"FAAAAACE!"

He doesn't hear Willie shout, doesn't sense Pickett's rage. He rushes outside, hands up, head turned to the clouds, rain drizzling on his upturned face.

The red coat.

For some reason, he's always wanted to wear the red coat.

To be good.

THE LIVE OAK grove is north of the house. It's perched at the top of a slope that overlooks the orchard and rice fields. Sura and Joe stand beneath sprawling limbs as thick as tree trunks. Freshly cut logs are scattered around the remains of a fallen limb.

"No, you make a fist with this hand." She demonstrates, pressing her fist to her midsection. "And then rest the other hand on top."

"Feels like my fist is wearing a hat."

Sura tries not to laugh. She straightens her back, opens her chest. "Smooth steps, slow steps. The body walks. The mind is open."

She breathes through her nose, counts her breath, and quickly rests into a meditative state.

"I can walk slower than that." He barely moves.

"Hey, you asked me how to do it."

"No, I asked what's the point."

"Well, I'm giving you the bonus answer. Aren't you lucky?"

"Charmed. Now is there a chant that'll make the sand fleas disappear?"

Joe's phone goes off. Jonah's face fills the screen. Joe gives several one-word answers, finishing with, "On my way."

He starts loading the firewood into the back of a utility vehicle. Sura helps with the smaller stuff, thinking about Jonah, wondering if he was always angry at the world. He looked just like Joe when he was the same age and Joe could never be as bitter as his dad. It's impossible.

Or is he destined to become like his dad?

"Has your dad always been like that?" she asks.

"Like what?"

"Cranky."

Joe rests in the driver seat, thinking a moment. "He's just quiet and to the point."

"You know, he looked just like you when he was your age."

"How do you know?"

Twilight hides her blushing. He doesn't know she stalked him on the school database. "I saw a picture," is all she says, resisting the urge to lie.

"You know you look just like your mom?"

"I get that all the time."

"No, I mean *exactly* like her."

Joe pulls out his phone, moves images around the glass, and taps through folders until a photo comes up. He holds the phone sideways. It's a picture of her mom and his dad standing in the sunken garden among the boxwoods. He's leaning on the end of a rake; her hands are clasped in front of her stomach.

Sura takes the phone.

She always knew they looked similar, but she didn't often see photos of her mom when she was sixteen. It's like looking at her identical twin. She spreads her fingers across the glass, zooms in on their faces, their heads tilted slightly, ever so slightly, towards each other.

Sura has a dreadful thought. Her mouth starts to move.

"No," he says. "He's not your dad and she's not my mom."

"How do you know?"

"Because I asked. You think he'd let me near you if they were?"

"He doesn't seem to like me."

"Proves my point, doesn't it? If you were his daughter, he wouldn't treat you that way."

"I don't like it." She hands back the phone.

"It's sweet."

"No, I mean, it's like looking at us twenty years ago."

The phone rings again. Maybe Jonah's watching. Or maybe his ears are burning.

"Hop on." Joe smacks the passenger seat. "Jonah is heating up."

"I think I'll walk."

"Why? You think he'll be mad?"

Yes. "No, I just don't want to hurry, that's all."

"You'd rather get thoroughly eaten by sand fleas than ride with me?"

"Maybe."

He reaches into the back of the vehicle and pulls out a small mistletoe bush. "Don't go back empty-handed."

Their fingers brush as they exchange the plant. He holds up his hand. They awkwardly high five. Better than a kiss or a hug because, honestly, if she starts kissing him, she won't stop.

Sand fleas or not.

"See you tomorrow?" he asks.

She nods, already pretending that the mistletoe is a bouquet. The vehicle revs up, slowly moving away in first gear. Tomorrow is such a long ways away and then she'll just have to say goodbye again. They'll high five again and she'll go home to an empty house.

"Joe!"

He slams the brakes. "Yeah?"

"Will you go to a school dance with me? It's a small one, a lot of people go out of town, but it'll be fun. I did the decorations and I'd like for you to see them—"

She puts her hand over her mouth, swears she doesn't feel nervous, but the words won't stop because if they do, he might say no, and now that she's asked, she wishes she hadn't.

"Love to," he says.

She did it. She asked him.

And he said yes.

And her heart floats twenty feet off the ground.

The vehicle speeds away, Joe waving. Sura waves back, smelling the mistletoe like it's roses, which is stupid, but maybe one day it'll be roses he's handing her instead of a parasitic plant.

She wanders out from beneath the live oak, stars filling the darkening sky. Her emotions keep her toasty. The house glows with holiday cheer. The worst day of her life happened when her mom died. *Was that only a month ago? Maybe that's why Mr. Frost brought me out here so soon. This feels like home.*

A cold breeze is ushered in on the night's wing and the sand fleas are crawling through her scalp. She wishes she would've taken the ride at least halfway. She could've gotten off before Jonah saw her and still enjoyed the long walk.

Sura walks to the back door, where she'll drop off the mistletoe and see if May needs any help. Someone's out back.

She can't see who it is, but he's way too short to be Templeton. He's even shorter than Mr. Frost, but just as round. It's hard to tell who it is with the long-tailed coat, wide boots, and tall, yellow hat. Sura hides in the bushes, watching the figure open the basement doors and climb inside. She's never used that entrance and May's never mentioned it.

Sura hurries for the house and starts up the steps. The basement door, however, is slightly ajar. A sliver of light flashes inside.

At the very least, I should close the door.

All she had to do was close it and she would've gone home to feed the horses and dreamed about marrying Joe one day. But when her fingers wrap around the handle, she has a second thought. She thinks maybe she'll take a peek.

The hinges creak.

Light seeps out along with a strange warbling sound. The bushes shake.

And that's the last thing she remembers.

MR. FROST gently touches the tank's cold surface, leaning closer. Inside, the eyes are closed and the whiskers are faintly green.

Less facial hair, that's good. His calculations estimated improved photosynthetic efficiency and, therefore, Jack would need less hair to start life.

Increase red and blue wavelengths, Mr. Frost thinks. *Also, boost carbon dioxide. If all goes well, I expect Jack to be ready for initiation within the week.*

Freeda agrees.

Mr. Frost slides away from the tank. *Project his image from inside the tank, Freeda. I want a better look.*

Light flickers on the incubation lab floor. Line by line, an image of

Jack's body, as it is in the tank, forms in front of him. A coat of silky, green fuzz covers most of the body. Only his palms and part of his face are exposed. He'll lose most of that before he's even out of the tank. Mr. Frost gives a command and the image lifts its feet to show him the scaly soles.

The root squirms. He takes a deep breath and lets it out slowly.

It looks just like him.

Aside from the hair, it's him: the fat belly, the protruding chin, and sharp nose. The proportions are correct, built to the specifications that were loaded into the root so many years ago.

Fear twists in Mr. Frost's stomach, trickling coldly into his legs. And beneath that lies the conflicting warmth of longing and love to see Jack like he was when Mr. Frost knew him.

When he was known as Pawn.

When Jack was blue.

His touch was cold and merciless, but no one saw him like Mr. Frost did. None of the elven on the North Pole saw the real Jack: the elven beneath the cold, blue exterior. Within those frozen eyes was a scared little elven. He was lonely, afraid, and he kept others from seeing that vulnerability by instilling fear in their hearts. He would freeze an elven with his deadly touch if they came close to seeing the real Jack.

"You're the only one I can trust," Jack would often tell Mr. Frost. "I need you."

Jack would sometimes be close to tears when he said that. Those tears froze in the corners of his eyes. The day the tears actually fell like tiny diamonds and bounced between his feet was the day Jack held up what looked like a grain of rice.

The root.

"I need you to hold this," he said to Mr. Frost. "To keep it safe."

Mr. Frost didn't ask what it was or why; he nodded because Jack needed him. Jack circled around him. Mr. Frost felt the cold aura that surrounded Jack at all times, a subzero body temperature that no other elven experienced, a coldness that gave Jack respect. A coldness that helped him cope with loneliness.

Jack reached behind Mr. Frost's head and numbed his neck. Even when Jack loaded the root into a pointed, silver cylinder, Mr. Frost didn't flinch. He didn't question Jack. He let him touch the gun to the cold spot on his neck.

He felt the pressure.

He heard Jack's tears dance on the floor. "Thank you."

And Mr. Frost was happy.

He didn't know what the root was for, just that it was important to Jack, so it was important to him. He never told Mr. Frost what it was for, but from time to time, Jack would visit the elven scientists and return to "update" the root with a small tin of grain. He'd put a few kernels in Mr. Frost's hand and tell him to eat.

They tasted stale.

Mr. Frost didn't know what the food was doing or how it was updating. Afterwards, the root would itch and Jack would blow his icy breath on his neck to make it go away.

It was like that for hundreds of years. And for hundreds of years, Mr. Frost happily allowed Jack—his mentor, his friend—to update the root, to soothe it when it squirmed.

But all that changed when Jack fell through the ice, when he sank to the bottom of the ocean with his mother and brother.

When Jack died.

And now there was no one left to soothe the itch.

Love and hate. When he sees Jack, he can't choose between love and hate, so he embraces them both.

Love and hate.

Sir, an intruder has compromised the lab.

What?

Your little pet followed one of the helpers into the lab.

You're supposed to monitor and report to me, Freeda. I'm tired of these lapses! Mr. Frost hides his satisfaction. He's counting on her missing things like that. *Where is she now?*

The toy factory.

The toy factory? She's not ready to see the toy factory!

She's sleeping.

Mr. Frost makes sure the red and blue lights are turned up in Jack's tank before sliding out of the room. He passes through the main room, around the elevator to the door on the opposite side.

The toy factory.

It always makes his head spin when he enters.

It's the wide open space. He's still not accustomed to subterranean rooms this size, a room that goes fifty feet into the earth. A room too wide to see the other side; a room filled with compartments, scaffolding, and dangling components. A cold room dank with the smell of moist earth and oily machinery.

Today, it's quiet.

Mr. Frost stops at the top of a steep ramp. At the bottom is a table surrounded by hundreds of tiny elven, with long-tailed coats and colorful hats—the helpers climb over each other for a glimpse of Sura. Their garbled conversation fills the emptiness of the dormant machinery.

Mr. Frost lets gravity pull him down the slick slope. The helpers scatter but only far enough for him to skid to a halt. Ice shavings flutter at his feet.

The helpers never sleep, never slow; they adapt to any temperature, build anything Mr. Frost can imagine, and would best a chameleon at hiding. There's very little they can't do and almost nothing they haven't seen.

But they've never had Sura in the toy factory.

One of them, wearing a yellow hat, slides out of the crowd. He stands no taller than Mr. Frost's knee. His nose is sharp and hooked over his mouth. He points at the table with a pudgy, but nimble, finger and a string of unintelligible sounds stream from his wrinkled lips.

He says they caught her sneaking through the back door, sir, Freeda interprets.

"I don't want her in here." Mr. Frost's voice echoes. The helpers back up. "She's not ready to see them."

The yellow-hat comes closer and replies. *He says she has not seen them,* Freeda says.

"Why is she in here?"

It wasn't necessary to bring her into the toy factory, but he knows why. Whether they'll be honest about it or not, he knows the real reason they brought her into the toy factory. It's the same reason Mr. Frost adores her.

She's special.

The helpers can't stop themselves from being around her. It has always been that way. Perhaps they sense the same thing he does, the warm essence of her kindness. The goodness of her emotions.

Mr. Frost moves a strand of hair from her eyes. *They just want to see her, that's all.*

All the conveyor belts and boxing machines, the wrappers, stackers, and envelope slappers have stalled. It's always in full production, 364 days a year, all of it getting ready for one day, sending out wishes and dreams, things that people want and need. Every kid will get something from Mr. Frost, something their parents will buy, their grandparents will purchase, or an aunt or uncle will order. No matter what the gizmo, no matter how long or how short, fat, or slim, he and the helpers have designed some part of it, manufactured a piece of it here in the toy factory.

Even the ideas that humans believe to be their own have, in one way or another, originated from Mr. Frost and the root inside his neck.

He made what Christmas is today.

Mr. Frost takes his hand from Sura's forehead. "Take her to the incubation lab," he whispers. "Let's insert false memories and get her ready to go home."

No less than twenty helpers—all with different colored hats—lean into the table, the soles of their leathery boots biting into the slick surface as they thrust the table up the ramp.

Mr. Frost looks at the rest of them, too many wrinkled and dour faces to see them all, but all of them disproportionately fitted with long noses and square chins. Their eyes, icy blue.

Jack wanted them that way.

"Christmas is coming!" Mr. Frost lifts his arms to rally their spirits. "HURRAY!"

Tiny fists pump in the air. They scramble away, soaring up ropes and climbing to their stations to make the next watch, the next doll, the next music player. The phone, the TV, the bicycle repairer.

They make it all. And so much more.

They have a life of servitude that very few humans would tolerate and yet, the helpers live with such joy. Bred to work—labor is in their DNA—perhaps they don't recognize this place as a prison.

To them, it's just home.

Mr. Frost pushes his way up the ramp. He looks back as the machines rev up like high-tech lasers, whine with heaters and compressors. A song starts somewhere deep within the recesses of the toy factory and spreads like a flame. All at once, they're singing.

Mr. Frost leaves the toy factory, realizing there is only one true prisoner on the plantation.

And he yearns to be free.

12

DECEMBER 14

Sunday

Bernie the cockatoo is talking.

Sura presses a pillow over her ear. She'd yell at him, but he's just a bird. He doesn't usually get worked up this early in the morning.

She sits up and rests her elbows on her knees. Her head feels like a fifty-pound bag of seed. The sun isn't up. She can't remember going to bed. She remembers walking back with mistletoe. She vaguely remembers driving home and feeding the horses. *Or was that the day before?*

Crenshaw strolls into the bedroom with his back arched, purring. Bernie's still pitching a fit. Sura can't remember feeding them. Her thoughts are like images on a foggy mirror.

She scratches Crenshaw behind the ear. "Did I feed—?"

Something crashes in the kitchen. Sura freezes. Her heart bangs in her throat. She's wide awake now.

She looks around the room and spies an old curtain rod in the corner. It's all she's got. The mess of clothes strewn on the floor dampens her footsteps. She stops at her doorway.

"Who's there?"

Bernie answers with a bunch of gibberish.

Sura reaches around the wall and turns on the living room light. She waits in her room, eyes wide. Nothing moves but Bernie. Crenshaw eventually slinks across the room. Sura follows the cat to the hallway and turns on another light. By the time she reaches the kitchen, every light in the house is on, including the floodlights in the backyard.

Crenshaw sways into the kitchen, meowing.

Sura's knuckles ache. She puts the curtain rod on the counter and picks up Crenshaw. The floor, counters, and table are clean. There's a pot turned over in the sink. She has a vague memory of cleaning the kitchen and washing the dishes. She also remembers Mr. Frost telling her to volunteer with her Helping Hands Horse Troupe after school instead of working.

Or maybe Templeton said something.

Sura carries Crenshaw to the living room. Bernie flaps his wings, stirring up white feathers. His bowl is filled with seeds. She sticks her fingers between the bars and rubs his head.

The horses are standing at the back fence, staring at the house. Or maybe they're staring at the yellow towel in the backyard. She thinks about picking it up before one of the horses starts chewing on it.

"Gottago,gottago,gottago," Bernie wails.

He sounds like an overwound toy, the words mashing together. Sura puts Crenshaw down to start working on chores before school.

Later, she realizes that the yellow towel is gone.

JACK'S CHILLY.

The red coat is heavy and the furry hat floppy. He unbuttons the coat to expose his thinning chest hair.

Jack targets a squishy-looking lady with his big, brass bell. She's thumb-punching her phone while a butt sizzles between her lips. She doesn't look up. There's a kid behind her, snot caked on his upper lip. He snerks back a payload and spits before waving at Santa.

There's a table on the other side of the Walmart entrance, some teenagers signing people up for something. Everyone that comes out of the store stops at their table to fill out tickets. The girls say thank you and smile each time someone drops one in a fishbowl.

Sometimes the people will look at Jack and sometimes they stare, but they never come over and they never put anything in his bucket. Actually, one guy emptied a pocketful of pennies into it an hour ago, along with lint and a bottle cap.

An old guy comes out of the store with two carts brimming with boxes.

"Excuse me." Jack swings the bell. "Do you have the time?"

"No."

"Would you like to make a donation?"

"No."

"Do you hate children?"

The old man shoves past Jack's outstretched hand, pushing one cart and pulling the other. Jack thinks about throwing the bell at the old buzzard. He didn't feel that way in the beginning of his Santa assignment, but hour after hour of rejection is wearing him down.

Claus should give out grades; let us know how we're doing. Do I have a C or an A+? How many good things do I have left to do, and how many points will I lose if I gong that old man on the back of the head?

If that table was to suddenly collapse and those tickets spontaneously catch on fire, maybe he'd stand a chance at making some real dough. They're getting all the attention. Jack needs to think this out. How can he make it look like an accident? If no one knows he did it, will Claus know? He would have to act very concerned when it happens, run over to help the poor girls, maybe even shed a couple tears.

Oh, you poor things. I can't believe someone would do this. Oh, the horror!

"Yeah, that's good," he mutters. "The horror."

"What?" a passing teen says.

"Shut up," Jack answers.

The teen shoves a gold coin in the slot. "Go buy yourself a new sled."

"Did you just..." Jack's arm stiffens.

The kid and his buddy look back with grins.

"Happy Chris... Merry hol..." Jack clears his throat; they're almost to their car. "Habby Lobiday!"

I'm an idiot... an idiot with a gold coin!

All it took was one good soul to see Jack needed a break and zooooom, he just flew up the good list because gold could buy some poor family a house or it could buy the shelter a year's worth of food or some poor slob a new coat. He couldn't be hasty, though. It's gold. And he's rich.

A+, baby.

He rings the bell with pleasure, without a care in the world. Nothing can stop him now. The sound of his annoying bell doesn't even bother him. In fact, if that old man comes back for another cart full of toys, Jack might even hug the old coot. He feels warm and bubbly. Joyous. *Yeah, that's it. Joyous. The spirit of Christmas is in me. The golden spirit of Christmas.*

He should probably take his bucket and leave just in case someone gets any funny ideas. There are some shady characters at Walmart. He doesn't want to lose the gold, but he has to act cool. Maybe hang around another ten minutes and then grab a cab.

And hope the cabby can make change.

People exit the megastore with armloads of stuff.

"Merry holiday, everybody! Happy Christmas, great New Year, silent night. Silent night, everyone! Silent night!"

He says it to everyone, no matter how tall, skinny, short, or fat. They all get his blessing. Each time, the words pass through his lips a little louder and a little more joyously. There's no stopping the spirit of Christmas.

He spreads his arms. "Siiiiilent night."

Several people turn at the sound of his lovely song. Jack heard it on the radio, but he likes his version better. It's simpler, gets to the point. He's not sure what the point is, but nonetheless he sings with joy.

"Siiiiilent night. Siiiiilent night."

"Don't you know the words?" A small kid is in front of him.

"What?"

"That's not how the song goes."

"Yes, it is."

"No, it ain't."

"The song goes how I sing it. So there."

"Because you don't know the words."

Jack chuckles. He looks around, ringing the bell. An old lady passes them but doesn't appear to belong to this little smart mouth. Jack waits until no one is looking. He's got a gold coin. An A+.

He's got a little wiggle room.

He leans forward, eye to eye. "Why don't you shut your mouth, you little booger-eater."

"You shut up."

"You shut up."

"You shut up."

"You're going on the naughty list," Jack says. "Guarantee it."

"Whatever, loser."

"Hope you like poop in your sock."

The kid laughs. Jack screwed something up. Santa puts something in bad boys' socks, but it's not poop. It should be.

"Come on, Bo." A large lady passes them. "Let's go."

"You're dumb." The little stinker races after her.

Jack almost throws the bell, considers the special one-finger wave, but then the lady holds out her hand and drops a fistful of gold into Bo's cupped hands. He peels off a cover and eats it.

A gold wrapper hits the ground.

The last tone fades from the bell hanging at Jack's side. He picks up the tin wrapper that's shiny gold on one side and smeared with mud on the other. He dabs it with his finger and puts it to his nose. It smells sugary. He licks it.

Chocolate.

The concrete starts to sway. Jack is losing his balance. There's another kid peeling a coin and popping it in his mouth. And the guy next to him is doing the same thing.

There are gold coins everywhere!

Jack goes to his bucket and tries to pry the lid off. He jams his finger through the slot and gets it stuck. He shakes the bucket and the pennies clang. People stop what they're doing as cuss words stream out of the short Santa that's punching the side of his donation pot.

He looks over his shoulder.

They look away, pretending they don't see him. Jack thinks about stomping the bucket flat—he's got the feet to do that—when he spies the guilty party.

I knew it!

Piled on the table next to the fishbowl is a mountain of gold coins. People are signing a piece of paper with a picture of a horse and grabbing the coins for free. They peel them and eat them!

Darkness fills Jack.

He's left with emptiness, left with a chasm of need and dashed hope. He's deep on the naughty list now. His heart shrinks to a cold clod of ice.

It's their fault. They gave out the gold coins. They made me call the kid a booger-eater.

The bell clangs on the ground.

Jack is going to flip that table, dash all their stuff in the parking lot, and stomp it with his fat, hairy feet until it resembles garbage from a compactor. If he's going to be on the naughty list, he may as well make it worth it.

Jack can't explain what happens next.

It's like the spirit of Christmas returns when a truck pulls up. Its mufflers are loud and obnoxious, but Jack suddenly feels warm and bubbly again. It's like he loves the world, and the world loves him back.

He feels like breaking out in song.

A boy is driving. A girl gets out of the passenger side. She skips around the front bumper, her rosy, round face beaming with a smile. Jack's foot slides toward her like she possesses gravity. He leans back so the force doesn't pull him through the crowd. It would be embarrassing if he landed on top of her and, right now, he just wants to bathe in the sweet sensation.

"What are you doing here?" one of the girls at the table says.

"I want to help," the chubby-cheeked, tractor-beam girl says.

"You need to be getting ready." The girl at the table waves at the boy in the truck. "We're doing just fine."

"Are you sure?"

A man and his family get between Jack and the girls. Jack shoves the kid out of the way and starts walking toward the table. The father confronts him, but he doesn't hear anything. The sweet vibrations fill his head. A tunnel wraps around his vision. The girls hug, smile, and laugh. Jack feels all giggly, too.

They look at him. He must've laughed out loud.

And then the girl of his dreams gets back in the truck.

"Have fun," the girls at the table shout.

They all wave to each other. Jack waves, too. He watches them drive away, the mufflers momentarily drowning out conversations.

And the resonating feeling fades. That beautiful Christmas spirit drives off in a four-wheel-drive truck and Jack feels colder.

Emptier.

Once again, his chest hardens.

And he wants to destroy that stupid horse table with the dumb coins. Jack picks up the bell and inspects a chip on the rim. He resists the urge to hammer the red pot with it, or shatter the dumb fishbowl. He wants that feeling back.

The Christmas spirit.

He waits for a gap in the crowd before wandering over to the table, while one of the girls tells someone about volunteer opportunities and disabled children and blah, blah, blah. Jack walks his fingers across the table and swipes a coin. It's soft and pliable.

"Hi," she says, wrinkling her nose. "Are you all right?"

"Oh, I'm awesome."

"I thought something was wrong with your donation can."

"Yeah, it malfunctioned. I fixed it."

"Good." She looks around, but no one is coming near them. Jack is staring. "Are you interested in signing up?" she asks.

"Oh, yeah. For sure."

She slides over a clipboard. "Just write your name with your phone number and email."

"Okay. I will." Jack picks it up and scribbles on the line. "Hey, by the way, I was just talking to... ummmm."

He whacks his head.

"What's the girl's name, the one that was in the cool truck with the kid?"

"Sura?"

Jack snaps his fingers. "That's it. I was talking to Sura about doing this, um, thing with the horses and stuff, you know, earlier... when you weren't looking. Anyway, she wanted some information about my bell and bucket."

Stupid. Jack shakes his head.

"Anyway, is she coming back?" Jack asks.

"Not today."

"Where she'd go?"

"The Blackwater High Christmas dance."

"That's right, she told me that." He pretends to fill out the form, not paying any attention to what he's writing. "Well, that's too bad. She was really, really, really interested in the bell, wanted to know where she could get one just like it. Maybe I can give this one to her since it's broke. Where does she live and what's her phone number and, um, email?"

"I don't know." The girl frowns.

"Yeah, you do."

"Can you just give me the clipboard back?"

"I'm almost done. Just tell me where she lives."

"Is everything all right?" The other girl stands up.

"He won't give me the clipboard."

"Yes. I will." Jack laughs, but people are staring. Something snaps. He looks down at the pencil clenched in his fist, now in two pieces.

Both girls hold out their hands.

"I don't like your attitude, missy." Jack drops the clipboard. "No one sign up!" he announces. "They're mean over here. They'll just be mean to you if you sign up."

The girls roll their eyes. One of them goes into the store, probably to tell on him. Jack goes back to ringing the bell. He'd walk off and leave all his crap if he had any idea where or what Blackwater High meant.

He'll find out when he's back at the shelter.

ANOTHER SHIRT LANDS on a growing pile. Several empty hangers swing in the closet. Sura digs into the blouses, things she's never worn, clothes she's never seen. For her, it's always been T-shirts and jeans.

But she's never been to a dance. *What do people wear?*

Sura drops on the chair, stares at the large mirror, and pouts into her hands. A picture of her mom is wedged into the frame.

It's too much pressure. Why don't they just build a fire and hang out with the horses? Why'd she even ask him to this stupid dance? It's not like she's friends with any of those people.

Because she wants to show him off, that's why. To come to the dance hanging on his arm, watch the girls drool.

Sura remembers sitting in that chair, staring into the same mirror when it was her mom's mirror. She remembers the time she found her makeup box and started playing with it, afraid she'd be in trouble. She tried to draw lines around her eyes and brush her cheeks.

Her mom had come inside the room just as Sura was twisting the lipstick. Her mom smiled, the corners of her mouth poking her chubby cheeks. She came back with a chair and sat next to her, rubbing the blush off her cheeks with a damp washcloth.

You remember something, her mom had said. *Your value is not here.*

She tickled Sura's face.

Who you are is here. She tapped her chest. *It's not who you look like—it's who you are. You are unique. Do you understand?*

Sura had closed her eyes. *Yes, Momma.*

She opens her eyes and sees her reflection. She brushes her

cheeks, like her mom taught her. She paints her lips pink. She digs through the drawers until she finds wire earrings with dangling beads, something she made for her mom when she was ten years old. They fit through her earlobes and brush against her jaws.

The back door opens and closes, rattling the walls. "You ready?" Joe calls.

"Just a second!"

Sura ties her hair back and finds exactly what to wear.

JOE IS at the dinner table, shuffling through a mess of old photos. He looks up when the boots clop on the hardwood. Without a word, his expression tells her exactly what she wants to hear.

Her cowboy boots have polished tips and the beaded belt matches the earrings. The loose-fitting top with the India collar exposes the leather necklace and pendant containing a small photo.

Joe stands. *"Belle dame!"*

"Merci." She curtsies.

His applause thunders throughout the house. He whistles, loudly. Sura feels her face heat up but doesn't hide.

"Um... *Je vais manger le chat,*" she says.

"You're going to *eat* the cat?"

"No, I said I'll feed the cat."

"You said eat."

Sura pulls the cat food from the kitchen cabinet, a smile chiseled into her cherub cheeks. Crenshaw comes out of hiding, rubbing against her leg. She hears the chickens squabbling. It's too dark to see the coop. *Better not be a possum.*

"You fed the chickens, right?" Sura asks.

"You ate the cat; I ate the chickens."

Sura washes her hands and grabs a water bottle, thinking she'll check the coop on the way out, just in case something dug under the fence.

"I like this picture."

"Which one?" she asks.

He holds up a grainy three-by-five photo. She didn't mean to leave that mess out. She happened to see the box in the bottom of her closet, thought it was in the attic. Sura takes the photo, struggling to make sense out of it. It was taken downtown near the water.

"Where'd you get this?"

"In here." He holds up a manila envelope. "I was just being nosy. Was I not supposed to look?"

"No, no. Mom printed all her digital photos. I was just…"

She trails off.

Sura liked having the photos out. It reminded her of what they did and where they went. But this photo, this one was developed from film and not printed at home. Its edges are thick and the corners sharp. Two people are standing on the pier. The younger girl looks about five.

"That's not me."

"It's your mom. I told you she looked just like you."

But Sura's not looking at the young girl. She's looking at the older woman. She never met her grandmother. She passed away before Sura was born. Her mom didn't talk much about her and Sura can't remember ever seeing any photos of her.

She looks exactly like Mom.

"Come on." Joe takes her hand. "Let's go dance."

Sura lets him lead her away from the table. She puts the photo on the refrigerator, a strange sense of déjà vu swirling in her head, that feeling that says, "Wake up! Look around!"

Wake up, her mom would say. *Don't sleep through the truth.*

Joe opens the back door. The chickens are quiet. "You coming?"

Sura turns on the outdoor lights and locks the door. She feels closer to normal once she's outside. Joe opens the passenger door like a chauffeur. While he jogs around the front, she hears the chickens squabble again and sees a bright color flash behind the coop.

It's yellow.

THE ARCTIC HORIZON IS SHARP.

The North Star sparkles white, red, and green while the Northern Lights dance around it with bands of similar colors. Mr. Frost remembers sights like this from the time he was born. The colors remind an elven he's home.

A light breeze ruffles his hair, the faint smell of the ocean on the wind; perhaps a polar bear with a fresh kill is nearby, staining the pristine snow as it fills its belly—a world so beautiful and so cruel.

He eyes a hole in the ice, water sloshing against the edges. The root begins fluttering beneath his skin with a steady beat. Freeda is calling. Her presence is not allowed in the wishing room unless he allows it.

The wishing room was forbidden for many, many years, but his nervous breakdowns were not an act. Mr. Frost was breaking under the pressure of her demands. The wishing room brought his sanity back. That's the only reason she allowed it.

Jack can't come back if I'm broken.

Yes, Freeda.

The helpers report that Sura has found a photograph of her grandmother.

How?

Sesi had evidently stashed a box of photos in the closet. Apparently, she taped an envelope of old photos beneath the lid.

How'd she handle it?

There didn't seem to be a problem, but it's too soon for her to know her truth. Her ego isn't stable enough to handle it. I don't really care if she loses her mind, but I know you feel differently.

Mr. Frost scoops a handful of snow and molds it into a sphere, trimming the imperfections with the edge of his bare hand. He knows his body is wearing the coolsuit to keep him insulated from the warmth. The wishing room makes him believe he's comfortable in the Arctic, but if he wasn't wearing the coolsuit, his body would overheat. He wouldn't last long.

Confiscate the photograph, he thinks.

What good would that do, since she's already seen it? Why not replace it with an altered version?

That would be easier, but it would throw her too far off the path of self-discovery. Deception can be far more damaging.

No. Have it removed.

She'll be suspicious, sir.

Curiosity is good.

Mr. Frost lets the snowball roll off his fingertips, careful not to let his thoughts roam freely now that he let Freeda in. It plunks in the water. Perhaps he'll plunge into the icy depths like he did as a youth.

He longs to feel the icy embrace of home.

Instruct the helpers to stop following Sura and Joe, he thinks.

Why?

I don't want to risk her seeing them, Freeda. She's been pushed to the limits. One more shove, and she could come unglued.

I disagree, sir. We need to watch them now more than ever.

Mr. Frost kneels. He pushes snow into a mound, molding two stout legs and a round belly. He sits back before finishing the rest of the snowman, pretending to consider her reply.

Okay, he relents.

Mr. Frost severs the connection.

He needs to be compliant. Freeda may be artificially intelligent, but her programming has evolved into a complex mind. Allowing her a victory curbs her suspicions.

And Mr. Frost needs to know what the kids are doing.

He finishes sculpting a snowman with a stout head and thick arms. It looks more intimidating than loving, but that is a misconception. A snowman of this sort is protective.

But there are no snowmen in Mr. Frost's life.

"I DIDN'T SAY I wanted to *go* to the dance—"

"Yeah, you did," Willie interrupts.

"No, I didn't." Jack chooses his words carefully. "I said I wanted to *see* the dance."

"And I said no."

The men at the next table laugh.

"Shut up." Jack spreads the map on the table, flattening the wrinkles with the edge of his hand. "Look, Willie. There's been a misunderstanding, let me start over. High schools have dances. It's normal. It's fun."

"Uh-huh. And where'd you hear this?"

"Just some crazy kids at Walmart. I like fun, you like fun. I'm just curious, where I might *seeeee* a dance?"

Willie starts organizing chairs around tables, prepping for dinner. "The answer's still no."

"Give me one good reason."

"I'll give you fifty, Jack. Blackwater High is in the country. It's late. You take the bus out there and you'll be stranded. Worse, you'll get arrested."

"That's only four."

"Look, why do you want to go, anyway, Jack? It's creepy, man. Trust me, a homeless dude like you showing up at a high school dance is going to end badly."

"Well, um." Jack hesitates, wondering how much he should say.

"You know how I don't remember stuff? It's just, I think I saw someone I know today."

"And that someone is going to the dance?" Willie stops wiping down a table and looks up incredulously.

"Yep."

"Still no. Go watch TV; I'm sure you can see a Christmas dance on the Disney Channel. You won't get arrested doing that, I promise."

Jack growls.

Willie shouts for someone to help move tables. One of the cooks calls him into the kitchen. Jack slumps into a chair and studies the map again. Nothing's labeled. If it just showed high schools, he could figure it out. Buses went all over the place.

It's not fair, really. Willie doesn't know what that resonating feeling is like. When he saw that girl, something rang inside him, and not like that stupid bell. This was warm and right, vibrating right down to the bone.

It felt like home.

"Hey, garbage man." Pickett sits across from him. "You want to go to Blackwater?"

"Yeah, duh."

"I'll show you, you furry little freak."

Jack studies his face and waits for the insult. Pickett nods all serious-like. Jack slowly slides the map across the table. Pickett points to the nearest bus line and explains.

Jack listens.

He never would've guessed Pickett would help.

THE PARKING LOT is half empty.

Sura can hear the music. Everyone is inside, dancing to it, except for the rednecks sitting on the tailgates of several fat-tire, jacked-up trucks. The door panels are decorated with mud.

They turn their heads, watching Joe's truck idle across the parking lot, the mufflers some kind of mating call. He parks near the front doors.

"Stay here." He climbs out.

Sura thinks, *No problem.* In fact, she'd be fine if she stayed in the truck all night, but her door opens and Joe holds up his hand.

"*Ma dame.*"

She doesn't budge. Joe waits patiently, hand out. The rednecks start laughing, but it doesn't bother him. *It's not safe out here, either.*

Ms. Wesley opens the doors as they approach. The music assaults them. "Why, Sura. What a pleasure to see you." She adjusts her glasses. "And who is this you've brought to our wonderful school?"

"I'm Joe." He shakes her hand firmly. "Nice to meet you, ma'am."

She asks where he's from, how old he is, what school he attends; the sort of questions a mother asks. Finally, she says over the sounds of Blake Shelton singing about snow, "And did you know your little sweetheart here decorated the entire hall?"

"Not the entire thing." Sura hangs her head.

"She's being modest, Joe."

"It's beautiful," Joe says. "No, seriously. We have dances and they don't look anything like this."

She blushes for two reasons. One, he's serious. She loves that. But, two, he's never been to a dance unless he was lying.

"I've never been to a dance," he whispers in her ear.

She smiles.

"Nice shirt." A tripod of *populars* walk past and give Joe a double take and a flirty wave, the kind where the fingers do the waving.

She thinks about dragging him back into the parking lot because this is all a big mistake. She doesn't belong here; she'd rather be snuggled up on the couch. Joe pulls her inside the gym, where they're doused with chest-thumping percussion. Red and green lights spin off a shiny globe. Most everyone is tucked into the dark corners, forming iron-clad cliques that would take a battering ram to break apart.

The chaperones are near the DJ's table, drinking from red cups and having more fun than the students. The center of the gym is empty.

Sura feels glued to the floor. Joe waits patiently. He hooks his finger around her pinky. She tries to be strong, thinks about how she should act. *What now? Go into a corner? Lean against the wall? Make fun of someone's shirt?* All she can think about is sitting at home, eating popcorn with Crenshaw.

The music stops.

"Can we go?" Sura mutters.

She turns for the door, but Joe hangs on like an anchor. The first chords of "Blue Christmas" strum through the speakers. Not the Elvis one, this one by Bright Eyes. A version she likes.

He walks backwards, pulling her with him.

She protests.

He's going toward the center where everyone will see her. One step, then two. She could pull away, break his grip, and run for cover—it's not too late—but then he smiles that smile, the one that's hardly on the lips but all in the eyes.

She falls in step.

He pulls her close.

Sura closes her eyes, cheek against his neck. The edge of his chin rests against her head. His hands are soft and warm. She feels herself merging into him, lost in a surreal cascade of goodness, where their energies mix like they did in the wishing room.

Two pieces become one.

The song falls over them, wraps around them, and protects them from prying eyes. She sways with his sway, moves with his moves. Their feet step gently, side to side, while he whispers the song to her.

When it ends and there's silence, the spell around them remains. She forgets all about her empty home and all the weird things in her life. All the strangeness, hurt, and confusion fall away.

There's clapping. It's the teachers. They applaud their dance. Joe curtsies and, to her surprise, Sura does too.

"We can go now," he says.

"Maybe just a little longer."

He smiles the smile.

JACK CAUGHT THE LAST BUS.

It's dark when he steps off, but he can read the signs pointing to Blackwater High School. He walks down the sidewalk, whistling. But then the sidewalk turns into grass and the buildings turn into trees. He almost steps on day-old roadkill. What looks like an armadillo has its guts steamrolled into maggot food.

His knees begin to ache. His feet begin to hurt. Joints stiffen.

It's darker in the country. No streetlights to keep him warm. It's not as bad as it used to be—in fact, the hair is falling off in shaggy clumps —but he still needs a little light just to keep the edge off.

He's shivering.

There's hardly room for him to walk, and the cars race down the road, whooshing inches away sometimes, honking as they pass. He marches into the trees when he gets so tired he can hardly walk, so cold he can't feel his big toes. He pulls out his flashlight to shine on his face long enough to stop the chattering.

Something is in the woods.

Jack swings the flashlight to scare it off. He doesn't want to be eaten by a bear. He walks some more, each time a shorter distance before having to get more light. Each time, hearing bears.

At some point, he's so cold and tired that he figures he's going to die. He's in the middle of nowhere. The batteries aren't going to last all night. He'll be a block of ice before the sun comes up. Even the thought of seeing the girl doesn't fill him with hope. Not anymore.

He's empty.

And, for the first time he can remember, he doesn't care.

Jack lies down in a soft bed of leaves to let the cold claim him. The shivering turns violent, but then tapers off. He feels numb all over.

Probably not good.

Still, he doesn't care.

He closes his eyes and dreams of a cold, white land that's flat as far as he can see. Even when he hears the bears come for him, he doesn't open his eyes. He won't stop them from gnawing on his legs. Jack is so numb he won't feel it. He's eaten many o' fish while they were still alive; he probably deserves it.

But then something vibrates, deeply.

Sura!

He opens his eyes. Too tired and stiff to sit up, he turns his head. It's dark, but she's not there. He felt that vibration, felt the goodness.

Twigs snap.

Jack looks closer to the ground and sees several lumps around him. It's difficult to see the details, but he sees they're fat little men wearing itty-bitty hats. Bite-sized people.

Jack can't move, can't feel his hand on the flashlight or his thumb on the switch. One of the tiny men shuffles through the detritus, turns the flashlight on, and points it at Jack's face.

He closes his eyes, seeing one big spot for several minutes as warmth ebbs back into his body.

"*Getup,*" one of them says, the language fast and slurred.

Jack understands; he just can't do it.

"*Comeonyoucandoit. Getup.*"

Jack grunts. No go.

They push him into a sitting position. They get leverage on his rump, heaving him upright. Jack teeters, but they hold him steady.

"*Youneedtogetontheroad.*"

Jack shakes his head, still seeing an orange glow where the flashlight hit his eyes. They want him on the road where the roadkill is. He'd rather freeze than become maggot food.

"*Gonow. Getontheroad.*"

They poke and prod, guiding him out of the trees. Jack protests but finds himself standing on a yellow dash painted over black asphalt, surrounded by a posse of very, very, very short little dudes with cute red, orange, and yellow hats.

The flashlight is still aimed at him.

And then a puzzle piece goes *click.*

"Helpers," he mutters. "You're the helpers."

He doesn't know how he remembers, just that there are hundreds of them. He's seen them before. They know him. And he knows them.

They feel like the girl.

The light goes off.

Jack's alone on the road when the headlights come around the bend: bright, intense, and loud as an angry beast. He's too tired to get out of the way. It's probably better to end it this way. He's seen polar bears eat; they take too long.

As the lights get brighter, he feels warmer.

THE NIGHT IS dark without a moon.

The truck sits alone near the curb. A few cars remain beneath the streetlights, while teachers close up. Joe opens the door for Sura. She scoots into the center, watching him go around the front, thinking about how differently the evening started.

How wonderful it ended.

She pulls the sprig of mistletoe from behind her ear and twirls it between her finger and thumb. Joe slides into the driver's seat and starts the truck. She collects a kiss, exhausted.

Content.

The tree-lined country road is curvy and dark; the headlights beam down the dashed line. Sura rests her head on his shoulder, closes her eyes, and sways with the turns. The vents exhale warm air and pull her into a heavy, hypnotic state, seconds from sleeping.

"What the...?" The truck slows.

Momentum heaves her forward. The truck jerks to a stop. The headlights engulf something dirty, ragged, and hairy.

"What is that?" she asks.

"I don't know."

It's a misshapen man. The pants are too big, the bottoms piled over his feet. Leaves and twigs are stuck to the sleeves. His face is blotchy with patches of whiskers. The halogen light casts a strange color on him, turning his skin bluish and the hair kind of green.

Joe puts the truck in park.

"What are you doing?" she asks.

"Stay here." His eyes lock on the weird little man.

"You're not going out there."

"It's all right; just let me talk to him."

"In the middle of the road?"

Joe pats her knee and opens the door. She doesn't let go of his arm until he gently touches her hand. He locks the door behind him.

The little man's arms are straight at his sides. They don't say anything at first, and then Joe asks something. The little man answers. There's a short conversation. Joe looks up and down the road, pointing toward town.

The little man nods.

Joe looks around again. He looks back at the truck. Sura feels her stomach drop like a trapdoor just opened. He comes around to the passenger side. Sura opens the door.

"Can you get in the backseat?" he asks.

"Why?"

"This guy..." Joe looks at him. "He's got some weird skin condition, something's really wrong with him, and he's lost. He needs a ride to the shelter. And we need to get out of the road."

Sura looks at the misshapen figure standing in the headlights' glare. "You sure?" she asks.

"We can't leave him."

He's right. Despite her fear, she agrees. The little man needs help.

"I want him up front," Joe says, "to keep an eye on him. I'd feel better if you were in back."

She slides out stiffly.

The little man shuffles out of the light, hiking his pants up beneath his enormous gut. He's about as tall as a third grader with a man-sized beer gut. She catches a whiff of fish. Joe helps him up. Sura covers her nose and mouth.

Dead fish.

He starts climbing into the backseat. "Whoa, no," Joe says. "You can get in front."

"I thought..." The little man points at Sura. "There's so much room back there."

"She's in back; you're in front."

"But I like backseats."

"You want a ride?"

The little man's bottom lip pouts like a kid who just got his sucker taken away. He climbs into the front, mumbling.

Joe guns the truck, the tailpipes rattling behind them. Sura looks out the window and catches sight of a swamp fox or feral pig in the trees. It looks like it's following.

"Sweet truck," the little man says.

JACK SPREADS his hands in front of the vents. Warm, dry air blows between his fingers, ruffling the fuzz on his knuckles. The girl gags.

He closes his eyes, wallowing in the Christmas spirit. He knew it would be in the truck. It's coming from the boy, too. He felt it when he came out to talk with him, felt it swirl inside him. But Joe doesn't have half the Christmas spirit as the girl.

Not even close.

"What's your name?" Jack turns and looks back.

She cringes behind Joe's seat and mutters.

"What?" Jack says. "I can't hear you."

"Sura."

"I'm Jack."

He holds out his hand, but she won't take it. His eyelids droop as the loving sensations course through him like a fountain of goodness. He just wants to hug her, squeeze her, and put her in his pocket, so he can feel like this forever and ever.

"What're you doing all the way out here?" Joe asks.

"Fishing."

"This late?"

"That's when they bite."

"No, they don't."

"Yes, they do."

"Where's your pole and tackle?" Joe asks.

"Where's *your* pole and tackle?" Jack snips.

"What?"

"What?" Jack starts humming, opening his mouth in front of the vent to inhale the warm air. He's tempted to take off his shirt, maybe rub some of this Christmas spirit under his arms. He sings his song, the silent night one, and wonders if Sura can hear it. She'd probably like it.

"Siiiiiilent night," he croons, over and over and over, waggling his eyebrows at the shrinking girl—

"Can you not do that?" Joe says.

"Oh, yeah. Sorry. I'm just happy... from fishing." Jack rubs his hands and hums along to the radio. He just lied. Those are naughty list points.

"Hey, I just want to thank you for taking me to the shelter. It's a long ways downtown and you probably don't live down there, you know, with the truck and all."

And those are good points.

"So what's your deal?" Jack asks.

Joe shakes his head. "What?"

"You know, where you live, work, and go to school... in case we become friends or something. I had a phone, but I lost it when it got ran over by a thing..."

More naughty points. He can't stop.

Joe flicks a glance in the rearview. Jack studies the chubby-cheeked teenager leaning back in the shadows, the dashboard lights turning her complexion orange. He wants to climb back there but feels like Joe will throw him out the window.

Jack slides a few inches towards the middle. "Sorry, seatbelt is binding my junk. So, where'd you say you live?"

"Not downtown," Joe says.

"That's not really an answer."

"Only one I got."

Jack adjusts his seatbelt and grunts. He'd like to argue that point a little further and remind Joe that lying will put him on the naughty list, but seeing as Jack is three fibs in the hole, he'll skip it.

"Go to school, do you?"

"High school," Joe says.

"And our dads are cops," Sura adds.

Jack turns, slowly. The girl's nodding, arms folded. He's really wishing he didn't start this lie-parade. Now everyone's doing it. He doesn't want to see her on the naughty list, might dampen the spirit.

Joe merges onto the interstate and turns up the music. The heater isn't doing Jack as much good as it was earlier. His guts are frigid and he's doing everything he can not to shiver. He needs light.

The truck is plenty dark and, fortunately, the occasional streetlight keeps him from chattering. He scratches the back of his hand and wipes the fuzz from his pants.

Jack turns the horrible music down.

"I just want to thank you again," he says sweetly. "Big sacrifice, taking me to the shelter. I don't have a job and all. It's the economy, you know. Not much out there. You two work? Mmm?" Jack looks back and forth, trying to include them both. "Do you?"

"Frost Plantation," Sura says.

Jack turns quickly with a smile reaching both ears. "Oh, really? That's wonderful! Are they hiring?"

"I don't think so. Mr. Frost doesn't like people, wouldn't you say, Joe?"

Joe changes lanes and nods.

Somewhere in the flow of Christmas spirit, there's a twinge of recognition, a memory that's swept in the current. He could likely remember what's nagging at him, but the Christmas spirit feels way too good to try.

Frost.

"Mr. Frost is protective of the ones that work out there, that sort of thing," Sura says. "Anything happens to employees like us and he finds them, if you know what I mean."

"No. What do you mean?"

"He finds them and hurts them."

So now we're all championship liars. Great.

She taps Joe on the shoulder. "I'm going to lie down."

"You don't have to sleep," Jack says. "I'll be quiet."

Sura curls against the seat with her back to him. Jack spins around. It doesn't matter if she talks, really. It still feels good. And there's always Joe. He's putting off some pretty good vibes, too. "Hey, I just want to say—"

"Shhhh." Joe puts his finger up and points to the back.

"Oh, right," Jack whispers. "I just want to say that it's really great..."

Joe turns the music up. Jack glowers at the backseat. She knew what she was doing. But then Joe gives Jack a thumbs-up, like he's a good guy. It's stupid, but Joe's approval rejuvenates him, intensifying the feel-good humming.

They near the end of the interstate. Jack rests his chin on the door, barely seeing over it. The scenery whizzes by, images of lit buildings and yellowish streetlights, billboards and railings. A car rushes past.

He soaks in Joe's energy, thinking about why this would even be happening, convinced this has to be a sign that maybe they know something. And, more importantly, how is he going to find them again without getting arrested?

Jack's eyes get heavy.

The vibrations rain down like big drops of delicious fish oil, freshly pressed and chilled. He licks his lips. The railing along the road turns into a flat line. Lights in the buildings twinkle like stars. The landscape blurs into a white blanket.

And Jack smiles.

The cold feels like home.

Faces emerge from the darkness: short, fat, and hairy. And a giant, icy mountain rises from the ground like an iceberg. He can see the short, fat, and hairy elven—yes, that's what they are, they're elven—all over the city... a city that has a name, something he should remember...

New Jack City. A city so nice, I named it after me.

Somehow, Joe's energy transported him home. He's back with his people on the North Pole where he belongs and not in this forgotten trash heap of smelly warmbloods and spongy, tasteless food. Yes, this is where he wants to be, how he wants to feel. It's not much to ask. He just doesn't want to feel lost anymore, unwanted, ashamed, and bad—

Sounds of war are all around. Footsteps are on the ice, and angry shouts and disapproval echo. It's all Jack's fault; he's to blame for thousands of years of grief, sadness, and suffering. He divided his people, dominated them with bitter anger. They hated him; they wanted him dead and gone because he was bad.

He is bad.

He's bad, bad, bad and cold, cold, cold—

"AHHHH!" Jack slams his head on the window.

Joe's shaking his shoulder. "You all right?"

"Am I..." Jack looks around. He's not on the North Pole. He's in the truck, parked next to a curb.

"We're here," Joe says. "That's the shelter, right?"

And so it is. They arrived just before midnight, just in time for Jack to get a bed. Just in time to get out of the truck. He takes a deep breath, shaking his head. He was dreaming about the ice and tunnels. Maybe he was dreaming about everyone hating him, too.

Jack unbuckles the seatbelt as slowly as possible. He opens the door even slower. "Hey, I just want to say—"

"It's all right." Joe holds up his hand. "Not a problem."

Jack slides out, feet on the pavement. Sura holds the door for him and takes his spot up front. Jack shuffles around the front of the truck and knocks on Joe's door. The window comes down.

"Say, if you ever want to hang out sometime, you know where I live." He points at the shelter. "Just call or something. Send me a text or email. Ask for Jack."

"Sure thing," Joe says. "Take care, Jack."

And the truck rolls away, loud exhaust rattling in Jack's chest, taking the beautiful vibrations with it, leaving him on the front steps, alone and empty.

Feeling as far away from home as ever.

13

DECEMBER 15

Monday

M r. Frost slides down the toy factory aisles, hands on his belly, idly watching the helpers hard at work. They hardly notice him. He passes through the main crosswalk—a wide thoroughfare that crisscrosses the toy factory where, previously, they had Sura on a table—and quickens his pace, sliding to the very back where the new release is being manufactured.

EyeTablets.

EyeTablets will be the toy of the decade, destined to ship all over the world. An estimated two billion will be activated by the New Year.

"May I?" Mr. Frost asks.

The helpers back up. He touches one of the contact lenses with the tip of his finger and places it against his eye. He blinks several times, lubricating the infinitesimal circuitry. Green lines stream over his vision. A grid takes shape.

Mr. Frost looks around.

Holographic images are displayed for his vision only. He focuses on an icon, blinks twice to activate a newslink, and video begins to stream. He'd need earbud implants to hear it, but that will be next year's big ticket.

He reaches out and rearranges the images. The eyeTablet senses the location of his hand and the tension in his imaginary grip, and responds. He spreads his fingers and expands one of the displays. He looks down to see his toes on a wooden raft rocking in the middle of the ocean. The helpers are faint figures in the illusion's scenery.

"Email," he says.

A keyboard hovers in front of him. He pecks at the air, typing out a reply, the words hovering over the blue waves.

"Voice activation," he says.

The keyboard disappears. The words appear as he says, "And thank you, once again, for your participation in this year's beta testing. Merry Christmas, Frost Enterprises. Send."

The words are sucked into the sky, on their way to cyberspace.

Christmas is so much easier in this day and age. Toys are tiny and shipping faster and more efficiently. It used to be that kids received plastic cars and stuffed animals; now it's laptops and smartphones.

And now this.

Mr. Frost anonymously leaked the eyeTablet technology to a start-up company in exchange for exclusive rights to produce and ship as long as he remained a silent partner. He could've gone with Google or Apple, but he'd leaked enough trade secrets to them.

The eyeTablets will be the greatest form of technology the general public will ever have experienced—the first step in phasing out phones and computers. However, it's still rudimentary compared to what Mr. Frost has planned for future generations. He would eventually release eyeTablets with neural capacity, tapping into the brain and nervous system, sensing thoughts and expanding intelligence. Humans will be able to send each other thoughts instead of texts. Schools will become obsolete when students can download lessons and have them integrated into their muscle memory within seconds.

Want to learn Italian? Done.

EyeTablets will eventually circumvent privacy at a level never thought possible. Governments will try to limit the technology to protect the general public, but people will want it, no matter the cost.

Mr. Frost could have the ability to know all their thoughts, to see through their eyes, hear their surroundings, touch their innermost desires, and experience their lives as if he lived them. He could tap into the entire human population at once, see them like a god.

He'll be able to make them do things. He doesn't like to think about that. After all, none of this is really his doing. In fact, it won't be

Mr. Frost eavesdropping on their thoughts and operating them like puppets.

Jack will.

Mr. Frost admits taking great pleasure in the creative aspect of inventing this technology. After all, the human population has done many wonderful things with his ingenuity. What they don't know is the insidious intent behind all these wonderful gadgets.

What's in store for them is beyond their imagination.

Mr. Frost finishes with the eyeTablets and slides down the main aisle.

Sir, I want to remind you that Jack's incarnation is ahead of schedule. He can be removed from the incubation tank in two days.

She sounds sullen. The photosynthetic fur still irritates her. Not only that, she sounds distracted. He expected her to check in with news of Jack last night.

What have the helpers reported about Sura and Joe?

Non-eventful, sir.

Mr. Frost veers too close to a blue-hat helper and almost knocks him over. He keeps his surprise in check. *Nothing happened?*

Nothing worth reporting. They danced, they kissed, and they went home.

Mr. Frost keeps his mind empty, avoiding entertaining thoughts of suspicion and shock. He didn't see this coming. His spies had already updated him. He's had to stay focused to keep those thoughts hidden from her. Maybe her unexpected deception is a ploy to rattle him into the open.

You should come to the incubation lab for an assessment, she says.

That won't be necessary.

You need to see if your creation—

"My creation?"

Some of the helpers look up. He must've blurted that out loud. Jack has been found and she's pushing him to awaken another incarnation? Serotonin leaks from the root and floods him warmly, but fails to soothe his emotions.

I am an unwilling participant in this madness, Freeda.

For a victim, you take a lot of pride.

I didn't say victim. You know things would be very different without the root. None of this would be here.

Her laughter is genuine. *You can't fool me, sir. I see inside you, remember. You pretend to hate this but, deep down, you enjoy it. You can't beat the root, so you go along with it and pretend like there's nothing you can do about it. You cope with the guilty pleasure by trying to understand the warmbloods, to empathize because it's not your fault.*

I take no pleasure in destroying the human race.

Jack is correct about the warmbloods, sir. They're self-destructive. All of your attempts to be like them, to experience their emotions, and empathize with their short-lived lives are all very noble, but you know you're just doing it to ease your guilt.

Mr. Frost pumps his arms as he climbs the steep ramp.

Stop fooling yourself, sir. You are an elven—they are human. If it makes you feel any better, you're doing nothing but letting them destroy themselves. You're not pulling the trigger, sir.

I'm putting the gun in their hands.

Very good, sir.

He said "I." He didn't say "Jack." *I'm putting the gun in their hands.*

If you're done spouting delusions, sir, would you come to the incubation lab for an inspection?

Later. He goes to the elevator and punches the top button. *Have Templeton bring me a drink. I'd like some conversation outside my own head.*

He feels her recede from his mind. His anger was genuine, but also intentional. Fierce emotion is an effective way to screen his true thoughts and motivation. He wanted to appear like an unwilling victim, but she convinced him that it was more than just a ruse.

Perhaps he really is willing.

14

DECEMBER 19

Friday

Green hair settles over the shower drain. Jack scrubs his arms and legs. Ever since Joe and Sura dropped him off, he's been itching like the truck seats were poison ivy. In the morning, his bed sheets looked like a leprechaun shaved. Bald patches of light blue skin are all over. He looks like a hallucination.

Jack tries to turn off the hot water, but it's already off. The pipes must be crossed because the cold knob feels like it's pumping water out of a geothermal hot spring.

He scrubs his head and face, lathering up and rinsing off, wishing the thoughts in his head would fall away like his hair. Joe and Sura's sweet vibrations haunt him along with memories.

He lived on the North Pole. *I already knew that.*

He ruled like a king. *Sweet.*

The elven hated him. *Okay, not so sure about that one.*

They wanted him gone. *That one's iffy, too.*

He was the coldest elven to ever live, which would explain the blue skin, but not the hair. He can't remember even having hair, not to mention curly, green hair.

And the naughty list? He couldn't care less about the naughty list anymore. He remembers something about Santa.

Claus is my brother. He always wore that dumb red coat.

It should be shocking, but the memory settles into place with no less disruption than if he remembered what he ate for breakfast that morning. Claus is his brother, no big deal. He thinks, for a moment, he'll tell Willie that he personally knows the fat man—they'd slid out of the same womb; they were tight—but even Jack can understand how crazy that would sound. He's already on thin ice covering Lake Sanity.

But delivering toys?

Sketchy.

He doesn't remember anything about toys. His memories are outdated—he can't remember anything he's done in the past two hundred years—but they weren't delivering free stuff to the warm-bloods. That's ludicrous. Then again, Jack's not in charge anymore. New management might see things differently.

They were always a little soft.

Still, he doubts the lists and the toys, but not entirely. He remembers sleighs and flying reindeer (turns out they are real), so maybe the toys are too. It all still feels like a dream. The idea of elven is too far-fetched, but all he has to do is look down at his giant feet and scaly soles to remind himself that the elven memories are as good an explanation as anything.

Right now he needs to find Sura to get another sweet jolt of her mojo or whatever she's dealing. That sweet essence emanates from her like distilled euphoria. He needs it to fill in the memory blanks and, more importantly, *so he doesn't feel so empty and alone!*

Now that he's had a taste, he wants more. He felt full and whole, no longer lacking or searching to fill the bottomless emptiness inside him. He felt like there was nowhere in the world he needed to be but right here. He didn't have to be anyone else but Jack.

He felt like he was home.

Jack doesn't care why those kids make him feel that way—he just needs it. His heart is dead without it.

"You need a dog groomer, man." Pickett kicks the wad of hair off the drain. It sticks on the wall. "Take your trash out."

Pickett and a few others hang their towels and turn on the showers far away from Jack. Pickett continues staring as Jack rinses the suds from his head. Jack gives him a full frontal view with a smile.

"You ain't human," Pickett says.

"Neither are you."

"I ain't shedding like a dog. I ain't got blue skin. I ain't got feet the size of flippers. You come from the ocean?"

"I come from your momma." Jack has no idea what that means, but it makes the others laugh. They try not to.

Pickett's lips get thin. "Two days, smelly. You getting kicked out of the shelter in two days without an ID, and this place can stop smelling like a bucket of fish."

"And start smelling like your butt," Jack says.

"Better than you, garbage man."

Jack gargles a mouthful of shower water and spits it on the wall. The hairball washes across the floor and finds the drain.

"Well, I got breaking news. I got my ID," Jack lies.

Pickett doesn't fall for it, but he's thinking. Jack's inside his head. That's where he wants to be. He wants to find Pickett's buttons and tap-dance all over them.

"I got that ID and I'm going to stay here forever and ever. And another thing, I talked to Willie, he's going to give me a bunk right next to you so we can work out our differences. Isn't that cool? We get to wake up next to each other like brothers. I got to warn you, though, I get the morning farts." Jack sort of whispers. "They smell like herring."

Jack's laughter bounces around the community shower. Pickett isn't moving. Jack feels his anger rise. He senses it prickle beneath his skin. He watches a lump swell in Pickett's throat. He hates Jack.

And Jack loves it.

Pickett crosses the shower. Sheldon comes with him but flinches when water spatters off Jack.

"Man, that's ice water," Sheldon says.

Something is hitting the floor, like a hole punched in a bucket of rocks. Little pellets of ice are bouncing off a patch of blue skin on Jack's shoulder.

"What the...?" Sheldon says.

Ice chips pile on the floor. Jack's shoulder is making ice, but that doesn't faze Pickett. He holds his ground. He doesn't care if gold coins are dropping out of Jack's butt. His hatred blinds him to the impossible.

Jack wants him to step closer. He wants Pickett to reach out, to give him all his rage. Jack doesn't feel the emptiness when there's hatred around him. Maybe he doesn't need the Christmas spirit after all.

He can fill the emptiness with this tasty treat.

"Jack!" One of the staff steps inside. "Willie wants to see you, pronto."

No one moves.

"Ice was coming off him," Sheldon says. "You got to see it, man— water just turning to ice."

Pickett trembles but restrains his fury even when Jack winks.

"Everything all right, Jack?" the staff member asks.

Jack grins. "Perfect."

He dries off while the staff member watches. The others move away. Pickett is silent. Jack hums a little Christmas tune while he gets dressed.

"Nipping at your nose," he sings.

"WILLIE." Jack holds out his fist. "Knuck it."

"Don't do that."

Jack falls into a chair across from the desk. He had the old, military-green jacket buttoned near his throat to hide the blue patches on his chest. Willie stares at the back of Jack's hand.

Unfortunately, he couldn't hide that.

"What's going on, Jack?"

"What? This?" He points to the bald spot on his hand. "I got stung by a bee... or wasp, I think. I can't tell them apart."

"It's blue."

"I know, right? Weird."

Willie pinches his nose and closes his eyes. He still looks exhausted when he opens them. "You got to leave in two days, Jack."

"I know."

"Look, I've done everything to help you. You're not doing much to help yourself. You have no ID, no record, and no history. We can't let you stay here. You could be dangerous."

"How can I have no history, Willie? I'm here, right?"

"You know what I mean." Willie straightens a pile of papers. "I like you, Jack. But I'm worried."

"You're so worried you're kicking me out?"

"Don't give me that; take some responsibility. I got a feeling you know exactly what's going on and, to be honest, I feel like a damn fool.

I'm giving you a few days to make some plans, but after that, you got to go."

"Okay, cool." Jack pulls open his collar. It feels like a steam room inside his jacket. "That it?"

"You all right?"

"Yeah, fine. This weather's crazy."

"Thermostat's at sixty-eight."

One hundred and sixty-eight.

Willie taps the desk, thinking. "I'm concerned about your health, Jack. You don't look well. Maybe now you got a fever…"

Willie wants to say something else. He is suspicious, of course. Everyone jokes Jack isn't human, but the joke is wearing thin. It's starting to look a lot like the truth.

Of course it is the truth, but no one ever heard of an elven outside of bedtime stories. And Jack looks mostly human—a very strange and odd-looking one, but human nonetheless.

"Your hair is falling out, Jack. Your skin is blue."

"You calling me a freak, Willie?"

"I didn't say that. You don't look right. Your hair is kind of green, your skin blue. Your feet are snowshoes."

"That's racist."

"Cut it out."

Willie shakes his head, the braided ropes swinging across his forehead. Jack can taste his anger; he can feel it in the back of his throat. It has a different flavor than Pickett's anger, no hate mixed with it. Willie's anger has more sadness and regret.

Jack doesn't get as much pleasure from it. Maybe because he likes Willie.

"I'm sending you to a doctor before you go." Willie slides the papers over to Jack. "I must be out of my mind for not doing this earlier. I gave you the benefit of the doubt, figured you just had a skin condition or big foot disease, hell, I don't know. I just wanted to help you, that's all."

"I'm leaving in the morning."

"You don't have to."

"I got a plan, Willie. I'm leaving whether you kick me out or not."

"Let the doctor look at you, at least," Willie says.

Jack picks up the papers that summarize the health benefits of regular exercise and eating right. He pretends to read it because Willie's a good dude.

"Hey, Willie."

"Yeah?"

"You ever heard of Frost Plantation?"

SURA SLIDES the last hay bale from the truck and pulls her glove off with her teeth. The dry taste of grass and leather lingers on her tongue. She looks at her phone.

Why aren't you working? Joe texts.

Who says I'm not working? she types.

Sura takes a drink of water and wipes her brow. Her phone sounds off.

Frost said you're fired, he texts back.

Sura gloves up, grabs the twine, and lugs the bale across the backyard. If she starts replying, she won't get a thing done. And there's plenty to do. Fences need mending, the horses need trimming and hayed. Just this morning, the autofill valve on the water trough broke.

Her boots squish through the mud. The two horses follow along, heads bobbing, necks craning. She waves them off and spreads the hay. If she could seed the front pasture, they could graze a little easier. *Add that to the list.*

The phone buzzes. Frost just hired you back.

Sura marches to the shed and comes back with a bucket of tools. It takes fifteen minutes to fix the autofill valve. She waits while it fills the trough, pulling her list from her front pocket.

The hinge is broken on the side pasture. She uses baling wire to keep it in place until she can pick up supplies. Gerty wanders over while she twists the wire. Hot air blows into Sura's ear. Gerty's nostrils flare. Sura puts the pliers down and plays with her rubbery lips.

"You getting lonely, girl?"

Gerty nudges her onto her butt. Sura gets up to scratch the old workhorse behind the ears and finds the soft spot that rolls Gerty's eyes. The horse sways with pleasure.

"How are those hooves?" Sura picks up Gerty's front leg and inspects the dirt packed inside. She needs to trim the horses before the hooves start splitting—

Gerty jumps back, snorting and stamping.

"Hey, hey, hey." She tries to calm her, but the horse thunders off.

A gust of wind passes through the treetops.

A strange sensation haunts her. Sura has lived in the country long enough to know that thoughts are her worst enemy. The mind can transform thoughts into seething monsters. She looks around the open space, smells the fresh air, and hears dogs bark in the distance. The horses are in the corner of the pasture, as far away as possible.

Something doesn't feel right.

There's movement near a rotten log in the woods just on the other side of the fence. Twigs snap in the rustling leaves. She remains as still as a turkey hunter, eyes on the log.

Chills grasp her heart and run up her neck.

Something is looking back.

She remains frozen, not swaying with a gust of wind, eyes locked on the hole in the log. There's something on the other side, holding as still as her. Sura looks around without moving and spies the rusty T-stake lying on the ground. Her movements are slow and deliberate.

She opens the gate with one hand, the T-stake in the other. The horses throw a fit. Nothing moves near the log, but she still has a sense of being watched. She's had that feeling ever since she pulled up to the Frost Plantation entrance the very first day. She didn't mind the noises at the plantation, but she's not happy to hear them close to home.

Sura wraps both hands around the T-stake, the rough edges biting into her palms. Her first step into the trees is noisy, dead branches snapping under her boot. She stops and waits. The log is ten steps away and she still swears it's looking right at her.

Her arms ache with tension. Her steps are slow and steady, breath shallow, muscles taut, arms coiled, stake back—

Her pocket buzzes.

Sura jumps back and yelps, gasping for air.

Joe's smiling face looks back from her phone. "Hey," she says.

"What are you doing?" he asks.

She pokes the log with the T-stake. It sinks through the decayed wood. Spongy chunks fall away. Sura peeks over the top and sees the gnarly cypress knee emerging from the ground.

"Hunting," she says.

"Hunting what? Rabbits? You sound like you're chasing them."

"I'm kidding. I just got myself all freaked out, thought something was watching me."

"What do you mean?" His tone becomes tense.

"It's nothing. What are you doing?"

Pause. "Working, like usual."

"Poor baby. You need some help?"

"Actually, I do. But since you're taking a vacation day, I'll settle for lunch. You want to meet in town?"

Sura sits on the log. "Sure, I need to pick up supplies anyhow. What do you have in mind?"

"Meet me at my house, I'll pick you up and buy you lunch. I've got the Christmas spirit."

"I got an appetite."

"I don't know if I've got that much spirit."

Sura leans closer to the cypress knee. The top is pointed, which isn't unusual, but the burgundy color is. It almost looks like a cap. And the bark is extremely knobby, kind of looks like a face.

"Sura?"

"Yeah, sure." She rubs the cypress knee, the bark flaking off. "Lunch sounds good."

They say goodbye. Sura stuffs the phone in her back pocket and stares the cypress knee in the distorted face. Maybe she'll come back and cut it down, put it by the front door. It'd make a cool ornament.

She finishes working on the gate and cleans out the horses' hooves before checking her list of materials. The chills of being watched never fade.

It never occurs to her there are no cypress trees on her property.

JOE'S BACKYARD IS SMALL, with an oak tree, a little bit of grass, and a million mosquitoes. For a gardener, it lacks... everything. Sura sits on the back steps next to a concrete garden gnome, the tip of its nose chipped off. Joe texted that he was running late.

Back door is open.

She rests her arm on the gnome's pointy hat, waving off the blood-sucking insects. She checks her supply list and figures there's still plenty of time to get everything done. There might even be enough time to run out to the plantation around dinner.

The feeling of being watched got in the car with her. She turned around at a stoplight and checked the backseat. If she thinks about it, the feeling had gotten really strong when they picked up the homeless guy. He was easily the strangest-looking man she'd ever met and, quite possibly, the smelliest. What she didn't notice at the time was the surreal sensation she experienced when he slid into the front seat, when he turned around and smiled at her.

It was a quiver that radiated from her belly, like a bell had been struck. It was unsettling, frightening. She thought it was just fear, whether that man was going to do something weird.

Sura tips the weighty gnome back and stares into its blank eyes. The scrapes around the cheeks look like it's tumbled down the steps a few times. The hat is stained yellow. Paranoia clenches her chest.

The concrete gnome looks sort of like the cypress knee.

"I'm losing it," she mutters. "You hear that? I'm losing it."

She swats another mosquito and stands up. She's had enough fun talking to the gnome and feeding the mosquitoes. Sura puts her hands against the glass and stares through the back door. She's looking through the kitchen, but the house beyond is dark. The door's unlocked.

"Hello?" She barely cracks it. "Mr. Jonah?"

There are no trucks in the driveway, but it doesn't hurt to make sure the old man isn't napping on the couch and Joe forgot to tell her.

The house smells like a musty aisle in a library. A clock ticks above a dripping sink. The kitchen table is smothered with newspapers, notebooks, and a stack of plates. A crust of pizza is on top. She's officially breaking and entering into Jonah's house, and this puts her head in a spin cycle. She steadies herself on the kitchen table.

She starts clearing the dirty dishes, running water in the sink. The empty pizza boxes go in the trash, along with a soda bottle. The dishwasher gets loaded. She starts hand-washing the rest of the bowls and cups, piling them in the sink. She has to hunt for a dishtowel. A clean one is hooked on the refrigerator handle.

There are pictures on the freezer door.

They are printed on bond paper, the edges curling around flexible magnets. It's mostly photos of trucks and flowers, pictures of Jonah and Joe.

There's one of Jonah and an older man.

Sura drops the dishtowel and plucks the picture from behind the magnet. She holds it close to her face while grabbing the handle. Memories are coming back, things she's been forgetting, like images tucked behind a screen, out of sight for her recall. This picture raises the curtain, refreshes her memory.

The old man has to be Joe's grandfather because... *they look exactly alike.*

The picture of my mom and grandmother is gone. It was on the refrigerator. Someone took it.

Something scuttles through the living room.

Sura hangs on to the sink to keep from falling. Vertigo swishes inside her head; paranoia smothers her like a blanket. She can't get enough air; no matter how deep she breathes, there's not enough oxygen. The floor heaves like a ship riding up a wave. Her head feels like it'll crack, but her brain feels soft, overheated. Waxy.

She takes half a step toward the door when something crashes in the front room. Sura presses against the refrigerator. A yellow broom leans in the corner. She holds the bristled end, the plastic-tipped handle in front of her like a toy sword. Whatever is out there shuffles across the carpet. It's not a dog or a cat.

It mutters.

The words are all crammed together. *Bernie was talking like that.*

When she woke up the other morning, when there was a noise in the kitchen, her cockatoo was talking at the wrong speed.

It was in my house. And now it's out there.

She slides to the floor. The picture is crushed against the broomstick, which remains pointed at the living room entrance. If it comes at her, she'll poke it at least once. After that, she'll be no good.

She should crawl. She should run.

Each time she moves, there's another noise.

Instead, giant tears roll down her cheeks. It's too much. She just wants to sit there until it goes away.

Until it all goes away.

Mufflers rattle outside. A truck pulls into the driveway.

Joe walks through the back door. The sink is half full of dishes soaking in cold, flat water. Sura is in the corner, broomstick in one hand. She holds a piece of paper in the other.

"Sura!"

"What is this?" she says.

"Where'd you get that?" He starts towards her.

"No." She points the broom. "Why do we look just like our parents and grandparents?"

"Just put the broom down, and have a drink of water. You've had a rough day; let's talk."

She shakes her head, crumpling the picture. The floor feels spongy, her legs soft and wet. At first, she thinks she wet herself, but she's sweating through her clothes. The world is still spinning and she can't make it stop. There's a dreadful feeling that the lens through which she understands reality is about to come into focus; that the curtain around her world, the wall that protects her, is about to drop, and she'll see monsters behind it. Everything is a lie.

"Sura." Joe slowly crawls near her and gently touches her hand. "Come here."

"Something's in the house."

Joe stiffens. "What?"

"Something is moving, making noise." She swallows a hard lump. "Talking."

"Where?"

"All over." She swings the broomstick. "I wanted to leave but was afraid I'd keep running if I did, and I've got nowhere to go, Joe. There's nowhere for me to go!"

Sura's holding back tears, but panic has swelled in her throat, blurring her voice. The broomstick taps against the floor. Joe brushes the hair from her cheeks and cups the back of her neck. His hand is firm and warm.

He gets up, holds out his hand for her to stay, and steps into the living room. Something scurries away. The steps creak. She waits for Joe to come back, tell her a squirrel got inside, or the radio alarm is running... but he follows it upstairs!

Sura puts both hands on the broomstick. There are voices. One is Joe's; the other's too fast to understand. They're talking. He's having a conversation with whatever is out there. Heavy footsteps take the stairs three at a time.

Joe hustles into the kitchen. "Come on."

He pulls her off the floor. The broom clatters. Sura's legs start out like noodles. Joe wraps his arm around her and guides her out of the house. The living room is silent this time. They rush through the yard.

"What were you doing up there?" she asks.

"Just hang on, I'll tell you in a minute." He doesn't let go of her until they're through the gate and in the driveway. He opens the truck door. "I'll be right back."

He opens the garage and searches the shelves, tossing rolled sleeping bags, duffel bags, and boxes into the back of the truck. He swipes one whole shelf into a bag and tosses that back there, too. The items scatter across the bed.

He looks under the truck before climbing in.

His frantic pace slows once he's in the driver's seat, his fingers twisting the steering wheel. He looks back at the house.

"Turn off your phone." He puts his phone on the dashboard.

"Why?"

"I'll tell you everything, Sura, just do what I say for now, okay? We can't talk for a while, all right? You just need to let me get us somewhere first, and then I'll tell you everything I know."

The picture is balled in her fist. "Okay."

Joe backs out of the driveway, pauses in the road, and looks at the house. Doubt passes through him a third time. He shakes it off. Sura notices something.

The concrete gnome is gone.

MR. FROST STANDS on the back steps. The coolsuit feels loose around his midsection. He hasn't been eating, not enough to keep up his blubber. He'd often thought of losing the fat layer since the added insulation is more of a hindrance than a necessity. But he's elven. His body had adapted to the weight. Losing it would alter his chemistry.

And he is already feeling out of sorts.

The helicopter's thumping introduces its arrival before emerging from the winter clouds, its slow descent ruffling the grassy field, tan waves rolling toward the house. Mr. Frost squints. Once the additional skinfolds shielded his eyes from Arctic glare and driving sleet, they now protect them from dust.

Templeton talks with the pilot while the crew attaches cables to the steel shipping container. He used to rely on horse, buggy, and railroad. When the combustion engine was invented (Mr. Frost had a little something to do with that), his product was pulled on trailers.

Now it flies.

Particle teleportation is in the near future, but he may not be there to see it.

Once appropriate documents are signed to ensure the destination of Frost Plantation Christmas products, the tandem rotors hum louder, pushing air across the ground. Mr. Frost's coat whips around his legs. He pulls it closed, cinching the belt tightly, suddenly remembering the days in the Arctic when Claus—leader of the elven—would stand on the ice, surveying the landscape even in the worst of weather.

Claus was a good elven.

In his final days, he'd become a beaten elven.

Jack was his twin brother and a formidable foe. He brought the elven under his rule with a cold fist. Had the warmblood Nicholas Santa not stumbled into the Arctic region at the turn of the nineteenth century, the world would look much different than it does today. There would be no choppers carrying gifts to children across the world, no strands of lights twinkling on rooftops, or stockings decorating fireplace mantels. No eggnog, no tinsel, no Christmas trees, or ornaments. No cheer, happiness, or joy to all mankind.

Then again, mankind might already be extinct.

The chopper lifts off with a final thumbs-up, the rotors drumming the air. Templeton returns to the back steps and watches it recede into the clouds.

"He will return within the hour," Templeton says. "One of the containers appears to have stalled in a port outside Windsor Alberta, Ontario, but outside of that, all shipments have reached their destinations. We are ahead of schedule."

Mr. Frost's neck itches. Just as the helicopter fades, another appears. This time of year, the plantation is rarely silent.

Sir, I have bad news.

Mr. Frost nods to Templeton and leisurely walks towards the garden. Not until he passes through the arbor, once the ice statue is in sight, does he answer.

Yes?

Joe has taken Sura.

Where?

We don't know, sir. He packed the truck with camping gear and left the house. They turned off their phones.

Did the helpers follow?

Yes. But he crossed the Cooper River Bridge. They're a bit sluggish across water, sir.

Have them wait at the bridge.

She pauses. *They're not coming back; I think you know that, sir. Sura saw another picture and Joe promised to tell her everything. They're running, sir.*

Mr. Frost meanders down the path and sits on a bench facing Jocah's continually weeping effigy. It always brought him comfort to see Jack's mother, reminding him of what the elven once were: peaceful, thoughtful, and kind. She embodied all of that, what every elven should strive to become. But she was not perfect, either.

Life is imperfect, she would say.

Mr. Frost closes his eyes, troubled by the events he knows were inevitable, focusing to keep his thoughts still, to not let his innermost motivations rise to the surface, to keep them hidden from Freeda's watchful presence. Instead, he only lets her see his concern and worry, which is legitimate. Everything he'd worked to achieve for the last hundred years will come to fruition in the next couple of days. Sura needed to be ready.

Joe will reveal everything. *What if it's too much?*

I'm going to make a suggestion. Freeda waits for him to acknowledge her. *Templeton and May are required to operate Frost Plantation and, to some extent, so is Jonah. Sura has become problematic.*

Mr. Frost bristles.

I allowed your experimentation with her because I sensed your loneliness. You have used her to establish an emotional understanding of humans and that has healed you, allowed you to function. She's become a distraction.

There are several billion humans in the world, Freeda. I think it's worthwhile to understand them.

I fail to understand why you should take such a vested interest in a species that will soon become extinct.

Perhaps it's best to know what the world will become without them.

We aren't destroying them, sir. They will do it to themselves.

WE are not doing it, Freeda. It's Jack. Jack plans to destroy them. He paces around the statue. *Not ME. This has never been me!*

This argument is moot, sir. I'm programmed to assist you in your destiny.

Jack inserted the root. That is not destiny.

I'm afraid it is, sir.

Mr. Frost exits the garden. It's senseless to argue with the voice in his head. He stands beneath the arbor, watching the arrival of another helicopter.

Another shipment.

Another step closer to the end.

An end he cannot resist.

What about the children, sir?

She is digging in, asserting her will. She can do what she wants, but she's learned to make him feel like he's making his own decisions. It's much easier on his psyche that way.

I'll consider suspending Sura and Joe at New Year's.

It'll be over before then.

❄

JACK SLEEPS with the lamp shining on his face. Once that light brought him comfort and warmth, now it feels like red-hot coals on his eyelids.

He's been shedding like a dog. He scratches his cheek and peels off a thin sheet of skin. *Good one.*

Onto the dead-skin pile he keeps under the bed.

His skin has gone from pale blue to just blue—not Blue Man Group blue, though; blue like winter sky. His skin is smooth and icy; the darker the blue, the colder it feels.

But the more hair he drops, the more skin he peels, the warmer he feels. The bed has become less of a mattress and more like a skillet. The sheets crackle like frozen blankets.

He doesn't have to stay in the shelter; he knows where he's going. There is just a little unfinished business to tidy up first, and then he'll be on his way.

He feigns sleep—sometimes snoring, sometimes farting—and around the wee hours, he thinks maybe he made a mistake. Maybe he should just leave now and stop wasting time. Or maybe he'll have to be assertive, go get what he wants. He doesn't want it to end that way, but time is money.

Somewhere, footsteps fall on the polished floor.

I knew you wouldn't let me down.

A thrill rushes through Jack's belly. He watches through narrow slits. A figure creeps up behind the lamp and reaches for the switch.

Click.

It takes a moment for Jack's eyes to adjust, to see Pickett twisting the pillowcase, soup cans knocking inside. He looks around, one last time, before reaching back. He is going to whack Jack in the fat belly. He means to hurt him, teach him a lesson, show him who is king.

The big dummy.

He grabs Pickett's bare thigh, just below the bottom of his boxers, and gets a good handful of flesh, all soft and hot.

Pickett doesn't yelp.

Or move.

Jack feels the cold leave his fingertips, creep through Pickett's flesh, penetrate the tissue and muscle, and paralyze the nervous system. Pickett's anger melts like a chocolate drop on summer asphalt. It dissolves into something much more tangible, something acrid, slightly bitter. Jack can taste it through his hand and feels it linger in the back of his throat. That's why he stayed. He wanted to taste fear.

Pickett is full of it.

The pillowcase slips from his fingers.

Frost creeps across his skin, beneath his shorts. Pickett lets out a whimper.

Jack closes his eyes. And savors.

15

DECEMBER 20

Saturday

Willie arrives for the morning shift.

He checks with the overnight staff, inspects the kitchen, and peeks into the bunkroom, where the men are already up and dressed.

Jack's bed is empty.

Willie feels guilty. He can't help it. Doesn't matter if a resident deserves it or not, he doesn't like to tell someone they're not welcome. Once they leave, their future is cold and short.

And it's Christmas.

He straightens an ornament on the artificial tree, thinking if Jack comes back, that he'll take him to the doctor. If something is diagnosed, maybe he can make an exception. At least until the holidays are over.

"There a phone over there?" Mark asks.

"On the tree?"

"No, on the floor or something. I can't find my phone."

"Want me to call it?"

"No, I'll find it. Probably left it in the kitchen. By the way." Mark holds up an envelope and slides it across the front counter. "Someone left you a note."

Willie adjusts the star at the top and steps back to ensure everything looks good and balanced before looking at the white envelope.

Willie, it says.

He has no idea who it's from. In fact, he's shocked to see Jack's name at the bottom when he opens it. The little man scrawled like a third grader when he first arrived.

Even his handwriting has changed.

You're a pal, Willie.

Seriously, you got a good heart for a warmblood. I'm not saying all warmbloods are bad, most of them, yeah, sure, but not you, Willie. You're one of the good ones. Probably the only one. I'd be dead if it wasn't for you.

But I'm not.

And you belong to the problem, Willie. Warmbloods, that is.

So nothing personal, pal.

Bye.

Willie turns it over, nothing on the back.

Nervously, he looks out the front door, aware that he's envisioning a short fat maniac marching up the steps shouting "WARMBLOODS!"

"Willie!" Mark rushes out of the bunkroom.

"What is it?"

"Call 911." His face is chalky. "Something's wrong with Pickett."

Willie doesn't move for a second, clenching the note.

Later, when no foul play was suspected, that Pickett simply blacked out and couldn't remember why he was lying next to Jack's empty bed, Willie still kept the note. It always bothered him there was frostbite on his leg.

A wave slides across the hard-packed sand, sloshing over Sura's bare feet. It recedes back into the ocean, disappearing into the foam. She remembers coming out to Edisto Beach with her mom in the winter months. They'd cuff their pants and walk in the wet sand. Her mom loved the horizon. She used to say there's mystery out there—that you don't know what's beyond the flat line or what life has in store for you.

"Why don't we just sail out there and see?" Sura would say.

"Patience," her mom would say. "Life will come to you."

Sura didn't like that answer. There was a sense of hopelessness when she said it, like she was trapped, that she didn't have a choice to explore her life, didn't have an option to see what was out there.

"Think of it this way," her mom would say, "if we sail in that direction long enough, where do we end up?"

She would make a circle.

"We end up right where we started. We end up here. So let's not run; let's be here."

"What if we take a right turn? Think of all the new things we'll discover."

"We still end up here." Her mom smoothed Sura's hair. "It's not that easy, child."

Sura's footsteps dent the sand, fading as the water rolls in. The sweater Joe gave her is moldy and oversized. She slept in her clothes, hunkered down in the sleeping bag, too afraid to poke her head out. Joe's breaths were easy and long. He wouldn't tell her why he brought her out to Edisto, why they were hiding. They sat by a fire until the sun went down, and then crawled into the tent until the next morning.

Sura doesn't know how far she's walked or how long she's been out there, just that she needs to keep moving. The world is steady again, as long as she keeps moving. If she stops, maybe a monster will appear.

And Joe knows what it looks like.

She faces the horizon, the cuffs of her pants wet with salty spray. A few beachcombers are far to her right. A boy is coming towards her, bearing gifts wrapped in plastic, his pants rolled to the knees, bare feet in the surf. Joe is chewing on a cinnamon roll. He offers her one. She shakes her head.

They watch the sun climb.

"Why'd you bring me out here?" she asks.

He struggles with the words. She'd asked him that when they were sitting at the campfire last night, but he just shook his head. This time, the words come out slow and unsteady.

"I grew up out there," he starts, not looking at her. "So I don't expect you to understand."

"Grew up where?"

"The plantation. Jonah and I lived on the first floor in the southwest corner of the house. I had my own room, May cooked all the meals, and Templeton did the laundry. That's all I knew. Honestly, I remember thinking that's how it is when you're born, that living on a plantation with other servants is normal."

"And that's why you brought me out here?"

He digs at the sand with his toes. "Our parents used to be together."

Her stomach sinks. "You said that wasn't true."

"It doesn't have anything to do with us." He pokes at the sand. "Jonah said you wouldn't know anything about the plantation and I wasn't supposed to tell you, either; he made that clear. So I guess when I got to the house and that picture somehow got on the refrigerator..."

"What do you mean 'somehow'?"

"Someone told me it was time you knew the truth."

He was talking to someone upstairs. "Someone?"

He waves his words off, like maybe he shouldn't have said that. "I figured you should know, that's all. It's not fair that your mother moved off the plantation and took you with her."

"I never lived there."

"Jonah says you were there in the beginning, but not for long. He says Sesi was too smart to play along, that she'd evolved some instinct to leave."

"Play along?" Sura hugs herself tighter. "What's that supposed to mean?"

"It means Jonah loved your mom. He says she loved him, too, but there was something wrong with it. At least, that's what Sesi told him. She didn't want to keep loving him, didn't want to be in a relationship until she knew who she was. It was the reason for the whole Zen thing."

Joe didn't say it spitefully, although there were bitter undercurrents in his words. He sits in the soft sand, arms propped on his knees.

Her mom never spoke about Jonah. She never mentioned living on the plantation, only that she wouldn't stop working there. Sura always assumed it paid well. Maybe she couldn't leave it for other reasons.

Joe is picking up washed-up reeds, breaking them into little pieces. "You don't know what it's like holding all these secrets," he says. "Mr. Frost... you've seen him. He's not normal. I don't think he's even human."

"You think he's an elven?"

Joe shrugs. He doesn't want to say it, but what other explanation is there?

"Elven don't exist," she adds.

He laughs. It's unsettling. Long minutes pass as sandpipers scurry across the sand.

"He does experiments," he says. "Down in the basement. It's the reason why Sesi left the plantation, Jonah says. The reason why she left him."

"What kind?"

He breaks apart another reed, flicking the pieces. He starts chuckling, shaking his head.

"Why do you keep laughing?" she says.

"Because I'm afraid you're going to start running." He glances up, as if she might already be down the beach. When he sees she's still there, he takes a deep breath. "There are these little people that help out around the plantation. It's how we get everything done. Think about the gardens and the crops, the entire plantation. Jonah can't do all that. The helpers do it."

"What do you mean 'little people'? You mean like dwarves?"

"No, not dwarves." Joe holds his hand a foot from the ground. "These are tiny, little wrinkled men that move fast and talk even faster. They all look the same and wear crumpled-up clothes and bright color hats."

Bright hats.

The cypress knee.

The concrete statue.

The plantation kitchen is big enough to feed an army.

Sura feels woozy again.

"I used to know their names when I was little," Joe says. "They used to play with me. We'd hike through the woods, climb trees, and hunt rabbits. Imagine wrestling a hundred of these little guys, all at the same time. It was like a mountain of puppies. They never slept, always laughing."

He breaks off a small piece and compares it to a long reed. His smile fades.

"They changed, though."

"How?"

"A couple of weeks ago, they got more serious and stopped talking to me. Jonah says that's what they're supposed to do, not treat me like a baby. Says I'm supposed to be normal, interact with other people, not the helpers. I guess it was the same for him."

"He grew up on the plantation?"

"We all grew up on the plantation."

"What's that mean? Who are 'we'?"

Joe takes a deep breath. "When it comes down to it, Jonah says the helpers work for Mr. Frost; they do what he says. Something's going on and I got a bad feeling. I think they've been following us. Watching us."

"They were in the house."

"They're not mean, just up to something. One of the yellow-hats was upstairs and told me we needed to run away."

"I thought you said they changed."

"The ones with the yellow hats haven't. That's why we left so quickly and turned off the phones, so the rest wouldn't follow. They can't cross bridges, at least not very quickly. We lost them on the bridge. They're probably waiting for us to come back."

"That's why we came out here? So you could tell me all this?"

He holds the sticks and looks up. "The helpers all look the same, Sura, because they are the same. Mr. Frost is trying to make someone in his basement. The helpers are part of the experiment, like practice. They do other things for him, too, but I think he's been practicing and he doesn't want us to know about it."

"Know what? That he's cloning little people, making them work like slaves?"

She's focused on the injustice, the crimes against nature. If the authorities knew what he was doing, they'd throw him in jail for life.

Joe doesn't say anything else. He's waiting.

Her knees weaken. Her feet are like bricks. It's the way Joe's looking at her, waiting for her to put it together.

The helpers all look the same.

He takes a big stick, breaks it in half, and holds the smaller pieces side by side.

My mom and grandmother.

He lines all the little pieces next to each other in the sand.

His dad and grandfather.

She takes half a step back. Numbness reaches her face, seeping into her brain.

They all look the same.

"You don't have a mother, Sura," he says softly, putting the last piece into place. "You never did."

Sura bolts away, blindly. She can't feel her legs. Tears brim on her eyelids. She runs and runs and runs.

Time to wake up.

JACK FALLS AGAINST A TREE.

"Someone kill me," he mutters. "Kill me, right now."

His tongue lolls like a workhorse driven daylong in July heat. He slides down the rough bark and hikes up his foot to inspect the burning sole. Some of the small scales have chipped away. His ankles feel like they were assembled with rusty bolts. If there was just an ice hole somewhere he could dip his feet.

He licks his parched lips.

Blindly, he searches the bag slung over his shoulder and pulls out a half-full plastic bottle of Coke he found on the road. The bottle swells as the contents freeze when he touches it, the plastic crackling with a frosty sheen.

He rolls it against his cheek, across his forehead, and over his bald scalp. The hair is all gone. The flaking skin sticks to the bottle. Despite the fact he feels like the glowing tip of a blacksmith's iron, his head is blue.

He rams the bottle on the tree's root flare. It takes ten pathetic attempts before the frozen plastic shatters, but then the block of soda rolls through the dirt and into the weeds.

"That's how it is?" He looks up at the gray sky. "I just wanted a lick and that's what I get? All right. Okay. I'll just not drink anything; how'd you like that?"

He throws the bag on his lap and continues to curse under his breath. When things go wrong, he curses at whoever did this to him (he's not sure who it is, but he looks up when he does it), and sings the stupid song about a silent night.

Song's not working!

He digs through the bag of stuff: empty cans, a few butts, a swollen magazine, and an old carton of Chinese food. He had licked the insides and it tasted fishy. He knew it'd take a while to walk to Frost Plantation—no one was going to give him a ride—just didn't realize it would be *in the belly of a furnace!*

The black case is at the bottom, just below a Skittles wrapper.

"All right, concentrate." He closes his eyes, draws a deep breath, and holds it. He pulls all the coldness into his core. The temperature of his hands equalize with the surrounding air.

His gut feels like he swallowed a campfire.

"Here we go."

He pulls the phone out of the bag. Delicately holding it with two fingers, he touches the screen. The map lights up. A blue dot illustrates where he's at, right now, leaning against a giant tree. The red dot isn't far. He looks at the dirt road disappearing into the thick forest.

The phone rings.

Mark's calling, again. He wants his phone back.

Jack releases the pent-up cold, engulfing the weeds in a crystal-lizing cloud. The phone turns into a block of ice. The glass cracks. Jack crushes it, shards trickling from his fist.

The sun is below the trees. Jack throws the bag in the ditch, stumbles to his feet, and waits for a filthy truck to pass. It honks.

Jack gives it the one-finger salute.

He crosses the boiling asphalt. "Ow. Ow. Ow. Ow. Ow. Ow."

The dirt road is rutted and slightly damp, a sliver of relief on his beaten feet.

His steps, though, are small and wobbly. It could be all night before he gets anywhere. He can't think about that, has to focus on moving ahead, going forward. Jack closes his eyes, follows the ruts, and occupies his mind with something good: his last memory.

A party. A big one.

The elven were throwing a party to honor Jack, to celebrate his victory. There'd been a long war called the Fracture. He dwells on this for several moments, the thrilling sensation of winning, of being good and right and on top of the world, offsetting the agony of this boilerplate.

Jack bumps into a tree and staggers back onto the road.

Not only that, it was his mother he beat. She was the one that caused the Fracture in the first place. She kept him down; she was the one that didn't believe in him.

She loved Claus.

She always liked him better. Right from the start, she wanted Claus to win and Jack to go away. She ignored him.

They all ignored him.

Well, he showed them. Jack *is* good. He's better.

He doesn't actually remember the party, just waiting for it. The last memory, the very last, final, end-of-the-line thing he can remember is giving another elven a little tin box. It was his friend. His only friend. Pawn.

Whatever happened to him?

Jack opens his eyes. "Hey, look. There's the ground—"

He hits the dirt.

Face first.

JACK'S SLIDING on his back.

The ice is rough. His face hurts. He can feel his heart beating in his nose. But it's not ice, he's not in the Arctic... it's mud.

Jack sits up. Actually, he doesn't do anything, but he feels his body sit up, feels something hold him upright.

He blinks.

The world is fuzzy. And blazing hot.

Tiny lights. Iron bars. A giant F. Lots of frilly branches and berries. Right now, he just wants to lie down, take a little nap. Won't hurt him if he sleeps, but something won't let him. Something holds him up.

"Hey." He looks lazily to his sides. "You guys look like me."

He's right. Pointy noses. Square chins. Not a single hair on their faces. The only difference is the skin color: dark yellow instead of blue. And the hats. They have floppy, colorful hats.

"You're handsome little buggers." Jack leans back, head swimming with thoughts, none of which make much sense. The little ones grunt to keep him upright and from getting squashed. Jack sways with the shifting weight.

"Like a massage," he says. "Feels good—hey, I remember. You helped me in the woods. That was you. 'Member when the bear was going to eat me?"

Maybe they answer. Maybe not.

Jack wants to sleep because the heat is killing him; it's cooking his brain like an egg. He can feel the yolk solidify.

Welcome back, sir.

"Aaahhhh!"

That voice is inside Jack's head.

JONAH IS SHEARING THE BOXWOODS. He's without helpers today and Joe never returned from lunch. There was no answer when he called. Later, he'll come home to an empty house. There will be no note, no message.

No Joe.

Jonah is not Joe's birth father. They may be clones, but they're human, they become attached. He won't sleep tonight and he'll mourn when Joe is still not home in the morning.

In the beginning, there was May and Templeton. Jonah came later. Their DNA was snatched from unsuspecting immigrants that came through the Charleston port—a sly prick of a needle was all that was needed. The three were approved by Freeda and did the sorts of things Mr. Frost didn't have time to do.

Sura, however, was a surprise.

When Mr. Frost escaped the North Pole, the Inuit took him into their village. The man that found him was named Pana. Mr. Frost was given a bed in his shelter. His wife had died giving birth to their only daughter.

Her name was Sesi. It meant "snow."

Day after day, they fed Mr. Frost and cared for him. Nighttime was the worst. That's when the root would ignite his brain and Mr. Frost would thrash away the animal skins and tear at the hair on the back of his head. Sesi would kneel next to him with a wet rag and dab his forehead, while spittle collected at the corners of his mouth. In the morning, he would be exhausted. Sesi would bring him something to eat.

It wasn't long before the village wanted him out. Clearly, he was possessed by demons. If he stayed, they would all become possessed. Pana, though, would not let them exile him. Mr. Frost was still too weak to survive on his own. It was Sesi, though, that argued with her father to keep Mr. Frost. She insisted they resist the village. Reluctantly, he listened.

Sesi fed Mr. Frost while Pana stood guard. She would hum a song while she dabbed his forehead. The wordless tune floated from her lips, soothed his aches, and filled his loneliness. Yet each night, the root raged with fury, demanding that he go south. The village elders were insistent. If Mr. Frost was not banished, Pana and Sesi would be.

On a night when Pana and Sesi slept soundly and the root remained quiet, Mr. Frost slipped from their shelter. He took with him furs and frozen seal meat to begin his journey. He also possessed skin cells that he'd scratched from their arms unexpectedly. At the time, he didn't know why he took them. It was much later that he retrieved Sesi's sample and fused it with a human egg cell.

Sesi was reborn.

Mr. Frost pretended it was a variation of May, but Freeda soon learned the truth. Her anger was furious. *This is not acceptable!* She punished Mr. Frost, reminding him how hotly the root could still burn. She threatened to flush all the tanks, to start over according to the plans laid out in the root.

But Mr. Frost convinced her otherwise.

I need her.

Freeda was not rigidly bound to the root's scripture. She had freedom to assess and modify. She needed Mr. Frost to operate efficiently and effectively. It was clear that he responded better to the carrot than the whip.

Now Mr. Frost had something to live for. He argued that Sesi would help him understand the human condition. Why did Pana and Sesi care for him against the village's wishes? Why did they risk their own well-being for a stranger?

This understanding would only help him complete Jack's mission.

Sesi also motivated the others, in particular Jonah. And she brought newfound life to an otherwise drab plantation. Productivity increased, cloning techniques advanced, spirits soared... all of which brought Jack that much closer, that much sooner. Freeda allowed Sesi to become part of the family.

Perhaps it was no accident that Sesi changed her daughter's name to Sura.

"New life," it meant.

And now Freeda wants to take her away. Perhaps she knows what Mr. Frost is planning.

Sullen, he slides away from the window, away from the view of Jonah bending to clean up his mess. If only his life were as simple as the gardener's.

Freeda?

She doesn't answer. She'd been quiet most of the day, said she was analyzing data. His spies have informed him why: she's bringing Jack home.

She's distracted.

He must act as if he doesn't know. He needs his spies, now more than ever. He slides near the center of the room, commanding the room to transform into a replication of the laboratory. Tables and tanks rise from the floor, monitors hover above him. A long, metal table takes shape in the center, a body flickering into view.

Jack's newest incarnation is breathing on its own.

There's less hair on this one. His cheeks are still moist from the immersion tank, lips swollen and saturated. Mr. Frost watches the data scroll on several monitors. They could start uploading memories tonight.

He could be awake by morning.

What if there are two of them?

He closes his eyes, taking a deep breath. Mr. Frost thought he'd be ready for this day—there were times he begged for it—but now he's not so sure. *What if I fail?*

He wipes the room empty with a thought. He'll go to the lab and get a closer look at the body. There's a chance he could tweak something, delay the maturation. Two fully awakened incarnations of Jack would create complications.

Sir, there's no need for you to come to the basement.

Mr. Frost is startled by the sudden voice. *I just want to see it.*

That's not necessary, sir. There's been a delay in the maturation of certain organs. I suggest we give the incarnation three days to develop before attempting an awakening.

That disagreed with his data. *Jack must be home!*

Are you sure? he quickly thinks.

You look haggard, sir. I suggest you relax today and return to the lab tomorrow. Let me monitor the basement. I've prepared the coolsuit. Would you care for a walk?

Mr. Frost hesitates. Her tone is unusually calm and placating, especially for this time of year. Especially concerning matters of Jack. Perhaps she's mocking him, and at some level she's known his plan all along and she's taking pleasure in its demise.

That sounds splendid. Please have Templeton meet me in the garden. I'd like to visit the wishing room.

He dons the coolsuit.

JACK REMEMBERED the day the cold tub was invented.

He had leaned over the square tub, the contents blue and bubbly. He wanted to believe it was as cold as they said it would be. *Salt water and isopropyl alcohol,* the elven scientists told him. *It's cold.*

Jack touched it with his toe. The solution was cool and frothy. He dropped his leg in, eased his body over the edge, and let its icy embrace wrap around him like a frozen blanket.

I don't remember it hurting my face.

His eyes snap open.

There's no cold tub. No beautiful, ice-blue water.

He's on a table, staring at a menacing hunk of metal suspended from a gray ceiling. But the room is *cooooold.*

It is minus fifty degrees. How does that feel, sir?

Jack jerks up. He's not alone.

There are fifty others in the room. Maybe more. Identical little squirts, good-looking fellows, all with bright hats of different colors. They're staring at Jack.

"Which one of you said that?" Jack said.

I did, sir.

He heard it again, only none of them moved their lips. He could squash them two at a time if he has to start stepping.

My name is Freeda, sir. You don't remember me, so let me take a moment to explain. I am an artificially intelligent organism currently residing in the home network. I am linked to your brain through a tiny processor that's embedded at the base of your skull and wired into your nervous system. You are my creator, sir.

"You're right. I don't remember."

I know, sir. We will remedy that.

"Okay, I'm down with that. First, make them stop staring. It's creepy."

We made them in your honor, sir.

"Great. Now make them leave in my honor."

Without hesitation, they march out. A few stay behind, still staring —two red-hats, one blue.

"You guys stuck to the floor? Follow the leaders and get out."

I will need them for the upload.

"Upload?"

Your memories, sir.

The menacing hunk of metal begins to lower from the ceiling. Things tick and hum inside its girth.

"Put a hold on the upload." Jack leaps off the table, away from the gleaming descent of metal. "Where am I?"

Frost Plantation.

"This is it?" He looks around a plain and relatively empty gray room. No windows, no chairs. Just three creepy little gnomes that look exactly like Jack and a giant weapon. And a table.

You are in a subterranean laboratory, one of several. We built it according to your instructions, sir. It is located in a warm climate.

"Yeah, I don't remember that."

Your assistant carried your plans, in a similarly imbedded processor, far away from the North Pole to hide, sir.

"Imbedded processor?"

Pawn calls it the root.

"Pawn is here?" Jack looks around like someone might be hiding behind his back. "Where is that little devil?"

He is occupied with other matters.

Jack vaguely remembers a rice-sized processor that his scientists had invented to carry all his memories. Jack wanted a backup, just in case things didn't work out. *Looks like they didn't.*

Your instructions were quite genius.

"Please continue."

I can't reveal more, sir. Your data, or memories, need to be uploaded in order to rapidly integrate with your psyche. Otherwise, you won't assimilate. Trust me, sir, we can't risk epileptic shock now. You've come too far.

"Shock, huh?" The floor is slick. He shoves off with his left foot, sliding around the perimeter of the room. It feels so good on his sole.

"I wake up with green hair in the middle of warmblood country and you think I can't take a little stress?" He continues sliding. "Talk, lady. Why the green hair?"

Green follicles were used for photosynthesis, adding additional carbohydrates while your body stabilized and evolved. They fell out as they were no longer needed.

"That was *my* plan?"

Mr. Frost improvised when there were... failures.

"I want to see... wait, who's Mr. Frost?"

You knew him as Pawn.

"Then why'd you call him Mr. Frost?"

He changed his name. It was a psychological move on his behalf. In effect, he wanted to forget his past. He's not happy with your plan, sir.

"Well, I'll make him happy." He slides to the door, but it's locked.

You can't leave, sir. It's imperative that you're uploaded first. These are your orders, sir. Your genius orders.

Perhaps if the uploader didn't look like it was going to lobotomize him, he would've been more easily swayed.

He crosses his arms and stands firmly.

Do you feel that, sir?

"Feel what?"

The vibration.

Jack notices the humming sensation in his belly. It's the same feeling he experienced around Sura. It's warm and sensuous. It feels good, feels right. And Jack likes that.

You're synchronizing with the energy around you, sir. You're home. This is where you're supposed to be. And I know what I'm doing. Trust me, sir. You invented me.

"I did?"

You want to remember everything before you leave this room.

Jack sighs. It can't be a coincidence that all the little guys look like him. He climbs onto the table. The little ones help him. A beam of light ignites from the bottom of the uploader. Crosshairs appear on his face. A little one with a red hat adjusts his head until the crosshairs line up between his eyes. The one wearing a blue hat holds up a rubber mouthpiece and taps it on Jack's lips.

"What's that?"

Precautions, sir.

"This better not hurt."

Blue-hat shakes his head. Taps again. Jack opens wide and the plastic fills his mouth. Perhaps the alarms in his head would be ringing louder if the vibrations in his belly didn't feel so good, convincing him this was the right thing to do.

A red-hat climbs next to the table.

"W'as 'at?" Jack jerks his eyes at the cord in his hand.

Fiber optics, sir.

"W'as it do?"

Connecting you to the uploader. You might feel a little pressure.

Pressure?

Before he can leap from the table and swat away the metal demon and its handsome little henchmen, the cable rams into the back of his head.

MR. FROST SLIDES around the circle of ice, the surface smooth and clear. Snow is piled around it. The sun hangs like a dull orb.

Elven like to have the sky over them during times of stress. They like to see the flatness of the polar ice caps and undisturbed snow that's white, pristine, and perfect, glittering in daylight.

They also like to keep moving.

Does she know my plans? Has she already planned a counterstrike?

Mr. Frost never thought Freeda would be so secretive if she discovered his elaborate plan. He'd always assumed she would strike as she always did when he broke the rules: swiftly and painfully.

A golden string suddenly dangles in midair just outside the circle of ice. A hand emerges from the center and parts the air. Templeton steps through the wishing room entrance, pocket watch in hand. He lets the opening close behind him and the golden string vanishes.

The snow is up to his knees. "If it's not asking too much..."

Mr. Frost waves his hand. The snow melts around Templeton to reveal a Persian carpet. A leather chair emerges from it along with a freestanding fireplace, logs already blazing.

Templeton sits without a word, crossing his legs and folding his hands.

"Jack has returned to the plantation." Mr. Frost continues his meditati
ve slide, hands folded on his belly.

"Are you positive?" Templeton asks.

"The yellow-hats confirmed it."

Templeton's composure is stiffer than usual. "This meeting is risky."

"She's distracted. This will be the only time to speak with you." He makes one complete circle. "The end is near."

Templeton nods thoughtfully. "You appear agitated. I assumed the end would bring relief."

"Freeda is behaving unexpectedly. She did not inform me that Jack had been located. In fact, she lied. I'm afraid she's up to something, Templeton. If she knows what I'm planning, this could end very differently."

"What do you think she's doing?"

"I don't know. There's another incarnation of Jack in the incubation lab that's close to awakening. Maybe she's going to use both of them."

Templeton drums his fingers across his knee, watching Mr. Frost go around and around. When he's near, Templeton says, "Perhaps we should kill them both."

Mr. Frost looks up. "That won't solve anything. The root will bring him back, bring Freeda back... even I can be reincarnated to continue the work. Death is only temporary. Transformation is the only solution, Templeton."

"Then let's destroy Freeda and Jack. It will buy us some time before you are forced to bring the operation back online."

Mr. Frost imagines the agony the root will put him through for such a transgression, forcing him to reinvest in another facility to bring back Freeda and start all over. He's too tired for that. Besides, Freeda will know what he did. She will adjust for it. Now is the best chance.

It must be now.

Mr. Frost stops. "Joe and Sura are safe. The helpers were directed to sequester them. I have reason to believe Freeda was planning to end them. Thankfully, the yellow-hats were there to inform Joe where to go."

"I see. And then what will they do?"

"Joe knows."

"They'll come back to the plantation?"

"When it's time."

"It's too risky," Templeton says. "You created them, but you don't have the right to put them in danger. They are human; they have a right to choose their fate."

"And they will. I cannot force them to return."

"But they will, you know it."

"I'm counting on it."

Templeton slowly walks to the fire. "Sura won't have the same effect on Jack as she does you. The human experience takes time to assimilate." He looks sternly at Mr. Frost and whispers, "He'll hurt her."

"No, he won't. He has synchronized with her energy, Templeton. He feels bonded to her, even Joe. If he's near them again with all his memories, I believe he will transform at that moment. He'll change."

Templeton remains quiet. Mr. Frost digs through his whiskers to scratch his chin, sliding in circles. It's risky, of course. All he needs to do is get them together, and he's certain Jack will change. It's what Mr. Frost has been counting on.

He turns his back on Templeton, sliding across the patch of ice. Four incubation tanks are now embedded in the once-pristine snow. The glass is frosted. Mr. Frost stops in front of them and looks up with his hands on his belly. If Jack doesn't change, well then, Mr. Frost has other plans.

Because nothing is certain.

"I want you to wait for Joe and Sura," he says, "and make sure they find me. Afterwards, take May and Jonah to the south end of the plantation until this is over."

Mr. Frost drags his fingers over one of the tanks, leaving trails on the glass. A vague form looks back from inside.

"You could hide with us, you know."

Mr. Frost touches the back of his head. "Jack must transform, but the root, Templeton, must be destroyed."

Templeton stands at the edge of the rug, hands at his sides. His chin is tipped up, his shoulders back. "Then I shall see you when this is over."

Mr. Frost looks up at Templeton. "Be safe, my friend."

"Of course."

"Don't make my only regret that I wasn't able to get more tanks into the wishing room."

"We aren't meant to live forever."

"If only everyone believed that."

"Perhaps you can remind Jack when you see him."

"I doubt he'll be in the listening mood."

Templeton takes the watch from his front pocket. It glows. The golden string appears. He parts the space. The dense foliage of the tunnel is visible.

Templeton turns before exiting. "It's been a pleasure serving you, sir."

"The pleasure has been mine."

Templeton steps through the opening. The space of the wishing room returns to an endless vista of snow.

And Mr. Frost continues sliding.

JACK DRINKS memories from a fire hose plugged into the back of his head. He has the urge to urinate, the sensation of bursting, the horror of panic. There's too much to make sense, data pouring inside his head, his skull cracking. Occasionally he catches a tidbit, a small snack of information, something that makes sense.

They hate me.

That's one. He didn't like that one, but it's true: the elven did hate him. They don't anymore because they don't know where he is. And they don't know where he is because...

I'm dead.

Jack feels like he's falling into a very deep, very dark, and very cold hole. Even for Jack, this feels cold.

Lonely.

Dark.

And somewhere in the bottom, he begins to understand what everything means. He's told that he died when he sank through the ice, holding his mother and brother; he died in their embrace and understood that they loved him.

He remembers planning for death.

The scientists showed him the tiny pellet, said it would hold all his memories—even the ones he forgot. It would also contain the blueprint of his DNA and the directions to escape in case he kicked the bucket.

You just need someone to carry it, they said. *Someone you trust with your life.*

That was easy. Jack knew exactly who would carry it. He didn't know what it would do to Pawn, didn't really care, just knew that if anything happened, Pawn would keep him safe and nothing would hurt him. Jack would come back.

The plan would bring him back.

It's a complex plan, only one a mastermind could understand and, thankfully, Jack is one. It's also one that might be construed as diabolical, dastardly, and mean-spirited. As vile, foul, and nasty.

And genius.

As the data continues filling him up, Jack settles at the bottom of this deep, dark, and cold hole. When all the memories are forced into his brain and find their rightful place, he understands.

His body is shaky and cold, bluer than blue. His heart, smaller than small, tiny as a pebble, and hard as folded steel. Cold as deep space.

He snaps open his bloodshot eyes.

He fully understands.

THE PUPPET

Her mother called it a marionette.

The girl didn't think she'd like it. Compared to the laptop and the bicycle, a puppet didn't look like that much fun. But when she got the hang of the control bar, when she learned to move the legs and arms, was able to make her puppet sit and walk, why, it was all she played with.

She made clothes for her puppet and named her. Her father made her a little bed to sleep next to her. When she did her plays, the puppet took on a life of its own.

But one day, when she wasn't looking, her brother cut the strings.

The puppet fell in a heap. Elbows and knees were bent the wrong directions, and the head cocked to the side. Her father said he could tie the strings, make it new again.

But the girl said no.

"Why?" the father asked.

"The puppet wants to be free."

16

DECEMBER 21

Sunday

om.

MThe word had changed. It had transformed into something stuck in Sura's throat. All her memories were a lie. Bedtime stories, late-night movies, days on the horses... lies, lies, lies.

Because she's not my mom. Never was.

All that talk of independence and truth, all that crap about enlightenment... the nights sitting at the dinner table when she'd say, "Wake up, Sura, and know yourself. You'll be set free."

How could her mom expect her to understand truth when it was disguised in words and fleeting meanings? Why couldn't her mom sit down and explain it like Jonah did with Joe?

Sura runs on the beach as far as she can. She can't feel her knees when she falls. That's when she pulls her legs against her body and cries.

Sand sticks to her. *A billion grains, each unique in color and shape.*

Did her mom say that? Sura remembers walking the beach and that line coming out of the blue—her mom telling her that there were a billion grains of sand, each one special.

Was she trying to tell me something?

She can't sit still or the surreal sense of vertigo will strangle her. She walks, suppressing the urge to run so she doesn't have to stop. As long as she's moving, she can tolerate the truth.

Maybe she's always known it, deep inside. Still, there's not enough space in the world to face it head-on. Not enough air to breathe the ugly truth.

I'm a clone.

❄

THE WIND DIES.

Sura's musty sweater is around her waist. The sun bites her cheeks, but her feet are still bare, much like her heart. The beach is empty except for an occasional beachcomber. The vacation homes look and feel empty.

She hasn't eaten since the day before, but hunger gives her something to grasp. She can't shake the sensation of falling, of spinning out of control.

Why am I here?

What's my purpose?

Who am I?

All those questions her mom used to ask now haunt and betray her.

Sura walks until the sand turns to swaths of seashells. She crosses mats of washed-up reeds and climbs over jetties meant to reduce erosion. She passes condominiums, abandoned sailboats, and broken surfboards. She finds a long stretch of empty beach that leads to a spit of sand, where someone stands with hands in pockets, watching the waves.

She's too tired to turn around. Too empty to run.

Joe doesn't turn as she nears. He doesn't watch her flop onto the sand. Exhaustion pulls her onto her elbows. Her cheeks are reddened by sun and wind. Joe pulls a water bottle from his pocket. She chugs it while he watches the waves roll, ceaselessly.

"She loved you," he says.

Sura dips her head, too tired to hold it up.

"That's why she left Jonah," he adds. "She loved you."

"She was made to love him." Sura notices the magnetic attraction intensify as they talk. "Just like I was made to love you."

"Imagine how hard it was for her to deny that love," he says. "Every day, her heart telling her one thing, but her mind something else. Every day she ignored her feelings for Jonah to do what's right—to search for the truth. She must've suffered greater than him."

Sura's mom always looked tired, always looked like she had been pulling extra weight. Sura always figured it was depression and sometimes asked her to look into medication. They learned in school depression could be treated chemically. Feelings are chemicals, someone said. *Love, too.*

"None of this is real," Sura says. "My feelings for you are just hormones interpreted by my brain. It's programmed into my DNA. I'm just a script that's programmed to be attracted to you for Mr. Frost's sick little entertainment. He designed us that way, assembled us like that."

"We're cloned, Sura. Not assembled."

"And the difference?"

"We're human. We're flesh, blood, and tissue. We're no different than everyone else, just conceived differently."

"We sprang from a petri dish and that makes us human? We're an experiment, Joe. We're Frankensteins that fooled everyone, including ourselves." She dips her head. "What's worse, you've known all along."

"Yeah, but I understand, Sura. It's not how we start that matters. It's who we are."

"You need to wake up."

She dips her head again. Tears swell without falling.

"It hurts me to see you this way," he says.

She resists the temptation to run to him, to get lost in his embrace, to forget the world, to erase the truth, and just fade back into ignorance and his sweet essence that hums so strongly inside her.

"Why'd he do this?" she says.

"Do what?"

"This." She pats her chest. "Why'd he create us?"

"Jonah said it had something to do with Jack."

"Who's that?"

He shrugs. "The entire plantation has to do with him."

We're cogs in a machine meant to build Jack, is that it? Just parts that click and clack and, in the end, out spits a clone named Jack?

"I don't want to be a cog," she whispers.

"We'll find out." He takes her hand. "The yellow-hat said we have to find Mr. Frost."

She's so tired, so bereft, that when he reaches for her, she falls into his arms, lets his warmth envelop her. She nuzzles into the crook of his neck.

I don't have the strength to resist him. Not like you, Mom.

Maybe, she wonders as they walk to the truck, she's not exactly like her mom after all.

MR. FROST EMERGES from the live oak grove. He stops to admire the Christmas lights. Each year, they add more. It's a reminder there is joy in this world.

He continues his late-night stroll, returning from deep in the trees where the land is mostly wet and wild, where alligators slumber for the winter and tree frogs happily sing. He'd grown accustomed to the green environment, never thinking he'd ever prefer it over the pure white Arctic.

His wide feet crush the dormant pasture as he slowly slogs toward the house, using the peaceful surroundings to process all these feelings, these difficult emotions that wrestle inside like baboons.

He hears a distant cheer, feels it beneath his feet. He's standing over the toy factory. The helpers must've accomplished quite a goal, all of them cheering at the same time.

Freeda? he thinks.

She hasn't responded for hours. Perhaps she's not pretending anymore.

A thick mug awaits him on the porch. Mr. Frost takes a sip of frothy fish oil, a blend of something exotic. Eel extract, his favorite. A light sensation passes from his taste buds into his head, lifting the worried thoughts. Suddenly, he finds Christmas cheer as accessible as an afternoon nap.

He walks around to the back of the house while downing the drink. He enters the basement doors, sliding down a slick ramp and unzipping the coolsuit before throwing open the toy factory doors.

The raucous noise is deafening.

Mr. Frost smiles, the exuberance contagious. He even feels his feet begin to shift, tiny little taps in time to the music. Someone is butchering the piano, but how can he not celebrate? Everyone is wildly dancing, standing on each other's shoulders, slinging mugs of drink, and rolling on the floor... where a blue elven pounds on an electric keyboard.

Mr. Frost's feet stop.

Jack throws his arms out and the music halts. A wide, toothy grin expands.

"PAWN!"

The helpers repeat after Jack. *Pawn! Pawn! Pawn!*

It's a name Mr. Frost hasn't heard for hundreds of years. A name Jack gave him when they were young. A name Mr. Frost secretly hoped never to hear again.

The dancing continues as Jack stutter-steps his way to the entrance, taking the time to do-si-do with helpers along the way. He pushes up the ramp and circles around Mr. Frost with his arms up. The helpers cheer madly.

"Hey there, old buddy, old pal," Jack whispers.

The helpers surge up the ramp, clinging to Jack's baggy pant legs, begging him not to leave, like they've been waiting a lifetime for him.

Which they have.

"Let me introduce you to a few friends." Jack slaps his arm over Mr. Frost's shoulders, biting cold sinking through the fabric. "They all look, well, pretty much the same, but the hats give them away. That's Crayman, that's Char, that's Gabbit, that's Farty... that's, um, Dummy... oh, I ain't got all day."

Jack raises his fist.

"To the tower!"

The cheers rattle Mr. Frost's eardrums.

"Not you!" Jack swings his hands, shooing them away. "Get back to work; make those toys, all of you. Christmas needs its workers and you're it."

They scramble like programmed slaves. *Which they are.*

The machines fire up, the production lines move along, and a song lifts into the air, a merry little number that keeps their spirits strong and productive.

"I love those handsome little devils," Jack says. "Now what do you say you and me do some catching up?"

THE ELEVATOR TAKES LONGER than usual to begin moving. The floor is crackling with veins of frost. Mr. Frost studies Jack's reflection in the shiny doors before a layer of frost creeps over it.

The smooth face and hairless scalp. The square chin and longish nose. Even the fingernails are bruised-purple as he picks his blocky, white teeth.

Jack is back.

Mr. Frost feels a chill creep inside him. His thoughts are tumbling into a pile of nonsense, tipping him off balance. He braces himself against the wall, the frosty surface numbing his hand.

"This is super awkward," Jack says. "You really need elevator music."

Mr. Frost doesn't face him.

"But it's your elevator, so whatever," Jack says.

Jack drums the wall with his fingernails. Debris showers the floor like an artisan carving a wall of marble. Maybe Mr. Frost is imagining the cold, that the hardening of his organs, the shrinking of his stomach, is just the result of his runaway thoughts and paralyzing fear.

Or maybe it's Jack's ability to freeze anything and everything.

Mr. Frost tries to muster the words, attempts to say anything that will make him seem less fearful. All these centuries and, in seconds, he's transformed back into that meek elven that followed Jack, doing as he pleased, whatever he said. Now he's standing next to Jack's incarnated body in a slow-moving elevator that's quickly turning into a death locker of ice. All his carefully laid plans seem like poorly constructed scaffolding.

The elevator stops.

The tower, dark and cluttered, is revealed.

Jack doesn't move. Mr. Frost is stuck in place, waiting to be told what to do. He feels a tickle on his ear, a huff of frigid air. Mr. Frost locks his knees.

"Love what you've done with the place," Jack says.

Jack slides around the desks and chairs, the monitors and tables. The fish tank. Max hides behind a pillow.

"It's so full of *stuff*, Pawn. So lived-in, so homey. It screams... *WARMBLOOD!*"

Jack displays a rainbow of jazz hands.

His pale blue jacket flutters behind him as he glides along. He studies the room, sniffing like a dog. He holds his fat foot out like a blunt joust and starts shoving furniture. A desk grinds against the wall. A monitor crashes on the floor. He races around the room, occasionally stopping to size up a vision or mutter an idea to no one. He even begins an argument with himself, eventually telling himself to shut up.

"Great job with the body, by the way," he shouts at Mr. Frost.

"Freeda had some doubts about you, but clearly you knew what you were doing." Jack licks his finger and touches his butt. "*Tssssssss.*"

Mr. Frost is still locked in place, his thoughts like squares of ice all stuck together.

"The green hair thing... have to admit, that was a little sketchy. I mean, I can't argue with the results, but do you know what I went through to get here?" Jack cruises behind Mr. Frost. "I was laughed at by warmbloods, Pawn. I got to tell you, it hurt. It's kind of like being the stupid one in a class of morons."

Jack slides past with his head tipped back.

"Oh, look. You did stars." He studies the constellations.

"Freeda!" he shouts. "Keep the stars, ditch the rest. I need to start over, the layout is horrible. No offense, Pawn. We just have different... tastes."

The floor quakes.

Jack skates along, biting his nails, while the furnishings melt away like sandcastles. Max scurries around the room.

"What's that?" Jack points.

Mr. Frost still can't get a word out.

"Here, boy." Jack pats his knees. "Come to me, now. I said now. Come to me now or else."

Max hides behind Mr. Frost. Jack's expression is placid, slightly annoyed. Fortunately, the room's transformation distracts him. The floor shimmers, reconfiguring the microscopic biocells that follow a magnetic matrix to construct objects and electronics at will.

An oversized desk, translucent and cold, spans one end of the room, with an extremely large chair. Various sculptures emerge like serpents, odes to the olden days of the Cold One, as Jack was known by those that feared him and those that... well, that's all there was. Just fear.

The room, once again, is crowded with icy, slick furnishings, the stuff that once inhabited Jack's room deep beneath the Arctic ice hundreds of years ago when he was king, as if the memory was plucked from his mind and made real.

The last vestige of the Cold One, the single most garish, most self-centered tribute to the reign of Jack's terror, formed in front of Mr. Frost: a round fountain with a life-sized carving of Yours Truly spitting in the center.

Jack takes his place at the desk, groaning with satisfaction. He looks down his pointed nose. "You don't talk much, Pawn."

"I..." Mr. Frost clears his throat, thawing the words. "I'm just... surprised, that's all. I didn't expect to see you."

"All you, buddy." He smacks his belly, waves coursing from the impact. "Wait, it was all *me*. I put the plans in the root and put the root in your head so, if you think about it, *I* did this. But I'll give you some credit, Pawn. You hung in there, persevered. Kept your chin up when the chips were down. You did that for me."

Jack says, in the most sincere tone, "I won't forget that, buddy. Now scoop out a fishy, I'm feeling a little woozy over here. Hypoglycemia acting up."

Mr. Frost bites his lip, refusing to let his thoughts out. There was no perseverance, no fight to bring him back; there was just the drudgery of being driven by the root and Freeda's daily voice. He slides to the fountain, the centerpiece reaching up like an icy dagger stabbing the heavens. The fish seem to be real, not manufactured by the room. Freeda was prepared. He swipes at the school of minnows, snagging a pair between his fingers, and tosses them on the desk.

Jack licks his lips, poking at the flipping fish gasping to breathe. They freeze into curled, fishy chips when he touches them, rocking on the hard surface.

"You know," he says, biting one in half, "you can't imagine what it's like out there. Warmblood food is like eating a pillow. The only thing worse is the smell. I'm tempted to punch you in the face for letting me escape before I had memories, but I'll hand it to you, Pawn."

Jack inhales sharply.

"The Claus myth is firmly in place. Christmas greed infects them all. I'm back and beautiful. You did a... great... JOB!"

Jack presses his face on the desk and pulls the other fish between his lips like a serpent. He sits back and savors the snack, gazing at the stars.

"Anywho," he finally says, "I'm back, so you got to move out. I got you set up in the basement with some sweet digs. The view sucks, but it beats living in this heat, right? It's the humidity that'll kill you."

The elevator walls slide up.

Jack flicks his fingers. "Off you go. I got some thinking to do, some planning to plan, that sort of thing. Christmas is in two days and there's still a lot to do."

He drifts into thought, as if Mr. Frost would merely disappear, like nothing existed if he didn't recognize it.

"What are you going to do?" Mr. Frost asks.

"What?"

"About Christmas. What are you going to do?"

A smile creeps across his darkening face. "First, I'm going to relax. Coming back to life after being dead a few hundred years takes a lot out of you. Second, I'm going to wipe out the warmbloods. But not necessarily in that order."

He hikes his feet on the desk.

"And then I'm going to celebrate Christmas. I'm not a heathen, you know."

"The eyeTablets just shipped. It'll take some time before they're integrated into society. My estimate before we—I mean, *you* can do anything is eight years, probably ten. However, if you wait—"

"I know, I know. Freeda told me. Listen, in case you haven't noticed, I like things now. Not later, but now. So I'm weighing my options."

"What options?"

"Just shut up, will you?"

The elevator hums.

Mr. Frost has pushed his luck as far as it'll give. But he had to know what Jack was thinking. He knows there are many options to achieve the master plan, and Mr. Frost has planned a way to counter all of them. However, he knows one will undoubtedly work.

Mr. Frost knows Jack. *Not later, but now.*

"Jack," Mr. Frost states.

"Hmm?"

"My name isn't Pawn. It's Jack."

Jack opens his eyes. "What's that supposed to mean?"

"You stole my elven name when we were little, Janack."

"Don't call me that."

"My mother and father named me Jack. You're the one that called me Pawn."

"You are what I call you."

The elevator closes on Mr. Frost. He waits for Jack to open it in a rage, maybe stick a finger up his nose until his brain crackles with ice crystals because that was a rash and stupid thing to do. He didn't plan on it, never had thought about it, not once. But suddenly it was there and he was saying it.

When Jack didn't come for him, Mr. Frost smiled.

My real name is Jack.

❄

JACK'S BRAIN feels like a bowl of hot noodles.

Freeda said he would just feel a little pressure and that was the lie of the century.

But he remembers almost everything.

He doesn't remember dying, but Freeda gave him the blow-by-blow, how he blubbered on his mother's shoulder before drowning with his brother. She told him they all died.

But who's alive now? Who's the winner?

Jack orchestrated the resurrection of all eternity. He always felt like a dummy—he hates to admit it, but compared to his brother, Claus, he was a little dim—but what he did with the root was brilliant. The scientists helped a little, but it was his idea, his genius.

Pawn couldn't deny what the root wanted him to do, but Jack gave him enough freedom to adapt creatively. Jack may have been green and grouchy when he woke up, but if that's what it took to bring him back, he won't complain.

Much.

He burps fish-scented fumes, thumps his chest, but it's not indigestion. It feels more like a halo of anger just below the sternum—two inches to the right where his tiny heart pumps antifreeze.

Jack.

Pawn just wanted to ruin his day. Jack attempts to soothe his heavy heart with cold thoughts, only to feel them melt.

Jack is Pawn's real name.

He slides past the fountain to a full-length mirror. Jack pulls off his clothes, dropping them in a pile. Black shorts are visible just below his doughy belly.

He's back. He's good. *Death ain't got nothing on me.*

And, yet, something's missing.

Jack works through the pile of clothes and pulls out a black pair of Oakley sunglasses. He slides them up his nose with one finger. The polarizing vision makes him look slightly rosy.

Almost tan.

His childhood dresser is on the far side of the room, the snow duster still in the top drawer. The candy cane press is on the low-rising coffee table, the one where you pour sugar and ice through a straw. The hinge is a bit sticky, but then again, it always was. And there, middle drawer, is the harmonica, still beaten and battered. Jack cups it, blowing all the notes.

It's all there. Everything he could remember, all the toys, all the inventions. And all the hatred, coldness, bitterness, and bile to go along with it.

Why didn't I erase that?

Not too late, sir.

"Quiet." He doesn't like her eavesdropping. He likes beating himself up when no one else is around. Fact is, everything is exactly the way it was hundreds of years ago, but something is missing.

Something.

A car door thumps. Jack leans on the window, hands pressed on the glass. Veins of ice crawl across the surface. Jonah's limping around the front of a pickup, dragging a tarp full of clippings from the garden. He goes back for another load, the blue tarp snaking behind him as he winds his way through the maze where a sculpture sparkles.

"What's that?" He pokes the glass.

A tribute to your mother.

"Mother?"

Mr. Frost thought it appropriate that she be memorialized for her wisdom.

"Uh-huh. First of all, no more 'Mr. Frost' crap. His name is Pawn, get with it. Second, there better be a big, fat, blue statue somewhere, if you know what I mean."

You are the tribute, sir. This entire plantation is in your honor.

"Uh..." He starts to object. "All right, I'll give you that one."

Pawn loved Jack's mother. Everyone did. The old lady spouted wisdom like a...

Fountain.

Pawn was one of those kid elven that sat at the back of the class and doodled on the desk, slunk down when the teacher wanted volunteers; one of those elven that never said a word. It had something to do with his parents dying when he was little, but boohoo—Jack didn't have a father and his mother was busy.

Jack made friends with him. Actually, no one wanted to be friends with Jack, either. They had that in common. Jack and Pawn became best friends.

Only Jack's name was really Janack. And Pawn's name was really Jack. It's confusing but not really.

Pawn did whatever Jack told him to do, so the name Pawn made sense. Besides, Janack was a stupid name and he sort of liked the name Jack. It was tough and sharp. He wanted it and they both couldn't be named Jack.

So Jack became Pawn and Janack became Jack.

Simple as that.

Jack fogs the glass with his breath and etches a name. *JACK.*

Sir, we need to discuss the options I gave you earlier—

"Oh my God." Jack clamps the sides of his head. "You can't tell me I approved your voice. If I have to listen to that for the next hundred years, I'm going to hang myself."

Freeda stutters.

"Make yourself useful and turn the temperature down; I'm sweating BBs over here."

The system is running at maximum power, sir. Her reply is terse. *Minus eighty is as low as it can go unless you want to remove all the replicated objects in the room.*

He rather doubts that. She's just making that up. Jack starts getting dressed.

As I was saying, depending on the option you'd like to initiate, we may have to act very soon, sir.

"Uh-huh."

Within the next hour.

"Okay."

Jack digs through his dresser and finds a black, long-tailed jacket that matches the sunglasses.

Sir, I don't understand. What are you doing?

"I'm going to party with the helpers. You're going to work."

You'll distract them, sir.

"Do you always make excuses?"

Sir, so much has changed from the original master plan. Earlier, you liked the meltdown option. Is that what you want?

"Uh, yeah. That's what I said. Why is that so hard to understand?"

Because initiating meltdown on such short notice is hasty, sir. The meltdown is an alternative to the eyeTablets that Mr. Fro—Pawn has prepared.

"Are you calling me hasty?"

The decision is, sir. It'll take time to communicate with all the toys we've manufactured and shipped around the world for the past two hundred years. Also, you should be aware that Pawn incarnated a fourth warmblood, who is now missing along with Joe. I hardly think now is the time to "party."

"Wait." He pulls the sunglasses off. "Did you say Joe?"

Yes. He's the boy that was driving the truck with—

"Sura."

She led him here. That energy of hers brought him to the plantation, gave him hope. She felt like home.

"Where is she?"

We don't know, sir. They're hiding.

"Well, find them. You have to find them. Now." Jack swaps the Oakleys for Ray-Bans and checks his reflection from three angles. "I want her back here before we blow up the world. No excuses. Call me as soon as you find her, and in the meantime, do what I designed you to do—compute. Look, I've been dead for two hundred years and I can't sit around all day, so chop-chop."

Jack wraps a skinny, black tie around his neck and slides the premade knot beneath his fat neck, a pound of blue flesh falling over it.

Sir, you want me to establish contact with billions of toys?

"Tonight."

There's not enough time. I really think we should—

"Call me when you're ready. I want to watch. Send Sura down when you find her."

Jack snatches the harmonica and wipes the spit off with his sleeve. He blows a few times and pockets the harp, determined to play. Determined they'll like it. Sura, too.

"By the way, what's that?"

That's Max, Pawn's pet. He's been feeding his memories to it.

"He's using a memory box?" Jack remembers that silver box he carried with him. The little nuggets were digestible memory chips. As long as the box was pressed against his skin, they absorbed everything he experienced.

"You're letting him do this?"

It's harmless, sir. Besides, it's a wise backup in case something goes wrong.

Max is curled on a pillow, baring his teeth when Jack slides his glasses down for a look. Jack thinks maybe he'll eat it. But that thing must be a hundred years old, probably taste like a leather boot.

"Send it down to him. He'll need something to talk to."

The elevator wall shimmies around the circle. Jack slides inside. His hand knifes through the gap just as the door closes.

"One more thing."

Yes?

"The statue."

17

DECEMBER 24

Wednesday

Sura huddles against the gas station. The late-day shadows are cool. She hasn't showered in days. Her sweatshirt will testify.

The boy in the silver pickup looks away from Joe, his eyes falling on Sura. The door is dented and the hood a different color. The driver climbs out and hands Joe the keys.

"Sure about this?" the kid says.

Joe calls him Bean. Sura doesn't care what his real name is, just as long as he gives them that rolling junk heap.

"Just till after the New Year," Joe says. "Then trade back."

Bean walks around Joe's truck, fingers trailing. "Still don't get it."

"Why you complaining, Bean?"

"Because I don't want no debt collector showing up at my house."

Joe clicks his tongue. "Come on, man. I just got to lay low for a bit, just till my old man cools off."

"Uh-huh. And what if he sees me in your truck?"

"Tell him the truth. You met me at Edisto and I was camping."

"Where you going to be?"

"North Carolina, probably." They both know he's lying, but at least they got their story straight.

Bean finally climbs into the truck. He tests the radio, nodding. It's a dumb move, but he can't pass it up. They shake hands before he drives off. The tailpipes can be heard growling a mile down the road.

"He's all right," Joe says, like this will make her feel better. "You ready?"

"What if we don't go?" Sura hugs herself tighter.

"What then?" Joe asks. "Where do we go?"

We find the nearest interstate, drive until the gas tank is empty, and call the nearest town home. We get jobs, buy a trailer, have kids, and spend the rest of our lives together, forever and ever and ever.

She can't stop the fantasies; they come to life when he's near her. She's afraid if they go back to Frost Plantation, it'll be the end. Her mom still loved Jonah. She denied that love to raise Sura, but she loved him.

"If we run," Joe says, "we'll never stop. We'll always be looking back. The yellow-hat helpers said we have to go back, that Mr. Frost needs us. I'm afraid if we don't, bad things are going to happen that we can't outrun."

"You trust the yellow-hats?"

He looks down the road. "Yeah. I trust them."

Bean's truck starts on the second turn. Joe throws the door open and waves Sura over. She kicks empty Red Bull cans off the floorboard and sinks into the sprung seat, arms still clamped around her chest. Her eyes ache with insomnia.

He takes her hand.

The ache subsides. She hates that it does, hates that it feels good to be near him, to touch him. To need him. She wants to love him, not feel compelled to. It feels like she's betraying herself, giving in to what Mr. Frost wants her to do, becoming the person he wants her to be, but she can't help it.

They hold hands until their palms sweat, and then he pulls her close. She leans in.

They take the country roads, drive north for an hour, and then circle around. Without a phone or a GPS, they get lost twice. The sun is setting when they turn on to a weed patch cut out of the trees. It might have been a road once, but now it's kudzu and pines.

Joe kills the lights. They listen to the engine tick as it cools.

"We're on the north end of the plantation," he says. "I used to come out this way when I was little, explore the woods, fish and hunt.

Helpers come out this way every once in a while, but this time of year, they're busy making toys."

"You mean like Christmas toys?"

"Yeah. It's weird, right?"

A week ago, she would've agreed. Not now. Nothing seems weird, not a short, fat man with engorged feet named Mr. Frost, not Christmas gnomes making presents, or secret gardens that transform into a Neverland. Normal has been redefined.

They start down the overgrown road.

Twilight is extinguished in the forest. Joe pushes through the brush, making a path for her to follow. The going gets slow, the nonexistent trail thicker and stickier. Thorns tug at Sura's sweatshirt and snag her jeans. Joe holds her hand.

The ground turns mucky. Water sloshes over her shoes, soaking her socks. The trees give way to marsh grasses and black water. Beyond, a hill slopes up to live oaks, their branches weeping with moss.

He looks up and down the tree line. The moon is bright.

They slog just inside the trees. Sometimes, the water reaches their knees. If she wasn't a Southern girl, she'd be thinking about alligators, but they're coldblooded. So are snakes.

Am I Southern?

Sura is an Inuit name that means "new life." She looked it up once for a class project but didn't think much of it. But now they're returning to the house of an elven from the North Pole.

"There." Joe points at a leaning tree with a thick rope. He splashes along the bank and pushes the weeds apart until an upside-down boat is revealed.

"Help me."

They flip it over. Joe stares at the beaten john boat. "I used to take this back and forth. The helpers put the rope up and we'd swing all day long. Can't believe the boat's still here."

"Can't believe it floats."

"It'll get us to the other side."

And it does. They paddle with their hands. The frigid water seeps through holes, but they make it before sinking.

Joe huffs on his quivering hands. "We'll climb the slope and slip through the sunken garden. The back door will be open. If we're fast enough, we can reach the elevator. The yellow-hat helper said Mr. Frost is expecting us."

Sura is grateful to be walking. Her knees are stiff. By the time they cross through the orchards and reach the north end of the gardens, she feels much better. Joe pries open the hedge and finds the hidden path inside. The wishing room is to the right, the garden to the left.

There's a dull thumping ahead.

"What's that?" Sura asks.

Joe listens. "It's late; no one should be in the gardens."

They creep along the darkened path. She stays close to Joe. The pounding gets louder. Joe puts his fingers to his lips, then peeks around the corner. His cautious expression turns to confusion. It takes a few moments to process what he's seeing. Confusion becomes shock. Sura reaches out for him, but he steps into the open.

"What are you doing?" Joe shouts.

"Joe!" Jonah's raspy voice calls from somewhere out there.

The bushes shake and gravel crunches as Jonah's bulky frame marches toward them with his arms spread, herding the teenagers back into the shadows.

"Back," Jonah hisses. "Quickly, both of you."

Joe tries to investigate what his father was doing in the garden, but Jonah is too insistent, too strong. His face is speckled with gray stubble, lines crunching the corners of his tired eyes. Sweat glistens on his cheeks.

Jonah pushes to the end of the path. He closes his eyes, lips fluttering, before prying the wall open. Orange light warmly illuminates the frozen specks on his face.

That's not sweat, that's ice.

"In you go," he says.

A bonfire roars in an open plain.

The salted ground is dry and hard. Sura thinks she can see the outline of distant mountains. The firelight only reaches so far into the abandoned land.

Jonah gestures to the fire. "Warm yourselves."

Sura's as close to the roaring fire as she can get, which is still quite far. She spreads her fingers, the warmth seeping through her cheeks. Steam rises from her pant legs.

Joe is shivering. He follows Jonah to the edge of darkness. They argue in French. The wood crackles in the flames while the two shout, point, and stomp the dusty earth. They argue like adults, not father and son. Occasionally, Sura hears her name.

Joe comes back to the fire. Jonah remains at the fringe of the fire's glow. Sura backs up to an abandoned log, its surface smooth and gray. Joe stays near the fire, still shivering. Jonah comes to him, a slight hitch on his right side, like he pulls his leg along. He rubs his grizzly jaw and drops a thick hand on Joe's shoulder.

Joe doesn't shrug him off. Instead, they warm themselves with outstretched hands. The shared moment of silence settles the tension between them. Joe sits next to Sura.

"I don't think we should yell," she says.

"No one can hear inside the wishing room," Jonah mutters.

That's not what she meant. For several minutes, the fire does all the talking, grinding the wood into glowing embers that spit into the dark.

"He's here." Jonah's voice is raw. "The man that Mr. Frost has been... building. He has arrived."

"We know," Joe says. "He's not a man."

Jonah doesn't seem surprised. He looks at his callused hands. "Where have you been?"

"Hiding," Joe says. "Helpers were at the house, and Sura was putting things together..." He looks for her response.

She squeezes his arm.

"A yellow-hat told me to get lost for a while."

Jonah nods like he's seeing distant images.

"We're supposed to find Mr. Frost," Joe says.

"Not yet. It's not safe." The light can't lift the shadows from his eyes. He returns to staring at his hands.

"What does he want with us?" Sura asks.

"I don't know." He studies the fire. "He's playing a very complex game that's taken hundreds of years. I couldn't possibly understand. I'm just a pawn."

"We're all pawns." Sura tenses.

"You don't understand," Jonah continues. "*Everything* hangs in the balance tonight. Come morning, this could be a whole new world. If Mr. Frost needs you, then you go."

"That's easy for you to say," Sura blurts. "You and Joe know what this place is—you've known about it since you were born. I'm still trying to believe that fire isn't real."

He shakes his head. The light glistens in his deep-set eyes. "Joe doesn't know everything."

Sura and Joe press closer. He's still shaking.

"This is our fate?" she asks. "We have no free will? We're victims of our biology, is that it? Mr. Frost programmed us like puppets so that we'll do what he says. That's not fair. It's not human."

Jonah is nodding. He doesn't disagree.

He grabs a twig from the dust and begins breaking it into smaller pieces, like Joe was doing on the beach. He groans when he stands, tossing the sticks into the blaze before walking away. He looks at the stars, hands on hips.

"I was sixteen when I met her," he says, without looking back. "I was hanging Christmas lights with my... father."

He doesn't know what else to call the man that raised him.

"We were in the garden when Sesi walked down the steps to collect flowers. I thought the lights were shining on her, but she was radiant everywhere she went. I felt her, right here."

He taps his chest.

"She was like a smile that held my heart, a blanket that warmed my soul. The sun would rise and set with her. She said she grew up on the plantation, although I'd never seen her before. As strange as that is, I never questioned why I'd never seen her before that day." His eyes twinkle in the shadows. "Later, I learned why."

"Why?" she asks.

"Within weeks, we talked about marriage," he says. "We were going to have three children and a farm. We were naïve enough to dream that Mr. Frost would one day give us the plantation and we'd raise our family with horses out back and crops in the fields. We'd live long and old and die happy."

Sura cringes. That's her fantasy.

A groan escapes him. He looks at the ground and kicks at the dust.

"We'd been together almost a year when the sun would set and never rise again. That's when she left. Sesi said she needed to wake up and break the cycle. I didn't know what that meant."

He shakes his head.

"The truth is sometimes hard and unforgiving."

Jonah reaches into his pocket and studies something flat and round, light reflecting off the edges. He reaches out, hand cupped. Joe lays his hand open and receives an antique pocket watch. The surface is nicked and worn. The etching is gone from years of friction, leaving behind a well-polished surface.

"Stay until eleven o'clock," he says. "Use the pocket watch to find the exit. Templeton will meet you at the back door and take you to Mr. Frost."

Jonah limps around the log and fades into the darkness, stopping just before he disappears. A golden string dangles in front of him. A clipped groan cuts short what he's thinking. Perhaps he has more to say. Maybe he wants to stay with them in the wishing room, huddle next to the fire, and just let the world go on without them. They'd talk about their shared fantasy, what they would name the kids, and what careers they'd have when they grew up. If they stayed in the wishing room long enough, they could transform it into a happy place where brides-to-be don't leave.

And Moms don't die.

The darkness parts like black curtains and Jonah slips out. Joe remains stone-faced, staring at the fire. They hold each other in silence. Jonah should've stayed to make them go when the time comes.

Perhaps they do have a choice.

FRIGID AIR HISSES down the walls.

Mr. Frost stands in the center, eschewing the bed despite the ache in his knees. He wants it to hurt; it distracts him from his thoughts.

Seeing Jack—the blue, fat, and bald elven—brought long-forgotten memories to the surface. There was no epic battle, no struggle for power, or clash of good versus evil. Jack slid into the tower and simply took everything from him.

Mr. Frost became Pawn.

Music thuds through the floor, penetrates his feet, tickles his joints. The root vibrates beneath his scalp. A song ends and another begins, faster and heavier.

Mr. Frost locks his knees.

The door cracks open. The earthy scent of the incubator lab wafts in from the other room. Music, too. The door swings open. There's a crash against the wall, followed by laughter. A crumpled blue-hat helper falls through the doorway. A red-hat helper stumbles down the hall. More laughter.

They pull themselves together and throw a sack into the room, slamming the door shut. Something yelps inside, kicking at the cloth. Mr. Frost drops to his knees and struggles to untie the knot. A white ball of fur leaps on the bed.

"Max!" Mr. Frost falls next to the Arctic fox.

Max's rough tongue kisses his nose. Mr. Frost pulls the silver tin from his pocket and fishes a few kernels from the bottom, leaving three in the box. He won't need a refill. Max gobbles them down.

Mr. Frost goes back to standing like a vigilant guard of nothing more than a thin mattress and a curled-up puffball. He stays that way for hours while the music drones on. He resists sleep. There's no way to know how much time has passed when the music stops. The silence feels strange.

It won't be long now.

"No!" Jack waves his arms. "You're terrible. Get off the stage!"

Jack shoves the bass player with his foot.

"I need a bass player; I can't do everything. My God, the instrument isn't that hard to play."

He takes a swig of fish oil while the guitar player tunes his instrument. The drink slides into his stomach, coating him with good feelings. Hundreds of helpers stumble around the toy factory. They'd cleared out the center and stacked machines on top of each other to make room for a round stage. Jack couldn't care less about toys.

There won't be a Christmas next year.

In fact, he decided he'd move into the toy factory. The tower is nice, the views are sweet, but there's just no room. The toy factory is more his style. After Christmas, all this equipment will go out on the lawn. He'd make the place his own.

"Nope." Jack shoves an orange-hat helper down the steps. "You've already been up here; I recognize the hat."

There are at least fifty orange hats.

"You know what, why don't all of you get off the stage?" he says to the band. "I'll go solo. First guitar, then drums, then trombone or something..."

He can't play any of those instruments. The helpers cheer, but they're faking it. He could fart into the mic and they'd applaud.

Sir?

"Oh, Freeda. Just the annoying voice I was thinking about. You reading my mind?"

No, sir. I need you in the tower.

"What you need to do is download a blues harmonica into these hands." He looks around and points at the helpers. They laugh. They have no idea why.

Sir, now's not the time to be playing games.

"These aren't games, Freeda. This is musical genius. I've got a lot of living to do; I want to start it off on the right foot." He shakes his right foot and gets a laugh. *It's sooo easy.*

Sir, there's a problem with the meltdown.

"What kind of problem?"

Something you should look at, sir.

Jack doesn't like vagary. If she couldn't handle this, he'd delete her —have Pawn write another artificial intelligence, one that could take care of the end of warmbloods while he got the band together.

"I'll be up in a sec."

Can't wait, sir.

Jack throws the guitar down and kicks the drums over. He storms up the ramp, thinking that maybe he'll have Pawn build Freeda a face. He needs something to yell at.

He takes the elevator up. Super-chilled air rushes inside when it opens. "What is it?" he shouts.

Sir, there appears to be—

"Hold that thought." Jack slides up to the fountain. The fish scatter. He thinks *net* and a fish net squirts from the floor. "Pawn did a super job with this place," he says to himself, combing the waters and trapping at least a dozen fish. "It's all about finding the right people, Freeda. You get good people, you get results."

That's what I want to speak about, sir.

Jack empties the net on the desk, throws his feet up, and begins munching. He spins in the chair, looking across the open field at the giant live oaks on the far side. He thought he hated the tower—he really wants to hate it—but just can't bring himself to do it.

The views are just too sweet.

"It's settled." He bangs the desk, squishing the last fish. "I'm staying in the tower, Freeda. We'll bring the band up here. It'll be a little tight, but I think we can do it. We'll need a bouncer to keep things in order, 'cause things are going to get nuts. I'm thinking Templeton—"

He snaps his fingers.

"May's the perfect hammer with that big, spongy gut and those bohemian arms; that woman was made to bounce—"

Focus, sir! You need to listen! You cannot run off and play. I need you to stop acting like a child.

Jack raises his fist.

That's why you died the first time.

He freezes.

Died the first time. Her words have an echoing effect. No one ever spoke that way to Jack. But, then again, she's not real. She's an artificially constructed intelligence. She doesn't know what it's like to have all this pressure to succeed, to be happy and make people like you. It's a lot.

Jack knows.

I'm the one that's real. I have a body, a brain, and memories. I am real.

He thinks about this a bit more. He can prove he's real and she's not. *As long as I remember who I am... wait.*

He didn't have memories at the shelter, but he was still real, still awake. It's not like he wasn't real until Freeda uploaded his memories.

As long as I have a body... hold on.

He didn't have a body for two hundred years. He was a DNA-script stored in the root. Was he not real then, but is now?

I'll answer that question later.

"You're right," he says. The words sound funny. He forces himself to say them. "My bad."

Jack shoves the desk. It slides across the floor and shatters the fountain. Water spills and fish flip around. He closes his eyes, imagining something more appropriate for the room. There's a ripple in the air. When he opens his eyes, there are floating monitors, tables, maps, and data; there are numbers and words.

Voices mutter in a dozen languages.

A chair rises from the floor. The armrests swell with little control panels at his fingers. The back of the chair fans out, worthy of a throne.

And in the center, where the fountain used to be, is Earth. It's six feet in diameter, tilted on its axis, and slowly rotating. Pinpricks of light are all around it, merging into a mass of golden hue where populations are dense. Toward the north, they become less frequent.

The North Pole is dark.

"Let's do this," he says. "Brief me."

Thank you, sir. Let me start at the beginning. Pawn seeded the thought of Christmas gift-giving into the warmblood population shortly after arriving in the United States in the early 1800s, and for a long time, he was the primary producer and distributor of toys, exactly as you planned.

"Thank you."

At first, it was simple toys, mostly wooden. As the years passed, they became plastic, but still simplistic. Regardless how modest they were, whether they were wood or plastic, everything was embedded with slave technology that would allow us to eventually control every toy we've ever manufactured.

The lights extinguish and begin to slowly reemerge on the globe, illustrating the spread of Christmas toys. The planet, once again, becomes fully illuminated.

Nonetheless, Mr. Frost—

"Pawn." Jack slides toward Earth. "His name is Pawn."

Freeda pauses.

Jack eases around the floating image of Earth, not knowing what to do with his hands. He tries to put them behind his back—he's seen very important warmbloods do that move—but his arms are too short. He opts for resting them on his belly.

What's exciting, sir, is that we are, for the first time, launching neural-integration technology that will communicate with warmblood nervous systems and, ultimately, brain activity.

"Yeah, I know, the eyeTablets. Stupid name."

Sir, your original plan was to use slave technology to gain control of products such as automobiles, phones, weapons... everything, sir. It was brilliant.

"I know."

However, the recent technology revolution has spawned a new opportunity, sir. Warmbloods now have smart phones and computers. Everything in the world is networked. With these new developments, the neural-integration technology will allow us to know warmblood thoughts. We'll connect with their nervous systems. We control them, sir. They'll be puppets.

Jack stops circling the globe and looks up at the star-speckled ceiling. "Do I eat boogers?"

Sir?

"Do I eat boogers?"

Freeda stammers. *I just... I'm not sure where you're going with this.*

"You just explained my plan like I'm a booger-eating first grader." He begins coasting around the room, hands locked over his belly. "I designed everything on greed, Freeda. No, I didn't know how you were going to do it, but I know warmbloods and, as a whole, they have one thing in common: self-indulgent, ravenous, gluttonous, insatiable greed."

He hesitates. Willie comes to mind. *He's the only exception.*

"They like to get stuff, Freeda. They like to have it, to own it, to stuff it in closets, attics, and basements. They rent storage containers so they have more room for more stuff. They won't stop, Freeda. Ever.

They'll build and collect until they figure out how to get to another planet, and then they'll fill that up with stuff."

He takes a breath.

"The eyeTablets sound great. I mean, marching those stupid warmbloods off a cliff sounds like my kind of party. But here's the deal: I don't want to wait twenty years. I want them gone *now*, so go with plan B, the one that turns slave technology into miniature nuclear reactors."

He points at the planet flickering with light.

"We'll use it to convert matter into energy but utilize the evaporating-microscopic-black-hole method to displace the energy somewhere else in the universe, preferably another galaxy, so we don't blow up our solar system. I like our sun."

What about other solar systems?

"Why would I care about that? Anyway, slave technology will become microscopic eating machines that devour all the warmblood stuff: cars, buildings, kitchens, and clothes... it all disappears. There will be chaos, mass destruction, and sadness. They'll sit in the dirt, cry, destroy each other, and eventually starve, and I'll sit back with a tub of sardines and watch. No more Christmas, Freeda, and no more warmbloods. All before summer."

He calls for the elevator.

It's a horrible plan, sir.

"Remind me not to make you so honest next time."

We'll have no control. There's no guarantee it'll work.

"There's no such thing as a guarantee, Freeda. Warmbloods invented guarantees. So do my plan. Do it now."

There's a risk, sir.

"My God, do you not run out of excuses? What risk?" Jack looks at the stars. "You better not say it's not working. I'll go ape on this place if you say that after two hundred years it's not working."

It's working, sir. I've already contacted over forty-two percent of toys in the world.

"I don't see the problem."

It's too fast, sir. If it doesn't work, the humans will figure it out and come after us. And they'll find us, sir. An anomaly could easily undo two hundred years of work.

"A what-aly?"

Something out of the ordinary, sir. Something unexpected.

"You're right." Jack rubs a layer of fuzzy frost off his chin. "If only I had a supercomputer to analyze everything beforehand."

I advise we move slower.

"And I advise you do it tonight. Any other questions?"

Jack glides around the tower, tapping his lower lip. All the monitors are filled with loathsome warmbloods arguing, complaining, whining, fighting, and lying. They're so stupid and they smell funny. Waiting would be a crime.

Two hundred years is long enough.

He pretends to check the time. "You have an hour to get things popping. I'll be in the factory. My fans can't wait."

You should talk to Pawn.

"Why?"

In case he knows about the nuclear reactor plan. It would reduce the chances of his tampering.

"Why are you asking me? You're in his head! Just look!"

He's become skilled at hiding thoughts.

"Do I have to do everything?" Jack throws up his arms. "Why would he do that? Why would he *not* want this to work? He doesn't love the warmbloods."

His words are lifeless. Even he doesn't believe them.

"Pawn loves me."

Of this, Jack is sure. Pawn would do anything Jack asked him to do. And his hatred of warmbloods is as pure as Jack's. He knows this because he told him to hate them.

I have my doubts.

"All right!" Jack shoves his fist into the Earth. The image shatters like an empty shell. The useless pieces melt away.

The elevator waits for him.

First Pawn. Then party.

JOE STAYS NEAR THE FIRE.

Sura can't sit still. She needs to walk, to keep moving.

Outside the firelight, there's nothing but baked earth and distant mountains. The North Star blinks its pattern of colors, signaling the falseness of this reality, that none of this really exists. It's all in her mind.

Wake up, Sura.

She keeps walking.

The mountains never get closer. The bonfire is just a spot of light glowing on the plain. Joe shouts. His voice travels effortlessly across the emptiness. He's waving.

"I'm coming!" Sura shouts.

Joe takes her hand when she arrives. His hand is freezing. He takes a shaky breath and holds up the pocket watch. It's almost eleven o'clock. He presses the button on top.

The golden string appears.

Joe slides his hand into it, pulling it open. Sura steps through the exit, where she's greeted with the smell of damp foliage. It's dark beneath the canopy. They move slowly, the mulched path dampening their footsteps, and pause at the entrance to the garden. Music thuds somewhere distant. It doesn't sound very Christmassy.

Joe's grip tightens.

They step into the garden and walk along the perimeter path until they reach the exit. Sura's heartbeat thumps in her throat. Joe exhales a long, cold cloud. Sura focuses on calming breaths.

The fountain is shattered. Large chunks of the statue are all that remain. A thin layer of ice has formed over the pool of water. Jonah was destroying it when they arrived.

The bad son has returned.

Joe squeezes her hand. She can feel him trembling. He puts a finger to his lips for silence and holds up three fingers... two... one.

They stumble across the road. The Christmas lights hang from the gutters and shine around the windows, not a dark corner in sight. They sneak along the house and pass the basement doors where the music rumbles. Templeton opens the back door. His robe is firmly pressed, the sash tightly knotted. His rigid lips part, his jaw opening like oiled hinges—

"Get in here, children." May shoves him aside. "Come on, hurry."

The doughy woman climbs down the steps, holding her robe with one hand. Sura resists hugging her and takes the steps two at a time. May chases them into the kitchen while Templeton closes the doors.

Sura doesn't resist once they're safe, sinking into May's soft, cookie-smelling embrace. May pulls Joe in, too, and she holds them tightly, making shooshing noises.

"All right." Templeton's hard-soled shoes click on the floor. "Enough with the pleasantries. You must go to Mr. Frost."

"Why?" Sura asks.

Templeton retrieves two coats from the rack and drapes them over his arms like he's delivering the king's clothing. He tugs at May's elbow. When she finally releases Sura and Joe, she turns around to wipe her eyes. Templeton puts his hand on her back and whispers in her ear.

May nods.

"You need these." Templeton gives Joe the puffy blue one and pulls a stocking cap down to his eyes. He holds the white coat for Sura.

She hesitates. "Why does he want to see us?"

Templeton appears stiffer than usual, but his expression is soft and confused. He glances at May before saying, "The world is not safe tonight, Sura."

"What's that mean?"

"It's all very complicated." Templeton sighs.

May can't hold back any longer. She smothers the teenagers in another embrace, her thick arms quivering each time she exhales a breath loaded with sobs. Templeton watches, coat hanging at his side.

"What if I don't want to go?" Sura asks.

"You don't have to go," Templeton says. "You can turn right, go wherever you want."

He lifts his free hand and traces a circle in the air.

If we sail in that direction long enough, her mom had said, *where do we end up?*

Sura asked what would happen if they turned right, but her mom seemed to believe they'd still end up right here and now.

Sura doesn't want to go, but calmness falls on her. She's exactly where she needs to be. She doesn't know where she's going or why, she just needs to be here.

So let's not run.

Templeton has to peel May's arms off them. She covers her face, inconsolable. Joe's complexion has paled. Templeton holds up the coat again. Sura slides her arms into the sleeves and pulls on the wool hat. He squeezes her hands. His fingers are not stiff and cold like she's always imagined.

The elevator door slides open. Four helpers waddle out, all wearing yellow hats.

Sura bumps into Joe.

"It's all right," Joe says, arm around her. "They belong to Mr. Frost."

Templeton kneels down and fastens spiky rubber soles to the bottom of Joe's boots. He does the same to Sura's shoes. "For walking," he says.

May cups Sura's cheek and then Joe's. Templeton grips her shoul-

ders, but she maintains control, despite the tearful slicks on her
cheeks. Her hand feels so much like home.

They step inside the cylindrical elevator. The helpers surround
them, the tips of their yellow hats reaching their knees. One of them
reaches for the buttons. The door slides shut; May's face is the last
thing Sura sees before her warped reflection looks back.

Joe takes her hand.

Her stomach rises as the elevator sinks down to the cold regions.

The yellow-hats talk like machine guns. They fire words at Joe.
"Yeah," he answers. "We can run."

Before Sura has a say, the door opens.

The frigid air steals their breath, waters their eyes. Sura holds onto
Joe and follows the blurry, yellow hats racing in front of them. The
spikes on the bottom of her shoes are flexible, grabbing the icy floor.

They run through a door on the right. The humidity rises. It's a
warmer room. An earthy scent fills her sinuses, reminiscent of the
garden. Joe leans against the wall to catch his breath. Sura wipes her
tears, rubbing the feeling back into her cheeks. There are rows of glass
tanks and a metal table in the center.

"Oh!" She backs against the wall.

There's a body on the table. It's shaped like an elven—short and fat
but covered with green hair. It looks like an autopsy, but the chest
slowly rises and falls. She waits for it to sit up or look at them.

The yellow-hats poke Sura and Joe like wranglers guiding cattle.

"Stop." Sura slaps at them.

They jabber at each other and keep pushing. "*Gogogogogo.*"

Sura's head is swimming. It's the weird body on the table and the
damp room that makes the room sway. It's the smell. The rich, organic
aroma fills her head.

Joe pushes off the wall. Two of the yellow-hats prod him to go
faster, but he ignores them. He stops at the table, staring at the body.

"What is it?" Sura asks.

"I don't know. It looks sort of like the Grinch, only shorter." He
leans over and sniffs. "Smells like algae."

Sura braces herself against the wall. The yellow-hats leave her
alone. They go to a door at the far end of the room that's between cluttered workbenches with glass tanks much smaller than the ones
standing in the room.

"You all right?" Joe asks, short of breath.

"It's something about this room." Sura steps carefully, the rubber spikes gripping the floor. "Have you been here?"

He shakes his head.

She approaches the table with short steps. The hair on the body is wet and matted. The lights above it are bright, the hairs sort of pointed at them.

"It's him." She steps back, hand over her mouth. "The guy we picked up after the dance, that's him."

Joe investigates again. The hair is shorter and there are no patches of blue skin. "I don't know," he says. "It looks sort of like him, but maybe elven all look the same."

"You're saying we picked up a different elven?"

But it's not the same guy, not exactly. He's different. He's newer, greener. More hair. Sura touches one of the tanks, the surface smooth and cold. There's a row on each side of the center aisle, and smaller ones lined up on shelves attached to the walls. Hundreds of them.

"What are these?" she asks.

"Come on." Joe touches her elbow, his hand quivering. "They want us to go."

The yellow-hats are pushing again. Sura ignores their gibberish and goes to one of the tanks. Their tiny hands feel like pool cues. She touches the glass tank nearest her. The inside is frosted. Some of the tanks are shorter than others. Some are slightly taller than her. There's something inside the one she's looking at: a dark form, like something standing up.

She cups her hands against the glass. The yellow-hats aggressively poke, knocking her off-balance. She kicks at them, but they deftly avoid her like martial artists, jabbing at her weak knees.

"It's all right," a voice says weakly. "She can look."

Sura jerks back.

Mr. Frost is standing in the doorway at the far end. The Arctic fox sits next to him, his bushy, white tail sweeping the floor. Mr. Frost's cheeks—what little can be seen between his beard and eyes—look haggard. His eyes, once sharp blue, are dull and gray. He slumps like a man that's carried a heavy weight all his life.

Sura puts her hand on the tank to steady herself. There's the man that created her and she can't form a single word. It takes all her strength just to stand up.

Joe grunts like he was kicked in the stomach. He's at one of the tanks, his face near a clear spot on the glass. His eyes are wide; his bluish lips flutter wordlessly.

"What is it?" Sura asks.

He shakes his head. The yellow-hats prod him away from the tank, but the shock remains. They come for Sura, but Mr. Frost lifts his hand.

"She wants to wake up," he says.

Wake up.

Is this what her mom meant? Discover who you are no matter what the answer. The truth doesn't always feel good. It's truth.

Sura turns to a tank behind her. She rises on her toes. The form looks like another clump of algae with shoulders. The facial features are subtle. The eyes closed.

This is where he grows us.

The yellow-hats keep her from falling. Mr. Frost says something. Sura slides to the floor. An acrid bulge rises in her throat. She forces it down while the room begins to spin.

"They're not awake, Sura." Mr. Frost's voice is out there, somewhere. "They are simply empty vessels. In fact, they are more like plants. The chlorophyll spliced into their DNA stabilizes their bodies while they remain in terrariums."

He says all this like a gardener explaining the workings of his greenhouse. Sura shakes her head to stop the room-spins. She pinches the skin on the back of her hand, twisting it like a key.

She grabs the edge of the table and puts a hand on Joe. He looks chalky, still no words. She crawls past the table and palms the tank behind him. The yellow-hats help her stand up.

They help her look inside it.

Joe.

It's him. Joe's inside the tank. A green-matted version of the way he is right now: same age, same size.

How can that be? He grew up on the plantation; he went to school and grew up with Jonah. He can't be in the tank like that. Not like that.

She remembers, in a haze of memories, when she looked him up in the database. It was like he just started school. She thought, maybe, he was just homeschooled before that.

Or maybe he just came out of the tank.

"Where am I?" Sura waves at the tanks. "Which one is me?"

"Are you your body?" Mr. Frost answers.

"You know what I mean! Where am I?"

The yellow-hats stand back. No one answers.

Sura walks numbly down the aisles, peering into tank after tank. Face after face looks back, vaguely human and unrecognizable. They could be her. They could be anyone. She slaps the tanks, pushes against them, but they're too solid to rock off their foundations.

"Where is it?" she shouts.

The yellow-hats and Mr. Frost watch. Behind them, on shelves above the workbenches, are the small tanks. They are slimmer and clear.

Something floats inside them.

Mr. Frost slowly closes his eyes. A nod.

Sura palms the tanks as she fumbles her way to the end of the room, her legs almost useless. She grasps one of the workbenches before losing her balance. A rack of beakers falls over. She leans closely.

Six little tanks. Six little, floating infants.

Infants with round faces.

Six of me.

"It has been a long journey, my dear," Mr. Frost says.

She towers over the portly elven. "Why would you do this?"

Mr. Frost nods slowly, like he understands. Her question makes perfect sense. He pushes with his left foot, slowly sliding away. The white fox follows.

"Once upon a time"—his voice floats around the room—"I tried to help a... man, shall we say."

"An elven," Sura says.

"Yes, an elven. This bit of lore I don't expect you to understand, but let's say he had not a friend in the world. And neither had I. Our friendship was not perfect, but it was better than being alone. Unfortunately, it brought us here."

He holds his arms out, palms up.

"When I arrived here, it was just me. I was being forced to do something that I couldn't do alone, so I gave birth."

"You grew us," Joe says before she can.

"Humans have been fertilizing embryos outside the womb for quite some time," Mr. Frost says. "I did not grow you."

"You called these terrariums!" Joe slaps the tank behind him. "You grew us!"

"No," Sura says, strangely calm. "You cloned us."

Mr. Frost grunts. "I gave birth," he says. "I needed help, not children. I developed adult bodies in vitro and then I gave them a mind."

"Memories." Joe stalks him, despite shaky legs. "You programmed us with memories, made us think we had a past. I remember growing up. I remember the helpers and... and..." He looks back at the tank. "And none of that's real."

"My boy, the mind is much more than memories."

"When did you take me out of the tank?"

"What matters is that you're here."

"WHEN DID YOU TAKE ME OUT?"

Joe punches the tank. Mr. Frost silently watches. The glass rings but doesn't move. He hits it again and again. His knuckles swell. The yellow-hats push him away, grabbing his arms. He tries to hit them.

Joe grabs the table, his chest heaving, head hung low.

"You are real," Mr. Frost says calmly. "You are as real as any human on this planet."

"We never left you," Joe says. "You programmed us to stay on the plantation like helpers."

"You have an instinct to stay here. This is home."

Joe shakes his head, glaring at the wet body on the table.

"What about me?" Sura asks. "Why am I an infant?"

A light returns to Mr. Frost's eyes, briefly and brightly. A smile grows somewhere beneath his whiskers. He bends over to pet the fox.

"Time had eroded my sense of being. Loneliness has that effect. I had lost touch with the essence of life; my identity was dying. I had been robbed of free will and was becoming numb. I still breathed, my heart still beat, but I was dead, child. I didn't care anymore and the world needed me to care."

He says it like a fact.

"You see, Jonah, May, and Templeton have a sense of duty, an unbending dedication to service. They are strong and dependable. But you, Sura... you were born with human frailty. You experience the full range of life, all the love and hate, the sadness and joy. You encompass the essence of humanity. You are vulnerable."

He opens his hand like releasing a dove.

"You are truth."

Joe looks at her blankly. She recognizes that look. It's one of alienation and abandonment. Now he wonders if he matters like she has all her life.

"And Joe?" she asks. "You wanted me to love him."

Mr. Frost looks at the boy. He smiles with the same degree of warmth.

"I am elven," he says. "We are vastly advanced in spirit and body. But we are not perfect. We are vulnerable to self-centeredness and self-pity. What I've done... well, it was not without a degree of self-indulgence. I needed to care again. I needed to understand humanity. I needed to feel what it's like to be human. I wanted to experience life through you. I watched you learn how to walk, struggle with your first words, suffer through sickness, and stumble your way through the human condition. It has been a gift. A selfish one."

Mr. Frost slides closer to the table. He says gently, as if the words would land softer, "But Joe arrived in consciousness about the age of... well, the age he is now, and you fall in love. I've watched your affection bloom and fade as you age. Your relationship encompasses the full spectrum of life."

That's why Joe just started going to high school. He wasn't home-schooled; he just came out of the tank with programmed memories. Joe just woke up in bed one day like it was another day.

Joe's anger fades.

He backs into the glass tank, his head hitting with a hollow bonk, and slides down, eyes glassy and distant. His world has turned into quicksand.

"This is sick," Sura says. "You pretended my clone was my mom. I raised myself."

He nods with a smile. "You are responsible for your own growth, my dear. You raised yourself."

"We didn't ask for this."

"No one asks to be born."

"This is wrong."

"Sometimes life is impossible."

"That doesn't give you the right to play God."

"You can't possibly understand the circumstances I have faced, and you don't know the peril the world faces right now. You should know that, despite all my actions, all my greed, you have been a gift to the world, Sura. Not just to me but to the world. You possess something the others don't."

He slides around the table.

"You have the ability to grow, my dear. Every time you woke into another life, you evolved and transformed." He throws out his hands. "Your understanding of life and the world around you increased, your presence of mind expanded. You denied your desire to love Jonah so that you could understand yourself."

"My mom did that, not me."

"Your growth isn't selfish. It has spread to the others. The others have transformed, too."

Mr. Frost stops a few feet away from her. His presence is chilly, but his face beaming. The color has returned to his cheeks; his eyes sparkle.

"You've changed us all, Sura."

Sura is numb. It's not the room or the temperature; it's the thoughts swirling in her head that steal her presence.

"Let's go." Joe is emotionless. He holds out his shivering hand. "Let's get out of here, Sura."

The yellow-hats are gone. Mr. Frost folds his hands on top of his belly.

"Come on, Sura!" Joe shouts.

She moves half a step. Mr. Frost doesn't try to stop her. Joe takes her by the wrist. His fear is palpable. She's seen that look before. She saw it on Jonah.

Hurt. Pain.

Maybe he's afraid Sura will leave him like her mom left Jonah. Maybe he's afraid of this place. Either way, Joe holds on tightly. He's never going to let go. He pulls her away from Mr. Frost, around the stainless steel table and the sleeping body. They won't make it far, but they'll try.

Frosty trails creep from under the door, racing across the floor like jagged snakes. Joe grabs the handle. Sura feels the temperature in his fingers plummet. Her foot turns painfully cold as one of the icy cracks runs beneath her shoe.

She catches Joe before he falls. His cheeks are stiff and shiny.

The door crashes open.

A blue elven looks down at them with a smile much different than Mr. Frost's.

JACK PLANTS his size-twenty-five foot on the door. It breaks open with ease. Subzero trails crackle across the floor, preceding his entrance into the room.

Smells like dirt.

He halts inside the doorway and almost tips over. A girl is on the floor with a boy across her lap. One sight of Jack and she tries to push away. She looks like a wounded animal.

"I know you." Jack snaps his fingers. "You had the sweet truck, right?"

But something's different. Something is missing. He doesn't feel her, not like when he saw her at the megastore or in the truck. Before, she lit him up with swirling currents of sweetness, branded him with a permanent smile, and filled him with the urge to hug every warmblood within reach. He had never felt that before.

Not ever.

Now she's just some dirty little warmblood giving him that look of fear and hate. She's just like all the others now. Just another warmblood.

"You!" she screams. "You did this!"

"Pipe down, fancy pants. Your boyfriend will be fine."

Joe's eyes are squeezed shut, his body rigid. His lips are sort of blue.

"Or not," Jack adds.

Sura's shoes squeak on the floor, the rubber-tipped soles giving her enough traction to scoot against a tank. She pulls Joe along, palming his cheek against her lips, whispering in his ear.

"Listen," Jack says, "if you didn't want to taste the cold, why'd you come down here?" He cocks his head, lifting an eyebrow. "Actually, how'd you get down here?"

"She's your daughter, Janack." Pawn stands in front of a table.

"What?"

"She's family," Pawn says. "So is Joe. They belong to you. They're your family."

"Pawn, you need a refresher on the birds and bees. How can I put this? I'm elven." Jack flattens his hand over his chest. "And they're warmblood. Two different species, see what I'm saying?"

"All of this is yours, Janack." Pawn spreads his arms. "The children were born because of you. They are part of you, and you are part of them. Can't you feel it?" Pawn thumps his chest. "The connection with them, I know you feel it."

Jack grimaces. He felt something in the truck and, come to think of it, there was no way he could harm her when he felt that. But it's gone now. He's empty. Dead inside.

"Wait!" Jack holds up a finger, looking for an idea on the ceiling.

"No, nothing. I've got nothing. They're warmbloods, Pawn. Just like the rest."

He claps twice.

"Haul them to the back," Jack calls. "Can't have her blubbering all over the place; I'd like to relax. Daddy's had a long day—long couple of centuries, really."

A brigade of twenty or so helpers slide into the room, their tiny hands snatching the girl's coat and pants. She fights them off, but they're persistent. Another twenty helpers file inside and soon lift the boy and girl off the floor.

Sura fights them and makes a move for Jack. She uses every cuss word Jack learned at the shelter.

"Honey, you ain't that tough," Jack says.

The helpers struggle to move them. They shove Pawn to the side and drag Joe in after Sura is in the back room. Her fists pound the locked door. Her profanity is distant but sharp.

"You teach her those words?" Jack asks. "Because I know I didn't."

"Why are you treating them like prisoners?"

"Why are they here?" Jack shouts. "Someone tell me how those punk kids got in my basement!"

I let them down there, sir, Freeda says.

"What?" Jack's eyes bulge.

They are Pawn's pets, sir. It was his plan to dissuade you from carrying out the master plan.

Pawn stays rooted in front of the table, looking at the floor, where he sees defeat fast approaching. There's a body behind him, lying as still as death on a metal slab. Jack cruises around to find his likeness breathing easy.

"What am I doing there?" Jack says.

It's taken some time for me to understand Pawn's motivation for raising children. I was fooled into believing that they brought him happiness and, as a result, he worked harder and more efficiently. He claimed to understand warmbloods now that he felt them, and that's when I understood what he was planning.

Jack waits. His body—the one on the table—breathes with a slight smile. Or maybe the lips are stuck.

"What? What was he planning?"

He wanted you to feel emotions for the children, sir. He thought it would change you the way it changed him.

"I don't feel anything," Jack says.

No, sir. Your incarnation on the table is without a mind, but it embodies all those feelings. I wanted it out of the tank when the children arrived to protect you from their influence. That mindless body has feelings, sir. It's protecting you from compassion, empathy, warmth, love, goodness, openness, kindness—

"All right, all right! I get it." Jack pushes the corners of the lips down so the face is frowning, but they curl back into a smile. Water pools over the eyelids. "Am I... I mean, is he crying?"

Sir, I want you to be free of any feeling so that you can think clearly. Please reconsider the meltdown—

"Shut up, please!" Jack covers his ears. "Go do your work and stop wasting time. And thank you for saving me from feelings."

Jack slides around the room, tapping his chin. The thumping from the back room has stopped; the cussing replaced by an occasional whimper. The fox stands at the door. Jack circles the lab while dragging his hand over the tanks.

Pawn is quiet and expressionless.

"That's it?" Jack stops in front of him. "Your whole mutiny was a girl and feelings? Why not a big gun or like a snaggletoothed swamp thing? A girl? Feelings?"

"I beg of you," Pawn whispers, "to put this incarnation away and open yourself to understanding again. If you see what I see, Janack—"

"Okay, timeout. See, that's where you're wrong. First of all, don't call me Janack. I've been telling you that for thousands of years and you're still doing it. Do it again and I turn your kidney into a tub of ice cream."

"I'd welcome that."

"Oh, don't get all sour grapes on me." Jack raps his knuckles on one of the tanks. "Freeda shoved a cable into the back of my head, so don't act all high and mighty. It itches, I get it. But you know why, dingbat? You know why it itches?"

Jack drags his fingernails across the steel table.

"All I wanted you to do was come here, amass a fortune, distribute slave technology, and reincarnate me. Is that too much to ask?"

Jack lifts Pawn's head up with the crook of his finger.

"But you had to build all these tanks for your warmblood pets. It's a waste of my time and money."

"It's called family, Janack."

"Don't call me that!" Jack puts his finger between Pawn's eyes. The color bleaches from his irises. Ice crystals form on his eyelashes. He slides away, shaking with anger. He makes a complete circle around the lab to give Pawn's ears time to thaw.

"You put green hair on me, Pawn."

Jack flattens his palm on the tank next to Pawn. The surface begins to crackle. The glass fractures beneath Jack's icy grip. He punches a hole through the suddenly brittle tank and the whole thing shatters.

A green lump slaps at Pawn's feet.

"GREEN HAIR!"

A layer of frost covers Jack's head, turning it from blue to a strange, very cold-looking coat of ice. The floor buckles as the temperature beneath his soles plummets. The fox runs to Mr. Frost's side. He picks him up.

Frigid air streams from Jack's nostrils, coating his jacket with crystals. His eyes bulge. He raises his fists, draws a deep breath, pulls his deep blue lips over pearly, white teeth...

"AaaaaaaaAAAAAAAAAAAAA!"

Icy lines race across the floor like tentacles, crawling up the walls and across the ceiling. Jagged lines wrap around the tanks.

Popping. Cracking.

Exploding.

Glass rains from all directions.

Green bodies tumble out of the shattered tanks, landing with wet thumps on the slick floor, limp and stagnant.

Jack wipes a thick layer of frost from his face, huffing to catch his breath. Air hisses between his teeth. He takes another lap to cool off. The bodies clog the aisles and force him to walk. When he returns, his flesh is baby blue.

Pawn remains at the table with the fox in his arms.

"What happened to us, buddy?" Jack asks. "We used to be on the same page, remember? Remember when we took control of the elven and tried to make the world a better place? Remember that? Remember when I was king and you were my right-hand man? Remember when you went everywhere with me, even took the root for me?"

Jack kicks a floppy arm.

"I'm gone a couple hundred years and look what happens. You have all this power, and you become a gardener? You put a statue of Jocah out there and build a wishing room? If that doesn't scream distraction, I don't know what does."

Jack frowns.

"And how did you build a wishing room where Freeda can't see or hear you?"

He had become despondent, sir. I was afraid we would lose him to madness and—

"Oh, my God. Are you still here?" Jack pulls upright. "Get to work! Besides, he's a grown man, let him answer."

Jack looks his friend in the cold, defeated eyes.

"I'm waiting."

"I, uh." Pawn puts the fox down. "I wasn't well. The itch and Freeda's voice made it hard to think. I wasn't able to function; I needed a place to recuperate. Freeda actually suggested it. It's a safe room; nothing can happen in there. It lets me visit home."

"I got news, buddy. You're already home."

Jack taps the table. His fingernails sound like rock hammers. He's thinking about what Freeda said. Maybe he's acting hastily. If Pawn could build that wishing room, maybe he could turn Freeda against him. Maybe a visit to the wishing room would ease his mind. He could delay the meltdown a day or two. No reason he couldn't do it on New Year's Eve, right when the ball drops in Times Square. Everyone in the world would be watching.

"You've changed," Pawn says.

Jack's startled. "No, I haven't changed, Pawn. This is exactly who I was two hundred years ago, you know that. There's nothing good about me."

Nothing good about me. Those words come out too easy.

"You don't remember the end. The last time you updated the root was just before you died. You planned a victory celebration where you confronted your mother, but something happened. Your brother came out, unexpectedly."

"First of all," Jack says, "their names are Jocah and Claus, not mother and brother. I cut them out of the will."

"Your mother asked for your forgiveness. Your brother did, too."

"Yeah, yeah. Freeda told me about it."

"But you don't remember. You transformed in that moment."

Jack chuckles and looks away. He doesn't really want to hear this.

"I saw it happen," Pawn says. "I was there, I saw you lose the coldness. I saw you filled with warmth, life, and love, that same experience you felt when you were near Sura—"

"All right, enough." Jack steps on a squishy leg. He can't slide away. He'd like to return to the tower now.

"Do you know how much it pains me to bring you back without that realization?" Pawn says. "To see you have that experience of being whole again and losing it? To see you return to your original elven self, right there on stage, and then have to bring you back without it? You're alone, again."

Jack climbs over a stack of wet bodies, their limbs tangled. His foot goes through the stomach of one. He stomps a path for the exit.

"Janack."

Jack stops against his will. For some reason, the name doesn't have the same sting.

"Let the kids go. They're innocent."

"They're warmbloods," Jack says, without looking back. "*You've* changed, Pawn."

"Yes, I have. And I owe it to them."

Jack plucks a mushy green foot from between his toes and tosses it. "You stay here with them. I'm going up to watch the show. And if anything goes wrong—and I mean anything—I'll be throwing your foot across the room."

Jack wants to slam the door, but there are too many body parts in the way. Instead, he races for the elevator.

Pawn better not ruin my Christmas.

MR. FROST WATCHES the green bodies freeze. They weren't human; they didn't have an identity; they were still plants. Still, his heart aches.

They will never be.

"It's almost over, Max." The furry white fox rubs against him.

The house shudders.

Mr. Frost climbs over the stiff botanical corpses. He reaches for the back door and hears the soft weeping. He hesitates. It's almost too much to bear.

JACK STEPS out of the elevator to applause.

The helpers are standing in stadium seating, clapping like they've been waiting for him to arrive, high-fiving each other when he looks in their direction. He's Elvis/Michael Jackson/Stevie Ray Vaughan all rolled into a fat, blue body.

"What's going on?" Jack says.

I sensed your loneliness, sir, and invited them to keep you company.

The helpers don't let up; they celebrate like the biggest game in history is only minutes away. The noise rattles his head. Maybe if they weren't whistling.

"Out," he says. "OUT!"

Silence.

"Get out, all of you! Get in the basement and stay there, every one of you. If I see one of your stupid hats before daylight, I'll punt you like volleyballs!"

The elevator opens. They politely file inside.

"There's only one trip down. Whoever's left behind becomes a footstool."

They pile into the elevator now, climbing on top of each other until it looks like a can of ugly, gummy gnomes. Jack shoves an arm and leg inside as the door closes with a groan.

The stadium seats fall flat.

"Status!" he shouts. "Tell me everything is good, Freeda. I mean it."

Sir, it's very good. Ninety-five percent of all toys along the East Coast will launch at midnight. That's in exactly fifteen minutes.

"Why not one hundred percent?"

We have to account for aging and a certain percentage of malfunctions. Sir, ninety-five percent is far beyond what I anticipated. My projections were closer to sixty percent.

"Sixty percent would've got you fired."

Jack looks out the window. The garden is lit with strands of white lights. The center glows around the remnants of the statue.

It wasn't supposed to be like this.

He thought Pawn would be happier to see him, thought maybe he'd be so thrilled that he'd hug Jack and Jack would push him off, tell him to stop, but not really. And when Pawn finally let go, he'd have tears in his eyes.

They were supposed to sit together, like the old days. Jack's big, comfy chair would be bigger because he was king. Pawn would slide the bucket of chum closer so Jack could reach it without getting up. They'd watch the master plan come full circle like old buddies. Old pals.

Pawn is in the basement. He doesn't have a chair down there. He's too grown up for chairs, so he can stay down there and think about what he's done.

He's grown. That's the dumbest thing Jack ever heard. He changed —he didn't grow up. He changed and Jack didn't, and he needed to get that through his hairy skull or he'd spend the rest of his life down there with those slimy, green bodies.

Sir, if you'd like, we can—

"Shhh."

Jack holds up his hand, cocking his head.

He swears he hears someone singing "Silent Night." He invented that song, at least the "silent night" part. He didn't have anything to do with the other words, but Freeda had told him how elven have influenced warmbloods. They stole the song from him.

That's Jack's song.

He sang it when he was little. It made him feel safe, like his mother was holding him. He liked that feeling, like everything was going to be all right, that the world loved him.

"Let's just say it's true," he says out loud. "Let's say I reconciled with my mother and brother at the end, that we hugged and kissed and everything was all peachy... that doesn't mean I changed. Maybe I was faking it. Maybe they were lying, trying to trap me, and I was pretending to warm up. Pawn doesn't know what I was *feeeeeling*; he just saw what was happening."

Sir?

Jack's lips snap shut. He said that out loud.

Five minutes until launch, sir. I've prepared a seat for you.

There's a chair in the room. Only one.

It's a big, comfy recliner with six snack buckets—krill, sardines, minnows, goldfish (the fat kind), tadpoles, and guppies—close enough he won't have to get up. The ceiling is stacked with monitors, each of them showing a scene from a living room somewhere in the world. They all have Christmas trees.

Jack's got the front row.

And if you wish, sir, you can choose one home to launch the first activation. Once we confirm success, we'll simultaneously launch on all the homes along the East Coast. You'll experience it firsthand.

He couldn't care less which one. He thought this would be a little more exhilarating, that maybe there'd be a tingly sensation in his belly, like the time he stuck it to Pickett. Now he feels dull and heavy.

He has a thought. Maybe he should wait, like she said. He'd have to admit she was right, though. And maybe Pawn might stop acting so selfish and next year he could be up there next to him.

"Umm..."

Yes, sir?

"Yeah, I was thinking..."

Yes?

Jack shakes a finger at one of the monitors and sneers. *Let's get this over with.*

The room transforms into a warmly lit living room.

The tower becomes four hideous walls splattered with family photos. There are two green couches to his left and a wall with a snow-crusted window. A coffee table is in front of him with a flickering candle. There are also pictures of Santa drawn with purple and red markers and a note and cell phone. A small plate of half-eaten cookies is on the floor. Beyond that are carpeted steps that lead upstairs, with garland wrapped around the banister.

Five minutes to launch, sir.

Jack yanks the note from beneath the cell phone. It's written in giant, ugly letters.

Santa,

I hope you like chocolate chip cookies. I made them. I hope you have a safe trip. I hope we are safe. I hope you got Mom a present.

I love you.

    From Cindy.

Jack wads it up.

The Christmas tree is surrounded by gifts, some wrapped better than others. Jack thinks about opening them and wonders if Freeda really knows what's inside them so that she can project an exact replica. He's never opened a present.

Far to Jack's right, about ten feet from the Christmas tree, is the fireplace, where blackened logs smolder. There are four giant socks hanging from the mantel, all bulging with stuff. Mom, Dad, Cindy, and Kooper are written on each one with glitter glue. Kooper must be a dog. Or he likes bones.

Two minutes, sir.

Jack pulls a box from one of the stockings. Pop-Tarts. Cindy got Pop-Tarts from Santa. Jack never had a stocking. He sort of wishes he could see what a Pop-Tart tastes like. Probably disgusting, but he still wonders.

The steps creak.

Little feet appear on the top step. A girl comes down wearing a long shirt. She's holding a ragged, pink blanket against her face and sucking her thumb. Her skin is brown. Jack wonders if Willie has a child and if she looks like that.

He watches her thump to the bottom step and stare at the mountain of presents. Her eyes are half-open, but her expression is filled with sleepy wonder. She basks in the magical colors dancing on the Christmas tree, the sparkly strips of tinsel hanging from the branches, draped over the gifts. She doesn't move.

Jack, either.

She goes to the nearest one, the biggest of them all, a present wrapped in glittery red paper, and drops on her knees. Sucking sounds escape her thumb-plugged lips. She picks at the paper without letting go of the blanket.

It's midnight, sir.

The cell phone vibrates. Not the intermittent buzz that indicates a text, just one long drone that slowly drives the phone across the table.

Cindy doesn't notice. She's turned the small hole into a long strip, exposing the box inside and colorful letters she's not old enough to read. The blankie hits the floor and the thumb comes out. Both hands attack the present—

A laptop begins to vibrate.

Cindy looks up. Computers don't vibrate.

The thumb goes back in the mouth. She grabs the blankie. She's not about to cry, not yet. But when the TV vibrates, well, that's enough to make anyone squeak a little.

Cindy squelches a cry, holding it inside her throat as she heads for the stairs. Just as she reaches the bottom step, the laptop falls off the desk. Cindy doesn't see it slap the floor like a wet towel.

Jack's still holding the Pop-Tarts.

The laptop melts like wax. The Apple logo spreads out like a stain and creeps through the carpet. The television slides off the entertainment center and eats through the bottom of the couch. The couch leans to one side as the TV goo consumes the leg.

The cellphone has eaten a hole through the table. The candle falls over. The flame catches the note on fire. The purple and red drawing of Santa crackles in the flame, black smoke curling at the edges.

The fire spreads to the wrapping paper.

Jack has crushed the Pop-Tarts.

It's working exactly like it's supposed to work. Slave technology consumes the room like roaming puddles of acid. And what it hasn't dissolved, the fire licks. Black smoke rises to the ceiling, setting off a piercing alarm. The floor vibrates as the television puddle merges with the laptop. The cellphone blob gnaws its way from beneath the burning table.

The room shudders.

Sir.

Jack drops the crumpled box and grabs onto the mantel. The walls are shaking. Ornaments roll across the carpet, stick to the oozing pools, and melt. Holes open in the floor as slave technology converts matter into energy and miniature black holes transport the resulting explosions to another place in the universe.

The Christmas tree falls over.

Sir! We have a problem!

Dad runs down the steps, a look of horror lighting up his face. Jack realizes he doesn't have long ropes of hair that dangle across his forehead, that that's not Willie. But still.

Dad doesn't notice the gray muck that's creeping up the walls. Mom comes down with Cindy, sobs leaking around her thumb.

Jack thought this would be more fun to watch. Maybe using live projection wasn't such a good idea. He's thinking a quick update would suffice. He doesn't need the blow-by-blow report.

A summary would be fine.

He's thinking, as the floor fractures and the furniture looks like poorly molded clay, that he'll take a nap, let Freeda handle the rest of this. He's tired. He'll wake in the morning and read about it—

"Stop!" Jack shouts. "Turn it off! I don't want to see it!"

The scene evaporates; the tower is once again empty but continues to shake. Jagged cracks form on the floor.

The elevator emerges.

Sir, you need to evacuate.

"What?" Jack tries to keep his balance.

Something happened. The launch somehow triggered micro-nuclear reactions inside the laboratories.

"What?"

The foundation of the house is being consumed, sir. You need to evacuate.

The tower sways.

"It's eating the house?"

Get out now, sir!

"But I... I don't have... where?"

Long pause. *You have to get out!*

Jack falls twice before getting inside the elevator. He lies on the floor, staring at a hole in the ceiling, as the elevator sinks towards ground level. He's afraid, but strangely he's not thinking of that. He's thinking Cindy will never get those Pop-Tarts. The beige color of the elevator ceiling fades to gray and bubbles at the margin. A blob hangs like melting plastic.

The elevator heaves to one side.

The gelatinous glob splatters on the wall and starts consuming the surface, revealing the shiny, metal tube that contains the elevator.

Don't touch it, sir.

"Okay."

The elevator opens.

A rack of pots crashes on the counter, metal tumbling across the floor like alarms. The house groans. A crack opens across the ceiling, spilling dust.

Get up, sir!

Jack wishes he never woke up.

Get! Up!

He plows through the kitchenware clutter. The door is jammed in the frame, but one mighty blow from Jack's adrenaline-fueled foot sends it off its hinges. In the hall, a mirror is facedown, reflective shards on the floor. Bad luck everywhere.

The house shifts in the other direction. Jack steadies himself and finds his stride as gray goo oozes from ventilation ducts. Half a credenza is cocked in the great room.

The back door is hanging on the bottom hinge. Jack runs full speed and leaps far enough to clear the gaping threshold. He rolls down the steps and into the brown grass like a giant ball.

It's below freezing, but not much.

It's hot.

Four yellow-hat helpers stop him from rolling across the field. The ground heaves like a beast is rising. The yellow-hats jump up and down, wave, and run toward the garden.

Sir... don't go...

She's breaking up.

Beams snap and the black, monolithic tower lurches like a tree about to fall in slow motion. Jack lets out a little squeak and pumps his fat arms, his wide feet slapping the earth, hot on the yellow-hats' trail.

The air feels like engine exhaust.

The tower follows him as it leans. A sudden shift in the foundation temporarily brings it back into balance. Jack gets to the road as the ground caves behind him. The underground laboratories and toy factory are collapsing like mine shafts. The Christmas lights illuminate the garden's entrance, where the yellow-hats jump and wave.

He misses the first step and rolls through the boxwoods, coming to rest on a thin scab of ice. The pedestal is still shaped like elven feet. Jack slips getting up.

SIR... SHOULDN'T...

He doesn't need that bodiless voice. It sounds like the Earth is grinding the house with massive molars. He runs after the yellow-hats bouncing up and down in the north exit, whimpering like a child stuck in a nightmare. He just wants to go home, wants to be back on the North Pole, where the world is flat, white, and cold.

Where the air doesn't bake his lungs.

He rushes into the tunnel, but there's nothing but thick branches and leathery leaves. It's a dead end. The yellow-hats pull the branches open. There's something white on the other side. They windmill their tiny arms, urging him to hurry, to keep going, to crawl through the hole.

The house lets out one final groan. An explosion of timber and steel rumbles the ground.

Jack's feet pound the mulch.

He gets momentum.

The ground heaves him forward. He throws his arms in front of him and dives into a layer of white powder.

Snow.

Snow everywhere. Nothing but.

He thinks he probably just died and went to heaven because if he designed heaven, it would be this. It would be just miles and miles of snow.

But he's not dead.

The air is crisp. The sky is dark and clear.

The wishing room.

Jack laughs, rolls, and hugs the snow, rubbing it on his face, putting it in his mouth. He makes a snow angel in the deep white blanket.

No more scary sounds.

He lies back in silence—sweet, sweet silence—and counts the stars. The North Star twinkles brighter than he's ever seen it, like it's welcoming him home.

"I don't know how you did it, Pawn. But you did it."

He rests easy and alone, feeling safe and happy, wishing Pawn was there to enjoy it. Maybe when it is all over, they could come back to the wishing room and plan their next move.

Surely Pawn would have a way out of the basement.

SURA SITS IN THE CORNER, her coat around Joe. His head is cradled in the crook of her arm. She strokes his pale cheek.

He isn't shivering. Not anymore.

"It'll be all right," Sura whispers. "It'll be all right."

Max whines.

The house groans. The doorframe cracks.

"Do something!" Sura looks up.

But there's nothing Mr. Frost can do, nothing he can say. Max runs to her side. He licks Joe's hand.

Sura rocks back and forth, humming a song that perhaps her mom once sang to her, a wordless tune that Mr. Frost recognizes—a song that's buried in her Inuit DNA. A song that Pana and Sesi hummed to Mr. Frost when he needed comforting.

Joe's lips move.

She lowers her ear to his cracked lips. He says something barely above a whisper. She squeezes tightly, crushing him against her. A moan escapes from deep inside her, long and primal.

Max begins to howl.

Joe's eyes are blank, a slight smile fixed at the corner of his mouth.

"Please don't go," Sura whispers, rocking again. "Please, please, please."

Mr. Frost gently takes Joe's body and slides it on the floor, careful to lay his head down. She fights him, at first, but then resigns. Hands to her mouth, eyes tearful.

"How could you let that monster do this?" she says.

"We cannot make people change or grow, Sura. We can only give them the opportunity."

Sura buries her face in her hands, shivering and wailing. Mr. Frost places Joe's hands over his stomach and adjusts his legs until he appears comfortable.

An explosion gives rise to panicked helpers stampeding through the incubation lab. The house thunders.

"You must go," Mr. Frost says.

"I'm not going."

"Your death will not serve him. You live, Sura. You must."

"I'm staying."

Mr. Frost wraps the coat around her, pulling the hood over her head. Her teeth chatter through sobs. She lets him cover her, either out of desperation or apathy.

"You should know," Mr. Frost says as he buttons the coat, "that I didn't create him to love you, or you to love him. I birthed you both out of love, and you came together on your own. None of what you feel is false, Sura. He loved you. He truly loved you, and I had nothing to do with that."

He puts his hand over hers and she reaches out, grabbing him tightly, pulling him closer, sobbing into his shoulder. Mr. Frost holds his own tears in check, comforting her while Max pushes between them, whining.

The ceiling buckles. Debris showers the bed.

He lifts her up. She lets him guide her from the room. Joe looks asleep and peaceful.

The incubator lab is dusted with debris drizzling from cracks. Fractures have opened on the walls. Gray stuff spills on the floor and sizzles. It pulses over frozen limbs, the stainless steel table, and fallen chunks of ceiling.

Mr. Frost guides Sura towards a hole in the back corner.

"Follow Max," he says. "Take it to the end, as far away as possible."

"You're not coming?"

"My place is here."

Mr. Frost digs the metal tin from his pocket and feeds Max one last time. The white fox dives through the opening, disappearing in the darkness.

"You must survive." He squeezes her hand. "You must."

The ceiling continues to rain. He wants to think that she leaves because he compelled her to, that he expressed his true feelings about her as a daughter. He always thought of her as such. But maybe, in the end, it was simply an impulse to survive.

It doesn't matter. As long as she does.

She looks back once, and then crawls into the darkness. Mr. Frost heaves a tank over the opening in case she thinks of coming back.

A loud crack knocks the main door off its hinges. Helpers are still searching for an escape. Most are already out of harm's way.

Mr. Frost feels the contraction of fear in his chest, the twist in his belly. He watches the ceiling ooze like faucets of matter-consuming bile. The house moans, shifting on its foundation. The eyeTablets were the obvious choice to execute the master plan—Mr. Frost had a counter for that, in case Jack wisely chose it—but Mr. Frost knew Jack was too impatient, that he'd want results as soon as he could get them. Slave technology used to consume matter would be too tempting; Jack couldn't say no to that any more than a child would refuse a marshmallow.

Mr. Frost knew it would end this way.

Wood splinters somewhere in the basement. Steel girders snap and a bright light flashes outside the incubator lab. Although he doesn't hear it, Mr. Frost feels her death.

"Goodbye, Freeda," he whispers.

And for the first time since fleeing the North Pole, the root falls silent. Completely silent.

In his last moments, he relishes peaceful emptiness.

SURA CAN'T SEE.

The ceiling isn't high enough to stand. She crawls on soft, some-times slimy, ground. When a cockroach crawls over her knuckles, she walks hunched over, hands out mummy-style. Max pants somewhere in front of her. Sometimes she brushes the side of the tunnel or feels something in her hair, but doesn't stop.

She can't go back.

Somewhere, in the dark distance behind her, something is grind-ing. She hums to blot out the sound, to distract her mind where the image of Joe, lying so still and quiet, demands her attention. Her thoughts try to turn her around, go back to the lab, and crawl up next to him.

The humming keeps her going.

She yearns for light, to see something, anything that will help her escape the haunting thought. The ground shudders, and she scrapes her head on the ceiling. Something crawls down her arm. Max begins to yip in the distant blackness. Sura swings her arms out to her sides, scrapes the concrete walls, and steps quickly and carelessly.

Another monstrous groan.

Max yips again.

The darkness begins to change. A gray form takes shape, getting lighter and lighter with each step. Max waits for her like a furry lump of ash. Sura scoops him up. He licks her wet cheeks.

There's a short ladder attached to a wall. Ten rungs up, there's a hole. Leaves blow inside. A head appears with a frumpy hat. Even in the dim light, it's yellow. Two more yellow-hats look down, their fingers urging her to climb. Their rapid words tell her to hurry.

Sura climbs the bottom rungs.

The tunnel exhales a mighty wind that swirls her hair. The yellow hats are caught in the draft, twirling out of sight as the crowd quakes. Dirt rains down. She stops on the third rung to cover up. A terrible crash of wood, glass, and metal is everywhere.

The helpers return with yellow hats back on their heads. Tea olives greet her at the top with their fragrant blooms. Sura peeks out from a hole wedged between the root flares of an enormous live oak. The yellow-hats take Max and help her up, covering the hole with an earthen lid.

The helpers made it out.

Blue hats, red hats, orange, purple, green, and every color in between, are huddled beneath the live oak grove. Some of them were probably the ones that threw her and Joe into the back room, but now they cling to each other, listening to the house snap like massive bones.

Max climbs onto her lap. The yellow-hats press against her, their bodies warm. More crowd around her. She feels the weight of their neediness, the quake of their fear. The house cries out and the tower— listing to the north—is sucked down. A final tremor rides across the ground where bottomless ruts have opened. All that remains are holes. The toy factory is gone.

And so, finally, is the house.

Sura feels another emotional hole inside her, one right next to her mom. This one is Joe. The fear that drove her through the tunnel and steeled her legs evaporates, leaving her with the messy emptiness of her life. She puts her head down, letting the waiting grief have its way with her. She sobs uncontrollably.

The yellow-hats put their small arms around her. She hugs them. When they climb off, more of them comfort her. Red-hats, blue-hats, green-hats... they all find their way to Sura and squeeze tightly. Some shake with fear, others sob with her. Some of them utter speedy little words that sound comforting. Apologetic.

Sura openly weeps.

And hugs them all.

18

DECEMBER 25

Thursday

J ack wakes in a soft bed.

He rolls over, reaches for a pillow, and rakes his arm through powdery snow.

He opens his eyes.

The sun is rising somewhere to his right, but the stars are not dampened, not entirely. The sky is deep blue. A barren landscape of snow and ice extends in every direction. He's on the North Pole. He's back home. It was all a dream and now he's home.

HOME!

Jack marches in a circle, stomping the snow and pumping his fist. "Snow! Snow! Snow!"

Wait.

A memory thuds. He jumped into the wishing room when the house tried to eat him. This is Pawn's special place, a room to fulfill his every desire. That means this isn't snow, not really. And if he's in here, that means what's out there...

Jack's heart lies heavy.

Little Cindy opening her present, the fire, the creeping gray goo. The Pop-Tarts.

"Freeda?" Jack jumps up. "Freeda!"

His voice evaporates in the open sky.

"Pawn!"

Jack wades through the snow, white dust up to his elbows, sticking to his chin. He shouts their names over and over, walking in circles, but it's snow forever and ever.

There's nothing out there.

"Free—"

A hole.

It wasn't there a second ago. Now there's an opening like space has been parted like curtains, dark shrubbery on the other side.

The door!

He's got to get out. He can't stay in the wishing room, he'll starve. Without a coolsuit, he'll overheat. At least, that's what Freeda told him.

"Freeda?"

No answer.

The vegetative alleyway is dim but, surprisingly, doesn't feel too bad. It must've cooled down overnight. He steps onto the mulched path, twigs snapping underfoot. The garden is ahead; he can see daylight. He stops and listens for someone. For anything.

He hears nothing—not a tree frog, not a bird or a bug.

Jack stops at the entrance to the garden. There are holes in the boxwoods where he rolled through them on his way from the house, and there are still chunks of ice in the center. Jack walks around the outside of the garden. Steam rises from the remains of the statue. He stops at the exit.

No wonder Freeda didn't answer.

The house is gone.

Vanished.

As if it never existed.

There's a hole in the earth and deep gullies in the field. The soil isn't scorched, nothing is damaged, just a big vacancy where the house, the labs, and the toy factory used to be. The slave technology consumed it, transformed metal and wood, plastic and glass, into pure energy.

Just... gone.

What's left is a massive vacancy, something that—it would seem—could never be filled again.

The sun isn't up, but all the stars have dimmed except for the

North Star. Jack is too jittery to notice it twinkling white, red, and green.

"Pawn!" Jack steps onto the road, hands cupped around his mouth. "Pawn! You there?"

He was in the basement, locked in the incubator lab. Why didn't he escape? Jack feels like he's falling, even though his feet are firmly on the ground.

"Pawn!"

His voice echoes off the distant trees. He resorts to Freeda's name, just in case there's a backup somewhere under the rubble. He'd love to hear her voice inside his head. So far, it's just his own. Each time he calls, it sounds shakier and a little higher pitched.

He stands at the edge of the chasm. Groundwater has filled it. He feels the depth of its hopelessness, how nothing is alive in that murky hole. He created it—this is *his* fault. He's the one responsible for this all-consuming hole in his life. He's been avoiding it for thousands of years and now he's staring into its depths. He always tried to fill the holes he felt inside himself, and now there's one big one he can't avoid.

And now what?

What does he have?

Nobody. It's just Jack and the hole.

"Janack?" someone calls.

He looks around. Maybe he's imagining it, but then he hears it again. It's coming from the garden. Jack steps tentatively across the road, trying not to make noise. He sneaks up to the entrance and slides one eye around the edge.

"Mother?"

There she is, standing on the pedestal where an ice statue chiseled into her likeness once stood. Her hands are folded on her belly, the white hair pulled back into the single braid.

"Janack," she says again.

Her face is soft, almost glowing. Her eyes, deeply set in fully rounded cheeks, are smiling blue.

Jack clears his throat. "Um, your statue... it fell over. There was a storm and, uh, we were going to do another one..."

She doesn't say anything. Jack gets the sense she doesn't care about the statue.

He looks up and sighs. He wasn't accustomed to taking responsibility. It's easier to lie. "It's just... you see, Pawn didn't tell me about you and me reconciling before I died, and I don't remember us, you know, that we were hugging and stuff, so if you think about it, it's kind of Pawn's fault."

This is hard.

"Oh, I don't remember what I said before I died." He swallows. "Or what you said or what Claus... so, I'm still a little..."

The words fall off his tongue like dead fish. He sounds stupid and embarrassed. His mother opens her arms. She smiles. That's all she does.

Smile.

Jack's belly softens. Without thinking about it, without forcing it, the words come out.

"This is all my fault." He looks down. "I did all this. I wrecked this whole place and everything in it. I was trying to help the world, you know. Seriously, I was. I don't like warmbloods..."

But that's not true. He knows it. And those words clog his throat until truer ones come out.

"I screwed up."

Something breaks loose. He feels it just below his heart, some silky essence spreading across his chest, rising to his throat. He's afraid to open his mouth or he'll...

"Come to me." Her arms are still open. Her face, still inviting.

Or I'll cry.

Jack steps through the boxwoods, taking a straight path toward the center. He stops short of the pool of water that surrounds Jocah. It's no longer ice, but he doesn't feel hot. He feels just right. His mother's love warms him.

He just... he has to say one more thing. He's got to say this, to admit it. To own it.

"I killed Pawn."

Warmth gushes through his throat and barks out sobs that rack his body.

"He was my only friend and I made him suffer with that root and then I shoved him in the basement and the house fell and I guess he couldn't swim or something..."

He runs out of breath. After that, the sobs take over.

He doesn't remember falling into her arms or splashing through the water, he just remembers the grief that fills him, that spills out of him. His feelings of hurt and abandonment rise up, feelings he's spent all his life trying to hide. He sees them, allows them space.

Pawn. My only friend.

And he did all that to him.

He tries to tell his mother more, tries to make sense of his thoughts, but the words are smeared with sniffles and sobs.

"What's wrong with me?" he blubbers.

His mother wraps him tightly, warmly, while he spills tears into the pool. Through blurry eyes, he sees his blue face.

"His name isn't Pawn," he says. "It's Jack."

He took that from his friend. It's time to give it back.

My name is Janack.

Another round of wailing fills the garden. He hangs onto his mother, her warmth protecting him, filling him, showing him that he's not bad.

He's lost.

Janack falls asleep in his mother's arms while the North Star twinkles white, red, and green. He doesn't feel his breath stop or his pulse silence. The end for the portly blue elven comes like a sweet lullaby.

THE CROW SOUNDS LIKE A HORN.

The sky is blemished only by fading white tracks left from airplanes crisscrossing at ten thousand feet.

The helpers are pressed all around Sura, keeping her toasty and comfortable. Their bite-sized snores merge like an endless mantra, tempting her to fall back asleep. She watches a commercial airliner slowly draw a white line across the blue sky, this one traveling south.

Max is gone. The crow calls again.

The tree root makes for a poor pillow, slightly bruising the side of her head. She sits up. Little bodies tumble off her but aren't roused from slumber. Sura rubs her eyes. The scene across the field quickly reminds her that reality can be cold and hard. A titan has taken a bite from the earth and stomped a hole in her life.

Joe is dead.

The image of his face will haunt her for the rest of her life: the waxy complexion, the vacant stare, his lips stiffly uttering his last words.

"N'ayez pas peur." Don't be afraid.

Those words will play in her dreams every night, will follow her every day. The hole in the earth is nothing compared to what she'll feel forever.

There are no tears left.

The truth shivers inside her. She thinks of crawling beneath the sleeping helpers, closing her eyes, and dreaming of some place warm, safe, and wanted. But that won't help.

And she's awake.

Sura stands up. She has to hopscotch her way through sleeping helpers. She steps out of the tree's shadow. Frost glitters on the grass where tracks lead away. Max must've left sometime during the night. It's not safe. The ground looks soft and the chasm deep. If he fell, there'll be no saving him, and she's lost so much already.

She exhales faint clouds.

How did this happen?

Where will the helpers go?

Where will I go?

Sura follows Max's path, the tracks etched in the frost. She hugs herself against the morning breeze, her clothes damp. She keeps her distance from the pit as clods break away from the sides and plunk into the deep water.

Birds flutter in the trees and squirrels dig through the fallen leaves. Whatever happened affected the house and laboratories. Even the barn is gone.

She slows as the space between the trees and the chasm narrows. The edge of the great hole stops short of the road that once circled the house. A flighty sensation of vertigo tugs at her. She brushes against the hedges as she approaches the garden entrance.

Voices.

Sura holds her breath. Her pulse is loud in her ears.

"We stayed at the southern end of the plantation," Templeton says. "There wasn't much sleeping."

Someone answers him, but it's too soft to understand.

"Sit down," Templeton says. "You're weak."

Sura crawls the final steps and peeks around the opening. She stays low enough to not be noticed. Templeton is near the center of the garden. He's wearing a puffy coat and a stocking cap. His face is smudged with dirt.

"The transfer," he says. "It was complete?"

She can't see the other person, but he speaks louder. "Missing memories," he says.

The voice trails off. Templeton listens patiently. Sura thinks about crawling closer, but that'll give her up, and she'd like to find out who is down there.

"What happened to Sura?" Templeton asks.

The other person says something. Templeton's expression doesn't change when he says, "We'll search for her when the others get here. What about Joe?"

Sura clutches the grass. She holds her breath, raises up slightly, but can't hear. Maybe he didn't say anything. Templeton, though, dips his head. It's not much, maybe he's just tired. He's not even standing upright.

"You're cold," Templeton finally says. "Take off your shirt."

Take off your shirt?

Templeton bends over to help. Max lets out a yip. The fox is down there. Templeton can't be talking to Mr. Frost. It doesn't sound like him. *And Mr. Frost doesn't get cold.*

There's mumbling. It goes on for quite a while this time.

"It's all complete," Templeton finally answers. "Everything worked as you planned. The house, the laboratories, everything. It's all been dissolved entirely. Janack's impatience and greed worked as you thought it would. He attempted to get it all and it backfired."

"Did Freeda survive?" the unknown person asks.

"Like I said, everything is gone," Templeton says.

"And the human race?"

"They are none the wiser. The initial launch harmed no one, including the family. However, they lost everything in a fire."

"I want—"

Templeton raises his hand. "Already taken care of. An anonymous donation will arrive this afternoon, along with presents for the young girl. I believe her name is Cindy."

Sura's elbows ache, her knees throb. It feels safe down there, but she can't take the chance. If she's wrong, if that's not Mr. Frost...

If only Joe was with her. They could get back in the truck and camp until they knew it was safe.

"So I must ask," Templeton says. "Jack is dead?"

Sura waits for the answer. There is none. Templeton is looking in the direction of the wishing room. He lets out a deep breath like he's held it for far too long. For the first time, he looks relaxed.

There's a squeal.

It comes from the south side of the garden. May is standing in the entrance, hands over her mouth. She's not bundled up like Templeton, but she's just as dirty.

"Is it true?" she asks.

Templeton almost smiles.

May runs carefully around the boxwoods, arms swinging to her sides, her squeal interrupted only by brief inhalations. She gets to the center and bends down, disappearing from Sura's view.

"Careful, May," Templeton says. "He's delicate. You'll snap him like a twig."

May finally stands up and hooks her arm around Templeton's elbow. She wipes her eyes.

"It's over," she says. "It's finally over."

Templeton pats her hand.

"Where's Sura?" she asks. "Joe?"

Sura can't hear the answer. She sits up and there's a sudden yip. Max shoots through the boxwoods and lands in Sura's arms. She falls over.

Templeton shades his eyes. May covers her mouth again. The squeal is twice as loud this time. She lifts her arms and doesn't bother with the path; this time, she pushes straight through the boxwoods. She struggles with the last row, so Sura goes to her to be crushed in a cookie-smelling embrace, smothered in May's heaving chest. She no longer cares if it's safe or not.

It smells like home.

"Come now, May," Templeton calls.

May releases Sura to wipe her cheeks. Sura blinks the world back into focus and sees Templeton waving them down. May clings to Sura's arm like she'll never let go. They wind their way to the center.

The mysterious guest is slumped on the bench. He's short, skinny, and his chest is covered with hair.

Green hair.

The face is vaguely familiar: the short nose and deep eyes. The whiskers, also green, are tightly curled against his face. His upper body is matted with thick, green hair.

He lifts his tired hand, beckoning her with a single curl of his finger. Templeton takes the shirt off the bench. Sura slowly takes a seat. He smells organic. Leafy.

He smiles weakly.

Sura recognizes the eyes set in the shadows of bushy brows. The icy blue twinkle.

"Mr. Frost?" she asks.

His smile grows.

May collapses on Templeton's shoulder, heaving great wallops of sobbing joy. Templeton hands her a handkerchief.

Mr. Frost takes Sura's hand. It's coarse, slightly damp. He holds out his other hand for Templeton. He takes it and holds May's hand. They form a ring—two of them standing, two sitting.

"I am so grateful." Mr. Frost's words are scratched and tearful. A breath wheezes into his lungs. "To call you family."

Their hands tighten.

"Joe isn't here," Sura says dryly, afraid to let her emotions rise.

Mr. Frost bows his head. Templeton and May do the same. They remain in silence for a full minute. Mr. Frost lets go and, with Templeton's assistance, he stands. Mr. Frost takes a moment to balance himself like a newborn calf before tenderly walking with Templeton at his side. Slowly, they go to the north side of the garden and stop at the entrance that leads to the wishing room.

Mr. Frost whispers to Templeton.

"Come along," Templeton says. "You, too, Jonah."

Jonah is standing in the southern entrance where May had entered.

Mr. Frost disappears into the tunnel. May starts to follow, but Sura's stuck to the bench, afraid to grasp the strange, tangible hope that seems to float around her. If they think seeing Joe in the wishing room will make her feel better, then they've lost their minds.

It'll only hurt worse.

"Come on, love." May gently takes her arm.

Sura walks with heavy feet. She reaches the north archway and refuses to go any farther. Jonah is at the end of the tunnel, facing the entrance to the wishing room. Light floods out of the opening.

Jonah steps inside. His wail is joyful.

"I'm not going, May." Sura steps back. "I don't want to see him in there. He won't be real; he'll just be in my mind and that's not... it's just an illusion, May."

May takes her hands to keep them from shaking, to keep her from running away. Nothing in that room is real. Joe will just be a dream and she doesn't have the strength to dream like that. Not right now.

If I see him in there, I'll never want to leave.

"I have to wake up," Sura says.

But May's expression never falters. In fact, it grows warmer. With tears brimming, May looks down the tunnel. Sura follows her gaze.

Jonah steps outside of the wishing room; a smile that looks foreign on his face is wide and toothy. He reaches back, helping someone step through the opening. He steps tenderly like Mr. Frost.

It's Joe.

Joe is outside.

A chill crawls over her, tingling her scalp. Her lower lip begins to flutter. She wants to believe it, wants to let go of May, but she's been fooled by dreams before. Sura looks up. The North Star is still visible, but it's not twinkling strange colors. It's not twinkling at all.

Jonah lets go of Joe. He walks on his own, stepping gingerly towards Sura. His arms and face have a thin coat of curly, green hair. Sura's afraid to move, afraid to blink, or he'll disappear. Afraid she'll wake up.

He steps into the sunlight and extends his hand. Sura hesitates.

"*N'ayez pas peur,*" he says.

I am awake.

MR. FROST SHIVERS.

"Let's get you into the sunlight," Templeton says.

The others have already left the garden, their voices shouting somewhere on the other side of the hedges. Max yips continuously. All of them, so happy.

Because it's over. It's finally over.

Templeton holds Mr. Frost's hand, guiding him away from the wishing room. The new body is so frail and light, the feet not half the size of what he's walked on his entire life. He will never slide on his soles again.

They step into the garden. He turns his face upward, searching for the sun. Green hair unfurls in the direction of light, warmth reaching his core. The photosynthetic gene splice was meant to temporarily stabilize the body. He could make it permanent, use it to help humans feed themselves with sunlight, but that would create a new species. Mr. Frost is done with that.

It's over.

He feigned surprise when Jack escaped the laboratory without his memories. He had the yellow-hats guide him outside when Freeda was occupied. They set him free.

Mr. Frost had won the yellow-hats' loyalty long ago. He accidently discovered the loyalty gene shortly after the helpers were first born. Freeda had programmed them to serve her. Mr. Frost made a slight alteration in the yellow-hats' gene sequence. It wasn't easy. In fact, it took decades to accomplish without Freeda knowing.

Without the yellow-hats, the ending would have been very different. They were the ones that put the pictures where Sura would see them—her mom's box and the one on Joe's refrigerator. They were the ones that lured her into the toy factory so that Mr. Frost could arrange for Jack to see her outside Walmart, to feel her presence.

Janack was right about one thing: Mr. Frost despised the warm-bloods when he still lived in the Arctic. Had Mr. Frost remained in the Arctic, had the root not forced him to live among the humans, to know them, to love them... well, again, the ending would have been different.

And if Janack lived with them, even for a short while, then he would know them, too. That's why Mr. Frost let him escape, to let him live with the humans. Perhaps, in the end, it had some effect. Mr. Frost will never know if Janack watched the attack with glee or horror. Did he try to stop it? Did he feel his heart grow? Did he feel love?

If he did, that will make all the difference.

Mr. Frost's feet feel like boat anchors. Templeton guides him around the perimeter of the garden. "Careful," he says, helping him up the stone steps. "This is your last body."

They stand at the crater's edge. On the other end, near the live oak grove, the others are mobbed by a sea of brightly hatted helpers. When Freeda went down, they were released from her command. They're all "yellow-hats" now. Max nips at their heels like a worried shepherd, keeping them from a watery drop.

A plane slowly crosses the blue sky.

Mr. Frost feels the sun rise above the trees. Light spreads across his shoulders. He reaches for the back of his neck, his fingers crawling through the short mop of coarse hair. No more itching.

No Freeda. No Janack. No root.

The end.

His memories are spotty. Mr. Frost had fed them to Max, where they were stored in a root imbedded between the fox's shoulder blades.

"May I ask where the blue elven's body is?" Templeton asks.

"Janack?"

"Do you know of another blue elven?"

Mr. Frost smiles. "It's still in the wishing room, beneath the leaves."

"You expended all that energy to hide the body?"

"In case Sura went inside the wishing room; I didn't want her to see it. She's been through enough."

They watch the celebration work its way toward them. Mr. Frost is no longer hunched over. The light is working wonders.

"What do you think happened?" Templeton asks.

"You mean how did he die?"

"I suppose."

Mr. Frost scratches his chin. "The wishing room provided Jack his deepest desire, but not so much what he wanted. It was what he needed. He reconnected with his mother, like he did the last time. I suspect that he transformed in that moment. Maybe he even realized he was stuck in the wishing room instead of actually resting in his mother's arms."

"Then why didn't he leave?"

"He didn't want to, Templeton. He preferred to die in the dream."

"Do you think he suffered in the end?" Templeton asks.

"I hope not."

"Well, let's not be rash. Perhaps he deserved a little suffering. After all..." Templeton doesn't finish the obvious thought. "Speaking of the blue elven, shall we go back to the wishing room and awaken the last body?"

"Mmm... perhaps we can enjoy this moment a while longer without it."

Mr. Frost takes Templeton's arm, urging him forward. "He has much to atone for, Templeton. Let's not waste time."

They start the slow journey back to the wishing room. Mr. Frost asks Templeton to first pass through the center. They circle around the garden to sit on the bench. The statue is still in shambles. Perhaps he'll replace it with something else.

"You were a great elven." Templeton sits next to him. "I believe you will be an even better man."

"Let's hope so, Templeton."

They rest a bit longer before returning to the wishing room.

To awaken the last human body.

19

DECEMBER 24

Sometime in the future...

The tickets are green and scarlet.

They're hard to come by at a reasonable price, but the chance to see Frost Plantation only comes on Christmas Eve. Shelly tucks the ticket into her back pocket. She'll keep it with the tickets from the last two events. Not many people can say they've been there three times.

Shelly knows people in high places.

The event started at six o'clock. It's almost midnight. Mr. Frost is finishing his annual telling of The Tale of Frost, a story that's become somewhat famous. "A Yarn for the Modern Day" *Time Magazine* called it. The story's not true, of course, but watching Mr. Frost tell it makes you wonder.

The great room has a domed ceiling that's three stories high, with long windows radiating from the center like spokes, the stars glittering inside the elongated panes, the moon fully lit in the northern glass. A Christmas tree—one worthy of Times Square—is near the north wall, with gifts wrapped in shiny, red paper and fat, green bows.

May and Jonah sit to the left of the tree, hands folded on their laps.

Templeton stands on the right, stiff as plaster, with their white dog, Max, at his side.

Mr. Frost performs in front of the tree.

Children—sitting on cushions that soften the marble floor—enclose the short, skinny man as he waves his arms and raises his voice for an hour, eliciting belly-clutching laughter and, soon, tissue-worthy tears.

At first, the children are transfixed by the gifts, wondering which one has their name on it. Mr. Frost soon makes them forget about the presents.

Shelly started volunteering at the horse therapy program when she started college. After four years of assisting Sura, they expanded its reach across the state of South Carolina. *The Frost Plantation's Telling of the Tale Extravaganza* tickets have always been distributed to charities, such as the horse therapy program. Shelly buys hers, of course. It's a privilege.

She leans on the doorway opposite the Christmas tree. She can't see much, but it doesn't matter, she just wants to hear it. Besides, the people in front of her are seeing it for the first time. It's a performance that's never been recorded and not because people haven't tried. All attempts come back blank. Rumor has it that there's a reward to the first hacker who can do it and, so far, it remains unclaimed.

The kids are slack-mouthed. Mr. Frost is telling the part where Joe walks out of the wishing room. Shelly's favorite part.

"Of course, it's all made up," Sura once told her. "My dad's been telling the Tale since we were little. He just added the part about Joe when we got married. Something for the grandkids."

Sura and Joe are sitting to the right of Templeton, listening like the story is new to them, too. Hallie, blonde with blue eyes, sits on Joe's lap, and Sunni, hair as red as a stop sign, sits on Sura's crossed legs. Riley, their third child, must be with her friends. If the tale was true and Joe and Sura really are clones, well, then their kids sure aren't.

"Hey."

Shelly jumps at the sound of her husband's voice. "Where have you been?"

"Shhh." His face is scratched. "I got to show you something."

"No. This is the best part."

"You got to see this."

Her eyes become circles. Henry knows what that face means, but it only makes him smile.

"Why didn't Santa save you?" a kid asks Mr. Frost.

The crowd erupts with laughter. Mr. Frost responds, "Why, he was busy, of course. It was Christmas!"

Another burst of laughter.

"You won't regret this," Henry says. "I swear."

"It's almost over, just wait."

"It just can't wait," he says too loudly, on purpose. "Now or never."

He never got like this.

Shelly looks up, thinking. He knows this look, too—that she'll give in because she doesn't want to have a whispering argument that's not too whispery.

"This better be good."

He pulls her out of the crowd that happily fills her vacancy. The hall is wide and tall, archways rising up to the ceiling. Mr. Frost's voice follows them down the hardwood.

An elaborate chandelier hangs above the massive doors strewn with garland and origami ornaments folded by children. There's a room to the right where a fire crackles in a wide fireplace, and a large painting of the family hangs above the hearth. Shelly knows almost all of them.

Dirt falls off Henry's shoes. It's also smudged on his knees. He pulls open the front door and rushes her down the steps.

"We got to hurry." He walks at a pace just short of running.

"Tell me," she whines.

"Shhh."

They cross the paved driveway, where a few people mill about, waiting for story time to end so they can get good seats on the night's final trolley tour around the plantation. The miniature train goes through the trees and near the old rice fields, around the live oak grove and past the guest houses. Jonah, the conductor, retells the story, pointing out where Sura woke up with the helpers on Christmas morning. Occasionally, guests see flashes of bright hats in the trees like little helpers are following.

The lake—where the story's first plantation house was built and, as the tale goes, disappeared—is glassy. The new house is on the northern end and facing south just in front of the live oak grove, the mossy branches reaching over it.

"All right." Henry slows down when every living soul is far behind them. "I started poking around because I've heard the story, like, a hundred times."

"You've heard it three times."

"Feels like a hundred. Anyway, I thought I'd look around where the original house was supposed to be."

"The story's made up, Henry."

He makes a face. "Yeah, I know. Converting matter to energy could evaporate the solar system. Even a high school physics teacher knows that, duh."

She smiles.

"I just thought it'd be more fun to pretend like it was real. And guess what?"

"You found a helper."

"Even better."

They reach the end of the lake, where an overgrown hedge reaches across a leafy archway. Henry quickly pulls her through the entrance.

The boxwoods are still neatly trimmed and the camellias are loaded with white blooms. "Seafoam," Sura once told her. A fountain trickles in the center where the tarnished form of a mother, her long braid down her back, comforts her son. Both are as round as cherubs. That's where Jack lay in his mother's arms, thinking he was in the garden when he was still inside the wishing room, where his body painlessly died in the South Carolina "heat."

Water dances over them.

"The garden," Shelly says. "This isn't a secret."

"I started thinking." Henry pulls her to the left, following the path. "The story talks about the wishing room on the north end of the garden, but there's no entrance."

"Because it's made up."

They walk halfway down the north side.

"Or they let it grow closed," he says.

The hedge is solid. There's no hint of an opening, just a wall of thorny firethorn. Henry gets on his knees.

"I'm not going in there," Shelly says.

He pushes through the bushes, disappearing like a rabbit. He holds open a hole from the inside. And despite what she just said, her body is tingling. Her heart, racing. *What if...*

No one is in the garden, no one will see. She'll make it quick. She scurries through the hedge. It's thicker than she thought and, for a moment, considers backing out.

She emerges in a dark tunnel. The branches arch overhead and twigs crisscross along the walls, like someone keeps it from collapsing.

"Oh my God," she utters, slack-mouthed like the children.

Henry uses his phone as a light and takes her hand, guiding her to the dead end. "I thought—"

"It's right there." Shelly points.

Even in the darkened passageway, she sees his expression of mock surprise. His hand tightens.

"I listen to the story," she says. "I know how it goes."

Henry sinks his arms into the dense growth and, rather easily, parts them like curtains.

And there it is.

The wishing room.

A small, circular opening is carved in the overgrown forest. The walls are just as thick as the tunnel, the ceiling much higher but just as dense. The ground is soft with leaves that crunch. Shelly drags her hand along the outside, imagining what it would be like if it worked. Would she be on the beach with her grandmother before she died? Or hiking with the family on Grandfather Mountain? Would the wishing room know her innermost desires, and would the North Star glitter white, red, and green?

"Wow," is all she can say.

"Yeah," Henry says in a told-you-so kind of way. "But that's not the best part. I figured maybe they just keep it like this for idiots like me. Then I found this."

He pulls wisteria vines—thick as mooring line—to the side. He aims the phone at the curved surfaces hidden beneath. Shelly kneels down, touching them to make sure they're real.

Glass tanks.

The surfaces are tinted green with moss and algae, rough with grime. It's how the tale ends. Joe is reborn in one of the tanks Mr. Frost stashed in the wishing room because that's the only place Freeda couldn't see. He doesn't remember much when he comes out, but he remembers Sura. True love never forgets.

The other tank is where Mr. Frost was incubated. A human body. Max is an Arctic fox in the tale. Mr. Frost used the special food to transfer his memories into his beloved pet, where they were stored in a special root imbedded just beneath the Arctic fox's skin. When the time came, Max carried them to the wishing room, where they were uploaded to a glass tank, where they were passed into a human body still green with hair.

"You think these are from the tale?" she asks.

"Heck yeah, they are. And maybe they just put them here, but it's a trip. Right?"

"Anything in them?"

Henry pries at a crease and the front of one opens, the inside filled with spiderwebs. "Nothing but arachnid condos."

"What's that?"

Henry pulls at the vines to her left. There's another tank tucked a little farther back, this one just as filthy as the others. The door is wide open.

"A third one," he says.

"There's not a third one in the tale."

Maybe Henry's right; they just put this stuff back there to give the tale life when people go snooping. *What am I thinking? The tale isn't true. There's no such thing as elven, Jack Frost, and incubators. Of course this is a goof.*

"Look." Henry plants his foot for leverage and pulls the vines back even further. "Is that another one?"

Shelly takes his phone and crawls deeper. A fourth tank is back there. Unlike the others, the door is sealed shut. She stands on her knees, the branches snagging her shirt. The surface is covered with algae and grime, but if she holds the light close enough, she can see the fauna inside like an upright terrarium.

Shelly gets to her feet and presses the phone against the rounded top. She can see a form inside. It has the vague shape of shoulders and a round head with wild strands of grassy foliage spraying around it. Shelly often wondered why the tale only had two tanks: one for Mr. Frost and the other for Joe.

"You don't think that's..." she says.

"What?" Henry says.

What if Sura died? Wouldn't he have prepared for that?

A train whistles.

Shelly jumps out with a short scream. Her heart is about to pound through her sternum. They laugh childishly. Henry helps her up.

"What was it?" he asks.

"Just another tank, but it's closed."

"Three open and one closed. What do you think the closed one was for?"

She shakes her head. If she says it out loud, it'll sound stupid. If she says it, it'll dispel the magic bubbling in her stomach.

"Two open for Mr. Frost and Joe, but what about the other open one?" Henry says.

"Yeah," she says. "No one ever said anything about that, either. Everyone was safe."

"I know what it is." Henry snaps his fingers and points at Shelly's expectant expression. "It's a tall tale."

She smacks his arm. It's more fun if they pretend it's real.

They sneak back out as quickly as they broke in. Henry exits first. He holds the hedge open. Shelly rushes through on her hands and knees, scratches already burning.

There are voices just outside the garden. *Just in time.*

"Come on," Henry says. "We can catch the trolley if we hurry."

They rush out the exit, still laughing like children, when they run into a man and child, frightening them as much as they scare themselves. The man falls to one knee, but the little girl hangs onto his hand.

"I'm so sorry," Henry exclaims, helping him up. "We were trying to catch the trolley."

"Quite all right." The man is short and slight, couldn't weigh more than a ten-year-old. The moon shines off his bald head. He brushes himself off, smiling.

"You all right?" Shelly asks the girl, and then recognizes her. "Are you Riley?"

"Yes, ma'am."

"I know Sura. She's your mother, right? I'm Miss Shelly."

She clings to the man's arm and doesn't care about her mom's friend.

The whistle blows again.

"You better hurry," the little man says.

"I'm so sorry." Henry pulls Shelly away. "Merry Christmas!"

The little man nods. "Merry Christmas."

Shelly waves. The little girl doesn't wave back, but Shelly hears her say something just before they're out of range. She hears something that, later that night when she's lying in bed, will give her cause to smack Henry on the arm and tell him that she knows who was in the third tank.

The little girl says, "Who was that, Uncle Janack?"

AFTERWORD

Now you know the tale of the Cold One and how his tiny little heart thawed and grew. Sounded a little like the Grinch, eh? Perhaps. Or maybe the snow miser? There's another story about someone who likes it hot.

But the heat miser is a tale for another day.

One more adventure awaits, the tale of a lonely boy with a secret to discover. And the great and powerful protection of something that will sacrifice everything to make things right. There's no top hat in this story. No button nose or eyes made out of coal.

This is the tale of Flury.

BOOK 3

———————

Flury: Journey of a Snowman

THE ARCTIC

Malcolm Toye fell.

He had seen nothing but ice for days, wandering the Arctic in search of the men that brought him this far north. Their ship crushed by the ice, they had struck out on foot, dragging boats over frozen snow and through open leads of water until landing upon Bennett Island. Ravaged by frostbite and scurvy, no one should've lived. But they continued south, and that's when Malcolm had become separated.

With rifle in hand, he had given chase to what he thought was a wounded seal, but had slipped into the icy water. Soaked and numb, he returned to camp to find that the men had already moved on. Shortly after, snow began to fall, and he was eternally alone.

And now he had fallen for the last time.

He couldn't feel his legs. He was certain that if a miracle occurred and the men found him, he would lose his feet to frostbite. At the very least, his toes.

It was a foolish journey, but men like Malcom Toye had always pursued such folly. The North Pole called to him, dared him to conquer it. He was eager to join the expedition, see parts of the world very few had witnessed with their own eyes. Only the dubious tales of explorers existed about the endless sheet of ice that topped the world. He wanted to be one of the first men to ever see it.

He had come close.

When he fell backwards, landing in the soft embrace of fresh snow, he didn't feel the impact. He was certain, as he gazed into the sky where, some-

where past his feet, the sun was just below the horizon, that he would not only lose his feet to frostbite, but his nose as well. That didn't bother him.

I will die alone.

He labored to breathe as he tore at the buttons of his U.S. Navy-issued coat, his fingers plastic things that refused to bend or grasp. Violent shivers made it difficult, but he managed to slip his hand inside his coat to find an inner pocket. Despite the numbness, he felt the cold metal fall into his palm.

A gold locket.

The latch was too tight for his stiff and senseless fingers. Instead, he clutched it tightly before the shivers tossed it from his hand. The attached chain pooled on the fabric of his frozen coat. He yearned to see, one last time, the photo of his bride, hope that she would be the last image he took with him in this unforgiving wasteland of ice. He imagined her green eyes and brown hair falling over her shoulders, the way she smiled when she woke.

As his breaths grew shallow, he let go of the pain squeezing his chest and melted into the snowy embrace. A warm sensation filled him. He drifted into sleep, where a sweet dream was promised and, perhaps, his wife would be waiting.

It was in these last moments that the wind began to swirl.

Malcolm didn't notice the ice shudder or the shadow pass over him. He had given himself to leaving the world. He opened his eyes one last time to look at the dark sky. Instead, he saw two massive legs straddling him.

A giant blotted out the stars.

GRANDMOTHER

Every once in a while, Santa skips a house.

1

———————

Oliver feels weird.

He drops his iPad. He'd been reading a zombie apocalypse where the guy lets his infected wife bite him so she's not alone. He got to the part where someone sees two zombies holding hands when his blood sugar crashed. He should test his blood. Instead, he sucks on a glucose tablet while leaning his forehead on the passenger window.

The curvy roads aren't helping. The hills and trees, endless.

Mom is strangling the steering wheel while grinding her teeth. A partially plowed road would turn most drivers' knuckles white, but that's not it. When they left Austin, it was sunny and warm, but that wasn't it, either.

Colorado is home.

Home doesn't welcome everyone.

She puts on the right-turn blinker and begins to slow.

The snow has been cleared from a nondescript opening in the trees. Mom pulls beneath the weeping branches. The wrought-iron gate is already open. She stops the car, lips silently moving, a private pep talk.

The black road beyond is plowed better than the main road, with swirling sweeper patterns on the asphalt. Mom eases down the private drive, the sunlight blotted out by overgrown trees. Oliver looks over the luggage in the backseat to watch the gates close behind them. The last time he was here he was five years old.

That was ten years ago.

His blood sugar is coming up, but the weird feeling remains as Mom steers down the curving road, her lips still moving. Her knuckles still white. The three-story house appears around the last turn. Several trees reach out like Nature is coming for the house.

Like zombies.

Mom stops in the patch of sunlight just short of the circle driveway. The steering wheel squeaks in her sweaty palms. She adjusts the wide headband that holds her thick hair off her face and takes in the three-story monstrosity. A round window looks down from the attic, snow frosting the lower half.

No sign of Christmas anywhere.

"This is just temporary," Mom says. "Okay?"

Oliver nods, but the last time she said that, the cable never came back on. Maybe this time she was telling herself this was temporary.

He takes her hands off the steering wheel before she tears it out of the dashboard. Her slender fingers squeeze his hand like a bear trap. She nods, compulsively, before letting her foot off the brake. The house's shadow falls over them. Mom adjusts the wide, paisley headband again and rubs her face before opening the door.

Oliver rubs his bristly short crop of brown hair. He can feel the heat leaking from his scalp. Snow-capped mountains rise above the trees. If they're going to live here, he'll have to grow some hair.

Even if it's temporary.

The weird thing about *the property*, as Mom calls it, isn't the gut-punching cold—it's the silence. Colorado is a mountain man's paradise, a place to hike and fish and sleep under the stars—commune with nature, that sort of thing. Not here.

Here, it's dead silent.

The attic window watches them approach. The entry walk has been brushed with a coarse broom. Mom stops on the top step, playing with one of the many hoop earrings piercing her cartilage. A small sign is embedded just above the doorbell.

Toye Residence.

She pushes the button.

A faint melody of bells echoes inside the house. Oliver can see distorted patterns of light and dark through a panel of ornamental glass set alongside the door. Long after the bells have gone quiet, a dark figure moves.

"Take off your shoes," Mom whispers.

She already has her shoes in one hand.

Oliver slides his shoes off. His toes are as stiff as the wooden porch. He's imagining the hot sands of South Padre Island when an eye— green with blue around the perimeter of the iris—appears in a diamond-cut section of the window.

The doorknob begins to turn.

The seal around the doorway breaks open to reveal an old woman plucked straight from the crypt of an ancient library. Her kinky gray hair is pulled back in a tight bun. Her posture, perfect. Vertical grooves dig around her joyless mouth.

"Debra," she says.

"Mother."

Oliver's mom steps over the threshold and hugs his grandmother. The old woman pats her on the shoulder and lets Debra hug her.

"Quickly now." Grandmother waves Oliver inside.

The foyer is expansive.

Sounds echo off the high ceiling. An immense stairwell is to the left of a dark hallway that leads deeper into the house. Photos of stodgy old men are hung in ornate frames. It doesn't feel cold inside— he can't see his breath, after all—but somehow it's no warmer. No sign of a Christmas tree, stocking or greeting card.

It's as if Christmas died at the wrought-iron gate.

"Oliver." Only she says *Olivah.*

"Grandmother."

He takes half a step toward her when she sticks out her hand. The knuckles are knobby, and the fingers slightly curled. He shakes it, careful not to crush it. It feels like paper, smells like medicine.

"You have grown."

She doesn't let go while looking him over: his hair, the stray whiskers on his chin, the insufficient winter clothing. She stares at the floor. His socks are loose at the ends of his frozen toes, specks of snow clinging to the fabric. Small puddles begin to bead on the polished floor.

"And how old are you?"

"Fifteen."

She purses her lips like he just lied. "And your health?"

"Good." That time he did. His blood sugar still isn't right. "I'll get the luggage."

"Nonsense. It's not going anywhere. You will come in and eat. Diabetics need a balanced meal."

If his memory is correct, she's called him "diabetic" more than she's called him "grandson."

She holds her hand out. Mom offers her elbow, and Grandmother takes it. They walk down the dim hallway. She's wearing big, puffy boots but doesn't slide them over the floor. Instead, her steps are carefully measured and silent. Dead silent.

Like outside.

Oliver quickly knocks the snow crystals off his feet and mops the water with his socks before following. The dim hallway feels like the house is swallowing him. Just past the stairway on the left is a doorway leading to the family room. A large picture window offers a panoramic view of the property. On the right side of the hallway, there's a long table with three table settings, including a teapot.

Grandmother opens a drawer in a small table against the wall and takes out a towel. "You may join us once your mess is cleaned up, Olivah."

His mom makes a silent apology as she guides Grandmother toward the dining table. He takes the towel to the front door and wipes up the little streaks of water. A gust of wind pushes against the door. A draft sneaks through the bottom. Oliver looks through the decorative pane of glass and sees the last wisps of snow swirling on the sidewalk.

A mess of twigs are scattered over the pavement.

He opens the door. The trees are still, and the silence is perfect. Not even the icicles hanging from the gutters are dripping.

"Close the door, Olivah. Come along."

With damp towel in hand, he returns to the dining room for bitter tea and dry muffins in the place he'll call home.

Temporary home.

2

Oliver hauls the last bit of luggage up the stairs.

The worn steps are slick beneath his socks. They're shallow for easy climbing. He holds the railing to keep from tumbling down three stories' worth.

The photos watch him trudge up the flights. Not photos, paintings —the kind you'd find in the back of a resale shop. It's mostly grizzled old men with sharp eyes and mirthless mouths. There are a few women in the mix, just as joyless. The last painting, just before the third floor, is of a ship. A small crowd of people are gathered at a ramp. With its bare rigging and leaning bow, it's as haunted as the old men.

All the doors are closed on the third floor, except the one to the far left. The floor creaks along the way. His breath puffs out in thin clouds, quickly dissipating. His room is in the front-left section of the house with windows looking east and south. There's a dresser and a night-stand with a lamp, along with a waist-high bed covered with a thick, white comforter.

Everything is dusted and wrinkle-free.

He drops the luggage and finds his kit. Rubbing his fingers together, he does a quick blood test to measure his blood sugar. It's too high. He should've done the test before tea. He quickly measures a dose of insulin and, pinching a fold of skin over his stomach, injects himself.

He checks his phone. No bars, no wifi.

All of his books are in cloud storage. It's doubtful Grandmother has Internet. Doubtful she's ever seen a computer.

Oliver drops his bag below the frosted window offering the same view as the picture window in the family room. There's a break in the forest and a view of the mountains. The sun has fallen behind the peaks, and the waning daylight casts a long shadow from a rustic windmill. The blades turn even though it seems calm. When a gust of wind hits it, the windwheel turns faster.

Lets loose an earsplitting squeal.

Something has crossed the clearing. The tracks are too far away to distinguish what kind of footsteps. He looks for binoculars—his dad used to sit around with binoculars when he lived on the beach—but the dresser drawers are empty and clean. But there's something in the bottom drawer of the nightstand.

A journal.

The cover is hardback, faded and worn at the corners. The yellowish pages, however, are blank. The binding cracks as he turns the stiff pages, finding not a spot of ink. He runs his fingers over the smooth cover, imagining a quill and a pot of ink that might've been used to record thoughts in something this old.

"Hey, kiddo."

"Ho!" The journal flips out of his grip, smacks the wall, and bounces on the floor.

Oliver's heart hammers his chest.

His mom is in the doorway with a black hoodie pulled over her head. She apologizes for scaring him.

"What'd you got there?" she asks.

Oliver retrieves the journal and assesses the damage to the corner, hoping Grandmother doesn't see it. He might have to hide it. His mom flips through the pages, but her mind is somewhere else.

"Sorry about freezing up on you when we got here," she says, twisting one of her earrings. "I thought I was ready for this. I didn't expect to...change."

She hasn't said much since they arrived. They ate a bland lunch mostly in silence. Grandmother cut her tuna salad sandwich with a knife and ate it with a fork.

"I felt like a kid when I walked through the doorway. I could feel my insides, like, churning and morphing back into a little girl...I'm sorry, you don't need to hear this."

"It's all right, I get it. You can't go home, right?"

He read that somewhere.

You can't go home because expectations get in the way. But his mom was sent to boarding school when she was ten. Strange she feels like this is home. Oliver would never have that problem. He's lived too many places. There'll never come a time he steps over a threshold and breathes the familiar essence of childhood.

"You test your sugar?"

He nods. She knows when he's being a bad diabetic.

"You get all your stuff?"

"Yeah." He kicks the duffel bag.

"You've got the third floor all to yourself. It's an old house your great-grandfather built. It's going to sound a little haunted. I'll be in the room below you, so if you need anything, you know where to find me. We'll make the best of it."

She pulls her headband around her neck and scratches her scalp. She notices him watching her.

"What's wrong?" she asks.

"I don't like seeing you this way."

"Change is hard." She sits on the bed and puts her hand on his. "We just need to be thankful we have a place to stay." She looks around the sterile room, then whispers, "Even if this is where Christmas came to die."

They lean into each other and laugh. His mom wipes tears from her eyes.

"I don't think Santa can find this place," he says.

"Trust me, he'll find it."

She scrubs his bristly hair, then pulls a stocking cap from the pouch on her hoodie. It's a North Face cap. She pulls it over his head and kisses his forehead.

"An early present," she says. Even her lips are cold.

He thanks her. "You think tomorrow we could go somewhere with service?" He holds up his phone. "I need to download books."

"There's a library in town. Maybe we can pick up a few Christmas ornaments and smuggle them into the house. I still have a few presents to get."

"Look, Mom, you don't need to buy me anything. I mean, this is plenty."

"Let me worry about that."

She kisses his forehead again and leaves. Her footsteps slide over the creaking floor like a kid with footy pajamas. The stairs groan with each descending thump.

Oliver plugs his ears with headphones and unpacks. He thumbs through the journal again. When he looks out the window, a full moon casts a glow over the property. Oliver cups his hands on the window and holds his breath to keep from fogging it.

There are more tracks.

"**G**ood morning, Olivah," Grandmother announces.

Oliver is startled.

He knew someone was awake, he could smell coffee, but didn't expect his grandmother to be standing in the kitchen waiting for him.

The floors broadcast every movement through the house—except for his stealthy grandmother with the padded Ugg boots. Her hair is tightly pulled back, as if attempting to stretch the wrinkles from her cheeks. Mom sits at the breakfast table, hovering over a steaming mug.

"You will find breakfast on the stove," Grandmother says. "Help yourself."

His hunger drags him around the island bar beneath a dangling rack of pots. A wisp of steam escapes a white teapot on the back burner. On the front, a cast-iron pan still sizzles with eggs and bacon. He can feel his grandmother's blue-green eyes on him like department store security as he fills a plate with bacon, eggs and a warm slice of toast.

When he turns around, she's gone.

He sits down to check his blood sugar. The plastic snap of the needle draws a tiny bead from his pinky. His mom watches him eat while sipping her coffee and smiling. A brown headband holds her hair back this morning. She doesn't look so frail. Maybe she just needed a good night's sleep. It had been months since she had one.

Oliver mentally calculates the carbs sitting on his plate and injects a dosage of insulin, this time in his leg. He thumbs through his phone while eating. The battery is almost drained.

"Did you hear the rumbling last night?"

Mom shakes her head. "I told you the house makes noise."

"This was out in the woods." He woke up to use the bathroom. It sounded like trees were falling in the distance, but when he looked out, nothing had fallen. The tracks were gone, even though it hadn't snowed.

"You slept well?" Grandmother asks.

The half-eaten toast leaves Oliver's hand and hits the floor. She looks down. Oliver finds a paper towel to wipe up the mess.

Grandmother doesn't move.

"I'm sorry." He looks for the trash.

"Pantry," Mom says.

He finds the pantry door opposite the oven. The trash can is beneath a shelf of canned goods. A small chalkboard is attached to the inside of the door, the green surface clean. The vertical wrinkles deepen around Grandmother's mouth. Oliver sits back down, and his mom winks, patting his hand, whispering, "It's all right."

"So, I trust you slept well?" Grandmother fills a teacup from the kettle.

"Yes."

"And you found the breakfast suitable?"

"Yes."

She brings her tea and saucer to the table and places a napkin next to Oliver's plate. Methodically, she spreads another napkin across her own lap and pauses. When he does the same, she resumes. Her posture is rigid as she stirs cream into the tea, as if she hasn't slouched since the day she was born.

Oliver takes small bites, but mostly pushes his food around.

"We're going into town, Mother. I was thinking of bringing back a Christmas tree."

"Absolutely not."

"Come now. This house could use some spirit."

"First thing's first."

She reaches into the sleeve of her white sweater and retrieves a crisply folded sheet of paper. Smoothing it open on the table, she slides it toward Oliver. The script is delicately handwritten.

"There are a few rules," Grandmother begins. "While at my house, you will tidy up after yourself. Whenever you leave a room, you will leave no trace that you were ever there."

He left clothes strewn on the bedroom floor and the bed unmade.

"Do you agree?" she asks. "Good. Next, a list will be posted inside the pantry door each morning. You are expected to complete your chores at the start of the day. When school begins, you will need to complete them before leaving in the morning. These chores will include repairs, cleaning, kitchen duty, etc."

"Mother, we'll be homeschooling while we're here. It's just easier. And Oliver is already a good student."

Grandmother's lips pinch together. Mom sips her coffee, waiting for the storm brewing on Grandmother's tongue.

Grandmother clears her throat, instead.

"Do you agree? Good. Given your condition, you will also be required to exercise outside for two hours every day."

"Your condition" must be diabetes.

"Dress appropriately, of course. When your chores consist of chopping wood or other such duties that will count toward your exercise quota. Otherwise, you are expected to be active on your own. You may explore the property as you wish, but you will be expected to be inside before the sun falls behind the mountains. Do you agree?"

"Why?"

"Do you agree, Olivah?"

"Yes. I'm just wondering...why can't I stay out later?"

Grandmother lets a few moments of silence be his answer. "We will eat our meals together. You are expected to have proper manners. Also, there will be no electronic devices in the house."

"At all?"

"Correct. I expect you to honor that rule while you are outside."

"Mother, he reads books with his iPad. They're called ebooks."

"There is a library in town. I believe they have books you can borrow. Do you agree to this, Olivah?"

He desperately wanted to say no. More than that, he wanted her to stop saying his name like it was something fancy to eat. Instead, he nodded. Anything else would make it harder on his mom. If he needed to work as an indentured servant to make this work, then he'd wax the car and paint the fence.

"You will also start referring to your mom as 'mother'."

"Now, wait a second, Mother."

"I see nothing wrong with cultivating manners into this impressionable young man."

"I've always called you 'mother', but to Oliver, I'm 'mom'. Don't interfere with our relationship."

"Your relationship is living under my roof. What you do outside this house is your business."

Mom pushes away from the table and stands, replacing the chair beneath the table before rinsing her cup in the sink. This is the person Oliver knows, the one that showed up at his school to argue, or refused to leave dealerships when they wouldn't agree to her offer. Not the one that drove up to the front door.

She offers a smile but doesn't agree.

"You may go wherever you wish," Grandmother continues. "However, if you find a door is locked, it is locked for a purpose."

Grandmother goes to the sink to rinse her cup, wipes the counter, and carefully folds the dishtowel. She stops at the doorway and says, before exiting, "Lunch will be served at noon. Have a pleasant morning."

Oliver pushes his plate away. His appetite has been murdered. He holds the list in both hands, the paper quivering. It has nothing to do with blood sugar.

His mom rubs his shoulders. "Let your *mother* take you shopping."

Despite covering their mouths, their laughter echoes down the hall. They clean the kitchen. When they leave, it satisfies rule number five. The wording, like the others, is odd. As if it's saying more than the obvious.

Rule #5: Leave rooms as if no human had ever passed through it.

4

Two nights later, it snows.

Six inches of fluff covers the land, including the sidewalk and driveway. Oliver clears it with a brand-new shovel.

They still hadn't made it to the library. Mom told him to sneak his phone into the bathroom or read the iPad beneath the covers. He just couldn't do it. It felt like Grandmother could read the guilt on his face.

They ate at the absurdly long table. At lunch, Grandmother instructed him on proper tea etiquette. It didn't help that the tea tasted like boiled cabbage water.

At dinner, they lit the massive candelabra and ate in silence while shadows danced on the walls. His mom made small talk, but Grandmother refused to open her mouth except for small, appropriately gauged spoonfuls of food. She chewed her food twenty times before swallowing, staring ahead as if she was counting.

His back aches from shoveling.

This will count for exercise. He's halfway around the circle drive in forty-five minutes when his mom calls from the front porch.

"Watch your sugar!"

Oliver waves. She's wearing an apron. He'd rather shovel out to the main road than help in the kitchen. A strand of white lights twinkles above the doorway, Mom's attempt to summon the Christmas spirit. When Grandmother saw them flashing, she set her jaw and narrowed her eyes like a bear had dropped a load on the porch. But she said nothing.

Christmas still has a pulse.

It takes almost an hour and a half to finish shoveling. He's sweating beneath new winter clothes. He could go inside and warm up, but that would require ten minutes of knocking snow off his pants, and then he'd just have to turn around for the remaining half hour of outside exercise.

Rule #22: Fulfill your duty to the second. He adds a thought. *Fulfill your duty before you take a doody.*

He chuckles, but then stops. Having those thoughts is dangerous. If she turns those blue-green x-ray eyes on him, she's sure to know what he's thinking.

He can warm up when he takes his mandatory five-minute tepid shower that fulfills the rule on personal hygiene.

He walks through the virgin snow to the decrepit windmill. The windwheel turns at a slow mechanic pace even though there's no wind. The artifact is as old as the house and just as solid, but something has to be done about the squeal. He can hear it in his sleep. He'd already gotten used to the thundering ruckus in the far-off trees. There must be construction somewhere, but at night?

He doesn't want to overanalyze.

The windmill, though—something has to be done. Maybe if he had some oil, he could lubricate the bearings. The struts are close enough to climb. And even if he falls, the snow will soften his landing. It may knock him out. Given the state of things, that doesn't sound so bad.

He grabs one of the four legs, thinking maybe he can gauge the sturdiness with a swift shake, when the world turns into a photo negative—black turns white, white turns black.

He lets go.

A strange tingle lingers in his arm, and his teeth feel numb. Suddenly, he feels weird. But his sugar isn't low.

The thing is wired.

Cattle ranches are hot-wired, he knows. He had gone to a friend's ranch and was told to watch out for the bare wire running along the top rail, but he got confused at the gate and grabbed the wrong one. The world turned inside-out.

So climbing the windmill is out.

Maybe Grandmother should know that it's electrified, but then he'd have to explain what he was doing touching it, and then she'd turn her x-ray eyes on him.

Rule #441: Don't climb rusty windmills full of electricity, dummy.

Oliver walks around the trees where the clearing opens up. The land slopes down. On the far side, the forest is dense. That's where the rumbling happens. The tracks he'd seen the last couple of nights have vanished. He looks back at the house and identifies his bedroom window on the third floor. Even with the fresh snow, it seems like there should be slight depressions.

But there are none.

He starts for the house and notices the orange snow shovel by the driveway. He's not sure where it goes, but it's definitely not the front yard. A detached garage is tucked into the trees. Oliver retrieves the shovel and takes it around the back.

The large garage door is locked. He finds a door on the back, out of view from the house. The doorknob turns easily. A wave of hot, dry air breathes out. A creepy sensation crawls under his skin.

If you find a door is locked, it is locked for a purpose.

This isn't locked, so he steps inside the dark confines of the heated garage, but not before stomping the snow off his boots.

It's so much warmer than the house.

A black Cadillac Eldorado is parked inside. Its trunk is massive, and the convertible top is down. Panels shine like it just came from the factory, but the red leather seats are worn like they'd seen a thousand road trips. He steps around the back end, careful not to touch the flared taillights.

Another oversized car could fit into the other half of the garage. The open floor is slightly darker than the concrete below the car, but both halves are clean—not a spot of oil, grain of sawdust or fleck of dirt anywhere. Large triangular blocks are wedged under the wheels as if it's on a slope, but the garage floor is level.

A workbench is attached to the wall with a pegboard above it. Hammers, screwdrivers, clamps, hoses, and things he's never seen are hung on hooks with their outlines painted behind them.

A single window faces the house, letting in diffuse light. A pair of binoculars hangs next to it. The view to the house is at an angle. No one can see him here. He pulls them off the nail and admires the cracked leather strap and well-oiled hinge. He brings the windmill into focus, the blades still turning.

He slings the strap over his shoulder.

A filing cabinet is to the right, nestled between larger shelves. Ducking below the window, he puts his hand on the top drawer.

His heart is pounding.

He looks at the window one last time and gives it a tug.

The drawer slides on lubricated rails. *It's not locked.* Manila folders are stuffed inside with bent tabs and scribbled notes. Oliver nervously swallows. His hand quivers as he pries them open, revealing endless pages of handwritten notes and sketches and schematics.

There's more of the same in the other drawers, each one so full that, it seems, another sheet of paper couldn't fit. Oliver's palms are sweaty. He tugs out a handful, carefully noting where their location is before placing them on the workbench.

In the dim light, the thrill of rebellion courses through him. Once he snooped through his dad's dresser drawers and found a pistol and a plastic baggie with white pills. That was nothing compared to now. His head fills with helium and threatens to lift him into the rafters.

He can't decipher any of the notes. It's all higher mathematics and engineered plans. One folder contains a folded map that appears to be a nautical chart with notes scribbled in the margins and lines drawn throughout the Arctic Ocean.

THUMP.

The snow shovel clatters on the concrete.

Oliver jumps back; his heart seizes for a full beat. His legs turn to jelly as he tries to catch his breath. He hurries to put the folders back together, shoving them into their correct slots, easing the drawers closed and then wiping his fingerprints from the handles.

He grabs the shovel and starts for the door...but notices something under the workbench. It's where the sound came from, like something hit the outside wall.

A large chest is hiding in the shadows.

His heart is still thumping. He should just take the shovel and go. Besides, the excitement is working on his blood sugar. He doesn't have his pack with him.

But maybe, next time, the door will be locked.

He squeezes the snow shovel with both hands until his knuckles ache. He lays it on the floor—if it fell again, he'd have a heart attack—and squats to get a better look. It's a green footlocker with a leather handle and brass rivets. He takes a deep breath before crawling underneath.

The buckles unlock with a sturdy tug. The lid cracks open,

releasing stale air. Oliver scoots closer. It looks like blankets. He digs his phone out and uses the flashlight app.

It's an old coat with a row of buttons. The material is coarse. Beneath it, though, are stacks of leather-bound books. Six of them. Oliver gently lifts the jacket out. The books are similar to the one in his bedroom, although, he discovers after prying one open, these are filled with words and not the kind written with a ballpoint pen. These appear to be quilled with a bottle of ink.

The binding cracks as he carefully opens the one on top. There's a date scribbled on the first page. He briefly flips through the pages, all dated and filled with notes and hand-drawn illustrations.

Next to the journals are miscellaneous items—a tattered long-sleeved undershirt, a sextant, a collapsible telescope, a jewelry box, and a weird key with a blue cube instead of teeth. There's also a small wooden sphere about the size of a golf ball.

Oliver picks up the sphere.

It hums in his hand. The vibrations drive up his arm and spread across his chest, but not like the windmill. This current, if that's what it is, feels warm and mild. It feels good.

Safe.

There are numerous lines carved into the surface—intricate shapes and designs that vary in width and depth, as if carefully crafted with fine instruments. It's heavier than he expected, too; perhaps the center is weighted.

He holds the phone closer, rubbing the smooth surface with this thumb, digging his thumbnail into the grooves. It reminds him of one of those drawings in the filing cabinet.

"Oliver!"

He bumps his head on the bottom of the workbench and scrambles to slam the footlocker. Mom shouts his name from the house again. The latches won't catch. He opens and closes the lid, and they snap this time. Oliver sweeps the shovel off the floor and slowly peeks out the window. She's on the back porch.

It's getting dark.

He rushes around the car, careful not to touch it, and sneaks out the back door, shutting it without a sound. He takes several breaths, afraid to let her see him coming from the garage. Instead, he flees into the forest and heads for the windmill, staying just inside the tree line and out of sight of the house.

To his right, the forest is dark and deep. He holds the shovel like a battle staff, breaking small, dead twigs. His heart bangs inside his head.

The squeal of the windmill calls from his left.

Just a little further and he can exit into the clearing. More twigs snap when he sees the dim light of the sunset ahead. He slows down, but the sound of breaking branches continues.

He spins around.

Something's back there, in the dark. Oliver stumbles into the open, tumbling into the snow with both hands on the shovel. The sun is behind the mountains. He scrambles around the trees until the house comes into view and stops with a stitch in his side and his breath burning in his throat, expecting a wolf or bear to come flying out, claws extended.

Nothing does.

He wouldn't have the strength to swing the shovel if it did.

The binoculars press against his ribs. When he shoves his hand into his coat pocket, he finds a small orb at the bottom.

The wooden sphere.

He doesn't remember taking it.

5

There's a small Christmas tree on the dresser.

Oliver stays beneath the thick comforter, watching the miniature lights glowing on the tips of plastic branches, splashing colors across the walls.

It's the smallest tree he's ever seen.

A black kit containing the blood test, injections and glucose tablets is next to the tree. It's too far to reach and too cold to get out of bed. He's sluggish and moody. His sugar is always low in the morning, but just a few more minutes.

He reaches under the bed. His phone is charging on the floor. He feels the binoculars wedged beneath the mattress. The wooden orb is next to them. He grabs the orb and holds it on his fingertips. He assumes it had been hand-carved, but the spherical shape is so perfect and the lines so precise that something had to fabricate it and certainly not those tools on the pegboard. Yet the footlocker looked a hundred years old.

The bedroom door begins to open.

If the hinges didn't creak, he never would've gotten the orb under the blankets before the gray-haired, tight-lipped old woman stepped inside. Oliver slides down until his nose perches on the comforter's edge.

Grandmother is momentarily distracted by the tiny tree. She tilts her head curiously.

"What are you doing?"

"You should knock."

"This is my house."

She takes a step into the room, glancing at the window. If she gets to it, she'll see the phone.

"I'm naked." He slinks lower. "I sleep that way."

"Well, I...Olivah, that is not appropriate." Color seeps into her ashy cheeks.

"I learned it camping. It's better for body heat."

"Well, then, you will have to wash the sheets."

Unexpectedly, she leaves the room, forgetting whatever she had come to do. Even her footsteps are loud, creaking all the way to the stairwell, where they stop. Mom must've been waiting. They begin muttering in low tones, but the words carry through the house.

"You didn't need to wake him."

"He cannot sleep all morning."

"Mother, he's been working ever since we got here. Let him rest."

"He's a diabetic, Debra."

"Yes, and let him manage it."

It had been three days since Oliver discovered the garage.

Every night, a few inches of snow would fall, and he would take the shovel out for another workout. Strangely, the road leading to the roundabout was always cleared, as if Grandmother paid someone to leave the roundabout for Oliver.

"Olivah should be on a schedule."

"He's not an infant." Mom's voice echoes.

"Don't raise your voice to me, Debra."

"Don't raise my son."

"He needs structure to shape his life."

"Structure worked wonders on me."

Footsteps come heavily toward the bedroom. Oliver doesn't hear his Grandmother's descent. His mom looks into the room. Her headband is around her neck, her brown locks falling over her eyes and ears, hiding her golden line of earrings.

"Sorry," she says. "Take your time."

"I need to shovel?"

She grimaces. "Yes, sorry. Your cousins are coming in a few days."

"Henry and Helen?"

"Remember them?"

Barely. They came down to Texas when he was seven. He doesn't remember that being fun.

"Grandmother wants to get the house ready. Once you get your chores done, you can do whatever you've been doing outside." She squeezes the lump at the end of the bed that happens to be his foot. "What have you been doing?"

"Exploring, that's all." He yawns to cover his lie. Grandmother and Mom have been around the backyard or calling for him too often to make another trip to the garage. "I've been, you know, just walking to the trees and stuff."

"Don't go too far. I don't want you stuck out there or lost."

"What happens when the sun goes down?"

"You know, the usual—monsters and trolls, things with teeth." She laughs, but not in the way she does when she's hiding something. It's not trolls she's worried about. It's her diabetic kid lost in the forest on a cold night.

"It's not so bad here, Mom."

She rolls her eyes.

"No, seriously. I mean, not the chores so much. Or the tea. But I don't mind having the third floor to myself and thousands of acres to explore."

"You're a good kid." She squeezes his foot again.

"What if I was bad?"

"I'd still love you, just not as much." She winks. "Now get your naked butt out of bed and get dressed."

"I'm not...you heard that?"

She swats his knee. "That was good thinking."

Oliver stays beneath the warm comforter, listening to his mom's large steps grow more confident. She's hardly the little girl that drove up to the house.

And they have a Christmas tree.

"Thanks for the tree!"

"You're welcome!" Mom's voice echoes throughout the house.

HE SHOVELS AFTER LUNCH.

The afternoon is sunny. The icicles drip from the gutters, and despite the ache in his back, Oliver hikes past the slow-churning windmill and out to the clearing. His kit is in one pocket, the orb in the other. Once out of sight, he enters the trees.

There's no path, but soon he finds the broken branches from his panicked escape. It's still dark in the deepest part of the forest, but nothing moves or snaps—it's just the calm, wintry silence that follows him to the garage.

Despite layers of sweaters and thermals, he's shivering. He's not made for the cold. "You're a skinny lad," a teacher once told him, "with not an ounce of meat."

The snow around the garage is undisturbed. He stops short, wondering where his footprints are from the other day. He pulls off his glove and wraps his fingers around the metal knob. It feels like a block of ice. He's afraid to turn it, to feel it refuse to open. He closes his eyes...

Pop.

Warm air heaves out.

Oliver jumps inside. He kicks the snow off his boots and opens his coat. The garage feels like the beach in July. If only the sun were overhead and the sand between his toes.

His distorted reflection follows him around the car, stretching his long face even thinner, turning his arms into noodles. The triangular blocks are still wedged under the wheels, although they seem to be slightly askew this time.

The afternoon sunlight beams through the only window, making the chrome gleam and black side panels shine. The seats are still worn. He always pictured Grandmother driving something more sensible.

Like a tank.

The wooden orb feels warm in his pocket. He places it on one of the little shelves above the workbench, next to a metal oil dispenser, and then turns his attention to the filing cabinet, careful to stay clear of the window.

He starts with the top drawer.

Most of the contents are handwritten. Portions have a large X over failures or wrong equations. Many of the folders are loaded with statistical calculations and circuit schematics. Occasionally, there are illustrations of gadgets that look more like large animals or flying wagons than anything practical: the daydreams of a fantasy world. None of it seems to jibe with his grandfather.

He was a mechanic.

It takes an hour to finish the top drawer. He starts on the next one and, after plowing halfway through it, finds himself bored with the tedium of details and indecipherable equations.

But then he strikes gold.

It's a folder with sketches, mostly; nothing out of the ordinary but this time he recognizes the object. Oliver rolls the wooden orb over the notes.

The designs match.

It's a schematic of weights and dimensions. The details of the lines illustrate exactly where they should be cut and how deep. There's also a cutaway of the internal mechanisms that shows circuits and finely manufactured components.

Oliver holds the orb up, examining the rough-hewn lines that don't exactly match the plan's precision. It's close, though. The plans, however, call for the shell to be constructed of aluminum, copper and an iron-nickel alloy. Maybe those metals are inside, but the outer portion is definitely wood.

Also, the sphere in the plans is thirty centimeters in circumference, about the size of a softball. The wooden one must be a prototype, but what are they for? Some kind of a game?

It doesn't feel like a game.

Oliver checks the time.

He puts the plans away before crawling under the workbench. He found the wooden orb in the footlocker; maybe there's a quick answer inside it. He leans deep into the dark recess beneath the bench and powers up his phone's flashlight.

He pulls the jacket out and places it across his lap. It delivers a one-two punch of mold and old and brings about a violent sneeze. Next, he takes out all six journals. He puts them in chronological order based on the date found on each of the first pages, ranging from 1881 to 1883.

With his phone perched near his chin, he opens the first one. The script is shaky and faded, as if penned with the opposite hand.

SEPTEMBER 10, 1881.
My name is Malcolm Toye. And I am a dead man.

OLIVER FUMBLES HIS LIGHT.
The garage, once warm and empty, feels crowded with ghosts.

Malcolm Toye was his great-grandfather. His mom once mentioned there were relatives in the navy, but there were no pictures to prove it. And rarely did they visit family.

When his heart rate nears normal, he turns on the light.

I HAVE SOMEHOW FOUND myself separated from my party. We reached a chain of Siberian islands. This, we suspect, being Bennett Island. The men are weak and frostbitten. Soon, we plan to take the boats in search of the mainland, in hopes of finding a native settlement.

And, somehow, I find myself alone.

There is no feeling in my toes and most of my legs after having fallen into an open lead. If I survive, which is doubtful, frostbite has already claimed these parts of my body. My nose, as well.

I write only with the hope that my love will know that, in these final hours, I am thinking of her. I was a fool to attempt this journey into the Arctic. No man will see the North Pole without perishing, this I am certain. Why would I think this expedition would be any different?

As I lay here, it is your love, my bride, which offers me the warmth and knowledge that I will pass through the gates of heaven with a smile.

THERE ARE several unintelligible passages that follow as his fingers appeared to stiffen on the water-stained pages. It ends with scribbles, like a man attempting to record his dreams long after he's fallen asleep.

There are several blank pages.

But then the entries resume, this time with sharp lines and fluent script, not the handwriting of frozen fingers. And oddly similar to the plans in the filing cabinets.

DECEMBER *10, 1881*

Is heaven a warm room? Is it a full belly and the comfort of a bed? If it is, my love, then I rest peacefully in the afterlife.

I can only guess the date at the time of this entry. It feels like months have passed since I last wrote, but I cannot be sure. I can only report what I see before me.

I write to you with not a quill and ink but an instrument much smoother. My belongings are heaped into the corner of this very small room, whose walls appear to be fashioned from blue ice, yet when I touch them, they feel no more frigid than a ship's deck. The floor, too, is ice, yet when I step on it, I do not slip.

What is more remarkable, if that is even possible, is that my fingers and toes are fully functioning. There is a slight discoloration on the smallest of my digits, but it appears that I have made a full recovery.

How is this possible?

My memories are scattered. I recall, with the help of this journal, wandering the frozen tundra and becoming separated from the party. I remember lying in wait of death, yet here I am, writing to you.

I have slept much. When I wake, there is little energy in my body, but I find food next to the bed. When I slumber, I hear voices that are never here when, once again, I wake. It is strange and impossible that I am still in the Arctic, but I have no other explanation.

I hesitate to record what is next, but feel certain you will understand if somehow you find these journals. I recall, in my final moments before waking in this room, there was someone with me. Or, perhaps I should say, something. When I was dying in the snow, I felt its shadow fall over me as my breath leaked from me. It was a large thing, an angel of sorts, that whisked me out of Death's clutches. Its body was massive, and its arms thick. My love, there is no other way to say it.

It was made of snow.

I am very aware of how this sounds, that these ramblings are the sort from a madman, that perhaps I damaged some part of the brain and tell you my dreams instead of reality. Perhaps I am still on the ice and dying after all, and these ramblings are a dream.

But I think not.

TAP, tap, tap.

The phone tumbles into Oliver's lap.

He finds it in the coat and scurries away from the noise. It wasn't a mouse or a branch. That was someone knocking. Something weird is about to happen. This is a different weird than low blood sugar weird. This is out there. He starts to climb out when the doorknob rattles.

Oliver slams into the footlocker and hides beneath the old, musty coat, fumbling to turn off the light.

A key slides into the lock.

The door opens, and someone kicks their boots on the doorjamb before coming inside. Oliver is as solid as granite. He squeezes his eyes shut, breathing as slowly as possible. Footsteps quietly cross the garage. Oliver dares a peek through the fuzzy slots of his eyelids. Grandmother's padded boots stand at the storage rack next to the filing cabinet.

She's humming.

It could be Mom wearing Grandmother's boots, but Mom shuffles. And she doesn't have an old, spotted left hand. Grandmother's right hand is clad in a strange metallic glove, something made of metal links and silver plates.

What's weirder is that she's humming.

He assumed she disapproved of all things fun and expressive, like music and dancing and laughing.

Rule #534: No joy.

She's tearing plastic wrapping, maybe opening paper towels. If she turns around and leaves, she'll never see him from that angle. But whatever she's got, she brings to the workbench.

Close enough he could grab her knee.

Oliver's fingernails dig into his palms. His head is getting light. He forces himself to breathe, trying to remember if he left anything open. Did he leave any papers out? Did he close the filing cabinet?

The wooden orb!

He stops breathing.

Hiding in the garage with great-grandfather's belongings on his lap, he's pretty sure will be breaking a rule, written or not.

Grandmother goes back to the shelves, humming a little louder, and then heads for the door, but not before unloading a three-step fart.

A moment later, she closes the door.

He takes a long breath just before things dim. He holds completely still, though, muffling his breathing with the coat. He stays that way for several minutes, just in case Sing-along Grandmother comes back with another dose of walking farts.

When he finally moves, it's in full-blown panic mode.

His legs are weak, but there's no time to check sugar. He shoves the items back in the footlocker. The wooden orb had rolled against the wall and wedged, luckily, behind a tin can of rusty nails. He grabs it and heads for the door.

He stops.

He might not come back for a while. He might not come back ever. He checks the window and sees Grandmother's tracks heading back to the house. Quickly, he digs into the footlocker and tucks three journals inside his coat.

He runs through the forest, sprinting out to the clearing as the long shadows begin to fade. He takes a moment to rub snow on his cheeks and forehead, pulling his gloves off to chill his fingers so that, when he returns, he's sure to look and feel like he's been exploring the property.

Just as he climbs onto the front porch, he realizes two things.

One, Grandmother had to unlock the door to get inside the garage, but he never locked it. But it's the second realization that sends chills down his neck.

Grandmother didn't notice his tracks leading into the garage.

Because they had been erased.

6

Oliver stands at the pantry door, stunned. Maybe he's asleep or Grandmother's alarm didn't go off. Like she has an alarm. *Like she sleeps.*

But two weeks until Christmas and there it is, a blank chore list. Christmas came early.

Oliver grabs a quick breakfast and returns to his bedroom. He listens at the door for a few minutes. When silence remains, he creeps to the dresser and leans into it, tilting it towards the wall and reaching underneath, where three leather-bound books are stashed. They barely fit. He's not going back to the garage anytime soon.

He should've grabbed all six of them.

He flops his backpack on the bed and shoves the journals inside, covering them with *Snowboarder Magazine*, something Mom picked up at a gas station. He'll need more magazines and books, just to make it look good. But what if Grandmother inspects the backpack?

Grandmother? What if Mom looks inside? How am I going to explain that?

This horrible plan worsens when footsteps come toward his room. He slams into the dresser like a linebacker. It thumps the wall just as a light knocking raps the door.

"Just a sec."

He can't fuss with the journals; it'll sound like he's up to something. Instead, he throws the backpack on the other side of the bed and takes several deep breaths before opening the door.

"Where've you been?" Mom's in a robe with a towel on her head.

"There are no chores. I was just, you know, relaxing."

A look crosses her face. She knows he's hiding something. He's as transparent as a glass of water. Then again, his lies are generally about how many bowls of cereal he ate or whether he checked his sugar, not hiding antiquated journals.

"Sorry, kiddo, no relaxing today. Your Aunt Rhonnie and cousins are coming today."

She slings a suit bag on the bed and pulls the zipper down the center, exposing a dark blue jacket and striped tie. A little handkerchief tufts out of the breast pocket.

"No, Mom. Please, no."

"It's not going to kill you."

"Yes, it will."

"I went to boarding school when I was ten and wore a uniform every day. It didn't kill me."

Yes, it did.

She holds the suit to his shoulders. He's heard her talk about boarding school, heard her say it did kill a part of her. She laughs when she says it, but it's only half a joke. Oliver feels like a part of her died before that.

"You've got two hours," she says. "Get a shower, get dressed, and you'll have time to sneak a few games on your phone."

"I don't know how to do the tie."

"Lucky you." She holds up a clip-on.

His friends back in Texas had dads that wore suits. Oliver was convinced it sucked out their souls. Oliver's dad never wore a tie. He made money with investments, but he was pretty sure his dad already sold his soul.

Oliver didn't want his soul sucked out by a suit or boarding school.

"Your chores for today are entertaining your cousins. Grandmother lives for this stuff, darling." She lathers the last word with stuffy English entitlement. "Be on your best behavior."

She turns at the door and, in bare feet, curtsies as if her robe were a ballroom gown.

❋

His shiny shoes are stark against the dull grain of the staircase.

Each step sends a hard-soled clack through the house, biting into his heels as he descends to the first floor, where Grandmother, dressed in pearls and dead animal fur, is waiting.

"Why good day, sir," Mom says.

"Debra, don't be foolish."

Mom curtsies, this time in a blue dress that hugs her neck. Her brown hair is off her face, except for a looping curl she pulls aside. She straightens his tie and fusses with his hair that's still too short to brush.

"Mom." Grandmother turns her steely stare on him. "I mean, Mother."

She doesn't stop fussing. She looks beautiful; he looks handsome. But, honestly, they look absurd. She must be thinking what Oliver is thinking. They try not to giggle and fail.

"Debra, behave yourself." Grandmother folds her hands beneath the draping fur. "What kind of example are you setting? Honestly, I expect more out of you. This is not how I taught you. If you had listened to me, Olivah would have a father to teach him these things."

That's when the light vanishes from Mom's eyes.

She rests her hand on Oliver's shoulder. The joy that a few moments earlier was bubbling out drains from her. She turns to Grandmother and lifts a finger.

"Don't," is all she can say.

Grandmother defiantly lifts her chin.

Beneath the rosy strokes of blush, her skin is the color of sun-bleached wood. Mom's complexion is a growing flame, and shallow creases form around her pursed lips, something he'd never noticed before. Oliver could swear that, despite the emotionless gaze, a tiny, infinitesimal twitch crinkles the corner of Grandmother's mouth.

A micro-smile.

Rule #575: Grind children under heel.

A silver car can be seen through the fractured panel of decorative glass. It eases up to the sidewalk. The tinted windows reflect the looming house.

"Olivah. Be so kind as to greet our guests."

He opens the large door, and a bitter breeze hits him.

Grandmother goes out to the porch.

Mom continues staring, as if the ghost of her mother is still in front of her. In a few words, Grandmother kicked the legs out from Mom's life, spilling her emotions all over the floor. She picks them up, though, and gives Oliver a half-empty smile before going to the porch.

A slender woman gets out of the driver's side, with a low-cut blouse. Round sunglasses, lenses the size of coasters, are perched on Aunt Rhonnie's pointy nose. She waves, fingers only, but her bright red lips don't move as she strides around the front of the car, her heels spiking the sidewalk, with a furry coat over her arm.

"Mother," she says.

They don't hug, but rather loosely take each other's arms and air-kiss each cheek. She's a stretched and younger version of Grandmother with a wrinkle-free complexion that's smooth, yet plump and expressionless—courtesy of her plastic surgeon.

Mom's twin sister—fraternal twin sister—approaches her.

"Welcome home, sister," she says. They embrace like normal people, without the fake kisses. Aunt Rhonnie holds her at arm's length. "Look at you with all your earrings and inner beauty. You look wonderful, you really do."

"And you, with your Michael Kors sunglasses and perfect skin."

"And who's your date?" She lowers her sunglasses. "Don't tell me... oh my Lord! This handsome young man can't be! It just can't be!"

Her lined lips form a circle that swoop in to plant a sticky kiss on Oliver's cheek. She wraps her bony arms around him, pulling him against her engorged chest until he smells like a cosmetics sampler.

"You look wonderful, Oliver," she says. "You really do. You remind me of your handsome father, all dressed up like a grown-up. Let's go inside before I catch pneumonia. I'm not made for this weather; I don't know why I live here."

She rushes into the foyer.

Grandmother and Mom follow. Oliver is last, wondering how long she's staying with the car still running.

"Where are the twins?" Mom asks.

"They're finishing their games. They'll be inside as soon as they're done. Oh my Lord, I am so happy to see you. It's so nice to have the family together. When's the last time we had tea?"

"A while," Mom says.

"Actually, never," Aunt Rhonnie says. "Oliver was too young. This is going to be so much fun, I can hardly stand it. Let me powder my nose. I must look dreadful after being in the car. Really, Mother, you need to move into the city. There's no point staying on the property."

Aunt Rhonnie, still wearing her sunglasses, sways down the hallway. Oliver waits for one of the pointy heels to hammer into the floor.

Grandmother goes to the kitchen.

Mom licks her finger to wipe the lipstick off Oliver's cheek.

"You wait here," she says, as if there's a war zone down the hallway. She rubs his hair, kisses his head, and goes headlong into the battle.

Oliver stays put as a draft creeps under the door and up the pant legs crumpled around his shiny shoes. A door slams outside, followed by another.

Henry adjusts his tie as he waits for Helen to come around the car. The twins open the front door without knocking. They stand across from Oliver, shoulder to shoulder like a pair of aliens. A few years older and just as many inches taller than Oliver, they have blond hair that, if he's not mistaken, is too blond. Almost gold.

Their features are angular, like Aunt Rhonnie's. Helen's hair is pulled back in a tight ponytail that, seventy years from now, will be gray and wrapped in a bun. She's sort of sucking in her cheeks.

They look like a commercial.

"Where's Mother?" Henry slicks his hair to the side without disturbing the part.

"They went that way."

And then the two, side by side, walk down the dim hallway. Oliver stays at the front door until his legs turn cold.

Mom is in the kitchen.

She's hyper-focused on arranging silver pots and bowls and miniature spoons on an oval silver tray with intricate etchings. Muscles are bunched on her shoulders. She doesn't notice him standing behind her as she fills one of the bowls with sugar cubes.

"Are you all right?" Oliver asks.

She drops the last sugar cube and curses. She covers her mouth and giggles, letting the tension fall away as she rubs her face and curses quietly again.

"Oooh." She sighs. "It feels like we've been in this house forever."

Strangely, this still feels like an adventure to Oliver. Parts of Mom, though, have never left this house.

"Can I help?" he asks.

She directs him to fill the other tray with scones and condiments from the refrigerator. He puts it together, but Mom starts methodically changing the placement of the little pitchers and plates.

"Grandmother's thing is tea," she says. "When I was little, I'd focus on the details to make it go faster. If I didn't think about it, just engaged in the action one hundred percent, no matter how I felt about it, then it was over before I knew it."

She tweaks the orientation of a small knife.

"We did this every time we had company. It's her ice breaker."

"More like ice maker."

Mom snorts.

She pinches her nose, but it doesn't help. Oliver smothers his laughter. She turns away, twice, before getting herself under control. Straightening the wrinkles in her dress, she says, "Let's get serious."

Once the trays are ready, they exit the kitchen and stop at the dining room, where company sits properly in their high-backed chairs. Grandmother is at the head of the table. Aunt Rhonnie and the twins are to the left.

"Tea," Mom announces, "is served."

The sarcasm is skillfully camouflaged, yet highlights the absurdity of bizarro world. Oliver waits for Mom to place her tray before putting his down.

"Very strong boy," Aunt Rhonnie says. Her sunglasses are hooked on the neckline of her blouse, exposing more of her very bony, very tan chest. Her eyes are intensely blue, like they've been Photoshopped.

Once they're seated to the right of Grandmother, tea begins.

They pass around the sterling silver decanter and pour the stringent, hot tea through a screen to filter the loose leaves. The small boats of lemon wedges and pitchers of milk are passed around. The twins, sitting ramrod straight with eyes cast down, drop three cubes of sugar with silver tongs into their cups and stir with miniature spoons without making a sound.

"You two, stop it," Aunt Rhonnie says. "Oliver can't have sugar."

She says it as if he's an alcoholic and they're guzzling booze. He pours creamer into his cup and remains unnoticed until his spoon clinks the porcelain.

Grandmother's lips tighten.

Rule #954: Don't clink your cup.

Everyone samples the tea with pinkies properly curled inward and not, as Grandmother explained, extended. That sort of nonsense is for the movies. They sip silently, staring down so as not to spill a drop. There's a long pause before the scones are passed around.

"So, Mother," Aunt Rhonnie says, "how do you like your new roommates?"

"There have been no surprises."

Oliver doesn't know what that means, but Mom flinches.

"Sometimes predictability is nice," Aunt Rhonnie says. "Lord knows, my life could use some. I was just saying that the other day."

She plies a scone with strawberry jam and talks about her divorce lawyer's counterproposal to her soon-to-be ex-husband's ridiculous offer. They'll just end up paying the lawyers more money, and, Lord knows, lawyers already make enough.

"I mean, what I offered the first time was more than fair. It could've ended right there. But if he wants to play games, then okay, let's play."

She tears a piece off the scone with her long, red fingernails.

"How's school?" Mom asks.

The twins look up, but Aunt Rhonnie answers. Helen had the lead in the school play and received a standing ovation. She posted pictures on Facebook, didn't they see them? Mom really needs to move into the twenty-first century and get an account. If she did, she'd also know that Helen just got her first modeling job. There's a chance that she'll end up in J. Crew's fall catalog.

Wouldn't that be wonderful?

Mom watches the twins dress their scones with jam and clotted cream and dab their mouths while Aunt Rhonnie describes Henry's violin concert.

"He received a standing ovation, and, believe me, he deserved it."

"School play, huh?" Mom says to Helen. "Was it hard memorizing your lines?"

"We practiced every night," Aunt Rhonnie says.

"Were you nervous?"

"Nervous?" Aunt Rhonnie says. "This girl has ice running through her veins."

Helen takes a carefully measured sip of the sugared tea while Aunt Rhonnie describes how much the costumes cost. Helen focuses on placing the cup back on the saucer without a clink. Is she doing the same as Mom, keeping her mind empty to get this over with?

"Henry." Mom pauses until he makes eye contact. "Did you bring your violin?"

"No, ma'am."

He hides behind his teacup, and Aunt Rhonnie describes the magical concert. They just have to come to the next; it has to be seen to be believed.

Mom exhales very slowly.

In the meantime, Grandmother cuts her scone into bite-sized pieces and chews twenty times apiece. She may as well be having tea alone.

Oliver's scone tastes like a clod of flour.

Against his will, he swallows a gulp of tea to wash it down and receives a glance from Grandmother. You don't wash down scones with tea.

"What do you do, Oliver?" Aunt Rhonnie asks.

All attention turns to him. He's slouching. This time, he pretends to sip from the cup.

"What do I do?" he replies.

"In your spare time."

"Mostly read, I guess."

"Smarty pants, huh? You hear that, Henry? Oliver likes to read. Henry read all of the Hunger Games books in a day and the Harry Potter books, all seven of them, in a week and, let me tell you, those last two were ridiculously thick. I mean, there's like 200,000 words or more in each one. Can you believe that?"

Oliver fakes another sip. He likes Aunt Rhonnie. No one looks at you when she's in the room.

"What else?" she asks.

"Ma'am?"

"What else besides reading? Surely, you've been doing something else in this house besides reading. What else do you like to do?"

"Oh, um." He thinks about the journals in his room and feels his face warm. "Chores."

Mom snorts. She quickly lifts her cup.

Aunt Rhonnie's perma-grin falters. "Chores? You like chores?"

"Yes, ma'am."

The funny thing is, he sort of meant it. He didn't mind the shoveling and making his bed and all the ritual that went with preparing meals and cleaning. Before they moved, he was glued to his phone. Maybe he wouldn't feel the same if he hadn't discovered the garage and the mystery in this bizarro world.

"How is our chore master, Mother?" Aunt Rhonnie asks.

Grandmother dabs her mouth. "Olivah has done a fine job."

And that's all she says. It's all she needs to say. It's as close to a compliment he's ever heard. It makes him feel warm and fuzzy.

"Chores and reading, then," Aunt Rhonnie says. "Good...that's good."

"Don't forget handsome," Mom adds.

They finish tea and learn more about Rhonnie's new career opportunity as a model consultant. Oliver doesn't have to talk. And that's just fine. Instead, he imitates the twins' mechanical tea performance, lifting and sipping, eyes cast down. He even finishes the scone by chopping uniform slices and chewing twenty times. Before he knows it, tea is over.

Later, he goes outside for exercise.

That's when he meets the real twins.

7

_____

Henry's on the back porch, dressed in a wool coat buttoned just past his waist. He tucks a black scarf around his neck and, looking up at the clear sky, slides on a dark pair of sunglasses. With his hands in his front pockets, he passes Oliver and peeks through the garage window.

"Wish we could go in there, right?" he says. "That's the one door the old lady never forgets to lock."

Oliver doesn't comment. *Maybe I got lucky.*

"You see that car?" Henry spits a hole in the snow. "We ever get the keys to that, Ollie, we're going on a road trip and never coming back."

The back door closes again. This time, Helen comes down the steps, pulling on gloves. Her sunglasses came off the same rack as her mom's.

Henry starts towards the windmill.

"Are we taking Ollie?"

"We can't leave him."

"We're not taking him with us, Henry." Helen still hasn't looked at Oliver. "I don't trust him."

"He's family."

"You're hilarious."

Henry looks back at the house, then at the windmill. "You a rat, Ollie?"

"What?"

"Can you keep a secret?"

"Yeah."

"Come on, walk with us."

Helen leads them toward the windmill that, mercifully, continues its silent mechanical churn. Despite the sunny day, the cold air pinches Oliver's nose and cheeks. Henry hooks his arm around Oliver's shoulders.

"We've been coming out here since we were born, Ollie. We've done more chores than indentured servants. You seem like a smart kid, doing your work without complaining. That's how you work the old lady, just do what she says and shut your mouth. But how long have you been out here? Two weeks?"

Oliver nods.

"That means you don't know squat. Am I right, Helen?"

She's ten steps ahead. Henry stops at the foot of the windmill and, with lips forming a circle, exhales a column of steam.

"I like your cap," he says. "Where'd you get it?"

"My mom."

"Yeah? Like an early Christmas present?"

"Something like that."

"Nice. Let me try it, see if it fits."

Oliver's legs get colder.

"Come on," Henry says. "I'm thinking about getting one. That's all. Don't be a selfish turd."

Oliver hesitates before pulling the cap off. He can feel the heat seep from his scalp. Henry pulls it over his product-stiff hair. He checks his reflection in his sunglasses.

"Helen, what'd you think?"

Now thirty steps away, she turns around, hugging herself. "You look like a douche."

Henry chuckles before scooping up a handful of snow and heaves a snowball at her. She starts for the open field again.

"Come on." Henry whacks Oliver in the chest. "You going to let her get away with insulting your hat? Nail her one, why don't you."

Oliver keeps his hands in his pockets. The cold fear seeps into his stomach. Henry smacks him again and points in his face.

"Don't leave me hanging, Ollie. You throw a snowball."

Oliver bends over slowly, giving Helen enough time to get well out of range before throwing one short.

Henry snatches two fistfuls of his coat.

"What are you doing, throwing a snowball at my sister?" His eyebrows furrow behind his sunglasses, his teeth clenched between tightly drawn lips. Oliver stares at his black reflection in the lenses, the cold fear creeping into his arms. They're still in view of the house.

Henry lightly slaps his cheek. "I'm just playing."

He drags Oliver with his arm hooked around his neck. They follow Helen's tracks around the trees. She's yelling at them to hurry up.

When the house is out of sight, Henry straightens Oliver's collar.

"You're a good kid. You're smart, you read and all that good stuff. I trust you can get lost for an hour. Don't let the old lady see you wandering around on your own."

"What if she comes outside?"

"Grandmother? You joking? Have you ever seen the old lady outside? Besides going to the garage, I've never seen her come off the front porch. And I mean *never*. Don't let any of them see you, for that matter."

Helen has already started across the open field, her shoulders hunched.

"We're going that way, Ollie. Don't follow us."

Oliver nods.

"I mean, don't follow us ever."

Pause. And nod.

"Good." Another playful slap. This time it stings. "This is your test. Don't disappoint me."

"Where are you going?"

"Don't worry about that."

Oliver stands near the trees, watching Henry catch up to his sister. The cold is feasting on his ears, but he doesn't move until they reach the other side and slip between the trees.

He has one hour to kill.

OLIVER HAD no intention of coming to the garage.

It would've been safer to wait. But Henry took his stocking cap, and his head feels like a block of ice. Oliver goes to the house and, after knocking off the snow, goes inside. He announces that he's just come to use the bathroom and do a quick blood test. Henry and Helen are waiting for him in the field.

He sneaks up to his room and, listening for footsteps, stuffs one of the journals down his pants.

Aunt Rhonnie is in the kitchen, pouring liqueur into a cup of coffee. Oliver rushes out before she starts talking, and finds himself, after wandering through the trees, going to the garage door.

Once again the doorknob turns easily.

Oliver opens his coat. He's got an hour before he needs to be at the field, pretending to wait for the twins to return. He sets the alarm on his phone and crawls under the bench.

The footlocker is just like he left it. Oliver takes the journal from under his belt and, with his phone illuminating the yellowed pages, looks for where he left off. There's not much time.

He turns the brittle page.

DATE? I don't know the date. I don't know how many days have passed, don't know if I'm still dreaming or awake.

Sleep feels like eternity.

I awake, or so I believe, with lotion on my hands and feet. My flesh still has an odd color, something closer to ash, and I've lost some sensation. But my toes wiggle and my fingers write, and someone seems to be making sure they do so.

Some mornings (I'm calling them mornings, but there is no way to know) there are fresh clothes stacked on the floor, clothes that I've never seen. They are newly tailored and warm, fitting perfectly over my pudgy frame. I can no longer see my ribs. And if I stand up straight, I can hardly see my toes.

I call out, but no one answers.

I feel buried, but awake with a full belly and salt on my lips. Someone is fattening me up. Perhaps I have fallen prey to a sea monster. I will wake, one morning, to find myself not walking the confines of a square cubicle but swimming in boiling soup!

Time has become my enemy. I am thankful for life, but what life is this? It is survival, I tell myself.

Survival until I see you, my love.

I pace the room and count my steps. And I do push-ups and sit-ups, fifty at a time. And then I start over.

Judging by the curly whiskers hiding my chin, I can guess that I have been here a month or so. Still, the unending silence, broken only by my own breath, pushes me toward madness.

Why am I alive? Why me?

And what of the crew? When I think of my mates, the room becomes smaller and the silence heavier. I can't think of them. Their fate has surely been cast. They either made it home or died on the ice.

   Either of those fates tortures me with envy.

THERE ARE pages torn from the journal and mad scribbles on the ones that follow—sketches of ships and desolation, of wistful clouds and sunrises in full array. Some of the entries are difficult to read, as if written on the brink of sleep or despair.

WHY?

   I shout after waking. I shout it to no avail.

   My captors tease me with compassion, but leave me only with the company of my thoughts. Dreams of you are all that I cling to. You reach for me in a field of green, and we walk the water's edge. We lie down in the summer and watch the clouds pass. I hold this locket to my heart, open it to see your loving face. I am tempted to touch your photo but too afraid it will blot the image.

   It is all I have.

   And just when I think I cannot wake another day without you, my savior appeared. With grizzled bush upon my face, I pushed curly locks from my eyes to see him enter the room

   And he is nothing what I expected.

AN ALARM GOES OFF.

Oliver drops the journal, accidentally prying the cover until the spine cracks. He touches the phone's screen, turning off the alarm. The time passed too fast.

It's the last entry in that journal.

There's no time to find the next one. He makes sure he's not leaving anything behind, squeezing the orb in his pocket and feeling the surge of confidence before closing the door behind him.

He makes it to the clearing, the sun hanging above the mountains.

A sharp whistle echoes off the trees.

Henry and Helen exit the far side from about the same spot they entered. One of them is waving. Oliver waits at the edge of the forest, rubbing his ears, watching them trek through the snow. Henry, with the black stocking cap pulled down to his eyes, starts running. He scoops up a ball of snow and throws it. It falls short of Oliver.

Oliver's head is already cold.

He starts to ask for his cap back, but Henry puts him in a headlock, thumping his scalp with his knuckle.

"Good doggie."

His coat smells like smoke.

Oliver pulls his frozen ears out of the arm-vise. He falls on his hands and knees. Just like a dog.

"Hey, come on." Henry yanks him up. "You did good, waited for us just like I said. Maybe you can come next time."

"Can I have my cap?"

"Not until we get back."

Oliver's ears are burning.

He can't stop frowning, but it doesn't bother Henry. It only makes the smile widen. Oliver can't wait until they're gone. He starts for the house, forcing himself not to run.

Helen is still behind them. Oliver isn't waiting for them. He's stomping a path back to the house, where he can get a shower and rinse the cold from his bones.

Maybe they'll be gone by the time he's out.

Henry shouts at his sister to hurry. Oliver buries his hands, now colder than his ears, deep into his pockets and hunches his shoulders when something moves in the trees near him.

The snow falls from branches just inside the tree line.

Something is lurking.

FOOP.

It shoots between the branches.

It arches high and hard.

A snowball, something the size of a basketball, rotates as it peaks. Oliver watches it fly over his head and descend.

All the way to Henry's face.

The stocking cap flies off, landing twenty feet behind him. He falls backwards, arms and legs out, landing flat in the snow. Oliver, with his hands in his pockets, watches his cousin rise up, his face as red as a flame. He shakes the dizziness away and looks around.

And finds Oliver.

His face turns a shade darker as he crawls to his feet and begins running. Oliver looks back at the trees, wondering if Henry saw it, too.

Although Oliver didn't see what threw it, maybe Henry did. *Why didn't he dodge it?*

Henry buries his shoulder into Oliver's chest.

Oliver goes down, eating snow all the way to the soil.

Henry lands on his back with all his weight, driving him into the frozen ground. Oliver can't draw a breath, struggles to find air as Henry rolls him like a log and drops his knees into Oliver's stomach.

Oliver gasps like a speared fish.

The side of Henry's face is starting to swell. Spittle bubbles in the corners of his mouth. He grabs handfuls of Oliver's coat.

"Stop!" Helen closes in on them. "Get off him!"

Henry slams Oliver's head off the ground.

The world is washed in light, but pain is overridden by the desperation to breathe. Snow falls over them as Helen slides into Henry, wrapping her arms around him. Oliver rolls onto his hands and knees and, finally, finds his first breath.

Drool dangles from his lower lip.

"He didn't throw it," Helen pleads. "Ollie didn't do it."

"What?"

"It came from the trees. I saw it, Henry. I swear, Ollie didn't throw it."

"Who did?"

"I think...I don't know."

Henry is huffing through clamped teeth, looking at the trees and back to Oliver. His gelled hair has been sculpted into a rogue wave. He starts toward Oliver, but Helen gets between them.

"Don't." She pushes him. "You drag him inside with a bloody nose and Grandmother will tie you to a stump."

He wipes his nose and checks the back of his hand. It's swiped with blood. He spits red, staining the snow.

"Who's over there?" he shouts.

He takes a step and stops, looking back at Helen. If someone is in there, he's not too eager.

"It came from the trees," she says.

"What's that mean, it came from the trees? Did you see him or not? *See him?*

"I don't know! I just saw it, that's all."

He spits again.

There's a long pause between them, unspoken words not meant for

Oliver. They know what's out there but don't want to admit it, not in front of Oliver. Or to themselves. Hands on his hips, he wanders over to the trees, but doesn't enter the forest. He points at the spot, and Helen nods. A few more steps. And that's it.

He doesn't say another thing, doesn't come to shake Oliver like a broken toy or kick snow in his face. He heads back to the house.

Helen helps Oliver stand, wiping the snow off his coat. He sees his reflection in her glasses, his cheeks pink and scuffed.

"Wipe your nose."

He rakes his hand across his upper lip. A faint red blur remains on his hand. She pinches his nose, then straightens his coat. Without saying a word, she follows her brother's footsteps leading to the house.

A headache begins to blossom while Oliver catches his breath. He feels shaky, too. It'd be good to get inside and check his sugar. First, he waits until both twins are in the house. Oliver trundles out to the clearing, his legs cold and nervous. He finds the buried stocking cap and knocks the snow off before pulling it over his ears.

Something looms in the tree's shadows, right where Henry's tracks stopped short. Snow falls from the branches.

And then it's gone.

8

————

Oliver finishes shoveling the circle drive.

The night of the mystery snowball brought a light dusting. He leans on the handle, looking down the spotless entry drive, contemplating where the snowball had come from. Someone had to throw it.

Once Aunt Rhonnie and the twins left, he realized the obvious hadn't freaked him out. *Someone had to throw it.* A snowball doesn't just spontaneously launch from the trees with the precision of a rifle. The thing that didn't occur to him until he was lying in bed was the obvious:

Henry and Helen weren't freaking out.

They were scared, but not freaked. Strangers don't come out to the property; they don't hang out in the woods and toss random snowballs. Henry and Helen weren't shocked at all. They were scared. They knew who was out there.

Or what.

Whatever threw the snowball meant to hit Henry, to knock the stocking cap off his head.

Holding the straps of his backpack around his shoulders, Oliver jogs to the side of the house and leans against the wall, just below the family room window. He'd like to hide in the garage and read another journal.

Who threw the snowball?

The thought causes his heart to work harder. He swallows the fear and clenches his fists, mumbling, "You can do it, Oliver. You can do it, you can do it, you can do it—"

He leaps before his thoughts change to *go to your room and hide.*

Eyes fixed on the trees, arms stiff at his sides, he marches across the backyard. His heart swells into his throat as he nears the darkness between the tree trunks. He ducks beneath the heavy branches, can hardly feel his legs as he forces his way into the shade.

Turning left, he forges toward the clearing like a nutcracker soldier, stepping quickly and stiffly. Nothing moves deep in the forest; snow doesn't fall from the branches. Nothing jumps out to greet him.

He reaches the forest's edge.

Nothing at all.

Oliver leans against a tree, staring into the shadows. There are no hulking figures, no snapping branches or mystery footsteps—just his raspy breath. He could go deeper, but he doubts his heart could take it. Besides, there's one more thing to find.

He looks across the wide field.

Their tracks have vanished as all tracks do on the property. It doesn't matter. Oliver starts across the open field, keeping his eyes on the sparse trees near the twins' exit point.

When he reaches the other side, he checks the compass app on his phone. He'd been camping enough to know that trees can all look alike. He gets his bearings, thinking north seemed a little more to the left the last time he checked the compass.

Maybe he didn't calibrate it.

The trees are long and stringy between hulking trunks of mammoth conifers. He makes a mental note of the bark chewed off a large poplar, maybe a woodchuck or a beaver. Still no tracks to follow. He moves side to side, searching for a trail or broken branches. The snow isn't as deep, but he grows weary and bored. This feels too far. The twins aren't nature lovers.

There's another poplar missing bark.

It looks just like the other one.

He gets closer and notices footprints. *It is the same one!*

He didn't turn around, he's sure of it. The compass is reading north slightly to the right this time. The app is broke. *That's great. Get lost in the woods looking for the twins' secret. If the weather doesn't kill me, Henry will.*

He takes a moment to consider which way leads back home when he hears something splash. In between the blood pumping in his ears, he hears it again.

He follows the sound instead of the compass, where the land begins to slope downward. He climbs over a fallen tree. Then another. Ahead, branches litter the ground, some the size of telephone poles. The tops of trees are broken in various locations, some dead, bent and hanging.

This is where the forest rumbles.

He'd been sleeping through the nightly ruckus lately, even wondering if he'd been imagining its odd nature. Maybe that's just how it was supposed to sound near the mountains.

The rushing water is beyond an uprooted cedar.

Oliver hikes around a tangle of vines and nearly steps in an over-sized hole.

Heart leaping, he looks down the gullet of a ten-foot-wide sinkhole —the smooth sides funneling deep into the ground.

Pebbles splash into a dark pool at the bottom.

No coming out of that.

He walks around, watching the ground for another potential death pit. The rushing water grows louder. Ahead, a deep trench is carved from the ground, snaking along the base of a steep slope like a scar. Oliver approaches warily, grabbing a sapling sprouted near the edge. An innocent stream runs across the bottom; debris caught in the rocky sides suggests stronger currents when snowmelt comes off the mountains. He leans forward, feeling the cool, humid updraft from the frigid waters.

Ice breaks under his boot.

Oliver's balance spills forward. He grabs the sapling with both hands and spins around as the backpack sways. His foot finds the sharp edge of a stone.

The young tree bends and cracks, but holds his weight. He hugs the tree and pulls himself onto solid footing, falling into the soft bed of needles.

His heart is full throttle.

That's a sign. As soon as the feeling returns to his legs, he's heading back to the house. Whatever the twins were doing can remain a secret.

He follows the stream, keeping a safe distance from the edge while watching for sinkholes until he's ready to turn south for the house. Tree debris increases. Up ahead, the gorge turns north where a fallen cottonwood spans the shores, its roots upturned on the opposite bank.

Oliver pauses.

He should go back to the house and warm up, that's the smart thing to do. It wouldn't hurt to look, though. He'd come all this way, braved two brushes with one-way trips into hypothermic water.

Just a look.

He makes his way to the broken tree.

The bark is smooth, and the leaves long fallen away. Rot has hollowed out several openings where branches once grew. He climbs through the debris and finds a clearing on the opposite side, a narrow trail that weaves to the foot of the shore, where flat stones lead up to the massive trunk.

He tests his footing.

The trunk is plenty wide and, strangely enough, somewhat flat. He wouldn't even have to step like a tight-rope walker, rather walk as if this were a sidewalk. The surface looks dry and tacky.

Oliver looks back. He knows he should turn around, play it safe. Let the twins do whatever it is they do. That would be the smart move.

Not this time.

He keeps his eyes on the radial roots fanning the opposite bank.

Oliver always follows directions. He's never had detention, never received a demerit or failed to apologize for a conflict regardless of who's at fault. If a sign says "Keep Off Lawn," he walks in the opposite direction.

Today, Oliver takes his first step on the forbidden lawn.

His legs become colder when he's over the water.

Refusing to look down, he feels the icy updraft. The water echoes from below, warning all warm-blooded animals to stay out.

Halfway across, with his arms out to the sides, he notices a stack of boulders on the rising slope. Across the river, the ground looks like jagged outcroppings over granite, but this pile is out of place—a pyramid of rounded stones.

There's another set of stone steps at the end of the natural foot-bridge. Oliver climbs down while holding onto stray roots until he's firmly on the ground.

Footprints.

The tracks lead around the array of root flares.

Oliver follows the skinny trail with convenient roots to grab. It goes up the hill, and then, without warning, the tracks vanish. He finds a snowless hollow beneath a rocky ledge where the base of the great tree was uprooted.

The pyramid of rocks is to the right of the opening.

His phone does little to illuminate the depths. He pauses after each step, looking behind him before taking another. The hollow is deeper and darker than expected, more than what the roots would've excavated.

Two more steps, he promises. *I'm not going to wake up a grizzly.*

The earthen cave continues beyond the light's reach. He's about to turn around when he sees the L-shaped root.

Maybe he wouldn't have noticed if there were other sticks or roots this far inside, but it's the only thing attached to the wall.

A light dizziness fills his head.

He lays his hand on the dry, gnarly root.

Click.

An earthen door swings on soundless hinges. Inside is a dark stone hearth with hand-carved chairs. The smell of soot lingers.

Oliver slams the door and runs to the foot of the upturned tree.

There's a room inside this hill.

A room!

He should leave. That's the smart thing.

He should go back to the house and hide in his room, check his blood sugar, take it easy, and no one gets hurt. That's what he always does.

Plays it safe.

This time there's something in his belly besides icy fear.

Excitement.

He squeezes the wooden orb.

Against every instinct he's accumulated his entire life, he turns around. He goes back to the door. Standing on the threshold, he stares into the warm confines, blinking rapidly as if, any moment, the illusion will vanish and he'll be staring at a mud hole instead of a furnished room.

Oliver steps inside.

It's a simple room with an arching ceiling that's just within reach.

Although the coarse walls and hand-carved furniture befits a hobbit, the space is almost full-sized but not quite. There's a small table with candles against the wall and a rug on the cedar floor.

A small window is to his right, a circular port that one would expect to see on a ship. He peers through the dusky glass. Mirrors are positioned to reflect the light through a short tunnel draped with cobwebs. He sees the fallen tree bridging the stream.

Henry and Helen couldn't have possibly built this place.

It's been carved from granite. And there's a fireplace that funnels up to the pyramid of stones that, individually, are too large for a grown man to lift.

His phone sounds off. A message has arrived.

A shiver slithers down his spine.

He hasn't heard that sound since they arrived on the property. Oliver pulls the phone out and slides his thumb across the glass.

151 unread messages.

He's getting five bars of reception.

The instinct to bolt out of this place overrides all other thoughts. Only the numbness in his knees keeps him from running.

And the excitement. The curiosity.

How is it that I'm getting reception in a place more remote than the house?

He falls into one of the chairs and scrolls through his messages.

He begins downloading his books.

He updates his apps and checks social media.

Occasionally, he gets up to look through the window and open the door. He's warm and alone with no chores to do or tea to drink. And now he knows why Henry and Helen trek out here.

And why they're keeping it secret.

OLIVER EMERGES from his phone trance. It takes a moment to realize his mistake.

The sun has set.

He fumbles toward the door but returns to put everything in order, just like he found it. In the dark alcove, he stops. The roots look like knobby claws in the dusky light, but that's not what sends a shiver up his throat.

Leaves are stirring, twigs snapping.

The forest is waking up.

He creeps to the edge, squeezing the wooden orb in his pocket for strength and confidence. For luck. Something quakes above him. Rocks trickle down the hill. His knees almost quit. Oliver pulls the backpack straps tight against his shoulders and eyes the stone steps leading around the tree. The next disturbance is closer.

Oliver shoots for the exit.

An avalanche of stems and leaves slide down the slope.

Oliver swiftly climbs the stones and swings onto the tree, speed-walking across the river with his arms held out to the sides.

His eyes fill with water.

He keeps focused on his steps. The water, cloaked in dying light, calls from below. He's almost across, only three steps to go, when the tree vibrates.

Something stepped onto the bridge.

Oliver takes one giant leap off the tree, stumbling down the stones and into a thicket of vines and branches. The wooden orb flies from his hand, disappearing into the snow.

The fallen tree groans behind him.

Oliver scrambles to his feet, blindly sprinting through a world blurred with tears and panic, pulling at ropey vines and tangled branches, tripping on stones. Ignoring where he's going or what's in front of him, he pushes ahead—

And slams into a wall.

If it was a tree or a boulder, he'd be unconscious. Oliver bounces on his backpack, flails to his knees, wiping the tears to see what's in front of him: two enormous stumps of snow.

Legs.

He grinds the heels of his hands into his eyes.

Ten feet tall.

Thick body and long arms.

Head like a turret.

It can't be.

A snowman looks down.

Branches are breaking. The ground trembles. Before Oliver sees what's coming, the snowman sweeps him off the ground. The wind shrieks in his ears, ripping the stocking cap from his head. A wintry blast hardens his cheeks and fills his head. Tree trunks fly past and disappear. Then the open field is all around.

The world is spinning.

It happens so fast that he's unaware of when the spinning stops or how he ends up lying in the snow, the screech of the windmill nearby.

The acrid taste of vomit stings his throat.

Oliver looks up at the massive form. Again, he wipes his eyes. Twilight highlights the hulking figure, snow like sparkling skin. It remains still, and, for a moment, sanity returns, and the thing looks like an intricately carved figure of snow, not something that picked him up and flew him across the forest.

I am not an "it."

Just like that, reality tilts back into fantasy.

The snowman is not an "it." Oliver thought that. No, he heard it. He thinks he heard it..."him"...think it...and Oliver heard him think it.

The weird fills his head.

It's the blood sugar weird feeling, a weird-weird feeling combined. It's falling off a cliff of reality and waiting to land.

The snowman's chest inflates.

Something's inside him, a source of light beaming through the snow, illuminating his body as he bends over, reaches out and wraps his hands around Oliver's arms and pulls him up.

The snowman opens Oliver's hand and drops the wooden orb into it. It vibrates through his arm.

"Oliver!" Mom calls.

The snowman straightens up and turns toward the windmill. It steps back and, just before dissolving into a shimmering flurry, tosses the stocking cap on Oliver's lap. The once massive form swirls into the forest like a sparkling cloud of diamonds, no footsteps left to follow. In the midst of the snowy dust, something glimmers.

A metallic sphere.

"Oliver!" Mom runs into the open field.

She sees him. Snow has filled her open-laced boots, and her coat is unbuttoned. "We've been looking for you. Where have you been?"

"I'm sorry. I got...turned around."

He keeps looking at the trees. There's a light, a shimmering light that lingers.

"Are you all right?"

"What?"

Mom looks where he's staring. "What is it?"

"I don't know."

She walks closer to the trees. The light goes out.

Grandmother is behind them. Her arm is tucked inside a long black coat. Mom takes Oliver's arm. Her fingers are cold and quivering. Grandmother waits for them to approach, silently scolding. He apologizes again.

She turns her back and leads the way home.

As she slides her arm out of her coat, he catches a glint of a metal glove.

9

Grandmother watches Oliver descend the staircase.

He slides his hand over the ornate post marking the end of the bannister. Arms crossed and lips chiseled, she nods.

Oliver turns around and begins his third ascent.

His legs are beginning to burn, but he's okay with that because none of this makes sense. The world has rules; existence has limits. The sun rises in the east, diabetes is incurable, *and snowmen aren't alive!*

The universe has laws. A snowman that can fly him across a field is not part of those laws. A snowman putting thoughts in his head, either. The world doesn't make sense anymore.

He's not an "it."

"What are you doing?" Mom is outside the second floor bathroom, toothbrush in mouth.

"Grandmother told me to walk the steps."

"Why?"

"Exercise." *Punishment. I'm not going outside anymore.*

"Ridiculous," she mutters. "Get your things. We're going to the library."

Oliver looks back. Grandmother can't see them, but Mom's voice carries through the house.

"Go on, get your backpack. I'll meet you at the car."

He picks up the pace, pushing through the muscle burn. The stairs squeal with glee. He packs books and magazines into his backpack. Checking the door, he grabs the journals from hiding and slides them between the magazines. He needs to get out of the house.

Off the property.

He returns to the staircase.

"What about lunch?" Grandmother says.

"We'll grab something," Mom says. "Do you need anything while we're out?"

Oliver pauses on the bottom step while Mom pulls on her coat, keys rattling in her hand.

"Do you need anything?" she repeats.

Grandmother shakes her head. Lips pursed.

"All right, then. We'll be back for supper. Come on, Oliver."

Oliver goes around his grandmother, turning so the backpack faces away, fearing her x-ray vision will see the journals.

"Bye, Grandmother."

He pulls the door behind him, but she follows him out. Oliver runs to the car. Mom drives around the turnabout, lines scraped across the icy windshield. Grandmother watches them leave from the front porch.

Mom twists one of her earrings. "You all right, kiddo?"

He nods. She sounds confident, but she's playing with her earrings. She'd be terrible at poker.

He looks out his window, feeling the rules of the universe come into balance the farther they get from the property. Maybe if he closes his eyes, he'll wake up in Texas and discover they never moved to Grandmother's, that he imagined secret journals and a hobbit house in the woods.

A snowman.

He feels the wooden orb in his coat pocket.

"Anything weird ever happen to you?" Oliver asks.

"What?"

"Have you ever seen anything, you know...weird?"

She's coming out of her driving trance, twisting her earring.

"Growing up on the property, I mean." He can't tell her the truth. She'd send him to therapy and blame Grandmother. "Did you ever, like, see anything in the woods? Anything strange."

"Strange."

Oliver stares through the windshield. She's frowning—confused not angry. "No," she says. "Have you?"

"No."

"Did something happen last night?"

"No, no. I just mean...it gets weird at night, you know? Funny noises and things, that's all." He glances at her. "You know what I mean?"

"You having bad dreams again? We can move you to the second floor. There's a room next to mine."

"No. I just wondered if, you know, you've seen anything weird. That's all."

"I have." She twists the steering wheel. "Your grandmother and Aunt Rhonnie."

Oliver chuckles.

Mom begins to laugh.

Before long, she's in a fit of laughter that's spilling pent-up emotions. She wipes away tears and, just when it seems like she's done, lets go of another round.

"Family is weird." She sighs.

THE LIBRARY IS OLD.

It's the kind with water-stained ceiling tiles and faded carpet. The air is thick with aging books.

Oliver checks his phone. His ebooks have already been downloaded, emails and texts received, reminding him that the hobbit house was not a dream. The memories of rushing water and woodland pursuit bring a wave of nausea.

"You look lost." A girl pushes a squeaking cart past him.

He holds up his phone. "Password?"

"You need an account to use the wifi."

"Oh, yeah. Sure. How do I...?"

"Come on."

The name tag on her *Doctor Who* T-shirt says Molly.

He follows her to the circulation desk. She abandons the squeaky cart and leans over one of the counters. Her braided brunette ponytail has a streak of candy-apple red weaved into it.

She slides a form at him.

"Bring it to me if Ms. Chatty Pants is still busy." She nods at the heavyset librarian. Before Oliver can say thanks, she's back at her cart.

He fills out the form and waits for Ms. Chatty Pants, who, without breaking away from her conversation about her gifted grandchildren, takes it to process.

Instead of waiting, Oliver scouts the library.

He goes through the nonfiction section and snags an oversized book on his way to a dark corner behind a rack of magazines. Settling in, he opens his backpack and, not without looking up and down the aisles, hides one of the journals in the oversized hardback.

Cracking the journal open, he's reminded of what really old paper smells like. He looks around before slumping deep into the chair.

The weird sensation he left on the property finds him.

NOG IS HIS NAME.

But I'm getting ahead of myself. My head is a storm of thoughts that blow like dust. The Arctic is not what we thought, my love.

People live here. Well, not people.

Nog is half my height and as round as the moon. His cherub cheeks are buried in his bushy beard, and his green eyes glitter beneath thick brows. He is more than short, my love, barely up to my waist. He slid into the room on bare feet as wide as paddles. He appeared to be a man.

An elven, he said he is. An elven.

THERE's a crude sketch of a cubicle with two men and a bed. One of them is twice as tall as the other. Several more sketches take up the next couple of pages. Some are abstract scribbles with resemblances to faces and bodies lost in a mess of static.

The last of the sketches is a very round man with a thick beard lying over his belly. His sausage fingers extend from fuzzy sleeves, and his wide feet have tufts of hair on the toes.

HE ASKED ME TO SIT.

A great peace fell over me. It was like an angel had spoken, his words filling me with love. He said to me, "Welcome to the North Pole, Malcolm Toye."

I was startled. "How do you know my name?"

"That is not for now," he said. But he told me, in great detail, of the Jeanette Arctic expedition with Lt. Cdr. DeLong. He knew of the ship becoming lodged in the ice and our hellish escape.

"You were dying of malnutrition," he told me. "And hypothermia."

"Where am I?" I demanded.

"Inside the Arctic ice."

I did not have the clarity to ask how that was possible. How could there be a perfectly square room cut from the ice floating on the Arctic Ocean? Where would this bed come from? Food and clothing?

Yet I stared at a person built more like a snowshoe hare than a man. "What are you?" I blurted in the most unapologetic way.

My manners did not harm his disposition. Perhaps he expected it. He folded his hands atop his plump belly and drew a deep breath before answering. He explained that he and others like him were an ancient race that evolved during the Ice Age. That is when I first heard him say elven.

I must admit, I felt a small sense of vertigo at that moment, yet I observed this short, fat, and hairy man that appeared to be built for the cold.

THERE ARE MORE RANDOM SKETCHES, as if he had been trying to clear his mind or make sense of his words. Much of the illustrations are, once again, lost in scribbles, but there's one of a very large foot. It's bent to reveal a sole covered with V-shaped lines. An arrow points at the sharp texture and is labeled "scales."

This would explain the ability to slide over the ice. The sharp ends of the scales, pointing at the heel, would grab the ice to shove forward. Lying flat, they would glide.

"WHERE ARE THE OTHERS?" I demanded.

"It is best that you talk with me," he said. "For now."

He took my hands and turned them over. I appeared to be a giant in his company, yet felt like a child. His pudgy fingers were smothered with wrinkles. Next, he inspected my feet. I let him examine the slightly numb and off-colored flesh.

"Frostbite," he said. My core temperature had dropped to fifty-seven degrees Fahrenheit. I never should have lived.

How did I?

I was rescued, was all he said.

And the others? The men on the journey? I had vague recollections of them suffering as I did. He confirmed the worst of my memories, that many had succumbed to the dire conditions. But not all of them, he claimed. Some had made it home. I know not if that filled me with hope or dread. I think, when I lie in bed, that his tone suggested I have lived, but am I going home?

He told me that human expeditions were venturing closer to the North Pole, that soon our race will traverse the ice with ease. I felt mild surprise that he referred to my "race" as if he was not human. Strange as he may be, I still considered him to be human.

This was my first mistake.

"Why?" I muttered. "Why save me?"

He stood to his fullest height. We were eye to eye, for I was sitting on the bed, when he reached for me, retrieving the locket from around my neck. It looked so large in his hand. He lifted it, as if to say this was the reason.

That you, my love, are the reason.

"DID YOU FIND THE DIRTY MAGAZINES?"

Oliver launches the book against the wall. The journal bounces on the carpet. For a moment, it feels like the entire library sees the open journal. Before he can sweep it into his backpack, Molly picks it up.

"This is really old. Did you get it here?"

"No. I mean, yes. I mean, I was just reading…" He takes it from her. One of the corners is dog-eared from the fall. "It's mine, I brought it. I swear."

"Don't forget your book on succulents in the Southwest." She holds out the oversized hardback he was using to hide the journal. "And you're pretending to read it? Cute."

Oliver accepts the botanical textbook and, despite being the property of the library, stuffs it into his book bag with the journal. When the bag is zipped, he sits back and stares, waiting for her to leave. A steady beat bleeds from the earbuds slung over her shoulders.

"You really live at the Toye property?"

"How did you…"

She holds a plastic card between her fingers. The library card is crisp and warm.

"I thought it was just the widow living there."

"That's my grandmother. It's just temporary."

"Temporary how?" she asks. "Days? Weeks?"

"So far."

Her funny look shifts to confusion. "You going to school?"

"Homeschool."

"So you stay there all the time?"

"So far."

Molly looks around, but no one's in sight. Still, she leans in. "What's it like out there? No one's seen the property in, like, thirty years, not even Google Maps. Check it out; there's like a distortion field blurring the details of that place."

"What?"

"I'm just saying, your grandmother keeps to herself. What's it like out there?"

What's it like?

How does he answer that? His tyrannical, choremaster grandmother is a shut-in. His lunatic aunt is a narcissist, and his cousin is most likely to be indicted on a future felony. There's no wireless service in the haunted house, but there's service in a hobbit hovel stashed in the woods surrounded by monster-things.

And there's the snowman.

"It's cool," he says. "So, you know."

Molly waits for more. Instead, she takes the hint. "Well, get back to your old dirty book."

"It's not a...dirty..."

But she's already plugged her ears with music buds. A few minutes later, a wheel squeaks across the library.

Oliver checks the time.

His mom won't be back for another hour. He sits quietly for a few minutes. He shouldn't let what just happened bother him. Besides, this is his chance to read the journals. Once he's back on the property, reality will blend with fantasy.

He might never find his way back.

He searches his coat pockets and finds the wooden orb, runs his thumbnail through the intricate grooves. The snowman saved him from whatever's across the river that comes out at night. *Is that why Grandmother won't let me stay out after dark? Of course it is. And that means she knows what's out there. But does she know about the snowman?*

He carried Oliver across the field and fled just before Mom got there, but not before revealing a glint of metal. And that reminds him of the plans from the filing cabinet, the ones that called for a metal sphere the size of a softball. It looked like the one in his hand.

It's all a dream.

But no matter how many times he thinks it, he just can't believe it's a dream.

Because this is happening.

Molly's crossing the library. The squeaky cart stops somewhere in the fiction section. Oliver swaps the orb for his phone and pulls up Google Earth. It takes a few minutes to find the location and load the graphics. He goes to Street View and scrolls down the main road until he finds the gates leading toward the property. From there, he zooms up to a satellite view and swipes toward the house.

It's a green blur of trees. The house is a nondescript blob centered in a patch of fuzzy snow.

Not even Google Earth knows.

Oliver packs up and begins looking down the aisles. He finds her filing novels in the K-L section. With her back turned and head bouncing to music, he waits for her to turn around. When she does, the books fly out of her hands.

She shouts in surprise, quickly covering her mouth.

"I'm sorry," Oliver says.

"Don't sneak up on me like that." She pulls out an earbud and playfully shoves him.

"Sorry, sorry." He squats down to pick up the books. "How did you know about Google Earth?"

"What?"

"My grandmother's property. You said it wasn't on Google Earth."

"Everyone knows." She begins shelving books and, like before, looks around before whispering, "No offense, but the place is haunted. I mean, ever since your grandfather disappeared, Ms. Toye hardly ever leaves the place."

"What do you mean 'disappeared'?"

"No one has seen him in decades. All I know is that people around here are a little weirded out about the Toye property. No one goes near it; no one knows what goes on out there. When she calls for groceries to be delivered, people say it's creepy. You know, like that feeling you get when you just know something's hiding around the corner."

Oliver's stomach drops.

"And then you can't see it on Google Earth. I mean, North Korea hasn't even figured out how to block satellite images. You all right?"

"Yeah. Low blood sugar. What else?"

"You need to sit?"

He waves her off even though the shelves are beginning to swish. "I'm fine, really. What else do you know?"

She studies him for a moment. Oliver watches her sway. She knows something about the property. Everybody does. Why didn't he think of that before? There must be stories about the Toye property. The house has been there for over a century. There have to be urban legends, too.

Every urban legend has a grain of truth.

"Come on." Molly abandons the cart. "You're turning into a ghost."

Not until he falls into a chair does he realize how wobbly his knees have become. She pulls a bottle of water from the fishnet pocket on his backpack.

"Are you diabetic?"

He nods while taking a sip.

"The shot kind?"

"Is there another kind?"

"My grandma controlled hers by diet, that's all I'm saying."

"Type 2."

"I guess." She watches him drink. He's thirstier than he thought. "Do they hurt?"

That's usually the first question. He shakes his head and returns the bottle. "So what else do you—"

"Molly?" Ms. Chatty Pants librarian approaches. "Is everything all right?"

Molly explains that Oliver needed help finding a book. Good call. People can get weird when they meet their first real diabetic. *The shot kind.*

The gold chains around her neck are wedged beneath her second chin. She suggests Molly finish shelving her cart.

"Can I help you find something?"

"No, thanks." Oliver holds up the succulents textbook. "I got it."

Ms. Chatty Pants raises an eyebrow. There's a long moment of uncomfortable silence before Molly says, "Okay, good. I'll see you later."

"Wait." Oliver grabs her arm. "Can I...I mean, I might need more help about...you know, what you were saying."

Molly pulls out her phone. A few seconds later, his phone buzzes. She goes back to her squeaky cart. Ms. Chatty Pants pauses long enough to make sure Molly doesn't return before going to the circulation desk.

He reads the text. *Smile Café. Tomorrow morning at 9.*

He punches the phone number into his address book, types "Molly." He still feels a little dizzy when he stands. He stays in Ms. Chatty Pants's line of sight while walking toward the fiction section. At the K-L aisle, he snaps a photo.

Molly bobbing her head.

10

Mom drops Oliver off at the town square in the morning.

He walks past storefronts, his reflection passing large plate glass windows with painted letters. Inside are dance studios and law offices, a bookstore and hairstylists. The Smile Café is on the far corner. Molly is in the front window, sunk into a low sofa chair.

A bell rings when he opens the door.

The smell of ground coffee beans and toasted bagels rides on a thick wave of Bob Dylan. Molly is wearing a Ramones T-shirt with black leggings and fuzzy wristbands. She looks up from her iPad and smiles. He hadn't noticed the gap between her front teeth in the library. Maybe she hadn't smiled quite like that.

"Get the chocolate pecan." She raises her cup.

Oliver goes to the counter and orders what she said. "You want room for cream?" the barista asks.

He doesn't know what that means, so he nods. She comes back with a tall, hot cup of coffee. Oliver passes a small platform, a miniature stage for poetry slams and acoustic guitarists, and places it on a small table. It smells better than Mom's coffee.

"I got you a present." Molly slides a gift bag across the table. She dumps out the contents. A book hits the table.

The Wonderful World of Succulents.

It takes a moment to make the connection with the book he was using in the library. "I saw it at The Little Professor. It was just sitting in the window, isn't that weird? I just had to buy it."

"Thanks."

He leafs through the glossy pages while Molly hums along to Dylan's "Like a Rolling Stone." She loves Dylan, she says, but doesn't think he really knows how to play the harmonica. Now Neil Young, she says, he can play. Oliver agrees without conviction. He streams radio for background noise, not deeper meaning.

Molly sinks into her low chair, duct tape hiding cracks in the vinyl armrests, and begins a countdown of her favorite folk singers.

"Things are weird," Oliver blurts.

The words exploded from his chest, shot off his tongue like lead weights. The admission lifts the suffocating feeling. His shoulders wilt, and, for a moment, he's afraid he'll tear up.

His whole life he's wanted to tell someone that.

He's always felt like an outcast. A weirdo. He didn't quite realize it until he blurted it out. He could never tell his mom, and he's only known this gap-toothed hipster for less than a day. But he said it, just like that.

"What kind of weird?"

He stutters as his filters engage. He can't tell her everything. People have their limits for weird, even Molly. But how to start? And where? He feels himself backtracking into panic.

"The journal," he spits out. "The book I was reading in the library, it's my great-grandfather's journal."

He pulls the leather-bound book from his backpack. He only brought the first one—the one that's mostly normal. Molly's eyes get big. She pulls her other earbud out and opens it, running her fingers over the worn cover and yellowed pages while Oliver tells her about the historic journey that ended in tragedy.

The words thaw his tongue, so he keeps going. He tells her about his grandmother's old mansion and the chores and exercise; how he's required to be in the house before dark and if you touch the frozen windmill, you get zapped.

She flips the pages, one at a time.

"Very cool," she says. "That's worth, like, a fortune."

"There's more."

He tells her about the garage and the car, the footlocker below, but not what's in the other journals. Despite what he's read, he's still not convinced these aren't simply diaries of a madman.

"I wish I had something like that. I didn't even know my grandparents." She sits back, twirling her candy-red swatch of hair. "I'm sorry about yesterday. I shouldn't have come up and asked all those questions. We're not supposed to be looking through people's personal information."

He fidgets. "I want to know about the property."

"Where you from?"

"All over. Florida, Georgia, Louisiana...just about every Southern state, really. Moved here from Texas."

"Why?"

"Mom lost her job."

"Sorry." She shakes her head. "I need to shut up now."

"No, please don't. I just...I want you to tell me everything you know. It's just...I'd like to find out what others think."

He can't tell her he doesn't trust anyone on the property to tell him the truth. His mom doesn't know it, and his grandmother is hiding it.

"Well, I don't know everything, but here's what most people think. In case you haven't noticed, it snows here a lot. Your grandmother orders out for supplies, and every deliveryperson says the entry road is always plowed, as in spotless."

"Okay."

"That's not so weird except that no one has a contract to plow her property. People have checked into it, and no one has ever admitted to helping her."

"Maybe it's someone with a truck and a snowblade."

"Nope."

"Maybe she made them swear to secrecy."

"Yeah, maybe. Only no one has ever seen equipment enter or leave her property. The county plow says that every time he does the main road, her drive is always clean and there are no tracks leaving. I mean, she could be plowing the road herself, sure. It's just everyone says it's always clean right down to the asphalt, like a snowflake never touched it."

"Maybe the road melts it, like heating coils."

"I suppose. Only folks say it's been like that for as long as they can remember, way before technology like that was ever thought about."

Oliver's heard weirder things, but she has a point. He shovels the roundabout, but the road is always clear no matter what time he wakes up. And why is it that tracks disappear in the field even when it doesn't snow?

"It used to be, way before you and me were born, that people just assumed your grandfather was doing all the work. But then twenty-seven years ago he went missing."

Oliver does the math. His mom would have been ten years old—about the time she went to boarding school.

"I don't think anyone would've known about it since he was just as reclusive as your grandmother, but he was always the one that picked up deliveries and signed checks and paid bills. One day, it all stopped. Not long after, your grandmother takes his name off all the accounts, changes her will, and pretty much erases his name off the deed. People in town got suspicious, so the police went out to see if everything was all right.

"When they kept asking questions, lawyers started threatening lawsuits for harassment. Add to that your grandmother owns half the buildings in town and funds most of the schools, well, folks left her alone. After a while, they all just forgot. Your grandparents never hurt anyone, and they left it at that. But no one's seen him since. And that road is still clean."

He doesn't know much about his grandfather. Mom didn't exactly carry family photos. But as far as he knows, there are no tractors on the property, and he'd never heard anything clearing the road. He always assumed that whoever was doing it arrived early.

Or at night.

"What do you think happens?" he asks.

She takes a long sip and thinks. For a moment, she looks lost in the music. "Well, some people think she's got zombies. Others think it's robots or slaves. There's one group that believes she hypnotizes animals to do it."

"What?"

"Yeah. And hunters swear the closer they get to her property, the fewer animals they see."

The perfect silence on the property hits that urban legend close to home. He's never seen a squirrel or heard a bird.

"But the weird thing," she continues, "is that every deliveryperson swears there's something watching them as they drive up the road. There's always an envelope waiting on the front porch where they dump the supplies, but no one ever comes out. But someone is always watching."

"The house has this window on the top floor. Sort of looks like an eye, maybe that's what they mean."

"Maybe. Doubt it." She shrugs. "Here's another thing: she doesn't receive power from the city, or propane or wood from local suppliers. And there are no records the house has ever been on the municipal power grid since it was built in 1901. That wouldn't be so strange if she had solar panels or wind turbines, but no one has ever seen one on her property. I mean, it's possible she's got them away from the house, but you said yourself the windmill was frozen."

Not frozen, but it's not supplying power. Something's supplying it with power.

She sits forward. "Have you ever seen anything?"

He searches his memory for any sign of a reflective solar panel or wires running from telephone poles, but the house seems normal.

Big, old and cold, but normal.

"The house is sort of heated. The garage definitely is."

"That's what I mean. No one knows how her lights work or how she keeps from freezing. And that Google Earth thing? It sounds like magic, right? I mean, no one has figured out how to block Google Earth—not movie stars, drug smugglers, or the military. It's all there, except your grandmother's property. You got to admit, something doesn't add up."

Oliver takes the journal off the table and squeezes it with both hands. *When something doesn't add up, that means there are missing numbers.*

"Why doesn't anyone go find out?" Oliver asks.

"Most people are scared, I guess. Hunters don't go near her property. They say a compass doesn't work."

She fiddles with the plastic lid on her coffee. Maybe that's why she doesn't notice him turn pale. Compasses don't work, he knows that.

"They sneak onto the property with their guns and ammo and end up walking right back to their trucks like the trees led them out."

Oliver puts the book on his lap to keep her from seeing his hands shake. He'd seen that beaver-gnawed tree twice, and he knows he didn't get turned around. Now the weird feeling he left on the property has followed him into the real world.

Molly looks up as an Eric Clapton song starts. She closes her eyes; her lips move with the lyrics.

Then she says, "Why doesn't she let you stay out after dark?"

"What?"

"You said earlier that you had to do chores and exercise, but you had to be inside before the sun went down."

Before he found the hobbit house, he could've told her he didn't know without lying. But now he can't tell her that when the sun goes down, things come out. *Things that mess with your compass and move trees. And chase you.*

He shoves his hands under his thighs, but the nervous energy flows into his feet. He closes his eyes, momentarily, and counts his breath, hoping he doesn't hyperventilate.

"Sorry," Molly says. "Sometimes I say too much."

The conversation hits a long pause, the silence filled with Clapton's guitar. Oliver gets his nervousness under control, but the floor is slowly moving. Good thing he's sitting. Molly, head back on her chair, comes out of her music reverie and announces she's grabbing a refill.

"Do you want to read the journals?" The words pop out of his mouth. There's no taking them back. It's a stupid thing to say, but for once he feels like there's an anchor keeping his life from capsizing, and it's wearing a Ramones T-shirt.

"Um, yeah. You have them?"

"No. But I can bring them, you know, next time."

"And when's that?"

"I don't know…"

She tilts her head, exposing the gap in a churlish smile. "Text me, then. When you're in town, text me and I'll come meet you."

"Okay."

Molly snaps a photo of him sitting in the chair. She shows him the thumbnail. He looks like a ghost. Oliver quickly gets his phone out and aims it.

Molly jumps on the miniature stage and grabs the empty mic stand, striking a silent but shrieking pose. Oliver captures her in his contacts. He tries a sip of lukewarm coffee. She returns, and they talk for another hour. The Toye property is forgotten.

For now.

11

———

Three days later, it snows.

Oliver has completed his chores, but still isn't allowed to go outside. He walks the staircase and not because Grandmother told him to. If he sits too long, he starts thinking, and too many thoughts are not his friends.

Walking keeps his mind engaged.

That night, Oliver goes to his room early. This time, he leaves his door open and listens. When the last footsteps are heard and the last door shut, he sets the timer on his phone and waits an hour.

Occasionally, tree branches break in the distance.

He doesn't want to read, that will put him to sleep. He can't pace; his footsteps will creak. Instead, he counts his breaths so the thoughts don't pile up. At ten thirty, his alarm goes off.

He stuffs a journal down the back of his sweatpants.

His footsteps announce his journey across the third floor. He stops in the bathroom and waits a minute before flushing. He runs the water in the sink and, while the toilet is refilling, walks to the room at the far end of the hallway.

A rope dangles from the ceiling.

He pulls down the attic door and unfolds the steps, carefully climbing them just as the toilet goes silent.

The ceiling is pitched at an angle.

Pale moonlight beams through the circular window that faces the driveway. He shivers as he waits for his eyes to adjust to the lumps surrounding him. The ghosts transform into dusty sheets draped over furniture and containers.

His phone illuminates uncovered boxes labeled *kitchen* or *dinnerware* or *office.* Most are sealed shut. There's a bookshelf to his left. He takes a couple of surprisingly silent steps to flip through stacks of *Newsweek, Life,* and *Popular Mechanics.* The dates are only ten years old.

Grandmother must still be hauling them up.

That's when he realizes how large everything is. It's not just the containers, but dressers, tables and chairs. He tugs the sheet from behind a bookshelf. It's an armoire. *How did that get up here?*

The door is cracked open.

He dares another step and pries it open further. The armoire doesn't look old, but the clothing hanging inside does. Most are small dresses for a little girl. Maybe these were Helen's? Or maybe a little girl that died fifty years ago and lives in the attic waiting for idiots like Oliver to come snooping around about midnight—

He closes his eyes.

Counts to ten.

When his thoughts are calm, he steps away from the armoire and doesn't look at it again.

He goes to the circular window, where a wide coffee table is positioned. He notices, as he sits down, it's a perfect setup to watch the driveway, which is exactly what he wants to do.

The circular drive is still clear—Oliver shoveled it after lunch—but the entry road is buried. His breath is puffing white clouds in the moonlight. He vows to stay awake until midnight. If nothing happens before then and the road is clear in the morning, then he'll bring a coat up the next night. He'll set his alarm to watch it at different times until he's got all the hours covered.

He could just ask Grandmother how the entry road gets plowed, but he wouldn't believe her and still come up.

It made sense not to ask.

The road is lonely. What starts out tranquil turns to cold boredom in fifteen minutes. The journal, still tucked in his waistband, sticks to his skin. He lays it on his lap. The leather cover is the same as all the other journals, aside from three dots of ink splashed near the corner. The yellowish pages turn frosty in the moonlight.

Random doodles fill the first couple of pages, followed by several pages torn from the binding. About a third of the way into the book, he finds the first entry.

FEBRUARY 14, 1882

Nog always arrived after I woke. He'd slide into the room wearing a different coat—sometimes long and furry, sometimes short and smooth. He'd slowly circle the room, staring at me like he had x-ray vision, looking right into my bones. He told me it was February.

Months have passed. It feels like weeks.

I think I'm losing my mind again. I just want out. If I'm going to die without seeing you, then let it be with the sky above me, the wind in my face. I told him this. Told him I thought he was a hallucination and that I wanted to die.

The next morning I awoke to a very different room.

It was bigger than when I had gone to sleep, perhaps three times as long and twice as wide. Ice shavings dusted the floor, as if it was freshly carved.

There was a pile of clothing in the corner that included heavy sweaters and a coat with a thick pair of boots. Next to the clothing, protruding from the wall, were steel rungs that led up to a hole in the ceiling.

Before excitement could drag me from bed, Nog slid into the room. He was wearing white this time. "Good morning," he started. "I'd like to begin with apologies, once again, for the lengthy adjustment period."

He paused. I nodded. It was the best I could do. They saved my life, as far as I could tell. I couldn't be indignant about that. But there was a hole in the ceiling that, I knew, exited to the outside.

"Trust," he said, "is essential. Power," he said, "is intoxicating. And you will find plenty of power amongst my people."

He paused again. Maybe he was letting the words sink in, I don't know. He can be long-winded and often used words I didn't understand. I didn't want to extend the conversation with a reply, but then he said, quite suddenly, "Let's stretch our legs today."

I got dressed very quickly and climbed the steel rungs. I emerged on top of the ice. Outside. In the world. Alive.

And tears filled my eyes.

I began weeping like a child. The stars shone in the frigid sky, and the ice was flat as far as I could see. It was clean and spacious and free. If I could not die in your arms, then I would have gladly laid my body to rest in that moment.

I began to laugh. My bellows carried long and far, perhaps all the way to the water beyond my eyes' reach. I must've looked like a madman. Nog popped out of the ice. He just shot up like a cork. Others did, too. Three of them of the same size and proportion. Two were females with clean faces, one with a long gray braid that reached her feet. Nog stood next to this one and held her hand.

All of them wore white.

I had assumed Nog was the leader, but when the one with the braid, the one known as Merry, spoke, it was clear they deferred to her.

"We knew this time would come," she said. "We have aided the human race in ways you cannot imagine, and have wished to remain anonymous and peaceful. Perhaps, though, now is the time that we reconsider and join the human race." She paused before saying, "We are not so different."

There was a strange current in the air. I could feel something was about to happen. Merry spread her arms and said, "Welcome to the Elven."

And when she said it, they all came up.

Thousands of them, my love.

They were just as round as they were joyful, squabbling as they pressed near me, reaching out to touch me as if I was not the one dreaming, but they were.

I was overwhelmed. Tears, once again, filled my eyes. Merry said, above the melee, "Perhaps you would like to meet the one that saved you."

I expected someone larger than the elven, a beast maybe, because my memory of lying on the ice was that of a large shadow and hulking arms, something large enough to carry me against its chest and certainly the elven were not large enough for that.

But I was not ready for this.

As the snow began to swirl, I felt my knees weaken. My savior made these words possible. Without this one, there would be no hope that I would see you again.

Merry held out her hand. She was wearing a strange glove. I looked around for my savior, but no one stood taller than the elven. Then I realized she had something in her hand. It was an ornament, my love. A big metal ornament with the most beautiful designs etched into its surface. Excitement was all around, but I didn't understand. How could the ornament save me?

She tossed it into the air.

The elven scrambled away, giving it room to land in the snow. But it never came down. Instead, a cyclone of snow swirled from the ice, a frosty cloud puffed across my eyes. And when it settled, when the air was clear, I saw him, my love. I saw the creature that saved my life.

He was made of snow.

· · ·

SOMETHING CRACKS OUTSIDE.

Someone's out there!

The person is wearing a long black coat dragging over the snow; the head is hidden beneath a heavy cowl. A faint layer of gray is on the shoulders and hood—snow that's trickled out of the trees. The person is staring down the entry drive, where a cloud billows like an approaching dust storm.

Oliver is frozen on the coffee table, his heart thudding in his chest.

His neck muscles, rigid.

The snow cloud gets denser. Branches snap and drag. The black figure steps back before the thickening cloud engulfs him. Oliver can hear something coming, like a distant train.

And then he sees it.

In the depths of the burgeoning snow cloud, he sees the whirling ball of branches. It spins like a bristled sphere made of a thousand twiggy arms that grind through the snow and scrape the asphalt as it moves back and forth, back and forth. It reaches the roundabout and stops.

The snow clears.

The thing rests in front of the cloaked figure. Its body is a dirty, slushy snowball, a pincushion of coniferous branches, the ends softened with pine and spruce needles. Short stumps emerge from the bottom, like legs, and another set grows where arms would be.

Oliver stops breathing.

It's a snowthing, sort of like the snowman that saved him but different. It's thicker, rounder and shorter. The snow slurpy and lumpy.

The black figure flicks his wrist.

Had Oliver not noticed the figure's hand, he would not have leaped up, the journal would not have slammed against the window. He would have remained an anonymous voyeur. It was a gleam of metal.

Moonlight reflecting off a glove.

Grandmother.

Oliver did leap.

The journal did slam.

And the figure turns toward him. The cowl, deep and dark, does not fall away. The snowthing, however, is gone in a cloud, the branches and slushy snow swishing into the trees.

Oliver closes his eyes and holds very still. When he opens his eyes, the driveway is empty. He runs to the steps and climbs down, paying no attention to noise.

He pauses.

Motionless, his ears filter out the natural ticks and creaks of the house in search of a door opening or a footstep falling. He goes to the bathroom and, once again, flushes the toilet and runs the sink. If anyone asks, he's having a bad night. On the way to the bedroom, passing the stairwell—

A ghostly figure watches.

Oliver actually shouts this time.

It sounds like a small dog stepping on a thorn.

The surprise flings him against the wall, and, he realizes, there's nothing to drop or throw.

The journal is still in the attic.

Grandmother, clad in a flowing beige robe and fuzzy slippers, methodically climbs the steps, crossing through a slice of moonlight. She looks like she should be carrying a lantern.

"What are you doing, Olivah?"

"I had the...the bathroom." He rubs his stomach. "My blood sugar was...I think it was something I ate."

She looks like she just climbed out of bed. It couldn't have been her out there. She couldn't have gotten up the stairs that fast. She's not even winded. But her hair is pulled back in a tight bun.

She doesn't sleep like that.

"What makes you so afraid?" she asks. "The things you see?"

She looks in the bathroom, then at Oliver. It sounds like something is caught in her throat. She returns to Oliver as silently as she walked away and takes both his hands, turning them over like she's checking for stolen goods.

Or dust from the attic.

"I washed my hands," Oliver says. "I always do when I...you know, go to the bathroom."

"Do you think I'm a tyrant?"

He shakes his head, but she can see the truth. That sound returns to her throat again. *Is that laughter?*

"We know nothing in our little worlds." She pats his hands. "Only when we know everything do we realize we know nothing."

"Okay."

He waits for her to leave, to return to her bedroom on the first floor, but she doesn't move. Her icy stare is fixed on him, her eyes like black marbles. She appears to smirk, but he can't be sure it's not just the wrinkles.

"Goodnight."

"Goodnight." He goes to his bedroom.

"Oh, Olivah."

He stops.

"Be not afraid. It's only your thoughts that have come to get you."

The moonlight through the window catches the side of her face. Even from this distance, he's sure he sees it.

She's smiling.

He climbs into bed and pulls the covers over his head, thinking she must be sleepwalking. What disturbs him most, though, was the feel of her hands.

They were very cold.

12

C hristmas arrives like any other day.
He opens presents with his mom. Grandmother joins them for breakfast. She wishes them a Merry Christmas, but no gifts are exchanged. Aunt Rhonnie and the twins arrive for tea. They all have new sunglasses and coats.

In the afternoon, the twins make their journey across the field.

Oliver says he's not feeling well, which he isn't. The weird has a stranglehold on him. He's woozy and dreamy. He tries not to think and sleeps as much as possible. The twins return before supper and leave early because Helen says there's a party that night and they must leave now.

Later, he realizes the chore board has been blank all day.

Merry Christmas, Olivah.

HE DOESN'T LEAVE the house for the next couple of days.

Oliver sleeps later than he should, and his blood sugar drops too low.

He does his chores.

He walks the steps.

And he avoids Grandmother.

Even at tea, he keeps his eyes forward, exerting perfect form and manners. On occasion, he glances at her when she looks away, careful not to make eye contact. But the old Grandmother is back. That smile he thought he saw in the moonlight is long buried. This is the one thing that gives him comfort.

Maybe I was dreaming.

Maybe he dreamed about everything, because pincushioned snowthings don't plow driveways, they don't take orders from old women...*they don't live!*

But no matter how much he throws himself into his chores or how long he sleeps, the world is still covered in snow. Every morning, he opens his eyes and he's still on the property. Things are not getting better.

Oliver thinks about Molly often, but it's so much easier to pretend none of this is happening. As the days wear on, the memories don't disappear, but they do fade.

In the middle of January, when normal kids have already gone back to school, Mom drops him off at the library. It was her idea. He waits for the car to leave. Instead of going inside, he clears the snow off a bench. With service, his phone downloads a list of emails and unread text messages. Five of them are from Molly.

The last one just before New Year's Eve.

Oliver can see the circulation desk through the sliding glass doors. Molly is helping someone check out. He stays outside long enough to become quite cold. When his phone buzzes, he pulls his gloves off with his teeth, but it's just an update reminder for one of his games.

He can't stop chattering.

It's late afternoon. Mom won't be back for another hour. Oliver wants to go inside, but if he does, he'll talk to her. If he talks to her, color and detail will return to the faded memories. He'll also get her in trouble with Ms. Chatty Pants. So he'll sit on the bench until his mom picks him up.

"Oliver? Is that you?"

Molly stands at the entrance without a coat. Her yellow and black rugby shirt is long-sleeved. She crosses her arms and walks beneath the awning. Oliver buries his hands in his pockets as his stomach drops twenty floors into fear and, for once, a little excitement.

"What are you doing?" she asks.

"Using the wifi."

"Out here?"

"My mom's picking me up. And I didn't want to get you in trouble."

"What are you talking about?"

He looks back. Ms. Chatty Pants is at the circulation desk. "There's no service at the property. That's why I didn't text you. I'm sorry."

"You're freezing. Come wait inside, at least. I know you're from Texas, but you know what cold is. Stay out here long enough and you'll be an ice cube."

Molly hunches her shoulders. She's already shivering.

"I...I'll go inside," he says. "In a minute. You should go before you get in trouble."

"You all right?"

He starts to answer, but words don't make it out. Just a funny sound. A knot lodges in his throat, pressure building in his chest. If he doesn't say something, he'll have to go home feeling like this. He'll have to sit in his room with it bottled up.

Still, the words don't form.

He looks at his boots, rocking back and forth.

"I'll be right back," Molly says.

She rushes for the doors. Maybe she's going to get a coat, or tell Ms. Chatty Pants to call 911. Or maybe she's not coming back.

"I saw a snowman!" He jumps to his feet. "I saw it. I saw all those things you talked about. You were right. And I saw a snowman."

The words had to get out.

He forced himself to say something, no matter what order they came out.

Before he exploded.

Molly stops under the parapet. Her cheeks are flush, but she's not shivering. Not like Oliver. Someone exits the library and goes to their car, looking back at the teenagers. Ms. Chatty Pants is looking at them from the desk, but he doesn't care.

He's got to get the words out.

He tells her about all the stuff in the attic and reading the journal and the snowthing cleaning the road. He tells her about his grandmother lurking in the cloak and the weird glove.

He doesn't stop there.

The hobbit house and the creatures and the snowman that saved him. When he's finished, when there are no more words left inside, Molly is still there. She hasn't moved. She just stares. He's afraid to say more, afraid he's already said too much. He's huffing to catch his breath.

"You think I'm crazy?"

She doesn't answer because this is the part where someone would ask if he's been dreaming or pat him on the shoulder or hand or, worse, the cheek and ask about his blood sugar because he's a diabetic, the shot kind. *There's no such thing as snowmen, Oliver. Not like the ones you're seeing.*

Molly walks over to the bench, arms still firmly crossed, and sits down. She says, "I believe you."

"You do?"

"You saw it, right?"

"But am I crazy?"

"Because you saw something? That's not crazy, Oliver. You had the balls to see crazy things and tell someone. That doesn't *make* you crazy."

He collapses next to her.

The words are out. He doesn't have to hide them anymore. Molly has them now. She heard them and believed them. And that, he thinks, is what will keep them from sticking in his throat again.

"There's more," he says.

"I know."

They stay on the bench until Molly begins to chatter. Oliver holds out his hand. She leads him inside where it's warm. They find a table at the back of the library. He tells the rest of his story, leaving no details unearthed.

Until he's empty.

13

February is warmer than usual.

Snow still covers the ground, but the melt glistens off the asphalt. That means no shoveling. Oliver walks down the middle of the road, listening to the trees drip until he reaches the main road. He shades his eyes.

The dashed line is visible on the main road.

He stands on the shoulder like a hitchhiker without a hope, waiting for a pickup truck to come over the hill. A red one. Eventually, he carves an indention in the snowbank and sits. He's almost asleep when the first vehicle passes.

It's not red. Not a pickup.

"You excited?" His mom is coming up the entry road, wearing a thick turtleneck and a long scarf.

"Just waiting."

Oliver shades his eyes to see her smiling. Casually, she walks onto the main road, standing on the dashed line to look in both directions. She looks like she expects something to come any moment.

"I used to come out here when I was little," she says. "I'd stare at the crest of that hill and wonder what was over it. How far did it go? Who was out there?"

She cups her eyes like binoculars.

"Sometimes, I'd pretend my real parents were out there, and if I waited long enough, they would drive by and recognize me, like they'd lost me when I was born and they'd been searching for me ever since."

She looks in the other direction.

"You ever feel that way?"

If he was honest, he'd tell her he felt that way once, when he stayed at his dad's in Los Angeles. But he couldn't tell Mom that. He couldn't tell her about the strangers that came to his house, the business meetings in the bedrooms, and all the times he turned on the television and told Oliver he'd be right back.

Sometimes the house was still empty in the morning.

She didn't need to know all that.

"I'm sorry, Oliver." She remains in the middle of the road. "I mean it."

What she meant was that she was sorry she was a bad mom.

Oliver made her stop saying that years ago. Now she just says sorry, like she's apologizing for his life. Somehow, she's responsible for his dad, for his diabetes, for his life. Somehow, if she could just get over that hill, she would find what she was looking for. But she'd gone over that hill, she'd seen what was over there. And she crested the next one and the next.

It was just more of the same.

More hills.

"What happened to Grandfather?" Oliver asks.

"Your grandfather?" She plops down next to him, sighing. "Well, my father, your grandfather, wasn't exactly warm and fuzzy. Ever since I can remember, he kept to himself. Usually, he was tinkering in the garage or hiking the property. He was a burly man, a real man's man. Definitely not a man for children.

"I had just gone to boarding school when Mother called, said she'd have someone pick me up at the bus station. I was at home a couple of days before I noticed he wasn't around. Mother never said anything until I asked. Then she just said he wasn't coming back."

She sculpts a snowball.

"It didn't matter, really. Another week and everything felt the same, with or without him."

She gets up and knocks the snow off her pants, clapping her hands. She was about to apologize again, but catches herself. Fact is, she had it just as rough. Maybe worse. She did the best she could.

She doesn't need to apologize.

A distant rumble comes from the left. They both hood their eyes to

see the truck. Oliver jumps to his feet. They wait by the road as it pulls
through the gate and stops.

Molly opens the door. "Need a ride?"

"Yeah." Oliver smiles. He opens the passenger door and waits.

His mom leans into the cab to introduce herself. It's the first time
she'd met one of his girlfriends, because she hadn't seen her yet. And
because Oliver's never had a girlfriend. Molly pushes the hair from her
eyes—the candy-red strand dyed brown like her normal hair—and
shakes her hand.

Mom steps back and squeezes Oliver's shoulder. "You go ahead."

"You sure?"

She's sure.

Oliver climbs into the cab, kicking empty Starbucks cups out of the
way. Molly turns the radio down. Oliver watches his mom in the sideview mirror. She closes the gate. Maybe she didn't see snowmen when
she grew up. Maybe she didn't see anything at all.

Maybe that was worse.

MOLLY SITS across the table from Oliver. She pulls at the stiff collar
rising from her wool sweater and catches Oliver's glance before casting
her eyes down.

"Tea is served," Mom sings.

Grandmother puckers her lips and reaches for a small plate of
scones. Tea is poured in silence. The awkward silence rings in his ears.
He stirs creamer into his tea and clinks the cup.

Molly, however, moves with precision as she pours her cup and lifts
it, eyes cast down and pinkie finger drawn in. The china doesn't make
a sound when she places it in the saucer.

"A lovely house, Ms. Toye. The orderliness is breathtaking."

A long pause hangs.

"Thank you, Molly," Mom finally says. "We work very hard to keep
it this way."

Grandmother draws another sip, passing a sidelong glance at her.

"We're happy to have you come out," Mom says. "Aren't we,
Mother?"

"Tell us about yourself," Grandmother says.

Molly takes a bite and doesn't speak until she swallows.

She grew up in town. So did her mom and dad. He's a cop. Her mom teaches high school history. "She'd kill to be sitting here, having tea with the Toye family. She says you're quite a mystery, Ms. Toye."

"Keeping to oneself is not outrageous," Grandmother says.

"Of course not."

"Why are you here?"

"Ma'am?"

"Your manners are perfect. Your flattery is charming. What do you want?"

"I don't want anything," Molly says without hesitation. "Your grandson invited me, and I like him."

Mom tries to interject. Grandmother holds up her hand. "Where did you get these manners?"

Molly swipes her scone with raspberry jam and chews slowly. She wipes the corners of her mouth while a knot grows in Oliver's gut.

"I learned about tea ceremony at the Zen Center of Denver. My mom would take me there when I was a kid. If I'm honest, it was boring. But now that I'm older, I appreciate the structure. As for the flattery, Ms. Toye, I was simply observing my surroundings. My hope is that you haven't lost sight of the historic beauty you have around you. I work in the library, so I appreciate order. It's where I met your grandson."

Mom hides a grin behind her teacup. Oliver sits on his hands. He taps his toe in a steady rhythm. Grandmother turns her head toward him.

He lifts his foot off the floor to fidget in silence.

"Honestly, I'm thrilled," Molly adds. "Very few people have seen the outside of your house. I would guess that fewer have seen the inside and had tea with you, Ms. Toye."

"Try none," Mom says.

"I'm honored to be here, sitting in the house your husband built in 1901 without any assistance from people in town."

Oliver didn't know his grandfather built this by himself.

"You are one of the largest donors to the Nature Conservancy," Molly continues, "and one of the largest private landowners in the state of Colorado. Like I said, I am honored. However, if I make you uncomfortable, I will leave."

Oliver is frozen.

His mom doesn't move.

Only Molly dares to sample her tea and take a bite while the silence hardens.

Fearless.

Grandmother stares ahead, then says, without looking at anyone in particular, "Very well. If we are to have company, it is perhaps nice to have someone that can appreciate what we do."

And that was it.

They talk about things like school and hobbies and hiking the countryside. When Grandmother finishes her tea, she wipes her mouth and announces tea is finished. She leaves the room in a way that Oliver has become accustomed to seeing. Strangers, he knew, would consider it rude.

Molly never flinches.

Mom lifts her teacup, finger hooked through the handle, and smiles at Molly. "It's so good to have you."

And she means it.

"THAT WAS AMAZING." Oliver holds the back door for Molly. "How did you know?"

"Know what?"

"All of that during tea! You nailed it, said everything she wants to hear, even the way she wants to hear it."

"It's easy. Just look at the place. You live in a museum. Your grand-mother donates to the community, half of it is done anonymously, but everyone knows it's her. She's a strong, assertive woman. I assumed she would respect strength and honesty. I just did the things that matter to her."

She made it sound easy.

They walk around the house. Before they reach the windmill, Oliver warns her. "It's electrified. Must be a loose wire or something."

"How do you know?"

"I touched it."

Molly's eyes wander to the top of the structure. Rust has chewed holes through the weather vane. A gust of wind hits the windmill's blades, and the squeal pierces their ears and gets under their skin. They both plug their ears with their little fingers.

"Well, it's not harvesting any wind," she says.

"Definitely not."

"No, I mean it keeps turning when there's no wind, so it must be using energy. But why?"

"Maybe Grandmother likes the way it looks."

Molly puts out her hand, lets it hover a few inches above the windmill's leg. She eases it closer. Oliver's fingers dance at his sides, but he resists the urge to pull her away. With a half-inch gap between her and the metal, her hair begins to rise. A few strands at first, then several fray out.

"That's weird," she says. "It's emitting a field or something. I don't think this is a loose wire."

Before Oliver can respond, she slaps her hand against it. Her hair flairs out below her stocking cap.

"Oh, wow," she says. "It's like I swallowed a tuning fork."

She sounds auto-tuned.

"I don't think that's a good idea." But when Oliver grabs her hand, the hairs stand on his arm. A current of helium fills the space between his eyes; he doesn't want to let go—can't let go—or he'll float away like a parade ornament.

Molly yanks her hand like a wet tongue stuck to cold metal. She examines her palm. Oliver feels planted on the ground, his head heavy again. She takes a lap around the antiquated structure and studies it from top to bottom.

"I don't think this is a windmill. Not anymore, at least."

"I don't care what it is; we shouldn't touch it."

"It's a disguise."

"For what?"

She shrugs. "Maybe this is why there's no Google Earth or cell phone reception. Maybe it creates a distortion field. You ever see it stop spinning?"

He shakes his head. "Why would she block cell phones? She's got a landline. What's the difference?"

"Maybe it's a side effect." She looks at the house and barely moves her lips, like someone might be watching. She whispers, "If you had a snowman, would you want the world to see?"

A chill wriggles down Oliver's neck that has nothing to do with the cold.

"What about the hobbit house?" he says. "There's reception in there."

"Maybe it has a deflector shield."

She chuckles, and he knows why. This all sounds like a Wachowski Brothers movie.

They venture out to the field but don't go very far—the hair still tingling on Oliver's arms—just far enough to get out of sight. He stops where the snowball had pulverized Henry, knocking the cap off his gel-sculpted head, and points to the exact spot where it was launched. Molly nods while he tells the story. Just as he gets to the part where Henry stops short of the trees, Molly wanders forward.

She touches the prickly needles.

"I swear he was right there," Oliver says.

"How do you know it's a 'he'?"

"It's a snow*man*. He, uh, told me."

She looks back. "He talks?"

"No, he doesn't talk. I just know."

"He wrote you a note?"

"No." Oliver sighs. This is when he feels the craziest. "I could feel it, like a thought."

"How do you know you weren't imagining it?"

"This was different, I swear. I was thinking about 'it' standing there watching me, and then I suddenly had this thought that told me he was a 'he,' not an 'it.'"

"Yeah, but maybe it's neither. It's like people call God a 'he.' Maybe God is both."

"You don't believe me?"

"I believe you." She means it. Mostly.

Molly steps into the dark between the trees like a foxhound with a scent.

"We won't find him."

"How far have you gone?"

"Pretty far," he lies. "I don't think we'll find him looking for him, I mean. He just showed up."

She's nodding, but looking as far as she can see. Which isn't far.

"I want to show you something."

Oliver walks just inside the trees. A few minutes pass before he sees the side of the garage. He waits for Molly to catch up, warning her to stay out of sight. The doorknob turns easily, and, as usual, a gust of warm, almost hot air greets them. The car is still spotless. Molly leans over the driver's door, inhaling the fragrant leather.

He warns her about the window, that if you stand in the right spot, someone might see her from the house.

"What will happen if she sees you?"

"I don't know." He knows. They both do.

Oliver pulls open the filing cabinet, third drawer from the top. It's packed with folders, the manila tabs bent and worn. They stack a handful on the bench and spread out the contents, Oliver keeping track of the order while Molly unfolds the plans. One of them looks like a space-age laboratory, the dome-shaped kind that could be erected on another planet.

"You sure he wasn't an inventor?" she asks. "These are like sophisticated plans."

"He was a mechanic."

She opens an eight-fold plan, smoothing out the wrinkles. The scale is larger, and the details easy to read. She studies it for several minutes while Oliver keeps the folders in order.

"Something's not right."

She slides her finger to the top right corner. The signature is dated back to 1920. The worn creases and yellowish color make it believable.

"He built this house before that," Oliver says.

"That's not it. This looks like plans for cold fusion and plasmic welding." She looks at the crescent wrenches and ball-peen hammers. "This garage is still in the 1940s. Besides, no one was thinking about cold fusion in the '20s and plasmic welding, whatever that is."

Oliver plunks the wooden orb on the plan. She compares it to the etching details on the paper. Oliver, however, doesn't tell her how the wooden orb feels when the snowman was near.

"This is a model." She rotates the wooden orb between her fingers and thumbs. "What do you think he was trying to invent?"

He knows what he was trying to invent. He knows what the wooden orb looks like—that drawing, too—but he's not ready to explain what he's read in the journal. *Did he invent a snowman?*

"No idea."

"You ever see anything like this around the house?"

"No."

She tosses it a few times before dropping it in his hand. "You know what I think it is? Some sort of power source. Look at the house. It's off the grid, remember? No solar panels and that windmill's not doing crap. Maybe this thing"—she thumps the plan—"is crammed in the basement or something."

But there's no basement door, not one Oliver's ever seen. And it's not in the attic.

"You see any plans for a metal glove?" she asks.

He hasn't. But there's a lot of paper in those drawers. Molly taps her chin, eyeballing the filing cabinet like a treasure chest.

"You want to read the journals?" he asks.

"They're out here?"

Oliver strips off his backpack and, stealing a glance through the window, digs out a journal from the inside of a *PC Gamer* magazine. "Come on."

She follows him beneath the workbench. Oliver shows her the footlocker, releasing the moldy smell of centuries-old fabric. Molly presses against him, looking over the rim as Oliver digs through the artifacts.

He hands her the journal.

She knows all the crazy things out there, but what's in the journals is the real test. *It's about to get nuts.*

She strokes the old cover. Oliver takes the phone and, while she's smells the leather, sets the timer.

"Just in case," he says.

The binding cracks like snapping twigs as she pulls the cover open. The pages are bright in the white light.

"Oh, man." Molly brushes the first page with her fingertips. "Oh, man."

He has the urge to put his arm around her, pull her warm body against his, but he's afraid. Her weight leans into his shoulder like she answers his thought.

"Read it." She puts the book on his lap.

"What?"

"I want to hear your voice. It's your great-grandfather; I want to hear it in your words."

Oliver sits up straighter, clearing his throat. Molly nuzzles up to him, tipping her head on his shoulder. An ache already throbs in his tailbone, but he doesn't move.

"Here we go." Oliver scans the page.

"What's wrong?"

"I just want to warn you. My great-grandfather was lost after his ship wrecked in the polar ice. He survived and wrote these journals. They're a little out there."

"I'm at the Toye Property. I expect it."

"I mean, like, *Alice in Wonderland* out there."

"Good. Stop stalling."

He feels her warmth. She leans her head back and closes her eyes. Oliver takes a deep breath.

And begins.

. . .

MARCH *19, 1882*

I grow weary, my love.

The elven have been most gracious, indeed. There is never a thing I want they don't provide—food, clothing, entertainment. Still, I grow weary. They cannot bring you to me.

There is discussion about me. Nog mentioned, when I asked the other day, they are considering chaperoning me back to civilization. They have been in hiding for 40,000 years. They roamed free during the Ice Age. I don't know why, all this time, they have chosen to remain separate, isolated in the Arctic Circle, hiding in the ice. Nonetheless, Nog said, they choose to watch the human race rather than join it.

What bothers me most is the implication of these discussions. I feel as if they are deciding whether I can return or not. I am in full health; there is no reason I should not return home, where I belong. In your arms.

I will be talking to the fat man very soon. If anyone should understand my plight, it will be him.

SKETCHES FILL THE PAGES. While still abstract, he's become quite good at drawing. There's a haunting tunnel of ice filled with short, round elven and a large, fat man among them with a grizzled beard, his thumbs hooked in his belt.

"Can you tell me something?" Molly asks. "What are elven?"

Oliver explains. Molly hums along, eyes still closed. He waits, tensely. When she doesn't immediately leave, he breathes easier.

"Then who's the fat man?" she asks.

"I don't know."

MARCH *22, 1882*

There was a celebration yesterday.

It was good timing. I was feeling quite melancholy. There was quite a stir amongst the elven, though. I could feel the excitement building. Nog informed me we would see the rising.

I climbed onto the ice with only a thin coat. I have grown quite large and find that, with this layer of blubber padding my flesh, I need less clothing to stay warm. If the captain could see me now, standing in the Arctic with one coat, he would perhaps cry.

Most of the colony was already on top. There are thousands. I don't think they all live where I am. Some must have migrated from other locations in grand sleighs. The gold rails were curled and the bodies shiny red. I cannot say how they would fabricate such items, but nothing surprises me any longer. While there were reins tethered to the fronts of these grand sleds, there was nothing to pull them.

I can say, without question, there could not be a jollier lot. Even the fat man was above the ice, towering over the elven, his distinctive laughter carried above the celebration. I have not met with him, but I have been promised our meeting will be soon. I considered confronting him right then, but he is very popular among the elven. They all want his attention, and the atmosphere for serious discussion was naught. After all, he arrived much like I did, only he never left. He made this his home. But he came with his wife.

I would do the same.

A sudden hush fell over them. They faced east. I stood next to Nog, watching the sky lighten until the first sliver of the sun rose above the horizon. It did so to raucous celebration. The elven hugged and kissed, throwing their short arms as far around their tubby bodies as possible. They exchanged gifts and plates of food—cookies being the most popular. Music began to play, and the elven danced and sang. Later, I saw the younger ones remove their clothing to plunge into the icy water, rising up with laughter.

I, however, did not join, my love. I watched the sun continue its ascent, remembering the time we spent on the wharf that early morning in July, the morning after we wed. How we watched the sun rise. I thought, naively, it would never end. I believed we would be together forever.

I never should have left.

THE FLAT LINE of a horizon bisects the page, a curved hump of the sun peeking above it. The scribbles of celebrating elven, spherical and jolly, arms raised, fill the landscape. Hovering above the sun is a mess of lines that, at first glance, appear to be a spray of clouds. Oliver begins turning the page when he recognizes the eyes, lips and a chin below the tip of a nose.

"Is there more?" Molly asks.

APRIL *18, 1882*

The fat man still won't see me.

My weariness has turned to worry. There are rumors that the colony is divided about my return. Some, I've heard, want me to remain in the Arctic, that life has been good without intervening with the human race. Others feel like now is the time to guide humanity, that our technology has become dangerous and without their wisdom we could cause irreversible damage.

I don't care about any of that.

I only want to see your face.

The claustrophobia has become unbearable. I can hardly sleep, but despite the fat that insulates me, I cannot remain above the ice indefinitely. I find myself wanting to tear down these icy walls, to be free.

Perhaps that is why Nog came to me yesterday. I believe he senses my unrest. He assures me, on a daily basis, that a decision about my fate will come soon. And daily, he brings no new news.

But yesterday, he suggested we do something different.

We journeyed topside. I thought, perhaps, we would ski the ice. I arrived on top of the ice in shock. I had to blink several times as the chill wind blew, but it did not dispel the mirage.

There, standing on four legs, was the largest reindeer in the world. Its rack of antlers spread the length of a full-grown horse. It pawed the ice while two elven stroked its front legs, as if they were the keepers.

"Where did it come from?" I asked.

The beast snorted, and its nose grew red as a flame, as if I had insulted it. When it shook its head, the antlers fanned the air. One of the attending elven said he lives on the mainland, where he feeds on lichen and such. That sounded impossible. How could a beast of this size reach the mainland? I asked that question, but secretive smiles were all I received in return.

I was not allowed to pet it. He can be temperamental, they said.

Nog asked that I step back. He pulled open his coat, revealing the magic bag on his hip. He still refuses to call it a magic bag; that is my name for it. Science, he insists always, is when you understand. Magic is when you don't.

But then he did something that explains why all those sleighs were at the equinox celebration. With the metal glove on, he reached—

"THE GLOVE!" Molly smacks Oliver's arm.

His heart begins to quiver. It wasn't just "glove" that was written. *Metal glove.* The entry sounds like his great-grandfather has already seen it, like he knows what it can do. There must be an explanation in one of the other journals.

Molly shakes him. "Keep reading."

. . .

WITH THE METAL GLOVE ON, *he reached into the magic bag. As he's done before, he pulled something out that defies the laws of physics. This time it was a red sleigh. The golden-railed sled emerged at first like stretchy fabric, but it shook the ice when it landed.*

They fed the reindeer another handful of green cubes. The beast minced the food without taking its wary eyes off me. They guided it to the front of the sled. Nog explained, while they tethered it, that the beast had modified organs, in particular a helium bladder. This had something to do with the webbed hide hanging loosely between its legs.

I suppose I had some idea of what was about to happen, but, at that moment, I could not think clearly. When Nog patted the seat, I sat without resistance. I still believed this thing would gallop over the ice like a stallion.

The attending elven stepped back, and a buzzing wave rolled around us, slightly distorting the horizon. "A shield," Nog said. "To protect us." Without warning, Nog called to the beast.

"Onward."

My stomach dropped.

The world blurred into two colors: white below, blue above; the two dissected by a fuzzy line.

The horizon, my love. I was looking at the horizon from above.

The reindeer soared in front of us, legs spread, the hide-webbing taut, and its belly swollen. My head spun. I clutched the railing.

We were flying.

THE ALARM GOES OFF.

There are illustrations of the reindeer, the sleigh and the flight. He closes the journal, and they sit quietly—Molly holding his arm with both hands.

She's still here.

"Did he ever write about eating wild berries," Molly asks. "In any of the earlier ones?"

"No. Why?"

"Elven. Flying reindeer. Maybe these are hallucinations. I'm just saying."

Oliver wonders the same thing, and, maybe, he'd believe his great-grandfather had written these in an insane asylum, that maybe his mom made all this up to keep him entertained while they lived here.

But he saw a snowman.

And he hadn't eaten any wild berries that day.

Before they trek back to the field to return to the house, before they even crawl out from under the bench, Oliver indulges one last nagging feeling. He flips back through the pages and stares at the face in the clouds.

My love.

14

Oliver wakes up at midnight.

It had become a habit, going to sleep at ten o'clock and waking up at midnight. He listens to the distant rumbling of the forest—branches snapping, ground thumping—thinking about Malcolm Toye's sketches and unrequited love.

It had been a week since he and Molly had sat under the workbench. She's coming for tea again. Grandmother even nodded and said, "That would be fine," when Mom told her. For normal people, that comment should be translated as, "That would be fantastic! I can't wait to see her!"

Oliver called her on Grandmother's landline, with her permission, of course. But without service, he can't text. He even began sketching her face into wispy clouds. He'd thrown all his attempts away. They were horrible, and he didn't need his mom seeing them. Grandmother, either.

What if she recognized it?

He's already read two of the three journals he took from the footlocker. The second one is still in the attic. He should've grabbed the other three when he was sitting right next to it with Molly, but he had other things on the brain.

It's windy everywhere, not just in the trees. The house pops and creaks with each gust. He tosses in bed as violently as the weather. Sleep is too far off, so he crawls out of bed and retrieves the two journals beneath the dresser. He reads them by the light of his cell phone, but he's been through them a dozen times. Nothing new.

It occurs to him that now is the perfect time to get the one in the attic. Why didn't he think of that before? Everyone's asleep. He'll get in, get out, and have something new to read.

He gets to his bedroom door in a few creaky steps and, with hand pressed around the metal doorknob, holds his breath. With an eye to the crack in the doorway, he searches for his grandmother waiting in the moonlight.

He walks to the bathroom, listening at the top step. Somewhere on the second floor, his mom softly snores. A gust of wind slams the house. Sleet smatters the roof like a handful of gravel.

A door slams.

Muscles coiled, ears tuned to every little tick—Oliver is catatonic. He can't be sure what he heard. It sounded like a door, but he's not certain. Maybe he left the snow shovel on the porch, and it fell over. Or an icicle dropped on the steps. He waits at the top step several minutes, counting his breaths. The distant noises seem right on top of the house.

Usually, he'd crawl right back in bed. But tonight, he refuses to run. It's just sounds he hears. Just thoughts that frighten. Now is the time to grab that journal.

He flushes the toilet, just in case, and hurries down the hall. His phone is back in the bedroom, and, without moonlight, the room is dark. He swings his hands like the rope's a piñata. He smacks the knob tied at the end and waits for it to swing back. When he has two hands on it, he begins to pull—

There's a flash outside.

Oliver jumps against the wall.

His heart swells with each beat.

At first, it seemed like lightning. But there's no thunder, just wind. Eyes wide, ears pricked, he watches the shadows play on the far wall. The light dims but doesn't go away. He slides toward the window. It's black outside, the night sky capped with clouds.

Light beams from the garage window.

Someone's in there.

His brain aches to remember if everything got put away. An errant paperclip could expose him. A cold emotion splashes down his spine.

The light brightens like a power surge.

For a moment, the entire backyard is lit up, and then it goes back to normal. Oliver watches until his body aches. Nothing happens. Not a shadow, not a form, not a sound. A thought occurs to him, one that wriggles down to his toes.

Who's out there?

"It's only your thoughts that have come to get you," Grandmother had said. And it's his thoughts that have locked his knees.

Just thoughts. There are no ghosts on the stairs, no wild things roaming the house. I'm just having thoughts something will happen. Just thoughts.

It could be those things from the river. It could be the snowman. It could be anything. He should go back to bed and pretend like nothing ever happened. That's what he gets for leaving the journal in the attic.

Not tonight.

He wants to know who's out there. If Grandmother catches him in the kitchen, he'll say he needed a snack. He's diabetic, after all.

He squeezes the wooden orb. Courage seeps up his arm.

It takes all that courage to not pass the stairwell and flee for the room, but he makes the turn. One step at a time, he descends.

Standing at the sink, he can see the garage. The light is still on. Other than that, there's nothing out of the ordinary. Maybe Grandmother left the light on by accident. Another ten minutes at the sink and still nothing.

It's during those ten minutes that Oliver has another thought.

Never in his life has he done something like this. When his dad had parties, Oliver hid in his bed. When there was a bully after school, he stayed in the classroom. He played it safe. The chances of getting hurt are slim if you stay in bed.

Just ask Malcolm Toye.

But he made it to the North Pole. He met the elven.

Stay in bed and nothing happens. Ever.

The journals.

There are three of them out there. He could wait until tomorrow and find a way to get them. There's always tomorrow. Oliver's lived his whole life waiting for tomorrow.

He goes to the mudroom and slides on his boots, carefully closing the back door behind him. The night air seeps beneath his shirt. He folds his arms, eyeing the square of light splashing across the lawn. Oliver follows the maze of exposed grass, avoiding the snow. He stops short of the window.

Nothing inside moves.

He moves to the left, taking tiny steps, almost shuffling, until the edge of his boot is touching snow. From here, he can see almost half of the garage. No one's in there.

The car is gone!

The door must've been Grandmother leaving the house. She must drive the car when no one is watching. Molly's right; she's a private person. Maybe she does her joyrides in the middle of the night.

Again, this would be a good time to beat a retreat back to bed.

Oliver races around the garage, past the large door to the entrance. He opens it quietly. It's strange to see the car missing. The garage seems so big without it. And the concrete where the car usually sits is so clean and smooth.

He wipes his boots and ducks beneath the workbench. His breath is loud, and his heartbeat thuds in his ears. He digs past the coat and yanks the remaining three journals out, stuffing them inside his pants. Without breaking stride, he races out of the garage, leaving on the lights.

Quickly, he returns to his bedroom and slips the journals beneath the dresser. Adrenaline pumps through him. He should check his blood sugar, just in case. But for now, he lays in bed.

Something bothers him, something's not right.

He assumes it was the risk he took. It was stupid, but it worked.

In the morning, looking out the kitchen window as he rinses his plate, he realizes what was nagging him before he fell asleep. It wasn't the danger of being caught or the journals hidden beneath his dresser. It's the snow around the garage, just outside the big garage door where the car would pull out.

There were no car tracks.

15

Molly dazzles at tea.

She tells a story about a dog named Peanut at the shelter where she volunteers on Saturdays that only poops when no one is looking. And when she cleans it up, Peanut barks at it.

She actually used the word "poop." During tea. And Grandmother smiled.

Remarkable.

They go for a walk afterwards. Oliver stops about halfway to the main road and, sort of whispering, tells her about the car. The next morning, it was in the garage like it had never moved. Molly starts asking questions, and he gives her the quiet sign.

"Let's go somewhere safe."

He leads her through the trees until they reach the field. The windmill churns behind them. Snow is drifted in the shadows, but the field is exposed and sloppy. April has arrived, but winter refuses to leave.

"I brought something." Molly's got a magnetic compass. "I saw it at the store, thought we might test the hunters' theory."

Oliver knows exactly how that test will go.

He warns her about the sinkholes. They hike through the trees, every once in a while checking the compass. North is never the same direction. Sometimes the needle settles in one spot and, before she puts it away, moves to another.

Molly stops at a pair of maple trees leaning against each other. The bark is misshapen and molded into a grafting kiss where the trunks touch.

"Test one more theory." She unties two friendship bracelets from her wrist, putting the red one around the smaller tree. Oliver attaches the blue one to the other.

She stands back. "The kissing trees."

It has been over a month since Oliver has been this far.

Snowmelt has transformed the stream into a river. The icy blue water crashes off the rocky shores, carrying debris in the white-tipped waves. The river speaks through the earth. They can hear it through their feet.

"Be careful." Oliver stops several feet short.

They walk parallel to the river until the bend appears up ahead. This part of the forest still looks like Nature's battle zone, with branches spearing the ground or hanging from above. Oliver points at the stack of stones across the water.

"The hobbit house."

"That's it?"

"Yeah." He can feel the water's draft from where they're standing. It was dangerous the last time he crossed. This time it would be fatal.

Molly slips her fingers between his. "We don't have to go."

"I know."

But she wants to go. And she's not afraid, he can tell. She's not shivering, not like he is.

One step at a time.

But this isn't the staircase, these aren't just scary sounds. Not this time. Fall and bad things happen.

Oliver leads her through the maze of branches and up the stone steps. He stands on solid ground, an icy breeze rushing past him. The tree bridge is solid and the footing tacky with moss. He's afraid, though, that his knees will lock up halfway across and his legs, now numb from his knees up, will fold.

Molly squeezes his hand and walks onto the bridge first. She stops halfway and, with plenty of room on both sides, reaches for him. He takes a step.

Another.

Together, they cross.

"The door's in there."

They enter the dark hollow, hand in hand, with phones guiding them to the gnarly handle. The door opens as easily as it did the first time. Musty odor, like wet blankets, greets them. The room hasn't changed. Firewood is stacked by the hearth, charred logs inside the fireplace.

"Someone lives here," Molly says.

"I don't think so. My cousins come out here for the service." His phone signals new messages. "The only place on the property. Look." He steps outside, only a few feet from the threshold. "A signal in there, but not here. Weird, right?"

"I can smell the weird. It's got like a…" She makes a swirling motion with her hand. "A smell of alloy, like metal beneath the mold. Can you smell it?"

He thought she was kidding, but she's taking deep breaths. He's not smelling it.

"Who do you think built it?" she asks.

"I don't know. It was just here."

She strokes the rough stubble of the plaster walls. Her fingers follow a crack running behind the table. She puts her ear to the wall and knocks, then moves the table and taps the floor.

"What are you doing?"

"Maybe there's a secret door somewhere. You know, push on the right spot and find a tunnel. The electronics are somewhere. You don't get cell phone service through a tree. If you ask me, this place is too empty. Who do you think stacked the wood?"

"My cousins, I guess."

"Someone lives here. They just don't want anyone to know."

"Maybe we should go."

She pulls the mesh screen on the fireplace and throws a log inside. "I say we stoke a fire and stay a while."

A lump is rising in his throat. Crossing the river was one thing; making themselves at home in the hobbit house had other consequences. *If Henry finds out.*

Molly finds matches in the table drawer. Before long, the room is warm enough to take off their coats. She pulls off her boots and socks, stretching in the chair. They listen to the wood pop. Oliver fishes through his backpack and pulls out the journal.

"You read my mind," she says.

Oliver sets his alarm so they have plenty of time to return. He can't make that mistake for a lot of reasons. He turns to the first page and begins to read aloud.

.   .   .

AUGUST 6, 1882

A decision has been reached.

The elven elders have debated my fate for far too long. Despite my protests, they urge for my patience. I suppose they saved my life, they have that right. But my patience has reached an inglorious end. It has been tested for an Arctic summer. So it is with great pleasure that I received the news that a decision has been made.

It has been several months since I woke in the ice. I'm afraid you would not recognize me. I am as round as a sow and hairy as a grizzly. This very morning, when Nog told me the news, I was on the ice with nothing more than a sweater. To avoid dwelling on the pace of life with the elven, I have dedicated myself to helping wherever I can. I discover something shocking every day. They know so much, my love, yet I feel I've learned little.

This morning, I was releasing solar dust. These are tiny particles, no larger than pollen, that hover hundreds of feet above the ice, absorbing the sun's heat and transferring it back to the colony in the form of energy. Can you believe this? They don't burn wood or fuel; they transfer it directly from the sun.

In fact, Nog let me use the magic glove. He still hates it when I call it that, and he shouldn't let me use it, but he, more than anyone, knows how difficult this is for me. He said he trusts me, and that is a sign the news of the elders' decision will be good. Or perhaps he was just trying to cheer me up.

I must say, the glove is more magical than scientific, I don't care what Nog says. It is made to fit an elven hand—not a full-grown man's hand—but when I slipped my fingers inside the small opening, it expanded in a way that swallowed my hand. The metal links squirmed across my palm, shifting and settling. There was a slight stinging, and then, just like that, I couldn't feel it anymore, as if it became a second layer of skin.

Nog taught me how to visualize what I wanted, to reach into the bag and find it. Energy cannot be destroyed, he said. The bag simply reorganizes it. On my first attempt, I retrieved a canister to store a batch of dead solar dust. Next, he showed me how to retrieve an abominable sphere. These metallic orbs do more than just allow a snowman to build a body, they store the memories of past elven. He described it as a computer, something that stores data. Then he tried to describe a computer, and I'm afraid I still don't understand. Nonetheless, the snowman orb can be dangerous. Elven can touch them without a glove, but humans he's not so sure. He thinks that one might absorb the memories out of me. I wasn't willing to test his theory, so I put on the glove.

Nog tossed one of the metallic spheres into the snow, and just as the body *began forming around it, I opened my hand and the orb slapped into the palm like the glove was a super magnet. It was quite empowering.*

"THAT WOULD EXPLAIN your grandmother's mystery power," Molly says. "Maybe your great-grandfather brought back solar dust. And if he didn't, maybe there's something else even more futuristic. You ever see a strange cloud hovering over the house?"

"No."

He had searched for a basement door, and there is none—none that he can see. *Would we even see solar dust?*

"What about a bag?" Molly asks. "Ever see anything like that?"

Oliver shakes his head. "I've only seen her wearing the glove. She might've had a bag under her coat or in her pocket, but I don't know."

Molly throws another log on the fire.

"Let's assume she's wearing the same glove," she says. "I understand why she'd keep it secret. I mean, you can't let everyone have a magic glove, but why would she wear it outside?"

Oliver reminds her how she pointed at the snowman clearing the road. She was wearing the glove. Maybe she was controlling it.

"But why the other times?" Molly says. "It's like she's using it for something other than pulling sleds out of magic bags."

Maybe it's a weapon.

Malcolm Toye pulled the sphere out of the forming body. Maybe Grandmother could do the same thing if she saw a snowman, or one of those things at the river.

Oliver flips past more drawings. The last one is of a gloved hand beautifully rendered to highlight the metal gleam.

SEPTEMBER 24, 1882

It has been a month.

It has taken me that long to record my thoughts. I'm afraid these words will never reach you.

I have not eaten. Food is tasteless. Even when I force it into my mouth, my stomach curdles it like spoiled milk. I have lost so much weight that I've had to wear heavy coats to keep warm. Even bundled up, the cold never really leaves.

To be honest, I have avoided this journal. To write the words will make their meaning real. I wake each morning hoping I dreamed the event, that my imagination is a magic bag that can rewrite history if I just visualize it. But each morning, I am still here.

You are still so far away.

I think Nog knew the decision. I should've known. The morning he led me to the elven elders, I sensed a change in the colony. We passed through the commons, where many elven come to eat. That morning, few were there.

Naively, I had assumed they were preparing for a celebration, that we would soon climb to the ice to welcome a new era where elven and humans walked the same sidewalks and lived as neighbors, that I would lead them out of the cold and introduce them like family.

My delusions were reinforced when I entered the great hall—a circular room with seats filled with elven. In the center was a raised dais, where the elders were seated along with Jessica and Nicholas Santa.

"DID YOU JUST SAY 'SANTA'?" Molly sits up. "As in St. Nick? As in Santa Claus?"

Oliver reads the paragraph again. "It says 'Nicholas Santa.'"

"Why didn't I see this coming? Did you see it?"

Oliver shakes his head. He hasn't seen anything.

"Elven on the North Pole, flying reindeer, and now Santa Claus?"

"It...it doesn't say Santa *Claus*."

"Is there another Santa?" She has a point.

"You want to hear more?"

She closes her eyes with a fixed grin. "Absolutely."

NICHOLAS DELIVERED *the message like he was cauterizing a wound. It was swift and clean. "We will not merge with the human race," he said. "It has been decided that the world is best served if the elven continue to exist anonymously. Humanity is still in its infancy. Elven technology would only thwart human growth."*

The fat man said 'we' like he was one of them. He is still human, like me. He still stands so much taller than the elven, but he speaks as if he's been one of them all his life. I, for one, don't wish for such delusion. I am human, and their attempts to mollify my pain are patronizing.

He continued to explain that the decision was difficult, that he knows I am lonely, that I yearn for home, for my love, but it is best for me, for the elven and humanity that I stay at the North Pole. Perhaps, he said, the decision will change in the near future. Does he realize dangling that temptation

before me is dripping lemons into the wound? A wound that's been open for
so long that it will never heal.

I have waited too long, my love. And while the jolly spirit has returned to
the elven colony, it is not contagious. Rather, it mocks my pain.

I would rather die in your arms than live long in the ice.

THE FIRE POPS, and the logs settle.

Silence between Oliver and Molly hangs for a minute. Then two.

"Oh, my God," Molly says. "Your great-grandfather may be wacked-out of his gourd on crazy berries, but this story is breaking my heart."

Oliver closes the journal. "It feels...*real.*"

"I know what you mean. The emotion is right there, on the pages. And those sketches are raw suffering."

"And the science behind solar harvesting, he wouldn't know about that in the late 1800s."

"Assuming the journals are authentic. I mean, your grandmother could've made those up before you got here."

"Why would she do that?"

"I don't know. I'm just putting it out there." She begins pacing, her bare feet quiet on the wood floor. "It's just the whole Santa Claus thing is throwing me."

"It didn't say Santa Claus."

"For some reason, the elven evolving during the Ice Age and the magic glove had me believing. But Santa Claus?"

"He said 'Nicholas Santa.'"

"What's the difference?"

She pinches her lower lip, walking back and forth, deciding whether to believe this or not. Her eyes have the intensity of a hungry owl. He can feel the doubts grinding in her head, this fantastic story colliding with reality. He's been there, too. He survived. *Or it altered me, and now I can't tell the difference between real and fantasy.*

The smell of weird is all over the property, but the mention of Santa somehow short-circuited everything.

Even the snowman.

"Do you still believe me?" Oliver asks.

"Yes, Oliver. I believe you."

There's a difference in how she said it, different than all the other times. A sliver of doubt had wedged its way between them. Oliver has had splinters. He knew if they weren't pulled out, they'd fester.

Oliver's alarm sounds off.

They snuff the fire and clean up, leaving the hobbit house exactly like they found it, even dragging wood from the forest and stacking it on the brick hearth. No one would know they had been there. Not the twins or anyone else.

Oliver leads her over the fallen tree, reaching back to hold her hand. The compass isn't much help, again. Oliver senses what direction to go, can feel the pull of home. A few minutes later, they spot the twin trees up ahead. The friendship bracelets are still attached.

"Look, Oliver!" Molly trots ahead. She loops her finger through one of the bracelets. "They switched!"

He's not sure what she means. The colorful braided bracelets are still tied to the branches, one on each side. But then he gets it: the blue one is on the wrong side, and the red is on the other.

He doubts his orientation, wondering if he's looking in the wrong direction, but he can hear the river at his back. *They switched.*

"Smell the weird." Molly pulls in a deep draught of air. When she exhales, Oliver feels her sliver of doubt wiggle free. Perhaps not all the way, but the weird has pushed it to the side.

Oliver leads the way, following a sense of direction emanating from his gut, pointing like a magnetic needle unaffected by the forest. He brushes aside hanging vines, jogs around saplings like a hound following a rabbit. And then he realizes, the pull isn't in his gut.

He pulls his hand out of his pocket.

The wooden orb is warm. It hums, but not like his phone on vibrate, more like a caffeinated buzz in the palm of his hand. Like the sun rising on a cold day to kiss his cheeks.

They reach the clearing.

Oliver stops just inside the trees, eyeing the windmill across patches of wet ground and dying snow. The orb burns in his palm, the vibrations shaking his hand. He holds it between his finger and thumb. It sounds like a summer cicada taking flight.

"What's wrong?" Molly asks.

It pulls Oliver's attention away from the windmill. He looks to the far left of the clearing, just about where the mysterious snowball was launched. Something moves in the shadows.

Something massive.

It steps into the light, revealing its thick legs and barrel-shaped torso. One powerful arm hangs at its side; the other holds the nearest tree.

Across the distance, Oliver feels the needles from the branch he's holding as if they're pricking his own hand. His heart, for once, isn't beating like the heart of a frightened rabbit. It's calm and still. For once, maybe the first time he can remember, strength fills him from the inside, pouring through his hand like the orb is a spigot turned wide open. At that moment, he could lift a fallen tree.

The snowman steps back and then dissolves like he had once before, this time in a slushy stream that sifts between the trees. The orb falls quiet.

"Do you believe?" Oliver asks.

Molly's eyes are glassy. She wets her lips and whispers, "I believe."

16

Green grass and May flowers replace the snow.
Oliver holds the wooden orb. Ever since they saw the
snowman, the day he took Molly out to the hobbit house, the
day she held his hand, the orb had fallen silent. Now it's just a piece of
wood. Oliver wishes for winter to return. Maybe not today.

Molly's coming.

Today they'll hike out to the forest flush with new growth and find
the bracelet tree. They'll cross the bridge to hike beyond the hobbit
house. If there's time, they can read another journal. Maybe the snow
is missing, but the magic can still happen. And not the science kind of
magic.

That boy-girl kind of magic.

He pulls on a sweatshirt and a clean pair of cargo pants, stuffing his
phone deep in the side pocket. His boots are on the back porch. The
backpack, though, isn't under the bed. He left it in the upstairs bathroom, tucked behind the toilet, to find the best journal entries to read.
The ones in his backpack had more sketches and boring details about
snow and daily chores—things about sustainable energy and food
sources. Once he got to a passage that addressed the fat man—the red-
coated man named Santa—he slid a square of paper between the
pages.

He promised not to read the last two journals without her. He
scanned the pages to find the good parts, but he kept his word and

didn't read them. Not all of them. But these are the last two. It was like coming to the end of a really good book: you want to read the end without the journey ending.

First things first.

Rule #1: Nothing happens unless the chores are done.

Oliver skips down the steps. Mom and Grandmother must be outside. There was talk about a garden and a shovel. Without a rototiller in sight, Oliver could guess who would be working the shovel. And what about mowing? Would he have to cut the pasture with a pair of dull scissors?

The chore board is clean.

Not a mark, not a letter. Nothing. His heart swells, but he holds his breath. Grandmother could be in the backyard, waiting to ambush him with a rusty pair of shears. *Get to mowing, Olivah.*

He'd have to think about this. Maybe it'd be wise to meet Molly at the entrance, hike through the trees to avoid the backyard; maybe load up his backpack for the day.

He closes the pantry door. *The backpack.*

It's sitting on the kitchen table, the flap flung open. The pockets are limp, the inside empty.

Oliver turns cold and not the kind nipping at your nose—the kind that reaches inside your belly, pulls your intestines into your throat, and wraps them around your heart like copper wire. Because it's not just the library books, the magazines and the *World of Succulents* that's missing.

"Where did you get these?"

Oliver jumps.

A sound escapes him, one reserved for cornered animals. Grandmother is wearing a black dress that reaches the floor, white frilly trim at the cuffs and hem. Clutched to her chest, her knuckles white around the spines, are the scuffed covers of the journals.

All five of them.

Oliver's chin begins to twitch. Lies tumble around his mind like a lottery wheel, but there are no words to get stuck in his throat. He's empty.

"*Where?*" Grandmother shouts. "Where did you find these? You tell me from where you took these books!"

Her voice has changed. It sounds small and scratchy.

The leather bindings creak under pressure, tendons stretching the thin and spotted skin on the backs of her hands. With them pressed to her breast, she reaches out with one hand, her fingers curled like talons, and crosses the kitchen. Her footsteps land like cinder blocks, shaking the dishes.

She catches his chin—her thumb plied to the left side of his jaw, her fingers clenching against the right. He falls back a step.

"This is not your property," she hisses. "I have locked doors in this house that you are not to open, places you are not to trespass. I made that very clear, Olivah. It was and is the first rule."

The pressure of her grip eases.

"How dare you violate my trust. Now tell me where you found these." Her eyes search his face. "Where are the other two?"

Other two?

She's holding five of them. If the one he dropped is still in the attic, that means there are seven journals. There were only six in the footlocker. He's sure of it.

"I want to know where you found these."

For a moment, it sounds as if she's asking, really asking where he got them. As if she doesn't know.

"Answer me!"

Her nails dig into his soft flesh.

"What's going on?" Mom is just inside the kitchen with dirt on the knees of her faded jeans.

"I have invited you to stay in my house, Debra. I opened up my life to you when you were in need, and now you have violated my trust."

"What are you talking about?"

"There are rules; I made that quite simple. All you had to do was follow them. Why is this so difficult? Why can't people simply *do what they promise?*"

It's not clear who she's talking to. Or about. A small squeak slips through her spastic attempts to swallow. She grabs the journals with both hands again, squeezing and pushing them up to her chin.

Mom looks at Oliver. "What happened?"

He clasps his hands behind his back to keep them from shaking. There's nothing he can do about his chin, still throbbing from Grandmother's claw.

"Answer your mother!"

"Mother." Oliver's mom holds out her hand. "Let's be calm."

"He took these. I found them in his bag."

"The blank diaries?"

The line between her thinning lips tightens. "No."

"What are they?" When Grandmother doesn't answer, she turns to Oliver, tells him to take a deep breath and relax. She just wants to know what's happening.

"Those are great-grandfather's journals...from the 1880s."

He adds more details about the journey. At first, his words blur together, but they become stronger the more he talks about the tragic journey and how great-grandfather survived because of the pendant around his neck.

He leaves out the weird parts.

Grandmother's eyes glitter as if a slick of tears has formed.

"Okay," Mom says. "Were they in your room with the blank one?"

"The garage."

"Liar," Grandmother seethes.

"Mother! That's enough!"

"That door is locked. It is always locked. No one is allowed in there, ever."

"I swear, it was unlocked," Oliver says. "I didn't do anything to—"

She starts for his chin. Oliver involuntarily steps back.

"Stop this!" Mom steps in front of her. "You will not touch him like that, Mother. And you will not speak to him like that, either. He is *my* son. I am *his* mother."

"Then act like it."

"And hit him? Berate him? Criticize him until he's nothing, is that what you mean?"

Grandmother turns her steely glare on him, the one that could pierce an armored tank. This time, though, it's lacking conviction. She walks to the other side of the kitchen, the books shielding her. The house is silent except for her wheezing and the covers squeaking beneath her palms.

"I know Grandmother's rules; I swear I never broke them." He winces, knowing he's broken more than a few, just not that one. "It was during the winter, when it was cold. I was looking for a place to store the snow shovel. The door was unlocked, I swear. I didn't think much of it. I wasn't snooping. But the garage was heated and I was cold, so I stayed until my exercise time was up. I didn't take anything."

He avoids looking at Grandmother because he *did* snoop—major league snooping—and he *did* take something. His hand moves over his pocket. Grandmother sees him feeling for the comfort of the wooden orb, reaching for the confidence that surges through his arm when he squeezes it.

"What do you have?" she says.

The blood drains from his cheeks, replaced by chilled antifreeze. Grandmother, walking silently this time, crosses the kitchen and pulls his hand away.

"What's in your pocket?" she asks.

He reaches to the bottom and pulls the pocket inside out. It's empty. *It's gone.* But he had it with him when he left his bedroom. He never goes anywhere without it.

"I just...I found the journals. They were interesting, that's all. I was bored."

"Why did you take them?"

He shrugs. "I was going to put them back when I was finished."

"Can I see them?" Mom asks.

"No," Grandmother says.

"Why not?"

"They are my property, Debra. Your son took them."

"If they're just diaries, why can't he read them, Mother? I'd like to know more about my grandfather. I'm sure that's why he read them."

Grandmother's grip tightens. Her chalky complexion turns pinkish then red like stage lights warming her face. She turns and, without a sound, leaves. The creaky floor tells them she's crossed the house.

Oliver explains to his mom, again, how the door wasn't locked. The door was indeed unlocked every time, the garage warm and inviting. As if waiting for him. Grandmother returns, her steps a little more forceful. She's pulling on a sweater. The journals are somewhere safe, unlikely to ever be found again.

"Come along." She gestures for them to follow as she trods—yes, actually trods—to the mudroom and out the back door. Mom watches her without moving.

A deep breath escapes her.

Grandmother is waiting in front of the garage, bare hands at her sides. No glove, this time. Oliver walks around the garage, his mom chaperoning like a prison guard. Nervous worms turn in Oliver's stomach as he steps into the shade. The mud squishes around his boots. Grandmother stands back, a grim frown pushing her chin forward.

Oliver reaches for the doorknob.

The metal knob is colder and harder than it should be. He squeezes it and closes his eyes. He turns it.

Click.

It hardly moves before catching the lock. It's followed by three more clicks as he tries again and again.

"Mom, I swear…"

Keys jiggle.

Grandmother pushes her way past them, avoiding the soft muddy spot where Oliver's standing. She removes his hand and, sorting through an old set of keys, some of them the old-fashioned skeleton type, finds a modern one. She slides it into the lock and, before opening it, drops the keys into her sweater pocket, but not before Oliver notices a smaller key sandwiched on the ring. This one is short and square, more like a peg with a glowing blue cube at the end, as if catching light in the shade. He's seen a key like that before.

In the footlocker.

Grandmother tells Oliver to remove his filthy boots. The garage is cold and dank.

"Grandmother, it was unlocked all the other times, I swear."

Her x-ray truth sensors tell her he's not lying about the door, and that's what bothers her. He was lying about something earlier.

"Where did you find the books?"

He points at the dark corner beneath the bench.

Grandmother investigates. "*Exactly* where?"

"In the footlocker. That was unlocked, too. I know I said I wasn't snooping, but I didn't come in here to do it. I was just looking for somewhere to put the shovel, and then I was going to leave. I just noticed the footlocker, and…and I got curious. I'm sorry, I really am. I didn't think I was hurting anything."

That's where the six journals were, he wants to say. *Not seven.*

A sick feeling fills his stomach. He was *curious* when he rifled through the filing cabinet and crouched beneath the workbench. But if he was honest, he was getting back at all the strict rules. The garage was his one safe place he could do stuff he knew he shouldn't be doing. He was hiding in the dark when she came into the garage wearing the metal glove, unlocking the door when she did and locking it when she left. But still, it was unlocked for Oliver. Somehow, it was always unlocked. This was his place to learn secrets.

Secrets no one was going to tell him.

He's not certain if that rotten sensation is guilt or sadness that it's over.

Grandmother walks away from the workbench and past the filing cabinets. The pinkish hue of anger fades from her cheeks. Her eyes dart around the room, her head turning like a bird listening for a worm. She pats her empty pockets. Her hand, the right one, the one that always wears the metal glove, flexes uncontrollably, like it's searching for something she can't reach.

Mom looks under the workbench. "What footlocker?"

"The old one." Oliver starts bending over, but now he knows. Maybe it's because the garage feels different—colder and darker. The look on Grandmother's face.

Something's wrong.

She walks around the shiny black car and pulls the garage door shut. Patting her pockets, Oliver thinks she's looking for the glove again, like the bulky thing was hiding in a secret pouch. Instead, she pulls out a cell phone and not an ordinary one.

A smartphone.

"Mother, what are you doing?" Mom asks.

Oliver doesn't notice that she's thumbing through contacts and searching for a number. He's still processing the vision of her holding a cell phone. And using it. She puts it to her ear, the black modern case clashing with the steel gray hair pulled back in a grandmotherly bun.

Grandmother answers his mom's questions, but Oliver is wondering how she's getting service. The rules prohibit Oliver from using electronics; he had assumed they applied to her, too. But if brought to a court of law, the rule clearly stated that *he* not use electronics.

"Hello," Grandmother says to someone. "Yes, it's Mother. I need you to come to the property tonight. Bring Henry and Helen."

That snaps Oliver back to the present moment like a fist in the midsection. It doesn't take long for the facts to tumble into place. If Henry knows he's been in the garage, when he finds out that he was reading the journals...

He'll know I've been other places.

17

Oliver adjusts his weight. The bottom step creaks.

Grandmother stands with her back to the front door. Despite spring's warmth, she hides her hands in the pockets of a dark wool coat.

"This isn't necessary," Mom says.

"Do you want to continue living here?" Grandmother takes her laser blue-green eyes off of Oliver. "If you do, there are rules to be followed. If you and Oliver do not follow the rules, people can be hurt. Or worse."

She puckers in consternation, lines of worry carving the flesh around her paper-thin lips.

"He said the garage was unlocked. He didn't take anything," Mom says. "I understand it can be dangerous if he gets lost on the property or stays out after dark, but you're overreacting, Mother. He was just reading journals about his great-grandfather. Maybe if the rules weren't so strict, if you let him use his phone and iPad, he wouldn't be looking for something to do."

Oliver shoves his hands deep into his pants pockets, searching for the comfort of the orb. He wishes he could find it. He'd squeeze it right in front of her, he wouldn't care. He needed it.

Grandmother turns her focused high-beam on him, as if sensing the untruth.

I did take something.

It never felt like he took it until she asked. The journals, those he took. But up until the moment she asked, the orb felt like it belonged to him.

"My property operates on rules. It is the sole reason I am alive today."

"What are you talking about?"

"Order, Debra. I'm talking about order and chaos. Without structure, there is chaos. You have to know your environment and the world you live in to survive. Despite your convictions, you know very little, my child. Chaos has not done you much good, I think you'll agree."

"Mother, can we just talk about the garage right now?"

"Do you want to stay in this house, Debra? Do you want to live under my roof?"

Mom's chin juts forward. She shakes her head, an expression Oliver has come to know as grim resignation. "I appreciate your hospitality," she says, the words being pushed out, "but there's no need to drag this out."

"Answer the question."

"Of course, Mother." Mom stands straighter. "We need a place for now."

"Then you shall follow the rules."

"And these are the same rules that Father followed before he left?"

Grandmother doesn't flinch. There's a long pause. Unspoken words hang between them, their long glares locking like horns.

"Your father broke the rules," she finally says. "And he is no longer with us."

Oliver fidgets, and the step sings.

"Olivah, keep your place and stand at attention. Keep your hands at your sides, no touching the bannister. You will remain here until further notice. Is that understood?"

He nods.

And then she says something that nearly buckles his knees. Not with fear, but shock and amazement.

"I love you both," she says.

Love. The word actually came from her mouth. Her lips formed it, her tongue spoke it. Hearing it was like swigging from a bottle of vinegar but tasting something sweet—it didn't compute. Even if she delivered the word with the synthetic emotionlessness of a computer, it still came out of her.

"But true love," she says, "has nothing to do with feeling good."

Oliver feels a wave of weird begin—his blood sugar is getting low. He'll let it drop. He used to do that when he was little, especially when he was mad at his mom. He'd let it go until he was shaking. It was his way of punishing her.

Grandmother slides her hands into her coat before walking to the kitchen. Mom watches from the front door, a grim smile dimpling her cheeks, her chin cocked sideways like she'd taken a right hook.

He knew this expression, too.

She's putting pieces together, hatching a plan. The last time he saw that look was in Texas, shortly after losing her job. Creditors had been calling, and the rent was due. There were few options for them, none of them good.

And then they came here.

She unlocks her jaw. With a brief nod, she climbs onto the bottom step, forcing him to move over. She takes a jagged breath, adjusting the kinks in her back before standing upright. A calm expression rises to the surface, placid and meditative.

Her next breath is smooth.

"We had to do this when we were in trouble," she says. "She would make us wait for our father. Sometimes it would be hours. When it was just me, the boredom was unbearable, but I became a pro at this. I learned to keep good posture. I hate to admit it, but it helps. Pretend there's a string pulling the crown of your head where your hair swirls. This will keep your back straight. Find a spot on the door and breathe through it."

She pulls an easy breath through her nostrils, lets it flow from her lips.

"And she always knew if we were touching the wall or the railing. And if we got the giggles, that was also more time on the step. The record was four hours, all the way until bedtime. And then we went back to the step first thing in the morning."

"What'd you do?"

"Doesn't matter." She shakes her head. "There are worse things than standing on this Godforsaken step, I suppose. Your grandmother never hit us, so there's that."

Oliver knew what it was like to be ignored. He knew what a fat lip was like, too. Given the choice, he'd take a shot to the mouth.

But neither was good.

Oliver tried her posture technique, imagining a string attached where the hair swirled on his head, picking a spot on the side panel of glass to breathe through. It wasn't long before his back ached. Worse, he thought about not seeing Molly.

That ached, too.

"Get off the step, Debra." Grandmother appears at their side. "Don't be silly."

Mom keeps her composure, quietly breathing. Oliver keeps his focus on the window. Several moments pass.

Grandmother stands at the side of the door, the sharp tip of her nose almost pressed to the glass. Oliver stares at the bun on the back of her head, not a single gray hair escaping the intricate web of pins and elastic bands. He inhales through his nostrils, imagining his breath pulling through her head like a cool breeze, her thoughts penetrating his sinuses like dust, swirling inside him.

Cold and empty.

He consumes her innermost secrets, or what he imagines them to be, picturing her up late at night, walking the property in search of something, the metal glove securely wrapped around her hand, the fingers arched like talons, the moon pale on her cheeks. Beneath her distant stare and hardened stance, he feels a great need, an unrequited desire for something she'd lost. Something she'd once had.

Once loved.

"What is love?" The words leap from his tongue, startling him like someone else said them.

Grandmother flinches. "Quiet."

"If it doesn't feel good," he continues, "then what is it?"

He was thinking about Molly, the way it felt when their hands were entwined, the warm swirl in his belly when they walked together. When he saw her, his chest opened and fireworks exploded. She was this star, this enormous field of gravity that he was hopelessly caught in, destined to forever orbit. If that's not love...

"It's a fair question." Mom spoke up.

Grandmother doesn't move, but her shoulders rise with a long, deep breath. "I didn't say it didn't feel good. The point of true love is not happy feelings. It's to do what is required in that moment. Good feelings may result, but that's not the point."

Colors spread across the distorted panes of glass as a car eases into the circle driveway.

"It is difficult to truly love." Grandmother opens the door.

Aunt Rhonnie is climbing the steps. The fair-headed blood-related duo is behind her. Henry is locked on him like crosshairs tracking a buck.

Breathing becomes difficult. It feels like a wool blanket has been pulled over Oliver's mouth. Each step his cousin takes, another layer is added.

"What's so urgent, Mother?" Aunt Rhonnie asks.

"Come inside."

She steps aside to let Henry and Helen go first. A smirk snarls deep into Henry's cheek, his eyes hooded like a viper. Aunt Rhonnie brings her open hand behind him, cuffing him in the back of the head.

"Stop smiling. Get in there."

Henry and Helen stand to the side, their shoes shiny and their clothes snug and wrinkle-free. Their fair skin appears to have avoided sunlight for too long, almost vampire-like in its paleness. Aunt Rhonnie lowers her movie-star glasses and peers at Oliver's mom.

"What are you doing?"

"Reliving old memories."

Aunt Rhonnie's eyes narrow.

"What do you know about the garage?" Grandmother asks. Aunt Rhonnie turns, but Grandmother is standing in front of Henry and Helen. The twins exchange confused looks.

"Tell me. Now."

"There's a car inside," Helen says. "Is that what you mean?"

"Have I not told you to stay away?" They agree, in unison. "Have you been inside the garage, then?"

"No," they say.

"Have you ever tried to go inside?"

There's a pause. Without looking at each other, they decide not to test Grandmother's truth detector. Together, they nod.

"Mother, really?" Aunt Rhonnie says. "This couldn't be done on the phone?"

Her death ray only works in person.

"Olivah says the garage was unlocked for him." Grandmother leans closer to Henry. Her nose twitches like she's smelling the truth. "He took something that belongs to me. Something very special. What do you know about this?"

A dark shade falls over Henry. The joyless smile is replaced with grim focus.

"Well?"

"Nothing, Grandmother," Henry says. "We've never even smelled the inside of the garage."

She stands in front of him. Oliver, once again staring at the tight bun, feels Henry's eyes as if they are boring through Grandmother to latch onto him.

"What's the big deal, Mother?" Aunt Rhonnie says. "So they want to see the car. I hardly think this deserves an investigation."

Grandmother steps away; her hands fold behind her back.

Henry, his stare once again fixed on Oliver, says, "If I may speak?"

"Continue," Grandmother says.

"What else has he done?"

A cold shank of fear drives down Oliver's legs, spiking his heels into the step. He can't feel his thighs and knows to keep his knees locked or he'll fall like a boneless bag.

"I'd like to have a word with Henry and Helen," Grandmother intones. "Alone."

"Oh, for God's sake," Aunt Rhonnie mutters.

"Come along." Grandmother exits the foyer, quietly padding down the hall. Henry lingers after Helen until Aunt Rhonnie tells him to get his butt in gear. Oliver avoids looking at them.

Once in the kitchen, their voices murmur. Oliver, Mom and Aunt Rhonnie concentrate to make out what is so top secret until the back door closes. Silence falls like heavy snow.

"Get off the step," Aunt Rhonnie says. "You look ridiculous, Deb."

"That's the point."

Aunt Rhonnie cusses. "I need a drink."

She slams the front door on the way outside. The pointy ends of her high heels hammer the steps and chisel the sidewalk. Several moments later, the base line of a synthesized beat vibrates through the front door. Aunt Rhonnie sits alone in the car.

Mom begins laughing. "Come on."

She steps off and stretches. Fear punches Oliver between the ribs. His ears prick for sound coming from the back of the house, aware that old ninja shoes can still be watching. Mom pulls him by the elbow.

Surprisingly, he doesn't fold like a book. His legs are still solid.

She walks to the kitchen, rifling through the cabinets for a glass, whistling while she does it. *She's done this before.*

When Oliver gets the courage, he follows. Mom is in the dining room, but a glass of tea is waiting next to the sink. He's not thirsty, but takes a sip. He grabs something to eat to bring his sugar up. He'll need a blood test.

Outside, standing in front of the garage window with her back to the house, Grandmother is talking to the twins. Oliver jumps to the side and, a few seconds later, eases in view.

Henry is looking at him.

But that's not why Oliver's knees go limp-noodle.

He's wearing a metal glove.

18

Aunt Rhonnie sits in the car for hours.

She's on her phone with a cup of Starbucks. A grande. Occasionally, she walks around the circle drive with cup in hand, waving it in a slow circle. Eventually, she goes home.

The twins stay.

That night, dinner is quiet. Almost silent. Oliver doesn't look up from his plate. Henry and Helen clear the table but leave the dishes for Oliver. He doesn't mind.

Oliver locks himself in his bedroom. He searches for the wooden orb, yearning to feel the vibrations in his arm like a fat beetle shaking its wings. It's gone. *Where could it be?*

He hears footsteps outside his door in the middle of the night.

The next morning, the twins are gone. There are chores by his name. Henry's and Helen's names aren't on the board. That afternoon he sees them returning from across the field. Dinner is almost as quiet as the first night.

This goes on for a week.

Oliver stays in bed the next morning. He eats his stash of energy bars to keep his sugar balanced. It's not quite lunch when he leaves. He pauses on the second floor. The bedroom doors are open. The house, a veritable motion detector, popping when someone yawns, is silent. He backs up a step, then two. The blood pushes through his veins in gushing waves. He clutches the railing.

His socks, hanging off the toes, allow him to slide quietly, not silently, but quietly toward Henry's and Helen's rooms. He stops midway at the bathroom, listening before continuing.

Henry's room is first.

Oliver peeks around the open door. His head vibrates with excitement. He takes a deep breath and steps inside. The bed is made, the corners tucked and the bedspread smooth. The top of the dresser is clean, like the floor. No one would know someone lived here.

Rule #980: Live like you don't exist.

Oliver looks under the bed, where dusty bunnies have been exterminated. He doesn't touch the bed, afraid a wrinkle will give him away. After listening for signs of life, he crosses over to the dresser and pulls open the top drawer.

It's full of clothes.

All the drawers are full. The shirts are neatly folded, the pants pressed and creased. Even the underwear is organized next to rows of socks lined up like soldiers. At first, Oliver hoped to see something without touching anything. There's one thing he wants to find more than anything else, even more than the wooden orb. Something that would ensure that he wasn't imagining, that this isn't a dream.

The metal glove.

Were they just pretending they couldn't go into the garage? It was one thing for Grandmother to get weird, but she acted like they were in on it. And Aunt Rhonnie and Mom still didn't seem to have a clue. But if I find that glove, it'd be proof the weird includes his cousins. If I find it, I could put it on.

But it's not there. And he's not going to move a single sock. He's already beginning to wonder if he's left footprints in the hall. He eases the last drawer closed.

"There you are."

Oliver's heart rockets into his throat, bulldozing blood into his head. Darkness spills into his vision, and he steadies himself on the dresser, turning to see someone in the doorway. His heartbeat slams past his eardrums.

"Looking for your cousins?" his mom says.

"No," he says. After several breaths, but still clutching the dresser, he adds, "Not really."

"I need to talk to you."

Oliver slides out of the bedroom while she adjusts the headband that holds her hair off her face. She's wearing fewer earrings than usual, just a couple in each lobe. Oliver uses the restroom first, just in case Henry or Helen come upstairs and see them standing outside their bedrooms. When he comes out, Mom has her shirt tucked in.

"How do I look?" she asks.

"Good. Are you going somewhere?"

"Sort of. I've got a job at the bookstore down the street from that café you go to."

"Little Professor?"

"That's the one. It's just shelving books and running the cash register, but it's something."

His mom was never good with real jobs. She always got bored. It was the whole punching a clock and taking orders and evaluations. She referenced Pink Floyd a lot when she complained, that humans weren't meant to sit in rows and march in lines. Sometimes she got fired, but mostly she just stopped going. They didn't have much money, but that never bothered Oliver. He didn't know he was poor until he got older.

Texas, though, was the first time his mom borrowed money. The lenders were coming for everything. Hard to start a career when you're standing in a hole. Oliver often wondered which one was deeper: the one back in Texas or the one Grandmother dug in her childhood.

"Is that what you wanted to talk about?"

"Yeah. That and moving out of here. I looked around for apartments and figured we could live in town. It'd take a few months to get enough for first and last months' rent, but we'd be out of here. How's that sound?"

"Great." He didn't shout or jump for joy, but a smile crossed his face.

"I know, I know. It wasn't fair to bring you here. I mean, I'm used to dealing with your grandmother. I won't be making much money, so we'll have to eat ramen noodles for a while."

"I'll eat paper for dinner, I don't care. I'll brush my teeth with soap."

"All right, relax. We're not moving into a dumpster. I want to stay in town, though. Your grandmother is getting older, and despite what she thinks, she'll need some help—"

Oliver wraps his arms around her, so elated that if he didn't hang on he'd float to the ceiling. They'll move to town, where he'll get phone service, where he can walk to the library. Where he'll see Molly.

He never thought he had much of a normal life compared to others. After living with Grandmother, he realized he was much closer than he thought. And he'd get back to that. Nothing could stop them from leaving. Nothing could change his mind. Least of all Henry.

He'll be happy we're leaving.

If only Oliver could avoid him until then. But the streak ends that night. Oliver thought Henry would be the last person to change his mind about leaving.

IT'S ALMOST MIDNIGHT.

Oliver can't sleep. He's imagining a two-bedroom apartment. He could put posters on the wall, not make his bed in the morning or do chores. Excitement trembles inside him like a surge of caffeine.

The silhouette of the windmill is dim in the open field. There's no snow to contrast against, not even patches in the shadows. Winter is officially over. The river must be swollen. Maybe it's even reached the bridge.

Oliver looks at the dresser, the outline barely visible in the dark room. There's still a journal in the attic. He hadn't thought about it since Grandmother snatched his book bag, afraid she'd see the thoughts in his eyes. *What must be in them that made her panic? Maybe she doesn't want us to know mental illness runs in the family. The world knows without those journals, trust me.*

And where's the seventh one?

Maybe now would be the time to go to the attic. He checks the time, thinking he could get down the hall and back within minutes—

Tap. Tap. Tap.

Oliver fumbles the phone. His teeth lock together, clamped by the raw grip of fear. Someone knocked on the door, but not with a knuckle. More like a fingernail, each rap separated by a long second. The last one sent gooseflesh across his shoulders as the nail dragged across the painted surface.

Tap. Tap. Tap.

…scratch.

The previous gooseflesh transforms into full-body shrink-wrap. Eyes wide, he stops breathing.

"Ollie."

Henry didn't so much as say his name as he breathed it. And not through the heavy door, but under it.

"Open the door, Ollie. I know you're in there. I know you're awake."

Oliver presses his hands over his ears. He could sit there all night. Henry couldn't get into the room unless he had a key. Which he probably does because it's just an old-fashioned lock.

"Olllllie."

If he's got a metal glove, he's got one of those keys.

"Open the dooooor."

Scratch.

With jerky movements, he slides across the room. The knob turns against the lock. Oliver gulps for air, drawing deep, smooth breaths, feeling his pulse flutter in his neck. He slides his feet—his dead cold feet—and holds the doorknob.

"Open," Henry says, "the door."

Oliver turns the oval end of the key. The latch tumbles in the assembly. He pulls it open. Henry stands upright in the doorway. Oliver can see the perfect posture of Grandmother possessing his body. The dim light from the bedroom window reveals a spreading grin.

"What do you want?" The words lack the quiver in Oliver's belly.

Henry, wearing a white robe with wide collars and soft-soled slippers, walks forward. Oliver steps aside. In the dark, he paces around the bed, hands in the square pockets of his robe. He looks around the room, tilting his head toward the dresser, the nightstand and bed, as if he might see something in the dark. Maybe he smells the binoculars still hidden under the bed.

"What do you know?" Henry flips the pillow and rubs his hand over the sheet beneath it.

"What?"

"What do you know, Ollie? What have you seen?"

"I don't know what you're talking about."

Henry sighs. With his back to the window, he's a silhouette. "I know you and your girlfriend have been out to the room, the one in the hill. When I specifically told you not to, you went out there, didn't you?"

Oliver hopes Henry can't see his chin quiver.

"You went into the garage. You read the journals. You snooped around."

Oliver shakes his head. Henry lets the seconds pile up. His breath leaks through his nostrils like steam.

"You don't know anything, Ollie. You know nothing about this family, about the property or Grandmother. You and your gypsy mother wander in here like homeless tramps and think, because we share DNA, you'll fit right in, but you're wrong. Tell me what you've seen."

"I don't know what you're talking about."

Henry moves a step closer, his features still hidden in the shadows.

"Was it magical? When you saw him, did it blow your mind? Did you think he'd have a corncob pipe and a carrot for a nose? He led you into that garage, took you right to the journals, didn't he? He put them right in your lap so that you'd know the story, and you ate it up. If you think he cares about you, you're wrong. He doesn't care about anyone."

"How do you know it's a *he*?"

"Kiss the journals goodbye. The snow is gone; he won't be back. It's just you, now. No more friends to protect you. No mystery snowballs flying out of the woods, no free rides to the open field. You're alone, Ollie."

"Why do you have a metal glove?" The cold quiver that usually buckles his knees is still there, but now there's an undercurrent of steel in his bones. His feet remain planted on the floor. He can feel the lines burning his palm as if he's squeezing the orb.

"It's not a *he*," Henry says. "Get it right; it's an *it*. And *it* doesn't like you."

"What's the metal glove for? Do you control them with it? I know Grandmother has one; I've seen her with it. Why does she have it? Why is the windmill charged and the forest shift and the garage locked? Why is all this a secret?"

The walls crackle. The momentum of courage pushes the questions out. He can't stop.

"What's the glove do?"

"You need to stop asking questions." Henry steps closer. Oliver can smell his mouthwash. "Nobody is ready for the answers, Ollie. Not you, not this town. Not the world. It's best if you and your mother be on your way. Before you get hurt, Ollie. It's not safe."

The menace dropped from the last line. There was no threat, like he actually meant it, he actually cared. Just for a moment. But the menace comes back in the very next breath.

"I know this is all wonderful and exciting. Everything is new and fun. There's so much mystery on the property, I get that. But it's not for you or your mother. You've got to go; it's for your own good. People disappear out here, and no one cares. You know that."

"I'm not scared of you."

"It's not me you should be scared of."

"We have a right to be here."

"I'm trying to help. Why can't you see that?"

"I don't think you are. The snowman doesn't, either. That's why he pulverized you with the snowball."

Henry hesitates. He doesn't move. And in that long moment, Oliver senses doubt covering something up.

"You're scared of him," Oliver says. "That's why you want us to leave."

"You have no idea what there is to fear."

"You're lying. He doesn't hate me, he hates you. And that scares the crap out of you."

It makes sense now. The snowman showed Oliver the journals. He kept Henry from taking his stocking cap and protected him from the things in the woods. Henry's not trying to protect Oliver; he's trying to save himself. Grandmother, too.

"You're forgetting something." Henry takes another step, and Oliver backs into the wall. His mouthwash smells like medicine. "Without snow, there is no snowman."

Oliver's hand is balled into a fist, aching to feel the grooves in his palm. He relaxes his hand, but reflexively squeezes. If he concentrates, he can feel the rough surface, sense the confidence surge through his arm. Cradle his chest.

Henry steps back and looks down.

Oliver doesn't realize he's staring at his clenching fist. Oliver finds himself cornered between the bed and window. He raises two fists and squares up.

He's never been in a fight, never thrown a punch. His dad taught him how to stand, how to hold his hands, but that was it. He smacked Oliver in the head, called him names, and laughed in his face. His dad bragged that Oliver couldn't even make him spill his drink.

Truth was, Henry was going to pound him, right there in the bedroom. Oliver could cry for help; his mom would come. She pulled him out of school and called the parents of a bully that took Oliver's lunch; she cussed out his dad when he came home with bruises on his arm. But for the first time, Oliver didn't want her to save him.

He was making a stand.

Henry catches Oliver's arm and, in one swift motion, twists it behind his back. Pressing his thumb into Oliver's wrist, he pries open his fingers to find an empty palm.

He shoves Oliver in the corner.

Oliver's huffing, fists in front again. He's bobbing on the balls of his feet. Next time Henry reaches, he'll crack the top of his head.

"Where is it?" Henry says.

"What?"

"You know. Hand it over."

"I don't have anything."

"Where'd it go?"

He shrugs. "Depends on what you want."

"Don't play, Ollie. You shouldn't have it."

"Have what?"

"The wood ball." Henry looks back at the door. "You don't know what you're doing, Ollie. You don't know anything. Now where is it?"

The truth would make this easy. It would be safe. Oliver shifts his feet, bends at the knees, and tightens his fists. He wishes he had the orb, wishes he had something to protect, a reason to tense for a battle. If he did have the orb, he'd like to see Henry try to take it from him.

Henry makes a move, but it's a feint to flush Oliver out of the corner. Oliver doesn't buy it; instead, he lunges. Henry's caught off guard but quickly regains his balance, avoiding Oliver's swing, shoving his face into the down comforter. With Henry's knee in his back and a mouthful of fabric, Oliver panics to breathe. He wasn't ready to hold his breath, and his chest is already on fire.

"You think you're special?" Henry says in his ear. "I've been out here since I was born. I've been waiting for that snowflake to give me the orb, and you come out here with your dirtbag mother two months and I get a snowball in the face..."

Oliver flails, but Henry holds him down. It's almost too easy.

"It's not going to work that way, Ollie. We'll decide where the magic happens."

His words are hot on Oliver's ear, but the air sizzles in his head as he tries to breathe. Henry twists Oliver's arm, and, automatically, his fist opens.

"Where is it?" Henry's knee thuds in Oliver's back. "Where is it!"

"Enough," someone says, drily.

Henry leaps off.

Oliver rolls onto his back, sucking air while tears stream over his cheeks. Grateful it's dark, that maybe they can't see him cry, he wipes his face.

Grandmother stands in the doorway; Henry's next to her. His hair isn't even messed up. He bends slightly. Grandmother whispers in his ear. Without a glance back, he swiftly leaves. Oliver, still laboring to breathe, listens to him descend the stairwell to the second floor.

Grandmother closes the door.

Calmly, she crosses the room to stand at the window. Her steps, silent as always, are shorter and slower—an old woman rather than a taskmaster faces the view of the open field. The moonlight highlights her stoic features. Tonight, however, her cheeks are burdened with emotional weight. Her eyes catch the bluish light.

"Does your mother know?" she says just above a whisper.

"About what?"

She turns at the shoulders, her neck stiff. It's clear what she means. *The snowman.* Oliver shakes his head.

"I need to know the truth, Olivah. Does she know?"

"No."

"Then you will do me a favor?"

"Yes."

"Keep it that way."

She contemplates the view with her hands balled in the pockets of her sweater. Henry came for the wooden orb. She was waiting for it.

"I know the stories," Oliver says. His voice is shaky. "I read about the elven and Santa in the North Pole. The snowman, too. Is it all true?"

"Do you have the orb?"

He pauses. "I had it. But it's gone now."

She doesn't bother asking where the orb is. She knows.

She knows what he's seen. When she found the journals, she thought, perhaps, he was just prying where he shouldn't be. She was angry at the betrayal, but something else, too. It wasn't just reading the journals, it was that he found them. And maybe what else he might've found, such as the orb.

Is she scared? For me or herself?

"I saw the glove," Oliver says. "I've seen you wear it when you're outside, when you go to the garage. I've seen you with it late at night, out by the driveway. I know something haunts the property, that the woods shift and animals don't live here. The old windmill is powered by something I can't explain, and the house doesn't get electricity from the city. None of this makes sense any more than the...what I've seen out there."

Snowman, he thinks. But he can't say it.

"It's best you don't know what happens out here. Trust me, Olivah. Your mother, too." And then she whispers, her lips barely moving, "He should not have come to you."

"Who?"

Her eyes darken. Lips purse.

"He saved my life." Oliver's breathing is normal, but his heart still racing. "That night I was out past dark, I found the little room in the hill, the one Henry and Helen go to. There were things that came to life, that chased me. The snowman saved me, I think. I don't know what they were, but they were going to hurt me. Is that what you mean? Is that what you're protecting us from?"

Her eyelids fall for a long moment. She shakes her head.

"He saved me. He picked me up and carried me to the field right before you found me." Oliver steps closer but resists the urge to reach out. "What is he?"

"There are things in this world better left alone. But once discovered, there is no going back." She turns to him, struggling to hold that perfect posture. Moonlight glistens in her eyes. "We can only limit the harm."

She crosses the room. With her hand on the doorway, she says without looking back, "You'll move out, Olivah. I'd prefer it that way."

Silently, she disappears into the dark hallway. Even the stairwell doesn't betray her descent.

Oliver remains at the side of his bed. There are lines pressed into his palm as if he had been squeezing the orb. *He should not have come for you.*

It doesn't feel like a bad thing. The snowman is anything but that. But Grandmother seemed so concerned, so worried for him.

And his mom.

Oliver never thought he'd feel this way. Staring out the window, he can't help feel the weight of sadness Grandmother left behind.

I'm not the only one that wants to leave.

GRANDFATHER

Not all grandfathers are great.

19

A little bell rings.

Oliver ties a bandana over his head. It keeps his hair—bleached by the summer sun—out of his eyes when he leans over the sink and the sweat from running down his cheeks. For a while, he tied it back in a small ponytail, but once, in the middle of July's heat wave, when temperatures reached one hundred degrees three days straight, he had to dump a cappuccino when sweat dripped in the foam.

"A large latte with soy." Cath slaps the order on the counter. "The double cap ready?"

"Almost," Oliver says.

"We're backing up, O."

He doesn't tell her the frother is partially clogged because she didn't clean it when she closed up the night before. Instead, he pours the espresso in a circle—his signature—in the white foam. Cath pops her gum, her gothic eyeliner giving her black eyes.

The line at the counter is five deep. Oliver grabs the next ticket in line.

"Need some help?" Ms. Megan, a short woman with bobbed black hair that has the texture of straw, is pulling on a second sweater. It's September—two-sweater weather.

Oliver slides over two tickets. He always feels funny passing work off to the owner of the Smile Café, but she once said she didn't open the place to stand around. Not many bosses work harder than their employees.

"Can you close tonight?" Ms. Megan asks. "I forgot about my daughter's recital. I'll make it up to you."

"Yes."

"You sure?"

"No problem, Ms. Megan." He and Molly were going to the movies, but they could do that tomorrow.

"You're a lifesaver, O. What would I do without you?"

Ms. Megan locks her elbow around his neck and pulls him down to plant one on his temple. She didn't kiss Cath like that. Maybe that's why the eyeliner queen always looked like she was sucking a lemonhead.

Not many bosses had an employee like Oliver.

Homeschooling let him work whenever he wanted. And living in the apartment above the café didn't hurt. They had lived there all summer and hadn't missed rent yet. Ten months without being late was the best they'd ever done. Now that he was working, too, they would shatter that record.

He texts Molly about the change of plans. She texts back a sad face. "Stop by," he texts.

A happy face comes back.

It takes half an hour to catch up with the morning rush. Once the tickets are cleared, Ms. Megan sneaks back into the office to catch up on paperwork. Cath files her black nails. Oliver cleans out the frother in time for the next wave of commuters.

At times, he misses the property. Even Grandmother.

When he was sweating in the July heat, he imagined hiking through the cool shade and the spring-fed waters of the stream. He had only been out there once since moving out last May. The open field was a wildflower wonderland. He didn't explore it. He had tea with Grandmother, instead.

She looked tired.

Her cheeks were rosy where she'd applied makeup, but ashen beneath. She made very little eye contact. When tea was finished, she escorted them to the door, said she was tired. Oliver watched the windmill churn its slow grind in the sideview mirror.

"Non-fat, no foam, chai tea latte. Make it hot," Cath says.

Oliver goes to work. He doesn't have to look at who placed the order—Ms. Vera had not changed her drink since late May. Even in July, she liked her drink smoking hot.

He puts it in the microwave for thirty seconds and burns his hand taking it out. His arm begins to tingle. At first, he thinks maybe he caught his elbow on the counter and hadn't noticed. He'd done that once before, so focused on what he was doing he didn't realize he'd cut himself.

Not this time.

The burning creeps past his elbow and into his shoulder. He rubs his biceps. The tingling spreads across his chest and begins to hum around his heart. He hasn't checked his blood sugar since he woke up, but he'd never felt this before. Not even the time he forgot his supply pack and the car broke down on the interstate. He went hypo when his blood sugar soared and woke up in the hospital.

This is more like a stroke.

"O." Cath waves a ticket in his face. "Wake up."

He hands her Ms. Vera's chai latte and swallows. His throat is slightly numb. The room feels darker and the windows brighter. He could definitely use a stocking cap instead of the bandana.

Art, a heavyset regular, stomps his feet at the door. "It's going to be a long winter."

Art greets everyone on his way to the counter, wiping sawdust off his sleeve. No need to write down his order—three shots of espresso and extra foam. Oliver's hand throbs like he pulled a metal pipe from a bed of coals.

"Summer was hot enough to melt the shingles off a tool shed," Art says. "Now Old Man Winter is in town like he's pissed."

The rotund litigator's bald head looks damp. He blows into his hands.

"They're talking six inches," he adds.

Cath turns around. The frother is still quiet.

"Take a break, O." Ms. Megan tickles his back. "I got this."

Oliver takes a deep breath. He goes to the bathroom, splashes water on his face, and washes his hands. The tingling fades, but it's still wrapped around his chest. Even the bathroom feels dim.

He grabs a small coffee and heads to the front of the shop to get some fresh air and test some blood. He was up late the night before, texting with Molly and scrolling through social media. He'd already had a cup of coffee that morning. Sometimes he gets the jitters. *This is different.*

He steps outside and realizes Art wasn't brushing sawdust off his sleeves; he wasn't sweating.

It's snowing.

Large snowflakes are coming down. Oliver brushes it off the small metal chair outside the door. First snow since he left Grandmother's. And now his chest humming. His hand burning. He packs a snowball and holds it until his fingers are numb.

His hand still burns.

THE LIGHTS ARE OFF.

The fluorescent closed sign reflects off the dark windows and The Black Keys thump in the café. Oliver cleans the frothing nozzles. The counters are cleared except for a skinny latte in a to-go cup.

He loves to close. It's his little secret. He likes to pretend Ms. Megan sold the place to him and he lives upstairs. He comes down whenever he wants, makes killer coffee for his mom, and hangs out after hours with the music turned up. He wouldn't change a thing about the place, except maybe add a few more loungers. If code would allow it, a fire pole would make it easy to slide down from the apartment.

He washes out a cup and turns it upside down in the sink. He's maxed out on caffeine for the day, especially after that burning episode. He feels normal except for his hand. He touched the frother while it was steaming.

That doesn't explain the lines.

There's a light rapping on the window.

Molly is at the front door, huffing on the glass and drawing a smiley face, her finger poking through brown gloves with the tips cut off. She dyed her hair black and frosted her pigtails pink. Large snowflakes stick to her coat.

Oliver goes to the front, drying his hands. "We're closed."

"I need to speak to the manager."

"Password?"

"The what?"

"The password."

She pinches her bottom lip, thinking. "The pearl is in the river?"

Oliver turns the locks and sticks his face in the narrow opening. "Do you mean 'zee pearl iz in zee river'?"

"Ahoy, matey."

She plants a kiss on him, her lips moist with chapstick. Oliver pulls the bandana off his head and opens the door. The streetlights glow in the halo of falling snow. Four inches cover the sidewalk.

"Love what you've done with the place," she says, unwinding her scarf.

Oliver returns to the sink. Molly cradles the to-go cup and inhales the latte before sipping. She closes her eyes, a foamy mustache on her lip.

She tells him about her day at school: an upcoming homecoming dance and the football cheerleaders and the jocks that love them. Afterwards, she worked a shift at the library. Oliver wipes down the counters and equipment as she tells him about a storyteller that entertained a bunch of grade schoolers.

She stops to sing along with the Pixies.

Oliver runs one last pitcher of water through the frother. Fueled on non-fat latte, Molly tells him the storyteller's story—"wide...mouth... frog." She's on the last chorus as the frother runs out of steam. He turns the knob—

And jerks his hand back.

Oliver massages his palm when the sensation crawls up his arm again. A tingling net falls over his chest and tightens around his heart —warm, protective but stifling. A storm thrums in his head.

"Oliver?"

Molly's by his side. He's missing a chunk of time, long enough for her to come around the counter. The storm continues howling in his ears. He rubs his chest and throat.

"What's wrong?" Molly asks. "Your blood sugar low?"

He dosed himself just before she got there. Besides, this isn't diabetes; at least nothing he's ever experienced. He describes the sensations, says it happened that morning, too. Maybe he's dehydrated. He hasn't had water, come to think of it. Or tinnitus, Molly says. She's heard of people getting hit with mysterious ringing.

"Maybe you need a doctor," she says.

"I'm all right. I'll drink water."

Molly helps turn over the last couple of chairs and hang the damp wash towels. He takes a breather, downs a bottle of water, and he's already feeling better. Besides, he doesn't want to ruin the night.

He stands up, gives it a second.

"Sounds like an allergic reaction," Molly says. "Better check what you're drinking."

She's got a point. They cracked open a new brand of coffee beans that morning. He needed to ask Ms. Megan if anyone else feels this way. It would kill business if they did.

Oliver grabs his book bag and slings it over his shoulder. Molly's waiting by the front door. The flap is unzipped and spills books.

He freezes in the grip of another tingling wave.

There's a book on the floor. One he didn't pack.

A book he hasn't seen since last winter.

He squats down to pick it up, staying on one knee as he brushes the leathery cover. The bottom corner is broken with three spots of spilled ink on the edge.

The journal from the attic.

"Where'd you get that?" Molly asks.

"I don't know."

His hand throbs. He turns it over. In the red glow of the CLOSED sign, they see a pattern in his palm.

The intricate lines of the orb.

20

The next day, the snow becomes slush.

Molly waits on the sidewalk. Snowmelt drips from the café awning. Oliver leaves with a dish towel over his shoulder. His hair curls from beneath the stocking cap.

"You all right?" she asks.

He turns his hands up. The redness has faded, but the lines are still there, like he'd been squeezing the orb. The warm tingles have disappeared, but the invisible net of claustrophobia remains. Oliver looks down the sidewalk. The Little Professor sign hangs four doors down. Mom won't get off work for another hour.

"You ready?" he asks.

Molly nods.

Oliver clutches the book bag in one hand. It hasn't left his sight.

There's a green door around the corner and a flight of noisy stairs. The oak door slams behind them as they run up the steps. The apartment is down a short hallway, first door on the left. He holds the door open for Molly. Inside, it smells like a coffee grinder. The couches and chair were all purchased from garage sales. To the left is the kitchen where the refrigerator rattles.

Nothing matches the olive green walls.

"There's not much time." He slings the book bag on the couch. A dust cloud wafts into a beam of light. Oliver slides the journal out. He feels slightly dizzy.

"I still don't get it," Molly says. "How'd it get in your backpack?"

He had told her that he recognized the journal. It's the one from the attic, the one he dropped when he saw Grandmother in the driveway. And this buzzing sensation, he says, that's what he felt whenever he squeezed the orb or when the snowman was nearby.

Without snow, there is no snowman.

"Snow." He turns toward her. "There hasn't been snow since we moved out, not until yesterday. I think my hand started burning when it started snowing."

"And the journal shows up?"

He shakes his head. "I don't know."

"I think he's looking for you. He wants you to know something."

He never should've come to you.

Grandmother said that, she thought the snowman had come for Oliver. Henry did, too. He was angry that he'd been out there all his life and never got the orb. Grandmother, though, wasn't jealous. She was worried. He didn't know if she meant for him to hear that. Maybe she thought once he was off the property, he'd be safe.

Maybe she's wrong.

The binding cracks as he opens the journal. The coarse pages are musty. Oliver reads aloud the portions he had seen while in the attic, about the day his great-grandfather, Malcolm Toye, first left the ice room. He went above to see the elven. And met the one that saved him.

Made of snow.

IT STOOD TEN FEET. Maybe fifteen.

Its legs were thick like timber, the long arms bowing from a stout chest that pulsed not from the beat of a heart but something more precise and mechanical. The head was wide like a turret and featureless except for two indentions where eyes would be.

I expected its steps to crack the ice or, at the very least, make the world shudder. But it was soft and silent. The elven reached for it as it passed, clinging to its legs and hanging from the swinging arms, laughing as they fell and rolled.

So powerful and intimidating, like a creature carved from a nightmare, that I expected to quiver as it neared, but I found myself smiling. A feeling of warmth radiated inside my chest, pulsing in waves corresponding with the thumping of its chest. There's no other way to describe what I felt when it stopped in front of me.

It was love.

"*He is an abominable,*" Merry said. "*He protects us, but he has limits. He risked his life to find you, Malcolm.*"

Life? I thought. It wasn't breathing, and it was made of snow, but she acted as if it was alive. How could I argue? It stood over me, filling me with a sense of belonging.

"*Why?*" *I asked.* "*Why would it do that?*"

"*Love is powerful,*" Merry said. "*Love is why we exist.*"

I remembered the locket when she said that, wishing I could see you one last time. Did the snowman know that?

"*Does it have a name?*" *I asked. It seemed a silly question, to ask if it had a name.*

"*Flury,*" *she said.*

"*Flury,*" *I repeated, and tears filled my eyes. He was a giant white blur when I reached for him and said,* "*Thank you, Flury.*"

He embraced my arm, and the wind began to whip around us. The elven began to cheer, and when I looked up, three more just like him had appeared as if the snow simply swirled up from the ice. They were distinctive in shape, but all massive.

And the feeling around my chest, the love that had ensnared my heart, made me think that whether they were made of snow or flesh, these creatures were more human than anything I had ever met.

"OH MY GOD." Molly is limp on Oliver's arm. "Not in my dreams, I never would've thought..."

She leaps up, fanning her face.

"I think I'm going to cry. Don't look, it's not pretty."

There's a lump in Oliver's throat. He's not about to cry or admit it, but the passage was devastating. The handwriting started crisp, as usual, and slowly turned shaky. At the end, it was almost illegible. He must've been crying when he wrote it.

What's more, Oliver knew what he felt. There was a connection inside him. It was that buzzing vibration that was netting his chest, as if synchronizing with the towering snowman that looked intimidating but, the closer it got, was soft and warm.

Love.

"I believe." Molly's hiding her face. "I believe all this. Do you?"

A snowman and mysterious burns are on his mind. And something about the quiet footsteps, the way the snowman walked so silently. It reminds him of Grandmother.

"Expect the unexpected," he mumbles.

The apartment walls shudder.

The door at the bottom of the stairwell had slammed. Mom's heavy steps echo in the hallway. Oliver shoves the journal under the couch cushion and scrambles to find the remote. Molly grabs it from beneath the coffee table, pushing the buttons as she collapses against him. The journal crackles beneath her.

Keys jingle.

The door opens.

"Hey," Mom says. "What's going on?"

Oliver and Molly, sitting upright and stiff, both say, "Nothing."

"Nothing? I thought you were working?"

"Lunch. Molly and I are just chilling, getting away from the café for a minute, you know."

"Oh, yeah?" She points at the television. "Just catching a little *Dr. Phil*?"

Dr. Phil was introducing owners and their pets to a psychic. And Molly was wiping her eyes.

"It's sad," Molly says. "They lost their beagle for a year, and now he's back, and...he said he missed them."

"Really."

"And I'm on my period."

"Okay."

Molly blows her nose. Oliver's arm is caught behind her at a weird angle, but he's not about to move. Mom goes to the bedroom. They can hear her laughing. She's smiling when she returns with a folder. "I'll be back in half an hour, just need to drop these off. You two be all right?"

"Yeah," Oliver says.

She grabs a bottle of water from the fridge. "Why don't you watch *Ellen*. It's a little more upbeat."

They remain still until the steps are quiet. The pictures on the walls shudder when the street door slams.

"Period?"

"I panicked. She thought we were doing stuff. I was under pressure. I think it worked."

Oliver knows it didn't, but if his mom thought they were getting down on the couch, he was all right with that. It was better than the truth. He stalks to the door and makes sure the stairwell is empty, swinging his arm around to get the feeling back. Molly blows her nose and balls up the tissue.

"I'm all right," she says. "Let's read before she gets back."

"You sure?"

She nods. They pull the journal from beneath the cushion. The cover is creased. Oddly, he's worried Grandmother will be mad. *That would be the least of my troubles.*

Oliver lays the journal open, and Molly leans into him.

The entries follow his daily life. He's rarely alone, always surrounded by elven that, apparently, are the happiest beings on the planet—constantly playing and singing. Malcolm soon yearns for solitude. *It's like living with puppies,* he says. He frequently complains about being trapped, how the elven never answer his questions about home. Once he mentions Santa, the fat man, but doesn't get to see him. *They don't trust me.*

His spirits pick up when he's assigned to different areas of the colony. To stay, he hopes that's not what they have in mind. Toward the end of the journal, he visits the energy production division, and things get interesting.

APRIL 6, 1882.

It's become clear that the human race knows nothing.

Whenever the elven explain something, they speak like it is common sense, yet I understand nothing. They push buttons and light appears. Magic happens. Nog continues to correct me, saying magic ceases when understanding arrives. Then it becomes science.

They don't burn coal or wood. They use the sun and wind and ocean currents, somehow converting these natural resources into power. I suppose that makes sense, but then they took me to the science lab.

In the science lab, I was hunched over to avoid the low ceiling, eventually getting on my knees while Nog slid next to me. Fascination kept the impending sense of claustrophia at bay. These elven wore long coats. They were much more serious than all the other elven, and I liked that. Too much joy only makes my heart heavier. Their efforts to raise my spirits only sink them deeper. Do they not understand you are my only happiness?

Our last stop, though, something felt strangely familiar. There were four spherical objects suspended in the air. They were about twice the size of my fist and gleamed like polished steel with intricate designs carved into their surfaces. They felt like the abominables.

"Each one is at the heart of their body," Nog said.

He went on to explain that the sphere creates an electromagnetic field that pulls snow around it, forming a body of sorts. The spheres also served as power storage, achieving enough density that their low-end gravitational field allows them to generate power and something about fusion. He pulled a sphere from his pocket, one small enough to fit in the palm of his hand.

"This," he said, "could power London." He claimed that houses could be automatically heated in the winter and cooled in the summer. He said there was more they could do with a power source like this, but it was beyond my imagination. Perhaps he doesn't realize they had already exceeded my imagination when I arrived.

Nog pocketed the smaller sphere and put on his special glove before extending his hand. One of the spheres floated to him. He held it like a crystal balll. "This is more than a snowman," he said. "When an elven passes from this world, he or she is absorbed inside. Their wisdom is contained in the heart of the abominable. It's what allows the elven to grow, to remain peaceful. To learn."

I will tell you this, my love. Standing in the presence of the spheres filled me with peace. I do not want to admit this, but in that moment, I wished for nothing. I felt no yearning to be anywhere else but here. That this moment was perfect, with or without you.

And I hate myself for feeling that.

THEY FLIP THROUGH THE PAGES, stopping at some of the sketches. Molly continues to sniffle. The apartment rattles. His mom returns, and they're sitting on the couch, the journal beneath the cushion and the television off.

She doesn't ask why.

Before he goes back to the café, Molly says, "I want a snowman."

Me too, he thinks.

21

Town Square is a long rectangle of paths and cozy benches beneath a grove of shade trees, where locals sat on a patchwork of blankets to listen to a string quartet on Wednesday nights in summer while kids played.

Oliver leans his bike—a beater with knobby tires he found in a dumpster—against a beech tree where initials are carved into the elephant-skin bark. He drops his book bag on a bench, the boards partially decayed with lichen clinging to the armrests.

Mom is at Grandmother's house for Sunday afternoon tea. "Grandmother," she said, "thinks you're too old for tea. I don't know what that means, but you don't have to go."

He knew exactly what it meant: *It's not safe.*

The trees are dripping. The four inches of snow had all but melted. Oliver leans forward, cold snowmelt thwapping the back of his weatherproof jacket as he kneads his palm. The pain is gone, but not the lines.

Thoughts rattle in his head. A landslide of ideas and emotions keep him buried. They roll him upside down until nothing makes sense.

"Hey." Molly's wearing a short-sleeved Clash concert T-shirt with a wool scarf dangling over the handlebars of her mountain bike. Her hair is tied beneath a red bandana. "How's the hand?"

He displays his palm, fingers spread. She bends over and squints, tracing the intricate pattern. "It looks like a brand. Does it hurt?"

He shakes his head.

Oliver pulls his stocking cap over his ears. Side by side, they pedal out of Town Square. A mile down the road, they turn onto a path and grind their way into the countryside. By the time they reach a meadow, their backs are spotted and their tired legs splattered with mud. They spread a blanket and lay out sandwiches, chips and dip with a thermos of dark roast coffee. The journal is placed in the middle like the guest of honor, a giant crease in the cover.

They eat in silence, letting the coffee hum through their exhaustion while staring at the Rockies, clouds sitting at the peaks like fluffy halos.

"I thought about your great-grandfather all night," Molly says. "I don't think I slept."

She digs a spiral-bound notebook from her backpack. The pages are filled with sketches and notes in bubbles and arrows connecting thoughts. It's half full. The first page is a diagram of the property, with house, garage, windmill and hobbit house all labeled, and the river running through it.

Oliver didn't sleep much, either, but he didn't write anything down. Wouldn't have made sense if he did.

"Let's start with the property." She drops a finger on a square. "There's the house and mysterious power and there's Flury. I think it's obvious, don't you?"

"What?"

"Your great-grandfather brought back one of those orbs."

"How?"

"I don't know, just saying one of those orbs solves the power mystery. The journal said one of those small ones would power London. That explains why your grandmother has never paid a power bill. It might also explain how the trees shift and compasses don't work."

"It does?"

"It seems like magic, right? Maybe that just means we don't understand, like Nog said."

"But my orb was made of wood."

"Prototype." She flips a few pages, taps a sketch. "All those plans in the garage looked like someone was designing an orb. Your grandfather was a mechanic or engineer or something, right?"

"Yeah, but those are my great-grandfather's journals. And maybe he built the orbs instead of stealing them."

"I didn't say he stole them. Maybe the elven gave them to him and sent him home."

Oliver retreats into his thoughts. Molly was being nice. She's thinking the same thing he is: there's no way they gave him an orb. They claimed to be reluctant to join the human race. It seemed unlikely they'd give him something that could power London and wish him a Merry Christmas.

That means he's a thief.

"Maybe he invented one," Oliver says.

"The journals are in the early 1880s. He built the house in 1901, so that means he returns within twenty years. People were still riding horses, so I doubt he invented a cold fusion power orb. Maybe he carved the orb you had, but it's more likely he brought back a functioning orb."

Oliver rubs his palm, wishing the evidence wasn't pointing in this direction.

"Look, we don't know if he stole one or not, so let's not assume." She rubs his shoulder.

"Okay."

"What we do know is that one of those orbs can power the house. It would also explain how a snowman can be running around the property."

"Abominable."

"Right. Abominable. Your great-grandfather brought back an orb and that explains Flury. So, the question is this: did he bring back more, and where are they?"

"Running around the woods."

"I doubt it. You read what that lab looked like when he saw them as power generators. I think they're hiding somewhere on the property."

"You think there's more than one."

"There's one in Flury, but I think there are others for power. It's just a guess, a weird guess. But I consider us experts in the weird. So let's assume there are more than one. Where would they be?"

"The woods. They chased me that one night."

"Maybe. But there's something different about them, I'm guessing. Your grandmother seems kind of scared of them."

He's not so sure she's not scared of Flury.

"The garage."

"Wrong." She turns to an elaborate sketch of the elven science lab. "I told you, I didn't sleep much. This is what I think the lab looked like. Those orbs were levitating on special equipment to generate power. I doubt she has them on a shelf behind a bag of peanuts."

Oliver describes the house. There's no basement that he knows of, and none of the rooms are suspicious. "It's got to be the garage."

"I know what you mean, I can smell the weird in there, too. But I think it's just a place your grandfather tinkered and kept the journals."

"But the footlocker wasn't there." It's logical, he knows, but his gut feeling tells him there's more to the garage. Grandmother didn't know those journals were under the bench.

"Right," Molly says. "Which makes me think..."

She goes back to her master sketch, accidentally smudging it with hummus. She thumps the far off circle.

"The hobbit house?" Oliver says. That nook definitely smells weird —a bunker in the trees with wifi. And the twins go out there most of the day. "I guess. But there's nothing out there, either. We searched for secret doors and didn't find one, remember?"

"I know, but maybe we missed something. Think we can get back out there?"

"Grandmother letting me explore the property?" He chuckles. "There's a better chance I'll turn into a snowman."

She lies her head on his lap, eating chips. "Maybe you're right, it was just your grandfather's man cave, a place a guy can go to hang with his snowman. You know, kick back, play a little catch...or whatever you do with an abominable. What would you do? I mean, besides throw snowballs and fly and pummel things."

"Protect," Oliver says.

"Protect what?"

"I don't know. That's what the snowmen did for the elven. Maybe grandfather has one to protect him against those things in the trees."

Silence stretches out as they recede into their own thoughts. At one time, Oliver would have wanted Flury to protect him from Grandmother, but he'd seen her when she was vulnerable. She was scared. *Maybe she's not scared of Flury. Maybe it's those things in the woods.*

"Last thing." Molly tosses the notebook on his lap. The windmill is circled with question marks. "What's that for? Because I know it's not about the wind. It turns like a clock."

"Maybe that's the power center."

"That's what I'm thinking. Maybe those orbs are under it. Is there a door or anything under it?"

He shakes his head. "Just dying grass."

"Maybe that's why it's dying."

They watch the clouds float past them, each one looking like a snowman. Her breathing turns heavy, and Oliver shuts his eyes. He's falling under the temptation of a dream, the sun on his cheeks and birdsong in his head.

"I know one thing," Molly says.

"Yeah?"

"Flury needs you."

Oliver remains awake with that thought, but sleep eventually pulls him under, and he dreams of dark rooms and silver orbs. When he wakes up, he's heavy with a thought, a realization that's finally come to the surface.

Flury needs help.

22

Oliver ends up reading the creased journal nine times.
He sneaks it into the bathroom in the mornings, takes it to work, and reads it on breaks. At night, he reads it by the light of his phone. Each time, he feels empty and sad when he finishes.

Helpless.

What good was a great discovery like the elven (and a man named Santa) if the price was separation from the one you love?

"Can I visit Grandmother with you?" he asks his mom one morning.

"Why?"

"No reason. Haven't seen her in a while."

Mom adjusts her headband. "Let me ask her. She hasn't been feeling well this summer."

This summer?

She's in her eighties, so it could be that. Or the lack of snow.

October is dry and warm; not a single snowflake falls. His hand returns to normal; the lines vanish. Oliver reads the journal five more times. He and Molly refine their theories, but there's little they can do when Grandmother "doesn't feel like company."

Halloween falls on a Thursday. Oliver is wiping down tables, a black eye patch to go along with his red bandana and the plastic sword on his hip, when Mom walks through the café door.

"Want to come?" she asks. "Just dropping off some groceries, we won't be long."

"Grandmother said it was okay?"

"No. But it'll be quick."

He takes an early lunch and grabs a few packets of pumpkin-flavored tea. Mom's car is parked at Town Square, where straw bales, scarecrows and various stuffed displays haunt the grounds. The roads are steep and curvy. He remembers feeling carsick when they first arrived.

It's almost been a year.

The gate is closed, but Mom has a remote. A chill crawls down his back. Unlike the vibrating hum back in the café, this sensation injects an inky cloud of fear beneath his skin. A second wave of creepy-crawlies hits him when the house comes into view. There's no need to decorate it—*it is Halloween.* The sunlight falls around it, not on it.

Mom swings around the circle drive and, unlike a year ago when she strangled the steering wheel, begins humming.

"Did you ever go into the garage when you were little?" Oliver asks.

"All the time."

"Anything weird?"

"Unless you consider tools weird." She finds a tube of chapstick in her purse. "She means well, Oliver. I think she had a hard life, a lot of buried pain. You got to remember, she grew up in a different era. Love was different back then."

"Is that what it is?"

"We all have unmet needs. Until we recognize them, life is hard."

"That doesn't make you angry?"

"No one can *make* me angry, only trigger angry thoughts."

"You don't have angry thoughts?"

"Oh, I have plenty."

She pats his knee and gets out. He grabs a box of groceries from the back seat. Mom rings the doorbell. A year ago, she waited for Grandmother to open it. Now she walks in.

"Mother?" The silent house answers with a groan.

Oliver takes the box to the kitchen. The smell of old wood mixed with shadows makes for a distinct brew, what Molly calls "the weird." *I smell it.*

Mom calls a few more times. She begins unpacking the box and finds the pumpkin tea.

"Did you bring this?"

"Yeah."

"Oh, that's sweet of you."

"I thought she might like it."

"She'll hate it."

"I know."

The house groans again, unfamiliar with the sound of laughter. Mom gives him a quick hug. "See if your grandmother is upstairs."

Oliver lets her finish unpacking the supplies. At the staircase, he stops on the bottom and looks at his hand—no redness or swelling. No lines.

No snow.

He studies the old framed photos on his way to the second floor, stopping at the illustration of a shipwreck. *How did he get back? And why doesn't anyone know about it?*

History books don't mention any survivors beyond the initial ones. No reports of a deckhand returning home months later—fat, healthy and hairy. It's like he snuck back.

And if he had an orb, why didn't he share it with the world?

Grandmother isn't on the second floor or the third. Oliver goes to his former bedroom. The bed is made without a wrinkle, as if no one ever slept in it. It seems like just yesterday he was trapped between the bed and the window, Henry pushing his face into the pillow, driving his knee into his back, searching for the orb.

What was he going to do with it?

The shrill cry of the windmill calls. The rusted blades make a quick turn in a rogue breeze before resuming their methodical rotation. Across the field behind the autumn foliage, the hobbit house is hidden and the stream runs cold and deep. There are no tracks in the snowless grassy field.

Oliver reaches under the bed blindly and finds the binoculars still wedged in the bedsprings. The trees are too far to see much, even with the binoculars. If the orbs were hidden in the hobbit house, why weren't there lights or heat? Molly and he decided one late night in the café, on their third latte, the orbs weren't out there; she had checked for secret doors. It had to be at the windmill since it carried the strange current.

He aims the binoculars at the corroded structure. A gust of wind comes across the grass and swings the windwheel one full turn. The windmill cries out. There's no room in the structure for a door. The grass around it is shorter and tanner than the surrounding field, like a blast of radiation. There could be a hidden entrance in the sod, but there are no outlines or handle. He could thump the ground for a hollow sound. It might be hard to explain what he's doing. *Just searching for a secret entrance, Grandmother. You know, where you hide the orbs great-grandfather stole.*

He focuses directly beneath the windmill, hoping to see the faint outline of a trapdoor or the loop of a handle. There's neither. He sweeps all around the legs. It's the third time around he sees something.

It's not what he's looking for.

There, leaning on the back side of the nearest footing, is the corner of something tan and rectangular. He checks the other legs for something similar, maybe a strut that's come loose or wooden block. It's hard to tell from the bedroom, even with the binoculars. It's the color of worn leather.

The sixth journal.

There are seven of them. Grandmother has four, the fifth one is in his backpack.

Oliver forces himself to walk quietly down the steps. He's halfway to the kitchen when he realizes he's still holding the binoculars and tucks them under his belt. The smell of pumpkin is in the kitchen.

"She's not upstairs." His voice is slightly pitched. "Have you seen her?"

"No, I haven't," she says from the pantry.

"I'll look outside."

"Check the garage."

He moves to the sink, keeping his back to the pantry so she doesn't see the binoculars bulging under his shirt. He can see the far wall of the garage. *The car is gone.*

"I'll go look."

Oliver rushes to the front of the house. After a quick scout around, he begins walking. Once he's in the open, in full view of the family room picture window, he sprints. The little square is still at the foot of the windmill, and the closer he gets, the more he's convinced.

It's a journal.

He picks it up. *Has it been out here since the last snow?* He slides it under the binoculars. Using the heel of his boot, he thumps the ground in search of a hollow sound or the hard panel of a hidden door. He doesn't quite make it to the center when something moves near the garage.

Oliver turns sideways behind a leg.

It's like trying to hide a jelly bean behind a toothpick, but the figure walking toward the house cuts across the grass in evenly measured steps. *Grandmother.*

Her head is slightly bowed, watching the grass in front of her. Oliver is too close to the coarse iron leg, the waves of power twisting his stomach like a carnival ride. He dry heaves but stays in place. She appears lost in thought, not looking up until she's reaching for the back door.

As soon as the door closes, he's on the run.

The windmill sucked the strength from his legs, and he stumbles. Regaining his momentum, he runs a crooked line to the car without another fall and stashes the journal and binoculars beneath the seat. He takes a moment to catch his breath. Thankfully, a bag of apples is still on the back seat. He can use that as an excuse for going to the car. With his heart pounding in his throat, he stops on the porch.

The car wasn't in the garage. And it didn't drive up.

Another frigid wave passes through him.

He goes around the right side of the house and stops before walking through the backyard. There's a stitching pain in his side. He takes several deep breaths with his hands on his hips. He's got to look normal, just a casual walk across the lawn. They'll see him from the kitchen. He counts to ten. Still slightly dizzy, he steps into the open with a bag of apples in one hand.

And stops in the middle of the yard.

He meant to just take a glance, like he was looking for Grandmother. But once he can see inside, his feet turn to concrete.

The car is there.

23

O liver parts the curtains.

Sleet ticks off the glass, settling on the window ledge and frosting the sidewalk around Town Square. Someone is parking right below their apartment. An older woman gets out and goes into the café.

The journal sits on the coffee table. *Number six.*

The leather is in worse shape than the previous ones, the surface water stained and scratched. *How long had it been out there?*

Oliver flips through pages. This one is thicker than the others. He resists the urge to turn the pages slower, to stop at random and read a page, just one. But he promised he wouldn't.

He looks at the time.

After another ten minutes of pacing, the apartment walls rattle. Having second thoughts, he stuffs the journal under the cushion. There's light tapping on the door.

Molly slowly opens the door.

"What took you so long?" he says.

"I got hung up. You didn't read it, did you?"

"No. No, I swear. I'm on break, but Ms. Megan's getting impatient."

"You closing tonight?"

"Yeah, but I've been taking a lot of breaks lately."

It has been a few days since his boss said, "What would I do without you, O?"

"Let me see." She strokes the cover like a delicate fossil. "I can't believe it."

He had texted her on the drive home. Molly made him swear not to read it. He hid it beneath his bed. It wasn't easy waiting.

"Did the windmill shock you?"

"Yeah." He explains the dry heaves and dizziness, stopping short of using the words *radiation sickness*. But they're both thinking it. "I don't think there's a trapdoor, though."

"It'd be hidden if it was, take more than your boot to find it." She places the journal on the coffee table. "And it was just leaning against one of the legs?"

"It was hidden pretty good. Lucky I saw it."

"I don't think it was luck, Oliver."

"I think it's been out there a while." He points at the water stains. "Anyone could've seen it."

"Who was going to see it?"

"The twins. Grandmother."

"I thought she didn't walk the property."

Not as far as Oliver knew, she didn't. And it took a pair of binoculars for Oliver to see it when he was looking directly at it. Grandmother could've been standing right next to it and missed it, especially the way she looks now.

They had stayed for tea. Grandmother took one look at the pumpkin tea and gave it back. It was Earl Grey or nothing. Her shoulders were slumped but not from a curvature of the spine. It was exhaustion, the same tiredness a coating of blush couldn't cover. Even her lips weren't as stiff as wire.

"And no car in the garage?" Molly asks.

"Not when we got there."

"Positive?"

"Stick a needle."

Molly continues petting the journal. She was thinking the same thing as Oliver: *Where did it go?* There was only one way into the garage, and he didn't hear or see the car. The trees on the other side were so dense a bicycle would have a hard time getting through. And what about those bright lights late at night.

"We got to get in that garage," Molly says.

"We?"

"Never mind. We're wasting time." She pats the couch cushion. "Let's read."

He's barely welcome out there. There's no hope for her.

Oliver props the journal on his legs and cracks it open. The smell of vintage paper fills his head.

And the weird escapes the pages.

November 15, 1883.

It has been quite some time since I last wrote, my love.

This is partly because I have been busy with this new life in the ice. The elven have gone out of their way to accommodate my needs. Summer was much more interesting. The sun never sets.

But that is not why I have avoided writing.

It aches too much to speak to you. Even though you are a world away, this parchment and ink spans the distance between us. These words bring you back to me. I see you in my dreams, hear you in my sleep, smell you when I wake. And yet, for all these blessings, I still cannot touch you.

And you are not here.

But to forget you is not my salvation. I think that is what the elven want, perhaps. They want me to file you in the past, to move on. Now that it is winter and the days are dark, I think of you more often. I dream of you in every step.

I spend my days walking the ice. The abominables come with me. The polar bears are hungry, and I would make quite a meal. Sometimes all of the abominables come, but most often it is just Flury. His footsteps are so stealthy that I forget he is with me at times.

He is an amazing creature. I have to remind myself, though, that he is not a creature at all. He is not the snow that makes up his massive body nor a mind inside it. He is a metallic sphere engineered in the science lab to contain elven memories. There is nothing real about him, yet when he is by my side, I don't feel so far away from home.

I worry that you would not recognize me, my love. I am the size of a walrus with a beard like tumbleweed. The Arctic cold affects me no more than a blustery autumn day in Colorado. Strange how relative experience is.

There are days Nog comes with me. Where ice is exposed, he slides with little effort. He has given me flexible soles to put on my feet that would allow me to do the same, but I resist. I'm afraid, as every day passes, I am becoming one of them. That worries me.

And that is why I am writing again.

· · ·

DECEMBER 5, 1883.

Something happened today, love.

I hesitate to write my thoughts, but Nog assured me there is no prying into my personal journals. And I have learned the elven are as honest as they are long-lived.

My walks above the ice have gotten longer. Sometimes I am just lost in thought and wander until someone comes for me. But lately I find myself walking with a purpose. I watch the horizon and pretend I see land. Each day, I walk farther, hoping that each step will bring something into view, a dash of terra firma, a shoreline besides ice. I fall into trances, I think, because hours feel like minutes. Sometimes Flury stops me to turn around.

And today, something happened.

I was focused on the horizon, placing one foot in front of the other, when a chill set upon my bones. I turned to see Flury a hundred steps behind me. He stood there, inanimate. I realized that it was the distance between us that brought about the biting cold, for I feel warmth when he is near. I went back for him, but no matter how much I coaxed him, he would not go further. It was today that I realized I had been walking for several hours. How far I had gone, I don't know.

But I reached Flury's limit.

I thought, perhaps, he had read my thoughts because, at that moment, I was thinking it was not possible for me to walk to land. No matter how well insulated my body has become, I still have human limits. But Flury could carry me. He brought me to the colony.

He could take me home.

I learned later the untruth of this. It was Nog that provided an explanation. Flury reached his limit, he said. The abominables can only venture so far away from the colony. What keeps them from going too far, he did not say. Nor did I ask. That would have certainly given away what I am thinking.

It was later I learned of the homing device kept at the colony that limits them. If they venture outside of it, they lose power. But if the homing device can keep them from leaving, there must be a way to turn it off.

And there will be no limit to where they can go.

"I GOT TO GET BACK," Oliver says.

"Oh my God, really? Call in sick or something. We can put a hot rag on your head, work up a fever. I've done it like a hundred times. You can't leave, not now."

He doesn't want to, but Ms. Megan will be upset. If he's honest, he likes those kisses on the forehead. He's also getting uncomfortable. This is his great-grandfather. His pain, for some reason, feels like Oliver's. It's nice having Molly to share all the weird, but he'd like to digest it alone. Get a grip.

He stashes the journal under his bed. "We can read the rest tomorrow."

When they get to the street, the sleet has turned into snow. That night, when he's closing the café and he's all alone, when it's just him and the journal, he breaks his promise.

THE LIGHTS ARE OFF. The music plays softly.

Oliver hikes his feet on the counter and leans back. No one sees him get the leather-bound journal from his backpack. Beneath a buzzing light, he reads the entries from that afternoon again, hoping the lonely ache of his great-grandfather's pain will settle. And like a fully loaded truck braking on ice, he blows right through the last entry he and Molly read.

And into the next.

DECEMBER 21, 1883.

I could hear them below.

The entire colony was celebrating the holiday season. Strange, they're a culture completely removed from the human race, arguably not even human, yet they have similar customs. They were exchanging gifts. They called it the Christmas season and why not. This is the North Pole, and they are elven. Nog once explained that many of our customs, habits and even language originates from the elven.

I have become numb to these propositions.

Some mornings I wake believing this is a dream. And then I walk onto the ice with Flury by my side to live another day. Have I lost my mind?

So I could not celebrate this holiday season without you. Nog and Merry had given me a pair of fur-lined mittens since my fingers are the only things that still get cold. I took them above the ice and watched the Northern Lights. The urge to walk had died inside me. Now that there are limits to Flury's range with no way to turn them off, as far as I know, I could only go so far. That took the life from my legs.

Killed my hopes.

I heard my name. It was a soft voice, and, for a moment, I thought the dream of you had come to visit me before slumber. But when I turned, I saw Jessica on the ice. Nicholas was with her.

The Santas are human.

I had gotten to know them in the summer. I didn't see them much. Nicholas is in some ways the leader of the colony. How he came to be that I have never understood, but it is clear that all the elven respect him.

They are as fat as me, my love. Nicholas maybe more so. His white beard and thick hair hang in large curls. Jessica's hair is gray. It is rare that I see them, but when I do, Nicholas wears a ceremonial red coat. There are sleigh and flying reindeer, my love. There is a man named Nicholas Santa that the elven sometimes call Claus. I haven't seen him deliver toys, but all the other stories are true.

They arrived at the colony seventy years ago by accident. The details of their journey are strange, indeed. But strange has become normal. Nonetheless, I thought perhaps I heard that wrong because they do not look old enough for that period of time to pass. Somehow, they have taken on the age-defying ability of the elven. Will they live thousands of years like the elven? They're not even sure why they have stopped aging like other humans. I plan to ask Nog how that is. And whether it's happening to me. Because if there's one thing worse than living without you, it is doing so for thousands of years.

They had come up to soothe my loneliness, I believe. They spoke of the wonders of living with the elven, the peace and wisdom that accompanies such living. Adjustment, they admitted, is difficult at first. But they insist it is essential to understand this life because of the potential the elven possess. I had assumed they meant the technology sitting next to me: the snowman whose body was drawing snowflakes to it like metal scraps to a magnet.

They encouraged me to come back to the celebration. After much talk, I relented. Afterwards, I journeyed back to the surface to be alone. The Santas had intended to set my heart at ease, to bring peace to my tangled mind. Instead, they brought clarity. I understand now, perhaps now more than ever, I am never going home.

I understand, now, what I must do.

OLIVER CLOSES THE JOURNAL.

He sits in the empty café, suppressing the urge to weep. Not in sadness for his great-grandfather and the long suffering he endured. Oliver fights back tears because clarity has come to him as well. After everything that's happened, and all that he's read, he knows something without a doubt.

Malcolm Toye stole Flury.

And there's a dreaded sense that his escape, in more ways than he can comprehend, has brought pain to everyone.

24

Wednesday evening at the library is busy.

Oliver stops inside the front doors with his thumbs hooked under his backpack straps. Molly's truck is in the parking lot. He sees her reshelving DVDs and walks down the adjacent aisle, dragging his fingers over the stacks of movies, stopping in front of the T section and checking out *Transformers*. She looks up for a moment, then goes back to her cart.

Oliver puts the movie back. "I'm sorry."

"You promised you wouldn't read it."

"It put a spell on me," he says with a chuckle.

Molly moves to the end of the row. There are two people in the aisle and another one behind them. Oliver drops the backpack and unzips it. Carelessly, he pulls out the battered leather-bound journal and holds it out.

"Take it."

"What are you doing?" She shoves it against his stomach. "Are you crazy?"

"No one knows what it is. You deserve it. I let you down."

Molly takes it and casually slides it back into his backpack, but not before stroking the cover. She remains kneeling, head down. "I can't take it."

"Yes, you can. We're in this together."

"It's yours, Oliver. Flury wants you to have it."

"No, I think he wants *us* to have it."

"Will you just let me be a baby for a minute?"

He doesn't know what that means.

Molly pushes the cart to the M section, slamming a copy of *The Matrix* into place. Two more movies abruptly find their rightful spots before she stops.

"I'm hurt." She doesn't look at him. "I'm hurt, and I'm jealous because you've got the family and the property and the journals." She points blindly at the backpack. "And I'm working in a library. Let me pout in peace."

Jealous?

No one in the history of humankind had ever been jealous of Oliver Toye, the kid with the hippy mom and the crappy dad. The kid with diabetes, the shot kind. They had no reason to be; he never had anything to covet. Still doesn't. His cousins are psychopaths, his great-grandfather is possibly a hallucinating bipolar hopeless romantic, and his grandmother a manic depressive. And there are things living in the trees that, he's pretty sure, want to eat him.

Jealousy is new ground.

"I need your help," he says.

"Not reading the journal, obviously." She stops the cart. "Sorry."

"It's all right."

"What do you need?"

"An obituary."

She files five more movies. Ms. Chatty Pants, the head librarian, is watching. Oliver is about to grab a copy of *Blade Runner* and thinks maybe he'll check it out, watch it for the fiftieth time, before hearing Molly whisper.

"Meet me in the computer room."

It's past dinner when a terminal opens up.

"You looking for your grandfather?" Molly pulls up a chair.

"Great-grandfather."

Her eyebrows arch. "Hadn't thought of that."

She leans into Oliver. One of her pigtails brushes his cheek like a feather duster, leaving a clean trail. She mutters while typing, pulling up a website that tracks obituaries through databases that include funeral homes, churches, guest books, death certificates, birth certificates, and census records.

"His name is Malcolm Toye?" she says.

"Yeah."

"That's your grandfather's name, right?"

"He was a junior."

Several Malcolm Toyes come up. Oliver doesn't remember if his grandfather had junior in his surname or a fancy Roman numeral. Molly narrows her search but doesn't find any birth or death certificates.

"Where was he born?

"I don't know."

"What about your grandfather?"

He shrugs. His family tree has been pruned many times over, and no one knows where the branches belong. She plays with the criteria, moving the cursor too fast for Oliver to follow.

"There." She taps enter. "That must be him. Look at the dates."

Malcolm Toye, 1860 to unknown.

"Definitely not your grandfather."

"There's no death certificate?"

Molly clicks the name and sorts through the following lists. "Doesn't look like it. Says here he was born in Charleston, South Carolina."

"Is that the right one?"

"I think so. I found his voter's registration in the local district in 1912. Says he joined the Navy in 1877 and was assigned to the historic journey to the North Pole. Doesn't say anything about him returning, which is weird." She clicks a few more times. "Think there was more than one Malcolm Toye that went to the North Pole in the late 1880s?"

Oliver points at the screen. Molly clicks the links. There's a brief summary of his duty in the navy, how he was selected for the journey. They follow another link to an account of the ship's disastrous destiny and the crew that survived. Malcolm Toye was not one of them.

"Look at that." Molly highlights a line of text. "'Malcolm Toye, originally thought to have perished during the journey, reappeared twenty years later in a small town in Denver. Initially, he eschewed questions pertaining to his whereabouts and how he returned, but eventually conceded that he had been back in the United States for nearly fifteen years and wished to have his privacy.'"

Molly flips her pigtails around and frowns.

"Maybe it's not him," she says. "Look at the citations."

There are several references to the source's legitimacy. One citation even questioned whether Malcolm Toye was ever on the voyage. *Rumors.*

"But he got here in about 1888?"

"That's what it says."

"Where's the death certificate?"

"There isn't one. But that just means it wasn't recognized by a doctor or church. Maybe he died at home and got buried out back. That's probably how he'd want it. You should ask your grandmother."

Rule #892: Mind your own business.

"I don't see a birth certificate for your grandfather." She clicks around. "I mean, if your great-grandfather lived here in the late 1800s, I'm guessing he was born here."

"Maybe he was born at the house."

"Maybe. No death certificate, either. That could just be country folk; you know, live and let live." She clicks around. "What's your grandmother's name?"

"Virginia."

"That's weird."

"What?" And then he sees where the cursor is hovering. He wishes, for a moment, he could turn the screen off and erase everything. But it's too late, he'd already seen it. And it felt like missing that last step at the bottom of a staircase, the sudden rise in your gut when the ground lurches up and you're not sure, for just a tiny moment, if you'll land on solid ground or just keep falling.

"It says here," Molly says, "Virginia married your great-grandfather."

"Look." She highlights the marriage announcement. *Malcolm and Virginia Toye were wed at the courthouse by a justice of the peace in 1905.*

Oliver keeps falling. "That's got to be wrong."

"I know."

"She'd have to be..."

"Like one hundred fifty years old."

"Oh, man." He sits back when the room spins inside his head and all he can smell is the weird. This feeling couldn't be cured with a dose of insulin. "Oh, man."

"What do you think?" Molly asks.

He knows what.

The pieces begin to click, and he knows. It bothered him the way

Grandmother tearfully cradled the journals after she found them in his backpack. There was a sense of longing and loss. Malcolm Toye was his grandfather's father. Grandmother was not blood-related to his great-grandfather. Her pain didn't make sense. Why would she care about great-grandfather?

Unless she loved him. His great-grandfather, not his grandfather.

And that was impossible.

Unless.

"I got to go." He shoves away from the computer.

"You all right?"

"No. I just...I got to think about this."

"Hey." She grabs his sleeve. "Call me. I'm in this with you."

"I know."

Oliver keeps from running, even though the lights feel dimmer and the air denser. Despite the falling temperatures outside, he opens his coat before he passes out. His bike is where he left it. He rides home in the dark without a light. Even if he had one, he would've left it off. He doesn't want anyone to see him. He can't keep a secret like Grandmother. If someone saw him, they'd know it just by looking at him.

Malcolm Toye isn't his great-grandfather. He came back from the North Pole. He stopped aging when he did.

Malcolm Toye is my grandfather.

And it didn't stop there. Oliver has a suspicion, a gut-feeling, his grandmother stopped aging, too.

25

"Of course I don't mind." Mom paces the faded kitchenette linoleum, never known to stand still when on the phone. She rolls her eyes and says, "I can pick up a pumpkin pie on the way, but Mother won't be happy with store-bought, you know that."

The scarecrows in Town Square have been replaced by bundles of cornstalks and Thanksgiving displays. Oliver stares through the television. His feet already ache in the dress shoes. The Dallas Cowboys take the opening kickoff to midfield when his phone sounds off.

"Wish I was with you," Molly texts.

It's Thanksgiving. He didn't want to go out to the property without her, but like every family in America, she'd eat turkey with her relatives. They'd stuff themselves and fall asleep in front of the television. They'd hug, they'd kiss, they'd say goodbye at the end of the day and give thanks for the company. They'd walk Molly's grandmother to the car because she's ninety years old. That's how old grandmothers are.

Not one hundred and fifty!

He didn't have proof his grandmother had been alive since the late 1800s, but he knew it in the pit of his stomach. It's the way she dresses, the way she never smiles, the way she talks. Great-grandfather...no, *Grandfather* returned from the North Pole with the elven's secret to aging. They lived thousands of years, he said in the journals. Somehow he brought that secret back home with a snowman and gave it to his love.

Grandmother.

He couldn't look at the journal, not since putting the pieces together. He just wanted to forget. Why was this the tipping point and not a walking, talking snowman? Because this is real, this hits home. Somehow, Flury and the journals and the hobbit house all felt like a dream, but a one-hundred-and-fifty-year-old grandmother?

That was the pebble that tipped the bucket.

"Okay, sure. I'll let her know." Mom wanders over to the window and pulls the curtain aside. "That shouldn't be a problem."

Oliver texts Molly. "Wish you were here, too."

"Aunt Rhonnie has car trouble," Mom says. "She's not going to make it, so it's just me and you, kiddo. What'd you say?"

"Good."

"You all right? You've seemed a little down the last couple of weeks." She places her hand on his forehead. "You feel a little warm."

"I'm all right."

"You've been working a lot; maybe you should take a few days off."

"No, that's not it. It's fine."

"You and Molly all right?"

"Yes, I swear. Just a little tired, that's all."

Mom gives him a chance to talk. He hugs her. When he needs space, that always works. She squeezes back and goes to the refrigerator to get a cherry pie, stuffing and casserole. It all fits in bags that Oliver can carry. He throws on his coat and takes the food to the door.

"We don't have to spend the night." Mom grabs his arm. "If you feel like coming back, just let me know."

That's good, because he's not positive he even wants to spend a minute out there. But he remembers something a teacher once taught in class. She believed in reincarnation, that when we die we come back to learn the lessons we missed. She figured that if she quit on life, committed suicide or just wasted away, she'd have to come back and do it again.

So she may as well do it now.

Flury was calling. Maybe he needed help. Maybe he needed Oliver. If the teacher was right, he'd have to go out there sooner or later. May as well do it now.

"Zip up, kiddo." Mom grabs her keys. She wraps a scarf around his neck. "It's really starting to snow out there."

❄

THE DRIVEWAY IS BURIED, including the circle. Oliver will shovel that before dark. The rest will be clean by morning.

His palm begins to warm as they approach the brooding house. It still looks like Halloween. The smell of turkey won't change that. Oliver kneads his palm without looking. Mom carries the cherry pie up the steps.

Oliver lags near the car, pulling the rest of the dinner from the back seat while staring across the field of snow. The silence is stifling, interrupted only by his breath. That familiar warmth tingles up his arm and gathers around his chest, this time not so sudden. This time it's a welcome embrace.

Welcome home.

The faint lines have returned to his palm. He traces them. The indentions are slight. He looks around, but nothing is watching except the window from the third floor.

And the old woman at the door.

Grandmother is wearing a black dress that brushes the floor. White buttons are snug on her neck. A tan shawl is draped over her shoulders. Her sense of style is outdated, but not for someone who once rode horses to town and pumped water from a well.

Oliver slides his shoes off on the porch.

"And what did you see?" Grandmother closes the door behind him.

"Snow."

Oliver tries not to make eye contact, but she doesn't move. Her complexion is still ashen, perhaps more pale than before. She's a grandmother, that's why. Grandmothers are old. *But one hundred and fifty?*

For a moment, all his convictions, his steel-cable theory about great-grandfather and anti-aging and elven all buckle and tilt.

"What do you see?" she asks again in that question-within-a-question sort of way.

"Nothing."

"Ignoring what you see doesn't change it, Olivah."

Is she telling herself that?

She points to the kitchen. Mom has the turkey on the stove. The smell does nothing for his appetite, but he helps prepare the side dishes and set the table. Later, they sit down to a traditional Thanksgiving.

They eat mostly in silence.

Oliver shovels the circle drive after cleaning the kitchen. It's dusk when he finishes, stopping just short of the drive that heads out to the road. He goes straight upstairs to shower and stay in the bedroom until morning. There will be chores, but he's due at the café by noon.

On the way up, he stops just short of the third floor. The creepy old pictures and paintings, as usual, seem slightly different, as if they're replications that someone didn't get quite right. The painting of the ship has been moved. It used to be closer to the second floor.

The rigging is barren, and the crowd of people at the bottom of the rampart appears to be travelers recently disembarking from a long trip.

He leans closer.

The painting seems significant, that's all. Something is calling to him, a detail out of place. *What is it?* One of those men must be Grandfather. He'd bet his life on it. The details are too vague to tell. Besides, he doesn't know what he looks like.

The child.

All the travelers are men, except for the fat little child. She's standing amongst them, not holding anyone's hand. As if she's a paying customer. She looks...familiar.

The bottom step creaks.

Oliver hustles up to the third floor. He gets to the shower before anyone comes up. By the time he returns to his room, the house is silent and the windows black.

A nearly full moon casts shadows over the snow. The skeletal frame of the windmill lays over solitary tracks already disturbing the pristine wonderland, wandering aimlessly into the field. The sun is down, and the weird is out.

Oliver sits on the edge of the bed. When he's certain everyone is asleep, he sneaks down the steps to look at the painting again. He knows why the little girl looks familiar. He saw that dress. It's short and wide, black with white frilly trim.

It's in the attic.

Tap, tap, tap.

He wakes up shivering.

His breath is foggy and his palm throbbing. He doesn't remember falling asleep. He had lain in bed trying to get the courage to wander down the hall and search the attic. That dress is hanging in one of the armoires, he's sure of it. He saw the strange clothes when he snuck up with the journal.

And now it's midnight.

What bothers him most isn't the dress or the painting of the ship with men and an obese child. It's the nagging feeling it isn't a child. *He brought back an elven. And her clothes are in the attic.*

But where would the elven be? Does she live in the hobbit house? Does she go with Flury? He's dozing again, the questions carrying him to sandy beaches and soft clouds, where the surf is warm and the water salty—

Tap, tap, tap.

He bolts up, sits quietly, wondering if he heard that or dreamed it. The house makes sounds all the time. Grandmother might be at the door. The house is still silent except for the occasional snaps and pops. And far away, deep in the trees, the branches crack.

He opens the door. The hallway is empty—

Tap, tap, tap.

The window.

Oliver feels like he's holding a glowing coal. The lines are raised on his palm like a brand. He holds still. The window, though, is still black with night. Anything that might be looking through his third-story window would mistake him for a shadow, but no frosty face is peeking inside. No Jack Frost tugging at the pane.

Tap, tap, tap.

It's the window frame, not the glass. It sounds like a stick, but there are no trees near this side of the house. He waits through another stretch of silence, and it happens again. Oliver creeps across the room, his steps so slow that the floorboards hardly creak. He leans near the window, searching the lunar darkness, cupping his hands to the glass. The moon is brighter, and the tracks across the field numerous. If someone, or something, knocked, it would have to climb—

Tap, tap, tap.

His heart thuds.

He sees it. There, lying in a track carved into a shelf of snow just outside the window, is a wooden sphere.

The orb.

It takes an aggressive shake to loosen the window frame in its tracks, but he lifts it a few inches. A draft blows snow on the floor. The orb rolls across the sill, and Oliver catches it.

It fits in his palm like a puzzle piece.

He feels the etchings fall in line with the marks on his hand, and like the turn of a key, his body hums. No more discomfort, no more swelling—just raw assurance that he's connected to something greater than himself.

How did it get here?

Oliver squeezes the orb. The house rattles. He's filled with a pulse of warmth. The pressure surges up his arm, emboldens his heart.

There's another sound, this one from downstairs. Oliver feels a slight change in air pressure, followed by a distant rattle.

The back door.

Oliver pulls open his door and, stepping ninja-silent, ventures down the empty hallway. Pausing at the top step, he listens for any signs of life. He dips into the bathroom and climbs onto the edge of the claw-footed tub to look out the window. The garage is dark, but, in the moon's glow, there are tracks in the snow.

He waits. Nothing stirs. No lights appear.

The orb heats up, and his hand tingles when the garage window illuminates like a square of light, for a moment hovering in the night. There's a bright flash.

And then, once again, darkness.

It takes a moment for his eyes to adjust. Nothing has changed. The tracks still lead to the garage. Oliver steps down. He stands in the bathroom with the orb humming in his palm. He knows why it appeared on his bedroom window, why it woke him up in time to hear the door close.

To see the light flash.

He leaves without flushing the toilet. With the orb in hand, with courage rushing through him, he races down the staircase.

He doesn't notice how silently he moves.

26

Oliver stands in the backyard.

His loosely tied boots are fitted into a lone set of tracks. The snow is several inches deep, and Grandmother dragged her feet, making it easy for him to follow. He remains solid and still, moonlight casting his shadow in front of him.

The seconds fall like drifting snowflakes that never seem to reach the ground. Minutes crawl past and accumulate too slowly for him to stay out much longer. He shivers in waves; his teeth chatter. Only his hand remains warm.

The orb is full blaze.

The garage appears abandoned. The moonlight, however, reveals the empty space where the car should be. Once again, there are no tire tracks leading out of the garage.

Oliver waits.

In the distance, a tree falls into water.

Just when he can take no more, when he can no longer feel the end of his nose or stand the sound of his teeth rattling in his head, the light returns. It bursts from the window like a spotlight. By the time he blinks the world back into focus, the light has dimmed. Grandmother is climbing out of the car's driver seat.

Like a two-legged gazelle, he lopes ahead, plunking his boots into every other hole. Snow tumbles into his boots and packs against his socks. He bounds around the corner and plunges into the trees' shadows just before light slices through the dark.

He holds his breath.

Grandmother emerges from the garage. Keys jingle in the lock. By the light of the moon, she steps around the garage a bit livelier than the sluggish tracks she made coming out of the house. Oliver lets his breath leak out, listening for the back door. It takes too long, and he imagines her coming back, following her footsteps and noticing the errant ones heading into the woods.

But then he hears it. The door closes.

Oliver waits.

He begins shivering again, thinking of the warmth of the garage. If it doesn't open, if he's locked out, how long will he be stuck outside? And what if the back door is locked? He hadn't thought of that. He cups the orb to his face, but the heat doesn't transfer like a hot coal.

Oliver comes out of hiding.

Without hesitating, he turns the doorknob, and like all those other times, it opens. He's greeted with warm, dry air.

He opens his coat and paces around, letting the chills settle. The triangular blocks are wedged against the car's wheels. The engine is quiet, not ticking as if it were cooling from a long drive. Or even a short one. Oliver touches the driver door, realizing he's in view of the house. If Grandmother were to look out the kitchen window, she'd see him opening the door.

The leather is warm.

There's nothing special about the dashboard. The speedometer and radio and gears are exactly where they should be. He considers pushing buttons. Maybe the radio raises a secret door. But the chocks against the wheels won't let it roll anywhere, and there's no key in the ignition.

The ignition!

That's the weird thing, the one weird thing about the car. It's not a slot for a standard key but a square. *Like something for a small cube.*

The corner of the footlocker is visible. He crawls under the workbench with his phone lit up, pulling the old coat out and pushing items aside. He finds the key in the corner and holds it up. The cube casts a blue glow like distilled moonlight.

With the orb in one hand and the key in the other, a current flows through his arms like positive and negative posts of a battery. Somewhere in the middle, right around his heart, the current chases the chill out of his chest.

Oliver climbs back into the driver's seat. The cube is no longer glowing but rather shining. The light streams between his fingers. And the ignition is glowing, too. The key gravitates toward it, pulling harder the closer it gets. It nearly slips from his fingers. The cube falls into the square hole.

Click.

He's thrown into the steering wheel as the car tips forward. For a moment, it felt like it was falling. A blinding light sears his vision, explodes inside his head. His ears ring.

The car begins rolling.

He can't see where he's going—he can't see anything—but the car is picking up speed. He's soaring downhill. Hair whipping across his forehead, Oliver latches onto the steering wheel as his stomach rises into his throat.

The car levels out. Images form in his visual whiteout.

A tunnel.

The walls are solid and gray—concrete, maybe—and curved like it was bored from the earth. Bands of light encircle the tunnel at intervals like he's flying down a particle collider. His hair snaps around his ears, and tears stream down his cheeks, but the engine isn't running, and none of the needles on the dashboard have moved. Oliver still has both hands on the steering wheel.

He's dropped the orb.

The tunnel begins to cool about the same time the car slows. The air feels heavy. Ahead is a steel wall. Oliver throws both feet on the brakes, but the car stops on its own. Oliver strains to see the outline of a door directly ahead. He rubs his eyes, head still thumping.

He clears his throat. The sound echoes behind him where alternating bands of light and dark vanish into the distance. *How far did I go?*

He went straight for quite some time, but how far and how deep? Time gets distorted when you have a death grip on a steering wheel. But there's a bigger question.

How am I going to get back?

This could be a one-way ride. There's not enough room to turn the car around. Besides, he didn't drive it. The thing moved on its own and stopped, too.

Something thuds on the floor mat. The orb rolls against his boot. He dropped it when the rollercoaster began. He sweeps it up and gets out. The sound of the door closing echoes deeper in the tunnel.

The dead-end wall is dull gray, the surface smooth and hard. At one time it might have been polished. The door is nothing more than an arching seam. What he thought was a doorknob is a spherical indention. Nothing to grab or turn. He reaches for it, his fingers brushing the inner surface.

"Ow!" He jerks his hand back, fingertips tingling.

It didn't exactly shock him, but there was some sort of charge inside it. At the same time, the orb begins vibrating. The indention in the door isn't smooth like he thought. There are imbedded lines that rotate and merge and divide into various designs.

Oliver holds the orb next to it.

Like the ignition pulled the blue-cubed key when it neared, the hemispherical indention grabs the orb and sucks it snugly inside, turning and shifting.

Pop.

The seal around the door jolts. The orb spits into his hand. Intense light seeps out. Oliver covers his eyes and steps back. The door swings away from him, opening into a larger room. Light bursts down the tunnel, and Oliver turns away to keep his retinas from frying.

He feels the light in his bones.

It's a higher form of tingling, similar to the orb.

He should be running away, screaming for help or, at the very least, struggling to breathe. But his heart isn't even thumping. He feels stronger. No, not stronger. There's an absence of quivering in his belly. He doesn't feel the weight on his chest, the lump in his throat, the weakness in his spine. He feels so present.

No fear.

That's what it is. He's not scared.

The light's intensity seems to diminish, or maybe he's adjusted. Oliver slowly turns toward the doorway. The room is a large dome, another hemispherical shape with equally burnished surfaces. He's seen this before. It was on one of the plans he pulled out of the filing cabinet in the garage.

Unlike the outer wall facing the car, these walls inside the dome are covered with wires and pipes snaking around like circuitry on a motherboard, sinking into random ports, each pulsing in synchronized rhythm. Somewhere beyond the wall, above the dome, water trickles.

Not circuits. Arteries.

They all reach the apex of the dome some twenty feet above him where a large metal post is attached.

The post, anchored into the shiny floor, gleams like newly forged steel, reflecting distorted images of the circuits and objects around the perimeter. There's a thin rod in front of the post, about the diameter of bamboo and pointed. Suspended inches above the needle-tip is a metallic sphere about the size of an overinflated basketball. The complex design of etched lines glow on its perimeter as it hovers in midair—a supersized version of the orb humming in his hand.

The elven sphere.

Each step closer to the sphere makes his bones sing louder. He stops a few feet away when his teeth vibrate; he tastes metal. He holds up the wooden orb, comparing the etchings. The metal sphere is different than the one in his hand. *Is this Flury, or another abominable? Why does Grandmother come here every night?*

If this is where she comes.

It is. This is it. He feels it.

His bones feel like forged iron, his skin like impenetrable fabric, his muscles like cords of steel. The weird feeling that hovers over him, the one from the threat of blood sugar imbalance, feels nonexistent. This is where she comes to stay young. She bathes in this room like a fountain of youth.

This is what makes her about one hundred and fifty years old.

He tries to get closer, reaching for the floating sphere, but a force repels him. The energy is too intense, pulsing inside the bones in his hand. Would it dissolve him if he grabbed it? Maybe that's what the metal glove is for.

He can't touch it. That's what one of the journals said, humans can't touch a sphere or it will...what? Suck their skin dry? Erase them?

He can't remember.

The rest of the room is a mad scientist's lab: workbenches cluttered with scattered parts and stacks of tools and crackling lights. There doesn't seem to be a light source, as if the walls are glowing. Water drips.

A small puddle is near his boot. He follows it to a bundle of conduit—veins or arteries or whatever they are—snaking across the dome's ceiling.

Pockets are set in the wall above the workbenches. Inside each one is a sphere similar to the super sphere, smaller in size and dull. While there are etchings, each one unique, they lack the glimmer and pulsing light. Oliver doesn't feel any life when he raises his hand over one of them, pulling it out of its display.

It's cold and heavy.

There are dozens of them, all lifeless metal spheres of various sizes. None are wood. Some of the pockets, however, are empty. He puts the cold, dead sphere back and trips over a plastic bucket filled with dented, scratched orbs. These are smaller, about the size of the wooden orb, but all metal. He finds an empty bucket next to it and, on a whim, slides it over the puddle.

The next drip thuds the bottom.

For the first time since arriving, his heart jumps with fear. The door is closed and sealed. But it's not the same door he entered. The dome is disorienting. The super sphere is on the other side of the post. The entrance is across from it, the door still open. The car is waiting.

This is another door. And another lock.

He didn't bring his phone. It's impossible to know the time, but he left the house about midnight. It's already late.

The orb fits snugly in the lock.

The door pops open, releasing a gush of cool air. Inside, a steel spiral staircase twirls up into the darkness, the quality dull like the walls of the dome. Oliver looks up, then steps back. Stepping into a lighted dome is one thing, climbing into the unknown is another.

Every instinct tells him to return to the car. Maybe if he puts it in reverse or inserts the key again, it'll take him back. He would've done just that—in fact, he might've run through the tunnel had the orb not hummed in his fist, sending a jolt through his chest. Warmth spills through him, relieving him of tension.

His boot lands on the first step and sends a clang into the darkness.

The railing quivers in his hand.

One step at a time, he pulls himself into the unknown, clenching the metal rail with one hand, the orb with the other.

The heavy, cool air becomes colder. The light is below him, but he can see his breath. There's a dim light above. He continues his ascent. *To the light,* he thinks. *Just to the light.*

But the light, like the lab, doesn't emit from a source but rather glows from the walls. He reaches up and scratches the metal surface. Below, the light reflects off the railing and bottom steps. He starts to descend—he'd kept his promise, after all—when he notices the steps above him have ended.

The top.

There's nothing there.

He feels around for a depression or knob, but the staircase appears to end at nothing. Perhaps, he thinks, this was a future project. His sweeping hand drags over a series of bumps.

The silence is broken.

The wall moves, and damp, earthy scents rustle his hair. Outside, the tunnel is dark. There's a dim opening several yards ahead. He takes a tentative step. Outside, the walls are no longer metal but crumble like clay. Roots dangle from the ceiling.

Foliage thrashes ahead.

Oliver takes a few more steps, waits and listens. He can see the trees beyond the opening and hear rushing water. There's something familiar about the smells and sounds, but it's not until he passes the L-shaped branch extending from the wall that he recognizes it.

The hobbit house.

The car went across the field. Of course it did. He didn't feel any turns, and it's pointed directly north. Once he put the key in, it dropped through a tunnel and raced underground. *But why so far?*

Debris showers the opening.

A cascade of leaves and snow whump down.

Oliver jumps back.

Among the twigs and sooty debris, something spherical catches the moonlight. *It's a sphere!*

He steps closer, but the pile begins to rise. Two legs raise the mass of dirty snow. Oliver backs up a step, then two. One of the legs—leaves falling from it—plods forward. The body undulates; broken branches, rocks and rotten wood ooze to the surface.

Arms extend.

Oliver turns for the staircase. He hears the sticks scratch the wall and leaps three steps at a time, spinning around the center pole as he descends. Above him, the door slams. Thuds echo down the spiral staircase chamber.

The thing hammers the other side.

Oliver jumps off the bottom step and collapses. The pounding fades. He curls against the wall, the orb cupped against his pounding chest.

The car is waiting.

The sphere hovering above the pointed rod vibrates through him but offers no confidence as he passes. He's prepared to run down the tunnel if that's what it takes. It would only take ten or twenty minutes.

He'd run an hour if he had to.

He slips into the driver's seat and turns the key. The car begins to move in reverse. Oliver watches the door close as it shrinks into the distance. It only takes minutes before he feels the ramp leading up to the garage. The floor lifts into place and the chock blocks slide under the wheels.

Oliver sits quite still, watching the house through the window, waiting for the kitchen light to turn on or the back door to slam.

His arms and legs are numb.

His head, spinning.

Now it makes sense why the concrete on that side of the garage is a slightly different color, why there are never any tracks outside the garage.

The back door to the house is unlocked.

Oliver turns the knob very slowly, knowing every click will echo. He closes it even slower. Tossing his boots and coat in the mudroom, he stops in the kitchen. If he hadn't stopped in the kitchen or dropped his things in the mudroom, maybe things would've been different. Maybe nothing bad would've happened and Christmas, a month away, would've passed without incident and no one would get hurt and everyone would be happy.

But standing at the open refrigerator with a carton of orange juice in his hand, he hears someone behind him. It's not the footsteps that give the person away. In fact, he didn't really hear anything.

He felt it.

"What are you doing?"

A month ago, if Grandmother had done exactly that, sneaking up behind him, the orange juice would've ended up on the ceiling. Instead, he pours a swallow into a glass and, after a sip, says, "Sugar a little low."

Grandmother watches him rinse the glass and place it in the sink. Oliver leaves her in the kitchen, wishing her goodnight. His steps make very little sound as he works his way up to the third floor and slips into bed. Staring at the ceiling, thinking about the jilted reality he's entered, he doesn't worry about whether Grandmother will see the snow on his boots or notice the distorted footsteps leading to the garage. He only thinks about the things in the woods and those pockets on the dome wall that contain spheres. It's the empty ones he thinks about as sleep falls on him. He knows where the missing ones are.

And why Grandmother doesn't let him stay out after dark.

27

"You sure?" Cath had shaved the sides of her head and dyed
them green.

"Positive," Oliver says. "I like closing."

"All right."

He wipes down the counters while Cath looks through her hand-
bag. She finds a tube of lipstick and applies a thick coat of bright red,
popping her lips in a small mirror. This goth queens celebrates
Christmas.

Only a week had passed since Thanksgiving. The stalks of dried
corn and all the hand-turkeys Ms. Megan's kids cut out and taped to
the window have been replaced with ornaments and garland. Red and
green strands of lights flash in the window; traditional Christmas
music plays.

"You sure you're okay?"

"Yeah." Oliver moves the miniature tree to wipe the counter. "I'm
fine."

"You don't seem fine."

"Well, I am."

"Fine." It takes another twenty seconds and half a dozen cuss
words for Cath to find her keys. "Merry Christmas, O."

The bell rings and the door slams.

Oliver turns the chairs and makes another pass over the counter.

Cath rarely leaves the café once, always forgetting something. This time, she doesn't return.

A Christmas miracle.

He drapes the damp rag on the counter and makes the last two cups of coffee for the night. Sliding them on a round table in the back corner, he leans back and lets the caffeine lift him from a long day.

He pulls the orb from his pocket.

It rolls across the table, gravitating to the other coffee mug. The wood never discolors in his pocket. Lint never wedges inside the etchings. He palms it, feeling the comforting warmth vibrate through his arm.

Molly's aunt passed away over Thanksgiving. Oliver got the text when he returned from Grandmother's. She would be staying in Illinois another week. "How'd things go at the property?" she had texted.

"Tell you later."

Bing Crosby is crooning when the bell rings again.

Molly slips inside.

Pausing at the unlocked door, she gives a short wave, the stiff-fingered kind that makes Oliver's heart thump. Her boots thump on the old wood floor. When Oliver stands up, she jumps into his arms.

She smells like Molly.

Bing Crosby is done singing when they finally let go.

"I missed you." A thick stocking cap hides her eyes.

He pulls her close again. It's clear how much he missed her.

They sit at the table, pulling their chairs closer. He asks about her family, the trip, and the weather. The talk is small and the pauses long. Their mugs are half empty when he says it.

"I found it."

"Tell me."

It takes longer to get started than he expected. He'd been holding it in all week, and now the details are stuck. Emotions swell in his throat, and for the longest time he rolls the orb between his fingers. She covers his hand and gently squeezes.

He tells her everything.

The more he talks, the more it feels like the trapdoor on reality that was sprung beneath his feet when he stepped into that car begins to close. With Molly to hold onto, his feet are back on the ground. She listens, just listens. When he's empty, when all the details of that surreal trip are in the light, he discovers something.

"Sadness."

"What do you mean?" Molly asks.

"The room, the...lab. It felt sad."

"How does a room feel sad?"

He shakes his head. When he stood in front of the super sphere, he felt something deep in his bones, something he couldn't identify. It was sadness.

The super sphere is sad.

"Does your grandmother know you found it?"

"I don't think so. We had tea the next day and went home. It all seemed so normal."

"It sounds serious, is what it sounds. That super sphere is a nuclear reactor or something. You remember the journals, where the elven used it for cold fusion. I think your great-grandfather has it wired up."

"Grandfather."

"What?"

"He's not my great-grandfather. He's my grandfather, remember?"

"Right." She hesitates. "Doesn't matter, that super sphere sounds dangerous. You felt it rattle inside like x-rays. I don't think you should go back."

She's right, he could feel it. And all the cables that looked like arteries, that had to be the power grid.

"This is no joke," Molly says. "If that thing ever becomes unstable, that could be a disaster on a national scale. We got to tell someone."

"What, that my grandmother's hiding a nuclear power plant stolen from the North Pole? Besides, Grandmother's not doing anything wrong."

"Tell them about Flury and the snowman-things..." She waves off. "Never mind. I just heard myself. What if you tell your mom?"

"No, I can't. Grandmother acted like she was protecting her."

"You can't do nothing."

They sit quietly through a bluesy version of "Baby, It's Cold Outside" and sip coffee. Oliver squeezes the orb like answers will leak out.

"If I ask you what needs to be done," Molly says, "what's the first thing that comes to you?"

Sadness.

That's what comes to mind, and that's what bothers him most. It's not the jilted reality or the crimes hidden on the property, it's palpable sadness. The essence saturated him, and he can't rinse it out.

"It's a prisoner."

"What is?"

"That super sphere. And so is Flury. They're sad because they're trapped."

"But Flury isn't."

"I think he is. I know he's running around, but somehow he's trapped on the property. The windmill is keeping him and everything else there."

"The windmill?"

He waves his hand. It's just a guess. "Just trust me, they're trapped."

"Well, maybe that's good, with those things on the other side of the river."

But that's the thing: that snowthing felt sad, too. That lumpy, dirty, leafy snowthing that rose up at the mouth of the cave and chased him down the spiral staircase was menacing, wanted to hurt him, but beneath the rage and hate there was a deep misunderstanding.

There were wounds it couldn't heal.

"We got to let them go," he says.

"We need to tell someone is what we need to do."

"First we got to release Flury."

"How?"

When he reached for the super sphere, it burned his hand like radiation. Malcolm Toye had written in one of the journals that he wasn't allowed to touch one with his bare hand or it would do something bad. But there was a way.

"We get a glove," he says. "If I get back down there, I can pull the super sphere off that rod. I think everything loses power after that, including the windmill. And the super sphere will be free."

"Why will it lose power?"

"Nuclear fusion, remember?" He describes the cables running across the ceiling. "That's got to be it."

"You could get hurt."

"Not with a glove. That's what he used in the journal. I can pull it out of the lab, and Flury can take it."

"Where?"

"Home."

"Where's that?"

He finishes the last swallow. "The North Pole."

28

T he snow begins coming down in the second week of
December.

By the third week, twenty-two inches accumulate.

When Oliver isn't working, he's sitting in the apartment watching snowplows search for asphalt. Unsuspecting parked cars become dormant lumps. Only the regulars within walking distance stop by the café for the morning grind.

Oliver keeps himself busy, but the coffee machines can only be cleaned so many times. Ms. Megan lets him put in hours even though she doesn't need him. The money is nice, but more importantly, his mind is occupied. Because when he's upstairs, he thinks about his plan.

And how flawed it is.

First, he has to find a metal glove. Grandmother doesn't exactly leave it around the house.

Next, he'll have to take another trip to the lab, assuming the key is still in the footlocker, assuming the footlocker is still under the bench, and assuming the garage is unlocked.

If all that comes together—the glove, the car, the lab—and he frees the super sphere and he doesn't kill himself with radiation or nuclear waste or whatever's cooking inside it, Flury will take it back home...*to the North Pole!*

In his mind, Flury would fly off like a magic unicorn while he and Molly stood next to the windmill and music played them into the sunset. She had asked about the magic bag; did he see one in the lab?

No.

Actually, he forgot about the magic bag. Even if he remembered to look, he'd still have to find a glove, still have to learn how to use it, still need a reindeer...

Yeah. The plan has flaws.

THREE DAYS BEFORE CHRISTMAS, Molly trundles across Town Square with her father's snowshoes. Mariah Carey sings through the café's speakers about what she wants for Christmas.

Molly will surely retch when she hears it.

Oliver considers walking to the back room to skip the song, but then the red and green strands of lights flicker out and the music dies. The café goes dark. So does the restaurant across the street.

The power outage lasts into the night.

By morning, half of the town gets their power back. Molly's house is one of the lucky ones. Town Square, however, is still cold. That's when Oliver and his mom pack up for the property.

The road is barricaded between walls of dirty snow. It's doubtful the car will make it. Colorado was built to withstand this snow—even small towns—but now power complicates matters.

Failed transformer, the gossip goes. *The backup, too. Waiting on parts.*

Here it is, two days before Christmas and it seems Grandmother has no choice but to let them stay over for the night. Or two.

They reach the property entrance.

The snow has been blown off the wrought-iron gate; the road beyond is clean. Just the slightest hump of snow runs along the pavement's edge. Grandmother waits on the porch, hands stuffed in a mink hand warmer. She looks shorter, her hair grayer.

Very few words are shared.

The chore board is long. At the top, in bold letters, is a statement. A rule.

NO GOING OUTSIDE.

That night, Oliver stands in his bedroom. The clouds turn the landscape ashy. He can't see the trees shake on the other side of the field, but hears the thumping, the limbs snapping. The wooden orb hums in his hand with each crushing blow. The fresh snow has renewed the battle of mystery.

Midnight, he goes to the bathroom.

The floor is unusually silent beneath his footsteps, as if he's somehow gained the ability to walk without sound. The garage, half-buried in a sloping drift, remains dark; no hints of a trail lead out to it.

Even Grandmother has abandoned the trek.

He wakes late the next morning feeling sugar-weird and injects insulin in his leg. Garland corkscrews around the bannister all the way to the bottom floor. Something smells good. Mom is whistling at the stove, and Oliver steals a muffin on his way to the chore board.

A new list is waiting.

In the living room, just below the wide picture window, is the miniature Christmas tree his mom bought last Christmas and had put on his dresser. Red, green and blue pinpoints glow on the tips. The tree is matched in height by six gifts, three on each side and brightly wrapped.

"You didn't think Santa forgot us, did you?" Mom says, drying her hands.

She goes back to baking and whistling.

Oliver stares out the window, a pristine field of white lays beyond the slow-churning windmill, not a single track spoiling its splendor. He spends the rest of the morning in that room, smelling the cookies and listening to Mom's happiness. Ever since he arrived at the property a year ago, the house has been a symbol of oppression and sadness, a place where joy withers in a never-ending winter. Yet, that day, this Christmas Eve, he had never felt so warm and comfortable.

So at home.

About midday, right before tea, a car door slams. A bean of excitement leaps in Oliver's stomach. He hadn't seen or heard from Molly since the power went out, which, according to Mom, has been restored. They'll go back Christmas day.

Tomorrow.

When a second and third door slam, his excitement turns frosty. Aunt Rhonnie's hollow laugh penetrates the door. When Grandmother opens it, his aunt has her phone against her head. She makes a grand entrance in a sleeveless top and tea-saucer-sized sunglasses. Her elbows are as sharp as window panes; more ribs push against him when they hug.

The twins follow like ducklings.

"Merry Christmas!" Aunt Rhonnie shouts. "Oh, Merry Christmas, Merry Christmas!"

The house silence is shattered by cackling laughter and the sharp command, "Put them in the living room, Henry. Now."

Helen is absorbed by her phone, and Henry carries presents while staring knives into the back of Oliver's head, shredding the magical spirit of Christmas Eve, killing the intoxicating cookie smell that dares to linger.

HENRY AND HELEN are putting on their boots.

"Where are you going?" Aunt Rhonnie says.

"A short walk," Henry says.

"No, you're not. It'll be dark soon, and we're opening presents."

Oliver is washing dishes when Henry comes through the kitchen, brushing against him on the way to the living room. Did they think they were going to cross the field and back before night? More importantly, do they know about the lab?

Of course they do. They go out to that hobbit house and sneak through the secret entrance, I'll bet. But do they have a key?

Oliver pats the bulge in his pocket, as if the orb could suddenly vanish. It had done so once before. He couldn't stop it from doing it again.

The doorbell rings.

Oliver's hands are deep in the sink. The front door opens, and his mom bursts out, "Oh, Merry Christmas!" There's shuffling in the foyer, shoes falling on the floor, and giggling. Oliver dries his hands.

"You're not going to open presents without me." Molly walks into the kitchen. Her hair is tied on top of her head, red and green striping her hair. A black scarf is wrapped once around her neck, hanging to the floor.

"Nice hair." Helen strolls through the kitchen.

"Nice scarf," Molly quips.

Helen stops in the doorway. They stare without blinking. Henry comes to his sister's side, like a shark smelling blood. His hair is stiffly sculpted into place.

"I think it escaped the zoo," Henry says.

Helen smirks. It's a deadly smile, the corner of her mouth jabbing into her cheek as her eyes darken. It turns Oliver's stomach cold.

Molly throws her arm around Oliver. "Better hide your eyes, kiddies. The animals are going to play rough."

She growls, biting Oliver's neck and tickling his ribs. They break out in laughter. The twins walk off.

"I missed you," she whispers.

He doesn't need to open presents.

Christmas is already perfect.

MOM LIGHTS CANDLES in the living room.

The warm light lifts the gray pall from the faded wallpaper. U2 is singing about Christmas on Helen's phone, the sound tinny and small on the built-in speaker but better than the silence. Grandmother sits in a rocking chair facing the window, the rails slowly creaking.

The field is still white. Still perfect.

The presents, meanwhile, have quadrupled. Aunt Rhonnie, with a Santa hat flopping over her ear, drinks her special coffee and sorts through the gifts. She claps as she hands them out. Mom has a matching Santa hat. For the first time, they look like sisters, act like twins. The wrapping paper is torn, folded and stuffed in a plastic bag as each gift is opened.

"Hug your cousin," Aunt Rhonnie says to Helen. Then, "Hug your grandmother."

Oliver barely makes contact with her.

Grandmother doesn't even bother hugging back.

The ritual continues until all the gifts are open. Aunt Rhonnie hugs them all, leaving a trail of expensive perfume that will need to be showered off.

The sun has dropped behind the mountains, and the day is quickly fading. The windmill is a skeletal figure. Oliver will have to risk leaving his room tonight if there's any chance of seeing the lab. He can't do it now for a lot of reasons, especially since Molly's here. The plan was bound to fail, he'd accepted that. She didn't need to be around when it did.

He can set his alarm for the middle of the night, long after everyone is asleep, during the hour Santa is laying presents under trees. If the footlocker is there, he can grab what he came to get. And go where he came to go, do what he came to do.

And hope he finds a metal glove somewhere along the way.

"What's that?" Aunt Rhonnie reaches behind the little tree. "Is this yours?"

"No," Mom says. "I didn't wrap that one."

"It's for Oliver."

"Maybe it's from Santa." Mom passes it across the room.

The gift is half the size of a shoebox. The wrapping paper is red. There's no ribbon or tag, just Oliver's name scrawled in the middle.

"Open it," Aunt Rhonnie says.

He pulls the tape from one end.

The windmill begins to squeal when he slides out a brown box. Oliver folds the wrapping paper and hands it to Mom. With eyes on the box, no one looks up when—out of nowhere—a gust of wind batters the window with sleet.

He pulls off the lid.

The candlelight captures the dull silver inside. Nestled in a fold of tissue paper, neatly lying flat, is a single glove.

A metal glove.

"Where'd you get that?" Helen asks. "Who is it from?"

Grandmother stops rocking. Expressionless, she watches him lift it from the box. It moves like thick silk, cool against his fingers.

"What's going on?" Helen asks.

A snow flurry blows across the open field.

The whiteout engulfs the singing windmill.

The house shifts in the blustering squall.

"Olivah." Grandmother is reaching, hand open. "Give it to me."

His hand aches to slide inside the smooth glove, to feel the snug fit, the metallic grip.

"Olivah."

Oliver rubs the interior, smooth on his fingertips, just like he thought. The glove's hem closes around his fingers and begins to work up to his knuckles.

"You don't know what you're doing. Hand it to me now."

The house shakes.

Nothing is visible past the window but a white cloud, bits of ice ticking off the glass.

"Honey, let me see it," Mom says.

Henry lunges.

Oliver twists away and gets to his feet.

Henry latches onto his wrist, but Oliver pulls away, backs against the wall. Effortlessly, almost of its own accord, the glove slides over his hand. The dull surface brightens like polished steel. A light warms him from the inside. The room flickers with candlelight, but the flames look bright, feel warmer.

And the wooden orb vibrates.

Henry gets to his feet.

Oliver reaches for his pocket.

"Stop," Grandmother says. Henry freezes, his knees bent and loaded. Grandmother leans forward and pauses before standing. "Olivah, listen to me. You do not know what you are about to do."

"He needs to be free."

"There are other things to consider."

"I can't leave him. He needs me."

"He needs all of us. Stop what you're doing. Hand the glove to me."

The raging squall rattles the window.

"I can't."

"Trust what I'm saying."

She takes half a step, hand extended. Even in candlelight, her cheeks are pale. Her eyes, tired.

"Olivah."

Strands of gray have pulled free from the eternal bun and wave over her forehead. She waits for him, openhanded. Oliver's fingers inch away from his pocket. He doesn't want the glove or the orb. He just wants to do what's right, wants to relieve Flury's suffering, wants to extinguish the sadness below ground.

"No!" Grandmother shouts.

Henry launches.

Oliver leaps backwards. His gloved hand instinctually seeks his pocket, sinking deep inside. Henry grabs his sleeve with one hand and thumps Oliver's chest with the other.

Oliver falls back.

His fingers dig deep.

The wooden orb leaps into his gloved palm.

A bolt, a current, a flash of energy fills him. Henry is knocked back. Grandmother falls back into the rocking chair. Aunt Rhonnie's Santa hat tumbles across the room. The miniature Christmas tree falls over, wrapping paper swirls in a sudden draft like the storm outside has found its way into the living room. Oliver swells with life, with energy.

Electrified.

His hair tingles.

Oliver pulls his hand out. The orb is locked into the glove. The storm dies inside the room, wads of bright paper wedged beneath the chairs, pushed against the walls.

The squall outside dies.

The flurry settles.

The windmill emerges from the whiteout. A path is dug from the field, wandering all the way to the distant trees. Walls of snow have been thrown to the sides like a commercial snowplow passed through. And in the middle, limping near the windmill, walking toward the house, is a figure hunched in a hooded cowl. Things move in the mist settling around the figure.

Disfigured lumps of snow.

"Henry," Grandmother says. "Let your grandfather inside."

29

"What?" Aunt Rhonnie says. "What did you say, Mother?"

The hooded figure makes his way toward the house with a slight limp. Oliver had assumed, when he snuck into the attic, that it was Grandmother in the driveway. Of course, there could be another black cloak, but the frail nature of the man she called his grandfather matches what he saw that night he watched from the attic. And those things in the field, the ones behind him, the creatures that chased him at night...*the snowthings*...they're with him.

A dozen of them line the gash cleaved across the field.

They don't march like soldiers but slide like half-baked snowmen, bodies slushy and gray. Leaves, branches and gravel are packed into their bodies; their throbbing heads are without features except for a single, dark hole.

"Tell me what is happening?" Aunt Rhonnie says. "Tell me who that man is and what those things are and what is happening, Mother!"

Her voice rises, each word building on the one before it until she sounds like something at the zoo. The long spikes of her heels hammer the floor. Her arms are inflatable appendages with lives of their own.

"Aaaaaanswer me!"

Grandmother turns. "Open the door, Henry."

Aunt Rhonnie storms out.

Molly's hand finds Oliver's. Their fingers entwine.

His mom stands behind them as the back door opens. There is a short bout of muttering, followed by boots hitting the mudroom floor. Henry returns to the living room. His pale face is as white as winter.

Oliver's fingers ache in Molly's hand.

The hooded figure stops in the doorway. He lifts his right arm; a spotted hand with knobby, curled fingers emerges from a hanging sleeve to push back the cowl, revealing a bushy gray beard and sagging eyes.

"Hello, Virginia," he says. There's a smile somewhere behind the whiskers.

Grandmother says nothing.

Aunt Rhonnie clops back into the room. Her drink tumbles on the floor. She lifts her hand, the painted nails trembling over her red lips. "Oh, my..."

"Father," Mom whispers.

"Hello, girls," Grandfather says. "It's been quite a long while."

"What are you...where have you..." Mom stutters.

"That, my dear, is a long story that I'm afraid I haven't time to tell."

"What are you doing here?" Aunt Rhonnie says.

He turns his stiff neck toward her. "Your mother knows why I'm here. I won't stay long, but some tea would warm these old bones, if you have some ready. And I know you do."

When no one moves, Oliver starts for the kitchen. "Not you, Olivah," Grandmother says. "Helen, prepare a cup for your grandfather."

"Bring sugar," he says.

He favors his right leg.

Stopping near Mom, he reaches with his right hand, the arthritic fingers incapable of straightening. He stops short of touching her cheek. Again, the grin returns somewhere behind his beard, his eyes scrunching.

"Debra," he whispers.

Mom's grip on Oliver's shoulders tightens.

Grandfather pauses at the picture window, running his curled fingers over his thinning scalp. The snowthings patiently wait near the windmill. Helen returns with a saucer and cup. He thanks her, dropping three sugar cubes into the tea. The tongs shake in his feeble grip.

He sips.

They watch him stir in three more cubes.

Wistfully, he stares outside. "I thought my gift might ruin your Christmas."

"You gave me the glove?"

"I've given you many gifts, my boy."

"The journals?" Oliver asks. "The footlocker?"

His eyes twinkle over the rim of the teacup.

"This, too?" Oliver raises the orb.

"Not that, my boy. I needed you to find that for me."

"Why?"

He reaches for another sugar cube and groans. "You look good, Virginia. Don't you agree, children? For her age, I mean. No one your grandmother's age looks that good."

The silence is filled with Grandfather sipping. The hidden grin dances in his eyes. He shares a thousand emotions with Grandmother without saying another word.

"Am I going crazy?" Aunt Rhonnie mutters. "Someone tell me what in the world *is happening!*"

"He left," Grandmother says.

"Wrong!" The word is surprisingly powerful, exploding from the frail old man's grizzled beard. Everyone jumps, including Grandmother. "I *never* left, Virginia. Now tell them what happened."

The silence swells.

"Tell them!"

Grandmother sits with perfect posture, hands folded on her lap.

"Mother?" Aunt Rhonnie asks. "Why would you send us to boarding school and not tell us Father was alive, and why is he here now, and what the hell is out there?" She jabs at the snowthings. "Will you talk for once in your life!"

"Mother?" Mom says. "What's happening?"

Grandmother remains unmoved.

The frail woman has hardened beyond anything Oliver has ever seen. She says little because she knows a lot. And they're about to find out what she knows.

"You never were very good at explaining things, Virginia." Grandfather sighs. "Perhaps you can explain it, Oliver?"

"Me?"

"Would you mind?"

All eyes land on him. Molly pulls closer. Mom throws her arm across his chest.

"I don't..." His throat tightens.

"Come now. You've read about it. You know the story. I believe you know why I'm here. Out with it, my boy."

The light that had twinkled in the old man's eyes is, once again, snuffed by sudden impatience. Oliver peels his mom's arm off and moves away from her and Molly, as if distance between them will keep them safer.

Because he knows why Grandfather is here.

He's come for someone.

Oliver squeezes the orb with the gloved hand, hoping the storm that shook the room will return and knock the old man through the window. But the power he felt earlier has diminished by his presence.

"Oliver?" he says.

"Grandfather was born in 1865."

If there was space for more shock to enter the room, it would have settled in between the pauses. But there is none.

There was nothing Oliver could say that could surprise anyone, not when snowthings are watching, not when a previously thought dead man is sipping tea.

Oliver continues.

He recounts the trip to the North Pole, the discovery of the elven and their advanced technology. He explains what the orb does and the glove he's wearing and the snowthings. Mom and Aunt Rhonnie are the only ones staring. Henry and Helen listen without watching him. Some of this they know.

Maybe all of it.

Grandfather nods along, occasionally sipping, but mostly staring at Grandmother.

"He stole from the elven," Oliver says. "He took their abominables and made those things out there."

The snowthings move closer, as if they heard. Aunt Rhonnie shuffles back.

"Very good, my boy. A quick study, you are. You are not a disappointment." Grandfather glances at Oliver's cousins. "I am over one hundred and fifty years old, but your grandmother is much, much older. I look like this because, if she had her way, I would be dead. That's what you had hoped for, isn't it, Virginia. You wanted death to solve your problems. But death has always been our problem, hasn't it?"

He swirls the cup. There couldn't be anything left but a slurry of sugar. Oliver's grandparents share a long, knowing glare. So much left unspoken.

"Girls," he says, "I know I just returned, but I have to go. Perhaps another time I can explain." He groans as his back refuses to straighten. "Come along, Oliver."

"You can't take him," Grandmother says.

"Nonsense."

"I will not allow it, Malcolm. Take what you want, but you will leave Olivah."

"You can't stop me, Virginia. Perhaps you should have been more active in seeking my death. It's too late now."

Mom pulls Oliver behind her.

Grandmother remains still.

They stare like gunslingers, fingers dancing, waiting for a move.

When it comes, Grandmother reaches for her sleeve, but Grandfather merely flicks open his hand to reveal a metal glove. Oliver's fingers are pulled open by some invisible force, releasing the wooden orb from his grip. Instead of bouncing on the floor, it shoots across the room and slams into Grandfather's palm with a dull clink of wood on metal.

Wrapping paper rustles.

Grandmother retrieves a metal glove from her sleeve. But it's too late.

Grandfather holds the orb between finger and thumb and sighs. He rotates it, admiring the intricate etchings.

"I made this, but it was Flury who put part of his soul into it." He squeezes, and a mild whirlwind tosses loose items across the room.

"You have it now," Grandmother says. "Now go."

"Oliver will come. I'll need him."

"It will work without him."

"No, it won't."

"I'll go." Henry steps closer. "I want to go, Grandfather. Take me with you."

"I'm sorry." He drops his bare hand on Henry's shoulder. "Flury knows your intentions are no better than mine. Your mother was always selfish, and she passed those traits onto you and your sister, I'm afraid."

"That's...well, that's just not true." Aunt Rhonnie raises her hand to her heart. "I'm very unselfish. I don't know what you're talking about."

"Flury picked Oliver," Grandfather says.

Aunt Rhonnie looks around. "Who the hell is Flury?"

Grandfather chuckles. Henry and Helen don't have that question in their eyes. They know. They've seen him.

"He is something you wouldn't understand, darling. He is someone that trusts youth and innocence. He sees the inherent goodness in a child of a certain age and offers his magic, gives his soul. Which, as it just so happens, is also the key to my freedom."

He displays the orb again.

"But he's a prisoner on this property, just like your mother and me. Right, Virginia?"

Grandmother flexes her gloved hand.

"We didn't mean to become prisoners," he says. "We brought him to the property and held him captive."

He gestures out the window. No one would guess he was referring to the slow-churning windmill except Grandmother. But Oliver knows what he means; he knows that the windmill is the homing device that limits where Flury can go.

"If he leaves, he melts, so he locked us out of the lab. Revenge, I suppose. Can't blame him." Grandfather shrugs. "That was a problem."

"You started aging," Oliver says.

"My boy, you are the smart one. We started aging"

Grandmother's shaking her head. Her lips remain tight.

"Truth is, if we leave, we become ordinary. As you know, ordinary people don't live to be one hundred and fifty. We are as much slaves to the windmill as he is, so you see I needed Flury to return, needed him to give me the *lab I built with my own hands.*"

The teacup shakes. He puts it down, grimacing, wiping away the memories that rise in his voice. He looks at the snowthings pulsing.

Waiting.

"We knew the key to Flury's heart was children. We knew he'd give his soul to one of you." He displays the orb. "And his soul would open the door. So we had kids."

He nods at Oliver's mom and Aunt Rhonnie.

"We had you to get the key, so that we could free ourselves from the windmill. But your mother had a change of heart just when you were about the right age. Not you, I'm afraid, Rhonnie. Flury wouldn't have trusted you. Your sister, though."

He nods at Oliver's mom.

"I think he would've come to you, Debra. Your mother knew it, and that's why she sent you away without my knowledge. And while I was gone, Flury betrayed me, tried to destroy me, and your mother watched. If it wasn't for my babies..."

The snowthings swell, drawing surrounding snow into their sloppy bodies.

Aunt Rhonnie tries to say something, to ask anything that would make sense. But she doesn't understand. How could she know what an abominable is and that Grandfather somehow used it to extend their lives like the elven? *How could she even understand what an elven is?*

But that technology, that power, turned dark. Maybe because he was never supposed to have it. Maybe that's why the elven didn't want him to have it. Flury must have known; he must've locked them out to stop them.

To stop Grandfather.

Grandfather reaches for Oliver.

Molly grabs Oliver's arm.

Mom stands in front of him, hand out to stop her father. Grandfather's dark laughter rattles in his throat. In the moment of distraction, Henry reaches for the wooden orb clutched loosely at Grandfather's side.

Grandfather doesn't try to elude his grasp, he simply squeezes the orb, and Henry turns solid, his outstretched fingers within inches of the gloved hand. Choking sounds gurgle from his throat; spittle rises on his lips.

Aunt Rhonnie screams.

Henry backs away, his feet sliding across the floor as if an invisible force drags him by the throat.

"Not all youth are innocent," Grandfather says. "Not all are good."

Henry falls next to his sister.

Aunt Rhonnie rushes to their sides. That's when Mom is pushed to the side by the invisible hand. Molly unwillingly lets go, shouting as her fingers untangle from Oliver's hand. Both women struggle, both curse, but the orb in Grandfather's gloved hand cannot be denied.

The candlelight flickers on Grandmother's softened expression, glinting in her eyes.

"I'm sorry," she says.

"You should be," Grandfather says. "You knew this day would come."

The snowthings begin their irregular sliding, advancing toward the window. Their forms loom in the dark.

Grandfather pulls a handful of objects from his pocket that clink in his palm. He drops them on the wood floor. The metal bearings roll in all directions. Once again, the wrapping paper begins to skid over the floor, only this time it wraps around the little metal balls.

Tiny spheres!

Tissues shoot from a box, envelopes slide off the coffee table, a scarf creeps over the couch. They collide with the metal balls, reform around them until several little forms rise up from the shuffling mess.

The oddball little creatures, no taller than a hiking boot, march to Grandfather's side.

"They'll stay," he says to Grandmother. "Until we're finished."

"I never wanted it to be this way."

"I think you did, Virginia."

"Flury is only trying to help."

"He's in the way."

"You don't have to do this."

"You know I do."

"We can end all this. It doesn't have to involve them."

"It's too late. I think you know that." Grandfather reaches for Oliver. "Help an old man, my boy."

Oliver takes his grandfather's arm and guides him to the kitchen. He's not forced to help him walk through the back door, where a path is carved through the snow. He walks willingly, knowingly.

He helps an old man limp to the garage.

30

————————

Grandfather stops behind the car, his eyes walking over the shiny exterior. It takes several short steps for him to reach the driver's side, exhaling like a dying engine. Oliver wonders if he might expire before falling into the red leather seat. He caresses the steering wheel, twisting the grip.

"Get in."

Oliver is obedient.

It would do him no good to disobey—Henry tried that—but a small part of him wants to get in the car, wants to go with him.

Flury picked me. Why me?

Grandfather begins to wheeze, coughing uncontrollably. Oliver thinks this time he'll crumple, but the old man recovers, pulling a key from his pocket—one with a glowing blue cube—and inserts it into the ignition.

Once again, the ride steals Oliver's breath.

When they stop, the wall is looming. Grandfather tries to get out but needs Oliver's help. The old man shuffles to the door. Ogling the wooden orb one last time, he hands it to Oliver.

"Go on."

Oliver knows what he means. When he takes the wooden orb, his body tingles. "It won't work for you?"

"Open the door, my boy."

"What if I say no?"

Grandfather guides him by the elbow. "I can take the orb back. You know what I can do with it."

Pressure closes around his throat just below the chin, triggering a fierce headache. He's released from the grip and, hunching over, gasps for air. The ache continues splitting his head.

The orb is pushed into his hand.

"Don't test my patience, my boy."

Oliver inserts the wooden orb.

Turn. *Click.*

Hands on his knees, he squints to see Grandfather inside the dome. The smile behind the beard returns, crinkling the corners of his eyes. The old man lifts his hands, tips his head, and begins to laugh. His joy echoes down the long tunnel.

"It's been a long time," he whispers. "A very long time."

He paces around the bucket now full of water. A droplet falls from the ceiling and plunks inside. Water streams over the sides.

The old man slides his boots over the floor. By the time he reaches the other side, the shuffles fade and each step echoes with a careful heel-to-toe clap.

He stands straighter, exhaling.

If we stay long enough, will his steps turn silent?

"What's its name?" Oliver steps inside and points at the super sphere humming at the end of the lance.

"No name, my boy. This one didn't come from the North Pole."

"You invented it?"

"I built all of them."

He gestures to the oddball orbs on display but gazes lovingly at his greatest achievement levitating in the center of the room, created in the likeness of Flury. All of those plans in the garage, the countless drawings of spheres and domes and circuits, they all had to do with the super sphere.

The snowthings were just practice.

"The magic bag."

"Hmmphff, the magic bag, yes. But even the imagination has limits, my boy. I created this"—he points at the super sphere—"for Flury, an upgrade of sorts. When he didn't cooperate, I locked it up."

"And then he locked you out."

"He did."

"So what is it now?"

"An empty vessel." For the first time, the old man looks away from the super sphere. His eyes fall on Oliver. "What it needs is a soul."

"A soul?"

"Yes, a soul. Memories, if you will. Structure, personality, a framework of thought and judgment. The elven did it to all their abominables, as they called them. It gave their snowmen stability and intelligence. Without a soul, it's just a power source. But with one, it becomes more than you can imagine."

"How're you going to give it a soul?"

Grandfather doesn't answer. He paces a few steps, eyes back on the super sphere. Already his steps fall quieter.

"Flury knew what I wanted to do with the super sphere. You see, abominables like him see reality more clearly than mere mortals; they see through the human distraction of thoughts and delusion. Our imagination makes us a great species, innovative and powerful, but it's also our Achilles' heel, the source of our self-centered delusion. I am no exception, my boy, and when he saw what I'd become, he locked the dome and left me out in the cold to age."

"I thought Grandmother did that."

"They both saw through me." He stretched out his arms like a man about to lift tremendous weight. "I have suffered on this property a long time, my boy."

It's hard to imagine the super sphere levitating over that sharp point is empty and mindless because the sadness is still in the room, radiating from its shiny, etched surface, filling Oliver's chest. Had Oliver not been in there once before, he would've thought it was Grandfather's misery. The suffering the old man spoke of hung like a scent, a vapor, a tainted haunt of despair sitting forever in the gut.

Nothing good has happened since he returned.

"Don't judge me, boy. You know the story, what I did to survive. There's no dishonor in my escape. I only wanted to be home, I deserved that much. I never intended for it to become this."

"You wanted to see Grandmother...your love."

"Mmm." He grunts, digging through his beard to find his chin. The light leaves his eyes. "If they had let me go, none of this ever would've happened. The elven are at fault."

His gaze turns faraway, as if the past plays out on the surface of the glittering super sphere spinning above the rod's tip. Grandfather appears distraught. When trapped in the North Pole, his love for

Grandmother was his only reason for living. Did that dream die when he returned? Was the dream better than reality?

My love.

"How'd you do it?" Oliver says. "How'd you get home?"

"It doesn't matter. The journals were for you to know why I did it. History is distorted too often, intended or not. I wanted someone to know the truth."

He stands upright.

The hunch between the old man's shoulders has vanished. The popping of his vertebrae resounds. Just being in the presence of the super sphere has straightened his back. Oliver can feel it, too. He feels stronger.

"Your grandmother hid the journals from you. She didn't want you to know what I was, only what I have become. I was not always this, my boy. There is a reason for who I am today."

"Is there a another one?"

"You know enough."

"Why didn't you give me the last journal?"

"I'm not evil, Oliver. I just want to live."

"You're already living."

"I died long ago, my boy."

The old man exhales.

The joy has receded beneath an onslaught of bitter memories. He didn't die, but something happened when he returned. He thought happiness was waiting for him.

What happened?

A drop of water lands in the bucket.

Another drip hangs from a bundle of conduit snaking into a hole. Somewhere above them, the river is leaking.

Something shimmers around the super sphere.

Tiny droplets are orbiting like electrons in slow motion. Grandfather didn't seem to notice. He was looking right at it, the luminescence reflecting in his eyes that don't seem as deep set as they once were, but not seeing what's in front of him.

He's been living in his thoughts far too long.

Our imagination makes us a great species, but it's also our Achilles' heel.

"Your grandmother has a good heart, my boy." He digs deep into his beard. Digs deeper into the memories. "Better than mine, I suppose. But, in the end, we're both flawed."

Ker-plunk.

Another drop.

The mist shimmers around the super sphere; a faint rainbow appears like a solar belt. The miniscule droplets orbit around it as if the super sphere is a planet, which in a way, it is. Those miniature spheres Grandfather dropped on the floor used wrapping paper and tissues, the snowthings attract slush, sticks and debris. Flury's sphere pulls snow around it to form a body.

An abominable attracts snow to make a body.

What about water?

Oliver steps toward the bucket. "What are you going to do with the super sphere?"

He nods. The hidden smile returns. "Start by feeding it memories."

"What memories?"

"Mine, of course."

"How?"

He grunts and stretches. Tendons flex along his neck. If Grandfather is going to put his memories into it...

"You want to become an abominable."

Grandfather is mesmerized again. It's three times the size of Flury's sphere. Imagine what it could do.

That's why Flury refused.

That's why he locked Grandfather out.

Too much power.

Oliver flexes his gloved hand. He can feel the subtle tug of the wooden orb wanting to come back to him, to feed him strength. To call for Flury. Oliver catches the next drop in his bare hand. It makes hardly a sound. Grandfather looks at the ceiling, unsurprised by the leak.

As if he's known all along.

"Those aren't sinkholes in the forest," Oliver says. "You've been trying to break inside, using the snowthings to tunnel to the dome."

"You can leave now, Oliver."

"But Flury stopped you, didn't he? That's what the battle in the trees is every night. Your snowthings are trying to crack through the ceiling, to let you in, but Flury stops them."

"I mean you no harm, my boy. You are still my grandson, but you must return to the house. Tell the family they must leave and not return. Your grandmother will have to stay, naturally. But she'll expect that."

"Are you going to make the elven pay for saving your life?"

"It's complicated, my boy. When you've lived as long as I have, you learn that nothing is ever straightforward."

"You should've died long ago. You're human. You're not supposed to live this long."

"Enough, Oliver." His hand clenches around the orb. Oliver feels the small hairs on his arms rise. "Return before I change my mind."

"Are you going to hurt the elven?"

"No more than they hurt me."

"I don't understand."

"Of course not."

"They saved you."

He nods absently. His hand relaxes, and the electrified air vanishes. He stares at the super sphere. The rainbow is vivid.

The wrinkles have vanished from the old man's eyes.

"I don't understand why you want to hurt them. You returned home to your love, you made grandmother live long like you; what else do you want? If you use the super sphere for revenge, you're going to prove the elven right, that humans don't deserve this much power. We don't deserve peace."

"Flury gave *you* the key to the dome"—Grandfather holds up the wooden orb—"in hopes that you'd change my mind, I know this. He knew that one day I would find a way back here. He knew I couldn't be stopped. I'm afraid, Oliver, that I've made up my mind. I did so a hundred years ago."

As the old man becomes younger, the sadness in the room becomes more potent. It feels heavier, more constricting. Grandfather thought Flury chose Oliver to convince him to do the right thing, but he was beyond changing. But maybe Flury chose him for another reason.

To feel the despair haunting his grandfather.

To experience the sadness of the empty super sphere.

Not to change his mind...*but to stop him.*

"I can't let you hurt anyone, Grandfather."

"My boy," he says, "I don't want to hurt you."

The old man focuses on Oliver, notices the heel of the young man's boot on the lip of the bucket, water sloshing over the edge.

He looks back at the rainbow-wrapped super sphere that's begun to rotate within the coalescing bands of water droplets. He understands what's about to happen and squeezes the wooden orb.

The atmosphere bristles, the air tightens around Oliver's forehead. The light dims in his periphery.

He kicks out.

Falls back.

Water splashes up his pant leg. The plastic bucket clonks on the concrete. Water spreads across the floor.

Then comes together.

A funnel rises, spinning toward the glowing super sphere.

The rainbow fractures.

Bands of light disperse off the walls as the water spout enters the gravitational pull of the super sphere.

Faster, it spins.

Grandfather is shouting.

Oliver's foot slips in the water. He rolls onto his side to crawl away, but something tugs his leg. He begins to slide toward the center.

"No! No! No!" Grandfather runs around the center post, unaffected by the force dragging Oliver across the wet concrete. The closer he gets to the center, the faster he's pulled. The super sphere wobbles on the rod's tip, a watery veil undulating over its surface. The floor quickly dries as every last drop is drawn into its gravitational field.

Oliver claws at the floor, peeling his fingernails back.

The smaller orbs pop from the wall pockets like artillery.

Grandfather's fingers brush against Oliver's outstretched hand as he's slurped into an electric white light.

And touches the super sphere.

Then perfect silence.

31

His body goes limp.

The boundaries that define Oliver—his flesh, his bones—flow like sand. Forms blur in unpredictable directions. Sounds are warped, unintelligible, punctuated by the watery impact of hardened cannonballs firing through him.

Colors smear across curved walls.

Round and round, round and round.

Hornets chase his watery tail.

I'm flying.

Time and space slow. Oliver begins to make sense of the hazy landscape with three-hundred-and-sixty-degree vision, seeing in all directions simultaneously. The hornets are not insects but a mass of orbs giving chase—the oddball spheres that were displayed in the wall pockets—nipping at Oliver's watery body. His grandfather is below, hands raised. A garbled sound roars from his open mouth.

There's an empty bucket on the floor and a body.

My body.

He's inside the sphere. He touched it. Humans are never supposed to touch a sphere...

It just needs a soul.

A wave of panic ripples through him. The watery mass quivers, and the orbs gain on him. It doesn't seem possible. His fleshly body has become a foreign object, a crumpled container, a discarded vehicle. He's inside the super sphere, a passenger flying through space.

How is this possible?

Grandfather, clenching the wood orb in his metal glove, aims his predatory spheres at Oliver. Each time one plunges into him, it takes a bite of water.

And Oliver slows down, becomes less.

They'll take me apart like parasites.

Each pass around the dome brings him closer to the old man's outstretched arm, closer to his grasp. More water. He needs more water.

The ceiling is still dripping.

With a thought, Oliver turns toward the leak. He focuses his attention, concentrates on the weakest point in the ceiling, and drives all his mass forward.

Crack!

He doesn't feel the impact. The super sphere rebounds.

Oliver's panaramic vision is jilted. A steady stream leaks from the conduit, splattering the floor. The parasitic spheres swarm him before he can circle the room, nipping away the watery body swirling around the super sphere. With each bite they take more water from him.

They feed on him, a frenzy in the air, sipping away the water that gave the super sphere a body, that allowed it to absorb Oliver. The room begins to dim. He's becoming less and less, going to sleep, going away.

Until he's barely floating above the floor.

I'll never see Molly again. Never feel her hand in mine.

The room's sadness floods inside him. The pain of loss, the fear of death. The orbs feast on the watery remains. The super sphere clinks on the concrete.

Begins to roll.

"You don't belong in there, my boy." The super sphere wedges against a boot. "Get back to your body."

Grandfather's callused palms grasp the super sphere. Oliver feels them against the etched surface, feels the weight of the old man's thoughts begin to pour inside.

His eyes pale.

He's coming inside.

Oliver feels the dense form of his own flesh against the floor, the steady thump of his heart pulses. His elbows burn where the skin is scuffed away.

He's coming to give the super sphere a soul.

Grandfather had planned, all along, to feed his memories into the super sphere. He wants to be inside it. He wants to become an abominable. He pushes Oliver out, throws him back into his limp body, where his chest rises and falls.

I can't let him.

The old man's grizzled body is on the floor.

The super sphere quivers beneath his old boot. The swarm of oddball orbs fall on the super sphere, throwing the water they stole from it back into the larger sphere's orbit, returning life to it now that their master is in control.

Oliver throws his hand out.

His fingernails scratch the concrete, crawl to the old man's pant leg, creep over his boot until he lays his palm on the super sphere's shimmering surface. Once again, the charge rips through him.

This time his memories—his awareness, his identity—remains in his body.

Oliver holds on, but his grasp is slipping. He can't get back inside. The etched lines slide under his fingertips. Grandfather is trying to keep him out. Oliver's hand goes numb. Then his arm. He closes his eyes and lets the super sphere absorb him once again.

Into the darkness he goes.

Into a bodiless space inside the super sphere that seems endless and welcome.

This time, he's not alone.

Grandfather struggles to push him back out, to put him in his body. *You don't belong here!* the old man shouts.

Oliver clings to the inner space, holding it with his thoughts, grasping with his presence. But Grandfather is too strong, too big. He feels the cold edge of the super sphere, the etched lines pressing into his awareness, the warmth of his hand lying limp on the metallic surface.

He begins to leak back into his skin—

The door is blown off its hinges.

It spins through the room, whooshes over Oliver's fleshly body, and snaps the levitating spire in half. A snowstorm fills the room. Oliver, clinging to the inner space of the super sphere, watches his fleshly body lift in the updraft and safety of powerful arms.

Flury!

The snowman pulls Oliver's fleshly body to his chest and crashes into the leaking ceiling like a wrecking ball. Water erodes the ceiling as the river above them finds a way inside. The swarm of orbs fall on Flury, nipping away his snowy body like flying piranha. They dart around the lab, the orbs gnawing at his arms and legs. Flury bounces off the floor, the ceiling and a workbench, soaring toward the exit.

The snowthings arrive.

Their slushy bodies ooze through the broken doorway.

They don't resume their grotesque forms that stood next to the windmill. They remain a neverending stream of gray slush that fills the room, surrounding Flury and plugging the leaking ceiling.

The slush streams toward the super sphere and enters the gravitational field.

Oliver grows.

But he's no longer just Oliver. His thoughts mingle with Grandfather's memories. Their minds, still separate, merge at the edges. They're becoming one.

Oliver-Grandfather.

Together, they're becoming an abominable.

And the gray slush surrounds them, gives them strength. As they fill the room, the cold torrent of partially melted snow cages Flury. The snowman eludes the super sphere's gravitational pull, cradling Oliver's limp and empty body in his arms.

Rage fills Oliver.

It pours into his being from the outside of his consciousness, radiating from Grandfather's awareness. It contaminates Oliver's mind as if they were one and the same. It fills him with seething anger, bitter vengeance. The urge to strike, to destroy, to fight the burning pain. He's consumed with the urge to crush Flury, to slurp him up like the streaming snowthings that have given themselves to the super sphere's vortex.

The amorphous gray slush spreads around the dome's perimeter. The empty space shrinks. The rage grows hotter. Flury will be digested in the pit of Grandfather's rage. The snowman risked his life; he came here to save Oliver. Flury doesn't know that his body is an empty husk.

I'll never walk again. Never kiss again. Never feel.

He'll be trapped in the super sphere forever. And ever.

Feed that, Grandfather's thoughts ring. *Give your sadness to the anger; let it burn the ashes of grief.*

The gelatinous slurry snatches Flury's leg. The snowman eludes the grasp by reforming his malleable body, but Oliver's flaccid body hinders his ability to elude the closing predator.

Grandfather's laughter echoes within the inner space. He's toying with the snowman, making him pay for locking him out of the dome all these years, for making him age in the cold wilderness.

It's just the beginning of the old man's trail of revenge.

Oliver relies on the memory of what it felt like to close his eyes and take a deep breath. He calms his thoughts. Outside his circle of awareness, Grandfather continues laughing.

Oliver concentrates.

He forms a thought, a single action. He protects it, hides it. He nurtures it with all his being, gives it purpose. He doesn't think about anything else, doesn't contemplate the consequences, what it will do to his own fleshly body. Oliver simply gives the thought all his strength. All his love.

Because he can't let Grandfather do this.

Because he won't give in to the fury.

When all of his intention fills this thought, he lets it go. It travels throughout the super sphere and into the gray body, quivering throughout the cold slurry. The slushy body that envelopes the super sphere is Oliver's body, too.

And he tells it what to do.

Grandfather hears it, but it's too late.

The thought directs the slush to part near the ceiling and expose the hole. Water begins dumping inside. The grip on Flury loosens. With Oliver's fleshly body safely tucked against his snowy chest, Flury bolts toward the ceiling and buries his fist in the gushing hole.

The floodgate opens.

Earth and water crash down.

32

U tter darkness.

No pain, no pressure. Just utter darkness.

Oliver moves with thoughts through the stillness. Despite the crushing earth that lay all around, it's not until he remembers his body is gone that panic sets in.

What am I if I have no body?

The super sphere is his body now, but he's not the only one inside it. Other thoughts are out there in the darkness. Grandfather's thoughts have wrapped around him, pushed him aside, enclosed him in a tiny corner of the sphere. Oliver can't feel the smothering weight of the soil, but he can taste the bitter thoughts that imprison him.

The anger. The rage.

It trickles like an elixir, feeds the vengeance he's nurtured for a hundred years. And now that he's in the sphere, it infects everything. Grandfather's mind flexes and roars.

The fury is out.

What is he avenging?

Beyond the echoes of Grandfather's thoughts, somewhere outside the confines of the super sphere, water trickles. A thousand rivulets are wicking through the soil. The super sphere is packed deep underground. Buried somewhere near is the angry swarm of orbs. Somewhere there are the dead orbs that once made up the snowthings.

Flury, too.

I'm dead.

His body has been crushed beneath a million tons of soil. Yet he feels no different in the inner space of the super sphere than he did in his flesh. How long will he survive inside it?

Forever.

Panic and fear ripple through the inner mind space.

If he could run, he would race away. If he could dig, he would climb out of this grave. But he's trapped.

The water continues to trickle toward the super sphere.

Oliver feels the strange weird of low blood sugar. Impossible, since he has no body. Hyperventilating, maybe? He's not breathing. He's pretending to breathe. It brings him comfort, breeds familiarity. He counts ten breaths and starts over.

Again and again.

When his thoughts cease to race, he reaches out like he did before, attempts to connect with the super sphere, to feel it like it is his body. If the trickling water continues to gravitate toward it, maybe he could climb. Maybe he could bring his fleshly body to the surface and breathe life into it.

Flury, too.

Grandfather has taken precautions. Oliver feels through the dark, his thoughts reaching out like appendages, but Grandfather's essence is everywhere, creating walls that contain Oliver, imprison him, keep him from interfering again.

Walls of pain and suffering.

He wants the world to feel his pain. He wants to be understood. Wants the world to hear him.

The earth moves.

A subtle quake rumbles through the dark. It feels like the soil is settling around them, packing tighter against the super sphere. It happens again.

This time the super sphere moves.

We're rising.

It's small jumps at first, but each successive attempt lightens the world around them. The trickling water is in the super sphere's gravitational field. Grandfather is building another body. He'll climb out of the earth. He'll find revenge.

Oliver spins through the dark. Grandfather's memories disorient him like a house of mirrors.

I can't stop him.

The rage is too great, the fury too potent. The old man has stoked this furnace for a century; it's too hot. Oliver can't possibly beat him.

So he begins digging through the old man's memories.

The most recent ones are saturated with loneliness. It's the years he spent on the property with only his snowthings and his thoughts. At night, he roamed the property, sending the snowthings digging through the earth to crack through the dome.

Flury always there to stop them.

When Oliver and his mom arrived, Grandfather knew his opportunity had come. He swept the entry road with the snowthings, had them dust the trails from the snow in the morning, and arranged for the footlocker to be found. Grandmother was helpless to stop him.

The world trembles.

The super sphere is rising faster. The surface is near. A cold sensation leaks through his thoughts. Darkness turns gray.

Then light.

Snow.

Water and fog are poor substitutes. The super sphere was built for snow, to gather it, to pack it. To be it. The water, having served its purpose, falls from the super sphere as the snow begins to swirl.

The world comes into focus.

The three-hundred-and-sixty-degree vision is restored. Images appear in the pale moonlight. Trees are toppled, and the river diverted. A whirlpool eddies below the fallen tree that served as Oliver's footbridge to the hobbit house. The stone chimney has toppled.

The sound of a locomotive begins to wail.

Oliver looks to the sky, expecting to see military jets, but the sound is all around. Snow is sliding across the ground and out of the trees.

Limbs snap, and tree trunks sway.

The howling continues.

A torso. Legs. Arms.

He's building a body.

Oliver dives back into Grandfather's memories. He tunnels beneath the hardened thoughts of recent past, digs deeper into his life. The memories are calcified and brittle. It takes great effort to push past the years of lonely bitterness. Back in time, he goes.

The birth of Mom and Aunt Rhonnie.

Late nights in the lab.

Building the house.

As the world outside the sphere continues to quake, Oliver digs past burning memories of hate and anger and finds the softer under-lying memories.

Pain and sorrow.

He had escaped the North Pole. He travelled with a companion back home to find the woman he'd survived to see, the woman that kept him alive through all the isolation in the North Pole. He yearned to see the woman whose photo was tucked into the locket, the woman he wrote to in his journals. His most dearest was waiting for him at the end of this long and impossible journey.

The woman that kept him alive.

My love.

He arrived to find an abandoned house. The furniture and belong-ings were covered in dust and rat droppings. Spider webs filled the corners. His heart broke cold. He thundered through the house, opened doors, cried her name. Fear had never gripped Malcolm Toye like it did that day. And when he found her, he fell on his knees.

She was in the backyard.

Malcolm Toye collapsed on the soft ground. A crudely assembled cross was askew in a mound of earth. Letters were scrawled into the wood.

Here lies Gayle Toye. Died of a broken heart.

Scarlet fever had claimed her life, he later discovered. It did not matter. His sorrow was unquenchable. His rage, endless.

He would never see his love again.

And he blamed the elven.

Had they not saved him, he would be united with his love in death. Had they released him, he would have returned sooner. They were to blame for his pain and suffering.

All of it.

Grandfather, the monstrous snowman, thunders through the forest. He doesn't bother pushing trees out of the way; he walks through them. The trunks crack like fireworks. They reach the open field. Beyond is the windmill.

And the house.

Rage radiates through the air like waves of heat. The snow is inhaled from the field, swirling into Grandfather's body. The legs become thicker, the arms stronger. The chest swells.

Grandfather roars.

The windows on the house shatter.

Oliver's awareness is ringing. He tries to find a place for Grandfather's memories as they merge into his awareness. The sadness, the agony, is torture. But a question continues to rise.

If the woman he loved died, then who is Grandmother?

There are three vibrating houses that finally come together as Oliver's focus returns. Snow swirls in the distance. A small storm has gathered at the back steps of the house. Someone is coming for them.

Flury! He made it out!

Oliver can't see through the shattered windows. There's no candlelight, no movement. No way to tell if anyone has stayed.

He hopes not.

Flury barrels across the field. Grandfather lifts his arms, casting moonlit shadows, and claps at the pesky snowman. Flury eludes the crushing blow and crushes Grandfather's knee.

The world tips.

Before Flury can deliver another strike, Grandfather rebuilds the leg and swats him. Flury tumbles across the field, his shiny orb temporarily dislodging from his chest. The snowman returns from the trees for another charge. The hopeless battle resumes.

Something moves at the house.

Someone descends the back steps. The movement is slow and careful. Her hands are folded over her stomach.

Grandmother.

Her path is clear.

No. No, no, no, no, no!

Grandfather doesn't notice the old woman. He catches Flury in his right hand and squeezes, but the snowman's orb slips between his fingers. Grandfather stomps the orb, and the earth rumbles like an approaching storm. He picks up his foot, expecting to see the pest flattened.

Flury's orb jettisons away.

Grandfather, fueled by hate, anger and revenge, begins to inhale again. This time it's not the snow he's drawing upon. Flury, still a naked orb with no snow to build his body, begins to slow before escaping into the trees.

Grandfather's going to absorb him.

Oliver turns his thoughts away and, once again, drives into Grandfather's memories. The deeper he goes, the softer they become. The emotions become like magma, warm and sticky.

Dense.

Oliver sinks deeper, letting the underlying emotions, the foundation of Grandfather's hatred, saturate his awareness and begins lifting it out of the depths. The memories have been buried so deep, packed away so that he would forget the pain.

Oliver brings it out of his subconscious for Grandfather to see.

Sadness, powerlessness. Aloneness.

There's so much of it.

It gushes to the surface like a tapped well, spewing through the hardened layers of hatred and bitterness. Sadness flows into the outer banks of Grandfather's mind.

The snowy titan hesitates.

Grandfather's thoughts turn toward Oliver. He feels the unearthed grief, the unresolved sorrow he buried all those years ago. For a moment, he seems curious to find so much, to discover that these memories have been the fuel driving the hatred, that his fear of being swallowed by his sadness drove him into anger.

And then he sees Grandmother.

The rage returns.

Oliver is scalded by an influx of vengeful thoughts. All the blame is focused on the old woman. Grandfather bats Flury deep into the forest and takes a giant step.

The ground trembles.

Grandmother falls to her knees.

Grandfather towers over the feeble old woman. Images of hate flit through Oliver's vision. Grandfather seeks to quench the ancient itch of revenge.

Oliver turns deeper into the old man's memories. The thoughts become hot. They boil like tar. There's one last wellspring of emotion he hasn't reached, a gold mine that's been feeding the hatred all these years, baking it into a hardened crust on which the old man has feasted until it was all he knew.

The old man lifts his colossal arms.

Grandmother gets to her feet.

With snow dusting her coat, she stares up. Her expression is a foreign one; a look that's never appeared in Oliver's presence. It's open and compassionate. Fearless.

Loving.

Flury emerges from the trees, but it's too late. The giant fists come arching down. The wind whistles. Grandfather howls.

And then Oliver reaches the bottom of his hidden feelings.

He finds the thoughts underlying Grandfather's mind, the pit of his emotions—the unresolved depth of his being. It is the foundation that supports everything he's become, a pool of resources buried deeply and soundly. Oliver feels it explode from hiding, feels it fill Grandfather's mind.

Fear.

Underneath all the hate is fear.

Perhaps if he'd reached it a second or two earlier, it would've made a difference. The lethal arms soften and slow, but they can't be stopped. The momentum carries them to the ground.

Grandmother disappears beneath their crushing weight.

A plume of snow swallows the sky.

Everything rings white.

33

Snow falls.

The engorged snowflakes flutter to the earth until the world is white.

The sound of Oliver's footsteps is soft and muffled. Mesmerized by winter's hypnotic dance, he's mildly surprised to discover he has hands and legs. His fleshly body is back.

Am I still in the super sphere?

The trees are gone.

The landscape is flat and white, the air choked with snow.

He starts in the direction that feels like home, but nothing ever materializes, no matter where or how far he goes. Despite the isolation, he's filled with peace. No panic or fear, no tension or worry. Just a peaceful world, wherever he is.

Even the distant rumble of thunder doesn't shake him.

A darkened blot forms on the horizon. *The house?* When it grows larger, wobbling as it nears, he's certain it's not the house. The person is as short as she is wide. A long braid of hair is slung over her shoulder. What he thought were snowshoes look more like wide boots.

Those aren't boots...they're her bare feet!

She waddles close enough to see her blue-green eyes, the snow squelching under each footstep. She's not even half his height.

"Who are you?" Oliver asks.

Her brow protrudes in concentration, staring through him.

"What's happening?" he asks. "Where am I?"

"You are still inside."

"The super sphere? But...how did my body get here?"

"Your thoughts have crystallized." Her fingers are short and fat. "Thoughts can be quite convincing."

He's seen her before. She's in one of the pictures along the stairwell, between the second and third floor. She was on the end of the pier, who he thought was a child the first time. She's the elven. Those are her clothes in the attic.

Something else is familiar.

"Are you my imagination?" he asks.

"I'm afraid not."

She pauses again, letting him explore the strange sense of familiarity. It's the way she's looking at him. The way the wrinkles bunch around her lips. Her eyes are blue, but green around the pupils. No one has eyes like that, except...

"Grandmother?"

She blinks heavily. Nods once.

"I...I don't understand."

"Of course not. No one would."

He thinks maybe his thoughts have made her appear shrunken, that she's a delusion. But just because your delusion tells you this is real doesn't make it so.

"Why do you look like that?"

"This is my true nature. The North Pole was my home." She opens her arms.

"You're elven? I...I don't..."

"Like I said, no one would understand. Sometimes, I don't know how I got here, but life is such. What you see around you is my home. Thousands of years ago, I was born an elven. Of course, you've read the journals, you know about the elven."

"But how could you be one?"

"I met a human long ago, a man in great pain. I sought to help him, but my compassion was misguided and brought us here today."

"But you're...or were...I thought you were human?"

"I transformed into human once it was clear I could not remain elven."

"The hobbit house."

A tiny house built into the earth, something that would resemble the ice caverns in the North Pole. That was built for her.

"It was not an easy process," she says. "Nor pleasant, but I could not go home, not after betraying my people. I was destined to live among humans. It was better that I become one. But here, inside the super sphere, you see me as I was born. You see my true nature. Inside here, our true intentions are exposed, our true nature embraced. Here, there is nowhere to hide."

Another round of thunder.

Grandmother looks up. Snowflakes melt on her cheeks.

"You accomplished something I failed to do for a hundred years," she says. "You showed your grandfather his true nature, helped him see past the bitterness and anger. You put him in touch with the sorrow and hurt beneath it all."

"He's still here?"

She smiles.

It's an expression Oliver doesn't associate with Grandmother, but one so infectious that he smiles, too.

"Of course he's here. His body is dead. So is mine."

There's no way she could survive the impact of that final blow. Grandfather's fists fell like military tanks.

"I'm sorry," he says.

"It was time for my body to rest. But you saved me."

"Me?"

"Yes, you. Your grandfather doubted his actions at the last moment, and that's what allowed the super sphere to absorb my awareness before my body passed. Elven never really die, you know that. We simply pass into the abominables when our bodies expire. We live in the inner world of our snowmen. As you can see, there's very little difference inside here."

Oliver wouldn't have known this was a dream. *Maybe the dream is outside the super sphere.*

"You, on the other hand," she says, "shouldn't be here."

"Too late for that." Panic clenches his heart and tears blur his vision. His body is in a deep grave.

"Your grandfather thought it was too late for him. His intentions, though, were misguided. I thought I could help him, save him from his thoughts and beliefs, but we can't live in the present when we're stuck in the past. And you can't help someone from themselves, no matter how much you love them.

"Your grandfather figured out a great many things, inventions that I thought would contribute to humanity. But when he created the super sphere"—she waves her arms—"I realized he was stuck on revenge. We were trapped on the property. The windmill, I'm sure you've noticed, always turns. As long as it does, none of us could leave. Not even Flury. Our lives had become stagnant. Your grandfather became angrier. Until you arrived.

"It took a beginner's mind, our grandson, to see with new eyes to resolve our beliefs. You freed us."

Grandmother slides forward and takes his hand.

"You did this. You saved us."

"I didn't do anything."

"You taught an old lady how to live and an old man how to love. You did everything."

Oliver grasps his grandmother's small hands. A smile broadens her cherub cheeks. Her grip is firm and warm. She doesn't say it, but he feels it.

Thank you.

Thunder pounds the heavens. This time the world quakes, the snow shudders.

"Ah," Grandmother says. "It looks like Flury has found us."

"What's happening?"

"The super sphere was buried in a mountain of snow when your grandfather collapsed. Flury has been searching for it. I believe he's close. He'll take you back."

"Back? Back where?"

"To your body, of course. You don't belong here."

"I don't have one. I'm..." He can't say it out loud. The word chokes him. *Dead.*

"Nonsense. Flury wouldn't let you die. Too many love you."

"I...I don't understand."

Wind comes out of nowhere.

The ground tips.

Oliver loses his balance. The snowflakes shriek past his ears, stinging his cheeks. He shields his eyes. Nausea curdles his stomach, and he begins to shiver. Electric shocks tremble beneath his skin.

His body feels like the jaws of a steel trap.

The storm swirls around him. The snow obscures her fading form. She's blurry.

Pain lances his sides.

Voices warble around him, some panicked and loud, others soothing. One voice is clear. It comes from the form fading in the sweeping snow.

Grandmother releases his hand. "Goodbye, Olivah."

He doubles over, falls backwards. The snow is hard like a wood floor. The weird feeling is back. It fills him, weighs him down, makes the world fuzzy and blurry and swirly.

His blood sugar is low.

34

"Where's his kit?" That's Mom's voice. She'd seen diabetic shock and knows what to do. She always remained calm, tested his blood, brought his sugar back up. She knows what to do.

Why isn't she doing it?

"He's dying!" That's Aunt Rhonnie.

"Look in his bedroom, Molly," Mom says.

"Are you joking?" Aunt Rhonnie shouts. "He's unconscious; he's barely breathing! He doesn't need an orange slice, for crying out loud. Give him one of those shots!"

"Stop it! Just stop it! Panic isn't helping. Just calm down." Mom repeats her request to Molly, but now her voice shakes. "We have to find out if his blood sugar is high or low. Do the wrong thing and we kill him."

"He's dying, sister."

"Rhonnie! Just shut it!"

Panic is in order. Oliver can barely feel his body. It's like he's received a transfusion of maple syrup. He can't move, not even his eyelids. So heavy, so tired. The wood floor is on his back, but the room is freezing.

Molly comes back. "I...I can't find it."

"Did you look in his book bag?"

There's an argument. Mom demands everyone start looking for it.

The bathroom. The diabetic kit bag is in the bathroom, on the floor.

The front door slams. "It's no good," Henry says, out of breath. "Trees are all over the entry road. There's no way we're getting out. We're trapped."

Aunt Rhonnie shrieks. "We're all going to die!"

"Did you get to the main road?" Mom asks.

"No," Henry says.

"I told you to get out there and see if you get a phone signal!"

"It doesn't matter. An ambulance can't make it to the house."

"We can carry him out," Mom says. "Or a helicopter can fly in. Go back out there and call 911, damn it!"

"Pour orange juice in his mouth."

"Rhonnie, shut up! He's unconscious; we need help now!"

Henry doesn't go. He didn't even try the first time because it's still dark and the forest is making strange sounds. And they just saw a snow titan crush their grandmother. No way in hell he's climbing over trees in the dark.

"Pick him up," Mom says. "Let's pick him up. We can't waste time; we'll call 911 when we get to the road. Come on, let's go."

Oliver focuses all his strength on his eyelids. They flutter open.

"Oh, my God, my God. He's awake," Aunt Rhonnie says. "Get the orange juice."

"Oliver? Honey?" Mom's hand is hot on his forehead. "Can you hear me?"

He moans.

"Sweetie, we're all here. Your blood sugar is off, all right? We're going to get you to a hospital, so just relax. Do you know where your kit is?"

Bathroom. He concentrates on the word. It sits on his tongue and moves to his lips. Mom lowers her ear—

Fffzzzzzzzzzzzt.

His body stiffens. The seizure is mild but lasts almost a minute.

Molly is squeezing his hand when he returns. "It's all right," she's whispering. "It'll be all right."

She sounds brave, but her voice is cracking.

"Get over here, everyone! Pick him up!"

"It won't do any good," Henry says. "Trees are everywhere. I couldn't climb through them, let alone carry him. It's just...impossible."

"We're carrying him out now, so get over here!" Mom throws Oliver's arm over her shoulder. "Now let's go. Helen, open the doors and keep looking for his kit. It's a little black bag with a zipper. Go back to his bedroom, then the bathroom. Now!"

Seizure number two makes number one look like a shiver.

Oliver had grabbed electrical lines on a dare in chemistry lab once. This was like that, only the electricity started in his brain.

About 10,000 volts worth.

He planks, shaking like a bell struck with a hammer. He floats somewhere near the ceiling. His body is bouncing on the floor.

The drab wallpaper flickers.

A fuzzy halo surrounds their heads.

Then he's back in his body, his eyes dry and burning. The voices around him slowly come up to speed.

Something is snapping.

The curtains around the picture window flap in the sudden wind. Jagged edges of glass are stuck in the pane like broken teeth.

A dark form fills the open window.

"Oliver?" Mom says. "Oliver? Listen to me, honey. We're going to give you some juice. Do you know where your kit is? Honey, please?"

Her hand is on his forehead.

Molly strokes his arm, holds his hand.

"Is it upstairs?" she asks. "Nod if you think it's—"

Aunt Rhonnie screams. There are words in it, but they're primitive. Helen returns and shrieks. Both back away from the window.

"It's back!" Helen manages to say. "It's back, it's back, it's back!"

They scuttle to the back of the dark room. Henry, too. A shadow grows in the open window. A large gray hand grabs the pane.

Flury barely fits through the opening.

"No! No, no, no! Get away!" Mom jumps up. "Get back out there! You can't have him. Get away!"

The snowman is too large to stand inside the room. Instead, he crawls toward Oliver. His eyes are darker in the dim room. Mom kicks his arm, punches his head. Molly stands over Oliver and chops at his arm. Snow sprays.

Flury ignores them.

Gently, he parts them with both arms. His frozen hands are cold but soft, sliding under Oliver. Like before, he holds Oliver to his chest like a child. Mom's grief is filled with rage as she chips away at his snow-molded forearms.

Molly hits him with a chair.

Snow spatters.

"Please," Mom begs. "Please don't take him."

Flury lifts him out of the house.

The wind howls around his hulking body, but Oliver's protected in his arms. Mom is at the window. Molly is climbing out to give chase. Oliver tries to lift his hand, to put his finger to his lips and tell them it will be all right. He knows where Flury is taking him. They can't get him to the hospital. The roads are blocked; the weather is bad.

But then the windmill squeals.

Trees lay all around it, but the windmill is still upright.

It's still churning.

Still working.

"No." His voice scratches his throat. "You can't...you can't..."

Oliver attempts to squirm from Flury's embrace. He's too weak, the snowman too strong. Oliver can't get the words out.

You can't leave the property!

The world is smudged with Flury's speed.

Oliver's eyes fill with tears. The frozen air steals his breath. He hunkers in the snowman's grip as the world speeds by. When the tears clear, Oliver can see pinpoints of light from distant towns. Treetops streak below.

Flying.

We're flying over the property.

The unbreathable wind is vicious, scouring his cheeks, numbing his face. Flury covers Oliver's head to protect him. In that pocket between his arms and chest, Oliver breathes easier.

They soar in perfect silence.

And peace fills him.

No. He knows the snowman can hear his thoughts. *I can't let you.*

The top of Oliver's head is numb. The arms aren't covering it anymore, not like they were minutes before. He holds his breath and turns his head. Through the streaming tears, the tiny lights are bigger. They're gaining on them. They must be off the property by now.

Oliver's stomach drops as they fall from the sky.

He clutches at the snowy arms. They're smaller and softer. Wetter.

Flury's footsteps thud on the ground.

Oliver breathes into his shoulder to keep the icy air from choking him. But it's not the wind that's grown more violent. He's more exposed because Flury's arms are thinner.

He's shrinking.

The highway is dark. The headlights distant.

Flury's footsteps grow heavy.

The wind begins to die. Lights no longer streak past them. Oliver scratches at the snowman's chest. The icy snow flutters away and doesn't return. A bright light burns inside his chest. Oliver can now see the orb pulsing, fighting the windmill's deteriorating effect.

With each step, it burns dimmer.

Pulses fainter.

When they reach the road outside the hospital, Flury is the size of an ordinary man. Oliver's legs dangle at his side. Like he'd done over a hundred years ago with his grandfather, Flury holds Oliver like a child.

It's no longer the wind filling Oliver's eyes with tears.

The snowman trots into the bright lights. By the time he reaches the emergency room entrance, he appears like a snow-crusted child carrying a teenage boy.

The doors slide open.

Oliver's weight heaves forward. He falls gently to the polished floor and slides across a pile of melted snow. He stops at the foot of an empty desk.

Nurses rush out.

"No, no, no," he mutters.

Several people hover. A woman gives urgent commands. "Who brought him in here?" she shouts.

Just before they lift him, Oliver opens his eyes. The ceiling lights are bright. He turns his head just as they begin wheeling him away.

He sees the weighted orb in a pile of slush.

The ornate etchings of Flury's heart glisten beneath the fluorescent lighting.

The metal surface is dull.

35

The delicate patterns of frost stretch over the window, their crystalline structures intersecting. Intertwining. Outside, the Christmas lights glow around the hospital courtyard, lending green and red halos to the frosty pane.

Oliver leans off the bed.

The floor is hard and cold on his feet. A draft sweeps into the back of the loosely tied gown as he brushes his fingers across the window. It's smooth and frigid, but his hand is warm.

He stares into his palm.

There are no lines besides the naturally occurring wrinkles. No tingling up his arm. He's warm because he's been in bed for days, not because the wooden orb is calling. That's somewhere on the property, buried beneath the river.

A lump rises in his throat.

Diabetic shock is a serious condition, but when he arrived at the hospital they diagnosed him with more than that: hypothermia, nutrient imbalance, exhaustion...all the signs of a drowning victim.

Each day he awoke in the hospital, a lump would rise from his stomach and rest in his throat. Oliver would lie in bed, staring at the ceiling tiles, trying to make it go away, trying to forget how he got here. But each day, he felt heavier. His stomach was filled with a weight about the size of the metal orb that's resting on the nightstand.

Flury.

Oliver picks it up with both hands. It's the size of a softball with the weight of a bowling ball. The nurse said he brought it with him. They thought it was a Christmas ornament.

He couldn't explain how he got there. When his mom and Molly arrived an hour later, having climbed out to the road and called for help, they couldn't explain it, either. Oliver woke the next morning with the metal orb at his side.

The sharp lines, once brilliant with light, are dark and recessed. The metal surface is foggy. If he could open the hospital window, he'd toss it in the snow and wait for his hero to pull the snow off the ground and stand in the courtyard. But the window won't open.

And his hero is gone.

The door opens. "I see your underwear," Molly says.

Oliver doesn't bother closing the back of his gown. He clutches the orb on his lap. Molly sits next to him, her weight sinking into the bed. Her hair hangs past her shoulders. No ponytails today. No makeup or jewelry.

"Where's Mom?" he asks.

"At the funeral parlor. Visitation is tomorrow. You wouldn't believe the response from all the charities your grandmother supported. For a recluse, she's real popular."

"No one knows what happened to her?"

"Coroner says she had a heart attack."

Grandmother's body was found in the backyard. After Flury took Oliver away, they found her in the backyard, hands folded over her stomach. Her complexion was pallid, eyes closed. It was as if she were sleeping between the house and garage.

Peace at last.

Flury had retrieved her after he returned Oliver to his body while Mom was desperately searching for the diabetic kit. Her body was unharmed by Grandfather's devastating blow. Maybe he didn't crush her after all, just invited her into the super sphere.

The lump rises into Oliver's throat, and, once again, he tries to swallow it down.

Molly goes to the helium balloons tied to a vase of flowers. Cards are propped on a table. "Ms. Megan wanted to come see you, but we told her you were getting out tomorrow."

She reads the cards, then tells him about Aunt Rhonnie asking about the will. Henry and Helen have told people what really happened, but no one believes them.

Because it's crazy.

Oliver traces the lines on the orb. The edges are crisp.

Molly puts the cards back and sits with him. They stare through the frosted glass. Somewhere out there, Christmas carols are sung.

He feels so heavy.

Nearly dying takes a lot out of you. It could also be the medication or the exhaustion, but he's slept for days, and his blood sugar is back to normal. And he's not tired. It's a heaviness that penetrates his gut, hovers in his throat. Every time he looks at the orb, it adds another pinch of sand to the weight.

Molly takes his hand. He cradles the orb with his other hand.

The lump won't swallow back this time.

And the frosty etchings on the window get blurry.

"It's not your fault," she says.

"Yes, it is." The words shake at the edges.

Oliver looks away so she doesn't see his lower lip quiver. She squeezes his hand. He hangs on like she's the ledge of sanity. But his fingers are slipping as he sniffles.

"I told him not to do it." His voice is blurry. "He shouldn't have. He didn't deserve this, not after everything he did. He's not just this."

He squeezes the metal orb.

"He was someone. He was better than me."

He tries to wipe the tears, but more come. The lump in his throat opens, and his chest begins to quake. It's no use swallowing. The sobs start as hiccups. He holds his breath and squeezes his eyes shut, but a river is flowing.

Oliver has always felt this way.

He's always felt like he didn't matter, like he was a burden. That weight was always in his belly, because everyone was better than him. And he knows it's not true, but it doesn't stop it from being there. Doesn't stop him from feeling that way.

And now he holds a true friend on his lap. Because of Oliver.

He tries to sob quietly. He covers his face, bawls into his hand. He's not just crying for Flury. It's his mom, his dad, his grandmother.

His grandfather.

It all weighs on him.

Molly wraps her arms around him. He drops the orb and buries his face in her hair, weeping openly.

"He chose you to help your family," she whispers. "You know why? Because he saw your heart, Oliver. He saw it was good."

They could hear him in the hall, but he didn't care. He had to get this out, had to let go of the weight. When he finally pulls away, he covers his face to wipe his puffy eyes. The aftershocks rattle his lower lip.

The tears begin to dry.

"He left you a gift," Molly says.

Oliver looks at the orb sunk in the bed. Molly shakes her head. She lays her hand over his chest.

Flury touched their lives. He changed his heart, his life. And that gift would last forever.

That night he sleeps deeply.

He dreams of snow in every direction. The wind swirls, but his heart warms. When he wakes, the orb is still dull and heavy.

But it is warm.

36

M olly turns the radio off.
The roads are still wet. April showers have been consistent for two weeks, and May flowers are already filling the ditches.

She pulls off the main road and stops in front of the gate. Weeds crowd around the brick pillars. Oliver expects it to open automatically, but the black gate sits still.

They sit quietly.

Neither of them has been out to the property since Christmas. Oliver runs his hand through his hair. It's almost as long as Molly's. He gets out of the truck to open the gate.

Most of the trees are still standing. The ones that had fallen have been removed, their enormous trunks squarely cut. Mom had trouble finding an arborist to clear the road in February. The rumors of the haunted property were persistent.

This place was dark and mysterious when he had first arrived a year and a half ago. Now light filters through the trees, highlighting the undergrowth.

No more secrets.

The house looks like a survivor.

Most of the windows are boarded. The attic window is still intact, watching them park behind Mom's car. Molly turns off the truck, and, once again, they sit quietly. She follows his lead, letting him go at his own pace. He tried to come out in March.

He just wasn't ready.

Oliver waits for Molly at the bottom step, their fingers entwine as she reaches for him. They start up the steps, but he stops and listens.

"What is it?" she asks.

"Listen."

They pause. "I don't hear anything."

"I know."

"And I don't smell the weird," she says.

And then he gets it. It's not the smell.

It's the sound.

Birds are singing. Squirrels are crossing limbs. Nature is rampant.

The property is open to the world again.

Footprints are stamped in a thin layer of sawdust on the porch. The contractors say the house will be habitable by autumn. They don't understand how the place worked. It's wired for power but never had any delivered. The contractors that ask too many questions usually end up quitting.

The glass panes alongside the door are intact. Oliver pauses, half-expecting a gray-haired woman to appear in the decorative glass. But no one is waiting for them when he opens it.

The house smells like mold, sawdust and plaster. A few of the pictures are on the steps, leaning against the wall. Above them are bright squares where they'd previously hung. The place still looks haunted, it just doesn't feel it.

Aunt Rhonnie wanted nothing to do with it, although the money she inherited apparently wasn't haunted. Mom let her have the majority of the investments. She wanted the property.

So did Oliver.

The kitchen is empty. The refrigerator is open and bare, so is the pantry. The chalkboard is still hanging inside the door. One chore is listed.

Rule #1: Finish your work.

There was a time when Oliver thought he'd never come back. There would be too much sadness out here. Flury wasn't just an invention. He contained a soul. Maybe it was a collection of memories, a soup of past elven that existed as one, whatever it was...he was real.

And now he's gone.

The cabinet above the sink is open, and the tea set missing. He finds it in the dining room, the table set. An empty teacup sits in a saucer at the head of the table.

Gooseflesh rises up his back.

"Look at this." Molly carries one of the framed photos from the steps. "I was putting it back on the wall and noticed this."

It's the photo of the ship at port with people gathered at the bottom of the ramp. The men wore bowlers. There are no women carrying umbrellas in what appeared to be a cloudless day, but there is the little girl.

Oliver rubs the dust away.

A very overweight child. *Not a child. An elven.*

Grandmother.

She looked exactly like he'd last seen her, inside the super sphere. They had arrived by ship as paying customers. Surely there were questions, but nothing they couldn't answer. She was a dwarf, they probably said. And once they arrived on the property, no one probably saw her again.

At least not looking like that.

The journals said the elven could transform humans into elven, and the process could be reversed. How long did she live in the hobbit house before deciding to become human? And why did she become human?

Why? Because she loved him.

She loved Malcolm Toye.

OUT BACK, the garage doors are gone.

They were blown off their hinges when Flury escaped the dome's collapse, when he whisked Oliver's body into the front room before charging across the field to confront the rising snow titan that Grandfather had become.

Something clatters on the concrete floor.

"I'll be right back," Oliver says.

Oliver peers around the corner of the garage.

Mom is squatting to the right of the filing cabinets, piling items into a box.

"Hey."

"Oh!" She lets a rag fly. "You scared me."

"Expecting a snowman?"

"I didn't hear you pull up."

She pushes a strand of hair under her headband. There are no earrings to twist. She stopped wearing those shortly after Christmas.

Never said why.

"What are you doing?" Oliver asks.

"Cleaning up. I've been putting it off forever." She spies Molly at the windmill. "Glad you came out."

He helps her lift the box onto the workbench. There are stacks of folders, old tools and miscellaneous cans. There are also mouse droppings on the shelves. *Nature's back.*

Oliver glances under the bench. The footlocker is missing.

He was never quite sure if Grandfather had been the one responsible for letting him have that. A part of him wonders if Grandmother put it there. Maybe she wanted him to find the wooden orb but Grandfather put the journals in it. She was genuinely shocked when she found them in his backpack.

The car is still there, but the shine is gone. Rust spots have already appeared on the bumper. The interior is water stained. When the dome collapsed, the car must've automatically found its way back. It hasn't moved since. Without a key, it would remain an ornament.

Mom is staring out the window, the glass missing.

"You all right?" Oliver asks.

She nods. "I've been avoiding the garage because I thought it would be too hard to remember my father. It was the only time I really spent time with him, watching him tinker with his toys while I played on the floor. But I keep looking at the house, expecting Mother to come out the back door. It's weird, but I miss her. And I never thought I'd ever say that."

He never told her about Grandmother's true elven nature.

Molly's the only one that knows what happened after he left the house with Grandfather. When Mom asks about it, he says he doesn't remember. It wouldn't change anything if he told her, but it seems like the right thing.

She was her mother. That's all that matters.

"The other day I stood on the bottom step of the staircase for half an hour. You believe that?" Mom's eyes turn glassy. "I just, uh, did it for her, I guess. I don't know."

"She loved us. In her weird way."

He cringes. He shouldn't have said "weird." She valued duty over feeling. She had to. He had a feeling there weren't many good feelings after she left home. Her home.

The North Pole.

"You want these?" She slides a stack of leather-bound journals across the bench.

"Where'd you find them?"

"Mother's room."

He opens the one on top. They're the ones she found in his backpack. He rubs the cover and slides them back.

He already knows the story.

THE WINDMILL IS STILL STANDING, but the blades locked in place.

"Do you want to walk out?" Molly asks.

"Your dad will be mad."

"I won't tell him if you don't."

Molly's dad wasn't happy with all the mystery after the event. She wasn't allowed to spend much time with Oliver, but Mom mended that fence when she went over to talk with him.

"They're good for each other," she insisted.

Many of the trees lay around the field.

They hike across the field and enter the forest where only a few trees have fallen. Oliver raises his phone and touches the screen. He only gets one bar of service. The compass, however, points north and doesn't shift. And neither do the trees.

Not anymore.

Halfway to the river, they come across a patch of fallen trees. In the middle, a pair of kissing trees still stands. Limp and faded, the bracelets still hang from the limbs.

They reach the river swollen with spring melt. Several new bridges have been created by fallen trees. They stay away from the river's edge, but when the path gets cluttered, Oliver suggests they stop.

"Maybe we shouldn't go any farther," he says.

"What?"

He's thinking of all the holes the snowthings drilled down to the lab. He can't remember where they are.

"I'll be right back," he says.

"Where are you going?"

"I just have to check on something."

Oliver climbs through a tangle of limbs and navigates to a cluster of fallen tree trunks. The crossing over the water is safer than the original tree. Molly promises to wait, but he's not even to the other side and she's already following.

She forgot she promised.

They hike up the slope where the trees appear unaffected. The ground is slippery, and several times they slide on their butts. Their clothes are caked with mud when they approach the bend in the river. The felled trees diverted the water in a new direction. The water twists into the newly formed pool. Somewhere beneath the swirling water are the remnants of the lab. Treetops rise above the water surface as if they simply sank in place.

"Look!" Molly points at the exposed roots of a fallen tree. The slope has eroded around a window.

The hobbit house.

The ground above is still intact.

Even a few of the chimney stones are still in place. They have to climb higher to safely reach it. Oliver uses exposed roots to slide down to the window. The river is only a few feet beneath him. He rubs the filth off the glass. A soft glow emanates from inside. There's no smoke from the chimney stones.

Gravel cascades on his head.

Molly is climbing toward the upturned roots of the great tree that served as the original bridge. Before he can say anything, she slides against it.

She's too close to the river.

"Oliver," she shouts. "I see it."

He crawls back to a safe spot and slowly slides down to meet her. A small hole is evident. Molly holds her phone inside it and illuminates the cavern leading back to the door. He opens his mouth to make her promise that she'll—

"I won't lie this time," she says. "You go first."

Oliver drops in.

The earthen cave is humid and stuffy.

The back of the cavern had collapsed, destroying the secret entrance to the lab. The rest must have been reinforced to remain open.

They shine both of their phones on the L-shaped root. The door, however, is jammed. The ground had shifted, wedging it into place. He uses both hands to pry it open just enough. Molly slides in sideways.

"Oh, my god," she exclaims.

Oliver sticks his head inside. The super sphere is in the center of the room. A soft glow pulses from the intricate etchings.

"Don't touch it!" he says.

Molly has her hand out. The super sphere is smaller than he remembers. In his memories, it's the size of the house. In reality, it's about knee-high.

He told her a hundred times how he'd been sucked into its inner space. Even now, this close, his stomach begins to twist in knots. But the dim glow suggests something is missing. He can feel the magnetic tug when he reaches for it, but it's weak and distant.

"This is it?" Molly asks. "That's what pulled you in?"

"Yeah. That's it."

His knees weaken. That's why he came out here. He had a feeling he'd find it.

Grandmother and Grandfather are still in there.

He tried to explain what it was like to exist without a body. He was pure awareness, just thoughts and emotions. There were no boundaries that defined him, no body to limit him.

But he still felt human.

And despite being interwoven with Grandfather, he still felt like an individual.

He could only assume Grandmother was right: *Grandfather had resolved his past.* If he hadn't, the river is right next to them. It wouldn't take much for the super sphere to become a watery titan.

"How'd it get in here?"

"I don't know."

The floor is water stained.

Maybe they did use the river, but only to move to higher ground, to hide inside the hobbit house until Oliver could find it. He should cover the super sphere so that no one does. They could hide the entrance and bury the window. It could exist here until he knew what to do with it.

Actually, Oliver knew what he wanted to do with it.

But at the moment, that seemed impossible.

It needs to be home.

"Oliver." Molly had wandered around the super sphere. "Come here."

She's standing in front of the fireplace. The hearth is open and clean. She's staring inside where something is propped against the wall.

The cover is leather.

The seventh journal.

37

J anuary 15, 1885
> *Time, my love.*
> *I have nothing but time.*
> *I have not written in this journal for over a year because, quite*
honestly, I never expected to see you again. It became quite clear that the
elven—despite my anguish, my tears and rage—were going to keep me
forever. But if all goes well, my words will soon touch your ears, my lips will
brush your lips, and I will feel your breath upon mine.

Home, my love. I am coming home.

I have lived almost two years beneath the ice, and today I stand on the
deck of a ship crossing into the Pacific Ocean, the salt spray dashing over the
bow and the sun warm on the boards. Water! So much water!

Now that we are safely en route, perhaps seven days from home, I am
relaxing into the wonderful boredom. I care not to sleep because dreams have
tempted my hopes for too long. I prefer to watch the stars at night, the sun
rise in the morning and glisten on the green waves. I want to taste every
second of this journey.

This impossible journey.

I have taken pen to paper, to finish this journal, because it was all that
kept me alive in those early days, for when I did so it brought me closer to
you. Even now, I can feel you at the end of my journey, a journey not
possible if not for the only elven that believed in me.

Ginny.

She stands, right now, at the front of the ship. Her unusual size and shape has made her the target of the crew's ridicule. I am quite a sight, as well, my love. I carry fat like a polar bear and a beard like a beast! But my feet, unlike Ginny's, are normal. But she seems to care not. Never in her life has she seen so much water uncapped by ice.

She is my savior. My hope.

When my pleas fell on the elven's deaf ears, she listened. Even when Claus, a human among the elven, agreed to keep me an unwilling citizen of the colony—a prisoner!—she listened.

She's not like the others.

When they celebrated, she was morose. When they sang, she was quiet. Untouched by a smile, she worked hard to support the colony, but not because she loved them. It is a very strong sense of duty that drives her.

And that is what led her to us.

Little did I know, she had been watching me. She approached me last August. I was on the ice, pushing Flury's limits as I did every day. It kept my mind occupied with dreams that, one day, he would get past their arbitrary border and fly me home.

Reality, though, was suffocating that dream.

It was that day she met me at the extent of Flury's range. I waited for the stout little elven to approach, wondering if someone had caught on to my intentions. We stared at each other for quite some time.

"You believe in love," she said. "I want to believe, too."

That was the beginning of our friendship.

We would meet on the ice at the perimeter of Flury's range and plan our escape. My desperation was not enough to bring me home. It required her raw determination, her dedication, her sense of duty of what she believed was right and just.

She learned the shipping routes of humans (elven know everything humans do). She knew when the solar flares would be greatest to interfere with the elven's ability to track us. On the shortest day of the year, we met on the ice.

We left on Christmas.

Flury obliged to take us to his farthest reaches. When he could go no more, Ginny pulled a glove from her pocket. Like a metal ball to a magnet, she extracted the orb from his chest, his body collapsed in a heap of snow.

I must say, it was quite disconcerting.

For a time, he seemed to be my only friend. To watch the heart drawn from him like a bullet brought tears to my eyes. He had saved me from death, and now he brings me to you. I cannot thank him enough. She assures me, though, that when we arrive at home, when snow is on the ground, we can bring him back.

You will love him.

You will love Ginny and Flury. Together, we'll become a family. A strange one, to say the least, but one that will remain bonded by eccentricities.

Time, my love.

It is all that separates us now.

For now, I will spend it watching the sun track the sky. I will spend it counting the stars as I draw closer. And when dreams and reality become one, when I stand upon the threshold where I left you before this journey, I will fall into your arms.

And I will weep.

WEEP, he did.

The following pages contain sketches of a ship, the ocean and a short, round elven near a thick mast. And countless drawings of a beautiful woman, Gayle Toye. His wife.

His love.

There are no more entries. Malcolm Toye had probably arrived home. There would be no reason to write.

Oliver closes the book.

Molly covers her mouth. Silently, tears track her cheeks. They remain in the hollow den as the light of the day diminishes, the weight of sadness filling the room. Behind them, trapped inside the super sphere, a man and an elven still exist because of love.

It's dark by the time they leave the subtle glow, crawling out of the mud and crossing the water. At the tree where the bracelets will remain forever locked, Oliver takes Molly's hand.

"I know what we have to do."

20 YEARS LATER

38

L arge maps bury the oak desk.
Notes are scribbled in the margins. Fresh ink—blue, red, and black—track various lines around the world, all leading to the white mass inside the Arctic Circle.

An X marks the North Pole.

Oliver pulls a stack of rolled maps off a keyboard, clicking through a website with one hand, a phone pressed against his ear with the other. When he gets an answering machine, the third one in ten minutes, he dials the number on the screen and waits at the window while it rings.

The second-floor bedroom, the one Mom used to sleep in, had been converted to an office ten years earlier. The frosted window faces the open field where the snow-covered windmill remains standing. The missing blades are the result of a severe thunderstorm. Beyond the wide open field, heavy construction equipment sits at the edge of the trees.

A wide path leads to the buried hobbit house.

A herd tramples down the steps, followed by children screaming.

"Hello?" someone says on the phone.

"Manuel?" Oliver trots across the room to close the door. "Manuel, it's Oliver Toye! I'm so sorry to call you on Christmas Day. How...how are you?"

Pause. "Fine, Mr. Toye. How can I help you?"

"Yes, I won't keep you. I've been going through the itinerary concerning the helicopter pickup. I'm afraid we've run into a bit of a delay on our end."

Manuel patiently listens to the explanation. He's become accustomed to changes in Oliver Toye's schedule.

"There's only so much I can do," he answers.

"I'll pay extra. Money's not a problem."

"Money can only do so much, Mr. Toye."

"I understand. I'm only talking two days, Manuel. I can email the change order this afternoon. It's the last one, I promise."

Manuel sighs. He heard that promise last year, and the year before that. And the year before that. Seven years this trip had been in the works. Seven times it had been cancelled. Oliver paid for every failed attempt.

That's the only reason Manuel picked up the phone.

Oliver searches through the papers and finds a set of designs to answer Manuel's questions. The children's screams are now outside the house. Five of them between the ages of five and ten are sufficiently bundled for winter, racing past the defunct windmill for the snow-covered field.

"Yes, yes," Oliver says. "Everything's the same; the extraction's just a little behind, that's all. No, the design is exactly the same."

Molly enters the office, wearing an apron with frilly edges. *Smile Café* is printed in block letters along with her logo design for the coffee shop when they bought it from Ms. Megan. Her pixie haircut is dyed red and green on the tips. She slides a coffee cup across the plan, lipstick staining the rim.

He lifts it, mouthing the words, *Thank you.*

Stop working, she mouths back.

He responds with a nod. Molly goes to the door and holds mistletoe over her head.

"I can send those right now." Oliver jogs over, kissing her passionately. "No, no, no..."

Molly giggles with his lower lip between her teeth.

"I promise, nothing's changed. It's the family time capsule. It's already been approved for transportation. We just had a few last minute delays."

Getting to the North Pole these days isn't difficult. You can ski up there, fly up there, or walk up there and spend as much time doing it as you want. Expedition companies did it all the time.

Dropping a box off at the North Pole, however, was a different story.

Flury's metal orb could fit in a backpack. He could drop that in the snow when they reached the top of the world.

The super sphere was a bit more difficult.

The transport company wanted to know what was in it. How could he explain what it was, and that no one could touch it? How could he ensure that once it was up there, it wouldn't present a danger to future adventurers?

It took seven years to design a box to contain the super sphere with a lock only elven could open. And in the event that elven didn't really exist, that his grandfather was indeed psychotic—although the evidence suggested otherwise—or the elven didn't find it, the box would melt its way through the polar ice cap and sink to the bottom of the ocean.

Oliver and Molly would ski up to the North Pole. A helicopter would carry the box—a time capsule dedicated to the family of Malcolm Toye—and pick up the expedition.

It was risky.

But it was the right thing to do. The elven would know what to do with it. And Grandmother deserved to be home.

Flury, too.

"Great, great," Oliver says. "I'll get that over to you, pronto. Thanks for being so helpful, Manuel. This means so much to us, really. I know...yes, I know you know. Have...yes, have a Merry Christmas, and sorry to call. All right, bye."

"Everything good?" Molly asks.

"Still on for March."

She plants another kiss on his lips, wiping the lipstick left behind. They watch the snow start to flutter down from a gray sky. The children squeal with delight somewhere near the trees.

"Give me a few minutes," he says. "I'll be right down."

Molly leaves him to finish. When the documentation is finished and sent, he turns the computer off. Someone is crying full steam when he gets to the steps. Madeline took a snowball to the face. By the time Oliver gets to the kitchen, she's already back outside for more action, coming inside just long enough to tell on Ben.

Mom is bent over the stove. Her hair, now white, is too short to pull back in a bun. Headbands are no longer necessary. Helen and Molly, both wearing aprons, are at the sink. He gets the update: Aunt

Rhonnie is running late for Christmas dinner (they plan for that). Henry won't make it. They plan for that, too.

Oliver volunteers to set the table.

"Can you check the living room, hon?" Molly asks. "I think something broke."

"What was it?"

"Something fell."

Their first child was born ten years ago. The last one, five years ago. Oliver had grown accustomed to collateral damage.

The living room is littered with stacks of opened gifts and errant bits of wrapping paper. The Christmas tree is to the left of the spacious bay window—the one Flury had climbed through to scoop Oliver up twenty years earlier. The snow has become thick. The children are racing toward the house, stumbling around the windmill as they lob snowballs at each other.

Nothing appears broken.

Oliver pushes boxes around to make sure a shattered ornament isn't hiding. He finds a plastic cup on the floor. Then another. When he's done scrambling through the Christmas carnage, there's five cups in all.

They're all empty.

Not a drop of juice or soda or flavored water is on the floor. The floor had its fair share of stains. Maybe a Christmas miracle had occurred.

The back door crashes open.

Helen and Oliver's mom stop the herd from pounding through the mudroom before shedding winter gear and stomping off the snow. Their laughter is contagious.

Oliver starts for the kitchen, but the Christmas tree catches his eye. There's a bare branch near the top. In most cases, something like that would go unnoticed.

Not on the Toye tree.

That branch is a place of honor, a branch inhabited by a special ornament that stays locked in a safe place all other times of the year. It's displayed for the family to recognize when they tell the story of elven and snowmen.

A wire hook dangles from it.

"Mom, Mom, Mom," Ben rattles. "You should've seen it. We were crushing the girls with, like, these big snowballs because, like, Cameron and Nicholas were on the sides and, and, and..."

Molly ushers Ben back to the mudroom. The kids stomp their boots, laughing and talking over each other.

"And then the snowball man took their side…"

Oliver wanders to the doorway. Molly doesn't hear them; she's busy keeping the snow out of the kitchen. He listens to the girls explain how the snowball man fought the boys, and then they all jumped on the snowball man's back.

"Snowball man?" Molly asks.

The children storm through the kitchen. Mom is passing out steaming cups of hot chocolate that they take to the dinner table. Oliver holds onto the doorframe. Mistletoe is taped above his head. Molly comes over to collect a kiss, but her gaze shifts over his shoulder.

Her mouth falls open.

Oliver turns.

The branch is still empty. The orb…the metal orb…the special metal orb called Flury…is still missing.

He goes to the picture window. Molly by his side.

In the field, far beyond the windmill, a figure emerges from a swirl of snow to stand near the trees. His body is thick and solid. Oliver feels a tingle in his arm, the heat in his palm.

The warmth in his chest.

They watch the figure made of snow pause before disappearing into a white cloud, swirling into the trees. The snowflakes settle to the ground like glittering diamonds, the sun catching the gleaming surface of a large metal object.

"Do you believe?" Oliver whispers.

Molly answers, "I believe."

AFTERWORD

Now you know the tales of a fat man, a cold elven and a thing made out of snow. It wasn't magic. Not fairytales but legends of true human nature and such.

But the tales don't end here.

Continue into the Claus Universe where a man of greed discovers technology can't fill an empty heart, a passionate mother can't cure a lonely heart, and the reindeer who protects the herd. Eb Scrooge, the heat miser and Ronin await.

Get Claus Boxed 2 (Vol. 2).

BERTAUSKI.COM/CLAUS

REVIEW CLAUS!

If you enjoyed this ride, please drop a review on your favorite vendor. It doesn't have to be long and complicated. Throw some stars on it and write *Loved it!* or *It was really, really okay!* or *Meh*.

Reviews make the difference.

YOU DONATED TO A WORTHY CAUSE!

By purchasing this book, you have donated to the development of mental health since 10% of the profits is annually donated to WINGS for Kids, a non-profit organization whose mission is to equip at-risk kids with the social and emotional skills to succeed in school, stay in school, and thrive in life.

CPSIA information can be obtained
at www.ICGtesting.com
Printed in the USA
LVHW021919141122
732651LV00011B/1065

9 781951 432447